C0-ATP-766

MODERN GREEK FOLKTALES

MODERN GREEK FOLKTALES

CHOSEN AND TRANSLATED BY

R. M. DAWKINS

GREENWOOD PRESS, PUBLISHERS
WESTPORT, CONNECTICUT

Library of Congress Cataloging in Publication Data

Dawkins, Richard McGillivray, 1871-1955, ed. and tr.
Modern Greek folktales.

Reprint of the 1953 ed. published by the Clarendon Press, Oxford.
Includes bibliographies.
1. Tales, Greek (Modern) I. Title.
[GR170.D3 1974] 398.2'09495 74-9217
ISBN 0-8371-7630-1

Originally published in 1953 by the Clarendon Press, Oxford

This reprint has been authorized by the Clarendon Press Oxford

Reprinted in 1974 by Greenwood Press,
a division of Williamhouse-Regency Inc.

Library of Congress Catalog Card Number 74-9217

ISBN 0-8371-7630-1

Printed in the United States of America

Preface

The intention of this book is to lay before the reader as large a collection as I could get together of the folktales commonly traditional in the contemporary Greek world. Each story I have tried to place in its general relation to the stories told in the other regions of a more or less common culture: that is to the stories told in Europe and in the nearer parts of Asia. My general conclusion will, I hope, appear fairly plainly. It is that the connexions of these Greek stories are in the main to be found not so much in western Europe or even more directly in Italy, nor yet in the Balkan peninsula and the Slav world, but rather in the lands lying to the east of the Greek area: all the way through Armenia, the Caucasus, Persia, and ultimately for many of the stories in India. In choosing what seemed the best variant of these Greek stories it is significant how often I have been led to the eastern regions of Hellenism; how very often to Asia Minor and Pontos and how very seldom to the western margins of the Greek world.

This field of widely spread traditional stories is, I hope, fairly covered by the eighty-four stories in this book. Yet it is often not easy to see where the line is to be drawn, for side by side with the stories whose range is so wide that their claim for admission is clear, there are not a few stories which, though truly oral and traditional, are, as far as we yet know, confined to some narrower area of Greece, though of course any day fresh collections of stories may enlarge the area over which any given story may be seen to be distributed. Nor in this connexion must we forget that the harvest of stories in Greece has been very irregularly reaped; the rich collections we now have from Zákynthos, from Thrace, and from Skyros are all contained in books that have only very recently been published. Among such stories of doubtful claims I would reckon Nos. 58, 59, 61, 62, 70, 74, and 84. In making my choice I have here allowed myself to be guided chiefly by intrinsic merit and interest.

Here is the place to record my numerous thanks for such of these translations as are taken from recent books. To begin with individual authors. To Madame Niki Pérdika I owe four stories,

Nos. 32, 43, 68, and 74, all taken from her book on Skyros. Professor M. G. Mikhaïlídis-Nouáros has given me two stories from his volumes on the Folklore of Karpathos, Nos. 13 and 27. By the kind help of the Maison Française here in Oxford I have leave from Madame Pernot to translate a story, No. 44, from the *Études de linguistique néo-hellénique* of her late husband Professor Hubert Pernot, and also from Professor Louis Roussel to take No. 54 from his book *Contes de Mycono.* From the book *Der heutige lesbische Dialekt* of Dr. Paul Kretschmer I borrow Nos. 9, 12, and 79. The Chian story No. 7 I owe to the kindness of Dr. Philip Argenti; it is from a manuscript collection of stories recorded by Kanellakis, and now in his possession.

Still heavier are my obligations to recent Greek local periodicals, and here my thanks are specially due to Professor Stilpon Kyriakídis of the University of Thessalonika. By his mediation I have the leave of Madame Giannópoulos—Maria Minótou—for a number of stories from Zákynthos, printed in *Laographía*—these are Nos. 2, 10, 41, 56, and 60—and of Madame Elpiníki Sarantí to use a long series of her Thracian stories printed in *Thrakiká*: these are Nos. 6, 11, 14, 16, 25, 26, 39, 40, 51, 58, 64, 77, 82, and 83. For three more stories from Thrace, Nos. 23, 35, and 71, I have the leave of Dr. Polýdoros Papakhristodoúlou; they were printed by Professor D. Petropoúlou in the *Arkheíon tou Thrakikoú laographikoú kai glossologikoú Thisauroú.* The periodical *Mikrasiatiká Khroniká*, published by the Enosis Smyrnaion, has given me No. 48, and *Kypriaká Khroniká* No. 84. For Pontic stories I have the kind leave of the Very Reverend Archimandrite Anthimos Papadópoulos, the President of the Commission for Pontic Studies, to print stories from the *Arkheíon Pontou*: these are Nos. 8, 18, 69, and 73, recorded by myself in 1914, and No. 79 recorded by Madame Déspoina Phostiropoúlou. Dr. Philon Ktenídis has given me leave to take No. 24 from the periodical *Pontiakí Estía*, and Dr. Xenophón Akoglou—Xénos Xenítas—to take No. 46 from the *Khroniká tou Pontou.* Dr. Akoglou has also allowed me to take No. 80 from his book on the folklore of Ordoú, *Laographiká Kotyóron.* With the editor of *Pontiaká Phylla* I have failed to make contact: I ask him to accept my thanks for Nos. 75 and 81. Nor have I been able to communicate with the Cretan periodical *Myson*, from which I have taken No. 59: here, too, all my thanks are due. I cannot say too much of the cordiality with which all these permissions have been granted: I was made to feel that it was I conferring a favour and not the authors.

For the older books, notably *Neoellinikà Andlekta*, Pio's *Contes grecs*, and the publications of the Sýllogos of Constantinople, my acknowledgements are in all cases appended to the story.

So much for the sources of my texts. My grateful thanks are due also to the authors whose works I have used in writing the notes to the stories: many of their names are found in the bibliographical note. Here, too, I must also acknowledge the special use I have made, as everyone working in this field must, of the five volumes of Bolte and Polivka's *Anmerkungen zu den Kinder- und Hausmärchen der Brüder Grimm.* My thanks are due also to Sir William Halliday for his learned advice and still more for the chapter he contributed as long ago as 1916 to my earlier book, *Modern Greek in Asia Minor*, and to Professor Stith Thompson whose *Motif-index of Folk-Literature* has been constantly in my hands. Dr. N. M. Penzer's book, *The Poison Maid*, 1952, reached me too late for me to make any use of his learned treatment of the subject.

Lastly, I would thank the Delegates of the Clarendon Press for undertaking the publication of this book, and the staff of the Press for their care and skill.

R. M. D.

Contents

Bibliographical Note

A FEW books have been referred to so often that it is convenient to use shortened titles. These are:

AARNE–THOMPSON: *The Types of Folk-Tales; Folklore Fellowship Communications*, No. 74.

BP.: Bolte and Polivka: *Anmerkungen zu den Kinder- und Hausmärchen der Brüder Grimm.*

CARNOY–NICOLAÏDES: *Traditions populaires de l'Asie Mineure.* Paris, 1889.

CRANE: *Italian Popular Tales*, by T. F. Crane.

CREWS: *Recherches sur le Judéo-Espagnol dans les pays balkaniques*, by C. M. Crews. Paris, 1935.

DELTÍON: see KAMBOÚROGLOU.

DIETERICH: *Sprache und Volksüberlieferungen der südlichen Sporaden*, by Karl Dieterich. Wien, 1908.

Forty-five Stories from the Dodekanese, by R. M. Dawkins, Cambridge, 1950.

GARNETT: *Greek Folk-Poesy*, ii, by Lucy Garnett.

GELDART: *The Folklore of Modern Greece*, by E. M. Geldart.

GUTERMAN: *Russian Fairy Tales*, translated by N. Guterman.

HAHN: *Griechische und albanesische Märchen*, by J. G. von Hahn.

Istanbul Masallari: Stanbul, 1938. Sixty-eight stories published by the Turkish Folklore Society at Constantinople.

KAMBOÚROGLOU: *Paramýthia*, by D. G. Kamboúroglou. These tales had appeared earlier in the Deltíon, *Δελτίον τ. ἱστορικῆς καὶ ἐθνολογικῆς ἑταιρείας τ. Ἑλλάδος*, and from this they are often quoted; e.g. by BP.

KANELLAKIS: an unpublished collection of tales from Chios.

KENT: *Fairy Tales from Turkey*, by Margery Kent, 1946. Thirty-three stories from *Istanbul Masallari.*

KUNOS: STAMBUL: *Türkische Volksmärchen aus Stambul* by Ignaz Kunos. Leiden.

KUNOS, ADAKALE: *Türkische Volksmärchen aus Adakale.*

LAWSON: *Modern Greek Folklore and Ancient Greek Religion*, by J. C. Lawson, 1910.

MEGAS: *Παραμύθια, ἐκλογαὶ Γ. Α. Μέγα.* Athens, 1927.

MIKH.-NOUÁROS: *L. S. Karpáthou. Λαογραφικὰ σύμμεικτα Καρπάθου*, by Mikhaïlídis-Nouáros, 1932–4; Athens.

M.G. in A.M.: *Modern Greek in Asia Minor*, by R. M. Dawkins, with a chapter by W. R. Halliday, 1916.

N.A.: *Νεοελληνικὰ 'Ανάλεκτα, ὑπὸ τοῦ συλλόγου "Παρνασσός"*, I, II, 1870–4. Athens.

PÉRDIKA: *Skyros*, by Niki L. Pérdika, Athens, 1943.

PIO: *Contes populaires grecs*, publiés par Jean Pio, Copenhagen, 1879. Translated from Hahn and sometimes referred to as Hahn, *Νεοελληνικὰ Παραμύθια*.

SAKELLARIOS: *Τὰ Κυπριακά*, by Athanasios A. Sakellarios, Athens, 1891.

Sýllogos: The volumes published from 1863 onwards by the Greek Literary Society (Sýllogos) of Constantinople, *'Ο ἐν Κωνσταντινοπόλει 'Ελληνικὸς Φιλολογικὸς Σύλλογος*.

Z.A.: *Ζωγραφεῖος 'Αγών*, published by the Constantinople Greek Literary Society (Sýllogos). Part I, 1891 and Part II, 1896.

Orthography, etc.

THE Greek character I have used as little as possible, and in transliterations I have marked the accent where any doubt is likely or possible. In general I have tried to reconcile consistency and common sense. The name Astypálaia presents a difficulty. I have accented it in accordance with the common Greek usage, Astypálaia, but the Zarraftis Manuscripts used in *Forty-five Stories* clearly indicate that the local forms are accented on the last syllable. Madame Tarsouli in her big book on the Dodekanese, *Δωδεκάνησα*, uses both forms, Astypálaia and Astypalaiá, indifferently.

Introduction

OF the very rich stores of Greek folktales many have now been printed, though for the most part in Greek only; many still remain in manuscript; many no doubt have not yet been recorded. In all this field there has in recent years been a very great activity, both by Greeks and by foreign scholars. Among Greeks national consciousness has played its part; that, and the very strong local patriotism natural to the Greeks, to whom the *patrís* is almost as much his own island or his own village as the country as a whole. Another line of approach has been the increasingly scientific study of the modern language, in which Adamantios Koraïs was more than a hundred years ago a pioneer. In more recent days the Cretan George Hatzidakis and a whole band of scholars have called attention to the local dialects of Greece, and it is these local idioms that are the vehicle of the Greek folktale. Thirdly, the late Professor Nikolaos Politis fully drew the attention of the Greeks to their own folklore, in 1909 founding the folklore periodical *Laographía*, now, under the guidance of Professor Stilpon Kyriakídis, in its thirteenth volume. With all this material at our disposal comparatively little has as yet been done on the relation of Greek folktales to those of the rest of the world; hardly more than is to be found in a chapter contributed by Sir William Halliday to my own book, *Modern Greek in Asia Minor*, and this was published in 1916. To show these relations and in this way to call attention to the special character of the Greek folktale has been one of the objects of the present book, and this I have hoped to attain by presenting in full translation, or in a few cases in not too short outline, every story which seems to me to be truly current among the Greek people. With the addition of a few seemingly local stories of special interest the total number admitted is eighty-four. Each of these I have aimed at giving in its most typically Greek form. The references, especially those to Bolte and Polivka's *Anmerkungen* to Grimm, will enable readers to go further in placing them in a still wider context. Also at the head of each story where it seemed practicable I have printed the type number of the Aarne–Thompson classification of folktales.[1]

Of all this material we have not much in English. The first book of translations was, I think, E. M. Geldart's *The Folklore of Modern Greece* published in 1884: it contained twenty-nine stories, none of them new but translated from texts in the Athenian periodical *Parnassós* and in the books of Hahn and Pio. Then in 1896 there appeared the second volume of Lucy M. J. Garnett's *Greek Folk Poesy*, and this contained folktales: from the Peloponnese and the islands, as printed in *Neoellinikà Anàlekta*; from Cyprus, taken from Sakellarios's *Ta Kypriaká*; and the Athenian stories published by Kamboúroglou from the dictation of his mother Marianna Kamboúroglou. Of stories not translated from already printed Greek texts we have in English hardly more than the tales collected in the eastern Aegean by W. R. Paton and printed in *Folklore*, vols. xi, xii, and the stories from Asia Minor, some ninety of them, printed with translations in my *Modern Greek in Asia Minor*.

Of translations into other languages the biggest collection is the earliest: the *Griechische und albanesische Märchen* published in 1864 by J. G. von Hahn. His stories are mostly from Epeiros; a very few only are Albanian. The next book was Bernhard Schmidt's *Griechische Märchen* in 1877; it contained twenty-five stories collected by himself, for the most part in Zákynthos. Later, in 1919, Kretschmer published his *Neugriechische Märchen*, a valuable collection drawn largely from unpublished texts. Roussel's *Contes de Mycono*, Leopol, 1929, are provided with French translations; and very fortunately, as the texts are written down in a highly scientific but maddeningly troublesome phonetic alphabet. The stories in Calabrian Greek printed in the Monteleone periodical *La Calabria*, in 1888 and following years, have Italian translations: but *La Calabria* is, I believe, a very rare book.

These translations, however, cover only a very small part of the field and for the most part Greek stories are available only to those who can read Modern Greek, and that not only as it is spoken by the generality of Greeks but in remote villages and districts. This is particularly true of Pontos from where many

[1] *The Types of Folk-Tales*, by Annti Aarne, translated and enlarged by Stith Thompson *FF C* (*Folklore Fellowship Communications*), No. 74. Helsinki, 1928.

of our best stories come. The local Greek there had become almost a separate language, and the same may perhaps be said of some of the more marked dialects, especially when the stories have been recorded with any approach to phonetic accuracy.

This material has increased enormously in recent years. Not only have we now the folklore periodical *Laographía* with its abundant texts, but many local periodicals have sprung up, and many of them have published folktales, thus carrying on the pioneer work done in the later years of the nineteenth century by the Literary Society, the *Philologikós Sýllogos*, of Constantinople, and the Athenian *Neoellinikà Análekta* of 1870 and 1882, in which we meet for the first time the honoured names of Politis and the historian Spyrídon Lambros. To such periodicals we owe rich collections from Thrace and from Zákynthos and still more from Pontos; these last gathered from the Pontic people who are now dispersed in the kingdom of Greece. In detail my sources will be found in the Bibliographical Note; yet I cannot here refrain from mentioning the very fine collection of stories from Skyros recently published by Madame Pérdika.

Besides all this published material there are many stories in manuscript in the collections belonging to the great lexicon of the contemporary language now being compiled at Athens. The Athens Folklore Archive also has collections, and how rich these are can be judged from the good stories from this source printed by Dr. George Megas in his *Paramýthia*, published at Athens in 1927.

With so much material before him and the consciousness that there is so much more not yet available, to say nothing of the unknown number of stories still unrecorded, the student may at first be inclined to think that the number of these tales must be unmanageably great. He will not, however, be long in discovering that so many stories fall into groups of variants of what is fundamentally one, that he may be inclined to take the opposite view, that the list is shorter than it really is. The field may be said to be represented fairly well by the stories collected in this book.

What may yet be in store no one can of course say; the possibilities are so great that any arguments *ex silentio* should be carefully avoided. For example: the large and prosperous island of Rhodes seems to be as yet an unharvested field: who can say that it may not prove to be as rich as Kos and Kárpathos, as Zákynthos and Skyros and Thrace? Yet whatever may come to us in the future, we have even now abundant material for such a book as this present one.

The first step in putting all this material into order is to do some sorting; first to bring together all the stories which can be seen to be varying versions of the same theme. It will soon become apparent that many episodes and elements, especially certain ways of opening and closing a story, appear again and again, in almost fixed forms but worked into stories completely different from one another. Such constant elements are therefore of no significance at all for the classification of stories. Thus for example: the latter part of our No. 26, *The Underworld Adventure*, appears again and again, not in its true setting but as a convenient piece of padding to lengthen out any story in which the hero can for any reason be brought into a well or underground cistern. A very common prelude to the adventure of a hero is the childless couple to whom a child is granted by some mysterious visitant, to be claimed after a definite term of years. Again, many stories end with the heroine telling the tale of her sufferings to a crowd of people all shut up together, the door being closed to prevent the escape of the conscience-stricken villain whose wickedness she is about to denounce. Such episodes form contacts, but merely accidental contacts, between widely different stories, and it is necessary to be careful not to use them as in any way a basis for classification. To take another example: the three gifts brought home to the rejected wife are used in the ending of No. 32, *The Prince in a Swoon*, and here they are logically in place: without them it would be a different story. Yet the three gifts have often found their way by an easy contact into No. 33, *The Ogre Schoolmaster*. In the same way the girl whose tears are pearls and her words as they fall from her lips turn into roses is properly in place in No. 11, the story which I have called *Roses and Pearls*, Yet an idea so pretty has easily strayed off into other stories. Again, if the plot demands that the heroine appear on successive occasions each time more dazzlingly beautiful, it is an obvious device to let her wear the well-known three dresses, worked one with the earth and its flowers, one with the sea and its fish, and the third, the most gorgeous, with the sky and the stars. Yet I believe that the three dresses are most truly in place in No. 26, *The Underworld Adventure*, where they appear not as a mere ornament but for the identification of the hero which is an essential part of the story. What we have always to do is to make a clear distinction between the plot which is the story itself and the episodes by means of which it is developed. Such episodes, found again and again in any number of quite different stories, are in fact part of the general outfit of any accomplished story-teller, and a feature of the local *ars narrandi* rather than any basis of classification of stories.

Further, if we seek to fix the descent and development of a story, again we see the importance of the plot. A real plot, a sequence of episodes following one another in a logical order, must, we may be sure, have been invented by one person and from him spread by diffusion, while single episodes, a young man for example falling in love at the sight of a picture or a shepherd picking up an outcast baby, are notions which might have been thought of many times quite independently.

In choosing what to translate I have tried to pick out the best variant of each type, always giving precedence to stories not yet translated and to the less accessible texts. In three cases only have I given fresh translations of stories already to be found in Garnett. These are Nos. 17 and 19 of which the versions in Garnett are very much the best, and No. 62, of which no other version at all is to be found. A certain difficulty has arisen in dealing with a few stories which, though clearly not literary, can hardly be called traditional because they appear no more than once only. These are not numerous, and I have omitted them, making an exception, however, in the case of the story from Skyros, No. 43, it must be admitted mainly for its special excellence. A good deal of space has been gained by not translating animal stories. These are never common in Greece. *Puss in Boots* is, indeed, widely spread, but this is not really an animal story: it is the story of a man in relation to an animal, which is quite a different thing.[1] As it appears in Greece it is

[1] *Puss in Boots* in Greece has been discussed by Halliday in *M.G. in A.M.*, p. 244. Penzer, *Pentamerone*, i. 158, has argued reasonably against its Indian origin.

the story of a fox which by its cunning makes a man rich. The fox, to test the man's sincerity, pretends to die and the man lets us know what his show of gratitude is worth by throwing out on the dunghill the supposedly dead body of his benefactor. From Pontos, where they are perhaps less rare than in most parts of our area, we have some real animal stories.[1] We hear, for instance, of three animals, a ewe, a donkey, and a rabbit, each explaining to a boy that of all animals man is the most wicked and malicious. There are, of course, plenty of stories in which animals, generally faithful dogs or devoted horses, very often with the gift of speech, or birds of magical power, play their part, but they are always subordinate to the human characters.

Next, I have left aside those stories which contain only one episode, and may perhaps be called more accurately anecdotes. These are the 'simple folktales' of Professor Stith Thompson's book *The Folktale*, and he has devoted to them many pages and an immense amount of learning. This leaving anecdotes aside largely frees this book from the necessity of dealing with the scatological element, which, though to the credit of the Greek peasant not common in these stories, cannot at all be said to be non-existent. It is never much to the fore because it is humour rather than wit which is apt to stray in this direction, and the Greek taste is much more for wit.

Also, of stories told to amuse children, and very probably often told by children, I have been sparing. Anyone who wants more may look at the notes which Halliday wrote in *Modern Greek in Asia Minor*, p. 250, to the Phárasa story of *The little Boy and the Markaltsa*—a kind of ogress found in the Taurus Mountains. Of such stories in which the hero is often the youngest child, one may suppose bullied in the nursery and comforted by his grandmother, or the little boy running about with his elder sister, I have put a few among the fairy-tales, early in the series. The typical Greek folktale, even what we are bound to call the fairy-tale, is intended for grown-up people; for hearers, certainly in many ways unsophisticated, but yet with a knowledge of the world in which they live; simple people, perhaps, but not with the simplicity of children.

A few good stories have been omitted as having been included in my *Forty-five Stories*. Here may be mentioned No. 6 in that

[1] *Arkheion Pontou*, xiv. 36.

book, *The Priest's Daughter*, or *The clever Girl and the Ogres*, and No. 11, *The Daughter of the Lady of the Sea*, or *The silent Bride*, this latter a good story and fairly widely current from the Islands to Epeiros. I omit it with the less regret as it seems to me a very Italianate story. *Forty-five Stories* also includes three pieces which, although so far as I know unique and so hardly to be called current stories, are yet of interest in so far as all three of them have some claim to be survivals from antiquity. These three are No. 34, *The wise Physician Askloup*, which can hardly be dissociated from the Coan cult of Aesculapius; No. 33, *Myrmidoniá and Pharaoniá*, or *the Fairy's Revenge*, in which I see an echo of the story of Erysichthon as found in Callimachus and Ovid; and lastly No. 45, *The Story of Jack*, which is very plainly a version of the Hellenistic romance of *Apollonios, Prince of Tyre*. There must be other omissions, stories in neither book, but I have tried to leave out no story of importance.

Winnowed in this way the stories generally certified by the number of their variants to be truly current among the Greek people seem to be about eighty. There is a large residue, but these are for the most part hardly traditional tales; rather they represent the efforts of single not very gifted tellers to produce a story out of their general knowledge of the usual repertory of episodes and motives. Such stories are apt to be fragmentary or confused or in some way deficient in true quality owing to the weakness of the thread of tradition, while strong individual talent to come to the rescue is hardly to be looked for. In these questions of selection and rejection personal taste must obviously play a large part: here I have done my best. It must always be readily admitted that many a story, of no particular merit or interest as it stands, might appear very different if some better variant should come to be recorded.

Although I have always given the first place to the truly traditional I have been unable to resist a few stories which have as yet been found only once or twice but yet seem of some special interest. Here come No. 59, *The Clerk Theophilos*; No. 61, *St. Alexios, the Man of God*; No. 43, *The young Man and his three Friends*: this story from Skyros though found nowhere else I have admitted as a well-told, well-constructed story, and all the more because of its relation to the widely spread story *The magic Brothers-in-law*; also No. 58, *The virtuous Wife*, because it is not only a good story in itself but is of interest as having been worked into the version of *Apollonios, Prince of Tyre,* which is No. 45, *The Story of Jack,* in *Forty-five Stories.* All the rest of the stories in the present book are found in so many places that they must be regarded as generally current in at least some region of Greece.

With regard to this diffusion the reader will observe that these eighty-four type stories have as a rule from four or five to as many as a dozen or more variants on Greek soil, and in drawing up the lists of variants I have been strict and admitted only those stories that really have the same plot. Some of these sets of variants are spread all the way from Pontos to Epeiros and the Ionian islands; some even to the Greek-speaking villages of Italy. Some sets are of much narrower distribution, not straying perhaps beyond Asia Minor and the Dodekanesian islands. The fundamentally traditional character of all these stories is supported by their still wider distribution, for many of them are stories found over the whole area of European folktales: that is from the western fringes of Europe all through the continent to the Near East and ultimately very often to the Middle East, and above all to India, the fruitful source of so many stories. Some stories again seem to belong by origin to the eastern Mediterranean area of which Greece is so important a part.

It is here the place to say that I cannot regard any one country or any one culture as the exclusive or even as the predominant source of the stories in this book: neither India nor the gypsies or any other place or people. Stories with a defined plot have, we may be pretty sure, been invented in some one place where there is a taste for this kind of art; yet as a rule the evidence is not sufficient to say where. Some stories Cosquin has clearly shown are from India, No. 57, *The Girl who was left at home,* Halliday has very plausibly suggested is a tale of Balkan origin, and so on. Each story has to be judged on its own merits and only too often the evidence can give us no clear answer. The object of this book is to pick out the specifically Greek form of each story: what von Sydow has called its Greek oikotype. These Greek variants, though they may tell us little of the origin of the stories, do by their unity enable us to see what shape each story has assumed in Greece, and it is these specifically local forms that clearly reflect the character and ways of thought of the people who tell them and like listening to them.

To get a general idea of these Greek stories it will not be a bad plan to look, even if only cursorily, at some of the collections of folktales gathered from neighbouring peoples. First we may turn to the East and look at a few stories gathered from the Arab world. The *Arabian Nights*, in spite of their reputation and their vast influence on the West, we may perhaps leave aside; the urban art of the Cairene professional story-tellers seems to have removed them from anything primitive or of the people. Quite recently we have had something more to the purpose. This is Major C. G. Campbell's *Tales from the Arab Tribes*, a collection of stories told by the Arabs of the Lower Euphrates and written down by the author with the occasional help of his Arab orderly, a man illiterate but seemingly very capable. The stories are thus directly taken down from the people themselves. At once we see work of a very different stamp from the Greek. A few of the stories are widely traditional and found in Greece: notably *The Story of Hajji Ali*, which is No. 36 in this book, *The Boy and his Guardian*, but whatever the subject the manner of narration is totally different. Wit is replaced by a certain rough, often cruel, humour; the feminine touch and the sympathetic view of women so marked among the Greeks are hardly here at all; they are very much men's stories and about the doings of men. They have also a strong leaning towards the macabre and horrible, qualities not at all to the sunnier Greek taste.[1]

The stories told by the Turks, of which we have now so many in the works of Kunos and in Mrs. Kent's translations from the *Istanbul Masallari*, *Tales from Constantinople*, are very much more akin to the Greek stories: the plots are often identical. In view of what we know from Radloff's collections of the stories of the eastern Turks of Asia and their wide difference from the Osmanli stories, I am inclined to think that here the influence has been from the Greeks upon the Turks rather than the other way. In any case the stories from Turkey have a certain difference from the Greek. They give the impression of a much

[1] *Tales from the Arab Tribes*, translated and set down by C. G. Campbell. Lindsay Drummond, London, 1949.

simpler people. The actors have less individuality. Love arises from no more than the chance vision of a beautiful girl, and apart from beauty all women are very much alike. Love is a passion, overmastering but childish. There is no wit but a special kind of humour, not cruel as with the Arabs, but generally akin to buffoonery. The Turks have the same feeling for the jolly simpleton that we find in the Russian stories. Romantic feeling is confined to a very real delight in flowers and gardens and streams and fountains of fresh water.

The stories from Persia and Georgia with their often chivalrous tone are too far away from the Greek world for it to be necessary to do more than mention them. The rich stores of India, except in the plots where the kinship is often very close, also belong to a world so remote that no detailed comparison is of much profit.

The stories nearest to the Greek are those from Italy. Many of the widely spread tales are naturally found in both countries, and there are also stories which have certainly reached Greece directly from Italy. Here may be reckoned *Lady Klera*, the first in *Forty-five Stories*, and *The Story of Fiorendino*, No. 49 below. Yet in general the Italian stories seem to me lighter and gayer in tone than the Greek: the search into the mysteries of human life, so marked in Greece, is hardly to be found in the Italian tales. There is a notable difference also in their mythological equipment. Both peoples have their popular mythology, their fairies and ogres, their women of the sea and their talking animals; but of that Christian mythology, so conspicuous in Italy and in the Spanish and Majorcan stories, the Greeks have almost nothing. The Greeks are unhesitatingly of the Orthodox Church; their religion is a part of their nationality; apostasy is an almost unheard of crime. Yet when God and the saints appear in folktales it is hardly in any Christian connexion at all. Christ appears as a sort of kindly, wandering prophet, interchangeable with St. Elias or even with his equivalent in Islam, Khidr, the Green Prophet of the Koran; God is often equated with fate or even with the sun who with his mother plays such a part in popular Greek ideas. St. George and St. Demetrius occur often enough, but as no more than the handsome warriors painted on icons or on the walls of churches.

Here I must leave aside the folktales of the Greek speakers

of Calabria and of the Terra d'Otranto: of the former we have a collection in the periodical *Calabria* and many of the latter were collected, but hardly anything published, by the late schoolmaster of Calimers, Vito Palumbo. Are these stories nearer to those of Greece proper, or to the Italian stories of Southern Italy?

After reading Rohlf's linguistic arguments I am inclined to suspect that, owing to the large admixture of Greek blood in all Italy south of Naples, the closest contacts of the *Calabrian* stories would be with the stories of southern Italy, both of them, however, as well as the stories of Sicily, having much in common with those of Greece proper. The stories of northern Italy I leave in this connexion entirely out of account.[1]

Of Albanian stories we now have a fair number. There are a few in Hahn's book; a few scattered pieces; twenty-five in French in Dozon's *Contes albanais*; nineteen in Albanian and German in M. Lambertz's *Albanische Märchen*; and besides these I have been able to read the translations made by Mrs. Hasluck of her great collection from all parts of Albania. This contains more than three hundred pieces; many of them are, however, rather anecdotes than truly folktales. In this material we have variants of the greater number of the really widely distributed Greek stories, but it cannot be said that any of them add much to our knowledge; indeed the style of narration is never very high, and is often very poor. What give the Albanian collections their greatest value are the novels and tales of social life, which throw a good deal of light on the Albanian manner of life and ideas in general.

Russian stories seem to me to be from a quite different world: very much simpler, much more entirely rustic than the Greek. The heroes are young, valorous, and hearty, quite free from subtlety of any sort. With them are the glorious Tsars and great nobles to whom all loyalty is due: romantic loyalty of a kind strange to the Greeks; in Greece its place is taken either by respect for the structure of society or by feelings of personal affection. The Greek stories give us merchants and traders; the Russian present peasant life with all its virtues and deficiencies, with its simplicity and coarse buffoonery. There is always an abundance of eating and drinking. In the houses fathers, and

[1] For the Calabrian question see of Rohlf's writings especially his *Scavi linguistici nella Magna Grecia.*

still more husbands, keep order and discourage faults not by good example or wise advice, but by a big stick. The village simpleton is always a favourite character. The people are infinitely less intelligent and have hardly the wits for the kind of clever rascality which a Greek audience finds so amusing. The general level of culture is much lower all round. A mark of the Greek story is the careful, perhaps over-mechanical, carpentry of the plot; notable examples are in No. 23, *The magic Brothers-in-law*, and in No. 45, *The three Measures of Salt*, and there are plenty more. These carefully thought out and logically arranged plots are not common in Russian stories; still less such an elaborately symmetrical structure as No. 48, *The silent Princess*, with its framework and neatly fitting subordinate stories.

If these impressions of folktales in various countries are to be summed up, I would say that the characteristic of the best of the Greek stories is that they have in the background that spirit of lively curiosity which marks the Greek genius. I have already quoted in *Forty-five Stories* the words of a Greek narrator, 'Man wants to know everything', and pointed out that with the addition of 'by nature', these are the very words with which Aristotle opens his *Metaphysics*. Here I find very much to the point all that Professor Adcock has said in an address, *The Cleverness of the Greeks*.[1] The general outlook is optimistic; the stories have happy endings. In fact I think a sad ending is rather a mark of the literary touch. Thus in No. 30, *The Girl shut up in a Tower*, the heroine, despite her bad beginning, ends in good fortune. It is only when the story reaches the *Pentamerone* that a kind of piquancy is sought for by the use of a tragic ending.

It is this congruity with their own national character that makes it easy and natural to discern in these Greek stories what A. H. Krappe recently called the psychological side of folklore.[2] In rather cumbrous terms he wrote of 'the psychological processes underlying many of the phenomenal factors of folklore'. This I take to mean that for a story to have the vitality to live over long periods of time and the adaptability to make itself

[1] Presidential Address, published in the *Proceedings of the Classical Association*, 1948, vol. xlv.

[2] Here I quote from an article which I recently published in *The Annual of the British School at Athens*, No. xlv, with a reference to Krappe's article in Funk and Wagnall's *Dictionary of Folklore*, i, p. 407.

welcome to peoples of very various dispositions and ways of thought, it must, beneath its outward dress of fantasy, contain a certain measure of psychological truth. It is precisely here that I see the greatest merit of Greek folktales: in this faculty for displaying truths of human nature behind the literal narrative. To take examples: the crystal tower in which the over-anxious father shuts his son, fearing for him the dangers of life in the world, is seen to reflect that over-exclusive love which is a weakness of parental affection. Under the veil of the *Cupid and Psyche* story we see in Greek versions very clearly the estrangement and the later reconciliation of lovers after long separation and toil. In *Forty-five Stories*, Chapter III, I have tried to show in a general way what in this book is pointed out in the comments on several stories, that in addition to their plain narrative interest they have a deeper import, conveying ideas on the general destiny and nature of man. Many of these widely spread and traditional stories have, as we find them in Greek hands, what may conveniently be called a mythical value.

Ruskin has somewhere said that in the graphic arts the grotesque, the good grotesque, is a product of the play of a noble mind: it is from the quality of the mind at play that in all cases the product derives its value. I feel that in the best of these stories we may see the workings of the Greek intelligence, frankly and on the surface entirely in playful mood, but in the background with always that spirit of inquiry and activity which marks the Greek genius.

In whatever way we look at these stories, whether we are content with the surface meaning or try to discern what may unconsciously be lying beneath it, we can see in them the general view of the world which I have tried to suggest in Chapter I of *Forty-five Stories*. We see a character on the whole kindly and optimistic but at the same time shrewd and witty; passion is there but always allied with a perhaps too strong current of plain common sense. A man to be of worth must be intelligent and sensible; moderate and kindly in all his actions; polite and civilized in his manners; if he is apt to seem a little cynical and too prone to admire nothing but worldly success, no great harm is done. His emotions should be powerful, but his heart never lose the guidance of his head. There is always much more regard for social morality than for the sanctions of religion; indeed some of the stories in this book, notably No. 59, *The Clerk Theophilos*, and the second form of No. 75, *The three Words of Advice*, show how people of this nature can take a story of religious import and transfer it entirely to the sphere of human values. Inside and beneath the fluent imagination of the Mediterranean man—here I am quoting Mr. Norman Douglas—lies a kernel of very hard reason. The northerner's hardness is apt to be on the surface rather than where it is more in place. This Greek character is too matter of fact, too little emotional, too little romantic, to please some readers; to others it is equally attractive because of its freedom from the self-deceptions of sentimentality and humbug: at this point I must leave it.

It is reasonable to ask how is it that the Greeks have put so much of their character, so much thought, into their folktales, so that what has among other peoples been so long an amusement of children has in Greece been and perhaps still is an occupation for grown-up people. The brothers Grimm called their book *Haus- und Kindermärchen*: it would not occur to anyone to give such a title to most of the Greek stories. The answer may perhaps be that the Greeks are a people of great natural intelligence and gifts, who lived for many centuries in a country governed by a people intellectually very much their inferiors. In their isolated islands and villages they lived far away from the general current of events which was all the time carrying the peoples of Europe into new ways of thought and life. Even in the revolutionary changes at the end of the eighteenth century Greece could do hardly more than turn in her sleep. For long the Greeks were ready for something new, but the nation lay always in chains. In their folktales we have, it seems, an art-product of a people naturally progressive and active but with no means of making progress. What they did was to develop the riches of their own home-grown culture, and the art of the folktale, in Europe entirely swept away except as an amusement for children, was in Greece developed until we reach such stories as those I have placed at the end of the present collection: stories in which the national philosophy of life shows itself so clearly.

Although I have not felt it necessary to divide these stories under formal headings, I believe that the reader who goes through them in order will feel that the arrangement is not entirely arbitrary. Of the first three-quarters of the whole, from No. 1 to No. 62, the interest is mainly narrative. Further, the stories are built up of two elements, the human and the supernatural; of the everyday world of men, and of another world of beings from Fairyland: powerful, sometimes kindly, sometimes cruel, most often capricious, at their best the guides and helpers of man. The stories are arranged in such an order that the human element gradually comes to the fore and the fantasies of fairyland lose in importance, becoming at last no more than a means of carrying on a story of predominantly human interest. This is to say that the fairy-stories at the beginning of the series give way insensibly but very really to what may be called the Fairy Romance. The narrative is now concerned, if not precisely with the real world, yet with a world in which grown-up people can easily take an interest, and in which they can even believe. The fantastic unrealities of Fairyland which mark such stories as *The three Oranges*, or *Snow White*, or *Cinderella*, give way to an interest in the doings of ordinary life, sharpened and made picturesque, but fundamentally the life of the everyday world. Here I would place Nos. 30 to 49. Very characteristic stories of this sort seem to me No. 38, *The younger Brother rescues the Elder*, and No. 46, *The Girl who went to War*. In none of these stories is the supernatural element essential to the narrative. Thus in the last of the group, No. 49, the Fiorendino story, the kiss of forgetfulness is no more than an explanation of why the hero forgot his bride: his forgetfulness might have been managed without any such recourse to the supernatural. In the earlier part of the story, too, Fiorendino and the princess might have escaped without any use of the magical flight: they might just have run faster than their pursuer. From the beginning of the series, all the way from No. 1 to the Fiorendino story, there is a gradual change in the atmosphere.

Of the Fairy Romances by far the most beautiful seems to me No. 43, *The young Man and his three Friends*. The Fair One in her tower 'at the very edge of the world', in the Wood of the Golden Boughs, has a good deal of the feeling of a William Morris Romance: *The Wood beyond the World*, or *The Well at the World's End*, although the sharp outline of the story is always more Greek than 'Gothic'.

With an audience of a slightly more sophisticated mood these romantic stories tend to shed almost entirely the altogether incredible and to develop into what may be called novels: often into the kind of thing which interested the Italian novelists; and if the art of story-telling had not been so much cut short by the spread of education, it seems likely that this genre would have been developed much further.

Any full account of these novels falls beyond the scope of this book, nor have I given any example of them. Such stories are indeed oral and of the people and so far they are a part of folk-lore, but they all seem to be rather a creation of individuals than any part of a corpus of tradition such as is here being examined. Products as far from tradition as these would form the subject of a quite different inquiry.

Yet I cannot entirely pass over this latest development of Greek story-telling. In the wide range of the art we can discern all the stages from the fairy-tales told to amuse children, in which not only the plots but even the actual words have been handed down by tradition, until at last we arrive at these novels which, however much they are carried out on the lines of a traditional art, are themselves free and original creations. They were perhaps commoner in Pontos than elsewhere. Thus in the *Pontic Archive* we find a long story called *The rich Youth.*[1] In it we have the adventures of a young man and a girl and their contests with a wicked moneychanger; it has nothing of the supernatural except a bird which plays a great part and it ends with the reunion of the lovers and their parents, quite in the style of an Alexandrian romance. This story covers thirteen octavo pages and is found nowhere else; it can hardly be doubted that it is a local creation.

In the same number of the *Pontic Archive* we have another story of the same kind: the subject is the confused identity of two men and the complications arising from it. Turkey under the older system was not a favourable field for the developments of modern life, and the popular arts and customs were in all the less danger of being swept away by the currents of modernism.

How closely these novels could model themselves on the old

[1] *Arkheion Pontou*, iii. 183. There are also six of these little novels in an unpublished collection of stories from Chios recorded perhaps fifty years ago by Kanellakis.

forms can be seen from a curious story of this sort recorded by Pio from Syra of which I would have liked to give the full text. Its interest is that it is entirely a story of possible contemporary life. In this it has all the qualities of a novel, yet the closely fitted mechanical structure of the narrative is exactly that of the most traditional of the fairy tales and romances. Here is the story in outline. There were once two friends, good friends. One of them married and at once became jealous of the other. For his security he built a house three storeys high. In the ground floor he put his mother; in the next floor his mother-in-law; in the top floor he made his wife live. By his orders no male creature, not even a tom-cat, might enter the house. Then his friend disguised himself as a rich travelling Englishman, a *lordos* as the Greek text puts it, and pretended that to satisfy his curiosity he wanted to make a plan of the house. He bribed the mother and with this excuse she admitted him. By the same means he gained admission to the next floor where the mother-in-law lived. Then he was admitted to the top floor where the young wife had to live. When he came to go down again the pretended *lordos* blackmailed the mother-in-law and the mother and made them return him the money he had given them for admitting him. The husband came home and found out what had happened and came to the sensible conclusion that to try to keep a wife shut up in this way was just impracticable nonsense. And so this Wit and Wisdom story ends: modern in its contents but truly of the ancient style in the manner of its construction.[1]

Here, after the fairy romances, seems to be the place to insert a miscellaneous group of stories, Nos. 50 to 62. Their wide diffusion, in Greece or in Europe or in both, and in several cases their actual history, show them to be much older than what I have called the novels. They are not fairy stories or romances; nor can they be classed among the moral stories. Some are from the ancient Greek world: No. 56, *The Thief in the King's Treasury*, has the oldest attested history of any story in the book. No 59, *The Clerk Theophilos*, and No. 61, *St. Alexios*, stories of eastern origin, seem to have reached Greece directly from medieval Europe. No. 50, *The Man born to be King*, is a European story. No. 52, *The forty Thieves*, is a widely-spread

[1] Text in Pio, p. 220; translated by Garnett, p. 397.

traditional tale. No. 60, *The Goldsmith's Wife*, has a very strong flavour of the *Arabian Nights*.

The stories which follow these show a notable change: they tend to be shorter and to have no particular plot; their object is not so much to interest us by a narrative as to embody an idea. Such narrative as they contain is in fact hardly more than a vehicle to exhibit some special view of life and its problems. First will be found a few stories, Nos. 63 to 69, of wit rather than humour, and for the most part with that touch of satire so congenial to the Greeks. The last stories, Nos. 70 to 84, present in a more serious vein a general outlook on life. Rather between the two is a story from Kos, printed as No. 18 in *Forty-five Stories*, with the title *Old Men and their Goods*. This story I found nowhere else, and like the novels it may be regarded, though oral, as hardly traditional. The subject is the thorny one of how an old man may deal honourably and generously with the younger generation, and yet not run into danger by placing himself too unreservedly in their hands. It is the work of a village philosopher and satirist who like many of his kind is apt to be severe upon women . It is in fact a satire on women just as our No. 66, *The foolish Women*, is a humorous exposure of their supposed folly.

In general we may say that the attitudes of mind implicit in the earlier stories are in these later ones presented explicitly, and the last stories of all sum up in a serious tone the whole matter. In No. 79, *The Search for Luck*, we see how a man, in spite of all his belief in luck and his resignation to fate, can bestir himself to better his own position and to help other people in their troubles: we have a mixture of enterprise, good will, and fatalism. Then No. 81, *God will provide*, enjoins the duty of reliance upon the divine goodness. From No. 82, *The greater Sinner*, we learn that nothing is more wicked than standing in the way of the kindly working of things; from No. 83, *The Mercy of God*, that resignation is rewarded, and the last story, No. 84, is a review of all the dealings of providence with man.

If we go on to ask if this attempt at classification has any historical or genetic value, it may be answered, first, that the fairy-tale does belong to an earlier stage of thought than the romances and the moralized stories of human life: we may suppose that the fairy-story and with it the animal-story were the first to come into existence. Yet all this development belongs to a time so remote that we can know nothing of it with real certainty. All the same, of the stories as we now have them, the fairy-tales may be regarded as the earliest typologically and the novels as the latest: not each of those in this book as absolutely so in time, but as belonging to genera which mark stages in the growth of human thought. And this relation holds of those who tell them and still more for those who listen to all these stories. The fairy-tales belong to the world of children and childlike people; light, irresponsible, and sometimes even cruel. The romances, with their extravagance and copious store of magical excitement to remove them from any too close contact with the prosaic world, appeal to the warm and sanguine feelings of the young. The novels and the moralizing tales of wit and wisdom, in close touch with the problems of human life, are made for men and women of more mature years or perhaps of more philosophic and inquiring temperament.

In such a collection as this, made to illustrate every kind of popular story, all these stages and varieties of the art find their place. In the same way on Mount Athos we find living examples of every kind of monastic life, from the solitary hermits fleeing to the deserts of Egypt from all contact with the world, down to the later coenobites, and finally to the modernized monks of the idiorhythmic houses, where every man leads very much his own individual life. For Athos we have in the records of the Church a guide by which we can sort out the several classes historically and genetically. In a collection of folktales we have no guide at all: we can distinguish fairly plainly the different kinds, but of their historical connexion we can have not much more than our own personal ideas. We can only be certain that as the social background alters, so fresh kinds of story become more congenial and are found more suitable and welcome, older kinds tending to drop out. At this point it is perhaps as well to leave the question.

Yet historical conceptions cannot be entirely set aside for it is hardly possible to present these stories to the reader without saying something of their connexion with the folktales of Ancient Greece, of which unfortunately we have so few. Working on what we have, and it is for most part no more than fragments and hints, Professor H. J. Rose has given us abundant examples from the literature of Ancient Greece of the appearance of folktale motives and episodes, and shown that they are found in modern folktales, though as a rule in the folktales of Europe rather than specifically of Modern Greece.[1] Of actual narratives, however, found both in Ancient and in Modern Greece, such as would lead us to believe that there has been any substantial local Greek transmission from the ancient to the modern world, there is a singular scarcity. I quote Sir William Halliday's summing-up of the matter and find myself in agreement with him on this point. His words are: 'Speaking generally, there are some instances . . . where stories told by the ancient Greeks are identical in plot with modern folktales, but there are not very many, indeed far fewer than is usually supposed.'[2] To give examples: The story in *Forty-five Stories*, No. 33,[3] to which I have given the name of *The Fairy's Revenge* and in which I would see a local reminiscence of the story of Erysicthon, is very exceptional. Cases like the Cupid and Psyche story in *The golden Ass* of Apuleius and the adventures of Odysseus with Polyphemos in the Odyssey are indeed commoner, but they are stories which belong to the general corpus of European folktales, and can hardly be claimed as specific survivals on Greek soil. Again to quote Halliday: 'There are certain incidents common to the ancient and the modern world of folktales, but they are incidents to be found in every collection of folktales from every country.'—'The wish,' he goes on, 'has been father to the thought.'[4] Here I must leave the subject; I have at least put my readers in a position to form their own ideas on this not very easy question.

Yet on one point I can speak with more decision. These folktales of today do suggest one very real inheritance from the ancient world, and that is the character of the Greeks themselves. This shows itself so plainly in the folktales that I have tried in Chapter I of my *Forty-five Stories* to give a short sketch of its main lines, and to this and to what I have already said by way of comparing the stories of the Greeks with those of their immediate neighbours,

[1] H. J. Rose, *A Handbook of Greek Mythology*, Chap. X, 'Märchen in Greece and Italy.'

[2] W. R. Halliday, *Greek and Roman Folklore*, Chap. III, 'Folktales and Fables': I quote from p. 87.

[3] *Forty-five Stories*, p. 347.

[4] *M.G. in A.M.*, p. 217.

I would now refer my readers. This Greek character is one that we may or may not like or admire, but it is as evident in their folktales as it is in all the products of the Greek imagination.

The reader of a folktale in a book is removed by several steps from the story at its best, and that best is on the lips of a good narrator; unless the narrator has had the proper skill the story has never had a good start. Narrators must naturally differ very much in quality; from *The young Man and his three Friends*, down to the children whom I met in the villages of Cappadocia—I have written of them in *Modern Greek in Asia Minor*—preserving among themselves the last traces and broken fragments of the art, each child telling his own special story to the others. Again, some narrators may preserve the story closely as they have heard it told; some by natural instinct may improve it, and by their skill bring out the points to more advantage. Many, too, by defect of memory or of intelligence or from lack of a stimulating audience may pass on what they have heard in a more or less degenerate form, sometimes omitting essential points, until the story, as they tell it, is so incoherent as to be almost nonsense. A good example of this is the version from Chios of No. 29, *The Sun rises in the West*, where one may suspect that the use of the phonograph as a recording instrument distracted the attention of the little girl who was telling the story. Yet the reader should remember that what may be obscure to him was not necessarily so to the auditors. To them the story is never likely to have been entirely new. Like stories told to children in this country today, a tale was none the worse for being old, and if a narrator's skill failed or his memory was not perfect, not much harm was done. The auditors were also helped all through by gestures and by the tone of the voice and the expression of the face: to us who read all this must be lost.

Then before it can be printed and set before the reader the tale as it was told must be recorded, and this can be done well or badly. The stories from Chios given us in such abundance by Pernot in his *Études de linguistique grecque* were recorded mechanically by the gramophone, and however much in some cases the machine may have embarrassed the narrator and cramped his freedom, we have in these records everything excepting always his gestures and facial expression. I know of no other stories recorded in this way. Elsewhere we have always the hand of the writer, and it is important to see how he went to work: did he take down the text as fully as he could from dictation, or did he listen to the story, probably more than once, and then write down what he could from memory and fill in the gaps afterwards? Greek recorders with a native's knowledge of the language will probably have followed the second method, and especially when they were working in their own district and were as familiar with the dialect as with the common language —here we may think probably of Valavánis at Kerasund and more recently of Madame Pérdika in Skyros—with results that no doubt reach a very high degree of excellence. It is interesting to note that the style of many of our best stories is so very close to that of Pernot's mechanical records that we cannot doubt the faithful closeness of the recorder. To be for a moment personal, I have myself always had to follow the former of these two methods: getting down what I could by following quite rapid dictation, and afterwards asking for explanations of dubious passages; above all things never interrupting by queries the flow of the speaker's words. When the ear is trained to the local manner of speech it is possible with a pencil to get down the words of a story which may at the moment even not be very intelligible: afterwards by study and by inquiry obscure points can be cleared up. Emendation is indeed dangerous. I have seen an unpublished collection of stories from Chios written down, and very well written, by Kanellakis, where the text has in many places been emended by someone with a blue ink-pencil, and invariably for the worse: fortunately the original text can in most places be made out. Too many people, however great their ignorance of the dialect and even of the story, find themselves fully competent to make these emendations. It is the first reading that one may safely take as being the better.

If a man writes from the dictation of a young person with a clear enunciation it is remarkable how very little subsequent emendation is needed. This method would, however, probably be impracticable with the blurred enunciation of elderly people, and it is from them that many of the best stories have been recorded. Here it is essential that the recorder himself should know the language well, and this means that hardly any foreigner can do really satisfactory work.

Lastly, for the non-Greek reader the translator has to be considered. The translations in this book are as close as English idiom permits: even to avoid tediousness I have made no omissions.[1] Two modifications only have been made. I have avoided the constant use of the historic present; natural enough in Greek, it is not pleasant in English. Also I have supplied the stories with titles. In the Greek texts often there are no titles; often the titles have no very clear relation to the story. Variants of the same story constantly have different titles, and I cannot think that what titles we have are any integral part of these stories. For all the stories I have recorded myself in Cappadocia and Pontos no titles were ever offered me. But to present stories without titles is very inconvenient, and I have done my best to fill the gap. In any case all responsibility for the titles as printed is mine.

Also, in dealing with Modern Greek the translator is faced with a language at present not at all adequately catered for by the dictionaries. He may get the thread of a story perfectly, yet every now and then come upon a word whose precise meaning is a baffling puzzle. The reader is asked to believe that the few words in this book at whose meaning only a guess can be made do not in any case affect the sense of the narrative.

In face of the comparatively small number of type stories and the great part played in village life by story-telling, it seems highly probable that it was only comparatively seldom that the story was entirely new to the auditors. In what then, we may ask, did their pleasure consist? With a people so eminently lovers of company and of life in common there was always the pleasure of the social occasion: the relaxation after the toils of the field or the fatigues of the road, the social jollity of the recurring festivals of secular and church life.

The Greeks are pre-eminently a critical people; seldom does a Greek peasant see any form of activity but he feels competent to criticize it and often that he could himself have done it a good deal better. The late Dimitrios Petroccochinos, so well known to all English people in Athens, once told me that in his

[1] Although the way in which so many episodes are repeated with only slight modifications in triplicate is often very tedious. Yet it is so characteristic of the style of these stories that it could not be removed. Once only, in No. 25, have I yielded to the temptation to omit.

young days in Chios there were in the villages numbers of people who, without being in any way men of learning or of any specially religious turn of mind, yet took keen pleasure in a critical appreciation of the details of the ritual of the Orthodox Church; they knew precisely how everything ought by tradition to be done, especially in the more elaborate services. To an audience of people of this sort there was not only the pleasure of recognizing the old stories, but of critically appraising the skill of the narrator. There is something of this spirit to be seen in a passage in a story from Kos.[1] The hero disguised in the rough clothes of a shepherd is dancing at a festival in the presence of the princess. At first, we are told, the audience looked at the youth to laugh at him: 'Just some drunken young shepherd.' But when he began to dance like a real master, the mocking faces changed and became full of interest; 'the eyes of all were gazing at him insatiably, and men were marvelling at the art, the dexterity, and the beauty of his dancing'. Such an audience would enjoy hearing stories told by a narrator who could use all the resources of his art: the proper management of the dialogue, the skill in descriptive passages, and not least seeing how well he could use a rather conventional versification at the more exciting or more emotional turns of the narrative; all thesc points would have their special appeal. Of this we get a glimpse in an account which Adamandíou has given of a famous story-teller in the island of Tenos, who boasted that a certain man, 'and a rich man too', used to send for him to tell him stories, and a servant carried a lantern to help him in the darkness over the rough paths. Some people said that the rich man invited him because it was the feast of St. Basil, but in fact 'he didn't care for St. Basil or for anything else: what he wanted was my stories'.[2] The story-teller was an artist who knew his business and the rich man was a patron who could understand his art and knew its value. Where there were such people the art flourished.

[1] *Forty-five Stories*, p. 491.

[2] Adamandíou in *Deltíon*, v, p. 279. In the Sir John Rhys lecture, *The Gaelic Storyteller*, by J. H. Delargy, we have a brilliant account of the art of story-telling as it was, and indeed still is, in Ireland. The lecturer brings out at length the character and art of the story-teller and his relation to his audience, and this part of the lecture applies not to Ireland only and certainly to Greece. The lecture is in the 1945 volume of the *Proceedings of the British Academy*.

1

The three Oranges

AARNE–THOMPSON TYPE 408

THIS somewhat elaborate story opens with a young man who in one way or another comes to a tree and plucks the three oranges; or lemons. He cut open the first one, then the second, and finally the third orange; from each of them there stepped a fair maiden. Each one demanded water, and as he had none at hand the two first girls died; for the third one he had water ready. Then she returned to her tree, but before the young man could send to fetch her to be his wife, her place was by a trick usurped by an ugly black woman. The man was over-persuaded, and accepted the black woman and married her. Thrown into the pool at the foot of the tree, the orange girl became a fish. The black woman had the fish killed, but a bone was left over and from this a tree sprang up: this tree also the bride had cut down. But a chip was saved, generally in the skirt of an old woman, and this again turned into the Orange Girl. She lived with the old woman, and the end of the story is brought about by her revealing her troubles; in the Zákynthos version I have chosen for translation, by working all her adventures into the design of a big piece of embroidery, which the man saw; at once he knew that it was she and not the black woman who was his true love.

This story has been studied by Halliday, who is inclined to think it originated in the Levant where indeed it is extremely common.[1] It is in the *Pentamerone*, v. 9, and BP. give an outline of the story with numerous references covering the ground from Portugal to Persia, but for the most part from Italy and the Balkan countries.[2] Their list may now be extended by two more recent references: from the Spanish Jews of Bitolj in Macedonia and from the Turks of Constantinople.[3]

There are two ways in these stories by which the hero falls in love with a girl he has not seen. Either he sees a picture and knows that this is the girl he must love, or, as here, he breaks an old woman's pot or plate and laughs at her; this makes the old woman curse him with

[1] *M.G. in A.M.*, p. 271.

[2] *Anmerkungen*, iv. 257; also ii. 125. More refs. in Penzer's *Pentamerone*, ii. 159.

[3] Crews, p. 83, and *Istanbul Masallari*, p. 32, translated by Mrs. Kent in her *Fairy Tales from Turkey*, p. 38.

a love that will either be hopeless to achieve, or, as here, unsuitable and disastrous. More of this is in the notes to No. 15 below.

The Greek references are:

1. CAPPADOCIA: from Delmesó, in *M.G. in A.M.*, p. 305.
2. AIVALÍ: Hahn, i. 268, No. 49.
3. CHIOS: Pernot, *Études de linguistique*, iii. 284.
4. MITYLENE: Kretschmer, *Heut. lesbische Dialekt*, p. 497.
5. THERA: *Deffner's Archiv*, i. 129.

6, 7. CRETE: *Epetirís et. kritikón spoudón*, iii. 314, and *Z.A.* ii. (1896), p. 55.

8. ATHENS: Kamboúroglou, p. 19; this is Garnett, p. 14.
9. THRACE: *Thrakiká*, xv. 337.
10. EPEIROS: *Sýllogos*, xiv. 259, No. 6.
11. NORTHERN GREECE: Höeg's *Les Saracatsans*, ii. 9.

12, 13, 14. ZÁKYNTHOS: Bernhard Schmidt, *Griechische Märchen*, p. 71, No. 5, and *Laographía*, xi. 431, No. 6, here translated, and 436, No. 7.

NO. 1. THE THREE ORANGES[1]

There was once an old woman; she was cooking on a brazier outside the house. Near by on the balcony a prince was standing. He let fall the golden apple he was holding in his hand and it fell on the brazier and broke the cooking-pot to pieces. The pot dropped on the old woman's foot and scalded her. With the pain she cried out: 'Oh, and no other wife may you have than the Girl bare in her Shift!' The nurse ran off and told the queen that the old woman had cursed the prince. Much annoyed, the queen at once ordered the old woman to be brought up before her. 'You wretched old woman,' she said, 'you must unsay your curse: whatever you ask I will give you.' 'Anything to please you, my lady: I meant no harm when I said it.' Then she said: 'My lady, do not be vexed; nothing will happen; my prayer is that he marry a princess.'

The boy grew bigger and bigger still until he came to the age of eighteen or twenty. One day he arranged with two of his friends to go shooting on an estate which belonged to him. While they were shooting, they ordered the servants to make them a meal; they went to take a drink of water. A lemon-tree stood there, and they saw it all loaded with lemons; each of

[1] Text from Zákynthos, in *Laographía*, xi. 431; with the title *The Girl bare in her Shift*.

them picked a lemon and so they went off. When they had done eating one of the prince's friends cut his lemon: he cut it and out jumped a fair girl, crying 'Water!' They had no water to give her, and so she died. The next youth said: 'And I too will cut my lemon.' The same thing happened. Then the prince said: 'I mean to have some water, and if the girl happens to ask me for some, I will give it to her and we shall see what she will do.' So he cut the lemon. Out leaped another girl, fair as the sun, a girl in her shift only. She said to him: 'Water!' 'Yes, my lady,' said he. So she remained alive. 'O my lady,' said he, 'for sure I must take you as my wife.' His friends were indeed filled with amazement at the sight of her. 'Yes,' said she, 'but you, how can you marry *me*, I who am here a girl in no more than my shift? Put me back up on the lemon-tree my mother, and go bring me clothes to fetch me away in.' This put the prince to shame, and in the evening he went home and had a talk with his mother the queen. 'O my son,' said she, clasping her head in her two hands, 'this must be the old woman's curse about the Girl bare in her Shift.' The prince pleaded this and pleaded that, and at last told her that if he could not marry the girl he would die. Then said the queen, 'Do as you please,' but a week had passed before he could persuade his mother. Then he filled a basket with shoes and gloves and dresses and all sorts of royal gear.

[NOTE. The following paragraph, down to the words 'was turned into a fish' are taken from the second Zákynthos version of the story in *Laographía*, xi. 436, which is much clearer than the version used for the rest of the story.]

One day an ogress went to the well to draw water, and in the well she saw the reflection of the girl; she thought it was her own reflection and was amazed at its beauty, She said: 'Only look what a girl I am! And to think that a girl like me should have to go and draw water!' So she smashed her pitcher and turned back home. Her sister scolded her because she had not brought any water to the house; she said that being such a beautiful girl never again would she go to the well to draw water. Then the second daughter took a pitcher and she too went to fetch water. She too saw the reflection of the girl and she too smashed her pitcher and turned back home. The third sister, the youngest, questioned her and to her she told the same story. Then the youngest took a pitcher and went for water. She too saw the reflection of the girl and said: 'See what a beautiful girl I am! And is it for such as me to go and draw water?' Then the girl up in the tree said: 'What you see in the water is not you at all but me.' Then the girl looked up into the tree and saw the Five Times Fair. She told her to come down and be devoured; she had to go to do her kneading. The girl told her to go and first do her kneading and then she could come back and eat her. The young ogress went back and told all this to her sisters, saying that when she had done her kneading she was going back to devour the girl in the tree. So after doing her kneading the ogress went back to the well and told the girl to come down and be eaten: she had to go back to heat her oven. 'Go then and heat the oven and then come back and eat me,' said the girl. The ogress went and heated the oven; then she came back and said: 'Now come down for me to eat you: I have to go and take the bread from the oven.' 'Go and empty the oven first and then come and devour me,' said the girl. So the ogress went and took the bread out of the oven and came back. 'Come now; come down; I have now no more work to do.' The girl would not come down, and the ogress began to climb up the tree. Then the girl came down to the water and was turned into a fish.

[NOTE. Here the translation goes back to the former version, in which we are told that the girl had changed not into a fish but into an eel.]

Next day the king came with his carriage and the clothes. When the youngest daughter of the ogress saw him she said: 'Why are you so late, my king?' 'Well, I had to persuade my mother,' said he, and he told her everything. Then said he: 'But how is it you have become as you are, you who were as white as foam when you came out of the lemon?' 'Don't you see? It is the wind and the sun here that have made me thus: I shall get all my fair whiteness back again.' At this what was the king to do? He dressed her and adorned her and brought her to his mother. His mother was amazed: 'Is this the girl you made such a story about with her beauty? Oh, alas! and what has happened to you, my son?' 'O mother, the rain and the sun and the wind have beaten upon her. But she will recover, she will recover.' Then with great rejoicings he was crowned in marriage and the time slipped by pleasantly.

One day the king told one of his servants to go and fetch him a bucket of water from the spring by the lemon-tree, because it was good water. So they took a bucket and as they were drawing the water the eel slipped into the bucket. They ran back to the king laughing and delighted because they had caught a golden eel. 'Oh,' said the king, 'we must put it into water in a glass vase and it will be a delight to us.' And this was in fact done. But the ogress's daughter, the queen that is, did not like the eel and she used to go to the vase to upset it: she ordered that the eel should be killed. The king did not want this, but she would have it. At last she persuaded him and the eel was killed and cooked and eaten. 'And you must command,' said the queen, 'that the bones be thrown into the sea and not one of them be left to fall upon the ground.' But as the people were going out by the gate of the garden a bone fell to the ground without their noticing it, and from that bone there sprang up a very beautiful tree. Well; the gardener saw it and said: 'This will be a tree that will be an ornament to the garden.' And in fact in a year's time it was a tree, a great delight to behold. As people coming from the palace passed through the garden, the tree showed no movement, but scarcely did the queen, the young one I mean, make to pass by than the tree showed as if it would cleave her in two and put out her eyes. Then said the queen: 'What a life is this when I can't even go down into the garden! We must cut down that tree.' When the gardener heard this, he was dashed to think that the tree should be cut down. Well; finally the queen gave orders to cut it down and to burn the wood in a certain place and not let a single chip of it be left anywhere else. As the men were on their way to do this, they met an old woman and she asked them for a bit of wood: 'My sons, I am a poor woman and be kind to me: I am going to do my cooking, and don't let the queen know.' The headman gave her a big piece of wood and the old woman started to split it up. As she was striking, she heard a voice coming from the wood: 'O my shoulders! O my foot! O my hand!' This happened three or four times and then a beautiful girl showed herself. The old woman was delighted: 'I will make you my daughter,' she said. 'And I take you for my mother.' So little by little the girl began to work and did embroidery and they made money to live on.

One day the girl said to the old woman: 'Mother, perhaps you can get me the silk and the cloth I need?' She said: 'Yes.' So the old woman went and bought a yard of satin and some thread. The girl sat down and made a design of everything that had happened to her in her life; everything; the banquet; the old woman and her cooking-pot; the table with the king's friends; the lemons; the ogress; everything, everything. Then she sat down and worked it all in embroidery. Then said she to the old woman: 'Take this and sell it in the king's palace; we shall get a lot of money.'

So the old woman went off with the embroidery. At the gate the soldier on guard stopped her, but he took the work up and gave it to the king. At once he had his suspicions as he examined it point by point. The man said: 'An old woman brought it.' The king said: 'Tell her to come up.' The queen too saw it: 'Bah, don't trouble yourself to buy it; send her away.' The young ogress said this and made a whole heap of pretexts because she understood what had happened. But what about the king? He went and said to the old woman: 'Who made this fine piece of work?' She said: 'It was my daughter. I have come to sell it to get some money to buy ourselves clothes.' 'All right,' said the king; 'I will buy it.' I don't know how much he paid: three or four pounds perhaps, and he said to her: 'Tomorrow you must come with your daughter and eat with me.' But the queen was left desolate to see the king so persistent.

Next day the old woman and the girl came and the king made a fine banquet. When they had done eating the king said: 'Everyone must now tell what has happened to him in his life. This it would please me to hear.' So everyone began, and they talked and they talked. The old woman's turn came and she told about the wood she had begged for, and this was much to the king's taste. Then the girl told her story. The king said: 'Ah!' said he. 'Ah, my lady; so it is you.' 'Yes, it is me.' And she took off the veil with which she was covered and all the banqueting hall shone brightly with her beauty. Then said he: 'Now what shall we do to this woman who has made you suffer so many things?' 'I wish nothing but that you send her away to her house.' And this is what he did and the king was then married to the Girl of the Lemon tree, the Girl bare in her Shift.

2

The little Boy and his elder Sister

By the aid of the nine Greek variants at least the first part of the full story of the brother and sister can be made out as follows, though no one version contains quite all the points. A man and his wife had two children; a girl and her little brother. One day the woman was cooking food for her husband and to be sure that it was properly seasoned she tasted it and so came bit by bit to eat it all: in the version from Crete the food was stolen by the cat. To cover up her lapse the woman cut off her breast and cooked it; the man liked it so much that the two of them determined to kill their daughter and eat her. Warned by her brother, or by a crow, the two children ran away. By the device of the magical flight by which objects, combs, soap, and so on, are thrown down by the fugitives and turn into obstacles to the pursuer, the children made their escape. In two versions the baulked mother cursed her son, threatening that he would be turned into an animal. This is from Crete and Karpathos: the curse is not needed and we shall see that these versions are not of those in which the story is logically developed. Then the little boy became thirsty, and in spite of his sister's warning drank the water from an animal's footprint: he was changed into the animal; as a rule a deer. At this point in the Cretan version he is carried off by the fairies: for no reason but to solve the difficulty of what to do with him. The girl climbed up a tree standing by the side of water. The king's horses came to drink, but seeing her reflection in the water were frightened and the girl was discovered. To induce her to come down from the tree the prince sent an old woman, who sat down at the foot of the tree and performed simple tasks so wrongheadedly that the girl came down to show how it ought to be done. For example, the old woman used a sieve but threw away what she ought to have kept and kept the rubbish, and this was too much for the girl's patience. The girl and her brother then came to the court and the girl was married to the prince, which exposed the girl and her brother to the jealousy of the queen his mother.

At this point two types of the story can be distinguished. In the first, and this is found in western and northern Greece, in Thrace, Epeiros, and Zákynthos, the children have the names Pleiad and Star of Dawn. In the palace we have the sister and her brother, the lamb or deer, the prince and his jealous mother, who gets the girl thrown into a fountain or well: as this does not interfere with her life, we may suppose that she was shut up in a dry cistern or well as often happens in these stories of jealousy and the ill-treated wife. The queen had the lamb killed, but the sister contrived to save his bones and from them there sprang up a tree. No one could pluck the fruit, and the girl climbed up to get it. God took them up from the tree and carried them off into the sky, and there they remain as a Pleiad and the Star of Dawn. My translation is of this type of the story as recorded in Zákynthos.

In the versions of the other type—those from Asia Minor, from Kárpathos, and from Crete—the children have not the star names at all, but in Pontos are called Johnnie and Polly (Maríka or Marítsa); in Cappadocia seemingly Sophia and Constantine or Anastasia and Anastasio; elsewhere having no names at all. The development of the story is never very clear. Sometimes we have again the jealous mother who persecutes the two children. Thus in the versions from Pontos and Crete the jealous queen makes a sister thirsty and as the price of a drink of water demands first one and then the other of her eyes. Her tears become pearls and her words roses, and by selling these to the queen a kindly shepherd buys back her eyes and restores her sight. This whole episode is borrowed from the story, No. 11, which I have called *Roses and Pearls*, and is not at all in place here. In the version from Ghoúrzone the girl is swallowed by a fish and by some means escapes in time to save her brother, who was on the point of being killed by the jealous queen, sometimes, as in Kárpathos, a negress usurps the place of the heroine, an episode seemingly borrowed from our story No. 1, *The three Oranges*, and this appears also in Pontos.

In none of the Greek versions is the ending very clear, especially as to the fate of the brother. We can conjecture that the heroine is thrown by her enemy into the water; swallowed by a fish, or perhaps becomes a fish, and escapes just in time to save her brother from being killed. A properly worked out form of this ending I can find only in a Turkish version from Constantinople.[1] Here the heroine and her brother, in this case a stag, lived in the palace with her husband the prince. When the girl was pregnant, a jealous negress pushed her into a stream and she was swallowed by a trout. The stag noticed her absence, and when the negress gave orders for him to be slaughtered he went to the stream and called for his sister, but she could not get out to him. The prince her husband listened to what the stag and the fish were saying to one another and called for

[1] *Istanbul Masallari*, p. 148.

his servants to drain the stream. The fish was caught and inside it the girl was found. So the negress was put to death and the prince and his wife, and the stag with them, lived happily.

There is another version like this given by Kunos, and Halliday gives further references;[1] also there is much material in BP.'s (i. 79) notes to Grimm No. 11, *Brüderchen und Schwesterchen*. These references cover a wide field and the remark, i. 89, that the Greek has much in common with the Slav forms of the story suggests that it may have come to the Greeks from the north. So far as I know the poetical idea of the two becoming stars is in Greece only, part of the Greek oikotype of this widely spread story.

The Greek references are:

1, 2. PONTOS: *Arkheíon Pontou*, i. 197 and viii. 191. The title of both is *Johnnie and Polly*.

3, 4. CAPPADOCIA: from Ghúrzono; *M.G. in A.M.*, p. 339; from ULAGHĀTSH, in Kesisoglon, *Idioma r. Oulagats*, p. 148.

5. TAURUS MOUNTAINS: from Phárasa; ibid., p. 505.

6. KÁRPATHOS: Mikh.-Nouáros, *L.S. Karpáthou*, i. 331, with the title *The wicked Stepmother*.

7. CRETE: *Parnassós*, ix. 233; called *The little Deer*.

8. EPEIROS: Pio, p. 1, which is Hahn, i. 65, No. 1; with the title *The Star and the Pleiad*, and Geldart, p. 31.

9. THRACE: *Thrakiká*, xvi. 180; with the title, *The Pleiad and the Star of Dawn*.

10. ZÁKYNTHOS: *Laographía*, xi. 423; *Pleiad and Star of Dawn*. This version translated below.

NO. 2. THE LITTLE BOY AND HIS ELDER SISTER[2]

Once upon a time there were a king and a queen and they had a daughter; they called her Pleiad. One day Pleiad's mother died and the king took another wife who had no love for Pleiad: the girl was so fair. One day the queen proposed to the king to sell Pleiad: they would get a high price for her, she was so fair. 'Of what use is she to us?' said the queen. 'And we have to feed her, all to no profit.' Not to vex the queen, the king resolved to do this, and he put her in the room below the house and fed her for some days on nuts and figs and sweets of all sorts to fatten her well and sell her as a most delicate piece. Pleiad saw

[1] Kunos, *Stambul*, p. 3 and *M.G. in A.M.*, p. 261.

[2] Text from Zákynthos, printed in *Laographía*, xi. 423, with the title, *Pleiad and Star of Dawn*.

all this but did not know what their object was. Star of Dawn also saw it: he was the son of the second wife, and was puzzled by it. He was very fond of his sister Pleiad.

One day Star of Dawn heard his mother say to the king that the time had come for them to sell Pleiad. They had a neighbour, an old woman, and Star of Dawn told her this: that their mother would sell his sister, and he asked her what he could do to save her. The old woman said: 'Listen, my son. On the day when your mother leads your sister out to sell her, when she is combing her hair, you must snatch the ribbons she will plait into her hair, and the two of you must run away. When your mother catches you up, you must throw the ribbons behind you; then when she catches you up again, then you must throw the comb behind you.' Then she gave him a little salt wrapped up in a paper and said: 'Finally you must throw down this salt.' When she had told him all this, Star of Dawn went to the window where Pleiad was sitting and told it all to her, saying: 'But do not be afraid; I will see you through safely. When your mother brings you out to comb your hair, I will snatch your ribbons, and you must run after me to get them back: all the rest is my affair.'

When the queen brought Pleiad out to comb her hair and sell her, Star of Dawn snatched the ribbons. Pleiad pretended to chase him all round and round the house. The queen said to her: 'Come back, my darling, and I will buy you some more ribbons.' 'I don't want them; I want my own ribbons,' said Pleiad, pretending to be vexed. In this way they came to the garden, and Star of Dawn said: 'If you can catch me, you can have them.' Pretending it was all in play the two came out into the road. When they were some way off Star of Dawn said to Pleiad: 'Run, sister, as fast as you can; we must get away from here.' When they were a long way off the queen saw that they were escaping, and began to cry out: 'Come back, my dear children.' The children stopped their ears not to hear her, and so until they were tired of running. Then Star of Dawn threw down the ribbons: the queen was chasing after them, and this was to prevent her from catching them. The ribbons all in a moment changed into a boundless plain behind them. From the far side of the plain the stepmother looked like a little black speck. But in a moment she was across the plain and would very soon have been up with them, if Star of Dawn had not thrown down the comb behind them. At once the comb behind them became an impenetrable wood; the stepmother lost her way in it and the children quite worn out rested to get their breath again. But at that moment yet once more the stepmother was seen in pursuit, and she would have caught them if Star of Dawn had not thrown down the salt which their old neighbour had given them. In a moment an impassable lake was spread out all round the children. The stepmother threw herself into its waves but she could not pass over.

The children came to a meadow. Star of Dawn was thirsty. 'Pleiad,' said he, 'I am thirsty.' 'Be patient, and wait till we come to a spring.' 'Pleiad, I can go no farther: I am thirsty.' The boy saw the footprint of a calf. 'I must drink, my sister,' said he. 'No, no; if you do, you will be turned into a calf.' So they went on and on, and the boy saw the footprint of a lamb. 'My sister, I must drink; I can endure no longer.' 'Do not, or you will be turned into a lamb.' But before Pleiad could hold him back, he stooped and drank and was turned into a lamb.

Pleiad took her lamb, and walking all day she came to the king's fountain. She drew water and drank herself and also gave water to her lamb. Close by the fountain there was a trough and by the trough there was a cypress. Pleiad climbed up it. The lamb grazed round about wherever he could find grass. Presently the king's horses were brought there to be watered. The horses saw the girl's reflection in the trough and would not drink. The grooms went off and told the king. The king would not believe them: 'I must go and see for myself.' The king took the horses to give them water and the horses stooped to drink: they saw the reflection and shied and refused to drink. Then the king too stooped down over the trough, and what did he see? A beautiful girl sitting up in the cypress. A thousand times he pleaded and a thousand promises he made her, but she would not come down. Then the king went and told an old woman of this, saying: 'If you can bring her down from the tree, I will make you rich.'

The old woman took a wooden kneading-trough and a sieve; also a pig and some flour, and she went up close to the fountain to knead dough. She set the kneading-trough and the sieve upside down, with the pig close to the flour, and made as though she were going to knead dough. Pleiad was watching her and cried out from her perch on the tree:

> 'Don't set the sieve like that, old dame
> Nor yet the trough below,
> And drive away the little pig,
> Or else he'll eat the dough.'

The old woman said: 'My daughter, come lower down, I can't hear you.' 'Oh,' said Pleiad to herself, 'the poor old lady is deaf.' So she came down lower.

> 'Don't set the sieve like that, old dame,
> Nor yet the trough below,
> And drive away the little pig,
> Or else he'll eat the dough.'

'What are you saying, my dear? Come down lower; I can't hear you.' And so the old woman went on until she had brought the girl down from the tree. The prince who was hidden close by seized her and set her on his horse and brought her to the palace. 'Oh, my lamb, my lamb!' cried Pleiad. At once by the king's orders her lamb was brought to her in the palace. Scarcely had the queen seen Pleiad than she became jealous of her and wanted to do away with her, for the girl was seven times more beautiful than she was.

One day the king and the prince were away and Pleiad and her mother-in-law were strolling in the garden. As they were passing by the fountain, the queen gave Pleiad a push and she fell into the water. In the evening the king and the prince came. 'Where is Pleiad?' they asked. 'I don't know,' said the queen angrily. The lamb was walking round the fountain, bleating 'Ba ba.' 'Oh, that lamb!' said the queen, 'will you be so good as to kill it? I can't bear to hear it; the sound splits my ears.' To stop her from complaining, the king ordered the lamb to be killed. The lamb understood this and began bleating: 'Ba ba, O sister Pleiad, they are going to kill me. Ba, O sister, they are sharpening the knives. Ba ba, O sister; they are laying the knife to my throat. Can't you hear me?' 'O God,' said Pleiad, 'grant me strength to go and save my brother.' Then at one bound she leaped out of the fountain: 'My lamb, my lamb!' cried Pleiad.

'Hush, lady,' said the king, 'I will buy you another lamb.' 'I don't want another lamb: I want my own lamb.'

So the lamb was cooked and they sat down to eat. Pleiad did not eat but she gathered up all the bones and put them into a pot and buried them in the garden. At the dawn of the morrow there was growing from the pot an orange-tree with an orange on it. Scarcely had the queen seen it that she wanted it to be picked. The prince went to pick it, and the twig with the orange shot up higher and higher and the other twigs of the tree bent down as if to scratch out the queen's eyes. 'I will try, mother-in-law,' said Pleiad. 'All these people have gone and failed; since you are willing, you go.' Pleiad went to the tree and the twig with the orange on it came down into her hands. 'Pleiad,' said a voice from the orange, 'hold on very tight.' And the twig shot up higher and higher. 'Goodbye, my dear father-in-law; Goodbye, my dear prince,' cried Pleiad. 'In this world no longer could I live. From the hands of my wicked stepmother I fall into the hands of my wicked mother-in-law.' And so the two went up into the sky, and there became shining stars, the Star of Dawn and the Pleiad.

3

The Boy called Thirteen

AARNE–THOMPSON TYPE 328

THIS is one of the stories designed to glorify and perhaps to comfort the junior to many, here to twelve brothers; hence his name Thirteen, often used as a title for the story. The example translated is from Thrace, and is the only variant I know with the incident at the beginning of the hero bringing his mother a tree for a spindle and a stone for a spindle whorl, and at the end the death of the ogre in a battle of magical transformations; for which see the note on No. 24, *Master and Pupil*. These are probably accretions due to the lively fancy of an individual narrator. Another notable variant is the one from Athens, in which the first demand made of the hero is that he bring the ogre's magic glass or mirror which has the property, common in such mirrors, that in it can be seen any war which is being waged anywhere. The rest of the incidents occur fairly regularly. The hero has to bring the ogre's horse, then his quilt, and lastly the ogre himself. In these three objects of quest we have a link with *The Master Thief*, Grimm, No. 192, where the thief is set to steal the well-guarded horse, then the sheet from the wife's bed and with it her wedding-ring, and lastly from the church he must carry off the priest and the grave-digger.

This story of the hero Thirteen and his thefts seems to be widely distributed all over Europe; references are in B.P., iii. 33 ff., where it is brought into connexion with Grimm, No. 126.

The 'kill bearer' letter sent by the ogre to the ogress is a buffoonish parody of the letter in No. 50, *The Man born to be King*.

The Greek variants are:

1. KÁLYMNOS: *Folklore*, xii. 93.
2. CHIOS: Argenti and Rose, *Folklore of Chios*, p. 466.
3. NÍSYROS: *Z.A.* i. 420, No. 6.
4. THERA: *Parnassós*, ix. 356.
5. TINOS: Pio, p. 196, which is Hahn i. 182 and Geldart, p. 174.
6. ATHENS: Kamboúroglou, p. 131.
7. NAUPLIA: Kretschmer, *Neugr. Märchen*, No. 48, p. 204.
8. THRACE: *Arkheíon Thrakikoú Laogr.* ix. 197, translated.

9, 10. EPEIROS: Hahn, i. 75, No. 3, and ii. 180, var. 2, which is Pio, p. 32.

11. ZÁKYNTHOS: *Laographía*, xi. 527.

NO. 3. THE BOY CALLED THIRTEEN[1]

Once upon a time there were twelve brothers. In the end another was born and him they called Number Thirteen. These brothers used to go out robbing. When Thirteen became a big boy, nine years old, he wanted to go out with them. Every evening when his brothers came back from robbing he would say: 'Wake me up too, because I want to go out with you.' But he used to oversleep, and every morning his brothers went off without him.

One morning he kept watch and followed them as they went out. They turned round and saw Thirteen following them. They caught him and tied him to a big poplar tree, so that when they came back they could take him back home with them. Thirteen was of the most manly strength. He tore up the poplar by the roots and brought it to the house. He called out to his mother: 'Mother, come and loose the rope by which they have tied me to the poplar.' His mother asked him: 'And why have you brought it here?' 'I brought it for you to use as a spindle.' When it was evening his brothers came back. They went to the place where they had tied him up and found the tree torn up by the roots and carried away. They went home and found the tree in the courtyard: they were amazed, and asked how it was. Thirteen was asleep. Their mother told them that Thirteen had brought the tree. They did not believe it. Next morning when the brothers had gone off Thirteen again followed them. They turned and saw Thirteen behind them. They took him and tied him to a millstone. Thirteen hoisted it on his shoulder and took it home, and cried out: 'Mother, today I have brought you a bob for your spindle.'

In the evening the brothers came back to pick up Thirteen. They could find neither Thirteen nor yet the millstone. They went home and found the millstone in the courtyard and Thirteen asleep. They asked their mother who had brought the millstone. 'It was Thirteen,' their mother answered.

In the morning when his brothers went off, Thirteen followed them. They went to reap one of their fields. On the way Thirteen was telling them that the day before he had been to the field and the corn was not yet ripe; his brothers did not believe this.

[1] Text from Thrace in *Arkheíon Thrakikoú Laogr.* ix. 197.

They went there and saw the corn all green; not ready for reaping. Close by there was a field belonging to an ogre. Thirteen said: 'Why should not we reap that field and he pay us for doing it?' So they began reaping. The ogre appeared. 'Whose leave did you ask to come into the field?' 'We came to reap our own field,' answered Thirteen, 'and since it was not ripe we are reaping yours and we want you to pay us.' 'Very well,' said the ogre. 'And I was looking out for harvesters. Why not make a wager?' said the ogre. 'And what wager?' said Thirteen. 'The thirteen of you shall reap and I will bind the sheaves and if I get ahead of you, then I may devour one of you.' To this they agreed and began their reaping. Thirteen looked behind and saw that the ogre was getting near them. Quick as the wind he went behind the ogre and untied all his sheaves. The ogre then had no more sheaves in front of him to bind and cried out: 'Well, now that plump one there can come and I will eat him.' Thirteen said: 'Why?' 'Because I have caught you up,' said the ogre. 'Look behind you: all the corn is lying loose,' said Thirteen. The ogre was puzzled and said no more.

Later the ogre asked them which of them knew his letters. Thirteen answered: 'They all do; but I don't.' The ogre wrote a little letter and sent it to his ogress wife. In it was written: 'The man whom I am sending to you, my lady ogress, you must kill and cook his head with garlic and the rest of him with onions.' Thirteen read the letter and tore it up. He wrote another letter to say: 'I am sending you this letter to tell you to kill the red cow; cook the head with garlic and the rest with onions.' Evening fell. The ogre took the others and went to the palace. Scarcely was the ogre there than he began to sniff for man's flesh and said: 'Bring me, O lady ogress, the liver of the man you have killed.' She answered: 'What man? Did you not send me a letter to tell me to kill the red cow?' The ogre saw what had happened and said: 'Number Thirteen must know letters.'

'Well, let them eat and grow fat,' said he to the ogress, 'and in the evening I will eat all of them.' After they had eaten he put the boys into a room with thirteen girls, for the terms of their wager had been that the reward for doing the reaping should be thirteen girls. On one side of the room the girls lay and on the other the young men. In good time the ogre had put an apple under each of the pillows. His calculation was that as he cut off each head he would take an apple, and in this way he would make no mistake and not leave out any of them.

When they lay down Thirteen smelled the apples; he lifted up his pillow and saw an apple underneath it. He saw that to each of his brothers there was an apple. He had suspicions and took and placed the apples where the girls were to sleep. When the ogre was sure that they were all asleep, he took his sword and came into the room. As he took each apple he cut off a head, and so he killed the thirteen girls. Thirteen was not asleep. When the ogre had killed the girls he left the room. Then Thirteen woke up his brothers and they went off. They crossed the ogre's boundary and there they rested. At dawn the ogre went and saw that he had killed the girls. He ran off furiously to come up with the boys. He came to his boundary and saw them and shouted out: 'What is this you have done, Thirteen? You have destroyed my fat cow; you have destroyed my thirteen girls.' Thirteen answered: 'What I *am* going to do to you, you have yet to learn.'

The brothers went off to work for a king. They were jealous of Number Thirteen, and said to the king: 'Our brother Thirteen is able to bring you the ogre's horse.' The king did not believe them: 'In this way I have lost so many men, and can it be that this young fellow will bring the horse?' The young men insisted. The king sent for Thirteen and said: 'I want you to go and get me the ogre's horse.' Thirteen answered: 'Since this is your command, I will go.' He started off. That horse could speak, and that moment it uttered a word: 'They are starting out to come and carry me off.' In the night Thirteen went into the stable where the ogre kept his horse, and when he was beginning to untie him, the horse spoke: 'They are carrying me off.' The ogre heard and went to the stable. He looked right and left but could see no one. Thirteen was hidden in the straw. When he heard that the ogre had gone he went to untie the horse. Again the horse spoke. The ogre came down and looked right and left; nothing to be seen, and he gave the horse a blow with a stick. 'Are you making game of me tonight, are you?' He went away, Thirteen came out to untie the horse and said to him: 'Don't cry out again; if you do I will kill you.' The horse said: 'Take the sheepskin on my shoulders and cut it into four pieces and tie them to my hooves until we are outside the courtyard.' Thirteen cut up the sheepskin and tied it to his hooves and mounted the horse. When he was right in the middle of the courtyard, the horse spoke: 'I am on my way off,' he said. The ogre took heed to this and ran up, but Thirteen had passed the boundary. The ogre came and said: 'O Thirteen, what is this you have done? You have been the death of the red cow; you have been the death of the thirteen girls, and now you have carried off the horse.' Thirteen made answer: 'What I *am* going to do to you, you have yet to learn.' So he went off.

When the king saw him he was greatly delighted, but the brothers were full of bitterness. They said to the king: 'Thirteen would be able to bring you the ogre's quilt.' The king did not believe them and said: 'How can he get the quilt? It has all those bells on it and when they ring it can be heard two hours away.' The brothers insisted. The king called for Thirteen and told him to go and get the quilt. 'Since this is your command, I will go,' said Thirteen. 'Take and fill me three reeds all full of fleas.' He filled the three reeds with fleas; Thirteen started off. At midnight when the ogre was asleep he loosed the three reeds full of fleas on him. When the fleas bit him, the ogre threw off the quilt and pitched it down the stairs. Thirteen took it up and went off. When Thirteen was out into the courtyard, the ogre saw what had happened and ran after him. Thirteen crossed the border and halted. The ogre called to him: 'What have you done to me, Thirteen? You have destroyed my cow and the thirteen girls. You took my horse and now you have taken my quilt.' 'What I *am* going to do to you, you have yet to learn,' said Thirteen.

When the king saw him he was delighted. The brothers were full of bitterness and said to the king: 'Most mighty king, our brother could bring you the ogre himself.' The king answered: 'How can that be? The ogre will devour him.' The brothers insisted. The king called for Thirteen and said: 'I want you to bring me the ogre.' Thirteen said: 'Give me two bags of gold coins and an axe and a sharp saw.' He took them and went to the ogre's place. He cut down a tree and made a chest. Lo, the ogre passed that way. 'Good day, my fine lad.' 'Good day, uncle.' 'What are you doing here?' 'About this chest I lay a wager; whoever can get into it, and then I hammer in two nails and the man can then heave up the lid, he wins the gold coins I have in the bags. Whoever cannot raise the lid loses two bags of money.' 'I will go into it,' said the ogre, and in he went. Instead of hammering in two nails, Thirteen knocked in a great number of nails and said: 'I have finished the nailing; now you can raise the lid.' The ogre tried to force the nails: the chest heaved, but the lid did not lift.

When Thirteen saw that he could not move the lid, he said: 'Well, ogre, I am Thirteen.' The ogre answered: 'Come, Thirteen, grant me my life and I will give you half my riches.' Thirteen would not listen to him. He took up the chest on his shoulder and carried it to the king. When the king saw him he was delighted.

Thirteen opened a hole in the chest and threw barley inside it. By magic art the ogre had turned into a hen with chickens and they ate the barley. Thirteen also knew magic arts and he turned into a fox and ate the ogre.

So Thirteen lived afterwards in the shape of a fox, and his brothers were workmen in the service of the king.

4

The Half Man

AARNE–THOMPSON TYPE 675

THIS is a curious story of which I find five examples: from Cyprus, from Kálymnos, from Epeiros, and two from Crete, the short one which is here translated and a much longer one, which is, however, a good deal padded out. The general idea is that if a man is kindly and merciful he will be abundantly rewarded, however miserable and feeble he may be; no more than half a man. In the Cretan version translated he is a little chap with a scabby head; in the other and longer Cretan version and in the version from Kálymnos he is the odd creature, a Half Man, granted at the prayer of his parents for a son of any sort whatever. This odd hero showed kindness to a fish or to several fishes by throwing them back into the sea; from the fish he learned a talismanic phrase: in the longer Cretan version this is *In the Name of God and by Favour of the Fish*; in the version from Cyprus *By the Word of God and by the Word of the Fish and of me who am a Sinner*. By the use of this phrase he won the hand of the princess. In the longer Cretan version, when her father discovered this, the Half Man contrived that a lost fork should be found in his pocket. The king said he did not know how it got there, and the princess said that neither did she know how she had come by her baby. The king was angry and shut up the Half Man and his wife and the child in a box and threw them into the sea. By the use of the magic words the hero escaped and went on with one success after another until at last we have him sharing the king's throne.

Halliday has discussed a closely parallel Welsh gipsy story where a lady who has been helped grants as a boon that every wish expressed should be fulfilled. The Half-Boy hero is found also in Persia, and Halliday is of the opinion that as a romantic hero he belongs not at all to western Europe but to the Middle East; by which he means the Middle and not the Near East.[1]

A story in Basile's *Pentamerone*, i. 3, of kindness rewarded has a general resemblance to this story, but the hero is not a Half Man but just a rather miserable sort of fellow of whom not much would be expected.

[1] References are to Lorimer's *Persian Tales*, p. 109; Ralston, *Russian Folktales*, p, 263; Straparola, iii. story 1. Also to Halliday in *Journal of the Gypsy Lore Society*, N.S. iii. 5 and iv. 8.

The references for *The Half Man* are:

1. CYPRUS: Sakellarios, ii. 335.
2. KÁLYMNOS: *Folklore*, xii. 197.
3, 4. CRETE: *Z.A.* ii (1896), 60, and *Syllogos*, xxxi. 136.
5. EPEIROS: Pio, p. 21, which is Hahn, i. 102, No. 8.

NOTE. The Half Man recalls a story of a child who was no bigger than half a pea and yet he helped all his elder brothers out of their troubles, although it is perhaps more akin to No. 3, the story I have called *The Boy called Thirteen*. I find it in Mitylene, Kretschmer, *Heut. lesbische Dialekt*, p. 532; in Skyros, Pérdika, ii. 165; and perhaps in Hahn, ii. 182, No. 3, version 4; there is also an Italo-Greek text from Roccaforte in Calabria in *Archivio p. lo studio d. trad. popolari*, v. 469. See also BP. i. 389. I venture to omit it as a very childish tale.

NO. 4. THE HALF MAN[1]

Once there was a king who had a servant, and one day he sent him off to get wood. The man went down to the shore looking for wood, and there on the beach he found four big fish. The fish said to him: 'If you throw us back into the sea, whatever you ask of us we will give you.' He threw them back into the sea. Then in about an hour he said to the fish: 'By the Power of God and of the Four Fishes, I should like down here to find four faggots of wood.' The faggots he then took home.

At that time the king had a daughter, and she told him she wanted to be married. The king brought together all the men in his realm and they went to a field. All round the field they made a circle, and in the middle of the circle they set the princess and gave her an apple. Then the king told her to choose whom she willed. And she threw the apple to the servant, a little man with a scabby head. The king said: 'Is this little scabby-headed man the one you will have?' 'Oh, father; I threw it, but it slipped and fell on him.' Then they formed the circle again, and she threw the apple to the little man with the scabby head. The king said: 'This man you shall marry.' The man accepted her and they were married.

Afterwards the pair wanted to go away to some other place. They journeyed and journeyed and went a very long journey

[1] Cretan text from *Z.A.* ii. (1896), p. 60, where it has the title *The little Man with the Scabby Head.*

indeed. As they were on their way the princess had a child. They were tired out and the man said to himself: 'By the Power of God and of the Four Fishes I would have two horses here with us.' Then out of the earth sprang two golden horses with saddles of gold. They mounted and journeyed on and on and on, and at last the princess was tired of carrying the baby. Again the man said to himself: 'By the Power of God and of the Four Fishes, I would have a woman here to serve us.' A serving-woman appeared and held the baby. Then they journeyed on and on and on and the servant grew tired, and again the man said to himself: 'By the Power of God and of the Four Fishes, I wish there were here a city and men could come here with drums and with soldiers to bring us on our way.' Then a city appeared and men came and brought them on their way with drums and with soldiers. So they were brought into the city. And when they were in the city the little man with the scabby head said: 'By the Power of God and of the Four Fishes, would there were here a palace.' Even as he was saying this a palace appeared all of gold; he went into it. Then came the king, his wife's father and he came into the palace and said: 'Are you the little man with the scabby head?' He saw the man seemed to have forgotten him. He said: 'I am the little man with the scabby head.' The king said: 'Oh no, surely you are not the man with the scabby head?' Then he set upon him the finest robes he had and recognized clearly that it was he. They shared the kingdom and all dwelled together.

5

The Ogre outwitted

AARNE–THOMPSON TYPES 1000–29

OGRES, for this is the word I think fits the Greek *drakos* better than any other, are often met with in Greek story-telling. They are always imagined as very big, very strong, and very stupid, generally living in companies of forty; often in caves. But they can easily be outwitted, especially by a man who has been warned that they sleep with their eyes open and keep watch with them closed, and by her cunning a girl can often get the better of them. The ogress-mother who devours men is particularly easy to appease by any hero who has the ready courage to hail her as mother and to suck at her breasts. The reader who wants to know more may read what Halliday and Lawson have written, and then go on to the traditions of *drakoi* collected by Politis.[1]

In addition to what is said of ogres in this book—see especially No. 33—it will be enough to outline a few stories. In a story from Chios with a close parallel in Epeiros we read of how an ogre is beguiled by an old man who pretends to great strength in carrying wood and fetching water, bringing home the whole forest and the whole fountain.[2]

In a story from Thrace with a close parallel from Astypálaia the clever daughter of a vizier lures ogres to their death. A similar story from Zákynthos tells of the contests of a boy with three ogres one after the other.[3]

A story from Tenos narrates the triumphs of a *spanós*, a beardless man, over an ogre: the victory of cunning over stupidity, for the beardless man is always in the stories a clever but cruel and unscrupulous villain; for whom see the note on 69.[4]

[1] Halliday in *M.G. in A.M.*, p. 225; Lawson, *Modern Greek Folklore*, p. 280; Politis, *Paradóseis*, Nos. 389 to 403; BP. i. 124, 499.

[2] Chios, in Pernot, *Études de linguistique*, iii. 271; with a parallel from Epeiros, in Pio, p. 34, which is Hahn, i. 173, No. 23, and Geldart, p. 47.

[3] Thrace in *Thrakiká*, xv. 358; Astypálaia, in *Forty-five Stories*, No. 6; Zákynthos, in *Laographía*, xi. 522.

[4] Pio, p. 203, which is Hahn ii. 211, No. 18, and Geldart, p. 185. Other references for such stories about ogres are Pio, p. 224; Kretschmer, *Neugr. Märchen*, p. 116; Hahn, i. 152, No. 18.

6

The Quest for the Fair One of the World

THE mysterious hidden beauty, the Fair One of the World, in Turkish stories the Dünya Güzeli, called also the Five Times Fair, with whose supposedly unattainable love the hero is so often cursed, plays her part in many Greek stories, and here we have a story from Thrace of which the whole subject is the quest for the Fair One by the usual three brothers. That the youngest of the three should succeed while the two elder ones fail is of course a commonplace; so is the falling in love with the girl by the sight of her picture: this is an alternative to being cursed by a hopeless love for her; for which see No. 1 *The three Oranges*. After the failure of the two elder brothers the youngest, instructed by an old woman, finds the Fair One in the last of the forty rooms of a palace reached by going down forty steps into the earth beneath her father's throne.

At the end of the story the hero has to pick out his bride at a sort of identity parade. When the girls were in the form of ducks his love signalled to him by wagging her tail; when they appeared as girls it was by moving her eyes: it may be supposed that they were wearing some kind of veil, a yashmak, which allowed only the eyes to be seen. In other stories the girl arranges that she shall be known by a bee alighting on her head, as in No. 34. In *The Master and Pupil*, as it appears in No. 43, a boy changed into a horse is picked out by his father, but I do not think that these identity parades are common in Greek stories.

When the hero has found the Fair One her father says to him: 'Either you are the son of a witch or the Fair One has guided you.' This and the hero's denial are a fixed formula found in other stories. In particular it marks many of the versions of our story No. 13, *The Girl who married an Animal*, for which see *Forty-five Stories*, p. 224.

NO. 6. THE QUEST FOR THE FAIR ONE OF THE WORLD[1]

Once upon a time there were a king and a queen and they had three royal sons. The queen died. Then the king said: 'When I too die, you are to take the keys of the palace and open the

[1] A Thracian text in *Thrakiká*, xvi. 130, with the title *The Princess or the Fair One of the World*.

rooms; but thirty-nine rooms only. The last room you must not open; if you do you shall have my curse.'

When the king died, after forty days the eldest prince took the keys and opened the thirty-nine rooms. In them there was stored up much gold coin. In the last room the key was still in the lock; he opened the door and saw a picture: it was of the Fair One of the World. Scarcely had he seen it than his eyes were dazzled, so beautiful was she. He marvelled at her and said: 'I must go and find her.' The room where the picture was was near the margin of the sea, and there was there a golden ship made fast with a golden cable. The prince went on board and the ship started of herself, for she was enchanted. So he was carried to a certain city.

When he landed at that city he asked: 'Where can I find the Fair One of the World?' They said to him: 'You can never find her. Her father the king has her hidden away and all the princes who have gone to find her have been slain by the king.' 'I shall go to find her.' The prince went to the king and said: 'O my king and many be your years, I have come to ask of you the princess, the Fair One of the World.' 'If you can find her, she is yours.' The king set him a term of forty days in which to find her. The prince searched all over the city; he could not find her. On the last day he went to the king and said: 'I have searched in all the city and I have not found her; now I must search in the palace.' He could not find her in the palace either, and the king gave orders for his head to be cut off.

Forty days passed and the second prince saw that his brother did not appear; he went round the rooms of the palace and opened also the fortieth. When he saw the picture of the Fair One of the World he was amazed and said: 'I must go to find her.' He went into the golden ship and she carried him to the city. He asked: 'Where can I find the princess, the Fair One of the World?' They said: 'You cannot find her. Her father the king has her hidden away closely: no prince has been able to find her, so her father kills them all.' 'I am off to find her.' The prince went to the palace and said to the king: 'O my king, and many be your years; I have come to ask you to give me as my wife the princess, the Fair One of the World.' 'If you can find her, she is yours.' The prince for forty days sought for her everywhere; then the king gave orders for his head to be cut off.

When time passed and the youngest prince saw that his brothers did not return, he took the keys and opened the thirty-nine rooms. When he opened the last room and saw the picture he went dizzy at the beauty of the Fair One of the World and said: 'It is for her my brothers have lost their lives.' He took with him much gold coin and embarked on the golden ship; the ship brought him to the same city. He made her fast at the margin of the sea and went and asked about the Fair One of the World. He was told: 'You cannot find her. It is for her that many princes have lost their lives.' What was the prince to do? He went to a witch; he gave her much gold and said: 'I desire to find the Fair One of the World.' 'You cannot find her. Yet you shall go to a goldsmith and order of him a gold camel. Inside the camel there must be room for a man to go with his food and his provision of bread. You must go into the camel and there play an instrument of music.' The prince went to the goldsmith and he made him the camel. The witch led him all round the city, and inside the camel the prince was making music. The king heard of the golden camel and its music and he commanded it to be brought to the palace for their pleasure.

Then said the princess: 'Father, you have held me all these years in slavery; will you not let this music be brought to me too?' Then by the king's orders the camel was brought to the princess's room. There was a hole in the camel for the prince to have air to breath and to see through. As soon as he saw the princess he marvelled at her beauty and said: 'You here are she whom I have been seeking so long.' Then the princess instructed the prince how he should proceed in order to win her. 'Underneath my father's throne is a plank with a brass handle. You must pull at the handle and then you will find forty steps; when you have gone down the steps you will come to forty rooms and the last one is mine. The king will say to you: "Either you are the son of a witch or the Fair One of the World has guided you." Then you must say: "Neither am I the son of a witch nor has the Fair One of the World guided me." Then he will bring before you forty ducks and will tell you to discover which of them is me. I shall shake my tail. Again he will say to you: "Either you are the son of a witch or the Fair One of the World has guided you." And you must say: "Neither am I the son of a witch nor has the Fair One of the World guided me." Afterwards he will let you see forty young girls, all of them alike. I will move my eyes and so you will know which of them is me.'

When the king had heard the camel play a number of tunes, he ordered it to be removed and gave money to the witch who owned the camel.

The prince went to the king to ask for the princess as his wife; the king granted him a term of forty days saying: 'If you do not find her, I shall take off your head.' 'Very well,' said the prince.

Thirty-nine days passed, and when the fortieth day came the prince went to the king and said: 'My king, and many be your years, I have sought everywhere and I have not found her; now let me look also in the palace.' He went this way and that and then he went right underneath the throne. The king said: 'There is nothing underneath the throne; not even a broom. The prince stooped down; he pulled at the brass handle; he went down the forty steps. Then he went in into the forty rooms and at last knocked at the room where the princess was. The king was astonished and said: 'Either you are the son of a witch or the Fair One of the World has guided you.' 'Neither am I the son of a witch nor has the Fair One of the World guided me.'

Afterwards the king brought out the forty ducks, all exactly alike: the duck who was the princess shook its tail. The prince knew that it was she. Then again the king said: 'Either you are the son of a witch or the Fair One of the World has guided you.' 'Neither am I the son of a witch nor has the Fair One of the World guided me.' Then the king showed him the forty girls all looking the same. The princess moved her eyes. 'This one,' said the prince, 'is the Fair One of the World.'

The king gave him the princess to be his wife; they held the wedding for forty days and forty nights and guests came from all parts of the realm. The king wanted to keep them there so that they should all live together. 'I thank you,' said the prince: 'I too have a palace and am the son of a king.' The king gave them his blessing and they went off to the golden ship. They ruled as king and queen for many years and had many children. I too was there and saw them living in fair prosperity and may we here live even better.

7

The Child from the Sea

THERE are in Greece four stories which, although quite separate and distinguishable, could yet all be ranged under a single rubric which might be phrased as *The Child given and claimed.* They all begin with a childless couple to whom in answer to their prayers a child is at last granted by some mysterious personage, often a dervish or a lady from the sea, who gives them an Apple of Fertility to eat and from eating it the wife has a son; often their mare eating the peel has a foal, afterwards the boy's favourite mount; a talking horse as a rule.[1] But with the gift of the child goes always one condition: after a term of so many years he must be given over to the strange personage who has been the means of his birth. These four sets of stories may be called, the first one *The Child from the Sea,* and it is placed at this point in the book because it can be reckoned as a fairy-tale. The second, No. 39, and third, No. 38, are here called *The Prince in Disguise* and *The younger Brother rescues the elder*: these are put, owing to their treatment and style, among the romances. The fourth type belongs rather to the Moral Tales: it may be called *The Mercy of God,* No. 83.

Lastly, this same beginning, the granting of a child to a childless couple, appears sometimes as the opening of stories with the thread of which it is in no way organically connected; such stories can be ranged according to their individual contents irrespective of the opening episode; No. 8, *The Boy and the Box,* is an example.

The general outline of *The Child from the Sea* is that there was a fisherman; an unlucky man for he had neither a child nor any success in his fishing. By the shore of the sea he lamented his fate, crying out 'Alas, alas.'[2] This brought from out of the sea a lady, a Sea Mother, who declared that Alas Alas or whatever word of lamentation the man had uttered was her own name. The lady promised that he should have a child, which must, however, when grown up be handed over to her. In the version from Chios here translated the fisherman saves the life of a fish, much as in the beginning of several versions of No. 36, and the fish grants him the child. When the time came the

[1] For which conceptions after eating an apple see *Forty-five Stories,* p. 54, and BP. i. 544.

[2] For which see note on No. 17.

boy ran away up a high mountain, in this way avoiding the grasp of the sea. Then by redistributing their food the boy won the favour of a lion, of an eagle, and of the ants;[1] changed into an ant he could enter the princess's room; as an eagle he could fly so swiftly as to bring her milk from the sheepfold still warm; changed into a lion he could defeat the attacks of the jealous suitors. But washing in the sea after the toils of battle he put himself in the power of the Lady from the Sea and she carried him away. His wife then fitted out a ship and took with her three golden apples. In the sight of the Lady from the Sea she played with the apples, tossing them in the air and throwing them to her one after the other in return for being allowed to see her husband, first his head only, then to the waist, and the third time entirely. This last brought him right up out of the grasp of the sea, and his wife was able to snatch him and carry him off to the discomfiture of the Lady from the Sea.

In the version from Epeiros it is an ogre who grants, wins, and at last loses the child. In the *Laographía* version from Thrace there is similarly no connexion with the sea; the boy is granted and claimed by a blackamoor, an *Arápis*.

The following versions are recorded:

1. Western Asia Minor: Pánormos, in *Mikrasiatiká Khroniká*, iv. 289.
2. Chios: unpublished version recorded by Kanellakis; here translated.
3. Mitylene: *Folklore*, xi. 113.
4. Naxos: *N.A.* ii. 122; translated by Garnett, p. 208.
5. Mýkonos: Roussel, *Contes de Mycono*, p. 59.

6, 7, 8. Thrace: *Thrakiká*, xvi. 117; *Arkheíon Thrakikoú Laogr.* viii. 185; *Laographía*, v. 452.

9. Epeiros: Hahn, i. 85, No. 5.

NO. 7. THE CHILD FROM THE SEA[2]

There was a man who fished with a casting-net and by this craft he made a living for his family. In the month of January when there are many notable days of festival people gave him many orders for fish, but just at that time he failed to catch even a single fish. One morning he rose up and took his net and went to a fresh place to fish, and here he came upon a beautiful big fish which the water had not floated off, and he set himself to catch it. The fish told him neither to touch him nor to injure him, but he should pick off two of his scales: one of them he

[1] For this common episode see No. 39.

[2] Unpublished text from Chios, recorded by Kanellakis.

should eat himself and one of them his wife should eat, and this would bring them a child, for it was a great grief to them that they had no child. But in return for this kindness which he would do him, the fish asked of him a favour in return, that he should push him farther out so that the water could float him off, for the fish said he was the Lady from the Sea. So the fisherman, grateful for the child which the fish said he should have, pushed it out into the deep water, and when the fish saw that the water was floating it off then it told the fisherman that the child whom he should have he must when he was eighteen years old bring to the Lady from the Sea.

The fisherman with delight took the two scales and went to his house and told his wife that they would have a child; he reckoned that after eighteen years who knew who would be alive and who would be dead.

By the mercy of God his wife became with child, and after the nine months she bore a son as the fish had said: the child was beautiful like gold seven times refined. Next day the man went down to the sea fishing and when he got there, before he could say that a child had been born, from a long way off the Lady from the Sea gave him the news. And from the day when the child was born the man became the first of fishermen, for the fish in shoals used to swim into his nets, and in a little while he became a man of great wealth.

When the boy grew big he was sent to school to learn letters, and his father used to pass on the finest fish to the schoolmaster to make him favour the boy. The master used to take him on his knees and teach him because he was the best of his pupils, and by the time he was twelve he was so forward that in learning he outwent the master. Well, his parents and all his own people and strangers too were proud of him, but when he was seventeen his parents began to consider that after a year they would lose him. And when he was eighteen as the fisherman was out fishing, the Lady from the Sea said to him: 'You must bring me our boy;' and this she said once and once again. But when she saw that the fisherman would not bring the boy, she lifted up her wave and smote the fisherman, nor would she let him have any fish, and the man went off weeping. When he came to his house he told his wife of his grief, and they were both of them crying because of the boy. And when the boy saw strangers taking delight in him and yet his parents full of grief, he asked them one day what was the matter and why they were all the day weeping. So when he asked them this, and again and again, they were forced to tell him what was happening. And when they had told him the story, he said to them that since the Lady from the Sea was asking for him, he must go to her, and if they would not let him go, then he would go of himself, because he no longer belonged to them.

Then his father took the boy and his net too and went to the Lady from the Sea; and when she saw them from a long way off she cried out to the boy: 'Welcome to you, my boy,' and the boy said to her: 'Welcome to you, my mother, the Lady from the Sea.' Then the Lady from the Sea told the fisherman that he must cast his net and take all the fish caught in it and then go away: and thus it was done. When the fisherman had gone the boy cried out: 'Mother.' And the Lady from the Sea said to him: 'Come now into the sea, my boy, for me to see you and to talk to you.' The boy could not make up his mind to obey the mother's word, and at last she asked him if he wanted her to make him a road by which to go into the sea. Then the sea divided into two, and there was a great wave on one side and another on the other, and these two waves were like mountains. But the boy was afraid to go in. Then as he walked along the margin of the sea he told her that he would go away. When he said this she cursed him: he could go if he chose, but never should he be able to cross lake or river, and if he were by the sea it would swallow him up.

As he was on his way he came upon a lion, an eagle and an ant; before them they had a carcase and they could not agree how to divide it. When they saw the boy the three said to him:

'Welcome, my lad, come hither
  and help us as you can;
Divide this meat between us,
  Faithfully like a man.'

The youth started and divided it into three; one part was the bones, one was the meat, and the third part was the entrails of the beast: the bones he gave to the lion, the flesh to the eagle, and the entrails to the ant, and this division pleased all three parties, and they were well satisfied.

Then the young man went on about his business, and when he was a long way off the three called to him and he turned back. They told him that he should have a gift from each one of them. From the lion it was to speak the word and become a lion, to go to war and fight, to conquer his foes and to scatter them without suffering any harm. The eagle told him to speak the word and become an eagle, and so fly off and go where he pleased. The ant too told him he could become an ant, very small indeed, and so when any enemy caught him he could slip out of his hands and creep into any place he chose. When he had heard all this, he started again in his way. Then when he had gone a long way he wanted to see and to make sure if all these good wishes they had given him were really true. So he went up on a high rock and said he would become an eagle and fly right to some city. And he had hardly said the word when he reached the city and became again as he was before. He went into a tavern, and when he had exchanged greetings, he observed that all the lads and all the young men had their noses cut off, and it was only the old men whose noses were not cut. Then he asked the reason but with great modesty and discretion, because he was afraid that this question might not be well received. The men told him that they did not want to tell him the reason for fear he might have his own nose cut off. But when he insisted and told them that this fear did not trouble him, at this they told him the story, saying that the king had a beautiful daughter and that she had proposed a test: whoever can go and fetch milk from her father's sheepfold and the milk be as warm as when the shepherd draws it from the udder, that man she will accept as her husband. The sheepfold they said was five hours from the city. And if he fails to bring the milk warm then his nose must be cut off.

When the youth heard all that they had to tell him, he went and visited the king and told him that he too wanted to undertake the wager which all the men with their noses cut off had undertaken. And when he saw him a youth so beautifully made, the king was sorry for him and told him not to do this because he too would lose his nose. But the youth said to him that since all the young men were in this plight, he too was ready to be the same. So he undertook the test and they gave him one of the king's milk cans. And when he had taken it in his hands and gone out of the palace, he spoke the word and turned into an eagle. At once he found himself by the king's sheep-fold, and when the shepherds had milked for him and he had taken the can in his hand, he changed into an eagle and before you could say Amen he was back at the stairs of the palace. He went and gave the milk to the king and it was still warm. And when the king saw that it was warm, he gave orders and the youth was detained, and he sent word to the shepherd to come to the palace. Then the king showed him the youth and asked if he recognized him. The shepherd said that this was the youth who had come to him on that very day and taken the milk. Then the king, who could do no otherwise because the king's word counts double, gave his daughter to this man who had won the test, and there was a wedding with gleeful rejoicings and all the fairest diversions.

Among the men with their noses cut off there were three king's sons, and when they saw that the test had been won by a stranger, they went away with sorrow in their hearts; each of them went to his father's kingdom. And when their fathers saw them, they were angry that their sons had been sent back to them thus with their noses cut off, and they sent word to the king that they would make war upon him. So one of them sent his ships suddenly to go to the city where the men with their noses cut off were. And when the king saw them he fell into great sorrow and care, and his son-in-law, seeing him sorrowful and heavy, asked him what was the matter. And he told him what was afoot, and his son-in-law pressed him to accept this challenge of war.

When the war began, this son-in-law turned into a lion and went in among the foe: he smote this side and he smote that side; he destroyed and conquered the enemy and as many as were not killed fled away as best they could. The same befell the second king and he too was overcome, but the third king had a great army and he had also a strong champion. Now since both the kings thus had champions, they made an agreement in writing that the armies should not fight but only the two champions, and whichever of the two should be overcome, his king should be led away as a slave to the other. And thus the two champions came to grips, and the one who had become a lion was the victor and killed the other and took the king as his slave. But he had had a hard battle, because his opponent was strong and had given him strokes both with sword and with lance, and so the soldiers came to help him wash in the sea. Then the Lady from the Sea found her chance to carry out her curse, and at once she engulfed him in the water and he was gone.

The soldiers were grieved at heart; hardly and with great fear did they tell this to the king and to the man's wife. She who knew him so well, for he had revealed to her all the conditions of his life, was sorely grieved and almost went out of her mind. She told her father to make her in the midst of the sea a palace of crystal with a terrace; also three golden apples. No long time passed before all was ready. In the evening she went and stayed in the palace and in the morning she went out on the terrace tossing one of the apples in her hands. When the Lady from the Sea saw her, she asked her what she was doing there: 'Have you come by chance to take my son?' 'Have you a son? If you have, lift him up breast high from the water that I may see him and I will throw you this golden apple.' The Lady from the Sea lifted him up out of the water to the breast, and when the princess saw him she threw the apple. And when the Lady from the Sea took it, she gave it to her eldest daughter. Then the other two were jealous and began to cry because they also wanted an apple.

Next morning she again came out on the terrace and walked there, and when the Lady from the Sea saw her she said: 'Perhaps you have come to take my son?' 'As you let me see him yesterday, so let him be seen by me today. If you are willing for me to see him, raise him from the water as far as the knees, and I will throw you this apple also.' And the Lady from the Sea took the second apple and gave it to her second daughter and so she was quieted. But the youngest was still crying; she too wanted an apple.

Then on the third morning the princess went out on the terrace and played and sported with the third apple. And when the Lady from the Sea saw her she said: 'Have you come to take my son away from me?' 'You granted me to see him yesterday and the day before; in the same way I would have him today. If you want me to give you the apple, raise him right up in your arms and bring him out of the water that I may see him, and at once I will throw you the apple.' Then the Lady from the Sea lifted him high up in her arms. And when she had brought him clean out of the water, he said the word and turned into an eagle and flew out of her hands and off to the palace. Scarcely had the princess come out on the dry land when the Lady from the Sea in raging stormy anger with a crash and a smash destroyed the palace of crystal and broke it to pieces.

And when the princess had come to the palace, the king held high festival, great rejoicings and delightful diversions, and he made a proclamation in his kingdom that he appointed his son-in-law his successor, for indeed it was fitting that he should wear a crown.

8

The Boy and the Box

THERE are many stories in the folklore of Greece, and indeed of most countries, in which talismans play a part, but this story is one entirely of the doings of the hero with a talismanic object.

The Boy and the Box, of which a Pontic version is here translated, is a variant of No. 39 in *Forty-five Stories*, where it is fully annotated. The story seems specifically Greek: the Turkish and Russian variants cited in *Forty-five Stories* are by no means close; in Greece there are these five real variants cited below. Two points may be noted: the talisman is either a lamp or a chandelier or is made to work by lighting a candle; and, what is not at all usual, the talisman will do its proper work only in the hands of its rightful owner: in anyone else's hands it is dangerous and destructive. The notes in *Forty-five Stories* add other details.

The references are:

1. PONTOS: in *Arkheíon Pontou,* vii. 89, translated here.
2, 3. ASTYPÁLAIA: Pio, p. 121, which is Geldart, p. 135; also Dieterich, p. 504.
4. SAMOS: Stamatiádis, *Samiaká,* v. 556.
5. CRETE: Kretschmer, *Neugr. Märchen,* No. 34.

Another talisman story is of sufficient interest for an outline of it to be given. It is of the doings of the hero with a series of talismans, of which one, the most serviceable of all, may be called *the Key Talisman*, an expression happily chosen by Stith Thompson which may be taken as the title of the story. I find it in Cyprus and in 1914 I wrote it down at Soúrmena in Pontos.[1] It begins with a gay youth, who can do nothing but just fiddle a little, going out to seek his fortune. He stole from an ogre a magic cup which at command brought food and drink of all sorts. The youth let a dervish have the cup in exchange for a knife, which at its owner's orders would strike and kill anyone. Using the knife talisman the youth killed the dervish and recovered the cup. He met a second dervish and gave him the cup in exchange

[1] Cyprus; Sakellarios, ii. 340 = Garnett, p. 130; Pontos in *Arkheíon Pontou,* iii. 89.

for shoes of invisibility. By means of the knife he killed the dervish and again got his cup, plus the shoes. From a third dervish in the same way he got a magic pipe which would restore the dead to life, again killing the dervish by means of the knife. The king made the youth drunk and took away his cup. Then by means of the knife the hero killed all the king's men, and by bringing them back to life by the music of the pipe so much delighted the king that he restored the cup and gave him his daughter in marriage. Thus by the aid of the key talisman, the knife, the youth had the cup and the shoes and the pipe, and in addition the princess.

The Key Talisman has been discussed by Stith Thompson in his book *The Folktale*, p. 72. He marks it as Type 563, and finds such stories spread over all Europe and Asia. It has been pointed out by Halliday that in these stories talismans may be acquired legitimately or by fraud: the fraudulent methods, of which in *The Key Talisman* the first is used, he and Penzer regard as of oriental origin.[1]

NO. 8. THE BOY AND THE BOX[2]

In the earliest times there was a king and he never had a son. One day as he was walking about sorrowfully a blackamoor came up and said to him: 'Why are you so full of care?' And the king told him why it was. Then the blackamoor said to him: 'If I bring it about that you have a son, will you let me have him?' The king said: 'Yes. I will.' Yet in his heart he was saying: 'He shall be the loser and not the boy.' After nine months the queen gave birth to a son, and when he was twelve years old the blackamoor came and asked for him. The king refused. At once the blackamoor gave the boy a buffet and immediately both he and the boy turned intc birds and flew off. Afterwards the blackamoor became a man again and he turned the boy back into a man, and they went their way. They went on and on until they came down into a great cave. Now by the power of God the door of this cave used to open once a year, and it stood open, but for half an hour only. At that time the hour was ripe and the door was to open. Then the blackamoor said to the boy: 'Go down in there; whatever treasures there are in the world, all of them are to be found there. But at them you must not look at all. Only inside a room there is a box; take that box

[1] *Journal of the Gypsy Lore Society*, N.S. iii. 154.

[2] Text from Argyrópolis in Pontos in *Arkheion Pontou*, vii. 89.

only and come back to me. Inside the cave there are also many fairies and you must not be beguiled into looking at them, because after half an hour the cave will close and you will have to stay inside it for a year.' The boy went into the cave and without looking at anything entered the room and took the box. When he was about to go out of the door of the cave, he saw inside the door three persons, fairies, two were dancing, and the other was singing very sweetly: it was only while the door of the cave stood open that the fairies played. The boy's eyes were fixed upon them and he forgot about the blackamoor. After a little while the door shut and the boy was left inside; the fairies were no longer to be seen; they had disappeared. As soon as the door shut the blackamoor rose up and went away. The boy ran here and there, up and down, and a long way off he saw a hole. He struck a match and lit the two tapers he had and behold, before him there were forty fairies: some were singing and some were dancing, and the boy gazed at the strange sight. Then he blew out the tapers and the fairies at once went out of sight.

The boy came to a place of men and there he stayed with a goldsmith. When he asked them the fairies used to bring him gold coins and these the boy used to give to the goldsmith. The goldsmith used to question the boy: 'How did you get these coins?' The boy would answer: 'What harm can this do you? Just eat the bread coming your way.' When there was no one by, the boy used to light the tapers and the forty fairies came again and danced and sang, and he would gaze at the strange sight. The king's daughter saw this, and one day when the boy was asleep the box fell from his pocket. She came up very quietly and took the box and went to their house. She said to her father: 'Stay; I will do something wonderful. Send for all the people to come here to look at the fairies.' The king called for all the people, and men gathered together, a happy crowd. The girl lit the tapers and out came forty persons, all of them blackamoors, and in their hands they held each of them a club, and then whack, whack, whack, on the men's heads, and many a man's soul departed from him. By chance a man in his stress puffed and blowed, and at his blowing the candles straight went out and the blackamoors disappeared.

The king said to his daughter: 'Oh, my daughter, what was all this?' And he sent out a crier: 'Whosever the box is let him come and take it.' The boy looked in his pocket; the box was not there. He ran up and said: 'It belongs to me.' Then the king said: 'If it be yours, make the forty fairies come out of it and then I will believe you.' The boy said: 'Tell everyone to come here.' The men were unwilling to come, but not to make the king's order of no effect, they came with fear in their hearts. The boy lit the tapers. Out came the forty fairies and danced and sang and the men were delighted, saying: 'We did eat stick but that is now all over.' The boy said to the fairies: 'Go and bring me my master's kerchief.'[1] The fairies went and were slow to come back. Afterwards they came and the boy said to them: 'Why have you been so long? Where is the kerchief?' The fairies said: 'And where is your master's house?' He said: 'The house over there,' pointing to the goldsmith's house. Then they said: 'O you mad fellow, your master is not here,' and they told him that the blackamoor had carried off his master the goldsmith. 'And now,' said they, 'your father and your mother from weeping for you have gone blind.' Then they gave him a fine horse, and he mounted and rode to the house where they were. His father and his mother were weeping and could see nothing. The fairies brought him a leaf and when he had rubbed it on their eyes at once they opened their eyes and looked upon the world. They embraced one another with delight. The king rose and got for his son a princess as his wife. They made a marriage for forty days and forty nights, and lived happily, and when they wished it the boy lit the tapers and the fairies came and danced.

[1] The point of this is obscure.

9

The grateful Animals and the Talisman

THE essential outline of this story is that a boy through mercifully saving animals from death first wins a talisman, and when he has lost it recovers it again. When he marries his wife takes a lover, and to please him steals the talisman. Then the grateful cat, and under her guidance the dog, win the talisman back for him, the cat inducing a mouse to tickle the lover's nose so that he sneezes and the talisman drops from his mouth where he is keeping it under his tongue. The dog swims off from the castle with the cat on his back, she carrying the talisman. Then by the dog's clumsiness the talisman is dropped into the sea but recovered, generally by being found by the cat inside a fish. Halliday has collected references which range from India to the Balkans, and he regards as proved Cosquin's view that the story originated in India.[1] This is accepted by Stith Thompson, who points out that the story is much commoner in eastern than in western Europe, though 'it is told, at least sometimes, in almost every country or province on the Continent'. He further remarks on its spread to the Farther East and to America, by French and Portuguese agency.[2] It is also found in North Africa. The most recently published version I find is from the Serbo-Bosnian gipsies.[3]

For translation I have chosen a version from Mitylene, though several other Greek versions have interesting details. In particular the variant from Astypálaia tells us how the mice live on an island of their own and are terrorized by the cat and forced to come to her help in recovering the talisman.

The references are:

1, 2. PONTOS: from Soúrmena in *Arkheíon Pontou*, iii. 91; and from Ordoú in Akoglou, *Laographiká Kotyóron*, p. 401.

3, 4. CAPPADOCIA: from Fertěk in *M.G. in A.M.*, p. 329; and from Potámia, ibid., p. 457.

5. CYPRUS: unpublished version.

[1] *M.G. in A.M.*, p. 264, with references for Indian origin to Cosquin, *Contes de Lorraine*, p. xi, and Jacobs, *Indian Fairy Tales*, i. 244. Also BP. ii. 451. In *Forty-five Stories*, No. 4, with further references: to Russian, Guterman, p. 31; to Turkish, *Istanbul Masallari*, p. 14; to the *Arabian Nights*, Burton's Lib. ed., xi. 113.

[2] Stith Thompson, *The Folktale*, p. 70.

[3] *Journal of the Gypsy Lore Society*, 3rd series, xxiv. 74.

6. Astypálaia: *Forty-five Stories*, p. 75.
7, 8, 9. Mitylene: Carnoy–Nicolaïdes, p. 57, but in part only; *Folklore*, xx. 201; Kretschmer, *Heut. lesbische Dialekt*, p. 524, translated below.
10. Crete: *Z.A.* ii (1896), p. 54.
11. Euboia: Hahn, ii. 202, No. 9.
12. Aigion: Megas, p. 76.
13. Epeiros: Hahn, i. 109, No. 9, which is Pio, p. 26, and in Geldart, p. 42.
14. Thrace: *Thrakiká*, xvii. 139.
15. Zákynthos: *Laographía*, x. 408.

NO. 9. THE GRATEFUL ANIMALS AND THE TALISMAN[1]

Once there was a woman, and she had an only child, a little boy. This boy never came out of the house at all, but sat on the dusty floor close by the ashes: so his mother called him Cinderello.

One day his mother said to him: 'Come, my little lad, go out for a while.' Cinderello said: 'Give me a farthing and I will.' His mother gave him a farthing; he took it and out he went. As soon as he came out into the road he came upon some children, who were about to kill a puppy. He said to them: 'Come, children, give the puppy to me and I will give you a farthing.' He gave them the farthing and took the puppy and brought it home.

Another day his mother again said: 'Come, my little lad, go out for a while.' Cinderello said: 'Give me another farthing and I will.' She gave him a farthing; Cinderello took it and went out. As he was passing along the road again he met some children about to kill a kitten. He said: 'Give the kitten to me and I will give you this farthing.' He took the kitten and paid over the farthing. The kitten he took home and there again he sat down in the dust.

One day his mother again said to him: 'Come, my little lad; you go out for a while.' Cinderello said: 'Give me another farthing and I will go.' His mother gave him a farthing and Cinderello went out. As he was walking he again met some children about to kill a snake. He said: 'Give the snake to me and I will give you this farthing.' He gave them the farthing and took the snake also to his house.

[1] Text from Mitylene in Kretschmer, *Heut. lesbische Dialekt*, p. 524 with the title *Cinderello*.

So he reared the three animals, and when they had grown big, one day the snake said to him: 'Come now, take me to my own country.' Cinderello rose up and, the snake in front and he following, they went off. On the way the snake turned round and said: 'I have a father, and he is the king of the snakes. Now when we go there, all the snakes will throw themselves upon you, but you must not be afraid. I will call out to them and they will leave you alone. Then when you go into my father's house, he will want to give you many gifts because you rescued me, but you must refuse to accept any of them and ask only for the ring which he has underneath his tongue.'

They went there, and the little snake gave one hiss and snakes started to come to them, more and more: the whole place was full of snakes. Among them was a big snake, as long as that: this was their king. When the snakes saw Cinderello they rushed upon him to devour him. He cried out to the little snake and they fell back. Then the snake went to his father and said: 'This boy, my father, saved me from death; by now I would have been all dead and forgotten. So today I have brought him here for you to give him whatever he may ask of you.' The great snake took him off to his house and said: 'What favour do you want from me for saving my little son?' Cinderello said: 'I do not want anything, except this: I would like the ring which you keep underneath your tongue.' Then said the king of the snakes: 'This is a great thing you ask, yet to please my son you may have it.' Cinderello took the ring and went off.

On the way he was thirsty. 'The snake,' said he, 'offered me all those things and I took nothing except only this ring, and now here I am dying of thirst.' In anger he dashed the ring down and ran on. As he did this there jumped out from the ring a black man, who said: 'What are your commands, master?' 'What commands?' said the boy. 'I want something to eat.' Quickly the black man set a table and served food and wine; all you could wish, my dear fellow. When Cinderello had done eating, the black man cleared everything away and went back again into the ring. The boy took up the ring and went to his village. He set his mother to go and make a proposal for his marriage to the king's daughter.

The king said: 'If in a certain place your son can satisfy with food all the men in my realm, then I will accept him as my daughter's husband. I grant him a term of forty days. If within the forty days he does not do this, I will have his head.' The mother went and told him. Now the days were passing by; Cinderello sat at ease paying no heed to the matter. At the end of the thirty-ninth day the king sent him a notice that the days were coming to an end and he must not pretend that he had forgotten about it. The boy sent a message back that he knew all about it and that the king was not to be uneasy. When the forty days were up, he took the ring and went to the place where he was to provide food for the multitude. He dashed down the ring; out came the black man and said: 'What are your commands, master?' 'I want you,' said he, 'to set out food to eat, everywhere here.' The black man started and set out food everywhere; the people went and ate and there was even food left over.

Then again the king said to Cinderello's mother: 'If,' said he, 'your son can cover with gold coins a straight path all the way from your door to my door, again within a term of forty days, then I will accept him as my son-in-law.' Again when the forty days were over the boy dashed the ring down and ordered the black man quickly to make a path from their door all the way to the palace and all laid with gold coin, and this to be done before the king rose up in the morning. The black man fell to the work and before you could count three he had done it. The king rose up and opened his window: lo, his eyes were dazzled by the brightness of the path.

Once more the king sent for the boy's mother and said: 'One more thing your son must do and then I will make him my son-in-law. I want him to make a tower finer than my own. Again I grant him a term of forty days. If he cannot do this, I will have his head.' Not to make a long story of it, at the end of the forty days the boy once more dashed down the ring; the black man came out and built a tower very much finer than the king's. In the morning the king opened his window and saw it: it was all made of gold. Then the king went and took Cinderello and married him to his daughter. In the tower he set a blackamoor to guard them.

In order not to lose the ring Cinderello kept it always in his mouth. Then the blackamoor who was their guard and Cinderello's wife made a pact between them. The blackamoor said to the wife; 'Can you,' said he, 'take the ring from his mouth and bring it here to me?' The wife went off and when her husband was asleep contrived to get the ring out of his mouth. Then she gave it to the guard. As soon as he had it in his hand he dashed it down, and the black man came out of it and said: 'What are your commands, master?' 'When he is asleep,' said the blackamoor, 'you must take this man up, bed and all, and put him out in the road without his being aware of it. Then you must pull down this tower and set it up in the midst of the sea and in it there must be no one but me and my wife.' The black man of the ring pulled down the tower, threw poor Cinderello out into the road and set up the tower in the midst of the sea, putting in it the blackamoor guard and Cinderello's wife. In the morning Cinderello woke up and found that he had been sleeping in the road and that he had no more with him either his wife or the ring. At once he rose up and with tears went to the king and made his complaints. Then the poor fellow went home lamenting.

Some days passed. 'This,' said Cinderello, 'I can endure no longer. I must go off and find what fate has in store for me.' He took the puppy and the little cat and went off. As he was passing by the shore of the sea, the cat saw a great wave in the midst of the sea. She said to Cinderello: 'Will you give us leave to go and see what this is showing in the sea?' Cinderello gave them leave. The dog with the cat on his back swam off over the sea and came to the tower. The cat climbed up to the roof. On that very evening the mice were celebrating a wedding. The cat made a dash at them and caught the bridegroom. He said: 'Let me go and whatever you want I will do.' 'Can you,' said the cat, 'get me the ring from out of the master's mouth?' 'I can,' said the mouse. So he went and dipped his tail into the honey and then went and rolled it about in the pepper. Then he went and stuck it into the blackamoor's nose as he lay asleep. The blackamoor sneezed; out flew the ring. The mouse carried it off to the cat, and the cat took it and went down from the roof and told the dog of her success.

Then the cat mounted on the dog's back, and he plunged in to swim; thus they would take the ring back to Cinderello. When they were nearly there, the dog said: 'Let me hold the ring too; I want to see it.' The cat would not and the dog threatened to let her fall into the sea. The cat was frightened and let him have it. How did they do then? Well, they let the ring slip and it fell into the sea. When they came to land, Cinderello asked them how they had fared. The cat said: 'We found the ring but by the fault of the dog here we lost it in the sea.' The dog said not a word. Again Cinderello began to weep. As he was weeping the cat saw men rowing a fishing boat that way: cats you know are fond of fish. She went near the fishermen and cried out *Miaou, miaou*. The fishermen were sorry for her and threw her some fish. As she was eating the fish, inside one of them she found the ring. With delight she took it and brought it to Cinderello.

Cinderello took the ring and went to the king and said: 'Do you want,' said he, 'me to bring you the blackamoor and your daughter in the tower and they be close by here?' 'Well, if you can,' said the king, 'will you not stay here and do this?' Then Cinderello dashed down the ring and the black man came out and said: 'What are you commands, master?' 'The tower,' he said, 'which is now in the sea you must take and bring it here just as it is and set it where it was at first.' The black man of the ring went off and took the tower and set it down outside the palace in the same place as it had been before. The king took his sword and went up to the tower, and slew his daughter and the blackamoor. The king had another daughter and afterwards he gave her to Cinderello as his wife. In the tower Cinderello kept the cat and the puppy and they all lived together happily.

10

Born of his Mother's Tears

IN many of these stories we hear of the magical conception of children by the gift, generally of an apple of fertility, to a childless wife. The birth of the hero of this story, Elias or John, is of a different kind. The child comes not as a gift to a childless couple, but to a mother left desolate; from her tears of sorrow a son is born to set things right and to bring her dead children to life again. Of this conception of a child from drinking tears I can find nothing further. Stith Thompson, in his *Motif-Index* Type 541. 1, gives only a Hindu reference, Keith 141, and this I cannot follow up, and another to stories of the North American Indians. In the note to their Chian version Argenti and Rose can only say that they cannot recall another instance in which conception is due to drinking tears. In his *Primitive Paternity* Hartland says (i. 13) that almost any part of a human body may be possessed of fructifying powers. but he makes no mention of tears. In Mrs. Hasluck's unpublished collection of Albanian stories I find a story which begins in this way. A mother loses her only son; she drinks her tears and from them conceives another son who becomes a great hero, but the rest of the story has no resemblance to the present stories, and at this I must leave the question with the suggestion that sorrow bringing about, or at least preceding, final consolation is very much in the symbolic tone of many of these Greek stories. In the mattins of Holy Saturday a verse is sung in which Christ addresses the Virgin: *Lament not for me, O Mother, seeing in the tomb the Son whom thou didst conceive.* Although naturally the church verse goes on with *ἄνευ σπορᾶς*, *as a Virgin*, it is the same chord of feeling that is touched: the destruction, the sorrow, and by the son born the final restoration.

In its simplest form the story appears in the version from Zákynthos translated below. The variants from Chios and Skyros are much the same. Those from Epeiros and from the Saracatsans, the nomad Greeks who roam over the mountains of Epeiros, begin with the hero's birth from his mother's tears and then continue like the latter part of the Strigla story, No. 27: the mother wickedly allies herself with some monster and plots the destruction of her son, who escapes only with the help of his lady love. The other version from Zákynthos develops into No. 26, *The Underworld Adventure*, although the hero is carried back into the Upper World by a fox and not by the usual eagle. With a similar lack of grasp of the lines of the story the teller has introduced several other odd scraps: the bay-tree girl who poisoned the food belongs to No. 25, *The Girl in the Bay-tree*, who in several versions salts the prince's food much too heavily; the questions asked the hero by the greedy youths who neglected to feed their animals belong rather to No. 79, *The Search for Luck*; and the thirsty girl demanding water is a clear touch from No. 1, *The three Oranges*. That the hero makes good his claim to have killed the monster by showing that he has its tongues is another common episode.

That voracious eating and savage manners are a mark of the vigorous hero is an idea found elsewhere. It is in a version of *The treacherous Brothers* from Kos, for which see *Forty-five Stories*, p. 180; in Lorimer's *Persian Tales*, p. 110, it marks the heroic vigour of Nim Tauck, the Half-Boy. In the same way Herakles showed what a fine fellow he was.

The references are:

1. CHIOS: Argenti and Rose, *Folklore of Chios*, p. 546. The hero is called Δακρυολιᾶς, *Elias of the Tears*, and this, surely by a blunder, appears also as *Ὁ Δράκος Ἐλιᾶς Elias the Drak, the Ogre.*
2. SKYROS, Pérdika, ii. 233; with the title *Johnnie, the Son of the desolate Woman.*
3. FROM THE SARACATSANS: Höeg, *Les Saracatsans*, ii. 16.
4, 5. ZÁKYNTHOS: *Laographía*, x. 394 and 398, the latter translated.

NO. 10. BORN OF HIS MOTHER'S TEARS[1]

There were twelve brothers and with them one sister; they all lived with their mother. Every morning very early the boys used to go and work in the fields. Their sister would bring them their dinner of cooked food from the house, and that she might not miss the path, when they went off in the morning they used to strew chaff on it. In his den the ogre was on the watch: 'Ah,' said he, 'I shall have some tender meat today.' Then he went and cleared away the chaff and laid it down on the path which led to his den. The poor unfortunate girl instead of finding her way to her brothers, fell into the snare. The ogre brought her into his den and heaped attentions on her: she was a pretty girl and he took her for his wife. Her poor brothers wept and lamented and they resolved that the eldest should go and find her and see what had happened to her. So he ordered an iron mace to be made for him and went straight forward on the way.

[1] Text from Zákynthos in *Laographía*, x. 398.

The ogre was sitting by the window, his wife cleansing his head. Scarcely had the ogre been aware of him than he asked: 'Is he eating our oranges, peel and all?' 'No,' said she. 'Then he is a lost man,' said the ogre, 'and I shall devour him.' And as soon as he came near the ogre did swallow him up, at a gulp. Not to make a long story of it, the twelve brothers all had the same fate: they came and the ogre made just one mouthful of each one of them.

All this time their poor mother was lamenting that she was left desolate: 'What a grief I have suffered!' said she. And so many were her tears that with them she filled a jug. The jug was full and in her despair the poor woman said: 'I shall drink of this and die; it is my poison; this is more than I can endure; it will be my death.' But what befell whoever could have expected? From her tears she became with child, and she gave birth to a boy, a strong boy, a real monster of a boy. His birth was from her tears and she called him Elias of the Tears.

Elias grew bigger and bigger and became a man fully grown. Talk came to his ears and he heard about his brothers. One, two, and the boy ordered an iron mace to be made thousands of times bigger than those of the others, and then, one, two, off he went to the ogre's place. There, I don't know how, he stole from the ogre's stable his finest horse. The ogre was sitting there and his wife was cleansing his head. 'Oh, wife,' said he, 'some one very strong is coming here; he is eating up our oranges, peel and all.' 'Never mind the oranges,' said she, 'he has stolen your horse. Now he is tearing up the stones and rooting up the orange-trees wherever he goes, and here you are doing no more than asking if he is eating our oranges, and is it with peel and all.' 'This is a bad business, wife.' Thus the ogre was overcome by Elias of the Tears.

Elias showed himself to his sister. 'Be not troubled, lady,' said he, 'and I will raise up all our twelve brothers.' From the top of the cupboard he took the Water of Life which the ogre kept to sprinkle himself with from time to time that he should never die. Then he went to the cellar where the twelve boys lay all stretched out dead. He cast on their heads a little of the Water of Life and they all began to come alive again. Then Elias of the Tears took them all and brought them to their house and from thenceforth they all lived happily.

11

Roses and Pearls

Cf. AARNE–THOMPSON TYPE 403

A GIRL was granted by the Fates that when she spoke roses should drop from her lips; when she wept pearls should fall from her eyes. In the versions from Crete and Zákynthos she cleanses the head of Christ and with so good a grace that she is granted this favour: her wicked stepsister does the same but so grudgingly that she is given no reward. The king asked in marriage the girl with this wonderful gift, but on the way her wicked stepmother, or her aunt, gave her nothing to eat but salt cake, and when the girl asked for water would give it her only on condition that she took out first one eye and then the other. Then she put her own daughter in the place of the blinded girl. But the girl of the roses and pearls always has in the background a mysterious old man to come to her help; he, with the very roses that had fallen from her lips, bought back her eyes and set them again in her head; as she had thus recovered her beauty the prince at the end of the story married her. The version translated mentions the roses only, not the pearls.

For this story BP. (ii. 278) give abundant references under Grimm, No. 89, *Die Gänsemagd*, and it appears to be spread all over Italy and the Balkans and Slav countries. To their Turkish reference, Kunos, *Stambul*, p. 29, we can now add *Istanbul Masallari*, p. 17, and *The Tale of a God* in Dora Yates's *Gypsy Tales*, p. 63. That in the two Turkish versions as well as in the Greek versions from Mitylene and Epeiros the heroine is the daughter of a bathman, speaks for the unity of the story. It is significant that the old man protector buys back the girl's eyes with the money gained by the sale of her roses. The grace of roses, hers either by fate or because of her kindly services to Christ, her special virtue that is, is in this way made the instrument by which she is delivered from her affliction, brought about not by any fault of her own but by the cruelty of her stepmother.

There is a story like this but without the salt cake and the roses and pearls from Pontos;[1] we have the daughter and the stepdaughter who is helped by the old man whose head she has cleansed with good will and not grudgingly; the old man gets her out of the troubles to

[1] *Arkheíon Pontou*, xiv. 196. From Santa.

which she is exposed by her wicked stepmother. It is the Roses and Pearls story with most of the savour taken from it.

The roses and pearls idea has spread into the Cretan version of No. 2, *The little Boy and his elder Sister*, and into No. 83, *The Mercy of God*. This same idea has, in Pontos, developed into a story of a woman who has an ugly and wicked daughter and a good and pretty stepdaughter.[1] The stepdaughter was given the usual salty cake to eat and was tormented with thirst, but rather than drink herself she gave the water to a succession of three old men, who blessed her and gave her the gift of roses and pearls from her lips and eyes. Her wicked sister unkindly refused water to the same three old men and was cursed by them: from her eyes should come snakes and from her mouth frogs. The mother got a husband for her wicked daughter, but he escaped and married the good girl with her gift of roses and pearls.

The references are:

1. PONTOS: from Ordoú in *Laographiká Kotyóron*, by Xenophon Akoglou, p. 387.
2. MITYLENE: Carnoy and Nicolaïdes, p. 107.
3. KÁRPATHOS: Mikh.-Nouáros, *L. S. Karpáthou*, i. 325.
4, 5. THRACE: *Thrakiká*, xvi. 177, translated; and ibid. xvii. 148, a poor version.
6. CRETE: *Z.A.* ii (1896), p. 58.
7, 8. EPEIROS: Hahn, i. 193, No. 28, which is in Kretschmer's *Neugr. Märchen*, p. 297; and a poor version in Hahn, ii. 81, No. 82.

NO. 11. ROSES AND PEARLS[2]

Once upon a time there was a stepmother; she had one daughter of her own, ugly and wicked; also she had a stepdaughter who was good and pretty. For her stepdaughter she had no love; she used to send her off to keep the sheep from morning to night, and when she came back in the evening, she set her to do all the work of the house. One day she sent her to wash clothes at the bridge. An old man was watching her and said: 'Why don't you go into the water, my girl, now that it is all water of gold?' The girl undressed and went in. She came out more beautiful than before, and when she laughed from her mouth there were roses falling. When she came home and her stepmother saw her fairer

[1] *Pontiakí Estía*, ii, Part 15, p. 857, from Oinoi.

[2] Text from Thrace in *Thrakiká*, xvi. 177, under the title, *The beautiful Stepdaughter*.

than ever and the roses falling from her mouth as she laughed, she turned sullen and questioned her: 'What have you been doing that you are so fair, and roses falling from your mouth?' 'When I was doing the washing an old man appeared; and he said to me: "Why don't you go into the water, my girl, now that it is all water of gold?" Then I went in.'

Next day the woman sent her own daughter to the bridge; the old man watching for her said: 'Why don't you go into the water, my girl, now that it is all water of gold?' The water was all mud, and the girl came out more sickeningly ugly than before. When her mother saw her, she turned still more sullen and used her stepdaughter even worse. The stepdaughter waited for God to bring the dawn of day when she could go out with the sheep and be free from the woman.

The prince heard that in his realm there was a beautiful girl; when she laughed roses fell from her mouth. He sent messengers to ask for her as his wife. The stepmother put her own daughter into the carriage, as well as her stepdaughter, and they went off to the city where the prince lived. On the way the stepdaughter grew thirsty and wanted water. 'Let me take your eye out and I will let you have some,' said her stepmother. So she took out the girl's eye and then gave her some water. The way was long; the stepdaughter again was thirsty and asked for water. The stepmother said: 'I will give you water, but I must have your other eye.' When she had pulled it out, she threw the girl down underneath the carriage. The prince came out to receive the bride. He was astonished when he saw that she was ugly and asked the stepmother: 'Is this the fair girl from whose mouth as she laughed the roses fell?' The mother answered: 'It is because she is tired that she looks like this.'

Now let us leave the prince and come to the stepdaughter, lying there crying where her stepmother had thrown her out of the carriage. An old man passing by asked her: 'What is the matter with you, my girl, that you are crying?' 'How can I not cry?' and so she told him all her troubles. 'Don't cry, my girl; for you too God has good in store. I will take you and you shall be as my own daughter.' He took her by the hand and led her to his cottage. In time the girl forgot her bitter grief and when she laughed the roses fell and when she washed herself, the bowl was all full of gold coins.

The prince's wife had a desire for roses and they were to be had nowhere. The old man heard of this and he collected his daughter's roses, and walked below the palace, crying: 'Roses, roses! Fine and dewy!' The servants came down to buy. The old man said if they would give him an eye he would sell to them. They went up again with this message; then they gave the old man the eye and took the roses. Full of joy the old man brought the girl her eye. Her delight cannot be told when she had her sight again; she laughed and the roses fell down like rain.

In a few days the old man went out again below the palace, crying: 'Roses, roses! Fine and dewy!' The serving women came came down to buy and he said: 'Roses you may have; the price is an eye.' The women went with this message and brought him down the other eye. The girl put the second eye in place; in her joy she became more beautiful than ever, and she lived happily with the old man loving him as if he had been her father.

From one mouth to another it came to the prince's ears that there was a girl whose beauty had no match; when she laughed, roses fell from her mouth, and when she washed herself the bowl was full of gold coins. 'This would be the girl whom I would have taken to be my wife.' He gave orders that all the girls in the town should come and tell him a story. The old man brought the girl to the palace, and the prince sent for his wife and his mother-in-law that they too should hear the story.

So then the girl began: 'Once upon a time there was a stepmother and she had a daughter of her own, ugly and wicked; also a stepdaughter. The stepdaughter was pretty and the mother had no love for her; she used to send her out to keep the sheep from morning to night, and in the evening she used to set her to do all the work of the house. One day she sent her out to wash clothes at the bridge. An old man watched her and said: "Why don't you go into the water, my girl, now that it is all water of gold?" The girl undressed and went in. She came out more beautiful than before, and when she laughed from her mouth roses were falling. When she came home and her stepmother saw her fairer than ever and the roses falling from her mouth as she laughed, she turned sullen and asked her what she had been doing. "When I was washing", said the stepdaughter, "an old man appeared and said to me: 'Why don't you go into the water, my girl, now that it is all water of gold?' And so I went in." Next day the stepmother sent her own daughter to the bridge. The old man watched her and said: "Why don't you go into the water, my girl, now that it is all water of gold?" The water was all muddy, and she came out more sickeningly ugly than before. When her mother saw this, she treated her stepdaughter even more despitefully. The stepdaughter waited for God to bring the dawn of day, when she could go out with the sheep and be free from the woman. Then the prince heard that in his realm there was a beautiful girl; when she laughed roses fell from her mouth. He sent messengers to ask for her in marriage. The stepmother put her own daughter into the carriage as well as her stepdaughter, and they went to the city where the prince lived. On the way the stepdaughter was thirsty and wanted water. "Let me take your eye out, and I will let you have some", said the stepmother. She took out the girl's eye and then gave her some water. The way was long; the stepdaughter again was thirsty and asked for water. The stepmother said: "I will give you water, but I must have your other eye." When she had pulled it out she threw the girl down beneath the carriage.'

The prince listened to all this thoughtfully, casting angry looks at his wife and his mother-in-law. 'As she stayed there weeping,' the girl went on, 'an old man passed by and asked her: "What is the matter with you, my girl, that you are crying?" "How could I not cry?" And she told him all her troubles. "Do not cry; for you too God has good in store. I will take you and hold you as my own daughter." The old man took her by the hand and led her to his cottage. In time the girl forgot her bitter grief, and when she laughed the roses fell, and when she washed herself the bowl was full of gold coins.

'The prince's wife had a desire for roses, and they were to be found nowhere. The old man heard of it and he collected the roses which fell from his daughter when she laughed and went below the palace and cried: "Roses, roses! Fine and dewy!" The servants came down to buy. The old man said if they will pay him with an eye, he will sell to them. Full of joy the old man took the girl her eye. Her joy cannot be told when she had her sight again; she laughed and the roses fell down like rain. In a few days the old man collected more roses; again he went out before the palace crying: "Here are roses, all fresh and dewy!"

The serving women came down to buy and he said: "You may have them; the price is an eye." The women went back with this message and so they brought him the other eye. The girl put this second eye in its place, and in her joy she became more beautiful than ever and lived happily with the old man and loved him as if he had been her father.'

Then the prince rose and embraced the girl and made her his wife. The good old man he kept in the palace, looking upon him as their father; the wicked witch of a stepmother with her daughter they ordered to be bound to two wild horses to be dragged all round the city.

Neither was I there nor are you to believe it.

12

Cupid and Psyche

THE essence of the Cupid and Psyche story may be taken to be that a girl wins the love of a mysterious husband from Fairyland who warns her that she must never reveal their marriage. The girl's jealous sisters tease her into letting out the secret, whereupon the husband disappears and is won back only by much toil and after many painful wanderings and expiations. A central type of this story is the tale of Cupid and Psyche as we have it in *The Golden Ass* of Apuleius, but in one form or another its distribution is world wide. The perennial attraction of the story is that it reflects in imagery so much of the relations of man and wife. That the husband or the bride is from Fairyland is an image of the wonder of love and the conviction in each case of its uniqueness. The loss of the mate through disobedience or by some misunderstanding or lack of sympathy reflects the quarrels of lovers and their alienation. That the lost mate can indeed be won back, but only after toil and sacrifice, presents equally a human truth. The factual and historical connexion of the story of Cupid and Psyche, even in its most ideally beautiful form, with the primitive tale and crude fancy of a human being marrying an animal does not impair its value as a myth: at some time and somewhere the creative imagination took up the old savage story and breathed into it the enduring life of the myth, of the joyous meeting, the sad parting, and the happy reunion of a pair of lovers.

The story from Mitylene here translated is clearly of this type, but the betrayal of the secret sends the husband back into his bondage with an ogress who holds him and two other youths under her enchantment, turning them into doves and apparently also into columns of stone. The wife learns that the eldest of the three has been betrayed by his mother; the second, that is her husband, by his wife; and the third by his sister. The word for column is *kolonna*, and it is a great temptation to think that there is here some confusion with *colomba*, the Italian word for a dove, and that the ogress's enchantment was simply to turn the youths to doves. But as earlier in the story the Greek word for a dove, *peristéri*, is used and it is always unsafe to be wise beyond what is written, it is better to suppose that the enchantment took now one form now another. The girl found out where her husband was and by performing the tasks set her by the ogress, who here plays the part assigned to Venus as Apuleius tells the story, won back her husband. The girl having to pick out the right column, the column which was her husband, is very like the identification parade of veiled girls and then of ducks where the hero must pick out his love in No. 6.

To this variant of the Cupid and Psyche story there is a very close parallel in *Forty-five Stories*, No. 8, *The Lily*, from Astypálaia. In this the husband is not one of three but one of twelve youths; not changed into doves but concealed in the shells of some kind of nut; the appearance of the husband as a handsome youth first on a black horse and then in a silver dress on a bay horse appears in the Astypálaia story as the riding-by of a horseman so splendid as to be taken the first time for St. George and the second time for St. Dimitrios; the inn and the tailor's shop where people are to meet is replaced by a bath-house; and the part of the old man and his boy is played in Astypálaia by an old woman. But in all essentials the stories are the same.

I find several variants which though never very close all contain elements of the Cupid and Psyche story.

They are:

1, 2. PONTOS: *Arkheíon Pontou*, iii. 99, and in Akoglou, *Laographiká Kotyóron*, p. 407.

3, 4. MITYLENE: *Folklore*, x. 501, and Kretschmer, *Heut. lesbische Dialekt*, p. 505. This is translated.

5. MÝKONOS: Roussel, *Contes de Mycono*, p. 199.

6. GREEK ISLANDS: Carnoy–Nicolaïdes, p. 127. The authors say this was told by a woman of 'Kia', which is probably Keos, *Τζιά*.

7, 8. THRACE: *Thrakiká*, xv. 362 and xvi. 156.

9. ZÁKYNTHOS: Bernhard Schmidt, *Griech. Märchen*, p. 83.

10. ALBANIAN FROM POROS: Hahn, ii. 116, No. 100.

11. ALSO ALBANIAN: in Hahn ii. 130, No. 102.

NO. 12. CUPID AND PSYCHE[1]

Once there was a woman who had no children. Opposite her house there was a palace and the woman used to go there and dandle the king's children. She would say: 'Oh, would that I had a baby were it only a crab.' This she said once and she said it again. God had mercy on her and she became with child. The time came for the birth. She bore a crab. After her forty days she began again to go to the palace dandling the king's

[1] Text from Mitylene in Kretschmer, *Heut. lesbische Dialekt*, p. 505, under the title *The Crab*.

children. The women began: 'You there who gave birth to a crab! We don't want mothers of crabs here dandling our children.' After this bitter pill the woman never again set her foot in the palace.

The crab day by day grew bigger. The woman at first kept him in her basket; then she made a little bag and put him in it. She used to go to church and leave the house with no one in it and dark, all dirty, and with the pots and pans anyhow, here and there. When she came back from church she used to find the house all swept clean, the pots washed and everything in its place. She was puzzled, saying: 'There is no end to this. I must just watch and see who is doing it all.' One day she left the house all dirty and went and hid underneath the stairs to see. The crab came out of his shell, and lo, what was before you? A youth like an angel. He started to pick up the broom. His mother came out. 'Oh, it is you, my son, and you have never told me. People are mocking and laughing at me for being the mother of a crab.' 'It is indeed I,' said he. 'Now you go to the palace and if they say anything to you, you must say: "My crab might well be the husband of your eldest daughter!" '

So the woman went to the palace. 'And how goes your crab? Near dead by now?' asked the queen. The woman said: 'Well might my crab be the husband of your eldest daughter.' The queen heard this and told the king. Again the woman went to the palace, and again they asked her: 'And how goes your crab?' Again she said: 'My crab might well be the husband of your eldest daughter.' Then the king said: 'When I rise in the morning and find close to the palace a garden and in it all the trees there are in the world and from all I eat fruit, then for sure he shall have my daughter in marriage.' The woman went home and told the crab. The crab had a talisman and now for the first of three times he made use of it:[1] suddenly there appeared three girls: 'What are your orders, master?' asked the girls. 'To-night', he said, 'you must go and make over against the king's palace a garden with all manner of trees laden with fruit.' In the morning the king rose up, and what did he see? A garden and all the trees in it laden with fruit. This was what he wanted. 'This man', said he, 'shall indeed have my daughter.'

When the old woman came he said: 'Good; the garden has

[1] The nature of the talisman and how it is used is not made plain in the text.

been made. Only this I must have: when I rise up early in the morning I must see the sun on the garden, because the sun does not strike this way; there are mountains and the place is not open to the sun.' Again the old woman went and told the crab. The crab used his talisman for the second time and out came the girls and asked him what he wanted. 'This I want,' said he. 'In the morning when the king rises he must find the sun shining there.' The king rose up; his eyes were dazzled by the brightness of the sunshine. 'What am I to do now?' said he. 'I will ask for something more, and he who will have my daughter must bring it.' So again he spoke to the woman: 'I want in the morning when I rise up to have a bath here and I can go and bathe in it.' Again the woman went and told the crab. For the third time the crab used his talisman: the girls came and asked what he wanted. He said: 'In the morning there must be a bath built for the king close to the palace.' The king rose up and saw a bath built close to the palace. He went down to it and took a bath.

Then he called to the woman and said: 'The crab must come to the palace to marry my daughter.' Could he come? Then the crab's mother came and took the girl and went back home. But her sisters were saying: 'There was no girl in the world to equal for our sister and is she to marry not a prince but this crab?' The girl said: 'To marry a crab was my destiny and a crab I must have for a husband.'

Some time passed and the two younger princesses wanted to go to a festival. They said to the eldest: 'Will you too come with us, dear?' She said: 'I must ask the crab. We will see if he will give me leave.' The crab said: 'You go and I will go too on a black steed. When your sisters see me, they will say: "There, my dear sister, is a youth for you," and a lot more of the same sort of talk.' The girls went to the festival. As they sat there eating and drinking, lo, in came a young man on the black steed. As soon as they saw him, the sisters began: 'There, sister, and keep your eyes shut. There is a fine youth for you, and you went and married the crab.' The girl said not a word, and the youth on his horse went away. They went up again to the village and her sisters went to their husbands.

Another festival came round; the sisters were ready to go and they told their sister. Again she said: 'I must ask the crab.' The crab said: 'Go, and I shall come on a bay horse, wearing clothes all set with silver. Again they will chatter nonsense to you, but you must say nothing at all about its being me; if you do, you will lose me.' So again they went to the feast, and as they were eating and drinking, lo, there came a youth on the bay horse. The sisters began again. Well, what do you suppose, my dears? They went on chattering and the girl said nothing at all. When the festival was over they went home again with their husbands.

Another feast came round. Again her sisters asked their elder: 'What do you say? Shall we go to the festival again?' She said: 'I must ask my dear crab and we will see what he says.' So again she asked the crab, and he said: 'Don't go, because this time you will make me known.' 'I won't make you known,' she said. 'No, no; you will,' said he, 'because your sisters will question you and tease you, and you will tell them that it is I, the crab, and then you will lose me and to find me again you will have to go to the place where are the three columns.' She paid no heed to this and went off with her sisters. So again as they were sitting and eating and drinking, lo, a young man passed by. The sisters again began chattering and then they took to teasing her. Then she said to them: 'See, that man is my husband the crab, turned into a fine youth.' As she said this, the youth disappeared.

The girl rose up and went home and questioned the crab's mother. She said that the girl must build an inn and a tailor's shop; then people could come and eat at the inn and tell each of them a story; then they could be given a dress to wear and so go off. The girl did this and many people came. There was a blind man with a child and he said: 'Come; we too will go and have a meal and have each of us a suit of clothes and then go off.' As they were on their way to the inn, they sat down by a stream to eat. The child took a morsel of biscuit to wet it and the river carried it off. The child ran along to get the biscuit and so they came to a tower. The boy wanted to go in; the door stopped him, barring his way. For a while they stayed outside. Then the child saw three doves going into the tower: they had said 'Let me come in, door,' and the door had not barred their way. When the doves had gone in, the child went up to the door and said: 'Door, let me go in.' So he went in. 'Stairs, let me go up.' He went up and found a table set with food. 'Table, let me sit down.' The boy ate a good meal. When he had done eating, the doves came. The boy went into a cupboard and hid. When the doves had done eating, they took wine to drink. The first one prayed for a curse on his mother: 'She it was who betrayed me into the hands of the ogress.' The second dove asked for a curse on his wife. The third one asked for a curse on his sister. When the doves had gone away the child went along the side of the river and found his father and told him what had happened to him. When the two of them came to the inn they had a meal and told their whole story, how they were on their way and the boy had come to a tower and saw three doves and heard what they said and saw what they did: to put it shortly, all that had happened to the child. When the girl heard this, she shut up the inn and with the child went straight off to the tower. When they came there: 'Door, let me in.' In they went. 'Stairs, let me go up,' and up they went. When they came up and saw the table, they felt hungry. 'Table, let me sit down,' and they had a meal. Then the child took the girl and set her in the cupboard and himself went back to his father.

When the doves came, they ate, and when they were drinking again they said: 'A curse on the traitor!' When the girl heard that it was the wife who was the traitor, she rushed out of the cupboard and said: 'Here I am, and I have come to deliver you from the hands of the ogress.' 'You cannot deliver me,' said the dove. 'Just come and I will show you.' He took her and showed her. 'Do you see that tower?' said he. 'You must go there and sweep out the tower. Then the ogress will stab at you and cry out, but you must not at all turn round and look at her; just go on sweeping. And when you have finished the sweeping, you must ask to have the column in the middle, for she will try to give you the column at the back.'

As soon as the girl came to the tower she began sweeping. The ogress pushed and teased her but she went on until she had finished sweeping. Then the ogress said: 'Will you not let me give you something for your trouble, for your sweeping? See; I will give you this column.' The girl said: 'If you will let me have one column, it would be better to give me the one in the middle.' So she had the column in the middle and this was her husband.

So they held a joyous wedding and a fine carnival.

13

The Girl who married an Animal

THE marriage of a girl of this world to a husband either from Fairyland, or an animal, or only partly human, and often under some enchantment, is a very common theme and several types may be distinguished though the lines are often not easy to trace.[1] In this book we have stories under the headings, *Cupid and Psyche*, *The Princess's Kerchief*, *The Gift to the youngest Daughter*, and all belong here. So also does the present story, *The Girl who married an Animal.*

The central theme of these animal bridegroom stories is that a girl is in love with some creature, half animal and half human. His mother sets herself against the human bride who escapes only because her husband shows her how to perform his mother's commands. Often the mother arranges another marriage for her son and the heroine's last task is to go and fetch from the mother's sister the instruments of music to be used at the wedding. In the end the second bride chosen by the hostile mother is driven away and the heroine and her strange husband are left to their happiness. In the Kárpathos version translated the husband is neither an animal nor yet quite a man: he is 'Moskambari', Musk and Amber, the son of an ogress who has made a marriage for him with the daughter of her sister, another ogress. The girl makes her escape from the ogress's wicked sister by disarming all her guardians, the lion, the barrier field, the fountain, the fig-tree, and so on by flattering them absurdly; softened by this they let her pass by. On this widely spread incident of the flattery of guardians, found also in Sicily, in Albania, and in Russia, there is a long note in *Forty-five Stories*, p. 171, to *The magic Brothers-in-law.*

In the Calabrian version the story is presented rather differently. The centre of it is not the bride but her animal husband, the Handsome Horse. The girl loses him, after the Cupid and Psyche manner, by revealing their marriage, and the horse gets betrothed to the squint-eyed daughter of a witch. The bulk of the story is concerned with the efforts of the witch to get rid of the horse's wife by setting her impossible tasks; in the fulfilment of which she is always helped by her husband the Handsome Horse. At the end the squinting bride is by an accident killed by her own mother the witch.

[1] BP. ii. 234, iii. 166.

The story may be regarded as Balkan; versions have been found in Turkey and among the Bulgarian gipsies,[1] and it has been studied in *Forty-five Stories*, p. 222. In Greece I find ten versions and also the one from Calabria, though how far the stories of these Greeks of Calabria belong to Greek and how far to Italian story-telling is not an easy question.

As in another story from Kárpathos, No. 27, the story is localized in the island: Menités is a large village in the southern part of the island; the other places I do not know.

The Greek references for this story are:

1, 2, 3. PONTOS: *Astír tou Pontou*, i. 247; unpublished version by Valavánis; *Arkheíon Pontou*, viii. 195.
4. KÁRPATHOS: Mikh.-Nouáros, *L. S. Karpáthou*, i. 292, translated below.
5. KOS: *Forty-five Stories*, No. 17, p. 213.
6. KÁLYMNOS: *Folklore*, xi. 115.
7. MITYLENE: *Folklore*, xii. 86.
8. CRETE (or Kasos): given me verbally by Professor Trypanis.
9, 10. THRACE: *Thrakiká*, xv. 362; and xvii. 97.
11. BOVA IN CALABRIA: *La Calabria*, v. 9.

NO. 13. THE GIRL WHO MARRIED AN ANIMAL[2]

There was an old woman with a one and only daughter. All the week they used to work at home, mother and daughter together, spinning and weaving; often too they went working in other people's houses, so that by Saturday they might have five or ten piastres to buy a little barley and grind it for flour and knead a cake to have food for two or three days. Then half-way through the week they would do the same thing, and so again and again. One Saturday they had no brushwood to bake the cake, and the mother said to her daughter: 'You stay here, my daughter, and look after the house, while I go and fetch from behind here a few twigs to heat the oven, that we may bake our cake.' The old woman went off, as far as right behind Aimona; she went about here and there but could find nothing. She went down, and down the hill as far as the streams, to find a few twigs to bring home. When the girl saw that her mother was

[1] Turkish from Kunos, *Forty-four Turkish Stories*, p. 70, and Kent, p. 79, which latter is *Istanbul Masallari*, p. 121. The Bulgarian gipsy version is in the *Journal of the Gypsy Lore Society*, N.S. v. 280.

[2] Text from Kárpathos, in Mikh.-Nouáros, i. 292, with the title *Musk and Amber*.

late, she said to herself: 'Who can say when my mother will come back? She must have run into some women talking and chattering and has forgotten all about it.' Then instead of waiting for her mother and to see what would happen, she sat down and ate the whole cake unbaked, the naughty girl! Then her mother came home with the twigs on her shoulder all sweaty and tired, and the daughter told the old dame that she had eaten the cake unbaked. The mother cursed her, saying: 'Away with you, my daughter, and may the kerchief on your head fly away to the house of the ogress.' The moment the old woman had done speaking, a mighty wind blew and carried away the kerchief from the girl's head right up into the sky. The girl ran after it crying: 'You women there, good luck be with you! Catch me my kerchief, for, alas! I have no other one to put on.' But how was anyone to catch it? She ran and ran, and when she got sight of it, the kerchief was caught on a fence. To recapture it, the girl jumped over into the courtyard, because the fence was very high and she could not reach over it. When the girl got into the courtyard, lo! the ogress suddenly appeared and said: 'How have you come here, girl? Here where no bird can come, no bird show itself in the sky? And what do you want here?' The girl said: 'O good woman, don't scold me for coming into your courtyard without your leave. The wind carried off my kerchief and I was running after it to catch it and in my trouble I did not know where I was going.' The ogress said: 'It is no matter, my girl, how you came into my courtyard for you are never to go out again.' The ogress was whetting her teeth to eat the girl. In her terror the girl trembled like a reed, and her tears ran down like the waters of the river we have here. But it seems that the ogress saw how beautiful she was and was sorry for her, for she said: 'To do you a favour and to help the good luck of my son Musk and Amber, I will not devour you, provided you can do what I tell you to do. Late tomorrow I am making a marriage for my son Musk and Amber. Now, look at my tower with its forty rooms! Here are the keys and you must go and sweep them all thoroughly; let me not find a single grain of dust for my tongue to lick up! If by evening you finish this work, good; you will be let go free. If not, look out; you understand?' So the girl took the keys and opened the rooms. Inside they were all choked with dust, and there she sat down and lamented her fate. As she sat, lo! there appeared a young man as fair as an angel. When he saw the girl—she was indeed five times fair—he was pleased with her, and said: 'Why are you crying, my girl? Has my mother her eye on you to get rid of you?' She told him all her troubles. Then the youth said: 'Come, let me give you a kiss, and I will tell you how to escape from my mother's hands.' She said: 'You mustn't kiss me; never mind if you don't tell me anything.' When Musk and Amber saw that the girl was resolute, he had pity on her and said: 'Early in the morning you must get up before the sun rises and turn to the east and say: "Come hither, you twelve winds, and blow and carry away all the dust from the tower of the ogress, for in the evening we shall make a wedding for Musk and Amber."' Even as Musk and Amber had told her, the girl did. She came forward and cried aloud: 'Come, you twelve winds, blow and sweep out the tower of the ogress, for in the evening a marriage will be made for Musk and Amber.' Then at once the twelve winds started to blow, and they made the ogress's tower spotless as crystal. Then came the old ogress and licked over the place with her tongue; she could not find a speck of dust. Then she said: 'Either your mother is a witch, or your father one who reads the stars, or you have had a counsel from my son Musk and Amber.' The girl said: 'Neither is my mother a witch, nor my father one who reads the stars; and your son Musk and Amber, where have I seen or known him?'

Then the ogress said to her: 'You must go and wash the clothes needed for the wedding and make them all as white as paper.' Then she gave her a cake and a bar of soap and a hungry dog and said: 'You must bring back the bar of soap untouched and the clothes all as white as paper and the cake uncut and the dog fed to the full. If you don't do all this, your end has come.' The girl took the clothes and the cake and the soap and the dog, and went to the brink of the river and sat down and lamented to think what would happen; what was she to do?

Then Musk and Amber again came and spoke to her just as before. 'Come, my girl, let me kiss you and I will tell you what you must do.' She said: 'You mustn't kiss me; never mind if you don't tell me anything.' Once more he had pity on her, and it seemed he was now in love with her, and so he said: 'You must turn in the direction where the sun sets and cry aloud:

"Come, ye good women, all of you together, and wash the clothes of Musk and Amber, because we are to make a marriage for him in the evening." So the good women gathered together, thousands and millions of them, and they brought bread in whole batches, and the dog ate till he was crammed, and the girl too. Then they washed the clothes and made them as white as starch, and the cake remained uncut and the bar of soap untouched. When she brought everything back in the evening, the ogress said the same thing.

Again the ogress said: 'Now you must go and stuff my son's mattresses all of them with feathers from the birds of God, and then we shall give them to Musk and Amber for his wedding.' Again Musk and Amber met her and told her to go up on the mountain and cry aloud: 'Come, all ye birds of heaven, and lament for Musk and Amber, for he is dead. Then they will come and shake out their feathers, and you must gather them together and stuff the mattresses with them and then bring them to the ogress.'

When the ogress saw how clever the girl was and that she had been able to do everything she had ordered, she then sent her to her sister, telling her as a pretext to bring the fiddles for Musk and Amber's wedding: but her intention was to be rid of her. This sister was even wickeder than she was, and even if a man had the strength of an ogre, he would not have escaped from her hands. So the girl went off, walking and walking and on and on, as one might say from here to Menités, all the way to the place where the ogress's sister was. When she got as far as, say, Pláka, where you have a view of Krámba, there she sat down to rest and to eat a crust of bread to get fresh strength to continue the journey. At that place, lo! Musk and Amber again showed himself, and said: 'Where are you going this way, my girl?' She said: 'Your mother has sent me to her sister.' To himself he said: 'What a bitch! What a wicked sinful woman!' Then he said: 'Come and let me kiss you,' and so on. She said: 'You mustn't kiss me,' and the rest. He said: 'Where you are now going, your eyes had better be four than two, for my aunt is far worse than my mother.' She said: 'What you tell me, I will do, and for all the good you do me, your reward will be from God.' He said: 'From here you must go down towards Krámba; the road is easy. On the road you will meet a crooked old woman, whose eyelashes you will see trailing down on the ground: you must ask her to show you the way. She will say that she cannot see to guide you, and you must take your scissors and clip her eyelashes, and then she will tell you what way you must go. And then as you go farther you will find a woman sweeping up the ashes in an oven with her breast. You must cut a strip off your dress and sweep up the ashes for her, and then go on again. Going farther you will find a fig-tree with a crop of wormy figs, and you must pick one and eat it and then say: "Oh, oh, what beautiful nice figs this fig-tree is bearing, and I wish I had known of them and come by every day to eat them." Farther on you will come to a fountain with water stinking and full of worms, and you will stoop down to drink and then say: "Oh, how cool this water is and how refreshing! I wish I were here every day to drink of it and slake my thirst." Then you will go farther, and come to a little church of the Virgin of Mercy, before whose picture men are burning ass's dung as incense. You must throw away the dung and take incense and offer it and do homage and kiss the picture of the Virgin of great Grace; then you will go on your way. Farther on you will find a field full of briars, and thistles for asses and prickly plants and poisonous thorns of all kinds. You will take off your shoes and walk in it and the thorns will prick your feet and draw blood from them, and you will say: "Ah, ah, how velvet soft are these thorns, and they have a scent too of basil; I wish I could have passed by here every day to pick them and enjoy their scent." Then you will see the tower, and outside the tower a lion and an ass tied up. In front of the lion is a sack of chaff and in front of the ass a pile of bones. You will change them over, and set the bones in front of the lion and the chaff in front of the ass. Then you will enter the tower. When the ogress sees you going into her courtyard she will receive you favourably and in cheerful mood will make you sit down, so that you may suspect no evil, and she will make out that she is about some business, but all the same going to whet her teeth. At that moment you must seize the fiddles from underneath the bed and go out and away.'

The girl kept all this in mind and did as Musk and Amber had told her; at last she came to the tower of the ogress. When the abominable creature saw her, her mouth ran with the slaver of desire; yet she spoke with gentle words. 'Sit down, my daughter, and rest after your journey and drink a little cold water; then you can tell me how it is you have done me this kindness, to come to my place.' She pretended that she was in a hurry to finish her work, and went out: it was to whet her teeth. Then the girl lost no time at all but put her head underneath the bed and saw the fiddles. She seized them and ran away as if she had four feet. By the time the ogress was aware of this, the girl was outside the door.

The ogress went in pursuit, but how could she come up to her? She cried out: 'Stop her, stop her, my lion!' The lion turned to her and said: 'All the years you have had me here always giving me chaff to eat! This girl came this way once only; she saw my ill luck and gave me the bones.' So the girl got past the lion safely and came to the field. The ogress cried out: 'Stop the girl, my field!' The field said: 'Why should I stop her? You pass by here every day and curse me saying that I am all thorns and weeds and she told me that my thorns are tender and fragrant like basil. Now why should I stop her for you?' The girl got past safely and ran off. The ogress came to the little church and said: 'O Virgin of Mercy, stop the girl, I beg.' The Virgin said: 'You pass this way every day and see men burning ass's dung for incense and you never cared at all; she passed by once only and threw out the dung and brought incense to please me; why should I stop her now?' The girl ran on and came to the fountain. The ogress said: 'Stop the girl, O fountain.' The fountain said: 'You come this way every day and curse my water, calling it nothing but stinking matter; she passed by once only and found it fair and good. Why now should I stop her?' The ogress ran on; so too did the girl. She came to the fig-tree; behind her was the ogress. She cried out: 'O fig-tree, stop the girl for me.' The tree said: 'Ten times a day you used to pass by here and always cursed me with ugly words: that my figs were full of worms and nasty. She came one day only and ate and thought them fine and juicy. Why should I now stop her?' Farther on the girl came to the house of the woman with the oven. The ogress was behind her and cried out: 'You with the oven, stop the girl.' The woman said: 'All these years I have been to the trouble of sweeping up the ashes in the oven with my breast and every day you came by here, but never did you give me any help to get free from my trouble. This girl passed by once only, and she cut a strip off her skirt and made it a mop to sweep out my oven.' Here too the girl passed freely. She went on to the old purblind woman. 'Ha Ha!' the ogress by now could come up with the girl, for she was tired and had no more strength to run. She called to the old woman: 'Stop me the girl, dame!' The old woman said: 'All those many years I was half blind and you never offered to take the scissors when I begged you every day to cut my eyelashes that I might have my sight; and this girl passing by once only had pity on me and trimmed them short.'

So the girl again escaped and passed beyond the limits of the ogress's power so that she could no longer chase after her and undo her. So the girl came to the first ogress, the sister of this one, and gave her the fiddles and the flutes. When the ogress saw that she had come back alive, which she had never thought could happen on earth or in heaven, once more she said to her: 'Either your mother was a witch and your father one who reads the stars, or you have had a counsel from my son Musk and Amber.' The girl answered: 'Neither was my mother a witch, nor my father one who reads the stars, and your son Musk and Amber, where have I seen or known him?'

Musk and Amber was by now in love with the girl and wanted to leave his betrothed and marry her, but how could he do this for no good reason? Also he was afraid of his mother. The time was now come for the wedding. The bride was dressed and adorned and the pair standing in their places. Then Musk and Amber said to the bride: 'Look now: after the crowning your mother-in-law will come and kiss the crowns and give you her wedding gift; you must be rude to her: this will amuse her and she will give you even a further gift.' So the wedding came to an end, and first of all the mother-in-law, Musk and Amber's mother, came to kiss her children's wedding crowns and to give her gift of congratulation: the bride insulted her; everybody stood amazed. But the bride laughed, for she was sure her mother-in-law would be amused and would perhaps give her yet another gold coin. The ogress, insulted at the very moment when she was about to kiss her daughter-in-law's crown, attacked her and would have torn her to pieces; pulled her limbs off her. 'O, evil be your years,' she cried; 'Hardly have we accepted you than you behave like this. Off with you to destruction, wicked shameless creature. And why should I not accept this worthy girl here; a girl like gold, she who has done so many things for me? Away with you! Never let my eyes light on you more!' And she drove away the wretched bride even when the crown was on her head, and set in her place the other girl with whom Musk and Amber was in love. Then they held a high wedding with many fair and joyous diversions. And I too had the fortune to be there, and for my trouble they gave me a piece of ham and I am still eating it and never come to the end of it.

14

The Girl with two Husbands

THIS is a story with a long plot, of the kind that could only have been invented by one person and spread by diffusion, although of the place of origin nothing more can be said than that it was probably in the Near East. In outline the story is that there was a little girl with a teacher; this teacher fell in love with her pupil's father and contrived the death of the girl's mother by getting her crushed by the lid of a chest.[1] Then she married the widower. To get rid of her stepdaughter she first got her married to a prince who had come into the world in the form of a snake; then by slanders she broke off the marriage and the heroine was driven out into the wilderness.[2] Here she met a second prince who was in the power of the fairies; he was delivered and the two were married. In the Thracian version here translated he is called Riga, *king*; in the version from Kos his name is Neros, in which I would recognize the ancient Eros, *Love*. Then her first husband came back from the war and discovered that his wife had been all the time innocent, and went in search of her. He found her and the question arose which of the two husbands was to keep her. The decision is made by a test. The three, the wife and the two husbands, go up a hill; she is to remain the wife of the one from whom she accepts a drink of water. In the version from Kos the first husband carries water and the second her baby; she chooses the water carried by her first husband, the snake prince. So too in the Epeiros version, and apparently in the Thracian version here translated. She prefers her first husband, though he is the one who has made her suffer so much: she would rather have him, the stronger character, than the second husband for whom she has done so much. In the Skyros version the point is not very clear, but the verses may easily be read in the same sense: though she needs her second husband, yet the first, the snake, is her true love.

This story plainly falls into two parts, of which the first, the marriage to the snake prince, is akin to No. 13, *The Girl who married an Animal*. The latter part of the story, about the second husband and the choice made between the two, is much rarer, and of the complete

[1] For the lid of the chest see BP. i. 422, with a reference to Gregory of Tours; and iv. 196. See also Penzer's *Pentamerone*, i. 62.

[2] Here changed letters often play a part, for which see BP. i. 286.

tale I find only four Greek variants: the one from Thrace here translated and others from Kos, Skyros, and Epeiros. Nor are full variants from other countries common. I find three only: one from Turkey, one from Armenia, and a Judaeo-Spanish version from Macedonia.[1]

In the Skyros version the second husband has the name Köroglou,[2] the Son of the Blind Man, and, a little altered, this appears in the Epeiros version in the form Kírigli or Kírikos. This Köroglou is the name of a sort of Turkish Robin Hood who is believed to have flourished in the latter part of the seventeenth century: a bandit hero, a Turkish Klepht, an accomplished minstrel, who became the hero of a Turcoman prose cycle.[3] His name here is perhaps a further sign of the eastern origin of the story. These and other points I have discussed in the notes to the Koan version of the story in *Forty-five Stories*, No. 36, where there is a different and much longer account of how the second husband was set free from his bondage to the fairies, with further notes on the subject. Here it is necessary only to give the references:

1. Kos: *Forty-five Stories*, p. 369.
2. Skyros: Pérdika, ii. 227.
3. Thrace: *Thrakiká*, xv. 347, translated below with the final episode added from the Skyros version.
4. Epeiros: Hahn, i. 212, No. 31, *Schlangenkind.*

NO. 14. THE GIRL WITH TWO HUSBANDS[4]

Once upon a time there were a king and a queen; for the princess their daughter they had a mistress to teach her letters. The mistress was a wicked and depraved woman, and she desired the death of the queen in order that she might marry the king. With this in mind she set to work with the princess: she could not do enough in giving her sweets and the most delicate food and in making her bed with twelve mattresses all piled one upon the other, and all to give her pleasure. Thus the princess began gradually to love her teacher more than her mother the queen, and she did everything which the teacher told her. One day the woman asked her: 'Which would you should rather die,

[1] Kunos, *Stambul*, p. 221; Macler, *Contes arméniens*, p. 167; Crews, p. 128.

[2] In the Greek of Skyros, *Τσιρογλές*.

[3] For Köroglou see the references in *Forty-five Stories*, p. 392, the best being to H. M. Chadwick, *The Growth of Literature*, iii. 49. For another possible appearance in Greek folktales see also Kirali in No. 54 below.

[4] Text from Thrace in *Thrakiká*, xv. 347, with the title *The Girl thrice accursed.*

I or your mother?' 'Indeed I love my mother, yet I would rather she should die than you.' 'As this is so, I will tell you something which you can do for your mother to be killed and for me to marry the king: then you will have me as your mother. You must start crying and ask for walnuts. The servant girls will be sent to bring you some; then you must say, "No, I want my mother to give them to me; it is from my mother's hand I want them." Then because she loves you, she will get up to find you the nuts, and at the very moment she is handing them to you, you must make the lid of the chest fall upon her and kill her.' The princess did just as she had been told. She cried and asked for walnuts: 'Walnuts, I want walnuts.' The servants were sent for them. The princess would not accept them: 'No,' she said, 'I want my mother to give me them; I want them from the hand of my mother.' The queen went to get her the nuts; the girl brought down the lid of the chest and killed her. There was much grief in the palace and wearing of black; the king wore black; the princess was given black to wear. Whoever could have thought that the princess had done this wicked thing; of set purpose?

The teacher then paid still greater attention to the princess: the twelve mattresses became fourteen. When she thought that the time had come, she said to the princess: 'Do you want me to become your mother?' The princess was full of delight at this, and the teacher gave her her instructions: 'You must go crying to your father the king, stamping your feet and saying: "I want my mistress, to make her my mother; I want my mistress; I want to make her my mother."' The princess began crying and saying: 'I want my mistress, to make her my mother; I want my mistress; I want to make her my mother.' 'Leave me in peace, child.' 'I won't. My mistress, my mistress, my mistress! I want her as my mother.' To be free of her, the father took a pair of iron shoes and an iron chain; he hung them from the ceiling, saying: 'When the shoes fall down from the ceiling, then I will marry your mistress.' The king never thought that such a thing could happen.

The princess went and told the mistress and she told her what to do. Every day (to make the chain rust) she must throw up against the ceiling stinking water and rotten lemons. The princess began as she had been told, every day to throw up the stinking water and rotten lemons,[1] saying nothing about it. Before forty days had passed, one day when the king was going into the room, he saw the shoes fallen to the ground. He had never imagined such a thing and was taken aback. 'This', said he, 'has come of destiny.' So he married the teacher. Before the wedding he said to the princess: 'I will take her as my wife since you wish it so much; you must not complain of any unkindness from your stepmother.' 'Good,' said the princess; 'let her do to me as she will.' The marriage took place, and in a few days the stepmother began to treat the princess unkindly; to take away her mattresses one by one, and by degrees to take everything from her. The princess shut herself up in her room, crying and beating her breast.

Let us now leave the stepmother and tell of another queen. This queen had no children, and one day as she was going for a walk in the mountains with the king, she saw a snake having young. 'Ah,' said she, 'it is a sin that I should suffer thus. All the beasts of the earth have young. Look at the very snake: it too has young. Oh, my God, out of your own mercifulness, give me a child, even if it be a snake.' God heard her and she became with child. The hour of birth came and the pains took her. Midwives were sent for, but as each of them put out her hand to take the child, the snake bit her and she died. The king made a proclamation that whoever could deliver the queen, the king would not know what to do to show his thanks. The stepmother heard of this and said: 'I must send my stepdaughter, the princess.' She sent to tell the king that she knew a woman who could deliver the queen. As soon as the princess heard this, she lamented: 'Indeed and how can I deliver the queen?' The king sent to fetch her. The evening before she had to go she went to the priest and confessed that she had killed her mother the queen; she confessed the whole affair. 'O unhappy woman, you have committed a very great sin, and there is no one with power to give you pardon. You must go to your mother's tomb and weep and lament and it may be she will have pity on you and tell you what to do.' She did the priest's bidding and went to the tomb, and began to make entreaty: 'I have sinned, O my mother; pardon me. Do not, I pray, do to me as I did to you.

[1] The acid of the lemons is to rot the iron, just as in No. 56 the boy uses water to soften the rings of bread.

Have pity on me.' And she wept and beat her breast over the tomb. Suddenly she heard a voice crying from the tomb: 'O woman cursed and thrice cursed, I will counsel you, because you are my child and I have pity on you, though indeed a curse must be on you. You must make a pair of iron gloves and set on the fire a cauldron of milk. When the hard pains seize the queen, the milk will be boiling, and you must set the queen over the steam. As soon as the snake smells the milk, he will fall from her. Then you must put on the iron gloves, and you will take the snake from the milk and attend to him as to a child.' The girl did as she was bidden. She went and got the iron gloves, and a cauldron of milk was set on to boil. A cruel pang seized the queen: she was set facing the cauldron and the snake fell from her right into the cauldron. The princess put on the iron gloves: she brought out the snake, tended it and carried it to the queen. The princess went off to her father's palace; as soon as her stepmother saw her, she said: 'She's come, has she? I will give her her deserts!'

When the snake was born, the people ran to fetch wet-nurses. All who were brought the snake bit, and they died. The stepmother heard of this and sent word to the king: 'She who delivered the queen, she it is who can suckle the child: I will send her to you.' Again the princess went to her mother's tomb and began to weep and lament. Again a voice was heard from within the tomb: 'O woman cursed and three times cursed, go and make breasts of iron and at the tip of them make holes; put on also your iron gloves: in this way you can give suck to the snake.' The princess went to nurse him. The queen was sorry for her, saying: 'You have brought the girl; yes, but how can she give suck to the snake?' As her mother had bidden her, the girl put on the iron breasts and gave him suck and so reared him up. When he was two years old, she was thanked and turned to go away home. Her stepmother saw her and said: 'She has come again then!' And she looked for some way to kill her.

The king wanted the snake to learn his letters, and they began to look for a teacher. All the teachers who came the snake bit, and they died. The stepmother heard of this and sent word to the king: 'She who brought him to birth, she who gave him suck; she is the one capable of teaching him his letters.' Again the girl was sent there. Before going she went to her mother's tomb to weep and lament. Again a voice was heard from the tomb saying: 'O woman cursed and three times cursed, you must make a dress out of iron and put it on; you must take also an iron wand with which you can keep the snake at a distance from you: in this way you can teach him his letters.' She went and got the iron dress and began teaching him letters. When the snake had learned his letters, the princess rose up and went back to her father's palace. The stepmother was much vexed: 'Look,' said she, 'she has again come back!' and she sought out an occasion to kill the girl.

Time passed and the snake grew big and began to go hissing all over the house, in at one door and out at the other. He wanted to be married, and the most beautiful princesses were brought for him. But he had only to be left alone with his bride, for the next day her bones to be found and the snake hissing still more furiously. No one knew what to do. A proclamation was made to find what girl could be got as a wife for the snake. The stepmother heard of this and again she sent word to the king: 'She who brought him to birth; she who gave him suck; she who taught him letters; it is she who is capable of taking him for her husband.' The princess heard this and it made her tremble to think that she should have the snake for her husband.

Again she went to her mother and began to weep and lament. Again the voice was heard: 'O woman cursed and three times cursed, the snake wears seven shirts. You shall go and accept him for your husband, and in the evening when you are to be alone with the snake, you must order a fire to be set in the middle of the room: you will go and sit in front of the fire on a chair. The snake will say to you "Undress!" and you must then say: "No; you undress!" Then you will take his shirt and burn it in the fire; then you will take off your own and so on till all his shirts are off.' The princess went and did as her mother had told her. The snake started to say to her: 'Undress!' 'No; you undress!' She took his shirt and burned it in the fire. Then she took off one of hers, until he was left in his last shirt. When the snake took off his very last shirt, he changed into a youth: for beauty there was none other such in the world. He kissed the princess and said: 'You have set me free from that torment.' And so they slept until the morning.

In the morning the queen was waiting for the door to be

opened, she weeping and lamenting for the girl. 'How can we open it? How can we open it?' Then her grief was such that she opened the door to look. Opening it, what did she see? The bed was shining brightly with the beauty of the youth: she stooped down and saw the two of them asleep. The queen fell to kissing them here and kissing them there; she was so joyful that she was like a mad woman. 'Ah,' said she, 'my daughter, what can I do in return for this benefit? To think that I should see my snake as a fine youth!' They started to make a marriage feast for forty days and forty nights; never was there such a joyful festival.

Now let us leave them all living thus happily and turn to the stepmother, who was near bursting with vexation. She could not rest: said she, 'I will destroy her utterly.' She dressed herself like a nun and went round visiting wizards to find means to undo the girl, but they were afraid of the king and would give her no advice.

The prince and the princess lived for two years very happily. Then there was a war and the prince made ready to go to it, saying to the queen: 'Mother, I am going to the war; let my wife be to you even as your eyes. If anything happens to her, I shall never come back home again.' The queen said: 'What are you saying, my son? We love you, and your wife we love doubly for turning you into a man and making you as you are today.' The prince went off, saying up to the very hour of his departure: 'Let my wife be to you as your eyes.'

The stepmother put on a monastic dress and said: 'Now for sure I shall be her ruin.' By paying money she got hold of the letters which the prince was sending them about his wife the princess. They were all of them fair and kind, but she changed them for letters for the king and the queen written by herself. Thus she wrote: 'My wife, that wicked woman, you must drive out of the palace; if you don't get rid of her, you will lose me too.' When the first of these letters reached the king and queen, they were at a loss: the prince who loved his wife so much! They did not know what to answer nor did they show the letters to their daughter-in-law. In this way a whole pile of letters was collected, bundles of them. The princess saw that the king and queen were troubled and did not know why. One day she asked them: 'There is something you are keeping from me;

can the prince have written you something bad about me? You are not as you were before the prince went away.'

One day as the princess was going about in the palace, she saw a pile of letters: 'From these letters I shall find out what is going on.' She read: 'This wife of mine, this wicked woman; when I come, I don't want to find her here'; and much more he had written. When she had read this she went to the king and queen, saying: 'Why do you not bid me go off to my death, now that your son no longer wants me? Even as he too must die.' 'But we want you, and even if *he* does not want you, we will keep you here.'

The princess rose up by night and went off, taking first one road and then another. She came to a place where there were men with flocks and herds, and said to the shepherds: 'Let me work for you and you can give me bread to eat and milk to drink.' To this they consented. There were in that place two very big middens. Evening fell, and she lay down on one of the middens to sleep for the night. She saw four fairies coming, and they dug up from the midden a dead prince. Hardly had they brought him out than he came to life. They let him go off where he pleased. When the cock crowed three times the prince came back and they buried him again.

When the princess saw this she trembled and did not know what to do. By degrees she became accustomed to it and every evening he used to come and sleep on the midden. At last they embraced and she became with child. When her nine months were fulfilled, she said to her husband: 'What am I to do? How can I have my child here in this wilderness?' 'You must go to such and such a city and ask which is the palace of Riga, and when they take you there, then you must say: "In the name of Riga, and may you have the happiness to meet him again! I pray you let me stay here in a corner to have my baby." Then you must say to them: "If you want to see your son Riga, every black cock must be driven away; not one must be left, even outside the king's land." '

The princess went off; she took one road and she took another; she passed through villages and through cities; then at last she came to the city of Riga. She found the palace and knocked at the door; it was opened and she told the people all her trouble. 'O my queen,' said she, 'so may you be happy and in a good hour see again your son Riga, let me stay in a corner here and have my baby.' As soon as the queen heard the name Riga, she said: 'Ah, my son Riga! it is now twelve years since I saw him; the fairies carried him off and I have lost him. Tell me, do you know where he is? Tell me what you know.' The girl said: 'No, my queen, I know nothing, but I have heard of him.' 'Since you speak to me in his name, come in.' The queen ordered her servants to give her a bath, and they gave her a change of fine clothes and cared for her. The pains came upon her and she bore a son. Then she stayed there and was lulling him:

'O hush, thou son of Riga, thou grandson of the king!
The queen if she but knew it, would make for such a son
The cradle all of silver, the swaddling bands of gold!'

This she repeated again and again, and one day the queen passing by heard the lullaby she was singing to the baby:

O hush, thou son of Riga, thou grandson of the king!
The queen if she but knew it, would make for such a son
The cradle all of silver, the swaddling bands of gold!'

The queen knocked at the door and said: 'Can this be the baby son of my son Riga?' 'Yes indeed, my queen. In such and such a place men dwell with their flocks and herds, and have certain midden heaps, and in these four fairies kept your son hidden. There I met him and he told me that if you want him to come to you, no black cock must be left in the whole realm and even beyond it; you must kill them all and the crowing of a black cock must nowhere be heard.' When the queen heard this, she gave orders and all the black cocks were killed. They dressed the girl in gold and fine gold work and the baby too; so they waited for the prince, the baby's father.

In the evening the fairies came and took the prince out of the midden; they waited for the cock to crow and waited and waited; no cock crew. The fairies burst with rage and the prince was left free; he ran off to his father's palace. Seeing Riga no one knew what to do with delight. The prince said: 'It is my wife who delivered me; it is my wife who delivered me.' A great wedding was held for forty days and forty nights, and they ate and enjoyed themselves, rich and poor.

Now we must leave them living thus happily, and return to the other prince, who came back from the war and asked for his wife. 'See,' said the king and the queen, 'here are the letters you sent us.' 'These letters from me? Some enemy wrote them.' He took a double satchel of money and went off to find her. He put goods of all sorts into a little cart and went round the towns from door to door so that the women should come out to buy: in this way he might find the princess. When he had been on these rounds for years and years, he came at last to the city where his wife was, and he went in front of the palace looking for her. He saw a woman dressed like a queen with a child in her arms. He knew her and his wife knew him, but she did not come down to him. Then she said: 'I have a child,' and so she sent down the nurse to buy a rattle. 'No,' said the hawker, 'such things I sell only to the ladies.' The princess understood that he wanted to see her and so she came down. She said: 'All is over; besides, I have a child.' 'What is this you say? You must come with me.' At that moment up came her husband, the second prince. They contested for her: 'No, I will take her.' The other said: 'No, it is for me to take her.'

At last they said they would refer the matter to the judge; yet for all that the judge could do, they were unable to agree. Then the judge gave the decision that they should give the girl a drug to send her to sleep for a while, and whichever of the two gave her water when she woke up that one should take her. After some days the princess woke up; she arose in the night and asked for water, and cried:

> 'My apricot, I dearly love; for him I long and sigh;
> Thou too, my noble husband: I thirst, I faint, I die.'

The princes had stayed awake night and day watching her; then from long sleeplessness they tired and fell deeply asleep. When they woke up they found the princess dead; this they could not endure and they died, both of them.

Neither was I there nor are you to believe it.

NOTE. The Skyros version of this story also ends with the wife's death. The situation is that the first husband, the Snake, and the second husband, Köroglou, have gathered together armies to fight for the lady. The Snake has come with his armies to the frontiers of Köroglou's country to invade and carry her off. The story goes on:

Köroglou sent heralds to ask the Snake why he had come to ravage his country. The Snake said: 'I want my wife and the child.' Köroglou said: 'She is my wife; it is she who delivered me from the enchantment and made me a man again, I who had been no more than a shade.' The Snake said: 'She is mine; did she not save me from death and from enchantment and has she not borne me a son?'

Thus they were set to give battle. Then an old man of great wisdom appeared and said: 'Instead of fighting and you and your armies being killed, is it not better to send for the queen to come here and she can tell us herself which of you she desires? Let her decide her fortune for herself.' So they agreed to this and Köroglou sent to the palace and the queen came. They told her to make her choice: the one of the two whom she loved the more, him she must ask to fetch her water from the fountain to drink. The other one, they said, will understand this and go away.

So the queen stood between them. She gazed at the Snake, the prince whom she had reared with her milk; she had made him a man; he was her first husband; she had loved him so dearly and yet he had given her bitter poison to drink and set men to drive her out of the palace. She gazed at Köroglou; they had loved and so he had ceased to be a shade and had become a man again; as she was wandering on the road he had saved her and brought her to his palace and made her his queen. What to do she knew not; with tears her eyes ran like a fountain. They pressed her for an answer, to tell them what she would do. She felt her heart faint and sat down by the edge of the fountain and said:

'Although the Snake is my true love, for Köroglou I sigh;
O Köroglou, water I beg; I am at point to die.'

While Köroglou was hastening to fetch water she fell down and her soul passed away.

15

The Gift to the youngest Daughter

THIS may serve as a general title for a group of stories of the mysterious otherworld husband with no very well-defined oikotype. The stories begin with a man, a king, who had three daughters; he had to go on a journey and told his daughters that on his return he will bring them whatever present they asked of him. The eldest and the second sister asked for the obvious presents, jewels and so on; the youngest asked only for a rose or some other flower, or a strange kerchief, or as in the story from Epeiros for a golden wand: objects all symbolic of her desire for a marriage with some unknown lover. This present the father sometimes forgets, but his ship then refuses to move until he has bought it or plucked the rose from the garden. The two elder sisters have asked for worldly wealth; the youngest has asked for love, and the sign of that love is a thing so trivial to the outside world that it may easily be forgotten. In the Epeiros version the kindly but not very understanding father has to be reminded by a mysterious countryman, for he has not seen that under the figure of the Wand of Gold the girl has foreseen in her heart her future lover. The lover knows in the same way from his own nature whom he must marry, and the picture he has of the girl is a symbol of this pre-established bond. It is an idea common in these Greek stories: in No. 33 of *Forty-five Stories* we read of a prince who carried the idea rather too far and had a regular gallery of girls' pictures.[1]

This symbolism of a picture revealing destiny I have met with in real life. At the monastery of Esphigménou on Mount Athos I met with an old monk, an American Greek, who had for much of his life been a bookmaker. Grown old and alone, he thought of the Holy Mountain; but to what monastery should he go? In a dream, or perhaps in a picture—the point is immaterial; what matters is that like the golden wand in the story he had an intimation of his destiny —he saw in full detail a monastery. He went to Athos and, either by instinct or by asking questions, discovered that the monastery of his vision was Esphigménou. It was there I saw him as a monk and he told me his story: no longer Khristos but the lay brother Khariton. He had had the same experience as Wand of Gold and many of the heroes of these stories.

[1] *Forty-five Stories*, p. 342.

Equally often in these stories the young man knows whom he must marry by the curse of an old woman whose pot he has broken; and she has cursed him with the love of someone supposedly unattainable.[1] Here the idea of love is that it is imposed by an external fate as a blessing or as a curse. When it is inspired by the picture, the idea is of some aspiration in the heart only to be satisfied in this way.

At this point the story develops in different ways. Most usually it becomes a Beauty and the Beast story, in which the girl is led to confess her love for the mysterious person to whom her father and the token he has bought lead her. He is at first in some monstrous form, and at her kiss turns into a beautiful youth, enchanted until he has in his bestial form won the love of a girl. The Nísyros story here translated is of this type and so very distinctly are the versions from Thera and Zákynthos. The version from Epeiros is more of the Cupid and Psyche type, with the jealousy of the sisters playing a great part: in the end the sisters are frustrated and the girl regains her husband, Here we have the Aarne–Thompson Type 432; see also the type 425C.

By far the best versions are those from Cyprus, Athens, and Epeiros, but these have been translated by Garnett and Geldart, and I find nothing better than the much curtailed version from Nísyros.

The references are:

1. CYPRUS: Sakellarios, ii. 325 = Garnett, p. 152.
2. NÍSYROS: *Z.A.* i. 420, No. 7, translated.
3. KOS: Dieterich, p. 456.
4. CHIOS: Pernot, *Études de linguistique*, iii. 301.
5. THERA: *Parnassós*, ix. 364.
6. MÝKONOS: Roussel, *Contes de Mycono*, p. 97.
7. ATHENS: Kamboúroglou, p. 85; Garnett, p. 3.
8. GALLIPOLI: Bernhard Schmidt, *Griech. Märchen*, No. 10.
9, 10, 11. THRACE: *Thrakiká*, iv. 334; xvi. 105; xvii. 97.
12. EPEIROS: Pio, p. 16, which is Hahn, i. 97, No. 7, and Geldart, p. 37.
13. ZÁKYNTHOS: *Laographía*, x. 433.

[1] For these curses see *Forty-five Stories*, p. 346, and notes on No. 1 above.

NO. 15. THE GIFT TO THE YOUNGEST DAUGHTER[1]

Once upon a time there was in a village a very rich man with two daughters. This man by degrees became utterly poverty-stricken and peddled wares in the street. One day he rose in the morning and said to one of his daughters: 'What would you like me to bring you in the evening, my daughter?' She said: 'A watch: I want one.' Then he asked the other one: she wanted a flower. So the man went out with his horse, for the road was long. He went off thus but from the morning to the evening he sold nothing so he could buy neither the watch nor yet the flower. Late in the evening when he was ready to go home he was caught in a violent storm of rain. The man had no money, neither to go and stop in some house nor to get any food. He let his horse go loose on the road and went wherever it took him. He went into an inn and dismounted and went upstairs; there he found a table set but no one was there. However he sat down and ate and lay down to sleep. At the third hour of the night he heard instruments of music being played in the garden, but he could see no one. He went to sleep and in the morning he woke up and mounted his horse and went off. On his way he saw a flower. Then he remembered what his daughter had said to him and went to pick it. A monster jumped out at him and said: 'Is it not enough that you have eaten and slept, but you now want flowers as well? Tell me what you want with them.' The man told him his story. Then the monster said: 'You must bring me the girl; I shall follow behind you and if you don't bring her, I shall devour you.' So the man went and took his daughter and brought her to the inn; he went away and left her there. When the sun had set she saw the monster coming up to her; he said 'Don't be afraid; I won't hurt you.' He said no more, and then went away. At the third hour the instruments of music began but no man was to be seen. After a month the girl saw in a dream that her sister was being married; rising in the morning she told this to the monster, and he gave her a day or two's leave to go to the wedding; he gave her also plenty of money. So she went and instead of staying two days she stayed three,

[1] Text from Nísyros, in *Z.A.* i. 420, No. 7.

because her sister would not let her go. She came back on the third day, but for those three days there had been neither music nor anything else.

In the morning she rose and went to the garden and saw the monster in the agony of death. She embraced him and kissed him and at once he turned into a prince; he was a boy who had been cursed by his father, who had said to him: 'unless some one soul can be found to love you, you shall never again become a man.' Then the girl's father saw the flags flying over the inn and knew what had happened; he went there and joined them in marriage and they ate and drank, and may we fare even better.

16

The Princess's Kerchief

THIS story belongs to the mysterious husband group but has an individuality of its own. I find only two versions: the one from Thrace here translated and another from Kos, recorded probably by Zarraftis and printed by Dieterich, p. 449. These versions are from places so far apart that it may be surmised that the story is not as uncommon as it might seem.

In the Thracian version the lover appears first as a crane and then in the dress of a dervish. In the longer version from Kos he is the son of the vizier, contracted in marriage as a child to the princess but later enchanted in the form of an eagle. The story has a close affinity to *Beauty and the Beast*.

It is by the agency of a mad girl that in this story the princess is brought to her lover, the prince who is turned by enchantment into a bird and appearing also as a dervish with the train of camels. It may be supposed that it was the girl's very madness that gave her the mysterious power to see the dervish: the mad are given these gifts of insight and the girl could see things hidden from saner mortals. She was in fact what the Greeks call 'one of a light or airy spirit'. There is a whole series of words to denote those persons who have the gift to see creatures of another world. They are all compounds of *elaphrós*, *light*, and the general idea seems to be that such persons must be of an 'airy' nature, not as earthbound as their more ordinary fellows. I am quoting a note from *Folklore*, xli. 36. See also No. 51 below.

NO. 16. THE PRINCESS'S KERCHIEF[1]

Once upon a time there was a princess and she was embroidering a kerchief all with gold; for twelve years she plied her needle and in the twelfth year she finished it. When she had finished it she called to all her friends to go out into the country for May Day. They climbed a little mountain and walked about, and as the princess was delighting in her kerchief, a crane came and flew off with it.

[1] Text from Thrace, in *Thrakiká*, xvi. 122, No. 17.

The princess began to cry; she beat her breast and refused comfort. The king said: 'Do not be vexed, my child; I will get you a finer one.' The princess would not listen: 'I want that one, embroidered with my own hands.'

The king wanted to have her married. The princess refused, saying: 'All I want is that you build me a bath and to it people can come and have a bath free and everyone who comes must tell me a story, and so I may perhaps hear something about my kerchief.' As the princess wished, the king built the bath and the princess was the bathwoman; she was at this for two years and heard nothing; but she never lost hope.

Now we must leave the princess waiting in hope, and I will tell of a mother who had three daughters; one of them was a mad girl with a craze for going out at night and walking about: her sisters would beat her, but she would go out all the same. Finally after beating her well they shut her up in the house. The girl went and slept by the front door and all night she looked out of the keyhole. She saw a dervish go by with a kerchief tied round his cap; he was riding on a horse and was followed by a train of camels; he held a pipe to his mouth and was playing on it. Being inquisitive she said she would follow him; so she broke open the door and went out to go after the dervish, the dervish in front and she behind. They came to a palace. Scarcely was he inside than he took off his robe, and lo, he was a youth like an angel. He sat down to eat but with no lust for his meat; then he went to bed. Before going to sleep he lifted up his pillow and brought out a gold kerchief and began weeping and saying:

'Ah, little hands which worked you
to wear on breast and head,
When will God grant the spell to break
that we two may be wed?'

This he said with tears and then fell asleep. As soon as the mad girl had seen him she went back home; her mother and sisters saw her and gave her a double dose of stick. When she had been beaten she lay down and went to sleep. In the morning she said to her sisters: 'Get ready and we will go to the bath.' They began to laugh at her; she went by herself and took a bath and went to tell the princess a story. 'My princess,' said she, 'Sleep did not hinder me last night from seeing pass by our door a dervish with a kerchief round his cap; he was on a horse and behind him there followed a long train of camels. The dervish held a pipe to his mouth and was playing on it. The dervish in front and I behind, we came to a palace. Scarcely was he inside when he stripped off his robe and there he stood, a young man like an angel. He went and sat down to eat but with no lust for his meat and then he went to bed. Before going to sleep, he lifted up his pillow and brought out a golden kerchief and began weeping and saying:

> "Ah, little hands which worked you
> to wear on breast and head,
> When will God grant the spell to break
> that we two may be wed?"

This he said with tears and then fell asleep.'

The princess said to the girl: 'If you will take me to that man I will give you freely the half of my kingdom.' In the evening the girl took the princess to her house and said: 'It is here you must sleep in front of the door.' So she made up a bed and the princess lay on it. At midnight they heard the pipe and rose up; the dervish was riding on his horse and behind him the train of many camels was following. Then the dervish and the camels passed on; following behind them were the princess and the mad girl. And so they came to the palace. Once more, scarcely had the dervish come in than he took off his robe and there he stood, a young man like an angel. He sat down and ate but with no lust for his meat; then he went to bed. Before going to sleep he lifted up the pillow and brought out a gold worked kerchief, and began weeping and saying:

> 'Ah, little hands which worked you
> to wear on breast and head,
> When will God grant the spell to break
> that we two may be wed?'

As the youth lay there weeping and beating his breast the princess showed herself and said: 'It was you who took my kerchief?' 'It was you whom I had been watching for so long.' The princess brought out a medicine which she had taken with her and loosed the enchantment, and he remained a youth as he had been aforetime. They went to the palace and kept their wedding for forty days and forty nights, with joy and feasting and many fair delights.

With the medicine she restored the mad girl and gave her half her kingdom, and so they lived in good hap, and I too was there in a pair of red breeches.

17

Human Flesh to eat

THIS story is a well-marked variant on the theme of the girl married to a demon lover. A blackamoor, a pasha, or some strange monster, offers marriage to three sisters successively, on condition of the girl eating a piece of human flesh, a hand or a foot, or a piece of tripe. The eldest sister and the second are caught pretending only to have eaten the loathsome morsel; the youngest avoids actually eating it, but by a cunning evasion makes him believe that she has. Then the story develops along two rather different lines.

In two versions, the one from Melos, which I have translated, and in Hahn's version from Crete the story follows the lines of Cupid and Psyche, though in rather a sinister style. In the version from Melos the heroine lives with her gruesome husband, the King of the World Below: here one is tempted to see some sort of reminiscence of Pluto and Persephone.

In the Cupid and Psyche story the mysterious husband when asleep is woken up by a drop of oil falling from the lamp which Psyche has in her hand when she comes to spy upon his secret form. In our versions from Melos and Crete she wakes him in a different way. In the Melian story we are told that at his navel the husband has a key; this his wife turns and in some unexplained way this gives her a sight of the whole world. She is betrayed into giving a loud cry, and this wakes up her husband who in his anger drives her away. She had cried out on seeing a river carrying away the yarn an old woman was bleaching. In the version from Crete, Filek Zelebi, printed in Hahn, the girl after turning the navel-key saw a river and women doing washing. A pig was about to seize one of the garments and the girl cried out to warn the woman who was doing the washing. This cry woke up her husband.

There is a Turkish story which contains much of the material of *Human Flesh to eat*. The youngest of three sisters is married to a mysterious husband, who after a test by pricking with a needle had rejected her two elder sisters. As he lay asleep the bride found a key projecting from her husband's navel. She turned it and opened the lock and 'went inside'. There she came upon a market where abundant clothes were being prepared: all of them, she was told, for the wedding of her husband with a mortal maiden. Then she came out and shut the door with the key. Her husband woke up and found that the navel-door had been opened and to punish the girl's curiosity drove her away.[1] Cosquin points out that there is a story in the *Pentamerone* in which the bride's jealous sisters tell her to open a padlock, *catenaccio*, which they give her, and this opening will break the spell under which her husband is labouring. The bride unlocks the padlock, which seems to have no physical connexion at all with her husband's body and has a sight of a number of women carrying packets of linen; one of them dropped her packet and the bride cried to her to pick it up, and this cry woke up her husband.[2] Basile had lived in Crete and may well have brought the story from there, but he plainly has the story in a much broken-down form. In the Greek and Turkish versions the navel is regarded as a kind of locked entrance to a land of further mysteries, and in it the girl sees always linen, either being washed or bleached or made into clothes, and with some connexion with her marriage. But the significance of this form of curiosity escapes me. In the Cretan story in Hahn the hero is called *Filek Zelebi* and if *Filek* is the Turco-Arabic *felek*, the name would mean *Lord Sky*, but this carries us no farther, except in the wrong direction; up to the sky and not down below the earth.

Among Mrs. Hasluck's unpublished Albanian stories is a version of our No. 15, *The Gift to the youngest Daughter*, in which the heroine has a mysterious husband, served by a black spirit. She finds out that he has a 'lock on his stomach,' and in spite of the servant's warning she turns the key. 'She put in her hand and saw a market-place surrounded by shops. One man was making a child's cradle, a second was making swaddling-bands, and some others were sewing clothes for the child she was about to bear.' For her indiscretion she loses her husband; then she regains him, and when her baby was born he too was found to have 'a lock on his stomach'.

This story makes it plain that as always what the girl saw by opening the lock were the preparations for the birth of her child, and beyond this I can go no further.

But in most of the versions, and these are from Mýkonos, Athens, continental Greece, Epeiros, and Zákynthos, the lover is frankly a demon and the latter part of the story recounts how the heroine escapes from him. In the Athens version, for instance, she is rescued by the Seven gifted Brothers, just as the girl is in *The Louse Skin*, the

[1] Kunos, *Stambul*, p. 326 and especially p. 329. The Turkish text is in *Oszmán-török népköltési gyüjtemény*, i. 168, and says very precisely that 'opening the lock she went inside (*ičine girer*) and saw a great market'.

[2] *Études folkloriques*, p. 539, and *Pentamerone*, Penzer's translation, i. 197. No. 9, with a good note. Cosquin quotes from Poitou (*Revue des traditions populaires*, 1888, p. 269) a story of a girl married to a goat and in his ear there is a magic key hidden.

second of the three sub-stories in *The silent Princess*, No. 48 below. In the version from Zákynthos she sprinkles the negro lover with the Water of Sleep, and then rouses his victims, 'a host of young men and young women, all turned to stone,' with the Water of Resurrection.

It is notable that often the demon is summoned involuntarily by someone crying out *Alas* or *Woe is me*, this being by chance the creature's name. This is found in many stories; in Nos. 7 and 24, for example, and is in the version from Melos of this story and in its non-Greek variants which I find in Turkey and Sicily.[1] This kind of involuntary invocation has been discussed by Cosquin.[2]

It is perhaps worth comparing this story with *The Underworld Marriage*.[3] For the World Below see the note on No. 41.

The references for *Human Flesh to eat* are:

1. MELOS: *N.A.* i. 7, translated below, and by Garnett, p. 277.
2. CRETE: Hahn, ii. 67, No. 73.
3. MÝKONOS: Roussel, *Contes de Mycono*, p. 96.
4. ATHENS: Kamboúroglou, p. 37.
5. MAINLAND OF GREECE: Buchon, *La Morée et la Grèce continentale*, p. 271.
6. EPEIROS: Hahn, i. 156, No. 19.
7. ZÁKYNTHOS: *Laographía*, ii. 528.

NO. 17. HUMAN FLESH TO EAT

There was once a poor gaffer. One day he rose up to go to cut wood. He got some together, and, when he was bringing it to the village, the poor fellow was as it were tired out. He sat down by the way and sighed from the bottom of his heart: 'Oh and alas and woe is me!' The moment he said this, a black man suddenly appeared and said: 'What do you want of me?' The poor old man shook with fear and said: 'I don't want anything of you; I did not call you.' Then the black man said: 'Have you any daughters?' 'I have three,' said the old man. 'To-morrow morning you must bring me the eldest here to this very place.' Next morning the old man brought his eldest daughter. The black man came, and he took the girl away to a place where there were great palaces and very fine gardens. Then at midday when it was time to eat, the black man set a table before her, and for food he gave her a man's foot, all rotten and wormy.

[1] These are in *Istanbul Masallari*, p. 132; in Kunos, *Adakale*, No. 26; and in Gonzenbach's *Sicilianische Märchen*, p. 23.

[2] Cosquin, *Études folkloriques*, pp. 536 ff. See also BP. ii. 63, 253.

[3] A text from Melos, in *N.A.* i. 7, with the title *The Lord of the World below.*

Then he said: 'If you eat this foot, you shall have as your husband the Lord of the World Below; if you don't, I shall take you back again to your father.' Only with looking at the foot the poor girl turned very sick indeed, and later, when the black man had gone away, she took it and threw it into the jakes. When the black man came to take away the table, he cried aloud: 'O my foot, O my little foot, where are you?' 'Into the jakes my lady threw me,' answered the foot. Then the black man said: 'Come, my girl; I must take you back to your father; you are not for us.' He took her back to her father and said: 'Bring me your second daughter.'

Next day the old man brought his second daughter. Again the black man brought her down below, and before her too he set a table. By way of food he served her with a man's hand to eat, all full of worms. Not to make a long story of it, she thought over this for some time; then she took the hand and threw it into the jakes. When the black man came to take away the table, he cried out to the hand: 'O my hand, O my little hand, where are you?' 'Into the jakes my lady threw me.' Then the black man took her too back to her father and told him he must bring him his third daughter. Next day the old man brought him the third daughter. The black man took her, and her too he set down at table and for food gave her man's tripes to eat, all stinking. Said he: 'If you avail to eat these tripes you shall have as your husband the Lord of the World Below; if not, you will fare as your sisters have.' But this girl was very cunning: 'With pleasure, my dear black man; all I ask is that you bring me two or three cloves and a little cinnamon to spice the tripes and then I will eat them.' So the black man with the tripes brought her the cloves and cinnamon. The she spiced the tripes and plastered them on her belly and made all fast with a belt. When the black man came to take away the table, he cried out 'O tripes, my tripes, where have you gone?' 'To my lady's belly,' answered the tripes. Then the black man was delighted and held her as the light of his eyes.

Yet the poor girl never saw her husband, because in the evening when she was finishing her meal, the black man gave her coffee, and in it he had put a sleepy drug. Thus she would go off to sleep, and when the Lord of the World Below came to bed, she was not aware of him. So the time passed by.

When the sisters saw that the black man did not come back at all, one day they took it into their heads to go and see how their sister was faring in the World Below. They told their old father. He came to the place and cried 'Oh and alas and woe is me!' Then lo and behold, the black man again. The old man said: 'My children have been remembering their sister, and if it is possible they would like to see her.' Then said the black man: 'Bring them here tomorrow.' Next morning the old man brought them and the black man took them off to their sister. She received them with great joy, and they sat down and chatted of this and that. At last one of them said to the youngest: 'My poor sister, you may think that you have the black man as your husband, but your husband is really a very beautiful young man. You have never seen him, because every evening the black man gives you a sleepy drug. But tonight when he gives you your coffee, pour it away secretly. When your husband comes to bed with you, you must know that by his navel there is a key: turn this key, and you will have sight of the whole world.' This her wicked sisters said and went away. In the evening she poured away the coffee and pretended to be asleep. The black man took her and placed her in her bed. Some time afterwards she saw a very handsome youth come into the room and lie down on her bed. When he left her and went to sleep, she fair and softly turned the key which he had at his navel: then what did she see? Constantinople, Smyrna, the whole world. She saw too an old woman bleaching her yarn by a river; the water carried away some of the yarn without the old woman being aware. Then the poor girl forgot where she was, and cried out: 'Old woman, old woman, the river has carried away your yarn.' When the youth in his sleep heard her voice, he woke up and said: 'You bitch, turn back the key; you are killing me.' In terror she turned the key again. But in the morning the Lord of the World Below said to his black man: 'Take her away. Clip two hairs from her head and put them into a flask and watch them day and night; when you see them sink to the bottom, come and tell me. Now give her a little bread, and put her out.' The black man did as his master told him, and the poor girl took her bread and went off.

So she went on and on, and on the way she met a shepherd. She said to him: 'O my man and luck be with you; won't you give me your clothes and I give you mine?' 'May this be to your pleasure,' said the shepherd. So she dressed herself in the shepherd's clothes and again went on. After going a long way she came to a big town and went along the streets crying: 'Here am I, a fine boy; a fine boy for service.' The king of the town heard her and saw a boy well-made and clean, so he took him for his servant. He asked the boy what he was called and he said 'John.' Then as time went on for John's sins the queen fell in love with him. One day the king went hunting and took John with him. Half-way the king saw that he had forgotten his watch; he said: 'My good John, I have forgotten my watch. Run and fetch it for me, but when you enter the room, go very quietly not to wake up your mistress.' So John went back and very quietly entered the room. But the lady was awake, still in bed. She seized him to do her wicked will; John resisted, and as they were struggling she scratched him with her nails and the poor fellow's face was all covered with blood. At last John pushed her away, snatched his master's watch, and went off. When he came his master saw him all covered with blood and said: 'My poor John, what has happened to you?' He said: 'Master, I was passing by a place where there were many brambles, and I was in such a hurry to come to you that I was brought to this sad state.' So in the evening they came back to the palace, but all on account of John the queen had become like a mad wild beast. She said to the king: 'Today, my king, you have very nearly found me no more alive. You sent that wicked fellow to fetch your watch, and he came here to put me to shame; I was still in bed, a poor weak woman; but I fought him off with my nails and made his face as you now see it, driving him away.'

Hearing a story like this, the king resolved to bring together all the kings of the land and in their presence to hang John. The appointed day came, and all the people were gathered together below the palace in the place where John was to be hanged. At that moment the black man cried out to the Lord of the World Below: 'Master, master, hurry; the hairs have begun to sink to the bottom.' Then the Lord of the World Below ran and mounted his horse, and riding as fast as he could made signs from afar off that they should wait for his coming. The queen was in the gallery of the palace looking on: she called to them to delay a little because someone was coming in the greatest haste. They waited until the man came. As soon as he arrived, he asked: 'Why are you hanging this man?' Then the queen said, allowing no one else to answer: 'This wretched man, my lord, attempted to put shame upon me.' Then said the Lord of the World Below: 'And suppose this man is a woman? In that case what ought to be done to you, my lady?' 'If that is so,' said the queen, 'then they may hang *me*.' The Lord of the World Below lost no time; he slit John's dress down to the breast, and at once the breasts of a woman were to be seen. 'There, my lords,' said he: 'and if you like I will slit it lower yet.' 'No, no; that's enough,' said the king. Then they left the Lord of the World Below to take John, now seen to be his wife, and the wicked queen they hanged.

But I was not there nor are you to believe it.

18

The Animal Wife

THIS title may be given to a well-marked story of a man with a mate either from the animal world or perhaps from Fairyland. It has been studied by Halliday and by Cosquin[1] and by BP. ii. 30, who bring it under the wide context of Grim, No. 63, *The Three Feathers*. Under the title of *The Tortoise or the Fairy Wife* it is No. 5 in *Forty-five Stories* where the Greek variants of the story are examined in detail. It is therefore not necessary here to do more than outline the story, of which there are in Greece no less than thirteen examples, stretching all the way from Pontos to Athens and over the whole Aegean area.

The general lines of the story are as follows. A man, a king, had three sons and when the time came for them to marry, their father bade them shoot each an arrow into the air at random, and where the arrows fell there they would find their wives. The eldest and the second son found very suitable brides; the arrow of the youngest son fell generally into some wild place, and there he came upon his destined bride: a frog or a monkey; in any case an animal of some sort. This animal is, however, discovered to be a girl of such beauty that the king claims her, and the bridegroom is allowed to keep her only by fulfilling a series of tasks imposed upon him by the king.[2] This he is enabled to do by the help of some odd little creature, some magical dwarfish monstrosity, who is found for him by his wife: he is sometimes her brother. So the story ends well. I print a translation of a text I recorded at Soúrmena in Pontos in 1914; the story is well brought up to date by the substitution of three bullets for the primitive three arrows.

Occasionally instead of the three arrows we find another opening. There is one young man only; he goes out and, as a rule by chance, brings the animal to his house and then discovers that it is really a fair girl. Versions of this type are from Astypálaia, Symi, Mýkonos, and Ainos in Thrace. In the Astypálaia version and in the version from Symi here translated the animal is a sea tortoise or turtle. The rest of the tale is on the same lines as when it has begun with the three arrows.

In versions from Syra, Athens, and Thrace, the story is developed

[1] Halliday in *M.G. in A.M.*, p. 258, and Cosquin in *Contes indiens*, p. 289.
[2] Here see Aarne–Thompson Type 465.

differently. The husband has sisters who are jealous of the animal bride and she shows that she is as good as they are or even better. In the Athens story she explains that she is of a family under a curse and this is why she appears as a frog in a marsh.

There is a Judaeo-Spanish version in Crews, p. 152.

The references are:

1, 2, 3. PONTOS: from Soúrmena, my own record in *Arkheíon Pontou*, iii. 84. Translated, 18*a*; from SANTÁ, my own record, unpublished; from ARGYRÓPOLIS, recorded by I. Valavanis in *Arkheíon Pontou*, vii. 91.
4. KASSABÁ: *Folklore*, xii. 207.
5. SYMI: in *Z.A.* i. 262, translated, 18*b*.
6. ASTYPÁLAIA: in *Forty-five Stories*, p. 84.
7. MÝKONOS: in *Μυκονιάτικα Χρονικά*, Jan. 1934, coming from a book *Τὰ Μυκονιάτικα*, by E. T. Monoyioú.
8. SYRA: Hahn, ii. 31, No. 67.
9. MITYLENE: Georgeakis et Pineau, *Folklore de Lesbos*, p. 1.
10. KÁRYSTOS: in Papakhadzís, *Δοκίμιον τοῦ ἰδιώματος Καρύστου*, p. 94.
11. ATHENS: Kamboúroglou, p. 76 = Garnett, p. 46.
12. AINOS: Megas, p. 46.
13. THRACE: *Thrakiká*, xvii. 134.

NO. 18*a*. THE ANIMAL WIFE[1]

A man had three sons and they wanted to be married. They asked their mother: 'Whose daughters shall we take?' Their mother said to them: 'Each of you must fire off a gun, and wherever each of the three bullets strikes, it is from that house that you must take your bride.' The first son fired and his bullet struck a rich man's house, and thence he took his bride. The second son fired, and he hit a poor man's house and so he too won a very fair bride. The youngest son fired and his bullet fell into the marsh. He searched there and found a frog: 'This is my fate,' said he, and brought the frog home to his house as though it were his wife, and put it to live under the foundation of the house.

He was taking a walk abroad and there was no one in the house. When he came back home he saw the cooking all done, the house swept out, the beds made; but he could see no one. One day he kept watch to see who it was did the cooking and swept the house and made the bed. He hid behind the door and

[1] Text from Soúrmena in Pontos; printed in *Arkheíon Pontou*, iii. 84.

watched. The frog came out from underneath the foundation and took off its skin and hung it on the peg high up in the corner and was revealed as a beautiful girl. Then the youth ran up from behind and caught hold of her back. The girl said: 'Let me go or your father will beat you.' He said: 'Let my father beat me; you shan't wear your frog skin any more.' Nor did the girl wear it any more.

When his father heard that his son had a beautiful wife—before that they used to laugh at him and say: 'Why, he has taken a frog to be his wife'—and when it was seen that his wife was a beautiful girl, his father was filled with passion and wanted to take the girl himself. So he said to his son: 'I demand of you to bring me a man whose height is one palm, and his beard must be two palms, and on his shoulder he must carry a gun weighing forty stone; you must also get a girdle which will wrap all round my house and half as much again and then there be some left.' The son was troubled and confused: how could he find an answer to this? His wife the frog asked him: 'Why are you in such confusion?' 'My father,' he said, 'wants of me a man a palm high and his beard must be of two palms and on his shoulder he must carry a gun weighing forty stone; he wants too a girdle which will wrap right round his house and more than half of it to be left over. And what am I to do? If I don't bring him what he asks my father will kill me.' His wife the frog said to him: 'Do not be afraid. Tell your father to come and I will have everything all ready.' The boy told his father and his father came and many people with him and he said to his son: 'Where is the man about whom I spoke to you?' Then the frog, that is his son's wife, went to the marsh and called for her father: 'Up! my father-in-law wants you.' The father rose up and started on his way with his gun on his shoulder and came to the house. He went up the stairs and so came to the frog's father-in-law. Then he said to him: 'What do you want me for?' The man said nothing. Then said he: 'I lay in the marsh all those many years and no one looked to find me, and what is it you want of me?' Then he fired off the forty-stone gun and shot the man and so delivered his son-in-law from him.

NO. 18*b*. THE ANIMAL WIFE[1]

Let me catch a buzzing gnat,
Gut him and take out his fat;
Fat enough to grease a boat
And two great frigates all afloat;
Grease them all and have in store
Five and forty okes and more.

The beginning of the story and a good evening to you.

It chanced there was once a fisherman, unmarried. He used to go fishing regularly with his rod and line. If he could catch one or two okes of fish, he would sell them and so could manage. This he did every day. After living like this for a long time, one morning he rose up very early and went let us say to the beach of Xinída. He baited his line and cast it. Then he drew it in and pulled out a sea tortoise. 'Anyhow I will take this,' said he, 'and put it into my cottage to eat the fleas; living alone I am eaten up with them.' Besides the tortoise he caught some two okes of fish and brought them all home. He left the tortoise there and some small quantity of fish for himself and took the rest off to sell.

When he had gone out, lo! from the shell of the tortoise there came a girl: there was not her like in the world. She tucked up her sleeves and took and scraped the fish; she cooked them, some stewed and some grilled, and set them aside in the cupboard. Then she went again into the shell of the tortoise. The fisherman came and opened the cupboard to take the fish and cook them. He found them all cooked and well cooked too; of a good savour. He said to himself: 'Some neighbour, I suppose, saw that I came back tired and cooked them for me; I wish I knew her to take her a couple of fish.' Well, he ate and lay down to sleep. In the morning he woke up and again went fishing: this was his business. He brought his fish home; left the share for himself and went again to sell the rest. The girl came out again and cooked the fish even better and again hid herself. The fisherman came back; again he found the fish cooked. Then he thought 'Oh, I wish I knew who this is; anyhow I could give her two or three fish.' To cut the story short, the tortoise did

[1] Text from Symi in *Z.A.* i. 262, with the title, *The Sea Tortoise.*

this for him several times. Then he thought of a cunning device: 'I must keep watch and catch her and see who it is.' So he went out fishing again, brought back the fish, left those he wanted to eat, and pretending to go away he hid himself to keep watch. The girl again came out of her shell to cook the fish. He saw her and opened the door and went and looked for the shell to try to burn it. She said: 'Do not burn it; if you do you will suffer much trouble.' He wanted to burn it but she stood in his way. Well, what would you expect? He threw it on the fire and it was burnt up. With no longer a shell to hide in she stood revealed. She went on serving him and was as his wife.

Let us now leave them and look at the king. He wanted to marry and sent out everywhere to find the most beautiful girl and to bring her to him to be his wife. They travelled over all the world but found no woman as fair as the fisherman's wife. This they went and told the king. So the king called together his council to consider and see how they could get the fisherman's wife for him. They said: 'There is no way but this. We must order him to overlay the whole palace with gold; that he cannot do and on this pretext we may do away with him and take his wife.' So they sent for the fisherman: the king wanted him. He said: 'And what does the king want of me? I am a poor man; what use can I be to him?' He went and the king said: 'You must take and overlay the whole palace with gold outside and inside, and do this by Sunday. If you don't, I shall cut off your head.' Said he: 'But, my lord king, where shall I find all that gold; I am but a poor man.' Thrown out of the palace, he went home weeping and sighing. His wife questioned him and he told her. She said: 'You see now? Did not I tell you not to burn my shell unless you would have much trouble? But sit down and eat and don't be troubled.' But could he even swallow his food? When he had finished, she said: 'You must go to the place where you used to fish and call for my mother and tell her to give you the little box on the hearth. She must give you the little box; not the big one: do you understand?' Her husband went to the place and cried out: 'Ho! mother of the tortoise!' At once she made answer: 'At your orders, my son.' He said: 'You must give me, so says your daughter, the little box which is, she says, on the hearth.' Behold, she brought it at once and gave it to him. He said to himself: 'And what is this?

Can it be some trick? What', said he, 'can be the use of this?' Well, he took it to his wife and she said 'Now you must go and tell the king to let you have men for the work.' Then the men started with brooms and brushes and gilded all the whole palace outside and inside with the stairs and the courts as well. Seeing all this the king said in astonishment: 'I say, this is a marvellously cunning fellow.' He summoned his council and after consideration they again sent for the fisherman and said: 'Tomorrow you must invite to dinner the whole army.' Said the fisherman: 'But, my lord king, how can I find food to entertain so many men? I am a poor man.' The king said: 'Do what I say; otherwise, off with your head.' Once more the fisherman was kicked out and thrown down the stairs. He went home weeping and beating his breast. His wife questioned him and he told her about it. She said: 'Did not I tell you not to burn my shell, or much trouble would come to you? Now come and sit down to eat and do not be troubled.' He sat down to eat but he could not swallow the food. His wife said: 'Once more you must go to the rock where you caught me and call upon my mother; she will answer you, and you must tell her to give you the little pot on the hearth; bring it here; that is all.' In the morning the poor fisherman rose and went to the rock and cried: 'Ho, mother of the tortoise.' At once she answered: 'At your orders, my son. What is it you want?' He said: 'Your daughter says you must give me the tiny little pot on the hearth.' She brought it and gave it to him. He took it and went off, saying to himself: 'But of what good can this be? It seems to me all nonsense: how can all those men be fed out of this tiny little pot?' However he brought it to his wife, and she said: 'You must now go to the king and tell him to send you plenty of men as servants and set the little pot on the hearth. Light a fire and call upon the pot and it will provide you with everything you need.' The king gave him servants in plenty. He went to the field, a big field, and there he built a hearth and lit a fire and set the little pot on it. Then he said: 'Bring me straw mats, bring me spoons, forks, knives, napkins, bread, and so on.' The little pot produced them all and the servants set the tables and the army was assembled and there they all sat down to eat; thousands of men. Then said he to the little pot: 'Bring out soup, boiled meats, food, this that and the other.' Then the pot brought out food of every possible kind and they all ate and were filled to bursting. The king saw this and was near to death.

Again the king assembled his council. They sent for the fisherman and said: 'You must get us a man, two spans high and his beard three spans.' The fisherman felt ready to die; weeping and bewailing himself he went off to his wife. She said: 'What is the matter?' He said: 'The other demands I have fulfilled, but look at this one; it is a thing which can never be done. Now for sure I shall perish. They will bring me to my death and when I leave you our wicked enemy will take you.' She said: 'But tell me what it is that the king said to you.' He said: 'He wants me to go and get him a man two spans high and his beard three spans.' She said: 'And does that trouble you? The man who keeps my hens, he is the man.' He said: 'Tell me then, my wife.' She said: 'Now sit down and eat and tomorrow you must go again to my mother and tell her to tell my hen-man that he must come here for we have need of him.' At dawn he rose and again went to the rock and cried: 'Ho! mother of the tortoise.' 'At your orders, my son: what is it you wish?' He said: 'Your daughter says you must tell her hen-man to come to her for she has need of him.' She said: 'The man is her brother: I will tell him and then if he is willing, . . .' He said: 'For sure he must come; the need is great.' She went off and said to the hen-man: 'You must go there, for your sister wants you and the need is great.' The man at once said: 'I will go, and I will take her a big basket full of eggs.' He filled a big linen basket with eggs; he put it on his head and went off. The poor fisherman saw him with amazement. They went off in procession one after another. On their way the little man was lost in the brushwood. He could see him here and then he saw him there; he could not be sure where he was. He shouted out to him: 'Come here.' The little man answered. Then he found him underneath a shrub, and tied him with his belt not to lose him again. Thus they came to the house. His sister received them. 'Let me see you, brother. You know where you must go? To the palace. Don't leave any breath in any of them; clear them right out.'

Next day the hen-man took a club and with the fisherman he went off to the king. The fisherman had sent a message so they were expecting them. The whole world ran there to see. The hen-man ran up the stairs of the palace and everybody was laughing at him. When he came before the king—the councillors too were there—they all laughed, ha ha ha. The hen-man made as though he were angry and said: 'But why are you laughing? Do you take me for a buffoon?' He smote with the club this way and he smote that way and cleared them all out and didn't leave alive either the king or anyone else.

Then he crowned his brother-in-law as king and his sister as queen.

They ate and drank their fill;
They died when they had no food.
Children they had at their will;
The land was full of their brood.

But I was not there, nor are you to believe the story.

19

The Mountain of Jewels and the Dove-Maiden

THIS is a long and complex story of a man's marriage with a fairy wife. Two of the versions, both from Epeiros, Nos. 4 and 5 in the list below, begin with the son shut up by his too-loving father in a tower: the same beginning as in No. 30, *The Girl shut up in a Tower*. In the food brought him the servants carelessly failed to remove a bone; by means of this bone he pierced the wall and made his escape into the outer world. The meaning of this opening I have discussed in No. 30, where the incident is really in place. The hero then met a Jew, and this is the beginning of the story proper. This Jew sewed him up in the skin of an animal; wrapped in this skin the eagles carried him up to the top of a mountain all covered with jewels; these he must gather and throw down to his master the Jew. The Jew having got his jewels abandoned the boy on the mountain and at this point the second part of the story begins. The boy found his way into a garden where three dove-maidens were bathing in a fountain. He won the youngest as his wife, but allowing her to regain her plumage he lost her; the rest of the story recounts his winning back his lost fairy wife.

The first part of this story, the boy and the Jew and the mountain of jewels, is by itself or in connexion with other developments a quite common episode. It occurs in No. 40 in *Forty-five Stories*, where on p. 437 a few references are given for its occurrence.[1]

The two separate and separable themes of the present story are closely welded together, and as we have this in several Greek versions we may take it that this combination is a fairly well-fixed form in Greece. And not in Greece only, for one of Laura Gonzenbach's Sicilian stories is on the same lines.[2] Here the hero regains his wife not by the aid of talismans, the carpet, the sword, and the cap, but by the help of ants and of an eagle and a lion, into whose shapes the animals have enabled him to change himself, like the hero of our No. 7, *The Child from the Sea*.

This same combination of the two themes is also in the Arabian Nights, where Hasan of Bassorah is an immensely extended version

[1] To Pio, p. 76; and Kunos, *Adakale*, ii. 74, No. 12.

[2] Gonzenbach, *Sizilianische Märchen*, i. p. 28, No. 6.

of our story. A good deal of this story with much else is also in *The Story of Janshah.*[1]

The Greek references are:

1. MITYLENE: *Folklore*, xiii. 452, with the opening of *The Son of the Hunter.*
2. MELOS: *N.A.* i. 56, here translated and also in Garnett, p. 219.
3. THRACE: *Thrakiká*, xvi. 183.
4, 5. EPEIROS: Hahn, i. 131, No. 15, reprinted in Kretschmer's *Neugr. Märchen*, p. 287, No. 61. Also Pio, p. 76, No. 25, which is in Geldart, p. 88. Pio's reference to Hahn, ii. 207 is not to a text but to several variants given in outline only.

NO. 19. THE MOUNTAIN OF JEWELS AND THE DOVE-MAIDEN[2]

Once upon a time and a long time ago, when the Turks were keeping Ramazán, with a hole in the pot and a hole in the pan:

There was an old woman many years a widow, and she had a one and only boy. All day from the very moment the sun showed himself to the hour when he sank in glory this boy used to shoulder his loads of wood to win his bread and to support his old mother. This went on a long time. Then one day on his way to the mountain to cut wood he heard the voice of a crier: he had been sent out by a Jew to make a proclamation along the roads: 'Whoever is fit to serve me for a day or two, to him I will give as much money as he wants.' These words struck pleasantly on his ears for he was thinking of his poverty and of his unlucky plight. Full of joy he ran off to his mother to ask her blessing. His mother did not stand in his way, and so he went to the Jew and took his money, which he handed over to his mother. Then he went off with the Jew. This Jew had ships and yet more ships at his service, and when the lad came to his house he took him down to the shore. They embarked in one of the ships, the others following behind. They had a very fine little trip; before their eyes on the one side there were mountains, high and all covered with greenery; on the other there were vineyards and trees and fields, all to rejoice their hearts.

[1] These references given by Gonzenbach, in a more accessible form are: for Hasan, Burton's library edition, vi. 166, and for *The Story of Janshah*, ibid. iv. 274.

[2] Text from Melos; printed in *N.A.*, i. 56, No. 11, under the title *The Son of the Widow.*

After a long voyage they found themselves below a very lofty mountain: its feet were washed by the foam of the sea and its head was hidden among the high white clouds. When they came there the Jew said to the widow's son that he must go up to the top of the mountain and there do what he was told to do. To the boy this seemed very strange and he asked him how he should do this. The Jew then bound weapons round his waist and sewed him up in the skin of an animal and gave him his instructions. When the boy was aware that the eagles had lifted him and carried him to the top of the mountain, then he should rip the skin open with his knife and come out; whatever he found up there he must throw down to the Jew. Thus he was told and thus he did. The birds of heaven came and lifted him up and brought him up on the mountain. Then with his sword he ripped open the skin and came out; and what did he see? Wherever he cast his eyes, diamonds in millions, jewels of gold and sapphires, all among myrtle bushes and rose trees drenched in musky fragrance. All your mind can fancy you would have seen in that place; instead of stones and pebbles, jewels of gold and diamonds scattered here and there, and on the rose trees before you not dewdrops but the quivering of pearls. When the youth saw all this he was amazed; he bit his lips and crossed his hands as though in awe to walk over all this brilliance and all these great treasures. Suddenly he heard the Jew shouting to him from below; then he began to gather up the jewels and to throw them down with both hands, as many as he could.

The Jew loaded his ships and sailed away, while the boy shouted to him from the mountain and asked what he was doing; the Jew made no answer. Again he shouted to him; there was no voice or any to hear him.[1] Left there all by himself, he walked about on the mountain in despair. The diamonds and the pearls were very fine, but what could you do with them? He had neither food to eat nor a drop of water to drink. By this time too he began to lament; he thought of his poor mother, deserted and alone. Then tired as he was, his eyes red and shining with tears, he stretched himself in the shade of a tree to get a little sleep. As he lay there his head was resting on a stone—a

[1] The Greek here uses a biblical phrase borrowed from the account of the prayers of the priests of Baal in 1 Kings xviii. 26. To judge from *Forty-five Stories*, p. 527, this is a common tag.

diamond perhaps or a lump of sapphire—and it seemed to him that the stone moved. Then he thought there might be some creature—who can say?—in underneath, and he raised the stone. Under it he saw a descent with steps leading downwards. He went down and down, forty, then fifty steps, I don't know how many, and then at the bottom he came to a palace. In this place to which he had come he could see no living creature, neither a man nor anything else. He was so hungry that he looked this way and he looked that to find something to eat. He saw a cupboard, and opened it and found a morsel of bread. He ate and abated his hunger a little. Then he went further on and looking this way and that he saw an ogre; the ogre was blind. At first he was afraid and began to tremble, but when he saw he was blind he took courage; yet he did not say anything to the ogre. He wanted to let the ogre know, but he was afraid and could not think how to address him. Well, the ogre was sitting down, and he came up quietly behind him: I beg your pardon, but he shouted out 'Father!' The ogre answered: 'And how are you my son?' The boy said: 'Born this very moment.' Then the ogre believed him and called to him and began to caress him as though he were really his son. Then he put into his hands forty keys and bade him open the rooms, thirty-nine of them; there was one he must not open. The boy went to and fro and opened all the rooms, and in them he found every gift of God to man, but that one room which the ogre had told him not to open he did not open. But after some days he began to be curious and to say to himself: 'But indeed why should I not open that room? There must be something fine there and the ogre is jealous and does not want me to see it.' So at last he found he could no longer refrain and he opened the door.

Inside he saw a beautiful garden, so fine that it dazzled his eyes. In it you would have seen brought together the choicest trees in all the world, and in the midst of all that greenery and among the branches, swaying under the weight of the lovely fruits decking them, there was built a marble cistern all white and shining. As the youth stood gazing at this garden not knowing where to look first, three doves came flying there, most beautiful doves: what can I say they were like? And just fancy! When the doves came near, at the edge of the cistern, they put off their plumage and turned into three girls all of them as fresh as flowers; at the sight of them even the Patriarch would have lost his head; so what of this boy, a fine young fellow? Then the doves entered the cistern swimming about all at their ease and thinking that there was no one looking at them. And how were they to know that the boy was at the door secretly looking at them? You would have seen his eye shining while a hot burning tear ran down his cheek. And how otherwise? This is what love is: cunningly it enters the heart and all at unawares. Well, of this enough has now been said.

So he was looking at the girls, at all three of them, and the three pleased him well, yet it was at the youngest he cast his eye most often, for his heart told him that she was the most beautiful. As he was gazing at them, suddenly they were no more; they picked up their plumage and put it on, and to his astonishment the youth saw these beautiful girls disappear from before him, and in their place three doves flying up into the sky. Imagine his sorrow. He shut the room and went back to the ogre grieved and downhearted. The ogre asked him what was the matter that he was sitting like that half-crying. 'What can I say?' said the boy. 'This is what happened. I opened the door and I saw . . .' so he told him all the story. 'Well; I am sorry, but can you be astonished that I am sad and that my heart cannot endure it?' When the ogre heard this he was sorry for him, and told him to go in the morning where the girls were swimming and take note where they left their plumage; he must take the plumage of the one who pleased him and hide it, for if she saw him she would snatch the plumage and fly away. So next day he went as the ogre had told him and took the plumage of the youngest girl: she it was who we have told you pleased him, and then went back to his own place. The other two girls when they had bathed put on their plumage and at once there they were, flying right up to the sky. The third girl looked about her and sought to find her plumage, but with no success: so she stayed there. Then the boy came out and approached her. She begged him to give her the plumage and promised that she would not go away. He said nothing and would not let her have it; in this way he took her for his wife.

Some time passed and the two lived together happily and had two children. Then the man, the son of the widow, told the ogre the story of how he came to be up on the mountain, and the ogre asked him if he would like to go back to his mother. On hearing this he was full of joy and said farewell to the ogre, who gave him plenty of money and opened a way for him through the mountain; so the boy went through it with his children and his wife, whom he loved as he did his eyes. They walked on and on until they came to the place where his old mother lived. Imagine the joy of the old woman when she saw her son and with him his wife, a goddess, and their two children full of grace and charm: you would have said they were little angels. After some time he gave the plumage to his mother and bade her hide it carefully lest his wife should chance to find it: if she did he would lose her. His mother hid the plumage in some easy place, so that some days afterwards when the young man was away, somehow, I don't know how, his wife managed to find it. Then right off she took the plumage; one feather she gave to one of the children and one to the other. Then she went up on the tiles of the roof and called aloud to her mother-in-law: 'Bid my husband take a pair of shoes of iron and a staff of iron and go off to find me, *Where all is green and all is red, and five white towers amongst it.* When she had said this, she took flight and was lost to the old woman's eyes. When the youth came home and found his wife not there, he began to weep and would not be comforted: his mother came and told him all that his wife had said when she flew away. Then all day and all night he pondered how he could find his wife, for he did not know where the place was where she had told his mother he must go.

He searched here and he searched there but he could find out nothing. So he made up his mind to go back to the ogre whom he held as his father; in case somehow or other he might know where the doves were to be found, the doves who used to bathe in the garden and turn into women. So he went again to the Jew just as he had done the first time when they had gone to the foot of the mountain, but this time he did not throw down diamonds to him or anything else, but just left him there confused and confounded. Then he went down the stairs to the ogre; he greeted him and told him all that had happened and questioned him about the command his wife had left for him. The ogre gave him the shoes and the iron staff and told him to start off and he would find a way to come to his sweetheart's palace. So he went on and on, and on the way he found in a desert place two men who were quarrelling and shouting at one another. He went near and asked them why they were shouting, and they said: 'Brother, see; here we have this carpet and this sword and this hat, and we don't know how to divide them.' The boy heard this and he thought to mock them as they sat there quarrelling about such trifles as these, so he said: 'Be at ease; are these things worth the trouble of all this shouting and quarrelling?' Then they explained to him that whoever put on the hat would become invisible; whoever stepped on the carpet and twitched it would be carried wheresoever was in his mind, and he who held the sword, however many men were facing him, he could cut them all down. He listened to all this as if it pleased him and bethought him how he could get possession of these things himself. So he said to the men: 'I will make the division between you. I will throw my staff over yonder and you must run to get it, and whoever is the first to come to the staff, to him I adjudge these things; it is he who shall have them.' While they were running to get the staff, the boy put on the hat and girded himself with the sword and stepped on the carpet: he had become invisible. The men looked this way and looked that: no, nothing indeed was to be seen. Then as soon as he was on the carpet, the boy told it to carry him, *Where all is green and all is red and five white towers amongst it*. Scarcely had he finished saying this, than, lo and behold! there he was where it was in his mind to go. There he left the carpet in a certain place and the sword with it and put on the hat so that he should not be seen when he went into the towers to find his wife and his children. He sought here and he sought there and at last he found his wife; she was in the stable among the straw with the fowls: her father had put her there when she came back to him. Then he went up to her and made himself known and told her that he would carry her off. She said: 'We must tell my father and then we can go.' Presently they heard her father coming down. She began to tremble, but he made a show of not heeding it and told her not to mind. So he then put on his hat and went out of sight, but without going away. Her father approached and asked her: 'Who is hidden here? There is a smell of man's flesh.' Then she explained to him that it was her husband who had come to take her away. Her father asked if he could see him because he wanted to understand what kind of man he was. But she would not let him show himself, because she was afraid her father might kill him, for this is how things are: when a man is uneasy at heart he is always full of fear. Her father then said he would give her back to her husband, if he could level a mountain there and turn it into a garden. We might put it this way: his meaning in saying this to her was: 'I will never give you back to him,' for he could not believe, and how could he? that the man would succeed in so great a task.

In the meanwhile the wife consented to this, and when her father had gone away, she called for her husband and gave him a piece of tile and told him to throw it into such and such a well: from it he would see a crowd of men come out and they would do whatever he ordered them. So the youth went off as his wife had told him and threw the tile into the well, and behold, there flew out of the well, what can I say? Men in thousands. The boy gave them his orders: 'By tomorrow morning I want this mountain levelled and in place of the mountain there must be gardens with trees and flowers of every kind.' He had not even finished speaking when the men girt themselves up and set to work. In the morning her father rose and opened his window; what did he see? The mountain was not there and in its place there were gardens: but what gardens! With trees and flowers and jets of water. How can I tell you of such things? How tell of them and again how tell of them? Things not to be recounted. He did not well believe it and he rubbed his eyes and rubbed them again until at last he saw that it was no deception. Then he went to his daughter and said to her: 'Well, this has been done. But now I demand that the garden be turned to sea, and in the sea ships.' Again his daughter gave her husband the tile, and to make a long story short all was done as it had been done the time before, and the gardens which I told you of were all turned into sea with three-masted ships and row-boats and whatever you please.

Then when this had been done, the young man appeared before the king girt with his sword and by his side stood his wife. When her father and her mother saw the husband of their daughter they made a dash at him to devour him. But he lost no time and said: 'O my little sword, slay them.' And the sword slew them. So they were left safe, and he and his wife and his children went off, and on the carpet they went back to the ogre and from him to his mother's house. Then his wife remembered how she and her sisters had taken out the ogre's eyes and had hidden them away in a cave; so with the carpet they went and got the ogre's eyes and went to the palace and restored them. Thus they abode there in all good health and may our state be yet better.

20

Snow White

AARNE–THOMPSON TYPE 709

Of this well-known story, spread over the whole of Europe, not much need be said. BP. i. 450 give full references under Grimm, No. 53, *Schneewittchen*; it has been studied by Halliday and by Cosquin and by Stith Thompson.[1] In the Greek field I find nineteen variants, stretching from Pontos to Zákynthos and including one (No. 14 in my list) from the Albanians of Poros. Most of the Greek versions are of the usual type beginning with the stepmother asking her mirror if there is anyone in the world as fair as she is; but four of them in the list below, No. 5 from Chios; No. 7 from Mitylene; No. 14 from the Albanians of Poros; No. 15 from Thrace; all have the opening of the story I have called *The Girl with two Husbands*, No. 14, in which the heroine is persuaded by a wicked teacher to get rid of her mother so that the teacher who proves a cruel stepmother may marry her father. The point of this opening is that it accounts in a natural manner for the heroine being at the mercy of a cruel and jealous stepmother; the usual opening, where the stepmother asks her mirror if there is anyone as fair as she, simply assumes that the heroine is a stepdaughter. No. 5 from Chios begins with the three girls and their wishes for a husband, which belongs to No. 31.

A typical Greek version of *Snow White* is from Skyros. The jealous stepmother drives out her too-beautiful stepdaughter who runs away with her brothers and they live in a tower. Disguised as a pedlar the stepmother sells the girl a ring which sends her into a sleep; her brothers put her into a crystal box and throw the key into the sea. The king gets the key and opens the chest. Taking the ring from her finger he brings Snow White to life again. Her three brothers, then monks on Athos, come to the wedding of the king and their sister Snow White. Then the jealous stepmother again hears of her and, coming as a wet-nurse for her baby, pierces her head with a pin and she became a bird, and the king took the stepmother as his wife, thinking that she is Snow White. The stepmother kills the bird but from its blood a tree sprang up and inside the trunk of the tree Snow

[1] Halliday in *M.G. in A.M.*, p. 269; Cosquin in *Contes indiens*, p. 95; Stith Thompson in *The Folktale*, p. 124.

White was found. Then the king and Snow White were reunited and the wicked stepmother put to death.

The Greek references for Snow White are:

1. Western Asia Minor, Kios: *Mikrasiatiká Khroniká*, iv. 296.
2, 3. Cappadocia: *M.G. in A.M.*; from Ulaghátsh, p. 347, and from Sílata, p. 441.
4. Cyprus: *Laographía*, iv. 716.
5, 6. Chios: Pernot, *Études de linguistique*, iii. 265, and Carnoy-Nicolaïdes, p. 91, No. V.
7, 8, 9. Mitylene: Kretschmer, *Heut. lesbische Dialekt*, p. 539; Anagnóstis, *Lesbiaká*, p. 183; Georgeakis et Pineau, *Folklore de Lesbos*, p. 57.
10. Samos: Stamatiádis, *Samiaká*, v. 580.
11. Skyros: Pérdika, ii. 205.
12. Crete: *Epetirís et. kritikón spoudón*, iii. 310.
13. Greek Mainland: Legrand, *Recueil de contes pop. grecs*, p. 133, taken from Buchon, *La Grèce continentale*, p. 263.
14. Poros: From the Albanians of Poros, Hahn, ii. 134, No. 103.
15, 16, 17. Thrace: *Thrakiká*, xvi. 165, 174, 176.
18, 19. Zákynthos: Bernhard Schmidt, *Griech. Märchen*, p. 110, No. 17, and *Laographía*, xi. 441.

21

Cinderella

FOR a story so well known and so widely spread, and over Greece as well as elsewhere, as that of Cinderella it is hardly necessary to do more than give an outline of the Greek oikotype and refer to BP.'s notes on Grimm, No. 21, *Aschenputtel*, and to M. R. Coxe's *Cinderella*. The Greek story always begins with the scene of the mother and her three daughters spinning, with the agreement that the first one who allows her thread to break shall be killed and eaten by the others. The mother's thread is the first to break, and the youngest daughter alone refuses to join in killing her. In the development of the story she of course plays the part of Cinderella and the carefully tended bones of her mother take by some magical means the place of the 'fairy godmother'. Cinderella shows herself in church; the prince picks up the slipper she drops, and finding to whom it belongs marries her.

Using Miss Coxe's analyses I can find this peculiar opening, with the mother and the three sisters and the killing of the mother, only in two places outside Greece, and they are both of them roughly Balkan; one of them is Spalato in Dalmatia, and the other is Bulgaria or rather south Slovenia.

Two of the Greek versions, those from Cyprus and from Chios, come to an end with the marriage of the prince to Cinderella, but the story as a rule develops along the lines of No. 31, *The three Sisters and their Wishes for a Husband*, and after the marriage the jealous sisters steal away Cinderella's babies and put kittens or puppies in their place; Cinderella is driven out and only at the end reconciled to her husband. Thus in the third of the Pontic versions in my list the babies are killed and from their graves spring up three cypresses. The jealous sisters then have the cypresses cut down and burnt, and from the ashes three plants grow up. A goat eats the plants and becomes pregnant with three little boys. The boys are saved and brought up by the sun and his mother, and at the end, when Cinderella tells her story, the children are recognized and their mother restored to favour.

The references for Cinderella are:

1, 2, 3, 4. PONTOS: *Astír tou Pontou*, i (1885), pp. 213, 234; *Arkheíon Pontou*, viii. 184; *Pontiaká Phylla*, ii, Part 15, p. 157; Akoglou's *Laographiká Kotyóron*, p. 397.

5. CYPRUS: Sakellarios, ii. 309 = Garnett, p. 112.
6. KASSAVÁ IN ASIA MINOR: *Folklore*, xii. 200.
7. CHIOS: Argenti and Rose, *Folklore of Chios*, p. 443.
8. CRETE: *Parnassós*, ix. 235.
9. THRACE: *Thrakiká*, xvi. 95.
10, 11. EPEIROS: *Sýllogos*, xiv. 256 = Garnett, p. 116; and Pio, p. 6, which is Hahn, i. 70, No. 2, translated by Geldart, p. 26.

22

The magic Bird

AARNE-THOMPSON TYPE 567

THIS story of the bird whose head, liver, and heart when eaten confer special qualities is found all over Greece and is generally well preserved. It has been discussed by Halliday with numerous references and by Stith Thompson.[1] Halliday thinks it probably came from the East into Europe, and more recently Aarne has formed the opinion that its home is in western Asia, perhaps in Persia. This is confirmed by its appearances in Turkey, south Siberia, and Persia.[2]

The outline of the story as found in Greece is much as follows. A man and his wife who had three sons found a golden bird which laid golden eggs. The wife had a lover, a Jew, and he killed the bird with the object of eating the head and the heart and the liver. Here he was forestalled by the three sons who thus gained the magic powers conferred by the flesh of the bird: the man who ate the head would become a king; the one who ate the heart would see into the hearts of men; and the one who ate the liver would find every morning money under his pillow. To escape the angry Jew the three boys ran away. The eldest, who had eaten the head, became a king, sometimes by the random perching of a bird on his head in a place where they were seeking a king by this method;[3] the youngest, who had eaten the heart and so gained the gift of wisdom, became his vizier; the second brother who ate the liver married a princess, using his wealth in this way one may suppose because the liver is the seat of the passion of love. She caused him much trouble but he got the better of her by giving her black figs to eat, and these destroyed her beauty by causing horns to grow on her head. He recovered her by giving her magical white figs to eat by which her horns fell off, after he had thus forced her to restore to him the liver. In some versions he also changed her to an ass by the water of a magic fountain. With his restored wealth he joined his two brothers and the three of them came home to their

[1] Halliday, *M.G. in A.M.*, p. 263, with many references. Stith Thompson, *The Folktale*, p. 75, quotes Aarne, *Vergleichende Märchenforschungen*, pp. 143–200.

[2] For Turkey it is in *Istanbul Masallari*, p. 154; for Siberia, in Radloff, *Süd-Sibirien*, iv. 477; for Persia, in Lorimer, *Persian Tales*, No. xxvi.

[3] For this choosing of a king by the random perching of a bird see a note on p. 522 of *Forty-five Stories* and BP. i. 325. In legend both St. Felix and Gerbert owed their election to the papacy by this perching of a bird on their heads.

father and put to death their wicked mother and her lover. In all these stories birds with their mysterious but surely significant language are the symbol of secret wisdom. The several virtues hidden in the body of the bird are those of men gifted in three several ways, each with the quality belonging to his own way of life: of the king who ate the head, from which he derives the art of ruling; of the second son, the common man, who ate the liver and derives from it the power of living successfully in the world of love and the human affections, the common human relations; of the third son, who ate the heart and became the vizier, for the bird's heart had given him the power of reading men's hearts and made him a good counsellor.

The Grimm story, No. 60, *The two Brothers*, has no more of *The magic Bird* than the bird which laid golden eggs and the luck of whoever ate the heart and the liver. So too the references to the Aarne–Thompson Type 567 suggests a simpler version in which only the heart is eaten and it brings riches. See also BP. iii. 3, on Grimm, No. 122.

The following are the Greek versions of this story:

1, 2. Pontos: *Arkheíon Pontou*, vii. 83 and 107.
3. Cappadocia: from Phloïtá, *M.G. in A.M.*, p. 411.
4. The Taurus: from Phárasa, ibid., p. 479.
5, 6. Chios: Pernot, *Études de linguistique*, iii. 228, 308.
7. Nísyros: *Z.A.* i. 417, translated below.
8. Mitylene: Kretschmer, *Heut. lesbische Dialekt*, p. 510.
9. Skyros: Pérdika, ii. 151.
10. Thrace: *Thrakiká*, xvii. 146.
11. Epeiros: Hahn, i. 227, No. 36.

NO. 22. THE MAGIC BIRD[1]

Once upon a time there were in a village a man and his wife; they had three children and one hen, and this hen laid golden eggs. The man went away on a journey and his wife fell in love with a Jew. The Jew said: 'I mean to come and live with you, but you must kill your children because they are now big and will tell your husband and he will kill me. You must also kill the hen and keep for me the head, the liver, and the heart.' So the woman killed the hen and put its head, liver, and heart into the cupboard for him to eat when he came in the evening. At midday when the children were let out of school they had

[1] Text from Nísyros, printed in *Z.A.* i. 417.

nothing to eat. They opened the cupboard and saw the pieces, and thought that their mother had put them there for them, and so they ate them. The child who ate the head became wiser than all men; the one who ate the liver, gold coins fell from his mouth; the one who ate the heart had the power of reading men's hearts.

When in the evening their mother came with the Jew she went to take the plate from the cupboard to give it to him; she found that it was not there. Then the Jew perceived that the children had eaten it all and he told their mother to kill them at once. So in front of the door they dug out a pit, so that the children should fall into it when they came back from school. The boy who could read men's hearts was aware of all this and he told his brothers what had been done: 'When you come into the house you must press always to one side.' The children went off and came to the house; they ate and drank and went to sleep. In the morning they rose up and went to school. Then the Jew came again and he told their mother that she must put poison into their food: and this she did. The reader of hearts saw what had happened and he told his brothers what was afoot: 'And you must not eat the food.' Thus they again escaped. Then a plot was made to kill them, but the reader of hearts again was aware of it and he would not let them go to the house at all, but they started off to go to another village.

As they were on the way they came upon a beautiful girl playing cards. The one from whose mouth gold coins fell stayed awhile to play with her. She saw him spitting out gold coins, so she made him drunk: he threw up the liver and she ate it. The boy wandered off at random and as he was passing by he saw a fig-tree—the season was winter and the tree had on it black figs. He ate two figs and two horns grew on his head. Then he gathered two more figs and put them into his pouch. Going farther he found another fig-tree and this one had white figs. He ate two of the figs and his horns disappeared. He picked two more and put them into his pouch. He walked below the house of the card-playing girl and cried: 'Figs for sale!' When she heard him cry figs for sale and in winter, she went down and bought. As soon as she ate the figs two horns grew on her head. Well: she sent for all the doctors but no one could put her right. Then the boy passed again by her house crying:

'Good doctor here!' She called for him and he went up to her. When he saw her he said: 'A great sin you have committed and you must confess it to me.' She began to tell him: 'I used to play cards and won much money from people. Then a man came who could spit gold from his mouth. I made him drunk and he threw up a liver and I ate it, and now I too can spit coins.' Then the doctor said to her: 'This is the sin you have done. You must give me the liver and I will make you well.' Then the girl let the boy have the liver, and he gave her the white figs and the horns fell from off her head.

Then the boy went and found his brothers: one was a vizier and one was a head man; this third one had become a chief elder. One evening as they were at supper the reader of hearts said: 'Tomorrow our parents will come here and we must in no way let it be seen that we are their sons. We can pretend to be playing ball with apples, and when the apples fall to the ground and we stoop as though to pick them up, then we shall be bowing down before them as it is fitting we should, but they will not be aware that we are.' So in the morning their parents came and under this pretext the children paid their due obeisance without the parents being aware that they were receiving the homage of their sons.

They went to the government house and there the father said: 'Two months ago I went away from my home and I left with my wife three sons and a hen which laid golden eggs: now I have returned and can find none of them.' Then he asked his wife where they were and she said: 'We had, my master, these three sons and they are dead; also we had a hen and she has been stolen. And what was I to do? Am I God to save my sons from dying?' Then her sons said to her: 'Did you now tell us that you had three sons and they are dead? Behold, we are your sons.' Then they tied her to horses and started them off and she was torn to pieces and the sons lived with their father.

23

The magic Brothers-in-law

AARNE–THOMPSON TYPE 552

THIS story varies a good deal in detail but the general situation is always the same. We have a man with three sons and three daughters; when the father came to die he ordered the sons to give their sisters in marriage to the first suitors who should present themselves. Three suitors came, persons of great and magical potency, but all presenting so sorry and unpromising an appearance that the two elder brothers were reluctant to carry out their father's wishes. The youngest son, however, insisted and the three sisters went off with their husbands. The theme of the rest of the story is the help given by the three husbands to the youngest brother who alone had befriended them in their suit for the three sisters, and of course their hostility to the two elder brothers.

In his study of this story Halliday has quoted Turkish, Magyar, Albanian, Servian, Russian, and gipsy variants, as well as one from Georgia, and regards the story as characteristic of the Balkan countries and the Near East.[1] This story is No. 12 in *Forty-five Stories*, where I have made a detailed study of it; in particular with a good deal of matter about what seems to me the most interesting episode of the story, the winding and unwinding of the skeins of night and day.

The story has two forms. In the simpler version the three brothers, after their sisters are married to the three magic brothers-in-law, set out one after the other in pursuit of the remote lady, the Fair One of the World, so common as the heroine of Greek and, as the Dünya Güzeli, of Turkish stories. On their way they each in succession came to castles where their three sisters were living with their husbands; these were naturally hostile to the two elder brothers, who met their death on their way to the castle of the Fair One. After them we find the youngest brother on the same quest and he, by the advice of his three grateful brothers-in-law, achieved the Fair One of the World.

Of this form of the story we have four variants: from Kos, Crete, Ainos, and Epeiros, and of these that from Kos is by far the best. It has already been printed in *Forty-five Stories*, and it seems hardly

[1] *M.G. in A.M.*, p. 272. We may refer also to Grimm No. 197 with BP.'s notes and references. The parallel in Basile's *Pentamerone*. iv. 3 is not very close.

worth while here to print one of the inferior versions, especially as the story is such a simple one.

In detail the references for this simpler form are:

1. Kos: *Forty-five Stories*, p. 157.
2. Crete: Kretschmer, *Neugr. Märchen*, p. 77.
3. Epeiros: Pio, p. 40, which is Hahn, i. 180, No. 25, and Geldart, p. 50.
4. Ainos: Megas, p. 103.

The second version is much more elaborate. It begins with the marriage of the three sisters insisted upon by the youngest brother: this episode essential to the structure of the story is omitted in the version from Pontos which, however, on account of its general interest I have chosen here for translation. After the marriages the three brothers go out on their adventures, and by night they are attacked by three successive snakes or monsters, each of them more formidable than the one before. These are sometimes killed by one after another of the brothers; sometimes all by the youngest. In any case the third combat is by the youngest brother, and in the course of it their camp fire is extinguished. The youngest brother sees a light and goes out towards it. There he finds an old man or an old woman who in some not very clear way is winding and unwinding skeins of white and black thread, bringing about by this the succession of day and night. The hero ties up the old man or the old woman to prevent the night from coming to an end before he has finished his adventure. Then he comes to a company of forty ogres or robbers who admit him to their fellowship. With them he goes to a king who lives in a castle with his three daughters, threatened by a monster. The hero takes an opportunity to kill the forty ogres, rescues the king from his peril, and marks his three daughters as brides for his brothers and himself. On his return from this adventure he releases the winder of the skeins of day and night and time is thus freed to resume its course.

The next episode relates how the hero's wife is carried off by some monster, in the version which I have chosen by a monstrous bird; in the Thracian version by a creature with a Turkish name, Demir Bouzan, 'He who makes Iron of no avail'. In this search for his lost wife the hero was, of course, helped by his three grateful brothers-in-law, the Bear and the Wolf and the King of the Birds. By the advice of the last—in stories birds are always the wisest of creatures—he found his way to the house of the monstrous bird and there he found his sister. He persuaded her to find out from the bird in what his strength lay, that curious part of a man's make-up outside himself; what is called his external soul. In this case it lay in three eggs in the head of a snake. The hero broke the eggs and the bird which had carried away his wife died, and so he had his wife again, and all by the help of the three magic brothers-in-law; in which help we may see a certain resemblance to No. 43, below, *The young Man and his three Friends*.

The variants of this form of the story are:

1. PONTOS: from Soúrmena in *Astír tou Pontou*, i. 360, translated.
2. CAPPADOCIA: two versions from Ulaghátsh, in *M.G. in A.M.*, pp. 355, 379.
3. MÝKONOS: Roussel, *Contes de Mycono*, p. 30.
4. THERA: *Parnassós*, x. 517. A very aberrant version, the main theme being the search by three sons for their mother, yet with most of the incidents proper to *The magic Brothers-in-law*.
5. EUBOIA: Hahn, i. 286, No. 52.
6. GREEK MAINLAND: Legrand, *Recueil de contes pop. grecs*, p. 145, taken from Buchon, *La Grèce continentale et la Morée*, p. 263.
7. THRACE: *Arkheíon Thrakikoú Laogr.* vi. 249. A very long version so disproportionately spun out that the brothers-in-law themselves are pushed out of the story.
8. CHIOS: there is a good deal of this story in a tale collected by Kanellakis, still unpublished.

NO. 23. THE MAGIC BROTHERS-IN-LAW[1]

There was a king with three sons and three daughters. One day the king was troubled in mind and said: 'Whoever comes and asks for my daughters, he must have them.'

One day the King of the Bears came and asked for the princess. The king could not go back on his word and he gave his eldest daughter to the bear. Afterwards came the King of the Wolves and he took in marriage the second daughter. Lastly the King of the Birds came, and he took the remaining daughter. And so the king's three sons-in-law went their ways.

When the king was old and about to die he said to his sons: 'You may go hunting on every mountain, but on the mountain yonder do not go hunting.' When their father was dead the sons went to all the mountains and found nothing to shoot. They said to one another: 'Let us go to the mountain yonder where our father told us not to go.' To this they all agreed and they went off. When they came up on the mountain they saw

[1] Text from Soúrmena in Pontos, published in *Astír tou Pontou*, i. 360, under the title *The three Princes*.

a great palace of three stories; very big with the doors open; the windows were narrow. They went in and saw tables set with food of all sorts. They sat down and ate and drank until the evening.

In the evening when they would go to sleep, the eldest one said: 'I will keep watch tonight; it may be that someone will come and attack us.' So the eldest brother watched and the others slept. At midnight he heard a rustling, and what did he see? All the mountain shook and trembled, and when he saw clearly, there was a great snake with one head coming into the palace. At once he took his sword in his hand and fought with the snake and cut off its head, and the blood ran out like a river. He killed the snake and threw it down a steep place; then he took water and washed away the blood. At dawn his brothers rose up and asked him: 'Did anyone come in here?' He said: 'Nothing; nor did I see anything.'

Next evening the second brother kept watch. There came a snake with two heads and, as I told you before, he killed it with his sword and then took water and washed away all the blood. When his brothers rose up in the morning he said to them what the elder brother had said.

Next evening the youngest brother kept watch. His brothers did not want him to, but he withstood them and said: 'I must keep guard.' So he did, and what did he see? There came a great snake with three heads trying to come into the palace. At once he seized his sword for the fight. The snake struck twice at the boy who fought and hit at the snake, but the snake had all but conquered him. Then the prince drew back and took a firm stand and drew his sword and hewed at it once and again. Then the snake started lashing with his tail and the prince smote him to the ground. The boy fought madly but cunningly, and when the snake rose up he ran back. The snake then hit out right and left and with his tail put out the light. The prince could not get a light again. He thought how he could get a light; then he saw a very long way off a light burning and he started to go to it to get a light and kill the snake and wash away the blood.

On his way he saw an old man who had two balls of thread one white and one black; he was winding up the black thread, and it was nearly at an end; then it would give way to the white. When he came near he said: 'Good evening, gaffer.'

'Good evening; and where are you going thus by night, my good lad?' 'I am taking a turn for the weather is fine. But what are you doing here?' 'Well,' said he, 'as you see, my dear boy, I am bringing the night to an end and bringing in the day. Know that many men in trouble long for the day.' 'No, gaffer, don't finish winding up the black ball; until I come back from going to that fire, do not bring on the day.' 'Oh no, my good boy,' said he, 'that I cannot do for the whole world is uneasy and is now expecting the day.' Then the boy was angry and he pulled at the black ball, though giving the old man the end of it to hold saying: 'Don't wind it up until I come back.' The old man refused, and the boy grew still more angry. He threw down the old man and set a heavy stone upon him so that he could not get up. When he got to the fire, what did he see? An old woman sitting there, and on the fire was a big cauldron boiling; it had forty handles. 'Good day, good mother,' said he. 'Good day to you,' said the old woman. 'If you had not called me good mother, I would have devoured you.' Said the prince: 'If you had not said good day to me, for sure I would have devoured *you*.' 'What do you want?' said the old woman. 'Fire,' said he. 'Whoever is to have fire from here, must lift up and move this cauldron.' The cauldron was always lifted by her forty sons, the ogres. 'Lift up the cauldron,' she said, 'and move it.' Then the boy lifted up the cauldron and set it down again in its place and took a light from the fire, and set the cauldron again on the fire and made ready to go. Then the old woman spoke again: 'Come and sit down here a little, my good boy, I have something to say to you.' And as he turned to her, her forty sons, the ogres, came; they saw the boy and wanted to devour him. But their mother said to them in a whisper: 'Hush hush; he can master you all. Why, all by himself he lifted up the cauldron and took fire from below it. He was just going away when I called to him. He will devour you all: hush hush.' Then the ogres said: 'Good evening, brother,' and the boy said: 'Good evening to you.' 'Will you become our brother?' said they. 'I will, and why not?' Then they sat down and ate and drank.

Now the forty ogres were at war with a king. They now wanted to take the prince to the war with them. The ogres fought and fought, but they could not conquer the king because his palace was on all four sides like a strong castle. Then said the ogres: 'Will you come with us to the war?' 'And against whom are you fighting?' he asked. 'With the son of the Rose of Delight; he is a most powerful king.' 'I will come,' said he. 'But you must first take with you a long chain.' Then the ogres took the chain and started off and came to the palace. The prince said: 'Drag the chain to the castle and make it fast to the castle wall.' They all pulled at the chain, but none of them could make it fast to the wall. Then the boy took the chain and pulled it up and attached it to the wall. Then he said: 'You stay here while I go up, and then you can come up one by one.' He went up and cried out: 'Now one of you come up.' Then one went up; the boy said: 'Come, and I will let you down on the other side.' Then the boy took the ogre and cut off his head and threw him down a well. Then he cried out: 'Another one of you come up, because I have let the first one down.' Then another ogre came up on the wall, and him too the boy killed. When he had killed this next one he threw him where he had thrown the other, and thus he killed and got rid of them all. Then by turning the chain over to the other side of the wall, he himself came down into the court of the palace. When he had come down, he went into the palace; he opened the first room and what did he see? The king and the queen in the room asleep. At that time the king's wife had a boy baby and he was lying in his cradle. Every year the king used to have a baby and a snake used to come and devour the child. Presently as he was looking this way and that, what did the boy see? There came a big snake, a real big one I tell you, and went to devour the child. The boy at once drew his sword and killed the snake. Then he saw the king's sword hung on the wall. He took the king's sword and in its place hung up his own; then he went out of the room and saw the king's eldest daughter where she was lying asleep. Then he took from his finger his eldest brother's ring and put it on her finger, and the girl's ring he put on his own finger; thus he betrothed her. Now all these three brothers had each of them a ring; he was wearing his own ring and the rings of his two brothers. Then he went to the next room and there he saw the middle sister asleep. He took her ring also, and put on her finger the ring of his second brother. Then he went to the next room, and there he found the youngest daughter asleep. He took her ring and put it on his own finger and his own ring he put on her finger, and in this way he made betrothals for himself and for his brothers. The king had only those three daughters and no other children because the snake had devoured them. Now he had also the baby boy whom the boy had saved from the mouth of the snake.

The prince then turned back and came to the old woman and took fire from her; then he came to the old man and loosed the stone saying: 'Now I am going to my house; you can bring forward the white ball of yarn.' Then he ran and went to his house and lit the fire and with water washed away all the blood where he had killed the snake. In the morning his brothers rose up and again questioned him, and he said: 'Nothing came here nor have I seen anything.' Now the story leaves them all there.

In the other land the king rose up, and what did he see? The snake lying dead and the baby alive. Then came his eldest daughter and said to him: 'Father; look; this ring of mine has been changed; what have you done that I have lost mine?' Then came the next daughter and the third, and said the same. The king was deep in thought: 'Some very fine man has been here in my palace.' To find who it was he sent a notice to all the country that everyone should come and tell him a story, anything they knew. They all came and no one failed to bring him a story, whatever he chose; then he asked: 'Is there anyone who has not come?' His servants said to him: 'There are in a certain place three youths and they have not come.' Then the king summoned them. The first one came, the eldest, and told how he had killed the snake with two heads. Then came the youngest and told everything that had happened to him. The king was amazed and said: 'So these girls of mine belong to you; take them and go with God's blessing.' And then the youth took his three girls out into the courtyard and he gave the two elder ones to his brothers and took the youngest for himself. So they went off.

As they were on their way there came a monstrous bird; in his claws he seized the youth's wife and flew off with her. He wept and cried and shouted but this did no good at all. His wife was gone. His brothers began giving him consolation and advice, but it was to no purpose: weeping and lamenting they took him off in the evening to their palace.

In the morning he got up and said to his brothers: 'I must go and look for her.' So he went off to his brother-in-law the Bear, and when he had told him all the story he asked him what he should do and if he knew where the monstrous bird was to be found. The Bear answered: 'How should I know? The bird is not to be seen, and how can I say where he is? I will convey you away from my realm and across my frontiers and bring you to the frontier of the Wolf, so that no bear shall devour you. Then you must question the Wolf and perhaps he may know.' So the Bear brought him to the Wolf and the Wolf said to him just what the Bear had said; and then he carried him to his brother-in-law the Bird. Then the youth made his lament to the Bird, and the Bird said: 'This affair of yours is very difficult, and it is not possible for you to recover her from the talons of the monstrous bird; if you go there the bird will devour you.' But the boy would not accept this. He said: 'Where is this monstrous bird and in what region?' Then he showed him where the monstrous bird was and gave him a horse, saying: 'When you go there you must say to your wife: "If the monstrous bird comes and devours me, then you must bind my bones on the back of my horse and give him a stroke and tell him to go to the place from which he came." ' Then the youth went off and came to the house of the monstrous bird and went in; the bird was then out hunting, and the boy said to his wife: 'When does the bird go out hunting?' This he was told, and he said: 'If he comes and devours me, you must bind my bones on the horse and give him a stroke and tell him to go back to the place whence he came.' And before the girl had time to say 'He is coming', the monstrous bird came into the house. And, when he saw the boy, gobble, gobble; at once he ate him right up. The girl wept and lamented to herself and without being seen gathered up all the bones and set them on the horse; she gave him a stroke and said: 'Go back whence you came.' The horse went to his sister's house, the wife of the King of the Birds: when his sister saw him she lamented and cried out. Then she took the bones and set them in order and then by her magic art poured a drug over the joints and put life into them. In ten days he became well again and once more wanted to go on his way. But his sister said: 'Do not go; if you go, I shall not be able to bring you again to health.' But he would not listen to her and again started on his way, and on and on and on.

When he came to the house of the monstrous bird, he went in and said to his wife: 'Ask the bird where his strength lies.' Then he went out. Knowing at what time the bird went out hunting, it was easy for him to come to the house. Next day he went there again and his wife said to him: 'He has told me that it is in the broom that he has his strength.' Then he said to her: 'This was a lie he told you. But you go and do worship to the broom.' She did worship to the broom; all round she lit candles and burned incense. The monstrous bird came back. When he saw the candles and the incense he said: 'That was a lie I told you; that is not it.' She made as though she were angry and said: 'Was it a lie you told me?' Then she wept and the bird said to her: 'My strength is in the wall.' Next day the boy went again and asked his wife what the monstrous bird had said to her. She said: 'He told me that his strength was in the wall.' 'Again he has told you a lie,' said the boy. 'You must do as you did before.' Then she lit the candles again in front of the wall and incensed it. When the bird came and saw her he said: 'You silly woman! What are you afraid of? My strength is what no man can take away from me.' Then she said: 'What is your strength and how is it placed that no one can take it from you?' Then he said to her: 'My strength is this. In the Katchan Dagh, the Terrible Mountain, there is a lake; in that lake there is a huge snake with two horns; between the horns there are three eggs. Of those eggs one is my sight, another is my strength, and the third is my life.' 'If that is so,' said she, 'I need no longer be afraid.' 'And that snake no sword can kill. The only sword that can kill him is one tempered in the milk of lions.' Next day the girl told all this to the prince and he went off and got lion's milk; he gave an order for a sword and said to the smith: 'When you temper the sword, let me know, and I will bring you the water; the reward I give you will be great.' Then the smith became all mad with delight to think of the reward he would get from the prince.

So when he had got the sword, the prince went to a village near the Terrible Mountain, to the house of an old woman; she had no kinsmen and was very poor indeed. He said to her: 'Come, my good mother, will you take me as your son?' 'I will,' said she. 'And surely I will make you my mother,' said he. After two or three days the boy said: 'My mother, perhaps there may be someone here with sheep and I could go and look after the dairy? For I am a shepherd.' Then said the old woman: 'There is, my dear lad. Go, take the sheep belonging to the village and go and graze them.' And the men in the village gave him their sheep and he went off to graze them. He led them to the lake of which his brother-in-law the Bird had told him. The pasture there was so rich that the sheep were very well fed; to that place nobody's sheep had ever been because the shepherds were all afraid of the snake.

Near by there was also a king; he saw the lad and was amazed to see him pasturing his sheep in that place. He sent for the lad and said to him: 'Will you look after my sheep too?' 'I will surely, and why not? But my pay is a gold piece a day, and you must give me my food as well.' The king consented. 'Well, in the morning,' said the boy to the king, 'I will come and take your sheep.' When the boy went off, the king privily killed a big sheep and took the fleece: the head was attached to it and so were the hoofs and the horns. In the morning when the boy came, the king went secretly to the space below the house and concealed himself inside the fleece. The shepherd drove the king's flock out to graze; among them was the king with the horns on his head; but how could the boy know that among the sheep was the king? The king went in order to hear and see what the shepherd was doing; all the time he kept close to the boy.

The prince took the sheep and went straight to the lake on the Terrible Mountain, and there he stayed by the lake. The king too was by the lake, his heart trembling within him. Suddenly the lake shivered and shook and out came the snake to devour the boy. At once the boy drew his sword to cut off the snake's head. The snake said: 'Ah, if only you had not that sword, then you would see what I would have done to you.' Then said the boy: 'If only the king's daughter were here! For one thing I would have taken a kiss off her, and for another, see, with a stroke of my sword I would have taken off your head.' Then the snake went back into the lake and did not come out again, because it was only once in the day that he showed himself. In the evening the shepherd went off with the sheep to their place.

Next day the king put his daughter into the sheep's fleece and told her what she must do: 'You must keep close to the boy; wherever he goes you must go too. Then when he says: "Oh, if only the king's daughter were here: then for one thing I would have a kiss from her, and for another with a stroke of my sword I would take off your head!" When he says this, you must come out of the sheepskin and say: "You are very welcome." For in this way only can the snake be killed.' All this the king knew well. Much grief had he suffered, for the snake had left in his land neither sheep nor herds and the king much desired that the snake should be killed.

Next day the shepherd took the sheep and went to the same place, but he did not know that with him he had the king's daughter. He went and again stayed by the lake, and the snake began to come out: the mountain and the lake shook and out he came. The boy at once drew his sword to cut off the snake's head. Then the snake said: 'Oh, if only you had not that sword there, then you would have seen what I would do to you!' The boy answered: 'Oh, if I had here the king's daughter, with one stroke of my sword I would have taken off your head!' Hardly had the prince said this, when the king's daughter showed herself and said: 'You are welcome.' Then at once he took a kiss from her and then with a stroke of his sword smote off the snake's head. He leapt forward and split the snake's head open and from it he took the three eggs and put them into his bosom. Then he went off with the sheep to bring them home again.

In the morning he started on his way to the palace of the monstrous bird. When the prince had seized the three eggs, the bird fell sick; he went to his house and called for the girl; he wanted to see her. But the girl was aware of this, and would not go to him. After this the prince came and the monstrous bird attacked him. The boy at once broke the first egg and the bird fell to the ground and began to entreat him: 'You have broken my strength; let me have the other eggs, my sight and my life.' But the boy was in a passion; at once he broke the other two eggs and the bird straightway died. Then the prince took his wedded wife and went to his brothers. They held a joyful wedding for forty days and forty nights, and as king the boy sat on his father's throne and lived with his wife for many years.

24

Master and Pupil

AARNE–THOMPSON TYPE 325

Of this story I give a version which I recorded in the summer of 1914—the precise date was the fateful fourth of August—from a young man in the Greek district of Santá in Pontis: the group of six or seven hamlets lies in a valley in the high pastures, the *parkhária*, between Trebizond and Argyropolis. Santá was a flourishing settlement with a special local coinage of its own: brass coins of one piastre and half a piastre with on one side a design, crude but bold, of St. Elias in his chariot. The *Master and Pupil* story has been discussed by Halliday with reference to Cosquin's study of *Le conte du magicien et son apprenti.*[1] They both hold that the story is 'undoubtedly of Indian origin'. As may be seen from the references given by BP., the European versions cover the whole continent.[2] Miss Wardrop has given a Georgian version.[3] In Greece the story is widely spread, from Pontos to Epeiros, but not common.

In one point very few of the versions of the story are quite clear. The reader may well ask why it is that the pupil must never admit having learned anything from his master. The answer is clearly given in a version from Vienna in BP.'s notes. The master wants a servant to help him, but the servant must never be allowed to pick up the magic art, specifically by knowing letters and so being able to read his master's secret books. The pupil conceals his knowledge of reading and so, without calling attention to what he is doing, acquires the master's skill, until one day the magician catches him reading his book of spells and he is driven out.

For the transformation fight at the end of the story I cannot do better than repeat Halliday's reference to E. S. Hartland's *Legend of Perseus*. The accidental calling up of the strange creature who calls himself 'Oh and Alas' is common in this story and well known elsewhere also, particularly in versions of No. 17, q.v.

The references are:

1. Pontic, from Santá: *Pontiakí Estía*, ii (1951), p. 956. Translated.

[1] *M.G. in A.M.*, p. 265, and Cosquin, *Études folkloriques*, pp. 502 ff.

[2] BP. ii. 60, in notes on Grimm, No. 68.

[3] Marjory Wardrop, *Georgian Folk Tales*, p. 1. Also in *Caucasian Folk Tales*, translated from A. Dion by Lucy Menzies, p. 13.

2. CAPPADOCIA: from Ulaghátsh, in *M.G. in A.M.*, p. 365.
3. SYRA: Hahn, ii. 33, No. 68.
4. SKYROS: Perdika, ii. 247, introduced into No. 43 below as a subsidiary story.
5. ATHENS: Kamboúroglou, p. 65, which is Garnett, p. 143.
6. EPEIROS: Hahn, ii. 286, as a variant of his No. 68.

NO. 24. MASTER AND PUPIL[1]

There was once a widow with a child. This child grew big and said to his mother: 'Mother, I want to marry the king's daughter. Rise up, and go and ask for her.' The first time his mother paid no heed to him. Later on the boy tried this way and that, and made his mother go into the king's presence. She said: 'My king, many be your years; may your royal realm prosper and may God give your sword a sharp edge: I have something to say to you. Will you give me your daughter to be my son's wife?' Then the king asked her: 'What is your son skilled to do?' She said: 'He is still young; nothing as yet; I have not had him taught.' Then the king said: 'Go away then, my good woman, and when he has learned every kind of skill there is, then let him come and ask for my daughter.' The mother went home and said to her son: 'My darling, if you want to marry and to have the king's daughter you must learn all crafts of every kind.' The boy wept day and night, saying: 'Mother, if I do not marry the king's daughter, I shall run mad.'

The poor mother, a staff in her hand, took her son and they went off. On her way she halted by a lake. She cried aloud: 'Oh and Alas for me, the poor widow!' She cried thus and out of the lake there came the Oh and Alas. He said to her: 'You have called me and I have come. My name is Oh and Alas.' At first the boy's mother would not tell him her trouble, but Oh and Alas would not let her go: 'Tell me,' said he: 'I am a herb to heal your wound.' Then the widow stayed there and told him all the story. Then said Oh and Alas: 'Have no fear. This is the very art I practise. I seek for men to teach them all skilful crafts. Let me have the boy. Then after three years come and take him again.' The mother went off and Oh and Alas took the boy and they went down under the water of the lake.

[1] Text from Santá in Pontos, in *Pontiakí Estía*, ii. 956.

When the daughter of Oh and Alas saw the boy, she loved him with all her heart, and was very grieved to think that he must perish, and to no purpose. When her father was going this way and that about his business, she came to the boy and said in his ear: 'Whatever you learn from my father, you must never let him know you have learned it. If you do, he will devour you.' Oh and Alas brought the boy to live there. From morning to evening he talked and talked and the boy understood. Then on the morrow he questioned him, but the boy would say to him nothing; nothing at all. The three years passed. The boy had gone on doing what the girl had counselled him: he was learning but would admit nothing.

Then after three years the boy's mother came to the lake and cried out 'Oh and Alas!' At once Oh and Alas came up out of the lake, bringing her son. Then the boy and his mother went on their way. 'Mother,' said he, 'have no fear; we are now rich people. If you wish, let the king give us his daughter; if you don't, why he may keep her. Mother, tonight I shall change myself into a big palace opposite the king's palace. In the morning you must offer me for sale, but be careful not to sell the key. If you sell the key, then you will have lost me.' They lay down to sleep. That night the boy changed himself into a palace, a palace finer than the king's. In the morning the woman rose up and looked out for a customer to whom to sell the palace. One was found and he paid her five thousand gold pieces. The mother let him have the house, but the key she did not let him have. 'I have lost it,' she said; she made some other excuses and kept the key. The unfortunate man conveyed all his furnishings and all his gear into the house: his folk ate and drank and made a great banquet for their friends with food and drink; then they lay down and went to sleep. But at dead of night they woke up, and just imagine! above them in the sky they saw the stars shining; their furnishings were all round them and they themselves were on the road; there on the road they had been sleeping. All the money they had paid was lost.

Next day the boy said to his mother: 'Mother, now I am going to turn myself into a horse, a finer horse than the king's. You shall sell me, but be careful not to sell the bridle. Then Oh and Alas found out that the boy had learned the art he had been teaching him and came out of the lake to buy the horse.

He came and questioned the woman: 'How much are you selling the horse for?' 'For five pounds,' said the woman. Oh and Alas counted out the five pounds and took the horse. But he wanted the bridle as well. 'The bridle,' said the woman, 'I am not selling.' 'Here are five more pounds; now let me have it.' When the woman looked at the money, it dazzled her and she let him have the bridle. He took the horse and went back into the lake. As he was going into the water, something happened to the horse; he swelled and swelled so that he was too big to pass through the gate. The daughter of Oh and Alas recognized the boy and to save him she seized her younger brother and threw him on the fire. Oh and Alas was busy with his son, and the horse took the opportunity and ran off and away. When Oh and Alas had rescued his son, he rushed off in pursuit of the horse. The horse turned into a bird. Oh and Alas turned into an eagle. The bird flew off; so did the eagle. The bird turned into a flower hanging from the king's cap. The eagle turned into a beggar and asked the king for the flower. The king handed it across to him, and the flower turned into a grain of corn and it fell from the king's hand. The beggar turned into a cock to eat the grain. The grain turned into a fox and the fox strangled the cock.

25

The Girl in the Bay-tree

THIS story is of a woman who had no children: she prayed for a child even if it were no more than the berry of a bay-tree. Such a child was born and from the berry there grew up a fine tree. From such an opening it might be supposed that the tree actually was the girl, but the story goes on as if the girl lived in the tree, among its branches or inside its trunk. The value of this distinction, of which the former idea seems to me rather oriental and the latter distinctively Greek, is discussed in the Kálymnos variant of the story in *Forty-five Stories*, No. 16, p. 211. The prince passed by and slept under the tree. He became aware that there was someone there, because either his food was found very much over-salted as though by some mischievous person, or the dishes had been touched. He found the girl and they fell in love. Then she being no more a maid, could not enter her tree again. In two versions from Thrace, one of which is translated here, she begged him never to allow himself to be kissed; this would be the kiss of forgetfulness and he would remember her no more. He did his best, but in his sleep his godfather kissed him and he forgot the girl of the tree. Then in the translated version he fell sick and the girl came to him in the disguise of a monk; she was recognized, and he married her. In other versions, again as a monk, she came to the church as he was being married to another girl, and the marriage was broken off in favour of the girl from the bay-tree.

The version from Mitylene is curious. It begins with a woman praying for a child even if she were to have to give it up and allow it to be taken from her by the bushes by the river: myrtle and bay. The bushes claimed her vow and the child was snatched away. The prince passed by the bushes and fell in love with her. Then, as in the other versions, she came to him dressed as a monk and found him being married to another girl. The wedding was not broken off and in the night she wrote him a letter to say what had happened. Next day they both killed themselves, an unhappy ending very rare in these stories.

The story seems not common. There is in Roumania a story of a girl who lives in a rose bush. In a Turkish version her abode is in a cypress, and when she follows the prince she disguises herself as a shepherd.[1]

[1] *Roumanian Fairy Tales and Legends*, by E. B. M., 1881, p. 42. The Turkish version

The kiss of forgetfulness we find again in No. 38, and in No. 49, *The Story of Fiorendino*, where there is a note on it. The circumstances are always the same: the man has married a wife in Fairyland or in some far country, and he is to pay a visit to his parents. But if he kissed them this would bring back to him his old ties of family affection, and he would forget his new obligations to his wife.

The Greek variants of this story are seven:

1, 2. MITYLENE: *Folklore*, xi. 339, and in Anagnóstou, *Lesbiaká*, p. 191.

3. KÁLYMNOS: *Forty-five Stories*, No. 16, p. 207.

4, 5. THRACE: *Thrakiká*, i. 214 and xvii. 100. The latter is translated below.

6. CRETE: *Epetirís et. kritikón spoudón*, iv. 202.

7. EPEIROS: Hahn, i. 163, No. 21, of which the Greek text is in Pio, p. 72; Geldart, p. 85.

NO. 25. THE GIRL IN THE BAY-TREE[1]

Once upon a time there was a woman; she had no children and she besought God to give her a child, were it only like the berry of a bay-tree, black and small. God heard her and gave her a child, small and like the berry of a bay-tree.

One day the mother took her clothes down to the stream to wash them; the child had been wrapped round with the clothes, but she could not be found. The mother searched here and searched there and could not find the child. She went back to her house crying.

Time went by and at the margin of the stream there grew up a tufted bay-tree. The prince coming back from the war passed by the stream and saw the bay-tree growing green. He sat down in its shade to refresh himself and ordered his table to be set ready underneath the tree. The prince was tired after his travelling and without eating fell asleep. When he woke up in the morning he saw that a fork had been thrust into all the dishes. Angrily he demanded who had dared to eat of the royal food. No one could be revealed as guilty. In the evening the table again was set; the prince pretended to be asleep and watched to see who it was who paid no heed to his commands. At midnight the branches of the bay-tree parted and out came a girl: never from mother earth had come a girl as fair as she

is in *Istanbul Masallari*, p. 62; and translated by Mrs. Kent, *Fairy Tales from Turkey*, p. 19.

[1] Text from Thrace in *Thrakiká*, xvii. 100.

was. She came quietly and ate a little from all the dishes and turned to go back into the bay-tree. When the prince saw her he was amazed; he caught her by the hair and said: 'Are you she who comes and eats of my food? I thought it was some one from my army who dared to do this. Tonight you must stay with me and tomorrow I will go with my people to my own land and then come back for you to make you my wife.' The girl was persuaded and stayed, saying: 'Be very careful that no one kisses you when you come to your country; otherwise you will forget me.'

Next day the prince said good-bye, mustered his company and went off. The king his father and the queen his mother, full of joy that their son had come back safe and sound from the war, were eager to kiss him; the prince drew away from them remembering what the girl had said: 'Be careful that no one kiss you; otherwise you will forget me.' His godfather heard that the boy he had christened had come back from the war and went to see him; the prince was asleep; the man bent down and kissed him. When he woke up he had forgotten the girl of the bay-tree: pensive and thoughtful he had no appetite to eat, none to speak, nor did he ask to be told any of the news. The queen in her grief did not know what to do; she sent for all the best doctors from the villages and the places near. To no purpose; day by day the prince was growing weaker.

Let us now leave the prince and tell of the bay-tree girl. When the prince went away she went back to the bay-tree and said: 'Open, my little bay-tree and let me enter in; open, my little bay-tree and let me enter in.' The bay-tree shut tight and would not open its branches to receive her; it said: 'Cuddled and kissed by royal lips, how can the bay-tree let you in?' The girl disconsolately wept and entreated; the bay-tree would not open and its twigs stirred lamentably as if they were saying, 'This is what befalls any girl who spends the night outside with a youth even if he be a prince.' A month passed; then two months; the prince did not come to take her; the bay-tree kept her shut out and the prince had forgotten her. Days and days she walked from village to village and so she came to the town where the prince was: she was told that he was very sick. She cut off her hair and put on a monk's robe and cap. She filled a bottle full of water and walked below the palace windows crying: 'A doctor for the sick to cure the sorrows of love; a doctor for the sick to cure the sorrows of love.' The prince heard this and told his mother to send for the doctor. 'But what can he do for you, my son? We have sent for all the best doctors and they have done you no good.' But this was the prince's wish and the queen ordered the doctor to be brought up. The prince questioned him: 'Where do you come from, monk?' 'From Bay-tree River.' 'And what have you seen or heard there?' 'I saw a girl weeping to make the trees wither. She was crying and what did she say? "O God, my good God, why did you put sleep upon me and take away my love?" ' The prince fell into a faint[1] and the monk sprinkled him with water from the bottle. This brought him round and again he asked: 'Where do you come from, monk?' 'From Bay-tree River.' 'And what have you seen or heard there?' 'I saw a girl weeping to make the trees wither.' 'Weeping was she? and what did she say?' ' "O my God, O my good God, why did you put sleep upon me and take away my love?" '

The girl put off her monk's gown and below it she had a woman's skirts. The prince recognized her and at once became well. In the palace there were rejoicings and high feasts as for Easter. Men came from all the realm to be present at the wedding of the prince and the fair girl of the bay-tree. The wedding was kept up for forty days and forty nights and they lived well and may we live even better.

[1] In the text this episode is repeated—'The prince again fell into a faint'—to the end of the paragraph.

26

The Underworld Adventure

THIS story has been studied by Crane and by Cosquin, who have notes on the European distribution of the variants, and lastly by Halliday in connexion with versions from Cappadocia.[1] He regards it as a story rather of the Near East than of western Europe. In Greek lands most versions run as follows. A king had three sons and by his palace there stood an apple-tree. The apples were always stolen and the sons one after the other undertook to catch the thief. The first two failed; the youngest wounded the thief, and following the traces of blood the brothers came to a well. The youngest son was let down the well and there he found three girls enslaved to the ogre who had been stealing the apples. The youngest girl gave him three nuts each one of them containing one of the three dresses so often heard of in these stories: one embroidered with the earth and its flowers, the second with the sea and the fish, and the third with the sky and the stars. She warned him that his elder brothers who had drawn up the other two girls and would presently draw her up too, would leave him in the well: here is an obvious contact with Nos. 34, 35, the stories of the treacherous brothers and of the servant who gets his master at a disadvantage. The hero left in the well came across two sheep, a white and a black; by mounting the black sheep instead of the white he was carried to a world below. Here he delivered the people and the princess from a monster which was cutting off the water, and as a reward he claimed to be carried up again into the Upper World. This is generally done by eagles whom he has to supply with water and meat. In the Thracian version here translated the boy won the favour of an eagle by saving her chicks from a snake, and she carried him up. But always on the way the meat runs short, and he has to keep the eagle going by cutting for him a piece of flesh from his own leg. In the Upper World the princess has all this time been seeking for the man to whom she gave the nuts with the three dresses. The hero working for a tailor undertakes to make the dresses demanded and as he has them already can spend the whole time he is supposed to be working at them drinking wine and eating nuts: this is an episode found in several other stories.

[1] Crane, *Italian popular Tales*; Cosquin, *Contes de Lorraine*, i. 1–27, ii. 135–46; Halliday in *M.G. in A.M.*, p. 274.

In the morning he produced the three dresses and the princess recognized him as the man she had seen in the well.

The story is often not well told and the details vary a good deal. For instance, in the version translated the stealing of apples is omitted. In particular there is sometimes, at least in non-Greek versions, some confusion between the interior of the well, which must be taken rather as a large cistern, and the actual underworld; in other words, the descent on the back of the black sheep is often omitted.

Halliday has pointed out that this story has sometimes quite a different beginning, and this he observed in Servian, Magyar, Russian, and Georgian variants, as well as in the Greek version from Ainos. I find this alternative opening also in Valavánis's unpublished version from Kerasund and in the underworld adventure as it is introduced at the end of a long, irrelevant, story from the island of Gavdos off Crete. The opening at Kerasund is typical. The hero is the well-known Strong Man, the Son of the Widow as he is very Akritically called. He has two companions, the Salt-man and the Stone-man. Their adversary called the Short-Man overcomes the companions and then the hero attacks him and cuts off his head. The head rolls away down into a cave or cistern. The three of them follow the trail, the head shouting: 'To him who can catch me I will give all the riches of the world.' The hero is left by his companions down in the well with the girls and the two sheep, and so the story follows the usual lines. The version from Ainos is much the same.

In the version from Ordoú in Pontos the story has been ingeniously used to make a kind of second chapter to the story of Faithful John; for which see the notes on No. 37. On this curious underworld, quite distinct from the world of the dead, I have written in a note to No. 41.

The references are:

1, 2. Pontos: an unpublished version from Kerasund recorded by I. Valavánis, and a version from Ordoú in Akoglou's *Laographiká Kotyóron*, p. 391.

3, 4. Cappadocia: from Ulaghátsh in *M.G. in A.M.*, p. 371, and from Sílata, ibid., p. 449.

5. Piiárasa in the Taurus: a poor version not published.

6. Cyprus: *Kypriaká Khroniká*, xii. 232.

7. Symi: *Z.A.* i. 241.

8, 9, 10, 11. Mitylene: *Folklore*, x. 495 and xi. 452; Carnoy–Nicolaïdes, p. 75; Georgeakis et Pineau, *Folklore de Lesbos*, No. 35.

12. Smyrna: Legrand, *Recueil de contes pop. grecs*, p. 191.

13. Syra: Hahn, ii. 49, No. 70, which is also Kretschmer, *Neugr. Märchen*, p. 267

14, 15. Mýkonos: Roussel, *Contes de Mycono*, pp. 27 and 43.

16. Thera: *Parnassós*, x. 517.

17. Crete, Island of Gavdos: *Sýllogos*, xxxi. 139.

18. THRACE: *Thrakiká*, xvii. 103. Translated below.
19. AINOS IN THRACE: *Sýllogos*, ix. 363.
20. MACEDONIA: Abbott, *Macedonian Folklore*, p. 351.

THE UNDERWORLD ADVENTURE[1]

Once upon a time there were three young men. They heard that down in a well there were three girls, and they went to bring them up. They said that the youngest of them should have as his wife the youngest girl, the middle brother the middle girl, and the eldest brother the eldest girl. The eldest brother went down into the well by a rope and he brought up first the youngest and then the middle sister. He was about to bring up the eldest sister when she said to him: 'You go up now and I will come up afterwards, for when your brothers see that I am the fairest of the three they will both want me for their wife, and they will pull up the rope and leave you here in the well.' The young man was unwilling to go up before her, and the girl then said: 'I know well that they will pull the rope up out of the well and leave you. Now you must take these two nuts: one has in it a dress worked with the sun and the stars, and the other a dress with the earth and the flowers: they are made without stitching or work of needle. Then two sheep will come by, one black and the other white. If you succeed in throwing yourself on the white sheep it will carry you to the Upper World and if you mount the black sheep it will carry you to the World Below.' The youths hauled at the rope and the girl was brought up out of the well. Hardly had the two brothers seen her than they marvelled at her beauty and wanted to take her in marriage themselves: they did not let the rope down the well again. The middle brother wanted very much to take the girl as his wife but she put him off with delays as long as she could. The days passed and so the girl said with a sad heart: 'Let our wedding take place, but first I must have two dresses, one to be worked with the sun and the stars and the other with the earth and its flowers; they must be without stitching or work of needle.' If he could bring her these dresses then she would know that her own lad was in the Upper World and to get him for her husband she would make even the impossible possible.

[1] Text from Thrace in *Thrakiká*, xvii. 103, with the title *The three Boys and the three Girls*.

Now let us leave the girl and return to the youth who was still down in the well, waiting for them to throw down the rope that he might catch it and be pulled up. He waited and waited: nothing. Then in the bottom of his pocket he hid the two nuts and waited and then he saw the two sheep. The white one passed by and he threw himself upon it, but not in time to get a grip. Then he flung himself upon the black sheep and seized it. The sheep carried him down to the World Below and there pitched him on a tree. Birds were perching on the tree and also he saw a snake approaching. In those days animals could talk. The birds said to the young man: 'O save us; the snake will devour us.' So he killed the snake. The mother bird came, a monstrous creature, and by the side of her chicks she saw the young man. She thought he had come to wring the necks of her chicks and attacked him furiously. The chicks besought her not to do him any harm, saying: 'This man is our deliverer: the snake was coming to devour us and see, he killed the snake.' Then the mother bird spread out her wings to make a shade over him and thanked him for the kindness he had done her: every year she hatched chicks and never saw them grow up; the snake used to come and devour them.

Then she asked him what favour he would like her to do him in return for this benefit. 'If you can carry me from down here up into the Upper World.' 'I can do it,' said the bird. Bring me forty sheep and forty skins of water and load them on my wings. Then you take your seat and we will be off.' The youth went and brought everything; the bird spread her wings and he set the sheep on them and the forty skins of water: then he himself took his seat. The bird soared up. She called out *Kra* and he gave her meat to eat; she cried out *Krou* and he gave her water: all the time they were flying on. Then the meat came to an end; the bird cried *Kra*, but what was the youth to do? He cut off a piece from his hip, the soft and fleshy part. The Upper World came in sight and the bird came to a stop outside the town. She took from her tongue the piece of man's flesh and set it back in its place so that there was no more pain. Then the bird thanked him for delivering her children and at once soared aloft and was out of sight. When the youth came to himself he entered the town. The first person he met was a merchant and he asked him to take him with him into his service. The merchant was in need of an assistant and took him. Time passed by and the youth saw the merchant in some trouble; he said: 'What is it grieving you, master?' 'What a story I have to tell you! Two dresses have been ordered of me, one worked with the sky and the stars, the other with the world and its flowers, and no stitchery or work of needle.' 'Is this what you are troubled about? Let me have a bottle of wine and sweets and some raisins and in the night I will make them.'

The merchant did not believe him but he brought him all he asked for. The boy shut himself up in the room; he ate the raisins and the sweets; he drank the wine and then he cracked one of his nuts: out of it there came a dress worked with the sun and the stars. The dress filled the room with light and the boy hung it on a nail. He cracked his second nut and out came the dress with the earth and its flowers: it had no stitchery or work with the needle. At its beauty the room laughed with joy, and this dress too the boy hung on a nail. In the morning the merchant saw the dresses and was amazed. When he took them to the bride she knew at once that her own youth was in the Upper World. For the wedding the crowns were ready; the wedding feast had begun with music and dancing and tables set out for a banquet. The youth went there with the merchant and they sat down at the table to eat: the bridegroom and the bride also sat down. The young man saw the girl and they recognized one another. When they had eaten, then the merchant spoke with words that came from God: 'If I take a vine branch and set it here on the table and it grows leaves and sets fruit and gives grapes for all of us to eat, then, oh then, we may give the bride to another husband.' All laughed to think of him making a vine twig grow leaves and set fruit and give grapes for them all to eat, and on this condition the bride being given to another husband. They consented to what he had said. Then the merchant took a vine twig and set it in the midst on the table; he blessed it and behold, it began to grow leaves, to set fruit, and to give grapes, hanging from it all as yellow as gold. All of them ate of the grapes, amazed at the marvel. Again the merchant spoke with words sent him by God: 'The bride is to be taken in marriage by the young man whom I have with me and I myself will set on their heads the crowns of marriage.' The wedding took place joyfully and they lived well and we yet better.

27

The Strigla

THE Greek word *strigla*, whatever its derivation may be and whether or not it has any connexion with a verb meaning *to utter loud cries*, has a quite definite use. The strigla is a female monster born of human parents, whose nature it is in secret and at night to suck the blood of and then devour first horses and then men; her activities are not unlike those of the vampire. The title of the version from Kárpathos here translated shows that she is confused with another Greek bogy, ancient and modern, the Gelló or Yiloú, who as a rule attacks babies. The general ideas of the Greeks about such creatures may be best learned from Politis's two volumes of *Traditions* (*Paradóseis*) or from Lawson's *Modern Greek Folklore and ancient Greek Religion*.

The folktale of the strigla is widely spread in the Greek islands; except for a version from Athens it has not been found elsewhere as yet.

The essential outline of the story is that in a family all of boys at last a much longed-for daughter was born. But it was soon found out from her dreadful doings that the girl at night became a strigla and was killing the horses in the stable. The elder brothers kept watch to kill her but they were themselves killed. The youngest brother then took flight with his mother. Soon the mother took to herself a lover, an ogre or sometimes a Jew, and the two set themselves to get rid of the boy. The mother pretended sickness and her son was sent off on dangerous quests to fetch her remedies: magic apples, the Water of Life, and so on. In all these tasks he was helped by his lady love and often by his horse, or his dogs, or his favourite lion cubs. At last his mother wheedled him into telling her where his 'external soul' was kept, so that-by destroying it she might bring him to his death: in the version translated below it is in three hairs on his head. In the end the hero escaped from the wicked pair or else killed them, and with his wife went back home and killed the strigla, still living among the ruins of the house.

There is also a strigla story from Aitolia in *Laographía*, ii. 385, but this records no more than the struggles of the hero against the strigla and has no connexion at all with the island story. In fact it does no more than tell us of the wideness of the belief in the monster herself.

If we put this story into the terms of a tale of real life, we see that the underlying theme is of a young man whose sister is born bad and whose mother, whom he has rescued and on whom he is ready to lavish all the trust and even credulity of affection, turns against him and allies herself with an unworthy lover. From these troubles he is rescued by the faithfulness of his horse and by the counsels of his lady love, with whom at the end he is left happy.

Although they are well knitted together the story plainly consists of two parts; we might say two chapters. The first contains the ravages of the strigla and the escape of the hero and his mother; the second the alliance of his mother with her wicked lover and their attempts to destroy him. With some suitable introduction this second part is quite enough to make a separate story in which the strigla plays no part, and we have only the wicked mother and her lover and their machinations against the hero and his lady. This second part is found over a much wider range than the complete story: in fact all the way from Pontos to Epeiros. On the question of whether we have here a splitting-up of a rather complex story or an ingenious welding together of the two themes I should rather say nothing. On the relation of this story with No. 28, *The three wonderful Dogs*, I have said something in discussing the latter story.

In the example from Kárpathos which I have chosen for translation it is interesting to note that the story is localized to Kárpathos by the mention of local names. Apeiri is a big village in the southern part of the island; Aphiarti is a locality somewhere near it, presumably with ancient remains, the name preserving the *Ephiálteion akron* of Ptolemy; and a few other names occur. This localization seems not common in Greek tales. It goes part way towards presenting a folk-tale as a local legend.

The references for the complete strigla story are:

1, 2. CHIOS: Argenti and Rose, *The Folklore of Chios*, p. 526, and an unpublished variant recorded by Kanellakis.
3. KÁLYMNOS: *Folklore*, xi. 240.
4. KÁRPATHOS: Mikh.-Nouáros, *L. S. Karpáthou*, i. 304; translated.
5. SKYROS: Pérdika, ii. 199.
6. TENOS: Four variants by Adamantíou in *Deltíon*, v. 293.
7. MÝKONOS: Roussel, *Contes de Mycono*, p. 44.
8. ATHENS: Kamboúroglou, p. 52 = Garnett, p. 245.

For the latter part of the story only:

1. PONTOS: *Arkheíon Pontou*, vii. 97.
2. CYPRUS: *Sakellarios*, ii. 330.
3. SYRA: Hahn, ii. 25, No. 65.
4. MÝKONOS: Roussel, *Contes de Mycono*, p. 77.

5, 6. THERA: *Parnassós*, v. 438, and Kretschmer, *Neugr. Märchen*, p. 194.
7, 8. EPEIROS: Pio, p. 9, which is Hahn, i. 90, No. 6, and Hahn, i. 215, No. 32.

NO. 27. THE STRIGLA[1]

Once upon a time there were a king and a queen and they had twelve sons, fine fellows, but they had no daughter, and for this they secretly grieved: every day they used to pray God to give them a daughter. After many prayers God heard them; the queen became with child and gave birth to a daughter. But the child was a strigla; at night she used to rise up and go to the stable and strangle the horses and drink their blood; then she lay down again without anyone knowing of it.

Every morning the king's servants used to go to the stable, and each time they found a horse strangled: next day the same thing and the next also. The king was told, and he ordered watchmen to be set to see who it was strangling the horses. When the eldest son heard this he went and said to his father: 'My lord king, give me a bow and your blessing and let me go and keep watch and kill the evil creature who is destroying our horses.' The king said: 'Go, and with my blessing.' So he went to the stable watching and waiting, and about midnight he saw a cloud filling all the stable so that a man could not even see his own finger: no, it was not the west wind with its shroud of mist. Into the midst of this cloud the prince shot an arrow: to no purpose. In the morning another horse was found dead. The second son heard of this, and he also went: to no purpose. The third and the fourth too: in a word eleven of them all kept guard and shot at the cloud, but in vain. Then the youngest son went and he shot an arrow at the cloud. He heard crying as a baby might cry who had cut his hand with a piece of glass. He lit a taper and went to see; he saw blood and drop by drop he traced it on and on till he came at last to the baby's cradle. Then the lad understood that the baby was a strigla and would devour them all one by one as soon as she had devoured the horses. He went and told his father: 'Father, we must go away from here;' and so he told him all the story. 'My sister is a strigla and she will be the death of all of us.' When the eleven brothers heard this, they

[1] Text from Mikh.-Nouáros, *L. S. Karpáthou*, i. 304 with the title *The Gelló*.

went off, each as he could: there were left only the king and the queen and the youngest brother. Then said the youth: 'Come, we too must go away; otherwise we are lost.' The old king said: 'I do not intend to run away. I shall stay here. In this way I may lose my life; the other way would be the death of me. You may take your mother and go off and save yourselves.'

So they took a horse for the mother to ride, and laid on it a saddle-bag full of money and a basket of dates to eat on the way, and so they went off. They went on and on and in the evening they came to a spring. The queen said to her son: 'Here in the open we can lodge for the night.' So they ate some dates and laid down their rugs and went to sleep. In the night their date stones, three apiece, sprouted up and grew into date-palms; very high trees, and when the sun rose up these gave them shade. When they had broken their fast in the morning they loaded up their gear and went on and on. At the setting of the sun they came to a tower and in the courtyard outside it they saw forty ogres and a huge cauldron with forty handles. The ogres were trying to lift the cauldron down but they could not. Then said the eldest of them: 'Brothers, today we had no good meat at midday; we could get no flesh of men and so our strength is failing us. But over there I see that a horse is coming with two people riding, so we shall have a nice little dish.' When the prince came up they cried out: 'Hi, friend, won't you come and help us to lift down the cauldron? We will give you your share.' Their intent was to pluck him like a fowl. He said: 'Go you to one side; I don't need your help at all.' Then he took hold of the cauldron by two handles and lifted it down. Then he said: 'Come this way one after the other and take your ration each one of you.' Then he attacked them with his bow and left not one of them alive.

Then said he to his mother: 'Let us stay here in the tower and I will go hunting and bring game for you to cook; thus we can live. And at your leisure drag away the ogres and throw them down into the ravine for the crows to eat them, and then you can sweep up the blood and set the house in order by the time I come back again.' So the prince went off hunting and he went as we might say down to Aphiarti; the place where in old days there stood a great city with palaces and towers. In the evening he brought back some game and the queen cooked it and so they did very well. At the very time you might say that the queen was dragging the ogres away out to throw them down into the ravine and rid the place of the stink, she went to sweep underneath the cauldron, and there she found an ogre curled up. He said: 'I am at your feet and in the hand of God, O my queen. Do not hand me over to your son for he will kill me; let me live and I will work for you and just ask to eat a morsel of bread.' The queen had pity on him and hid him from her son. By day the ogre did all the queen's work and by night he hid himself underneath the cauldron and no one knew anything about it. As soon as it was morning the prince used to go out hunting and in the evening he would return: he went always to the same place, Aphiarti. It seems that he had fallen in love with a princess who lived there and he told his mother that they were betrothed. But love does not seize hold only of the young but old people as well it drives out of their minds, and the queen started an affair with the ogre. The prince at that time began every now and then to spend a night away in the tower of his betrothed, and sometimes it was two or three nights before he came back. The queen pretended to be angry because her son was thus leaving her by herself, but this was all for a show, because she too had her lover and passed her time very pleasantly. But however much this was so, she was uneasy, because the prince might learn of it and before one could count three put an end to both of them. So they found in this a good excuse to kill the prince so that in this way their opportunities for pleasure might be even fuller.

The ogre said to the queen: 'Now when your son comes, you must pretend to be sick and when he asks you what is the matter, you must tell him that you will die if he does not go and bring you the Water of Life, for you to drink and be whole.' So when her son came in the evening, she told him all this and he said: 'For your pleasure, my dear mother, I will go to the very end of the world to make you well.' Then he went off to his betrothed and told her that this and that had happened. She said: 'Go; do not be afraid and I will guide you what to do. The Water of Life is in such a place'—let us say at Katodio near Apeiri—'and it is guarded by forty ogres. You must go there on your horse and get a look at them from above. If the ogres have their eyes staring wide, that means they are asleep, and you can dismount and take the water from the cistern and go off. But if they have their eyes shut, then they are awake and you must run off: if you don't you are lost.'

So the youth mounted his horse, and, one, two, he came to Katodio. By his good fortune the ogres were there lying down, their eyes open and staring. 'What a chance,' said he and plunged a jug into the cistern and took of the Water of Life and off he went. The Water began to shout and cry: 'They are carrying me off; they are carrying me off.' The ogres woke up and went in pursuit. The horse went like the wind and before they could turn and see where he had gone, the youth had reached Aphiarti and the tower of his betrothed. But he was so tired he lay down to recover his strength, and his betrothed emptied out the Water of Life and set it aside and filled up the jug with water from the pitcher she had there. When the prince rose up he took the water to his mother to make her well. She had of course nothing the matter with her, but was shamming sick, so that by sending her son on this quest she might get rid of him. But when she saw that he had come back alive from the quest for the Water of Life, she said: 'Look, my boy, the Water of Life has done me no good. If you want me to be well, for I see that my sickness grows worse and worse, you must go and fetch me the Apples of Life for me to eat and be cured.' He said: 'All to give you pleasure, my mother.'

So off he went again and came to his betrothed and told her the story: 'My mother is asking for the Apples of Life and is sending me off to fetch them.' She said: 'Be easy; you need have no fear. You must go and find the forty ogres who guard the tree with the Apples of Life. To get there you must pass in between two great rocks which open and then shut again. The tree with the apples is in a garden which lies in there beyond the rocks. If you succeed in passing through with your horse and the rocks don't catch you, then you will get the apples and come back safely. But if the rocks catch you, then you are lost.' So the youth went off and came to that place. He passed through with his horse before the rocks closed. He came to the apple-tree and found the forty ogres all of them asleep: in a moment he gathered the apples and ran off. At the moment he was going out, the rocks shut and caught the tail of his horse, and tore off half of it. The horse lamented the loss of his beautiful tufted tail and the prince consoled him saying: 'Don't be vexed, my dear little horse. I will deck your tail with gold when we come to the tower.' I forgot to tell you that at the moment when the prince was plucking the apples, the tree began to cry out: 'They are carrying off my apples, my apples.' At this the ogres woke up and chased the youth, but by that time he had passed the rocks and he took no mischief from the ogres. So he came to his betrothed and showed her the apples. She did as before and kept back the Apples of Life and put in exchange others like them and these he took to his mother. When she saw them she ate them and pretended to be now in sevenfold health: O, may her years be few. By this she understood that she could not easily rid herself of him, so she said: 'Now that I am well, you must go to our palace and see what your poor unhappy father is doing, for he is now an old man; and you must also see what our daughter is doing, whom we left a baby when we went away.' The wicked woman's object was to send him off and have him devoured by the strigla. The youth again went to his betrothed, saying: 'My mother is sending me to our house where my sister the strigla is, and when you see three drops of blood falling from my bow hung up here and my dogs tied up here turning the place upside down, then you must let the dogs loose, for I shall be in great danger.' So the prince went off to the town where they had once had their palace. The palace was standing there but no soul born of woman was to be seen there anywhere; neither master nor servant, neither horse nor horse-fly was anywhere there: the strigla had devoured them all and had grown to such a monstrous size that she filled the whole house from the very top down to the courtyard. When she saw the youth with his horse she knew him at once and said: 'Welcome, my little brother, for I have had nothing to eat for two or three days; this will be a fine day for me.' All trembling with fear the youth said: 'First, tonight you may eat my horse and in the morning you can eat me.' She said: 'So be it: I won't thwart your pleasure.' So out she rushed and with one bite nipped off one of the horse's feet. Then she came and asked him: 'How many feet has your horse, brother?' He said: 'Four.' She said: 'As I see it he has but three.'

Then presently she ate another foot and again asked the same question; by dawn she had devoured the whole horse. Then she came and asked: 'How many horses have you, brother?' He said: 'One.' 'But now you haven't any horse at all.' Then she said: 'Now your turn has come, because with one horse only I have not yet had my fill.' He said: 'Before you devour me, do me a kindness and bring me a jug of fresh water from the well in the courtyard that I may drink and not go on my way thirsty.' She said: 'Don't you see I have not slept all night guarding you and keeping you from running away? And now I don't trust you.' He said: 'If you like you can bring me a sheepbell to hold and I can ring it so you will hear that I have not run away while you are going to fetch the water.' 'Very well,' she said. So the prince rang the bell and the strigla could hear it and was at ease, saying: 'I have you here all right.' When she had filled the jug, she said: 'It would be a good thing to wash myself a little: I was all night without sleep.' So she washed and freshened herself. Then she said: 'O for a whetstone! Would it not be a good thing for me to whet my teeth a little for I have been all this time without whetting them and now I want to enjoy my food.' Now while the youth was ringing the bell for the strigla to hear him, a mouse with no tail also heard the noise and came out from his hole: he saw a youth ringing the bell. The mouse said: 'What are you doing here, my young man? The strigla will break all your bones. Do you not see that she has even nipped off my tail?' He said: 'What am I to do?' The mouse said: 'Tie the bell to my foot and I will ring it for you and you can run off.' So the prince ran off and disappeared. Right at this point the strigla returned. She heard the bell but could see no man at all: the mouse had hidden himself in his hole and was ringing the bell there. In her rage the strigla pulled down the wall and swallowed it all down and the bell as well. Then she ran off to catch her brother and chased him and chased him, and the hills and mountains echoed with the noise she made. When she saw him two or three miles away she shouted out: 'Oho, my lad, and where are you off to? I mean to drink your blood.' Then presently she had all but caught him. When he saw the danger he climbed up a little palm-tree: you remember that he and his mother had eaten three dates and that three date-palms had sprung up from the stones? The strigla came below him and said: 'Come down or I shall cut the tree and so you will be brought down.' Then she made one snap with her jaws and bit through the palm-tree as though it had been less than a stalk of asphodel. Just in time the prince jumped across to the next palm-tree. The strigla came up crying: 'Come down.' 'I won't come down.' Then the second palm-tree was cut through and now there was but one left. When the prince saw the strait he was in he said to the strigla: 'Now indeed my end has come, but let me shout three times and whistle three times and then I will come down for you to eat me.' She said: 'You may shout and whistle as much as you like, but no longer can you escape from my teeth.' Then he cried out: 'Lion, Tiger, and my good Little Fox,' and whistled three times for his dogs. At that moment his betrothed saw his bow and it was distilling three drops of blood, and the dogs were gnawing at their chains and baying. So she at once let them loose and before you could rub your eyes, there they were at the foot of the date palm. 'What are your orders, master?' said they. He said: 'See the strigla up there; tear her to pieces.' And they threw themselves upon her. At the very moment when they were tearing her to pieces and devouring her she cried out, O the cursed creature: 'For sure some finger-nail will be left of me and that shall grow to my full stature once more and devour you.' The prince from up above in the tree shouted to the dogs: 'Let me see you at work. Not a nail, not an ear, not a hair must you leave of her. If you do we are lost.' Then Little Fox saw that one of her toe-nails had been pushed into the earth; at once he scratched with his paws and then swallowed that too.

Then the prince came down from the tree and went to his betrothed. She hardly knew him so like a wild man had he become in his fight with the strigla. Then he went back to his mother and told her all that had happened to him. In the evening the queen and the ogre talked together. She said: 'To have escaped from the strigla he must have some power somewhere to help him and we must find it and get it away from him. So when it was dawn his mother said to him: 'Come, my son, my golden son, show me where you have your manly power for I want to do homage to it and to burn incense to it every day, for it has done so many things for us.' No word came from his lips, but his mother was so persistent that to get rid of her he said: 'See, my manly power resides in the broom by our door.' Then she took the broom and decorated it with ribbons and other adornments and set it among the icons and incensed it and made as though she were worshipping it as the source of her son's manly strength. Some days later when her son had gone hunting she talked with the ogre. 'See, now is a time for us to burn the broom in the oven; then his strength will be lost and the wild beasts will devour him and he will never come back here again.' So they went and threw the broom into the fire and thought they had got the dog by the foot so great was their delight. Late in the evening, behold, the prince bringing two horses laden with lion cubs and tigers: he had not even had a bad dream.

In the morning again his mother said to him: 'Come, my son, my golden son, don't you love me? Why won't you tell me in what your manly strength is lodged?' He said: 'In the kerchief round my neck.' Then she took the kerchief and washed it and ironed it and hung it up where the icons were. She burned incense before it morning and evening and prostrated herself and saluted it with reverence praying God to guard her son and his manly power. At that time two kings were making war and the prince too went with his army to fight. Then the queen said to the ogre: 'Now is the time for us to see if he is telling us lies when he says that his manly strength is lodged in this kerchief.' They took the kerchief and tore it to bits and threw it into the fire. Then they fried a pan full of eggs and ate them.

In two or three days, behold, the prince appeared with all his banners and with cries of victory. 'Again he has managed to cheat us,' said the wicked woman. In the morning, weeping and beating her breast, again she began saying: 'I am by now an old woman and must die, and you won't trust me with your secret that I may know it and rejoice over my son's bravery?' This and many other wheedling words. The youth was moved to see his mother weeping—how could he guess that the shameless woman was acting with a lover?—and so this time he told her the whole truth saying: 'On the crown of my head there are three golden hairs, and in them is lodged my manly strength. If anyone cuts these three hairs, all is over with me.' Two or three days passed and they were sitting there one evening on the balcony of the tower talking together. Then the queen said to her son: 'Come hither, my son, to my knees that I may cleanse your head and tell you a story too and pass the time.' And while she was pretending to cleanse his head and the prince had gone off to sleep, she took a little pair of scissors out of her pocket and cut the three golden hairs at the root. At once the prince woke up but he had now no strength, not even to rise up. Then the bitch knew for sure that her son had lost his strength; she called for the ogre and with his billhook they cut him into forty pieces. They dug a grave forty fathoms deep and put him into a sack and threw him in; then they filled it up with stones and earth.

At the moment of this murder the prince's dogs in the tower of his betrothed were biting at their chains and turning everything upside down. The girl was then aware that something evil had befallen her betrothed and she let them loose. The dogs went and scratched at the grave with their nails whining. Then they turned back to the tower of the betrothed and then again back to the grave. Then the girl went off with them. She saw the grave and brought men to dig it up. They found the sack and the forty little pieces of her betrothed. Who ever wept, who ever was filled with longing but this girl? She took the sack and brought out the pieces one by one and set each of them in its place as they were in the man's body. Then she took the Water of Life which she had laid by safely and sprinkled it all over the pieces. They came together and the youth stood there alive as he had been at first. Then she laid the Apples of Life upon his eyes and his sight came to him. The only thing lacking was the manly strength he had before. But day by day as the hairs grew longer his strength came again. Then when he was fully recovered, he went back to his mother's house and found her sitting there with the ogre; each of them had a child in their arms and was caressing it. He seized the same billhook with which they had cut him to pieces; one blow for his mother; one blow for the ogre; and one for the little bastards: he cut them all into pieces. Then he threw them to his dogs and the dogs ate them at one gulp, and so they were rid of them.

Then he went to his betrothed and they held their wedding with festivities and joy and fair diversions, and they had heirs to their line who filled all the world. Yet for all that I was not there and you are not to believe the story.

28

The three wonderful Dogs

OF this story I find in Greece only two real examples; one is from Chios and one from Zákynthos.[1] As recorded in Chios the story is that there were a brother and a sister, the brother being the owner of three wonderful dogs, with names expressing their strange powers: Hill-splitter, Iron-eater, and Star-gazer. They found themselves in the tower of an ogre and the sister allied herself with the ogre against her brother. To get rid of him the girl pretended to be sick; thus she and her ogre lover found a pretext to send him off on the dangerous search for rare medicaments: in Chios for the Water of Life; in the Zákynthos version for a curative apple. They hoped that in these quests he would lose his life, but he was always saved by the three dogs, and the ogre and the sister discomfited. The last part of the story tells how the brother rescued a princess from a monster and married her. Like Andromeda, she was being offered to a monster to be devoured, for without such sacrifices the monster would allow no one to go to draw water from the spring. This is a motive very common in these stories.

The version from Zákynthos is very much less complete. Of the love of the sister for the ogre we have hardly a hint; the dogs, Digger, Iron-biter, and One who could run like a Camel, have no special roles to play and the story is clumsily told. It seems hardly worth while to translate such a bad version, especially as the story seems of Italian origin. I therefore content myself with the reference to the Chian version and add a few notes on the general relations of the story.

Two other Greek stories are akin to this one of the three dogs. One is from Thera and appeared in *Parnassós*, vii. 551. A childless king was ready to hand over to the Iron Wolf any son he might have; just like the parents in *The Child given and claimed*: Nos. 7, 38, 39, 83. The story consists of the boy's adventures in fleeing from the Iron Wolf. He is helped by his three dogs and the Iron Wolf is helped by the hero's treacherous wife. Finally the dogs devour both the queen and the Iron Wolf.

The other similar story is from Euboia in Hahn i. 79, No. 4, and

[1] From Chios in Argenti and Rose, *Folklore of Chios*, p. 483, and from Zákynthos in *Laographía*, xi. 525.

in Kretschmer, *Neugr. Märchen*, p. 281. A childless queen was given three sons by a dervish; the youngest was carried off by the wicked dervish but escaped. He was helped by a lamia, by three ogres, and finally by three lions who take the place of the three dogs of the other stories. His wife then allied herself with the dervish against him, but their plans were frustrated by the three lions.

This story, rare in Greece, has many parallels in Italy. Pitrè has published a version from Tuscany where the three dogs are called Ferro, Acciaio and Più-forte-di-tutti. From Sicily also he has printed a variant, and the only substantial difference between this and the Greek versions is that the disturber of the happiness of the hero and his sister is a wicked miller.[1] All the rest of the story is closely the same, and Pitrè gives so many variants from Italy that in the face of the rarity of Greek examples, and all of them being from parts of Greece largely under influence from Italy, it may be taken as probable that the story has passed into Greece from Italy during, it may be suggested, the post-crusade period of Italian occupation and rule.

It is at once plain that this story, though pretty clearly of Italian origin, is in some points very close to the latter part of the strigla story, No. 27 above. The only real difference is that in the strigla story it is the hero's unnatural mother who conspires against him, while in the present story it is his sister with her monstrous lover. Also in the strigla story he is helped by his horse and his lady love; here by the three dogs. But the full strigla story belongs, as we have seen, rather to the eastern part of the Greek world, while *The three Dogs* seems to have reached Greece from the west, from Italy. It seems to me therefore that there are no reasons for seeing a genetic connexion between the two stories. Both are based on the same theme, that under the influence of a base love a woman may forget her natural family affections, but the idea is fairly obvious, and the working out is so different, in one case with the hero's mother and in the other with his sister, and the means of his deliverance are so different, that the two stories must, I believe, stand apart. The method of trying to get rid of the hero by sending him on dangerous quests is, it is true, the same in both, but this method is a commonplace in very many stories; for example notably in No. 42, *The Son of the Hunter*.

[1] Pitrè's texts are in *Novelle popolari toscane*, p. 9, and *Fiabe e leggende popolari siciliane*, i, p. 15, No. iii.

29

The Sun rises in the West

IN a long and important paper, *The Sun in popular Story*, Politis has given in outline a tale picked up in Smyrna.[1] A man was swindled by a Jew and lost not only his property but his wife and child. He wandered off in despair and came to a tower. This was the tower of the Sun and the woman who admitted him was the Sun's wife. The Sun came and wanted to devour the man, but the wife appeased his appetite by an abundant meal and the Sun was ready to help the man. He told him he must go and make a bet with the Jew that the sun would rise not in the east but in the west; and this the Sun promised to do. The Jew jumped at the idea of betting on a certainty: the sun did rise in the west; the man won his bet and the Jew had to give him back his wife and his child and all his property.

Kretschmer gives a similar story from Thera.[2] A man had a tree given him by a snake and this tree would bear, as its owner wished, either quinces or pomegranates. By betting on what fruit it would bear the man won first a ship and then the stock of glass-ware belonging to a Jew. The Jew then contrived a bet with the man and won everything he possessed. The man then went to ask the help of the Sun who promised to help him by rising in the wrong quarter, and on this he could make a bet with the Jew. The Jew betting on what seemed a certainty lost, and the man won back everything.

Pernot in his *Études de linguistique*, iii. 273, has printed a rather confused story from Chios beginning with two brothers, one of whom saved a cat from death. The cat by killing all the rats brought them to great prosperity and they built themselves a magnificent palace. Then one of them brought home a snake, which they kept in a cage and tended kindly. What would be in a cage would naturally be a bird, and we are told that a Jew, finding out that the creature was really a snake, could guess what it was although the brothers were betting that he could not. In this way the Jew won all their money and their palace as well which, like the villain in *The grateful Animals and the Talisman*, he at once conveyed into the middle of the sea. By the Greeks the cooing of a dove and the hissing of a snake are

[1] The paper is now reprinted in *Laographikà Sýmmeikta*, ii; reference to p. 120.

[2] Kretschmer, *Neugr. Märchen*, p. 202, No. 47.

supposed to sound much the same, and we must suppose that the brothers enticed people to guess and back their guess as to what the creature was, and the Jew had by some means found out that the cooing was not that of a bird and so was able to guess right.

If we ask why it is so easily accepted that the dove and the snake make the same noise, the answer is in a story I heard in Crete. When the flood was upon the earth the ark of Noah sprang a leak; the water was coming in through the hole made by a knot in a plank. The snake stopped the leak with his tail. But his tail grew cold and he threatened to pull it out. The dove came to the rescue and by crouching on the snake kept him warm and the snake could go on with his tail in the hole. From the snake's hissing the dove learned to coo.

Beginning in this way Pernot's story has a close contact with No. 9, *The grateful Animals*, but it continues on quite different lines. The man, swindled by the Jew, went off and found the Mother of the Sun; she was kneading her dough not with water but with spittle. He went off and killed the monster who was preventing people from getting water, and the Sun to show his gratitude told him to make a bet with the Jew in what quarter the sun would rise. The Jew naturally betted on the east, but lost when the sun on that day did in fact rise in the south.

Of the Smyrna version we have only an outline; the Thera version is badly told, and this third version from Chios is very incoherent: for all that we can see clearly that there does exist in the Greek islands a story of a man helped against a Jew by the sun, who enabled him to win a bet by rising to please him not in the east but in some other quarter. A good version might appear any day.

There is a very curious story from Mitylene called *The Snake-Cypress*: a snake was killed and was reincarnated in a cypress-tree. At the end there is this same episode; to bring about the winning of what seems to be an impossible wager the sun appears to rise in the west.[1]

There is an Imeretian story that is to the point here.[2] A servant of Solomon the Wise was content with three words of advice instead of his wages: *Tell no one your secrets*; *Do not lend anything without being asked for it*; *draw the skin of a serpent over a little stick and set it up in your courtyard*. From the stick grew a tree with golden fruit, which tree was wheedled from his wife by three Armenians. To get it back the man was told by Solomon to get them to bet where the sun would rise;

[1] In *Folklore*, vii. 151.

[2] *Caucasian Folk Tales*, translated by Lucy Garnett from Adolf Dirr, p. 268.

they betted on the east; by his art Solomon made it rise in the west and the man got his tree back again. This is plainly a variant to the Greek stories: note that the Thera version turns in the same way on a wonderful tree.

I find no European references for any such story, and the fact that in Greece it belongs to the islands and is found in the Caucasus suggests that it has reached Greece from the east.

30

The Girl shut up in a Tower

THE tower in which the too fondly loved child is shut up to be secure from all danger is not uncommon; in particular it is the opening of the Epeiros versions of No. 19, *The Mountain of Jewels and the Dove-Maiden.* Of the present story of the love adventures of the girl shut up I find two variants: one from Samos here translated and one from Thera, published in *Parnassós*, iv. 901. The stories begin with a father who loved his daughter so dearly that he shut her up in a crystal tower, allowing her to see nothing of the world outside. Her food had to be prepared with such dainty care that not even a fragment of bone should be left in the dish. But fate cannot be outwitted and servants are careless, and one day a bit of bone was passed over. The girl was by this distressed and disturbed; her sheltered life was, she felt, in some way broken in upon. Partly in anger, partly to amuse herself, she threw the bone about, and it broke the window of the tower. After first troubling her so much, the bone thus enabled her to see through the window the world outside her tower, and she made her escape. At this point the story follows two lines, though both narrate the girl's adventures in love. In the Samian story here translated she hears of the great beauty of a youth called Sir Nerak,[1] and falls in love and finally marries him. Sometimes by an obvious error the lover is called not 'Sir Nerak' but 'the son of Sir Nerak': this I have tacitly corrected.

The crystal tower is easily seen to be a symbol of the excessive and exclusive love of the father, which causes him to try, but of course in vain, to keep the child entirely to himself, shielded also from the dangers of the natural life of freedom. In fact it corresponds in this fairyland to the sofa in the half-darkened drawing-room in Wimpole Street in which Mr. Barrett succeeded in shutting up his daughter, but only until the moment when Browning appeared to carry her off. That the window or wall of the tower should be pierced by the bone accidentally left in the food indicates that it is by the means of the very knowledge brought her by the bone that there is a world outside that the captive child wins her way out into the world of natural love. In a story with a tragic ending in Basile's *Pentamerone*, iii. 3, a bone plays a similar part. It is destined to bring about the death of

[1] In Greek *Σὶρ Νεράκ.*

an imprisoned girl; again it is the instrument by which she breaks her way out of the tower. Then she finds her lover already married and at this she dies of grief.

As for the name Sir Nerak, *Σὶρ Νεράκ*: I have tried to show in No. 36 of *Forty-five Stories*, p. 389, that the name Neros is a form of the ancient *Eros*, *Love*. In *Nerak* I would see *Neráki*, the diminutive of *Neros*. To call the lover Dan Cupid would be a literal translation, but it would invoke medieval European associations, here hardly in place. That Sir Nerak is to be explained in this way is made the more likely from a story from Zákynthos given by Bernhard Schmidt: *Griechische Märchen*, No. 16, p. 109. This is a short story of a girl who fell in love with a youth much above her in station and wealth. She wandered away and found the Mother of Erotas, which is the modern form of *Eros*, *Love*. She told her trouble and the lady made a marriage between the girl and her son Erotas, who it is implied was the youth with whom she had fallen in love. In this Zákynthos story the Mother of Erotas or Eros takes the place of the Sister of Sir Nerak, who in the story from Samos has mercy on the lovelorn girl.

NO. 30. THE GIRL SHUT UP IN A TOWER[1]

Once there was a king and he had a daughter. But what a daughter! Her beauty shone as brightly as the sun. Now since he loved her well, her father built her a tower of crystal and set her in it and there he kept her. As she sat in the tower, every morning her serving women used to bring her coffee and every midday her dinner, first preparing it with great care: never did they leave a bit of bone in it, for such were the princess's orders. One day as usual they brought her her dinner, but it seems they had not prepared it carefully, and when the princess began to eat she found in it a little bit of bone. At once she grew angry; outcries and reproaches; an ugly business; the serving women were in utter confusion. In her anger the princess threw the bone up against the window and broke the pane of glass. When she had broken the glass her anger dropped a little, and she said: 'Well, now that the glass is once broken, I must make a bigger hole and look down and see what is going on in the world, since my father will not let me go out.' When she had made the hole large enough to put her head out, she looked down and saw

[1] Text from Samos, in Stamatiádis, *Samiaká*, v. 610.

below her a crier, holding in his hand three very fine feathers: one was white, one was black, and one was red. The man was shouting: 'Like this white feather is the countenance of Sir Nerak; like this black feather is his moustache; and like this red one are his lips.' When the princess heard this she was as in a faint and fell to the ground very sick. Her father the king came, and seeing her in this state asked her what was the matter. At first she would not tell him the truth, but kept telling him lies, one thing after another. Then after a long time she said: 'My father, either you will give me Sir Nerak for my husband or I shall take poison and die.' When the king heard what she said, he said to her, for he loved his daughter very much: 'My dear daughter, do not act thus. See, now I will send envoys with abundant gifts to Sir Nerak for him to come and take you for his wife.'

The man lived in another realm and the king sent to ask him to be his son-in-law. Now Sir Nerak was an extremely haughty man, and what did he do? He put into a gold tobacco box a toothpick and a hair and a pearl, and sent them to the king with a letter saying: 'Were your daughter to become slender as the toothpick; were she to grow as lissom as the hair; were she to be as delicate as the pearl; yet I would not take her for my wife.' When the king received this letter, he showed it to his daughter. She began to cry and nothing could soothe her: indeed she wished she could kill herself. 'Never mind, my daughter, I will give you a finer husband,' said her father, but she would not listen. 'Since you won't have me kill myself, failing to win the man I love, even though I know him not, order them to make me a coffer and put me into it and throw me into the sea, and so let come what will. Otherwise I shall slay myself; there is no strength in me to do otherwise.' When he saw that he could not shift her resolution, her poor father said to himself: 'Rather than that she should kill herself, it is better to put her in the coffer in the sea, and who knows what may happen? For sometimes it comes about that from where a man can see no hope his good may come to him.' So the king gave orders and the coffer was made; they put the girl into it dressed in her finest clothes; then they threw her into the sea. Washing her this way and that, the waves carried her to the place where the palace of Sir Nerak stood. Her fortune carried her there and at that very time Sir

Nerak's sister was sitting on the shore. When she saw a coffer being floated towards her by the sea, she rose and laid hands on it and called for one of her servants to send it to their palace. There she took a little axe, but as she began to strike at the nails to open it, she heard from inside a voice saying: 'Gently, gently; do not strike me.' 'What voice is this? It sounds like a woman's voice,' said Sir Nerak's sister. 'There must be some human creature inside,' and she began very carefully to open the coffer. Finally, to cut the story short, she opened the coffer, and what did she see in it? A girl, and with her beauty the house shone brightly. 'But who are you, my fair lady?' said she, 'and how did you come here?' Then the princess began to tell of her love for Sir Nerak, and how he had scorned her and how for this she had resolved to die. 'Be at ease,' said Sir Nerak's sister. 'He is my brother and tomorrow he will come back from hunting and I will manage things for you.'

Then, in fact, next day he came back from hunting, and when he had changed his clothes he went into his sister's room to ask her how she had fared. When the princess saw that her beloved had come she went and put on her finest clothes and took the tray with the sweets and went to serve him. When Sir Nerak saw such a beautiful girl standing before him with the tray, he was near to fainting. So when the princess had gone out he asked his sister where this beautiful girl had been found. 'I will send her to you and then you can ask her,' said his sister. So when he called for the princess and asked her who she was and where she came from, she brought out the gold tobacco box and said: 'I am she to whom you sent word that were she to become slender as the toothpick and as lissom as the hair and as delicate as the pearl, yet you would not have her for your wife.' When he heard her say this he began to treat her lovingly, saying: 'I did not know that it was you. If I had known, I would not have written such a letter. Now I love you and want to take you for my wife.' So they sent word to her father and in a few days he came and they held the wedding, with feasting and drinking and rejoicing.

But I was not there and I bid you not to believe the story.

31

The three Sisters and their Wishes for a Husband

AARNE–THOMPSON TYPE 707

THE countless BP. references, ii. 380, to Grimm No. 96, show the wide range of stories of this type: the earliest example is in Straparola,[1] and our twenty-three versions show how common it is all over Greece and its general Greek form. As found at Delmesó in Cappadocia it has been studied by Halliday under the title of *The two Sisters who envied their Cadette*; he found it of worldwide distribution from Brazil to India and from Iceland to Egypt.[2] It has also been studied in some detail by Pernot in his *Mythes astrals et traditions littéraires*, who brings under his survey a number of tales and ballads, some of which seem to me very little to the point: nor can I recognize in the story anything at all of the astral myth.

In the Greek examples there are considerable variations in detail, mainly because in its full form there are two questing brothers and three objects of their quests, and omissions are naturally frequent, but the general outline is as follows. There were three hard-working sisters, and when the king issued an order that no one should have a light burning at night, they shut their shutters but still kept a light in order to continue their handiwork. The king spied on them and heard them talking. The eldest sister said she would like to marry the king's baker and the second sister his cook: thus each would have plenty to eat. The youngest said she would marry the king himself and bring him three children, in beauty like the sun and the moon and the star of morning. It is this detail which tempted Pernot to regard the story as an astral myth. The king married the girl and the three children were born.

The sisters were jealous of the young queen and by the help of the midwife at every birth they substituted an animal, a puppy and a cat and a snake, for the children, who were thrown away: often put into boxes and sunk in the cistern or in the sea. They were saved by a fisherman or a shepherd or the king's gardener, but their mother was put away by her husband and confined in some miserable way.

[1] *Le piacevoli notti*, iv. 3.

[2] *M.G. in A.M.*, p. 271. I find also an Indian version in L. B. Day's *Folk Tales of Bengal*, p. 227, and a very recently published Albanian version from Prizren is in *Folklore*, lix. 39.

The three children, two boys and a girl, were put to live in a castle or a tower, but their mother's jealous sisters, or in some versions, the king's jealous mother, found out where they were and sent the wicked midwife to bring about their destruction. This she did by persuading the sister to make demands on her brothers which would lead them into danger: here we have a clear contact with the story of Snow White. The demands vary a good deal but the third and last is almost always for a magical speaking bird. The version from Cappadocia is exceptional in having only one brother and him going on only one quest: to fetch as a companion for his sister a very beautiful girl who lives with her magic mirror in a palace all made of glass. Like the Tsitsínena below she can turn men into stone and this she does to anyone whom she has seen by the aid of her mirror before he has seen her. But as a rule there are three quests, the first brother being turned to stone by the magic bird. In the Melos version here translated the first quest is for a Golden Apple, the second for a Golden Bough, and the third for the magical bird, the Tsitsínena, who knows the language of all birds and so has all their wisdom. On this final quest the brothers meet with some helper; in the Melos version a monk; in the Cretan a friendly ogress, to guide them on their way. But the strange bird turns each of them successively into stone. In the Melos version the turning to stone of the first brother has been omitted; we hear only of the turning back into flesh of a lost brother.

Then the sister, warned by the sympathetic withering of a branch or, as in the Cretan version, by the turning of the water in a flask into blood, that her brothers are in danger set out to rescue them. In the Melos version it is the second brother who invokes the aid of the monk who had helped him and the monk rescues the brothers. In any case they were saved from the enchantment of the bird who is now their good helper, and all four of them, the brothers, the sister, and the bird, went off together to find their father and force him to restore their ill-treated mother.

In all these Greek stories the monk, or whoever it is has helped the brothers in their quest, seems to represent a kindly providence helping the unfortunate, and the bird to be a symbol perhaps of wisdom, anyhow of some power which, except under the kindly mastery of providence, is as dangerous as it is now powerful. We shall see presently that it is only the advice of the bird which saved the children from a last danger of being poisoned by their jealous enemy.

The wind-up of the story is that the three children and the bird found their father. He invited them to a meal, but the bird warned them than the food would be poisoned, in the Melos version by the king's mother. In the version from Crete the three children put sand into the food they offered to their father. When he complained, they told him that he had no cause to complain of what they did seeing that he had treated their mother so cruelly. The mother was restored to favour; the wicked sisters are often punished, and so the story ends.

The Greek references are:

1. PONTOS: *Pontiakí Estía*, i. 154.
2. CAPPADOCIA, AT DELMESÓ: *M.G. in A.M.*, p. 316.
3. WESTERN ASIA MINOR (Siyí): *Mikrasiatiká Khroniká*, iv. 287.
4–8. CHIOS: Pernot, *Études de linguistique*, iii. 252 and 259; Pernot-Hesseling, *Chrestomathie*, p. 169; Argenti and Rose, *Folklore of Chios*, p. 492; also an unpublished version recorded by Kanellakis.
9. NÍSYROS: *Z.A.* i. 425.
10. KÁRPATHOS: Mikh.-Nouáros, *L. S. Karpáthou*, i. 287.
11. SYRA: Hahn, ii. 40, No. 69; which is Kretschmer's *Neugr. Märchen*, No. 50, p. 257.
12. MITYLENE: *Folklore*, x. 499.
13. CYCLADES: almost certainly Melos; *N.A.* i. 17, translated.
14. CRETE: *Epetirís et. kritikón spoudón*, iii. 317.
15. ATHENS: Kamboúroglou, p. 124 = Garnett, p. 185.
16. EUBOIA: résumé in Hahn, ii. 291.
17. AITOLIA: *Laographía*, ii. 388.
18, 19, 20. THRACE: *Thrakiká*, xvi. 185, and *Arkheíon Thrakikóu Laogr.* v. 171 and vi. 258.
21, 22. ZÁKYNTHOS: *Laographía*, x. 381 and xi. 427.
23. EPEIROS: Hahn, ii. 287, No. 69.

NO. 31. THE THREE SISTERS AND THEIR WISHES FOR A HUSBAND[1]

Once upon a time there was an old woman who had three daughters; they used to go out to work. The king of that land issued a decree that no one should have a light in the evening for oil was scarce. When they heard the decree the old woman's daughters said: 'What will become of us if we can't work in the evenings? It is winter and the days are short; how shall we make our living?' So they blocked up all the holes in their doors and windows so that they were dark and the light could not be seen. In this way they continued to work.

One day they had worked very hard and in the evening they were hungry. The eldest sister said: 'I wish I were married to

[1] Text in *N.A.* i. 17.

the king's baker and then I could have a roll to eat, all nice and hot.' The second sister said: 'Oh, my poor dear, and do you fancy the baker? I would like to marry the cook, and then I could eat of all the king's dishes.' The third sister said: 'O my poor dears, what things you want! I would like to be married to the king, and thus I could have all good things. And I would bear him three children: the Sun and the Moon and the Star of Morning.' The king was standing in disguise outside their house, for he wanted to see who had a lamp burning and who had not. Well, he was passing outside the door at the very moment when they were talking in this way. Without saying a word he went off, but in the morning he sent for them to the palace and asked them, one by one, what they had been saying the night before. First he questioned the eldest: 'What were you saying last night when you were sitting and working?' The poor girl said: 'My lord king, we said nothing at all.' 'No, no, you must tell me what you were saying.' So she said: 'How can I tell you, my king? We were sitting in the evening over our work and I said that I wished I were married to the king's baker, and then I could have a roll to eat all nice and hot, for the way we were sitting and working I had become hungry.' 'Oh, very well,' and the king took her and married her to his baker and sent her off home. Then he started to ask the second sister: 'What were you doing yesterday evening?' 'Well, my king, we were working and talking.' 'No no, there was something you said yesterday.' She said: 'How can I tell you, my king? I said I would like to be married to the king's cook, and then I could eat of all the royal dishes.' The king dismissed her too and sent her to be married to the cook. He called for the youngest sister and said: 'What were you saying yesterday evening when you were sitting at work?' 'My lord king,' said she, 'here you have your sword and here I have my throat, and you may take off my head, but I cannot tell you what I was saying.' He said: 'I will not kill you. I want you to tell me; I don't want to kill you.' She said: 'And how can I tell you this thing, my king, and many be your years? My sisters said, one that she wanted the baker, and the other the king's cook, and then I said: "O my poor dears, what things to want! I should like to be married to the king and then I should have all good things. Also I would bear him three children, the Sun and the Moon and the Star of Morning."' 'And could you be the mother of such children?' She said: 'Indeed I could, my king.' Then the king crowned her in marriage and made her his queen.

This marriage made by the king his mother was not willing to accept, but since her son had chosen the girl, what could she do about it? She said nothing, but always she hated the bride. Now when the girl was with child and was about to bear the boy like the sun, word was sent to the king that he must go to the war. So he gave his orders to his mother: 'Mother, I must go off to the war, and you must guard my wife, now that she is to be a mother, like your own eyes.' 'Be easy, my son; go about your business and have no care about your wife: I will look after her.' Well, the day came for the child to be born. Then the king's mother sent for the midwife and they agreed together: 'When my daughter-in-law has the baby, we must throw it out, and I will pay you handsomely.' So they took and made a coffer and put the queen's child into it and threw it into the sea, and by the side of the mother they set a puppy. The king came back from the war and asked his mother: 'Tell me, mother, what like was my wife's baby?' 'It was a dog, my son.' Well, he said not a word and did nothing. Again his wife was with child and again tidings came that he must go to the war. Again the same thing happened. He instructed his mother: 'Mother, you must guard my wife as your own head. She will now bear me the child like the moon.' And again his mother made the same answer. When he had gone off she arranged with the midwife to put a kitten by the side of the mother. Again they made a coffer and threw the baby into the sea and in its place put a cat. Again the king came and asked: 'What like is my wife's baby?' She said: 'She has born a cat.' Again he said nothing and went on living with his wife. Again his wife conceived; it was the time for her to bear the child like the star of morning. Again word came to him that he must go to the war and again he gave his mother the same commands. Again she arranged it with the midwife, and a snake was brought in and the baby they threw into the sea. The husband came from the war and asked: 'What like is my wife's baby?' 'It was a snake, and would have strangled you, my son. Ah, such a wife as you have and you still keep her in the palace and don't drive her out to go and live in some hut and rot!' Then he said to his wife: 'You promised me that you would bring me the Sun and the Moon and the Star of Morning, and you have brought me a dog and a cat and a snake. Go away then; I don't want you.' He took the poor woman and walled her up in the jakes.

Now we must leave them all and tell of the children. Every time when the coffers were thrown into the sea the children were carried straight to a little hill where there was a monastery in which a monk lived. Now every day this monk used to go down to the sea and catch a fish and in this way he lived. On that special day two fish came. Then the monk prayed to God: 'O God, did I ever complain to you and ask for more food?' But when he was on his way to his dwelling he found the coffer and in it the baby. 'Oh,' cried he, 'and this is why God sent me the fish, because He sent me this child as well, and the fish is for his food.' So he kept the child with him for a year and fed him with the fish. A year later he went to the shore and caught three fish. Again he prayed to God, and again on his way back to his dwelling he found a little coffer; he opened it and found a child in it. 'Oh, so that is why God sent me two more fish.' Again after a year he caught four fish and found the third baby. The monk kept the three children, going here and there always looking for things to bring them: thus he reared them up. When they had grown big he said: 'My children, you cannot live here on the mountain.' To the eldest he said: 'You must take your brother and your sister'—for Star of Morning was a girl—'and take them to the city and thus you will learn the habits and ways of the world, because here you can learn nothing.' They came to the city and with the money which the monk had given them they rented a house. Then they looked about to find out how the world lived and to learn the ways of men.

One day the eldest went down to the market and there he met a Jew who had a little box for sale. The Jew was saying: 'Whoever buys this box will change his mind and wish he hadn't; but whoever refuses to buy it, he too will change his mind.' Then the prince—for the boy was a prince—said: 'Whoever buys it will change his mind and wish he hadn't and whoever refuses to buy it, he too will change his mind: well, it seems better then to buy it.' So he bought the box and went home. When he came to the house he found his sister sitting crying. He asked her: 'What is the matter, sister, that you are sitting crying?' She said: 'Why do you lock me up in here and let me have nothing to amuse myself with?' Well, and what would you like to amuse yourself with?' She said: 'An old woman came by and told me that I am pretty,'—now this old woman was the midwife but the children did not know this; she had found out that the children were alone and she was trying to destroy them: again because the mother-in-law had paid her to do this.—'but if only I had the Golden Apple, the one which forty ogres keep guarded in a garden, then I should be still prettier.' Her brother said: 'I must open this little box, the one I was told that whoever bought it would be sorry for it, and whoever refused to buy it he too would change his mind and be sorry.' So he opened the box and in it he found a winged horse, all green. Then said he: 'Ah ha! This is the right horse for me to ride and I can go and fetch my sister the apple.' He mounted the horse and rode out of the gate. Then his horse questioned him: 'Good day, master; and now where are we going?' He said: 'We are going to fetch my sister the Golden Apple, guarded by forty ogres.' 'Well,' said the horse, 'my poor master; this is very difficult but I will travel like a flash of lightning and like a clap of thunder and so I shall come into the garden. If you are able to snatch the apple, then all will be well. If not, it will be the death of both of us if the ogres catch us'. And so they went forward and when they were near they dashed forward like lightning and thunder after it to seize the apple. They brought it back to the girl and she kept it to play with.

One day the old woman again passed by. She said: 'A pretty girl you are, my daughter, and now you have the Golden Apple, but if only you had the Golden Bough to which all the birds in the world gather together to sing, then you would be more lovely still.' Her brother came and again he found her crying. 'What is the matter, sister?' 'That old woman passed here again and she told me that if I had the Golden Bough to which all the birds in the world gather together to sing, then I should be even more fair.' He said: 'See, I will go and bring it for you'' He rose up and took his horse and rode out. Again his horse said: 'Good day, master, and where are we going?' 'I am going to fetch my sister the Golden Bough, to which all the birds in the world gather together to sing.' The horse said: 'Oh, my poor fellow! After the Golden Apple we did escape; but after this? All the same, let us go; I will move even like a flash of lightning and like a clap of thunder, and you must carry an axe and cut a branch of the tree.' Off they went like thunder and lightning; the youth cut the Golden Bough and they started back with it. He brought it to his sister. All the birds of the world gathered to it and sang: a heavenly delight.

Again the old woman passed by. 'Ah,' she said, 'how pretty you are with the Golden Apple and the Golden Bough, to which all the birds of the world gather together to sing. Yet if you had also with you Tsitsínena, she who knows the languages of all birds and could tell you what they are saying, then you would be fairer still.' Again her brother came and she said: 'Again the old woman has passed by and she told me that if I had also Tsitsínena, she who knows the languages of all birds, then should I be yet more beautiful.' He said: 'I will go and fetch her for you.' Again he mounted his horse and they rode out. The horse said: 'Good day, master, and where are we going?' He said: 'We are going to fetch for my sister Tsitsínena, she who knows the languages of all birds, that she may tell her what the birds are saying.' 'My poor master, from the other tasks we escaped; from Tsitsínena we cannot escape, for she will turn us to stone.' 'Well, let her do what she can to us; we are going and may God be our helper.' So off they went and came to below the house of Tsitsínena; it was a long way off. The horse said: 'Now call to her.' The boy shouted: 'Tsitsínena.' From up above them she cried: 'Marble! Turn him to marble, even to the knees.' Again he cried: 'Tsitsínena.' Again she cried out: 'Marble! turn him to marble even to the thighs.' Yet once more he cried out: 'Tsitsínena.' Again she cried: 'Marble! Turn him to marble even to the waist.' Then he began to bethink him and the horse said: 'Why are you waiting? Cry out to her to change us back from marble, because now we can move neither forwards nor backwards; here we shall have to stop.' Then the boy remembered that the monk when they went off had given him some hairs from his beard and said, 'When you have need of me, burn one of these hairs and I will come to help you.' Then he struck a spark and burned a hair. Behold, the monk stood there before him: 'What do you want, my boy?' He said: 'Look and see the plight I am in: I remembered that you would help me.' Then he told him all his story. The monk cried out:

'Tsitsínena.' 'At your service, master.' 'Come quickly and help my children.' 'At once, master.' She came down with in her hands a bottle of the Water of Life; she sprinkled it over them and brought back to life all the body of the youth which had been turned to stone. She had in that place a whole crowd of people all turned to stone. So she turned them all from stone back into flesh and among them was the other prince, the boy's lost brother. Then they all started to go off, and the monk said to Tsitsínena: 'Now you are travelling with my lads, you must take good heed; be as if you were their mother or even the Holy Virgin herself.' So Tsitsínena went off with them.

As she travelled with them she told them all that the birds were saying and all the doings of the world; she knew them all. One day the boys wanted to go for a walk. Tsitsínena said to them: 'Today you will meet the king on the way. He will see you and come up to you and invite you for tomorrow to his table and you must tell him that you will come.' The boys therefore went out and they did meet the king. The king said: 'How like these children are to the children that woman said she would bear me!' So he went up to them and said: 'How much I loved you the very first moment I saw you! I should like us to have a meal together. Will you come?' The children said: 'Yes, we will.' They went home and Tsitsínena asked them all that had happened. 'Tomorrow' she said, 'when you sit down at table to eat, you must have a puppy with you and give it a spoonful of the food.' So when the children went they took the puppy with them and gave it a spoonful of the food: it ate; the food was poisoned and it died. The children said: 'My king, we have not come here for you to poison us. You see the puppy how it died after eating. But if it please you, come tomorrow to eat at our house.' Loving the children so much the king did not refuse and said he would come. The children went and told Tsitsínena that they had invited the king as she had instructed them. They told her to get ready plenty of food because on the morrow he would come; and on the morrow the king came. The children were expecting Tsitsínena to have the food ready, but she neither served any food nor had a table set nor anything. They said: 'But, Tsitsínena, the king has come and haven't you got a table set ready or anything?' She said: 'What o'clock is it, children?' They told her that it was a quarter of an hour before they should sit down at table. Then as the king was sitting on the sofa and Tsitsínena was conversing with him, she clapped her hands three times and before the king there was set a table; more than a table for kings; a splendid set-out. The king was amazed suddenly to see such a table. However he ate of all the dishes and was highly pleased. When they had finished he said to them: 'My children, what favour would you like me to do you?' Now Tsitsínena had told them not to ask any other favour than that he should deliver the woman whom he had shut up in the jakes. The king sent at once and she was brought out and taken to the bath and washed and dressed and brought before him. When she had been brought Tsitsínena rushed forward and said to the king: 'Do you want to know of the children whom this woman bore to you? See, here is your wife and here too are your children.' Then Tsitsínena told him the whole story: what his mother and the midwife had done. 'These are your children: the Sun and the Moon and the Star of Morning; now accept them as your own.' The king embraced them all and they kissed one another and he took his wife and went with her to the palace. After this he took his mother and the midwife and bound them to four horses and set them in the street and all the world declared that they were wicked women. Then the horses were whipped up and the women torn to pieces.

32

The Prince in a Swoon

THIS very well-marked story has been studied by Cosquin in conjunction with *The Ogre Schoolmaster* and the reader is also referred to what it is said of both stories in a paper published in *Folklore*,[1] and to the notes to No. 33 in this book, *The Ogre Schoolmaster*. In Greece I find seven versions, very uniform and all well told, scattered from the Islands to Epeiros: for translation I have chosen the version from Skyros, although it omits the prophecy at the beginning of the story.

Cosquin considers the story of Indian origin and that it has moved westwards;[2] to his references may now be added a Persian example given by Lorimer.[3] Farther west Cosquin quotes examples from southern Arabia and Egypt and so along the African coast to Morocco. From the northern shore he gives a Turkish version[4] and now we may add these seven versions from Greece.

The essence of the story is that it is prophesied of a girl that she will marry a dead man; by which is meant a man who has already in a manner passed from life to death in a magic swoon. In a story a prophecy is not merely a declaration of what will happen; it is still more a revelation of what by decree of fate must happen, and the heroine lives under this dismal doom. She is brought into a castle and there in a room she finds the prince lying in his strange swoon. The ways in which she reaches the castle are significant. In one of the Thracian versions she is carried off by a whirlwind. In the Epeiros version she is caught by the rain. So too in Skópelos and Skyros, where she is presented as out in the country with her mother gathering herbs and the two of them take refuge from the rain. In the Athenian version she is carried off by an eagle. Always she comes to the castle by some means which show her as the passive pawn of what is beyond her power to resist or control. From the fulfilling of a prophecy no escape is possible.

By the side of the prince she finds a paper on which it is written that whoever watches over him for a certain time shall be his bride.

[1] *The Story of Griselda. Folklore*, lx. 363.

[2] Cosquin, *Contes indiens*, pp. 95–154. Refs. for these magic swoons are in BP. iii. 426.

[3] Lorimer, *Persian Tales*, p. 19; *The Story of the Marten-Stone.*

[4] Kunos, *Stambul* p. 215; *Stone of Patience, Knife of Patience.*

The girl carries out her vigil almost to the last when a slave girl presents herself and is allowed to take her place for a moment. But in that very moment the prince wakes up and it is the slave girl whom he marries, the rejected heroine being kept in the house in some wretched state. The prince then went off on a journey and for a present the rejected bride asked for a Rope of Hanging, a Knife of Slaughter, and a Stone of Patience. The prince overheard what the outcast said to these three objects and at once recognized his error.

The Knife, we are told, said: 'Kill yourself.' The Rope said: 'Hang yourself,' and the Stone said: 'Be patient.' It is a great temptation, probably to be resisted, to think of the Knife as saying: 'Kill him.' This brings in an attractive symmetry, for a knife is as much fitted for murder as a rope is for suicide.

Both dealing with a rejected bride, this story and *The Ogre Schoolmaster* naturally have many contacts and contaminations as has been remarked by Cosquin. The most obvious is the episode of the three gifts which, however, seem to me more in place here than in the ogre story. A slighter contact is in the Skópelos version in which at the beginning we are for no reason told that the girl was on her way to school when she met the bird who prophesied that she would marry a dead man: 'school' is an echo of *The Ogre Schoolmaster*. The version from Chios and the second of the two from Thrace contain a good deal of matter which belongs properly to No. 1, the story of *The three Oranges*.

In a story in Basile's *Pentamerone*, ii. 8, the three symbolic gifts form the ending of a quite different story of a persecuted girl.

In the version from Athens there is more than a suggestion that the prince's castle lies in a kind of World Below, for which see the notes on No. 41, *The Underworld Marriage*. Perhaps also No. 17, *Human Flesh to eat*, with its lord of the underworld should here be considered.

There is a Sicilian story that begins with *The Ogre Schoolmaster* and passes into *The Prince in a Swoon*.[1] The wicked schoolmaster, discovering that the girl had been spying on his cannibalistic doings, threatened her and beat her, and said that after seven years seven months and seven days a cloud would carry her off to the Hill of Calvary. At the time appointed the cloud carried her off. With difficulty she came down from the hill and came to a castle; it was empty; no one was in it. Then she saw a youth lying as if dead, and a writing that if a girl would rub him—again for the same period—with the herb of Calvary he would come to life and marry her. Again she climbed the hill to get the herb and set herself to rub him. The herb we may

[1] Gonzenbach, *Sizilianische Märchen*, i. 59, No. 11.

guess was basil, *origanum*, for it is a Greek idea that basil sprang up at the foot of the Cross. As usual she was tricked out of her reward by a slave woman, and asked for and was given a knife and the Stone of Patience. She told the Stone all her sad story, which when the Stone heard, it swelled up and broke in two. As she was taking the knife to kill herself, the prince came forward and took her to himself, and the slave was put to death.

The Greek references for *The Prince in a Swoon* are:

1. CHIOS: Pernot, *Études de linguistique*, iii. 285.
2. SKYROS: Pérdika, ii. 167, translated.
3. SKÓPELOS: Kretschmer, *Heut. lesbische Dialekt*, p. 543.
4. ATHENS: Kamboúroglou, p. 93 = Garnett, p. 40.
5, 6. THRACE: *Thrakiká*, xvi. 125, and *Arkheíon Thrakikoú Laogr.*, iv. 154.
7. EPEIROS: Pio, p. 49, which is Hahn, i. 121, No. 12, and Geldart, p. 62.

NO. 32. THE PRINCE IN A SWOON[1]

Once there was an old woman and she had a granddaughter. One day they set out for the mountain to gather herbs. There they collected whatever they could find, sowthistle, partridge-foot, windwort, bryony, lamb's lettuce; to eat that day and the next, so very poor were they.

A sleety blast blew with heavy rain and thunder; thunder-bolts as well. Where to take refuge they did not know. They saw a mountain a long way off and on it a light burning. The old woman said: 'Run, my dear child; we must go there to escape from the rain.' When they got there, they saw a door, and the girl went in. The old woman was at the point of entering when the door shut; it was of marble; she was left outside. The old woman and her granddaughter wept and cried aloud, but all in vain; they were lost to one another. They cried and shouted but there was nothing to be heard. Then the girl said: 'I must go and look to see if there is any other door by which I can get out.' She went off and came to a stair. Up and up she went and she came to a palace; it all lay open. Lights were burning every-where, but there was no one to be seen. She went into a room and found a shrine with icons; there was nothing there; all the rooms were empty.

Then she went into thirty-nine of the rooms—the whole

[1] Text from Skyros, in Pérdika, *Skyros*, ii. 167.

palace was of forty rooms—all of them were empty. In the last room she found an old woman keeping watch over a dead man, a prince. Such was his beauty that a glance only and one would desire him. Above his head was a paper with writing: 'Whatever woman can be found to sit burning incense at my head for forty days and forty nights, forty full days, her I will take as my wife.' The girl knew letters and read the writing and then sat down with her incense at the prince's head and censed him.

The forty full days passed, and on the evening when she was to see the dead prince rise up, the old woman said to the girl in a whisper: 'Come, my daughter, you go and lie down for a little while and the moment the prince awakes I will call you. You will make yourself ill with all this watching and no sleep.' The girl trusted her and went and lay down at the feet of the prince.

Presently the prince woke up and he saw the dirty old woman; by this time she was burning incense over him. 'Are you she who has been watching over me and incensing me for all these days?' he asked her. 'And who else has it been, my darling?' said the wicked old woman. 'And who is this girl,' the prince then asked. 'She is my adopted daughter,' said the old woman. 'I have had her here to keep me company.' Then the prince took the old woman as his wife and the girl they kept there as though she were their daughter. The prince, poor fellow, was in misery all day, and when it was time to go to bed, he used to lock himself up in his room and weep. He grew weak and lost all his colour; in sad plight he had no further use for his life.

A little time went by and the prince went off on a journey. He asked his wife what she wanted him to bring her; he asked also the daughter. She would not tell him. He pressed her and she bade him bring her, if he could find them, the Knife of Slaughter, the Rope of Hanging, and the Stone of Patience. The prince was very curious to know what she wanted these things for, but she told him nothing. He got them for her and when he came back he gave her them. She thanked him and as soon as the time came for them to lie down, she took the presents he had brought her and went into her room.

Very quietly the prince came up outside the room to see what she was doing. Privily he looked in and saw that she had set the things in a row on the shelf above the hearth; he heard her crying and beating her breast and saying: 'What God can have willed this? What a fate and what a fortune is this of mine! For me to watch him and burn incense over him for forty nights and forty days! to look upon him and to have him for my own for forty full days, and then the moment he awoke for him to mock me, and the dirty old woman have him, and he leave me all desolate like a reed standing in the field! Such torments I cannot endure. What can I do with such a life? Come tell me, my Knife, what I am to do? Shall I slay myself?' Then the prince heard the Knife speak and say to her: 'Slay yourself, my lady, slay yourself.' Then the girl wept and wept and to the Rope she said: 'O my Rope, and what will you tell me? Am I to hang myself?' Then the prince heard the Rope speak and say to her: 'Hang yourself, my lady, hang yourself.' Then the third question; the girl asked the Stone: 'O my Stone, you too tell me what I must do.' 'Patience, my lady, patience.'

The prince left no dust on his feet; there was no time to be lost! He marvelled at what he had heard; he was enraged with the old woman who had deceived him; he could not restrain himself; he pushed at the door and went in. 'You must tell me your story; I want to hear everything from the beginning.' So said he to the girl they had as their daughter. As soon as he had heard from her mouth how the stricken donkey of an old woman had beguiled him, he ordered her to be tied to two savage horses, to be torn to pieces: she was to be thrown out on a rocky place—Bássale here—so that not even her bones should be found. Then he took the girl and made her his queen and they laughed and were happy and all with many fine diversions.

Neither was I there nor are you to believe the story.

33

The Ogre Schoolmaster

UNDER this title Cosquin has discussed a story which he has found on both shores of the Mediterranean, on the south from Egypt to Morocco, on the north in Turkey, in Sicily, and among the Greeks of the island of Syra.[1] In a paper in *Folklore* I have discussed *The Ogre Schoolmaster* at some length in connexion with *The Prince in a Swoon*, coming to the conclusion that these stories of a distressed and persecuted wife at last restored to the affection of her husband are a counterpart in the world of folktale to the literary story of Griselda as found in Boccaccio, in Petrarch, and in Chaucer's story put into the mouth of the Clerk of Oxford.[2] In these stories in praise of patience the sufferings of the heroine are sometimes due to human wickedness or wantonness, and sometimes are presented as a wholesome discipline sent by some agent of heaven, a saint, or even the Virgin.

Cosquin found only one Greek version, the one from Syra. Since he wrote three more have appeared; from Athens, from Mitylene, and from Chios. The Chian version translated by Argenti and Rose, is so very much the best that it seems unnecessary to print another translation: I therefore content myself with giving a general outline of the story:

A monstrous demoniac creature, the ogre of Cosquin, in the Athenian version the Devil himself, kept a school; a day school for girls. One of his pupils, coming to school early, saw him devouring the body of one of her companions. In the Sicilian version he was seen through the keyhole doing something, we are not told what, to a dead body.[3] The little girl said nothing of what she had seen, but after this had happened several times, ran away. In the Athenian version the monster, the Thrice Accursed, in the guise of a whirlwind carried her off and set her down in front of a palace. In due course the heroine was married; in the Athenian version to the king of the palace. Then her husband had to go away to the war; in his absence a child was born. The ogre appeared and carried off the baby; in some versions he devoured it. After three such happenings the husband lost patience and drove his wife out, shutting her up in some miserable hole. In a Turkish version from Constantinople the hus-

[1] Cosquin, *Contes indiens*, pp. 112–21, with full references.

[2] In *Folklore*, lx. 363. [3] Gonzenbach, *Sizilianische Märchen*, p. 59, No. 11.

band proposed to take a second wife, and, like Chaucer's Griselda, the poor wife was called upon to suffer the humiliation of serving this second bride, her supplanter.[1] Then comes the dénouement of the story. The husband had again to go away, and, as often in folktales, asked every woman of his household what present she would like him to bring back for her. The rejected wife asked for three things; for the Knife of Slaughter, for the Rope of Hanging, and for the Stone of Patience. If he forgot them his ship would not be able to move; this is a motive found in many tales.[2] The husband of course did forget; some wise person suggested the cause of the trouble and he bought the presents and so came safely home. Curious to see what his wife would do with such strange gifts, he kept a watch and heard her speaking to them in turn and asking their advice in her troubles. The Knife said: 'Kill yourself.' The Rope said: 'Hang yourself.' The Stone said: 'Be patient.' The underlying idea is that no one should ever despair: she must meet her troubles like the stone, firm and patient to endure everything. At this point the husband declared himself; the ogre reappeared bringing the children with him; the patient wife was restored and so the story ends happily.

This story has clearly points of contact with *The Prince in a Swoon*; in both the central idea is the duty and virtue of patience. The stories have in several points affected one another and in particular in both the happy ending is brought about by the three presents, the Knife, the Rope, and the Stone. Yet I think that the presents more properly belong to *The Prince in a Swoon*, where the episode is more clearly set out; where it is also more logically necessary for bringing about the happy ending of the story. Quite without the three gifts the reappearance of the ogre with the heroine's children is a sufficient motive for the girl's restoration to her husband in *The Ogre Schoolmaster*.

There is an unpublished story from Chios collected by Kanellakis which seems a much mutilated form of *The Ogre Schoolmaster*. We have a persecuted wife who has been deprived of her children and then called upon to be a servant to her supplanter. Her husband hears her lamenting her fate to a stone column: nothing else will have any feeling for her sorrows. Then she is restored to favour.

The references are:

1. Chios: Argenti and Rose, *Folklore of Chios*, p. 457.
2. Mitylene: *Folklore*, xii. 84.
3. Athens: Kamboúroglou, p. 37.
4. Syra: Hahn, ii. 27, No. 66.

[1] *Istanbul Masallari*, p. 57: *Sabur Tashi*, *The Stone of Patience*. There is also a Turkish version taken from a text of Radloff in Kunos, *Stambul*, p. 181.

[2] See notes to No. 15 above.

34

The Servant who took the Place of his Master

THIS story has been discussed by Halliday who quotes Balkan variants. References given by Cosquin for a wider area cover stories in which the oath not to speak as long as life lasts is not included. I do not reckon these as true variants of this Greek story, the outline of which I quote from Halliday; he calls it *The King's Son and his treacherous Servant.*[1] The servant, in Greece generally a beardless man, the usual villainous *spanós*, for whom see No. 69, got his master at a disadvantage by inducing him to go down a well; he granted him his life on condition of their changing places and the master swearing that as long as he lives he will not reveal the change of personalities. At the king's court the servant then played the role of master, and for his own safety tried to get rid of his master by inducing the king to send him on various quests. The last was to fetch the Fair One of the World. When all the tasks had been performed the villainous servant killed his master, but the Fair One of the World, generally with the Water of Immortality, restored him to life, and in this way the master was absolved from his oath, which now that he had once died was no longer binding. So he revealed who he was and the servant was put to death.

This story is clearly very close to No. 35, *The treacherous Brothers*, and the prominence of the quests is a contact with No. 42, *The Son of the Hunter*.

The version here translated has the identity parade with the help of the bee; the bee marked the right girl by smearing some honey on her head. For these parades see the note on No. 6.

At the beginning of the version from the Peloponnesos the mother says to her son that if he meets a man with no beard he must turn back. For the ill luck brought by these men see No. 69.

The following seven versions are found in Greece:

1. CAPPADOCIA: at Ulaghátsh, *M.G. in A.M.*, p. 353.
2. TAURUS MOUNTAINS: at Phárasa. Ibid., p. 469.
3. CYPRUS: *Kypriaká Khroniká*, ix. 293.
4. CHIOS: an unpublished version recorded by Kanellakis, translated.

[1] *M.G. in A.M.*, p. 268, and Cosquin *Contes de Lorraine*, i. 32.

5. PELOPONNESOS: *N.A.* i. 46. It is in Garnett, p. 28.

6, 7. EPEIROS: Hahn, i. 233, No. 37, and *Sýllogos*, xiv. 255; the latter strays a good deal from the type.

NO. 34. THE SERVANT WHO TOOK THE PLACE OF HIS MASTER[1]

There was once a prince and he wanted to make a journey somewhere to see the world a little; so he spoke to his father the king and begged him to give him a ship with all its necessary fittings. In her he embarked with all the men for the service of the ship to keep him company. So they journeyed for many days until they came to land. There in that country, his head being dizzy with so much sailing, the prince chose to put on shore. So he disembarked and found it a desert place where there was neither beast nor man. After he had been going for a long time far into that land he saw a shepherd. The man led the prince to his sheepfold and gave him of what he had as is the custom with shepherds.

It happened on that very evening when the prince was lodging at the sheepfold, that the shepherd's wife had a baby, and the prince became his godfather and gave him the name of Johnnie. And when the time came for the prince to go away to his father's kingdom, he told the shepherd to guard the child well, and when he was big to send him to school to learn letters: when he got a little bigger, he should send him to his kingdom. And in order to be able to recognize him he left him a locket, saying: 'This locket you must hang on his neck so that I can recognize the boy when he comes to my kingdom, that he is my godson, the boy whom I held at the font.'

When the boy was a little grown, his father made him ready and hung the locket on him and bade him farewell, telling him to be obedient and well behaved; and so the boy went off.

As he was going on his way there met him a man with no beard, and the man asked him where he was going. The boy told him the truth, that he was going to find his godfather; in order that he might recognize him, he had left him a locket, and he had it hung on his neck that he might not lose it.

Like the cunning fellow he was, from that moment the beardless man thought out all sorts of tunes to play to Johnnie, and

[1] Unpublished text from Chios, recorded by Kanellakis.

he told him that he too was going to the same place. As they were going on the way they became thirsty and they came upon a well. The man proposed to the boy that as the younger he should go down the well to fill the jar which the beardless man had with him, and then he would draw him up again. Then Johnnie, who had no cunning about him, went down. The beardless man then told him that he would leave him down there to die, and the boy began to beseech him to pull him up. After he had for a long time treated him thus cruelly, the beardless man asked him to give him the locket so that he himself could pass as the boy, the prince's godson; Johnnie being only a young boy consented to this. And again the beardless man made a proposal, that Johnnie as the younger should let himself appear to be the servant and should so present himself before the prince. Also he was to swear that, then and then only if he should die and come to life again, would he reveal what the beardless man had done to him.

Poor Johnnie was in a sad fix and consented to all the demands of the beardless man, and he took an oath to God: 'Then and then only if I die and come to life again, will I reveal what you have done to me.' And on these terms the beardless man drew him up out of the well.

So the two of them went on together and came to the city where the prince was. They appeared before him, and the beardless man gave the locket into his hand and said that he was the boy to whom he had been godfather. But the eye of the prince was on the boy and he asked the beardless man who the boy was whom he had with him. He replied that he had taken him for company on the way. The prince kept him there because he had a liking for him.

One day in summer at midday the swallows, birds who never tire, were flying in and out of the men's room: it was there they had their nests. One swallow was late in coming and her mate scolded her and hit her with his wing. The son of the shepherd, who had learned the language of birds, began to smile at what they were saying. Then the beardless man who had been seeking a cause to drive the boy away, gave him a buffet. The king was sorely vexed at his conduct and asked the beardless man why he had hit the boy. He answered that Johnnie had smiled to mock him. The king asked Johnnie if this were true, and he said that his laughter had been about the birds, the pair of swallows, because the cock bird with his wing had struck at his mate and had scolded her because she was so late, and she had told him that she had been tarrying to collect the hair combings of a beautiful girl. These were all of gold, and she wanted to bring them for their nest, for they would be very soft for their chicks. The girl, said the swallow, was called the Girl with golden Hair.

When the beardless man heard this, he told the prince to order Johnnie to go and fetch the Girl with golden Hair because for the prince she would be the most beautiful wife who could ever be found. So the boy was ordered to go to fetch her. Then the boy, who held by his father's counsel not to be disobedient although the command might cost him much, took a fine strong horse and went off to go to look for the Girl with golden Hair. As he was going on his way, he met an ogress, a Lamia, and greeted her in a way that pleased her,[1] and she told him in answer that she would not devour him, for he was the godson of a prince, and she asked him what he had come out to seek. He answered that he had come to seek the Girl with golden Hair. Then she said: 'And have you come out with empty hands?' And she gave him this counsel, to go back and get forty sheep killed and flayed and forty skins of honey, for on the way he would come to a place crowded and black with ants, and farther on to a great swarm of bees; to be able to get by he must throw the sheep to the ants and the honey to the bees, and the ants will betake themselves to the sheep and the bees to the honey.

So the boy turned back and went and asked for everything the Lamia had said, and when he had been given them he started on his way. Then from a long way off he saw a place black all over: a little hill, to his amazement. When he came closer he perceived that it was the ant-hill, and the horse laid back his ears and was reluctant to pass it. The boy went forward and at some distance away threw down the sheep, and when the ants had the smell of them they all ran to the place and so the boy had a chance to get past. And as he went by the king of the ants called upon him to stop, and in his little voice he told him that the great ones among them had held a council and because

[1] The correct way for a young hero to appease an ogress whom he may meet is to hail her as Mother and to suck at her breast; no doubt this is what Johnnie did.

of the good he had done them in bringing them food they had resolved that they too would do him some benefit. Then the king gave him a wing and told him that if he had any need of them he must singe it in the fire and they would go to him wherever he was. The boy took the wing and put it away safely, and then he went on his way. Going farther he came upon a great swarm of bees so that he could not pass by. Then near them he poured out the honey. At once the swarm broke up and made for the honey and thus he got past there also without the horse taking fright. But the bees also called a council just like the ants, and they resolved to do him a kindness. The king of the bees flew out and caught up with Johnnie and gave him a wing, telling him to put it away as a treasure to be guarded, because all their great ones had resolved to do him a benefit. If he were in need, he had nothing to do but to singe the wing a little in the fire. Saying this to him, the bee went away. And thus the boy was again able to pass, and he reached the place of the Girl with golden Hair. And when the people saw him, they asked him where he was coming from and where he was going, and he told them he had come there with the intention to fetch away the Girl with golden Hair.

Then they told him that as for the Girl with golden Hair, it was only by performing certain tasks that a man could win her, and that if he was willing to wager on these tasks, she would propound them to him, and that if he could not succeed in them his head would be cut off. Then they pointed out to him a tower built all of the heads of young men of every sort, men who had undertaken the wagers and had failed, and now only one head was lacking for the tower to be complete: 'Well, think it over and make up your mind.' Johnnie heard all this paying very good heed, yet for all that he consented to engage in the test. They showed him a very big granary, full of wheat, barley, oats, and other grains, but all the sorts were mixed up together, and they told him that if he could in one night empty that store and not a grain escape him and then set each sort apart, then the Girl with golden Hair should be his.

Well, when he heard of this test he began to think how he could succeed in it, and he remembered what the ant had said: he took out the wing and singed it and before you could say Amen the ant appeared and asked him what were his orders.

'I want you to empty this granary in one night and this very evening, and each kind must be put separate and you must not miss out even one grain.' At once all the ants came, going in and going out like an army when in full array it is exercising on the field, and by the morning they had shifted all the grain just as he had said. One of the ants who was lame was late in coming out of the granary, and they went to see what had happened, because they were uneasy about her, and when they went in the ant was coming out carrying a grain of wild barley, which had rolled down into a crack, and she had been working at it all night before she could get it out. For all that the others had done, it was only the lame ant who had saved the head of the poor lad. When men rose up in the morning and saw the granary all cleared, swept out, and washed, and every grain set in its separate place, they were all amazed and could not imagine how this had happened.

The Girl with golden Hair also heard of this to her great displeasure, and she set before him yet another test. She sent word to him that she would come down with her serving women, and they would all be wearing clothes of one cut and pattern, and all of them would be veiled; if he could recognize her, she swore that she would follow him wherever he took her and he should have her for his wife and marry her. When he heard this he fell into great thought and great confusion. Dizzy with care and trouble, it came into his mind what the bee had said. He brought out the wing and singed it, and at once the bee appeared before him. 'What are your orders, master?' So he told her what was happening to him. Then the bee told him that she would go to the place where the girls were to be dressing themselves, and she would put a mark on the Girl with golden Hair, and that when the girls went downstairs she would follow her. When they reached the place where the girls would be brought for him to pick her out, then she would come round to her and alight on her head and on the covering of her head she would lay some honey. He must be careful not to be confused with his happiness and pick upon another girl.

So when the time came for the girls to dress the bee was there and she made a clear mark on the Girl with golden Hair, and when the girls were dressed and had gone down from the palace to the place where the king was and with him all the first men of the palace and of the realm, there was Johnnie with his eyes cast down. When the bee saw him she went and buzzed and tickled him, and at once he came to himself and lifted up his eyes. He kept them alert and watched the bee to see where she went and alighted, going and coming back again, and on the head of which girl she left some honey. The girls all passed in front of him three times, and at the third time he took one of them by the hand: it was the Girl with golden Hair. She at once showed her face and by her beauty bright as the sun he saw who it was.

Now when he had succeeded in the second test also fireworks and illuminations of all sorts were prepared so that the night was as bright as the day. Everybody was delighted for by then they had had too much of seeing so many young men brought to death and the tower built of their heads.

Next day the two of them were sent off on their way with all good wishes. The boy took her and they went off to the country of the prince who had been Johnnie's godfather. The prince marvelled at her, but the beardless man was jealous of the boy's bravery and at his fine achievements, and he wanted to kill him, so he gave him a drink which brought him to his death. When the Girl with golden Hair saw him fallen down dead, she gave him a draught of the Water of Immortality and raised him up again. Johnnie uttered a sigh and said: 'Ah, how sweetly I was sleeping; why did you awake me?' Then the girl told him the story of how the beardless man had poisoned him and how she with the Water of Immortality had raised him up again.

The youth remembered the oath that he had sworn, and that now that he had been dead and was alive again the bond was loosed, because he had sworn: 'Then and then only will I reveal what this man has done to me if I die and come to life again.' So now was the time and now he had a right to reveal to his godfather the hidden secret. Therefore very fully and point by point he told all that we have narrated from the beginning to the end. And when she heard it the girl told what Johnnie had endured for her sake, and how if he had not been able to find how to pass the tests she set him he would have lost his head, and how she had sworn to him to take him for her husband and to be married to him. The young man too said that to her he owed his life and he was hers.

When the king and the prince heard all this, in order to show the world that they were just judges they gave orders that the beardless man should be hanged, and Johnnie they married to the Girl with golden Hair, and the wedding was celebrated with joy and with many fair diversions.

35

The treacherous Brothers

THE general outline of this common story as it appears in Greece, where thirteen versions have been recorded, is as follows: A king desired some rare object to complete and make perfect a church or a mosque or a palace which he had built. This rare object is very often a bird of some kind; this is in the version from Amisós in Pontos and in the version from Thrace here translated; also in the version from Kydoniá. In Hahn's version from Euboia the object sought for is a magic mirror. In the other Thracian version the brothers are sent to seek a cure for their father's blindness. In the version from Skyros which I have also translated an ill-omened and mysterious monk makes a demand for a lamp which never goes out, and it is for this that the three brothers must seek.

Whatever the search may be it is always the youngest of the three brothers who is successful. The elder brothers become jealous and entrap him in a well, which of course does not prevent his final vindication. In the version recorded by Legrand from Smyrna this incident of the well is made the occasion to insert No. 26, *The Underworld Adventure*; This might be regarded as a piece of personal padding if it were not that the same insertion is found in an Armenian version in *Folklore*, xxii. 351. Other contacts are with No. 34, *The Servant who took the Place of his Master*, and with No. 42, *The Son of the Hunter*. All of these are essentially quest stories.

From the references given by BP. in their notes to Grimm's No. 57, *The golden Bird*, it is plain that the central line of the story as widely diffused over Europe is that a sick king needs to cure his troubles some kind of magic bird which the youngest of his three sons is successful in fetching him, and is then the object of his envious brother's treachery. The Greek oikotype of the story has a definite character of its own, markedly in the fact that the object sought for is not to cure the king's illness but to perfect the decoration of a building. The bird as the object of the quest is a feature which the Greek oikotype has in common with the European version of the story. The cure of the father's blindness in the Thracian version not translated is rather of the European type of the story, for which consult the references given for Aarne-Thompson's Type 550.

The Thracian text translated shows the neatness of construction very characteristic of the artistry of folktales. The youngest brother in pursuit of the golden nightingale comes first to the bird's forty guardians. They will give him the bird, but he must bring them the horse with wings. The forty guardians of the horse demand as their price the king's daughter. He wins the girl and the guardians give him the horse; by a trick when he takes the horse he carries off the girl as well. The first set of guardians in return for the horse give him the golden bird; again by a similar trick he carries away from their house not only the bird but the horse they have demanded as its price. Thus he has not only the bird but the horse and the girl.[1] The rest of the story is much curtailed.

The use of the three dresses by the heroine is a borrowing from *The Underworld Adventure*. In the version from Skyros the refusal of the hero to strike a second blow and his making his way by means of flattery are commonplaces.[2] That ogres are asleep when their eyes are staring open and vice versa is well known.[3]

The references for *The treacherous Brothers* are:

1, 2. PONTOS: *Astír tou Pontou*, i. 472, and from Samsoun, *Arkheíon Pontou*, vi. 233.

3. KYDONIÁ: Hahn, ii. 64, No. 72.

4. SMYRNA: Legrand, *Recueil de contes pop. grecs*, p. 191.

5. SAMOS: Stamatiádis, *Samiaká*, v. 539.

6. KOS: *Forty-five Stories*, p. 173.

7, 8. MÝKONOS: Roussel, *Contes de Mycono*, pp. 21, 25.

9, 10. SKYROS: Pérdika, ii. 170 and 252, the latter translated.

11 EUBOIA: Hahn, i. 254, No. 51.

12, 13. THRACE: *Arkheíon Thrakikoú Laogr.*, iv. 177 and viii. 187, the latter translated.

NO. 35*a*. THE TREACHEROUS BROTHERS[4]

Once upon a time there was a king and he had three sons; to each of them he gave a pot of gold coins. The three agreed together to build a mosque. They built the mosque and invited everyone to come to see it. Among them there came an old man from Bulgaria. 'A fine mosque; a lovely mosque; but it has one thing lacking,' said the old man. The people all went outside

[1] These tricks rather recall the key talisman story in No. 8 above.

[2] For the second blow see *M.G. in A.M.*, p. 226, and for the successful flattery of objects which might have been obstacles see *Forty-five Stories*, p. 171.

[3] See *M.G. in A.M.*, p. 226.

[4] Text from Thrace in *Arkheíon Thrakikoú Laogr.* viii. 187, with the title *The Golden Nightingale*.

and the mosque fell down. Again they built up the mosque. Again they invited everyone; they came and with them came the old man who again said the same thing. The people all went outside and the mosque fell down. They built it up again and still more finely. They invited the people and they came and the old man came and said the same thing. The youngest brother was present and he said: 'What is the one thing lacking?' 'It ought to have a golden nightingale in it.' The three brothers agreed to go to find one and off they went to get the bird. They came to a fountain where there were three roads: on one a man might go but never come back. They took off their rings and laid them under the slab that was by the fountain: whichever of them came there first, he should wait for the others; he would know by the rings.

The youngest brother took the road on which there is no returning. He went on and on; growing tired he sat down to rest; he lit a fire and put on the pot to make a cup of coffee to drink. An old man also came there. 'Good day, my fair youth.' Good day to you, old man.' 'Be so good, old man, as to take a coffee.' 'And where are you going like this, my boy?' 'I am on my way to find the golden nightingale.' 'But, my boy, on this road there is no returning. On this road where you are now going, my boy, there are forty ogres. There in the field you will find their mother doing the washing, with her breasts hanging over her shoulders. You must suck them and call her mother. She will say: "My lad, even before saying good evening, here you are sucking my breasts. I have forty fine lads and when they come they will devour you and devour me too." "Look here, mother; you hide me and later on you can say that I am your son." This is what you must say to her.' So the boy went and sucked her and did everything the old man had told him. She gave him a buffet and this turned him into a broom; she leaned him up against the wall. The forty young men arrived. 'Mother, we can smell man's flesh here.' 'You have been off to the frontiers, eating and eating, and that is why you smell man's flesh here.' 'No, no,' said they, 'a man has been here.' 'But, boys, suppose a man does come here; if he sucks the same milk as yourselves, surely he is a brother to you.' The thirty-nine of them said: 'He is our brother,' but the youngest of them all said: 'No, here we are forty and can have no other brother.' The others said: 'Whatever our mother says, that stands.' They went into the house and their mother set the table for them to eat. She gave the broom a buffet and it turned into a youth. 'You are very welcome, brother,' said they. 'I have come,' said the boy, 'for you to grant me the golden nightingale.' 'We will give it to you,' said they. 'Yet you must go yet farther and you will find forty youths; we go but can never overcome them; if you can fetch us from there the horse with wings, then we will let you have the golden nightingale.'

The boy went off and crossed the frontier. He became tired and sat down to boil up a coffee to drink. Again an old man came up. 'Good morning, fair son.' 'Good day, old man, be pleased to drink a coffee.' 'Where are you going, my boy?' He said he was going to fetch the horse with wings. 'If you go this way,' said he, 'you will lose your life. As soon as you are in the house, the old woman will be baking bread with her breasts over her shoulders; you must suck them and say to her: "Mother, hide me." ' The boy went and sucked, and she gave him a buffet and he was turned into an apple; she put the apple on the shelf. The forty youths came in. 'A smell of man's flesh!' said they. They sat down to eat and the mother rapped the apple and it turned into a boy. 'Welcome, brother,' said they. 'Why have you come here?' 'I have come for the horse,' said he. 'We will give him to you,' said they, 'but there is a certain king's daughter, and it is for you to go and bring her to us.'

The boy went his way to fetch the king's daughter. On the road he again lit a fire and again the old man came and said: 'Take this gun with two barrels; whatever you find, you will be able to shoot.'

The boy went on. At the frontier he saw a vulture. He made to shoot it, but the vulture came and perched by him. 'If you will not shoot me, what can I do to help you?' The bird plucked out a feather and gave it to him saying: 'When you are in any trouble, set light to the feather and I will be with you.' Again the boy went on his way. He saw a fish in the sea. 'This fish anyhow I will shoot.' The fish came out before him. 'Do not shoot me; take one of my scales and when you are in any trouble set it alight and I will be with you.' The boy went on farther and met a fox. 'Anyhow I will shoot this fox.' 'Oh, don't shoot me,' said the fox, and gave him a hair. 'Take this hair; set it alight and I will be with you if you are in any trouble.' He went on farther and came upon an ant. 'Anyhow I will shoot this ant.' 'No, don't shoot me,' said the ant 'Take this foot of mine and when you are in any trouble, set it alight and I will be with you.' So he came to the king. 'My king, I have come here for your daughter.' 'You see that tower,' said the king. 'It is built all of men's heads. For three hours you are to stay in hiding. My daughter will go out to find you and if she finds you I will have your life. If she does not find you then you may have her.'

The boy set light to the vulture's feather and the vulture came and carried him away up into the clouds. The king's daughter came and looked, looked here and looked there; she caught sight of him up among the clouds. The vulture brought him down to earth. 'And what do you expect now?' said the king. 'Better wait for the third time,' said the boy.

Then he set light to the fish scale and the fish came to him. 'Hide me,' said the boy; 'if I am to save my head from them.' The fish carried him down into the sea. The princess came out and looked and she saw him in the sea, and brought him out. Then the boy set light to the fox's hair, and the fox hid him right down in the earth, and came into the king's garden. The king's daughter came out and the fox began to play tricks. The men went about to kill the fox and so three hours passed; then the fox brought the boy up out of the earth. 'You have done well,' said the king; 'yet for all that I have a granary full of all kinds of grain. If you can in one evening sort them out, then I will give you my daughter.' The boy set the ant's foot alight and the ant came to him. 'Well,' said the boy, 'see if you can set the granary all in good order.' The ants came and each sort of grain they set apart by itself. Said the king: 'You are worthy for me to give you my daughter.' So he took the girl, and on the way he told her where he was taking her. He told her too that there he would take the horse and start for a ride and that she too should mount and so they would go off together. They went to the place; he mounted the horse and rode and the brothers shook hands with him in farewell. The girl was about to shake his hand in farewell when he snatched her up and they rode off quickly to the place where the golden nightingale was. The brothers there wanted to keep the girl with them and he to take the horse and the nightingale. He put the nightingale into his saddle-bag and began to say farewell to the brothers. The girl too started to say farewell to the brothers, and as she was doing this the boy snatched her away from them.

So they came to the fountain. He lifted the slab and under it he found the rings. He bought a second horse and dressed the girl like a man and took her off to a certain city. There he found one of his brothers selling biscuits. 'Baker,' cried he, 'will you not come with me for a monthly wage and we will go and buy sheep together.' The man dropped his biscuits and went off with the two of them. They came to a village and there they saw the other brother; he was grazing calves. 'Can't you leave the calves', said they, 'and come with us and we can buy cows together.' The man left his calves and went with them. So they went on all of them together and came to the fountain. The princess took off her man's clothes, and there she was, a beautiful girl. 'Well, my good brothers,' said the youngest, 'We started off to fetch the golden nightingale, and here am I, and with the beautiful girl and the horse.' He lifted up the slab and brought out the rings.

The two brothers were jealous of the youngest and they attacked him and put out his eyes, and took the girl and the nightingale too; they tried to take the horse but it would not come, so with the girl and the nightingale they went off to the mosque. They set the nightingale in the temple and men of religion and students all assembled there. The nightingale would not sing at all. Then they wanted to make a marriage between the eldest brother and the girl. The horse right where he was spoke and said to the blind man: 'If you can you must come and untie me from here and catch hold of the bridle, and thus we can go to the well of holy water. You shall bathe there and set a leaf on your eyes and they shall be opened.' The blind youth obeyed: he loosed the horse, took it by the bridle and went to the well of holy water. Then he bathed and laid a leaf on his eyes and they were opened. Then he mounted the horse and rode to the mosque. In it prayers were being read to make the nightingale sing, and the wedding was being prepared. The youngest brother, his clothes all torn, passed into the mosque. The nightingale began to sing. Everyone was amazed; who was it made the nightingale sing? Everyone went out and the youngest brother went out. No one could see who it was made the bird sing. The people again went into the mosque and the boy too went in: again the nightingale sang. One by one the people went out of the temple. The youngest brother stayed there in a place, the last of them all. The police came to make him go out. Scarcely had they made him move from his place than the bird's voice broke and they had hardly got him outside when the bird stopped singing. The boy was brought forward and declared that it was he who had brought the nightingale and that he was the prince. He took the girl in marriage; the others were put to death and he became king.

I was there and they gave me a plate of rice. Then I passed by the side of a lake and in it were some frogs crying out *brak, brak, brak*, and I thought they were shouting *drop it, drop it, drop it*, so I dropped the rice and went off.[1]

NO. 35*b*. THE TREACHEROUS BROTHERS[2]

Once upon a time there were a king and a queen, and they had three boys. The king and the queen were good and all their people loved them; they took a proud delight in them when they walked abroad with their three sons, handsome and lively as they were, all three of them. But the king was not a man of good luck: he and all the people with him lived in fear and distress, for the realm was haunted by an evil spirit. Every now and then from a cave opposite to the palace a little old monk used to come out; he would stand at the mouth of the cave and lift up his hands and cry aloud three times: 'I must have the Lamp which never goes out.' Everyone could see him, but no one could get close to him to catch him, however many might try. The monk would stand there for a little as if he were waiting for them to bring him that for which he was seeking. When it was not brought, he would appoint a set period: twice more he would show himself and cry this aloud: if they did not bring him the Lamp, all the men in the palace would die; not even a fly would be left. And this in fact had come to pass.

So everywhere the realm had the name of being a place haunted; no one wanted to be king there; they were afraid. This

[1] *Brak* is in Turkish the imperative of the verb *brakmak*, to leave. I venture to translate *drop it*.

[2] Text from Skyros in Pérdika, ii. 252, with the title *The Lamp which never went out.*

latest king was a good man; he had pity on the people, for if they had no king, they would be ruined and carried off as slaves. So he made up his mind and to that realm he went. 'Anyhow we shall all die some day,' he said. 'At least let me die as a king.'

He married and had these three sons. The sons grew up. The monk made no further appearance. All were then saying that he would not show himself any more; that even the evil spirit was having compassion on the king and the queen and their three sons, such good folk as they all were. Then suddenly one evening people again heard that the monk had come out with his cry; all fell as if dead with sorrow and distress. Then they all assembled below the palace weeping, the young men calling upon the king to come forward and summon his Council of Twelve to look into the matter, and find out and tell them where the Lamp which never went out was to be found: they would go and fetch it to deliver their much loved king and the queen and the princes from the power of death. The king embraced his wife the queen to comfort her, for she was weeping and nothing would sooth her, nor could he himself recover; in his grief his eyes were running like a fountain. The princes at first were confused by all this weeping and the loud cries; until then no one had told them anything about the monk. When they understood the reason of all this trouble, the youngest spoke out from his heart; he was a lad not easily to be frightened; he was also the handsomest of the three. 'Brothers, I say that this business is for us and we by ourselves must go and take thought to find this Lamp, that so we may deliver our father and our mother, and deliver ourselves too, once and for all from this monk and his threats.'

The brothers whetted their swords and took their weapons; thus they mounted their horses and went off to find the Lamp which never goes out. All the people escorted them, and they received the blessing of their mother and their father and so went off. They rode on and on, and after a while they came to a place where the road forked. They dismounted to refresh themselves a little and to decide which road each of them would follow.

Over one road they read a notice: 'Who goes this way returns again.' Over the other was written: 'Who goes this way does not return.' They took counsel which of them should follow this road. The youngest said: 'My brothers, I shall take the road by which there is no returning, to see if I can find anything. Let us take off our rings and leave them under this stone here in the corner, and whoever comes back first will find the rings; he must sit down here and wait for the others until this same time next year. If I have not come back within a year, do not wait for me any longer, but go away back to the palace and our parents.'

Now we must leave the two who went on the level road, asking everyone whom they met about the Lamp which never goes out, and see what the other one did, the youngest, he who took the road on which there was no returning. He went on and on and saw no one at all. Then it befell that a long way off he saw a tower, and he said: 'Glory be to Thee, O God, for now I shall find someone to ask.' He went up and knocked at the door: no one there. He opened and went in, into one room and then into another. He found a girl Five Times Fair. When she saw him she was amazed and threw herself upon him, saying: 'How have you come here? What is it you seek? Do you not know that on this road of yours there is no returning? An ogre will come presently and he will devour you. No; go away, and go quickly.' For she was grieved that he should lose his life; such a fine youth and so handsome as he was!

The youth said: 'No, I will not go. I have come for the Lamp which never goes out, that so I may deliver my people, and I am determined to find it, and to win it I will wrestle even with Death.' Then the princess said that she would help him as much as she could to conquer the ogre who held her enslaved, her and her two sisters; only he must not leave her there, forsaken, but take her with him when he went back to his kingdom. On this they agreed, and the princess said: 'I will now by my magic turn you into a broom, so that the ogre may not find you; he will be coming now. When he has eaten and laid down to sleep, I will make you into a man again; then you shall go and kill him if you can. But know that if you do not cut off his head with the first blow of your sword, you are lost. If you try to give him a second blow, instead of being killed he will wax even more savage and will devour you.' Then she raised her hand and gave him a slap on the face and turned him into a broom and set him behind the door. Presently, behold the ogre! He began to sniff, saying: 'There is a smell of man's flesh here.' 'How can that be?' said she. 'No, no,' said the ogre,' there is a smell here of man's flesh; I cannot be deceived.' He searched all the rooms but found nothing. Then he sat down to eat and lay down to sleep.

The princess went out and gave a tap to the broom: it became a man again. 'Now,' said she 'the time has come. But you must know that if he has his eyes open, then he is asleep; if he has them shut, don't go near him at all.' The prince took his sword and, one two, in he went; he took his resolve; he saw the ogre with his eyes open and he struck him a blow with his sword: he cut his throat right across. The ogre began to howl, and cried out: 'Strike me another blow.' 'No; this is enough; you're all right,' said the prince. 'Who are you, you who have conquered me?' said the ogre. 'My kingdom is now all yours. Yet you will have to reckon with my brother, and whatever you do, you will never go back, and this I tell you for sure.' He knew well that the youth was determined to go forward. With these words it was the end of the ogre.

The prince went off into the tower. There he found the Five Times Fair. He embraced and kissed her and told her that he had killed the ogre and that now she was free. He begged her to help him to go forward on his way. Then the Five Times Fair took him down to the stable and saddled the ogre's horse: his name was Thunder. The prince mounted and she gave him two great bags full of pieces of meat and said to him: 'My brother, Thunder will now carry you to the next tower where the second ogre dwells. There you will find my sister; she too is held in slavery. You will tell her that I have sent you and she will guide you what you must do as you go on farther. Only don't forget the promise you gave me that, when you return after conquering the ogres and winning the Lamp which never goes out, you will take us too along with you. Take also this meat, for on your way you will come to a field all full of beasts under enchantment; they will throw themselves upon Thunder to devour you. Then you must throw them the meat saying: "Oh, what lovely beasts; never in my life have I seen more beautiful animals!" By the time they have eaten the meat, Thunder will have carried you past and will take you where you will.'

The prince spurred Thunder and was off like the wind. He came to the field and threw down the meat; passed by and came to the second tower. Thunder came to a halt. The Five Times Fair had told him that this tower had no door, and he must leap up and get in by way of the balcony. He scrambled up a tree; with one jump he leaped from it to the balcony, and there was the girl. When she saw him she was astonished. 'How did you come here? Have you seen my sister? How came the ogre to let you pass?' She asked these questions, and he told her how he had killed the first ogre; that her sister had helped him; that his resolve was to kill all the ogres and so win the Lamp which never goes out; that if he succeeded in winning it, on his return he would take both of them along with him. Also that he had pledged the first Five Times Fair to be the bride of his eldest brother, and herself, if she were willing, he would marry to his second brother. He begged her to guide him, what he must do to overcome this ogre also and so go forward on his way. Then the Five Times Fair said to him: 'The first ogre you have conquered: yet this one is far more powerful. His strength is in his knees. He will say to you that he will cleanse your head, and if you are beguiled by this and rest your head on his lap, he will crush it between his knees. You must not let him do this; you must make him fight with you, and see that you break his sword with one blow of yours: if you strike him a second blow with the sword, he will grow furious and kill you.'

Then the ogre came, and when he saw the youth he was aware that he had killed his brother and this made him afraid. He received him kindly and asked him to sit down and they would eat together. When they had finished eating, he said: 'Stoop down, and let me cleanse your head.' The prince said: 'No, I don't want you to.' They began the fight. The prince drew his sword and struck a blow against the ogre's sword; he broke it in the midst, all but a hair. The ogre shook with rage. 'So that is what you have done! Strike again and divide it right in two.' 'No,' said the prince: 'it is better thus. Now it is your turn.' He gave the ogre a stroke and cut his throat from one side to the other.

He went to the princess: rejoicings, embraces, kisses! 'Now let us go to the stable,' said the princess. 'You shall leave Thunder and take the horse called Lightning, who is even faster and also knows the way to bring you to the third tower. On the way you will come to an enchanted field full of snakes; you will spur Lightning three times, and he will dart forward without putting hoof to the ground and will bring you over like a real flash of lightning, and no ill will befall you. When the snakes dart forward to bite you, you must stoop over Lightning's neck and say: "Oh, what lovely snakes!" '

He mounted on Lightning. He said farewell to the Five Times Fair and told her that she must be ready for him to take her with him on his return. So he went off. He came to the snakes, and said: 'Oh, what lovely snakes!' He spurred Lightning forward and reached the third tower. This one too had no door; he leaped up to the balcony and so went in. He found the third sister, and what beauty was hers! He felt mad for love of her as soon as ever he saw her. She trembled and said: 'Are you a man? And how have you come here?' 'It is when a man has no will, that he cannot succeed,' said he. 'I am resolved to go through to the end. If God grant me to succeed, your sisters shall be for my brothers, and you I will take as a wife for myself.' She consented, saying: 'Have a care; with his arms this ogre will fight; it is in them he has his strength. He will try to force you down into the earth. See that you force him first, and with one shove, because if you give him a second, instead of being pushed in deeper, he will fly upwards and strangle you. If you overcome him, then as a last test you will have to struggle with the man-devouring monster Méaina; she is their mother and has the three ogres all in her service.'

Presently the ogre came and saw him: he began to grind his teeth. 'Who is this man? How did he come here? I shall kill him.' The youth drew his sword. The ogre said: 'No fighting with swords! Wrestling with arms to grip!' He seized the boy by the waist, gave him one shove and forced him down into the earth to his ankles. The ogre shoved: the boy shoved, and drove the ogre down into the earth to above his knees. The ogre said: 'Give me one more shove.' 'No,' said the boy; 'it is well as you are. I have now conquered you.' The ogre disappeared from view.

The Five Times Fair said to him: 'Go off at once; go to Méaina's tower before her sons the ogres get there and tell her that a man has set his foot here; afterwards it will be too late.

On the way you will come to a lake with bitter water all full of worms; you must stoop down and take water in your hand three times and drink and say: "Oh, what sweet water! never have I drunk such sweet water as this." You will pass by and go on your way. When you come to Méaina's tower you must first go and find the monster's horse, a talking horse: he alone it is who can carry you back again. Take these sugared cakes to give him to make him gentle and quiet and to prevent him from crying out. At any outcry the horse may make: "Mistress, they are carrying me off!" you must go and hide yourself in a cave where there is a holy well opposite the place where the horse is kept: in there Méaina cannot go. She will change into a spirit of the air, to go in and feel about everywhere. When she fails to find you in your hiding place and goes away, then you must go back and again give cakes to the horse to make him know you and not make any more outcry when he sees you. Then you will take him and saddle him to have him all ready; then you will go forward into the tower. At twelve o'clock Méaina lies down to sleep. If you find her asleep you must snatch the key from her throat and the Lamp which she has at her feet and you must go away at once, to get off before the monster wakes up.'

The youth went off like lightning; he passed by the lake and drank some water. Then he went to the tower and found the horse and gave him the cakes. The horse began crying out; the boy hid himself in the cave. Méaina came out and went to the horse: 'Who is carrying you off?' she asked. She turned into a spirit of the air and searched everywhere but found nothing. She went to the mouth of the cave, grinding her teeth: 'O thou cursed cave, what are you hiding from me? Is there anyone inside you?' The cave said nothing. Then the monster went to the horse and said: 'How does it seem to you tonight? Isn't there someone here?' She went inside and lay down to sleep. The prince again went to the horse and gave him some more cakes. This time he took the cakes and ate them; then he began crying out. Again Méaina came down and searched everywhere; the prince was hidden, and she found nothing. She went to the horse all in a lather of rage and said: 'What has happened to you today? Are you dreaming? Don't talk any more and wake me up for nothing, or I'll cut you to pieces.' She went off.

The prince went there again and caressed the horse and gave

him cakes. The horse ate them and kept silence; he did not make any more noise. The prince put on his girth and made him all ready. Then very quietly he approached Méaina; he saw she was snoring and with her eyes open. He cut the cord and took the key and snatched up the Lamp. Then he ran to the stable and mounted the horse and they were off like smoke. Before long Méaina woke up. Hardly had the monster seen that the key had been taken and the Lamp which never went out, than she became a wild beast. Down she went to the stable. Not finding the horse, she changed herself into a spirit of the air and with a rush started to chase after him. One moment she saw him near the lake with the bitter water. She cried out: 'A curse upon you, my lake, if you do not drown him, now that he has to cross over you.' 'Never will I do that', said the lake; 'the man drank of my water and found it refreshing.' Then the monster threw down a magic comb; the earth split open to swallow the man. The lake took him up on her waters and carried him to the farther side. He went forward and came to the tower. He seized the Five Times Fair and set her on the horse: they were off like the wind.

The monster puffed and panted and once more came up to them by the field with the snakes; she cried aloud 'O my snakes, devour him; poison him with your venom, him and the Five Times Fair with him.' The snakes said: 'Never will we do this: he stooped down and looked well at us and marvelled at our beauty; and shall we poison him?' They then coiled themselves round Méaina, whom they knew as their mistress, and lifted up their heads for her to caress them. She in her wrath tore at them and dashed them to the ground. As soon as he was free from them, the prince went forward and came to the tower. The Five Times Fair mounted on the horse Lightning, who had been left in the stable. They all went off together.

Near the field where the wild beasts were they again saw the monster coming to attack them: her eyes were bursting from her head in her rage; foam was coming from her mouth; she was terrible to look at; at the sight of her you would tremble. 'O my beasts, devour him; tear him to pieces, him and the girl with him.' But as soon as the beasts saw the prince, they said: 'This man gave us food when you had kept us so long fasting, also he marvelled at our beauty: can we then devour him?

Never will we do that.' Then the monster fell to the ground and burst herself with rage. The time allowed her was at an end; after this she could do nothing against them.

They reached the last tower; there they sat and ate and rested themselves. The three sisters, the Five Times Fairs, could never have enough of kissing and embracing one another: they had been so long without seeing one another. They were weeping for joy to be delivered from the ogres, and that they would now go back, all of them together. When they had well rested from their toils, they started to go away, taking with them all the ogre's golden jewels and coin; all the riches which they found in his chests and cupboards they loaded on horses, and themselves mounted and went off.

The Five Times Fair, the one who was betrothed to the prince, gave him three walnuts and told him to guard them well in his pocket and let no one see them; she wanted to make two of them presents to her sisters and the third she would keep for herself. In them were three dresses: one was worked with the field and its flowers; the second with the sea and its fish; and the third, the finest of all, with the sky and the stars. She wanted them to wear them as their wedding dresses.

Now we may leave these on their way in all joy to the place appointed by the three brothers, and see what the other two princes had been doing all this time. When they had gone round from city to city and found nothing, they turned back, thinking sadly that they too must die and with them their father and their mother, just as they were saying that their brother must have done. They reached the place where the road divided and found him waiting for them with the Lamp which never went out and the princesses. Then they all of them together took the road back, the prince rejoicing that he had with him the Lamp and would deliver his father and his mother and his brothers. But the other two were jealous and wanted to kill him, and themselves take the Lamp which never went out and bring it to the king.

As they were on their way they came to a well; they were thirsty and had no bucket to let down to draw up water. They persuaded the youngest of them to go down into the well himself and fetch them water. Then they began to throw down stones on him from above to kill him. He drew to one side of the well so that the stones should not reach him. There he saw a hole in the wall of the well and in it he took refuge. The two brothers stooped down and looked, but they did not see him. 'He is drowned,' they said. Then with the Five Times Fairs they went off to their father.

Presently a shepherd went to draw water up from the well to water his kids. The prince caught at the rope and came up; bruised and bloody, in a sad state. The shepherd tended him and washed off the blood. Then the prince stayed with him and helped with the grazing and the milking. In order that he might not be recognized, when he went round selling the milk, he put the skin of a newly born kid over his head, and so he looked as though his head was scabby.

One day as he was selling milk to the tailor, he heard it being said that the eldest son of the king had sent out a crier to proclaim that whoever could make him three dresses, worked with the sky and the stars, with the field and its flowers, and with the sea and the fish, and each one of them to go into a walnut, to that man he would give a thousand gold pieces.

The eldest brother had intended to take as his wife the Five Times Fair who was betrothed to his youngest brother; she would in no way consent to this, always weeping for her betrothed, but to the king she could not even say anything, because he never left her a moment by herself. At last to get rid of him and to see if her beloved were still alive, she had said: 'I will take you for my husband if you will bring me those three dresses,' she knowing well that no one could make such things.

When the prince heard all this, he went to the palace and said: 'I can make the dresses, but first I must be taken to the princess to have her measures.' As soon as this was told to the Five Times Fair, she understood that this was the man, her betrothed. She ordered leave to be given him to come up to her. When she saw him she recognized him at once. She fell into his arms and took him with her to the king and the queen, who were lamenting and weeping for the death of their son. He said: 'Do not weep; I am not dead.' They did not recognize him in the sad state in which he was. Then the Five Times Fair sprinkled a powder upon him and cleansed his face: once more his beauty shone out as before.

Then he told his father that it was he who had found the

Lamp which never goes out: of his brothers he told him how they had sought to kill him. The eldest brother denied this and the king did not know which of them to believe. At that moment the cry of the monk was heard: he was coming out for the third time, and if they did not bring him the Lamp which never went out they would all die.

The prince ran to take it to the monk. The eldest brother snatched it from him: 'I found it and I shall take it,' he said. But when he came to the cave, the monk would not accept it from him and cried out: 'I must have the key too; what is the use of the Lamp without its key?' Then the youngest brother rushed up to the cave and gave him the key. The monk disappeared and was never seen again.

Then everyone understood that it was the youngest brother who had brought the Lamp also. They drove out the elder brothers who had tried to kill the youngest. Shortly his marriage with the Five Times Fair took place, and the king handed over to him his kingdom and himself with his wife withdrew to an estate they had and there lived at their ease. The prince and his wife had many children and lived in great love for many happy years.

36

The Boy and his Guardian or *Kindness rewarded*

AARNE–THOMPSON TYPES 505–8

In one form or another this story is found all over Europe, and further east as well, as may be seen from BP.'s references, iii. 94, to Grimm, No. 136, *Der Eisen-Hans*, *Iron John*. A version from Kos has been printed with notes in *Forty-five Stories*, No. 41, *The Boy and his Elder*, and a special form of the story, in which a dead man is the beneficiary is the subject of Gerould's book, *The grateful Dead*. The most recently published version is *The Story of Hajji Ali* in Major C. G. Campbell's *Tales from the Arab Tribes*, 1950, and from the same part of the world is the version in Lorimer's *Persian Tales*, p. 169.[1]

The essence of the story is that the hero does an act of kindness or mercy, and the beneficiary in some unexpected form appears later and acts as his devoted guide and helper. To pass to the Greek versions: sometimes, as at Vourla, in Pontos, and in Cyprus, the hero spares the life of a fish which might have been used as a remedy for a sick man; in the form of a servant the fish comes to serve and save him. In another set of versions the hero is again connected with the sea, but in this case by a special devotion to St. Nicholas, the patron of all sailors; in return the saint as an old man protects him and brings him prosperity. Here come the versions from Chios, the second from Mýkonos and the first of the two from Thrace. In a separate and important set of versions the hero has shown compassion for a dead man. In the Mitylene version, here translated, he gives burial to an abandoned corpse, and the dead man appears later as a 'Naked Man', a sort of savage who serves him with devotion. With no special service mentioned the 'Wild Man' appears again in Astypálaia, in a version a little like the Faithful John story. In the first Mýkonos version also the hero gives burial to a dead man. In Dieterich's version from Kos a man is saved from the gallows and afterwards helps his benefactor. It is with stories of this type that Gerould's book, *The grateful Dead*, is concerned. The other variants in my list are either vague about the service rendered or in some way diverge from what may be called the two central types of the story.

[1] A Mingrelian story in Wardrop's *Georgian Folk Tales*, p. 124, is hardly a parallel. It begins with the kindness to a fish and then goes on to the hero's kindness to a deer, the general idea being just kindness to animals.

After having earned the services of his guardian the story goes on that the hero in due time sought the hand of a girl, but he had a rival. The two youths set out in ships to trade and the one who made most money it was agreed should have the lady. By the help and advice of his guardian, who often directs him to load his ship with salt and make a great profit by selling it where salt is not known, the hero returned much the richer of the two, and the girl was his. To his great alarm the guardian appeared in the bridal chamber saying the time had come for them to part; they must go shares in all their wealth, including the bride, whom he proposed to cut in two with the sword he had in his hand. And he did indeed slash at her body, from which he cut a brood of snakes, snakes which would have been the death of the bridegroom. Then the guardian disappeared and the hero was left alone with his wife.

We are left asking: what are the snakes and how did they get into the woman's body? The guardian's last service is to save the hero from this element of danger in his wife. We may think at once of the Poison Maid of the *Gesta Romanorum*, the girl who had been dieted on poisons to such an extent that her embrace, or even her touch or her breath, would be fatal to any lover. From the danger of such a bride Alexander, we are told, was saved by his tutor Aristotle. It should however be noted that in our story no reason is given for the snakes and the danger of the wife's embrace; it seems to be no more than the idea of a general danger latent in women. In short, our present story and the Poison Maid have nothing more in common than the dangerous embrace. On what kinship this may betoken between the two stories it is not easy to be precise; for myself I think it small.[1] Yet there are two versions of our story in which the bride is a real Poison Maid. One is from Ovatchouk near Nikopolis in Pontos and the other is a gipsy version from Constantinople. In both of these we are told that the bride had been fatal to previous husbands.[2]

Especially in the form of *The grateful Fish* the story seems to be of Indian Buddhist origin, and this is the version we find in the Chinese book *Monkey*,[3] where we have a fish caught to serve as a meal for a sick parent and then out of mercy and kindness let go free. Then the fish in the guise of a 'Dragon King' helps the hero in his adventures. The book *Monkey* concerns a mission to India to bring Buddhist scriptures to China, and that it should contain *The grateful Fish*

[1] The kinship of our story to the Poison Maid, I would prefer to say to the idea of the dangerous embrace, has been worked out by G. H. Gerould in chap. iv of his book *The grateful Dead*. The *Gesta Romanorum*, reference is chap. 11, p. 288, of Oesterley's edition.

[2] See '*Αστὴρ τοῦ Πόντου*, i. 169; Paspati, *Études sur les Tchinghianés*, p. 601; *Forty-five Stories*, p. 462. [3] *Monkey* by Ch'êng-ên, translated by Arthur Waley, chap. ix.

suggests that we have here an Indian Buddhist story caught as it were, on the wing, on its way to China.

That in *Monkey* the beneficiary is a fish and that this marks the Indian and the two most eastern Greek versions, the ones from Cyprus and Pontos, suggest that this is the earliest form of the story and its Indian and eastern oikotype. St. Nicholas, the saint of the sea, is akin to the fish, and him we have found in the Greek islands in Chios and Mýkonos, as also in Thrace. The granting of burial to the dead man found at its farthest east in the islands in Mitylene, Kos, and Mýkonos, may be regarded rather as the European oikotype, although it occurs in the Persian variant in Lorimer's book. Major Campbell's Arab version has the mercy shown to the fish and so goes with the eastern stories.

Between this story and the next one, No. 37, *Faithful John*, there is a certain contact in as much as in both of them we have a youth served and guarded by a faithful adherent. But they differ essentially in that Faithful John is always a servant, while the elder or guide of the present story is a being of superior quality and nature, to whom the hero has had an opportunity of showing kindness.

That a man who has killed a monster should cut out and preserve its tongue—or its teeth—as a proof that he has been the killer is a commonplace; it is found again in No. 37, and for references see Stith Thompson's *Motif-Index*, H. 105, 1.

The references are:

1. PONTOS: *Astír tou Pontou*, i. 169.
2. VOURLA, near Smyrna: *Mikrasiatiká Khroniká*, iv. 239.
3. CYPRUS: Sakellarios, ii. 337.
4. MITYLENE: Anagnóstis, *Lesbiaká*, p. 161, translated.
5. CHIOS: Pernot, *Études de linguistique*, iii. 299.

6, 7. KOS: *Forty-five Stories*, p. 438, and Dieterich, p. 464.

8. ASTYPÁLAIA: Pio, p. 179 = Garnett, p. 261.

9, 10. MÝKONOS: Roussel, *Contes de Mycono*, p. 13, Nos. 6, 7.

11. EUBOIA: Hahn, i. 288, No. 53, which is Kretschmer, *Neugr. Märchen*, p. 233.

12, 13. THRACE: *Arkheíon Thrakikoú Laogr.* iv. 163 and vi. 245.

NO. 36. THE BOY AND HIS GUARDIAN[1]

In the days of old a king one day called his three sons to him and said: 'Listen, my boys, to what I have to say to you. Now that we have our kingdom in our hands we live well. But if some day

[1] Text from Mitylene in Anagnóstis, *Lesbiaká*, p. 161, with the title of *The Naked Man.*

a stronger king should come with his armies and overpower us and take away from us our kingdom and our treasures, have you ever thought what would become of us then?' This made the king's three sons very thoughtful and they did not know what to say. Presently their father spoke to them again: 'This matter, my dear boys, I have in my thoughts every day, and I will tell you what it is in the back of my mind that we should do, so that we be not left one day with our throats dry, and we, as the saying goes, breathing on our porridge and it never get cool. Now that you are all three of you still young fellows and are men of repute and wealth, you should begin to take up some work so that one day when we find ourselves in great stress you may have the means of living. There is nothing to be ashamed of in working. It may be any work you please, only it must be something from which a man can earn his keep, that you may not have the shame of running into debt, now to one man now to another. So tomorrow morning rise up early and come to me that I may give you as much money as each of you needs, and so start on the work which each of you likes best: first with the blessing of God and then with mine. If a man will work, God will never let him go hungry.'

When the king's sons heard this they made answer to their father. The eldest said that he wanted to be a merchant and deal in corn; the second that he would sell oil; the youngest brother however was ashamed to say what it was he wanted to do. When his father and his brothers pressed him, he said he wanted to deal in cattle, to buy oxen, and then either to sell them again or to feed them up for the butcher. When the three had made an end, their father said: 'Well, my boys, have you talked over this matter together? In the tasks which you undertake are you aware how many obstacles there are to overcome? Do you know what unkind things the world will have to say? Now, my sons, when other men see you coming as strangers with a good sum of money in your hands, they will fall upon you like crows to pick your bones, to eat you up. Now do you know what you must do? Each of you go off and find a partner and have him to work with you. One of you will, let us say, contribute the capital and the other whatever craft he may have.' So with this the sons agreed and they went off to find each of them his partner.

Before many days were over each of the two elder sons found a partner and they went to their father and took what money they needed and went to carry on their business. But all this time the youngest brother however much he tried could find no one at all to be his partner or his companion. He went to the poor; he went to the rich; he displayed all his money: to no profit! No one wanted to join with him.

When the king his father heard of this, he was on the one hand grieved that his youngest son was of so sour a nature that no one in the world liked him, and on the other he was angry with his son who could not in all those years find a friend for himself. So he sent for him and said: 'Listen to what I am saying. If before next Saturday you do not find a partner, then I will have your head off.'

When the poor boy heard this he was ready to die of fright, for he knew that his father was not in jest. So he went off with a sad heart and in tears; he went down the stairs and so off. He did not know what to do. At one last attempt he took courage and went round to all the butchers and told them what his father meant to do, standing before them in tears, to see if he could persuade any one of them to have mercy upon him and be his partner. In vain, in vain! all in vain! No one would even turn to look at him. The boy was in such grief that he was like a dead body; prick him with a needle and from him would flow stinking matter.

When the days were nearly over which the king had set for his son to find a partner, the boy resolved to go for this business to some other village, seeing that he could do nothing where he was. So he started and, one two! there he was in another village, a place where there were many butchers, thinking to himself that there he might bring off something.

When he came to that village the prince went into a tavern. He sat down and took a coffee and poured drinks for men he knew and for men he didn't know, and then said why he had come. Then they sent and called for the butchers of the village to come to the tavern, and to each of them the prince told his trouble. But what do you think? Not one would consent. One said that he was now tired of that business; another said that he did not want a partner, and not to make a long story of it, no one accepted his offer. Now consider the boy's position. He had two days left. When he thought of this, that in two days his head would be cut off, he had it in mind to run off to the mountains.

Then he broke out: 'Bring me an oke of raki,' he cried to the tavern keeper. 'Come, boys; let us drink and never trouble about partnerships and partners.' All those in the tavern joined in and they began all of them drinking together.

After this some voices were heard outside the tavern, and they saw many people passing along and four men were bearing a dead man on a carpet. The shouting of the children brought all the company to their feet. When the prince saw such doings from the window of the tavern he went out and asked what was going on. Then the men carrying the body halted and told him that it was a poor man and a stranger who had been that day begging in the village; he had been found dead and they were carrying off the body to throw it on the midden, and they did not know who the man was. 'But why do we not give him burial?' said the prince. 'Is it not a sin to throw him out on the midden?' 'It is, master,' said the men, 'but we found in his pockets nothing, not even a halfpenny'. 'What does that matter?' said the prince. 'Set the body down and one of you run and fetch the bishop and bring the priests from all the villages round here, and so we shall bury the man as it is fitting.' All the men stopped there to listen when they heard this, one of them saying to another: 'Why, the prince must have lost his senses to want to bury a beggar with such pomp.' But when they saw him fling a handful of gold pieces down on the bar of the tavern, and tell the tavern keeper to pay the men, and all the expenses arising from the burial, and if the money were not enough, to keep an account and he would pay the rest, then everyone of them went this way and that as fast as he could to do what the prince had told them.

Before six or it may be eight hours everything was there; everything in place and ready: the bishop and the priests and the processional cherubim and the coffin for the body; all before you could count three. What cannot money do? When all was ready, down came all the village and there was such a funeral as had never been before. When they had buried the dead man everyone began to go back to his work and the prince again went into the tavern, and ordered some brandy for men to drink for the pardon of the dead.

After this as they were drinking and all saying 'May God pardon him!' and to the prince 'A long life to you!' lo, there came forward into the tavern a Naked Man with in his hand a knife. His face was fierce and swarthy. His eyes were black and the whites of his eyes seemed swimming in dirty rheum. Clothes he had none whatever but was simply stark naked. He never laughed. If he opened his mouth to speak or say anything, it showed itself all full of teeth: to count them would take you all Tuesday and all Wednesday too.

Well, when the Naked Man came into the tavern he greeted the company, and then it happened that he sat down next to the prince. At first the boy shrank from him, but presently he gave an order and a drink was poured out for the Naked Man. Then one of the company asked him what man he was. The Naked Man said that he was a poor man and had no share in the light of the sun: his work, he said, in his own country was no success and so he had gone away from home to see if he could find someone who would be his partner, doing one thing and another. 'But what was your work?' they asked him. 'By the knife I carry,' said the Naked Man, 'you can see what my business is: I am a butcher. But see, I have no money. Alas! At one time I had my shop, but now one man and another have devoured my goods, and look, here I am, out on the five roads of the world and as naked as I came from my mother. When the prince heard this, he came to life again. 'So you are a butcher?' he turned and said to the Naked Man, 'and you want to carry on business and have no money? Will you not come and let us be partners; I will put down the money and you know the business.' 'Surely I will come;' said the Naked Man, 'whenever you want me, I am ready.' Then everyone was delighted that the prince had found a partner and they started drinking and singing because now the prince would not have his head cut off. Also at this very time the prince with the Naked Man started out to go to his village. When they arrived the prince presented himself before his father and told him his news, that he had found a partner. You cannot imagine the delight of the poor king on hearing this, for he too, as he saw the days passing by without his son being able to find a partner, was vexed even to death. For by that time all the world had heard of his intention that if his son did not find a partner, he would kill him, and in order to keep his word and to make an example he would have had to do it. So at once he said. 'Where is he? Bring him here at once for me to see him.' Then the prince turned to his father with an objection: 'My dear father,' said he, 'I have found a partner, but he is rather an unusual person, and I am afraid that you may not like him.' 'What kind of man is he?' said the king. 'He has an oddity, shall I say a fancy? that he always goes about naked and with a knife in his hand.' 'Never mind,' said the king, 'Bring him up here and we can come to an agreement with him, and then early next morning you can get up and go about your business.' Then they went and shouted out from the courtyard for the Naked Man to come. The man who I have told you never laughed any more than Lazaros[1]—savage too he was and swarthy—came up and presented himself before the king. Then they talked over the whole matter and agreed that the prince should pay down all the money needed and the Naked Man should contribute his skill, and that they should divide between them the profits of their venture. They drew up an agreement and sealed it, the king with his own seal and with the seal of the realm. The Naked Man knowing no letters set on it the imprint of his finger. Then the king paid out to them a great sum of money, as much let us say as they needed, and bad them go their way.

When they were starting off the Naked Man turned once more and said to them: 'Boys,' he said, 'we have, so to say, signed papers and we have no fear of making a quarrel, but now I repeat this to you in order that we may have no confusion about it: What we win from our journey that we will share half and half.' 'In this we are at one,' said the king and the prince, and so they went down the stairs and were off.

At dawn all the people who had come very early out from the palace to see the prince hanged saw him with the Naked Man riding down to the harbour to find a ship to cross over to Anatolia, there to buy cattle.

Now we must leave these people all asking who was this man whom the prince had found to be his partner, one man making a short and the other a very long story of it all, and we must go with our pair of friends, the Naked Man and the prince, who found a ship to ferry them over to Anatolia.

[1] Who when dead saw such terrible things.

The kingdom where they wanted to go to buy oxen lay a distance of four days from the sea and all the road by which they would go was through very wild country. When they disembarked they mounted their horses and began to travel over this wilderness. All day they found not even a span of clear ground where they could rest, nor was there water to drink, or any place to sit and eat a little. Only at the time of the evening bell they found a little green grass and here, as I tell you, you may see them staying.

In this place where the green grass was there were two or three big plane trees, and underneath them there was a stream cold and refreshing. When the prince saw such a fine place he wanted to stay there for that night and sleep. But the Naked Man said they should go on. Not to make a long story of it, the prince persuaded him, and they dismounted and refreshed themselves. As the sun was setting they had a meal and then when it was fully night they lay down underneath the plane trees to go to sleep.

The prince at once fell asleep because he had been delicately brought up, you see, and also because that day he had had no chance to get a sleep. The Naked Man too lay down on one side of the place and made as if he were snoring, but he was not asleep. Then at midnight, lo, a noise was heard, and at once a seven-headed monster came out. When he saw the Naked Man and the prince and the horses, he rushed at them at once to devour them. Then, good gracious, the Naked Man who was pretending to be asleep, lost not a moment. He flew at the monster, and began, O my dear Sir, with his knife to hew first at one and then at another of the monster's heads, and so on until two or three o'clock in the morning. When the monster was quite dead he dragged him to one side and dug a pit. He laid aside the monster's tongues after putting salt to them that they might not stink; then he washed his knife in the fountain and went and lay down by the side of his fellow. The prince was quite unaware of what had happened, and so when he rose up in the morning and found the Naked Man still asleep, he sat up and mocked him and scolded him for being sleepy, saying: 'You see; this place did not please you, and now I see you want to stay here and go on sleeping.'

Well, the Naked Man presently got up, and they washed and ate a little, signed themselves with the cross and mounted and went off. When they had gone forward for some quarter of an hour they again came upon a desert region. All day it was the same: all pines and brushwood and cistus (?) bushes. The place was, you see, scorched and hot, they were fainting with the heat. Late in the evening they were lucky and again came upon a place that was fresh and cool like the one they had come to the evening before. When the prince saw a place like this he began to beg the Naked Man that they should sleep there that night.

They dismounted and washed in the stream, and cut a little clover for the beasts; then they prepared food and ate. When they had done eating and the prince still saw that the Naked Man was always downcast, he wanted to ask him to say what had happened, but he would say nothing. When the prince saw that he could not bring him to say anything, he again lay down and went to sleep. The Naked Man withdrew to one side and pretended to be asleep. Suddenly, lo, a monster came as on the evening before. The Naked Man arose and did as he had done to the other one, and again the prince knew nothing of it. When the prince woke up in the morning, again he mocked at the Naked Man, saying that he has been delicately brought up and could not rouse up in the morning. Ah, and how could he know what had happened those last two evenings! To cut the story short the Naked Man rose up and they went on.

At sunset again they came to a pleasant region, and the same thing happened. The prince wanted to stay there and the Naked Man was unwilling, but again the prince's will prevailed. Well; it is a tiresome tale, but we cannot but tell the whole story: at midnight again a noise was heard. But that evening it was not a monster making the noise, but an ogress, we might call her a mother ogress, and with sons who were ogres.

The ogress was riding astride on a jar: no, I don't mean that;[1] she was riding not on a jar but on a hare, and she was carrying a jar on her shoulder to go and fetch water from the spring. When she saw the men and the animals underneath the plane-tree, she said nothing but filled her jar and went to the cave where her sons were, the forty ogres, to tell them that there was something fine for them at the spring, and they should run and devour the two men. But the Naked Man, who again was not asleep, followed the ogress, and when she went in he stood out-

[1] Here in the Greek is a pun between *layíni*, a jar, and *layína*, a female hare.

side the cave. When the ogress told her sons this news, they began to go out one by one; the Naked Man stood there with his knife in his hand, and as each one of them came out, whack and down he went. And thus, my lad, he killed all the forty of them. Afterwards when their mother came out to see what had become of them, he killed her as well, and then he went down into the cave. And, Oh, what did he see there? And what did he find? Whatever I were to say, never never could I give you an idea. Going down there he saw rooms and rooms, one after the other; he counted them; there were forty. One by one he opened them, and inside there were things he had never seen, not even in his dreams. In one of them he found piles of gold coins and heaps of diamonds. In another he found golden sovereigns, pieces of three hundred, stones to stay the flow of blood, and many other lordly possessions; all you could imagine. In another room he found men, men slain and men strangled, and slaughtered beasts, all there for the ogres to eat. In another he found their provender, biscuits and so on; boiled food and porridge: complete household stores. In behind he opened a room and what did he see? In it he found three girls hung up by their hair and the three of them princesses. The ogres had stolen them away and were demanding money from the kings, their fathers, if they wished to have them back again.

When the poor princesses saw him, they broke out into weeping, loud enough to reach heaven, and they begged him to set them free. Then the Naked Man started to take them down, asking them who they were. Each of them told him where she came from and what she had endured. It chanced that one of the girls was the daughter of that very king to whose realm they were going to buy oxen. The Naked Man said nothing of this, but treated them kindly and showed them where all the provisions were and told them to stay in the cave and have no fear and that he would do everything he could to set them free. Then he went up out of the cave and pulled out the teeth of the ogres and the ogress. Then at dawn he went and lay down to sleep by the side of the prince. In the morning when the sun struck the mountains, they woke up. The Naked Man said not a word of what he had done in the night, and again they mounted and went their way.

At the hour when shepherds come home, they saw from a

long way off the city they were going to, and at the time the lamps were being lit they were there and dismounted in front of a tavern. When they had stabled their horses and drunk their coffee, they called one or two men and told them why they had come to their town, and asked that anyone who had oxen for sale should let them know and they could meet in the morning. After this talk they heard a crier making a proclamation. Everyone in the tavern stayed to hear and to see what he would say. The crier proclaimed: 'Listen, you men of the village and round about. Listen well. Tonight close your doors early; block any chinks in your houses; shut the doors and the windows, because the king's daughter is to come abroad for a walk. Don't have to be sorry for your doings and then say that you have not heard.' When the crier had finished the villagers started talking again, but the Naked Man and the prince could not rest after what the crier had said.

You smash an egg and it all spills out. The prince turned and said very quietly to the Naked Man: 'What does this mean? Because the king's daughter is going out for a walk, is that a reason why men must shut their doors and their windows and block up the chinks in their houses?' Then for the very first time the prince saw the Naked Man smile when he heard this: not that he said anything, and who knows what he had in his mind? Well, the prince sat down on his chair again, but all his mind was on what the crier had said: my dear fellow, he could not be at rest. At last he could refrain no longer, and turned and said to all the people in the tavern: 'I say,' said he, 'why is it that when the daughter of your king goes for a walk the whole village has to be turned upside down?' At first the men laughed because the prince's question seemed to them rude. Then presently they said: 'You are a stranger here; that is why you do not know. This is what happens. The daughter of our king, and many be his years! is so beautiful that when anyone sees her at once he runs mad. To save people from this, it is managed in this way: notice is given beforehand that everyone may go into hiding and come to no harm.' 'What, and is she then so beautiful?' said the prince. 'Ah, my poor lad, you who live on bread, just you see her!' said a man in the tavern, a man with a broken heart.

When the prince heard this he said nothing but in his heart he resolved that he would have a good look at this beautiful princess. The Naked Man made as though he did not care a farthing for such things.

Meanwhile the people went off to the village and shut their houses and the taverns. One by one the men got up and went away. The Naked Man and the prince with him were left there, just the two of them with the tavern keeper. The tavern keeper than started to shut up the place carefully and closed as well as he could all the chinks in the house. Then he laid down a mattress and a pillow on the floor of the tavern, and left them. 'Good night,' said he and bade them go to sleep. It was about the third hour of the night.

When they had lain down the prince turned on his bed this way and that, and all his mind and his thought were on this: what he could do to see the beautiful princess. Now see what he devised. He took from his pocket a knife he had and very quietly began to cut out a big hole so that he could see who was passing by outside. When he had finished doing this, he heard a stir and he thought he saw something shining. He glued his eye to the hole and what did he see? Some hundred girls fair and fresh as water were coming down the way and in the midst of them was the princess. Ah, what beauty was hers! When the poor prince saw her he fainted, and when he came out of his faint she had passed by. He lay stricken on his bed. Until dawn his mind was on the princess; you would have said that she had enchanted the poor fellow.

When they rose in the morning the Naked Man began to say to the prince that they should go and meet the men who had oxen and strike a bargain with them. But the prince was as it might be drenched with rain and dead with thunder: the poor fellow was undone with love for the princess. When the Naked Man had done speaking the prince stayed thinking a little. Then he said to the Naked Man: 'Listen to what I say, partner. I have no one else but you to whom I can tell my sorrow. Last night I did a foolish thing. When you were asleep, I opened a chink in the wall and saw the princess when she was out for her walk.' 'Well, and what of that?' said the Naked Man. 'What of that!' said the prince. 'Ah, she is so beautiful I fell in love with her at once and I want her for my wife. Unless I win her I can never live. I shall be nailed up in my coffin. I shall be carried off to the grave yard. You don't know, my dear comrade, how goodly she is, what a fine girl. Such beauty has never been before. Ah, what shall I do? Tell me, tell me.' Thus he went on talking to the Naked Man. But that honest fellow made as though he did not care, saying: 'I don't know about that. We have come here for business; not for these vanities. Leave all this, I tell you, and let us go and see about the oxen.' Now you can fancy the feelings in the prince's heart when he heard these harsh words. His eyes at once were dimmed with tears and he began to cry like a child. Love is a heavy business. Is there not a song that goes:

> A curse is laid on love; a curse on lovers too;
> Whoever trusts in love, that man is sure to rue.

When the Naked Man saw the youth in this state he was sorry for him and turned and said: 'Don't weep, my lad, in this childish way; it breaks my heart. What has happened, has happened. It is a pity you were so foolish as to look at her. Now what do you say we should do? For me, whatever my hand can do to pleasure you, I will not fail to do.' This in truth was what the prince wanted. At once he fell to beseeching the Naked Man to go straight to the father of the princess and make a proposal of marriage on his behalf. At first the Naked Man would not, but presently he consented.

So our fine fellow, the Naked Man, rose up and went at once to the king's palace. When the people in the palace saw him, a savage naked figure with a knife in his hand, they did not want to admit him, but the king who happened to be sitting in the balcony and heard them talking, learned what was going on and ordered them to let the man come upstairs. When the Naked Man came up he presented himself before the king and said: 'O my king, many be your years! Yesterday evening when your young daughter was taking a walk, it happened that the young son of my own king saw her. She pleased him and his heart is set upon having her for his wife. Now he has sent me to make this proposal to you and to ask you: will you let him have her or not?' The Naked Man made his speech just like this, uncouthly and with no polish at all; then he stood up and waited to hear what the king would say. Then the king said: 'Very well. But even I cannot give my daughter to whomever I choose, for I have made a vow that no man shall have her who cannot perform the three following tasks; it does not matter who he is. Now listen to me and tell him, and if he is able then he may come here and at once he shall be my son-in-law. In a certain place there is a monster with seven heads; then in another place there is another monster and he too has seven heads; in a certain place too there are forty ogres and their mother. Now these monsters and the ogres stand at watch to prevent anyone coming into my kingdom to buy beasts: such a man they will devour. Now you can understand what an injury this is to our realm. No one can come into our country to buy oxen, or cows either. Nor is this all that these ogres have done; they have also carried away my eldest daughter, and now they are demanding a huge sum of money to give her back to me. This is what is being done. Now whatever man can kill these monsters and the ogres and deliver our country from this trouble and get my eldest daughter and bring her back to me, that man shall be my son-in-law and have my youngest daughter.' So said the king. Now as soon as the Naked Man had heard him say all this, he was very well pleased, for he saw that the king was speaking of exactly those very monsters and those very ogres whom he had himself killed. He said nothing but saluted the king and went down the stairs and was off.

Then he came to the prince who was wearing out his eyes with watching and waiting for his coming. The Naked Man sat down and told him everything. When the poor prince heard it he was much set aback; he did not know what to do. For his part the Naked Man did not console him by saying: 'Cheer up, my lad; don't be troubled; I have killed those monsters,' and telling him all about it, and in a word that it need not trouble him. No; rather he said: 'Well, what do you say? Can you do what the king demands and win his daughter?' The youth again began weeping and entreating him: 'Oh, my dear comrade, I do beg of you: and can you do all this task?' And the tears ran down his cheeks.

To put it briefly, the Naked Man again took pity on him and rose up as if to go and kill the monsters: monsters whom he had already killed. The Naked Man went off and produced the tongues of the first monster whom he had killed. When he came back in the evening he took the prince with him and at once they went to find the king. When they were near the palace the Naked Man called the boy aside and brought out the tongues of the monster and gave them to him and directed him to go to the king and say that it was he who had killed the monster.

When they came before the king the prince took the monster's tongues from his pocket and gave them to the king and started to tell him how he had killed the monster; how hard the struggle had been and how the monster had been near to wearing him out, and a whole lot more lies that the king might believe that it was he who had killed the monster. The king believed him and told him to go and deal with the next monster.

In the morning the Naked Man went and produced the tongues of the next monster, and he and the prince went again to the king. Again the king believed that the youth had killed that monster also, and ordered him next to go to the ogres, and when he had been successful there also, he would for sure make him his son-in-law.

Early in the morning our fine friend the Naked Man went and fetched the ogres' teeth and with the prince brought them to the king. When the boy gave him the teeth, the king told him that his eldest daughter was there in the ogres' cave, and he would give him a great number of mules and a force of soldiers, that they should go all together and make up loads of gold and diamonds, when they went to fetch the princess in the cave: she with the two others, and bring them to their fathers.

When the poor king heard that his child had now been set free and that the country was rid of the monsters and of the ogres, he wept with delight and hardly knew what to do. At once he took the prince in his arms and kissed him and called him his son, the husband of his daughter. Then he sent and called for his daughter, the beautiful one, and told her to bow down and kiss the prince's hand; then he said: 'This man here is the husband whom I shall give you, because he has freed your sister from the claws of the ogres and has delivered our country from the monsters.' The fair princess laughing and with delight sat down by the prince. Then she took a pure silver dish and crystal cups and served him with drink. Then she cut herb basil and other herbs and carnations and made a nosegay and tied it up with red silk and gold wire and gave it to him. Then the serving woman started and laid a table with a tablecloth of fine striped stuff and embroidered napkins, and served food of all sorts: everything was there; the very milk of birds. Then the king gave an order that all the world should come and everyone sit and eat and drink and take his pleasure as long as he liked, because the eldest princess had been delivered and the land set free from those monsters.

In the morning the prince and the Naked Man too went with soldiers and many beasts to ride, to go and fetch the enslaved princesses, and with them much gold treasure and jewels. Late in the evening everyone was outside the city waiting for them. Presently they saw in front the Naked Man and behind him the three princesses and the prince, and in a long train two hundred beasts of burden laden all of them with gold coin and jewels; behind them again were the soldiers. When the people saw this they went mad with delight, and all together they proceeded to the palace and there in front they sat and ate and drank the whole night. The prince was now full of joy. With his betrothed bride he was shouting and dancing and could never look at her enough.

At dawn the king sent for them and told them to get ready to travel: the wedding, you must know, had to be held in the city of the bridegroom. When everything was ready the king sat down and wrote a letter to the prince's father, the king to whom he was to be allied by this marriage, and sent him also a great number of presents. From then the Naked Man and the prince took in their charge the princess, the girl so fair that whoever saw her went mad for her beauty. Also they took their prize, the two hundred loads of coin, and said farewell to the king and with his blessing went to their own village to hold the wedding.

One day when the king and the queen, the prince's parents, rose up in the morning and sat to drink their coffee, the queen saw a horse-fly sitting on the king's robe. She turned and said to the king: 'Look, husband, we shall be having congratulations on good news. I don't know which of our children will have written to us, but it will surely be for good, let it be whoever it is.' The queen had not finished speaking when a man with no shoes came rushing into the room and told them that their youngest son was coming bringing what he had won, two hundred loads of gold and diamonds too, and that he had with him a girl whom he was to make his wife, and her beauty was such as the sun had never before seen. When the king and the queen heard all this, they rubbed their eyes. What! Their youngest son! The one who had no energy and no luck, he who could never find a partner with whom to set up his business! Could it be he who was bringing home such treasures?' As the man went away, the king turned and said to his wife: 'If this is indeed he! But look you, as men here say and as my father now in bliss used to say so often: A castaway ship has come fairly into harbour. If it be he, we must go out to meet him and in all haste.'

At that moment another man came into the room and gave him letters from his son and from the other king, his son's father-in-law. Then the king fully believed it was his son. He rose up with great joy, and with soldiers and instruments of music went down to the shore with all the rest of them to be in time to meet his son, the son whom at one time he used to kick and beat and had pretty nearly hanged him too. Now he had turned out better than all his brothers and more adventurous. When the men came to the ship and saw the treasure and the beautiful girl and heard that she was a princess and that the prince had brought her with him to marry her, they were all much delighted.

Well then, the music made a brave show and they went up to the town. In the morning they were married. But such a wedding as this was I cannot describe to you. The bride had brought her dowry with her, and I have not the skill to tell you of her ornaments and of the bridal songs and of the rejoicings there were.

On the third day the guests started to depart. That same evening when it was time to leave the bridegroom alone with the bride, and the cocks had begun crowing, and men were leaving the place of the wedding, and the only people left were the groom's kinswomen, and the serving women had begun to put out the lights to make all those who remained start to go away, then at that moment a heavy step was heard on the stair. They turned and what did they see? It was the Naked Man with the knife in his hand, but in what a state! Holy Virgin, save us! He was in a savage passion; you would have thought his eyes were running out with blood. Like a cloud he came into the room, and casting his savage glance at them he came and stood in front of the bridegroom like a pillar. From his fury he could not speak but stood gaping. They all stayed staring at him, not knowing what he would do. Then he turned looking askance at them and his angry eyes fixed upon the bridegroom, and he cried with a voice that quivered as it came from his mouth: 'How long,' said he, 'have we been here! You, lucky fellow, have spent the time in pleasure and in amusing yourself! But I say now we have something to talk about: when shall we make a reckoning? You have plenty to eat and to drink, but do you ever ask how I fare? We must look to our reckoning; and at once too!' Thus spoke the Naked Man, stamping his feet and shaking his knife and foam flying from his mouth. Then the prince turned to him and said: 'My good partner, is this a time for us to make our reckoning? Come tomorrow and we can sit down like men and see what is between us.' 'Tomorrow?' said the Naked Man. 'And that will be a fine tomorrow! No ending to this business! Now is the time, let me tell you, for this job: now!' Then the prince too grew angry. 'Very well,' said he. 'If you want it now, let it be now. Our reckoning is very simple. We brought here two hundred loads of diamonds and gold; you go down now and take a hundred and go about your business.' 'Oh, if that were all,' said the Naked man, 'then it would be easy, as you work out our reckoning, but was there nothing but the treasure that we brought back from our journey?' 'Well, and what else?' said the prince. 'And this girl?' said the Naked Man, and he pointed to the bride, the princess, the prince's wife. At this every one smiled and said to themselves that the poor Naked Man was now in the wrong.

'Yes indeed,' continued the Naked Man angrily. 'Was it not our agreement that whatever we won on our journey we should go shares, half and half? And did we not bring her back from our journey? Half of her falls to me and I won't give up my due share: I must have it. Do you think that it was just for the bright blackness of your eyes that I went running over the waste world and broke my strength, and all just to give you a wife?' 'But as you love God,' said the prince, 'whatever can your demand be? Has it ever been heard of that men should divide a woman? Was our bond for this? Are we talking fairy-tales? Surely you don't mean it.' 'I don't care,' said the Naked Man, 'One half of her is mine and I mean to have it.'

The prince could contain himself no longer. 'But what will you be leaving for me?' said he to the Naked Man. 'If you win, will you take my wife for five days and then I have her for another five? Or what? Oh, clear out and get away from here.'

Then he made a sign to the men there to seize the Naked Man and to drive him out of the house. But before he could say a word, the Naked Man said: 'This is not the way I meant we should divide her, but like this.' And with these words before anybody could seize him, he rushed at the bride and caught her by one leg and threw her down, and then he raised his knife to hew her in two at the waist. The poor girl had only time to cry out and then she fainted; and at once out of her mouth there ran a whole tangle of snakes. Then the Naked Man left the girl on one side and with his knife cutting this way and that he began to kill all the snakes one after the other.

When he had killed them he turned to the other men there who were standing frightened to death to see such a thing, and said to them with a gentle voice to go straight to a man's heart: you could see he was no longer the savage Naked Man: 'Listen, and you first of all, my dear prince; we have eaten together bread and salt and have lived so long together in fair love like brothers. This girl whom you took as your wife was under the curse of her old mother that no man should live happily with her on the pillow, and that the first evening when she would lie with her husband, these snakes should come from her and bite him and he die. Now if we had left these snakes in her and had not killed them and you had lain down with your bride, in the morning we should no more have seen you alive. And now do you know why I did this for you and so many other good things which are known to us two only? I did them for this reason: only to show you that I am not ungrateful, and that a good deed even if it be done to a man who is dead is a thing which is never lost. For I am that dead man whom you came upon when they were taking him off to throw him on the midden, and you stayed and gave him a burial with so much honour. Farewell.' And at that moment the Naked Man disappeared from their sight, and from that time he was never seen again or heard of anywhere.

37

Faithful John

FAITHFUL JOHN *Der getreue Johannes* of Grimm's No. 6, is the best title for this story, of which a version from Symi, called in the Greek *The Slave*, is here given. The story is discussed in *Forty-five Stories*, p. 53, and BP.'s references, i. 42, show its diffusion over the whole of Europe: it appears not to be over-common in the Balkans, and two Turkish versions are certainly not very close to the Greek.[1] Benfey, as probably too often, thought it of Indian origin.[2] The outline of the story is that a servant helps and guides his master to good fortune, though the master is often both stupid and incompetent. The variant from Athens is rather off the usual lines, because the master is not stupid but malicious, and tries to destroy his helper, the son of the vizier, by setting him impossible tasks.

To emphasize the close link between the master and the faithful servant the story, as in the Astypálaia version printed in *Forty-five Stories*, sometimes begins with the miraculous birth of both of the boys from an Apple of Fertility. The adventures of the pair in search of the Fair Lady, in this Symi version introduced by the prince seeing her portrait, naturally vary a good deal, but the scene in the marriage chamber and the turning into stone and the bringing to life again of the servant by the blood of the master's child are essential parts of the story.

The Zákynthos version of No. 60, *The Goldsmith's Wife*, printed in this book, has been brought very close to the story of Faithful John by being made to start with the miraculous birth of the two young men from an Apple of Fertility, and an ending in which the one friend delivers the other, in this case by warning him against his mother's quite unmotivated jealousy and being turned gradually to stone for divulging the danger. At the end he is brought back to life again by the sacrifice of his friend's three children. In short, *The Goldsmith's Wife* is made to begin and end like the story of Faithful John.

The final episode in the story when the hero and his wife sacrifice their son to bring back to life the faithful servant deserves a further note. There is a whole series of stories originating in India of which the central episode is either the willing self-sacrifice of his own life

[1] These are in *Istanbul Masallari*, p. 190, and in Kunos, *Forty-four Turkish Folktales*, p. 217.

[2] There is a version of it in L. B. Day's *Folk Tales of Bengal*, p. 16.

by a child, or the sacrifice by the parents of their little son in order by the use of his blood to bring to life again a friend or one to whom gratitude is owing. These stories have been studied by Dr. Winstedt,[1] who points out that this idea of a blood sacrifice has travelled from India to Europe, where it appears in both forms. The child as a willing sacrifice is the theme of Hartman von Aue's *Der arme Heinrich*. The baby sacrificed by the parents to save a friend is best known in the French story of Amis and Amile, translated by William Morris; and it is in this latter form that we have the sacrifice in the story of Faithful John.

Although there is this contact between the two stories, *The Sacrifice of the Child* and *Faithful John* are entirely different, each with a thread of its own; the sacrifice of the child is no more than an episode in the story of the Faithful Servant. It occurs also in the story to which I have given the name *Only one Brother was grateful*, No. 70.

A contaminated version from Ordoú—Kotýora—in Pontos has some interest. It is called *The good Brothers*, and begins in the Faithful John style with the son of a king and his humbler friend who wins a wife for his master. In the palace of the ogres who are the bride's brothers the pair open a forbidden door. Inside they find a giant and cut off his head. This head rolls off down a well and the story then follows the lines of *The Underworld Adventure*. But the prince who rescues the girl does not leave her there in the Underworld when he is carried up again by the bird to the world of men, as he as a rule does; he brings her up with him and gives her to his faithful servant for his wife. By this ingenious welding together of the two stories the hero is made to return his friend's service; his friend found him a wife and from the Underworld he provides a wife for his friend. The story is printed in Xenophón Akoglou's *Folklore of Ordou, Laographiká Kotyóron*, pp. 391.

BP. points out that there is an allied story in which a sister takes the part of the faithful servant and that this stretches from Greece where it appears in Bernhard Schmidt's collection from the Ionian islands and so eastwards to Armenia and the Caucasus.[2]

The versions of the Faithful John story are these:

1. SYMI: *Z.A.* i. 254, here translated.
2, 3. ASTYPÁLAIA: *Forty-five Stories*, p. 41, and Pio, p. 80, which latter has been translated by Geldart, p. 92.
4. KÁRPATHOS: Mikh.-Nouáros *L. S. Karpáthou*, i. 322. This story and the one from Mýkonos are very doubtful variants.
5. MÝKONOS: Roussel, *Contes de Mycono*, p. 119.
6. ATHENS: Kamboúroglou, p. 46 = Garnett, p. 229.

[1] In *Folklore*, lvii. 139.

[2] *Griech. Märchen*, p. 68.

NO. 37. FAITHFUL JOHN[1]

There was once, though perhaps there never was, a king, and this king had no son. Afraid that he might never have a son he got a son by his slave girl. At that time it befell that the queen herself was with child and she too had a baby, a little son. The boys grew big; they played together; together they went to school and together they took their holidays. The slave boy was lively and of good wit; the prince was thickheaded and disorderly. All the same the slave boy loved the prince dearly. The prince frequented taverns. The slave boy gave him good advice, yet he consorted always with worthless ragamuffins.

It happened that one time the prince came upon a framed picture; it was of the Fair One of the World, and he went mad for her. He fell sick and took to his bed. Doctors went in; doctors came out; the prince could never be cured. He resolved to go off to find the Fair One of the World, and this he told the slave. The slave loved the prince and he knew well what this journey meant, so he resolved to go with him to keep him safe. They went to their lord the king to ask his permission, saying: 'My father, we want to travel and see the world and learn of fresh matters, and so we beg you to give us your blessing that we may go on our journey in all prosperity.' The king gave them his leave and his blessing; also he said to them: 'Do you know, my sons, the course of your journey and where it will take you? First of all on your way you will come upon a pavilion; you will go in and sit down and eat and drink: food and drink will come to you of themselves. But unless you will have my curse, do not stay and sleep there; you must go outside to sleep and so you need have no fear. Close by you will find a tall tree; sit down beneath it. There will be couches there and you may eat and drink; the victuals will come of themselves. But unless you will have my curse, do not lie down to sleep underneath that tree. You must go some furlongs away for your sleep. Close by you will find a great field and in the midst of it there is a tower; the door will be open. Go in and sit down and there too you may eat and drink. Only beware: unless you will have my curse, inside that tower you must not lie down to sleep. Go outside and there sleep. After that, go where you will and have no fear.'

[1] Text from Symi in *Z.A.* i. p. 254, with the title *The Slave.*

The king gave them his blessing and the boys went off. They journeyed on for five or ten days, for nineteen days or twenty, and one evening they came to a place and saw a very fair pavilion. They went in and looked; and what did they see? Couches laid with coverings so soft that if you stretched yourself on them you would sink in; carpets, rugs, pillows! Not a man to be seen! The boys sat down. At once there came all of themselves sweets and coffee and pipes. Then the table was set all of itself, complete with foods and drinks of very many kinds. They sat down and ate and drank; again there came coffee and pipes, and they drank and smoked.

The prince became drowsy and seemed as though he would fall asleep. The slave saw this and said: 'But, brother, what did our father say to us? Did he not tell us to eat and drink, but unless we would have his curse, not to sleep in the house, but to go outside to lie down to sleep?' The prince said: 'Be at ease. With beds like these why should we go outside to sleep? I shall lie down here; you go outside it you want to, and be frozen and devoured by wild beasts.' The slave said: 'No, I will not lie down to sleep.' Well, and what do you expect? The prince lay down on that soft bedding, and sleep came upon him: he snored too.

The slave did not sleep, saying to himself: 'Something for sure will happen here.' He went and sat in front of the prince, on the stairs opposite the door. He brought out his bow and strung it tightly and laid it by his side, as he sat smoking. Then lo, the pavilion was shaken; an ogre appeared, a monster with three heads. The ogre saw the slave and the sleeping prince and said: 'Was it not enough for you to sit here and eat and drink, but you must needs lie down to sleep in my bed?' The slave said: 'And what are you going to do?' The ogre said: 'I shall eat you.' The slave said: 'Go, eat your own heads.' He took his bow and an arrow; drew the bow and right off shot at the three heads of the ogre, one after the other. This was the death of the ogre, but still writhing he said to the slave: 'Ah, you rascal, if ever you boast that you have slain such a monster as me, then up to the knees you shall be turned to stone.' The slave said: 'So long as I have killed you, that's enough.' Then he took his sword and hewed off the ogre's heads and cut out the tongues and tied them up and put them away in his wallet. Then he cut the monster into pieces; gathered all up and threw it far out of the way and washed away the blood. Then he lay down to sleep. By then it was dawn.

In the morning the prince rose and called out to the slave: 'Hullo! Get up, we must be off; it is dawn. Oh, what a fool to want to keep watch!' The slave, to make a good show of being soundly asleep, opened his eyes and rubbed them and said: 'Yes, indeed, brother; I sleep very heavily and you must excuse me.' So he rose up. They waited expecting coffee and pipes, but nothing came. The prince said: 'Come, let us be off; it seems it is not the custom here to bring one anything in the morning.' The slave knew that it was because the monster had been killed that nothing was coming any more. So they rose up and went off.

They went on and on and so they came to a tree, tall and beautiful, and beneath it there were couches set out. They were tired and went and sat down. At once, behold, there came all of themselves sweets and coffee and pipes; the trays were silver; the cups were silver. Then dishes of food came all by themselves; the table was laid all of itself; the spoons were silver; there were knives and silver forks. The boys ate and drank. To make a short story of it, the prince saw the soft couches and lay down to sleep. The slave urged that they should go some way from the tree and there lie down. The prince would not and laughed at the slave. Then the slave again took his bow and strung it and set it by his side with his two-edged sword: again he sat to keep watch. Then at midnight, lo, the whole tree was shaken, and at once a monster with six heads appeared, saying: 'You rascals, was it not enough to sit and eat and drink but you must lie down to sleep in my bed?' The slave said: 'And what is it you will do, rascal?' 'I shall eat you.' 'Go, eat your own heads,' and he took his bow and drew it and at one shot carried away four of the ogre's heads. Then he drew his sword and hewed off the other two. When the monster was about to die he said: 'Ah, you rascal if you should ever boast that you have killed such a monster as me, up to the waist you shall be turned to stone.' The boy said: 'So long as I have killed you, that is enough.' Then he hewed off his heads and cut out the tongues and put them away in his bag. He cut the monster into pieces and threw it all far away from the tree; he washed away the blood and he too then lay down to sleep. After a little it was dawn, and the prince woke up and called to the slave and again mocked at him. The slave did as before and pretended to be sound asleep and rose up. And then? Again they went off on their way.

For some days they went on and on and in nineteen or twenty days they found themselves in a field. In the middle of it there was a tower; in the evening they came to this tower. The door was open and they went in. What did they see before their eyes? Oh, what rugs, what carpets, what couches those were! They sat down. Then this happened: all of themselves there came sweets and coffee and pipes. The trays were of gold and what trays! The table was set all of itself; plates and cups and knives and forks and spoons; all were of gold. The food came all of itself, and Oh, what food! They ate and drank. Again the prince made as though he would lie down to sleep. The slave said: 'What are you trying to do, brother?' The prince said: 'Such fine couches, and can I leave them and not go to sleep on them?' The slave said: 'But what was the command we have from our father? Did he not say that unless we would have his curse, we must not sleep here inside but must go outside to sleep?' The prince said: 'Our father is an old man now and has lost his wits. Did anything happen to us in the other places where he told us not to sleep?' 'Come, brother; be sensible.' 'And are you crazy? I intend to lie down here: I will not leave such fine rugs and go outside to sleep. If you want to, you may.' Well, the prince lay down and at once sleep came upon him. The slave made ready and again sat there on guard. Lo! there at the door appeared an ill-omened monster with nine heads. The tower shook and the earth trembled and you would have thought that all the world was ready to fall in ruins. Inside the tower everything was shaking. The monster looked at them and foamed with rage: 'Ah, you rascals, was it not enough for you to eat and drink but you must needs also go to sleep in my tower?' 'Well, fellow, and what does it matter? What are you going to do?' 'I mean to eat you.' 'If you want to eat, go and eat your own heads.' The boy shot with his bow and at one shot knocked off six of the heads. Then he drew his sword, striking this way and that, and took off the other three heads. Then said the monster as he lay writhing and roaring, 'Oh, you rascal, if ever you boast that you have killed such a monster as me, up to the neck you shall be turned to stone.' The slave said: 'As long as I have killed you, that's enough.' Then he took and cut the monster into little pieces; gathered it all up and threw it outside. He wiped up the blood and then set himself to go to sleep.

In that place he saw a bunch of keys hanging up. He counted them and they were forty: they opened the forty rooms in the tower. The boy took them and opened one room. What did he see? The room was full of Venetian florins. He opened another: full of coins of Sultan Mahmoud. He opened another: full of roubles. And so on: every room was full of some sort of coin. He opened the room at the back: it was full of diamonds. He took and filled one pocket of his bag with diamonds and the other with coins of Venice. Some too he put into his pockets. He shut the door and hid the keys. Then he went and fell into a sleep like death, for he was very tired after the struggle he had had before he could destroy such a monster.

In a very short time it was dawn. The prince woke up and again mocked at the slave. The poor slave did not let him know anything and again pretended to be sound asleep; then he woke up with a show of stretching himself and yawning. They looked to see if by chance any coffee would come, any pipes; but nothing came. The boys went out, the slave shutting the door and hiding the key in a window opening. So they went off.

In the evening they came to a city and went to the house of an old woman. The slave said to her: 'Say, mother, we are strangers; will you not let us sleep here in your house?' She said: 'You may sleep, my boys, but I have neither rug nor bed for you to cover yourselves.' 'Are they not to be bought somewhere here?' 'To be bought! Of course they are: rugs, coverlets, quilts, carpets, mats; the shops are full of them.' The slave brought out some money and gave it to her, saying: 'Here you are; go and buy some.' The old woman saw the money and nearly went off her head. Then she went and brought them rugs and coverlets of all sorts; she gave them also her own. The slave gave her some more money and she went to buy food of all sorts, and wine too. They sat down and ate and drank with the old woman and poured out to her health: 'To our happy meeting, mother!' 'Your health, my boys!' Thus they ate and drank and lay down to sleep. In the morning God brought the day; the slave knew the town, what town it was; he knew too that in it there dwelled the Fair One of the World, but of this he said nothing to the prince: searching for her the prince did not know that she was there. He went out and all up and down the place, but how could he find out anything? On the very first day the slave found out which was the café to which the king of the place resorted. He took the prince there and they made friends with the king: whenever they wanted they used to go and meet him and talk together.

One day the slave sat down and closely questioned the old woman: 'What place is this? What fine things has it?' The old woman said: 'This is the place, my boy, where she is whom men call the Fair One of the World.' The slave said: 'Then, mother, does not this Fair One of the World ever leave her house? Never mind about that, mother, but I should like to see her and not go home and say that I have been here and never seen her.' Then said she: 'Good gracious, my boy, how can anyone see her? She stays always shut up in the palace. See, it is only at night when all passers-by are at home and at rest that they bring her out, so closely is she guarded. Forty soldiers go in front of her and forty behind her and so they bring her to the house of her teacher: she goes in and the soldiers mount guard outside. The teacher gives her her lessons, reading and sewing and knitting, and then some two hours after midnight they take their stations round her and bring her back to the palace. And this happens every night.' The slave said: 'And where is the teacher's house?' She said: 'Good gracious, my boy, and what can you do with the teacher's house? Even if you do know it, you can't go in there to see her either by day or by night. She lets no one else come in but only the princess.' Well, he set a bait for the old woman and fished out where the teacher's house was. He went there when it was day and found the house and looked at the neighbourhood, and then he went to the prince: they sat down together, but of all this the slave said nothing.

When it was fully night the slave put some diamonds into his wallet, and went and climbed up on the wall round the courtyard of the teacher's house. He threw a handful of diamonds down into the court and then dropped down off the wall and went away. The princess came and her people knocked at the teacher's door. The teacher came out to open the door and saw in her courtyard something shining brightly. In amazement she picked it up and what did she see? Diamonds. She gathered them up and put them away. To continue: she opened the door and in came the well-guarded princess. The teacher gave her her lesson and the soldiers escorted her back again to the palace. Next night the slave again waited till the same hour and went and scattered another handful of diamonds in the teacher's courtyard. Again the teacher saw them and gathered them up saying to herself: 'I must keep a look-out and see who it is who throws the diamonds in here.' On the third night when the slave had climbed up on the wall and was on the point of throwing the diamonds into the courtyard, the teacher seized him by the hand. This was exactly what he wanted and he dropped down into the yard and said: 'I have some of these to give you, as many as you like; only you must hide me in here that I may see the princess.' But the teacher was afraid and said: 'Good gracious! this is not a thing which can be done. If the king hears of it, it will be off with our heads, and that for both of us.' Well; the slave persuaded her and she brought him into the house and dressed him like a woman and set him in a corner and gave him a piece of cloth and a needle, as if he were beginning to learn to sew.

At midnight the princess came into the house. She saw the slave and was troubled: it was the first time she had seen any other woman in the teacher's house. She said: 'But, my teacher, how is this? And afterwards, when my father hears of it?' The teacher said: 'It is no matter, my dear; she is a cousin of mine, a shepherdess, and she has come to stay with me for a few days that she may learn to ply her needle a little to do her mending.' Well, the teacher kept the princess quiet and every now and then she would scold the slave: 'Ah, shepherdess, ah, my girl; work the needle this way; do it thus.' To put it shortly, from one night to another the princess and the slave became more and more friendly: the slave too was a very handsome fellow. Then they began to sport with one another and one night as they were playing the princess became aware that it was a boy. Whatever the reason, the princess at first was much disturbed, though later the slave found it not difficult to reassure her. The teacher played her part and said: 'This boy is a prince and a finer fellow you will not find.' What else was bound to happen? The princess fell in love with the slave. He said: 'Now, what shall we do to escape from here?' The princess said: 'As for me, in a few days they are going to have me married. The wedding will go on for forty days and forty nights, and we have a custom in our country that on the fortieth day the bride with other women goes out of the town and they all offer incense at the graves of the dead. I too shall do this and I shall go a little way aside out of the road; then you must be there ready with your horse and you must catch me up and we will be off.' The slave said: 'Very well; we will do this.' The princess went away and in the morning the slave went off to the old woman.

The prince had lost sight of the slave now for some days; he did not know where he was and he grew angry. Then when he saw him again he said: 'Friend, where have you been? What were you doing?' The slave said: 'Alas, brother, I was held all these days in a tavern, and for your sake I suffered all the trouble fate appointed for me; what I saw and what I suffered to get away, pray do not ask me.'

Some days passed by, and lo! one day a proclamation was made that the princess was to be married to the son of the vizier, and all the world was invited to the wedding. The prince heard of this and when he inquired was told that the bride was the Fair One of the World. He ran and told the slave: 'I say, brother, she lives here and they are marrying her too.' Said the slave: 'True enough.'—'But what now, brother? This will kill me; I shall go and drown myself.' Said the slave: 'Do not let this trouble you.' Well; the prince was nigh to going mad, and what was the slave to do? He said: 'Now this is what we must do to carry her off; but don't say a word about it.' Hearing this the prince seemed to come to himself a little, and neither of them were uneasy about the matter.

The slave asked the old woman: 'Tell us, mother; what is the custom at marriages here in your country?' She said: 'Listen, my sons. When there is to be a wedding, the bride comes forward with her golden tray to pour wine to the healths of guests, and each man puts into the tray a gift according to his capacity; whatever he chooses, money or something else of value.' To be brief, the day came, let us say Sunday, and the wedding began. The prince and the slave with him were invited as though they had both been princes. The slave gave the prince all the diamonds he could hold and he himself put a handful into his wallet and so they went to the wedding. When the prince saw the princess, he nearly went out of his mind. The slave kept elbowing him: 'Steady, brother, steady: be at your ease.' The princess stepped forward to pour out to the company. The king threw into the tray a handful of gold coins; the vizier threw down some more. Then she came to the slave and the prince; each of them cast in a handful of diamonds. The tray was bright with them and all eyes were dazzled. Seeing this the king said to himself: 'See, what princes! I wish one of them had been my son-in-law. I must say I wish I had managed to get such a son-in-law.' So every day the company ate and drank and made merry: all the music you could desire and dances too!

The fortieth day came, and the slave said to the prince: 'The time has come; now you must be ready to be off.' As the sun was setting they gave the old woman her present, some diamonds. 'We wish you good health, mother.' 'Good-bye, my sons; may your journey be for good.' They mounted their horses and were off. When they had left the city and came near the tombs, they went a little aside from the road and stayed there waiting. When the light failed, the princess was seen coming; her sister-in-law and other women with her. They went to offer incense over their dead kinsmen. The princess saw them and with her sister-in-law went a little way aside off the road and came straight to where the slave was. He caught up the princess and set her on his horse, saying to the prince: 'What are you staring at? You take up the other girl.' Then the prince took up the sister-in-law on his own horse and they went off at a trot. The horses were good and they were soon out of sight. The other women missed the princess and her sister-in-law; they cried out and searched for them but they could not find them. They went and told the king and the bridegroom. The king saw who had stolen her and did not trouble himself at all. The bridegroom almost burst with rage and sent to pursue them, and that is what he and his men are doing at this moment.

Now we must leave the bridegroom and the king and turn to the slave and the prince. They went riding on and on and on, and so they came to the tower. They dismounted and sat and refreshed themselves. The slave opened the rooms and they took money and diamonds as much as they could. Then they re-mounted and went to their father, the girls with them, and told the story. The king received them well. The slave said to the princess: 'You are to marry the prince.' At this the princess said with anger: 'No; it is you I want. If it had been to please him, I should never have done as I have. It was for your sake I ran away.' Then said the slave: 'It comes to the same thing, I or he. He is my good brother; he is the prince and he came specially for you and it is for this very purpose that I am now with him. You shall marry the prince and I will marry the other girl, your sister-in-law.' Well; he persuaded her and she married the prince and the slave took her sister-in-law, she who had escaped with the princess: she too was very beautiful. So they held the marriage festivities and all the people came to be present.

When night came and they would go to bed, the prince with the princess, the slave knew that some great evil would come upon them; it would be the death of both of them. Then said he to the prince: 'Brother, I want to sleep in the same room as you. You make me a bed a little way off yours so that I can be sleeping there.' The prince made as though he did not like this, but the slave was very urgent. He plied the prince this way and that, and at last persuaded him. A bed was made up for him close to theirs. The prince went and lay down with his wife; the slave too lay down on his own mattress. The prince and the princess fell into a very deep sleep. The young slave sat there keeping watch; he strung his bow and kept it by him and his sword also. Then at midnight there was a noise as of thunder. The roof split open and down there fell upon them an ogre, a huge monster come to devour the prince and the princess. At once the slave shot an arrow and slew him. The monster said: 'If you boast that you have killed so great a monster you shall be turned all to stone.' The slave said: 'So long as I have killed you, that is enough.' Then with his sword he cut the monster in pieces and carried it all out and in front of the door he dug a pit and buried the pieces. Yet he was still afraid lest some other monster might come and devour them, and so he went and sat near their bed with his sword lifted up in his hand so that if anything should happen he would be ready. The shock and the struggle had been so great that sleep came upon him there as he sat with his sword drawn. When the prince woke up he saw the slave by their side with his sword drawn, and his mind was so much confused that he thought the slave wanted to kill him and so take his wife. He started shouting for people to come. 'Fellow, have you come to kill me? If you wanted her you should have taken her and not come trying to kill me.' His cries brought men running from the palace. The slave also woke up in confusion and saw that the foolish prince was in a fright. Much against his will he could say nothing of what had happened, because he knew he must not boast of it. So he said to the prince: 'Hush, brother; had I wanted to, could I not have taken your wife? But I love you and strive always for your good.' The prince could understand nothing of this talk but kept crying out. The princess understood it all, but what could she say?

To put it shortly, the king heard of what had happened and ordered his men to go and hang the slave. The executioner came and led him to the place where he was to be hanged. The crowd collected. The king too went and the princess and the prince and the Council of Twelve. The slave asked them to bring him a priest for him to make his confession. The Council found a priest and commanded his presence. The slave began to speak out loud. He was told to speak secretly to the priest in whispers. He said: 'I do not wish to speak in secret; I want to say it all out loud for the people to hear me.'

So the slave began: 'My royal father.' The king said: 'You bastard, don't go calling me your father.' The slave said: 'Very well then; I am a bastard. However, when we went off on our journey, what was it you said to us, father?' Again the king in a boiling rage said: 'I tell you not to call me father.' The slave went on: 'Did you not say to us: "When you go off, you will find first a pavilion; go into it and eat and drink, but unless you will have my curse, don't lie down to sleep in it; you must go outside to sleep; have no fear." Close by there, did you not tell us, father.' . . . The king said: 'Don't call me father, I tell you.' The slave said: 'Very well; Did you not tell us that there is in that place a tree and we must sit under it and eat and drink but, unless we would have your curse, not lie down to sleep under it? Did you not tell me, "in that place you will find a tower in a field and you may go into it and eat and drink, but, unless you will have my curse, you must not lie down to sleep in it, but go outside to sleep; then be not afraid." We went off on our way and came to the pavilion and went in and found the couches finely set out; everything came to us of itself; coffee, pipes, food, drinks of all kinds. We sat down and ate and drank and then my brother wanted us to lie down to sleep there. I did not lie down; he lay down and slept. I tried to prevent him, saying: "Did not our father lay his curse upon us if we should lie down to sleep inside? What then are you doing?" Is it not so brother?' His brother said to him: 'I am not your brother.' And the king kept shouting to him: 'Don't call me father, fellow; don't call me father. I am not your father.' The slave went on: 'Sleep came upon you. I did not lie down; I sat watching. Then at midnight the pavilion was shaken, and behold an ogre with three heads appeared, saying: "You rascals, is it not enough for you to come here and drink, but you must also lie down to sleep in my bed?" I said: "Well, and what are you going to do?" He said: "Now I shall eat you." I wasted no time but shot my arrow and hit the ogre's three heads. As he was writhing the monster said: "If you boast, you rascal, that you have killed so great a monster, up to your knees you shall be turned to stone." And if you don't believe me, here are the tongues of the monster.' He brought them out and showed them. Then at once the youth up to the knees was turned to white stone. When the people saw this they cried: 'Alas, for the lad!' and upbraided the king. The prince and the king bitterly repented of what they had done and cried out: 'Alas, my brother!' cried one; 'Alas, my son!' cried the other. The slave was saying: 'And now am I your son? Now am I your brother? I cut that monster to pieces and I threw him out. And so we went along that road and came to a tree.' The king and the prince cried and besought him: 'Don't tell us, O my son, O my brother; it is enough, my son, my brother. Now it will be for us to give you your living, all your drink and your food.' The slave cried: 'I must tell you the rest. We came to the tree and again we sat down and ate and drank. Again you wanted to lie down to sleep below it. I wanted you not to; you would have none of that; once more you lay down and sleep came upon you and I kept watch. At midnight there came a still greater monster and with six heads. Him too I killed. The monster said: "If you boast, you rascal, that you have killed so great a monster, up to the waist you shall turn to stone." And if you don't believe me, look at his tongues here.' At once up to the waist he turned to stone. Again they cried out: 'Enough, my son; enough, my brother. Say no more.' But to this he paid no heed. The king and the prince were weeping; by this time everyone was crying out against them. The slave said: 'We went on that road and came to a tower; we went in and ate and drank; again my brother lay down to sleep: I sat watching. There came an ogre with nine heads; I killed him; see, here are his tongues. He too said to me that if I should boast of this, I should up to the neck be turned to stone.' Then still more they fell to weeping. The slave would not stop his story. 'We went on and found the Fair One of the World. Is not that true? I told her to marry you. If I had wanted, could not I have killed you at the beginning? But I did not, and when you were married, in the night when you went and laid down with your wife, I knew what would come upon you, and I did not go to lie down with my wife to sleep, but again I sat and kept watch. Then at midnight there was a noise of thunder and the roof split open. Down upon you came an ogre, a huge monster, intent to devour the two of you. I shot at him with my bow and killed him. Then I cut him into little pieces and gathered them up and buried all in a pit in front of the door. But when he was still writhing he too told me that if I were to boast I had slain so huge a monster, I should be turned all of me to stone.' Then men went and dug outside the door of the palace and they brought out the monster all cut in pieces. Then everyone believed his story. The prince wept and beat his breast. Then he took up the stone figure and carried it to his room and set it up and kept it there, and morning and evening burned incense before it as though it had been a holy icon.

Some time passed: the princess bore a little boy and had him lying in a cradle. One night at dawn—it was Easter Sunday—she saw in her sleep a woman dressed in white: it was the All-holy Virgin, and she said to her: 'If you want your husband's brother to come to life again, you must kill your son and anoint the marble all over with his blood. Then you must put the baby into the oven till he be burned to ashes. Take the ashes and scatter them over the marble and then all the marble will fall away and he will be as he was before.'

Well, the princess was by now aware that it was for her sake that the slave had endured all that he had endured, and she felt a great kindness for him and was much grieved for him. She woke from her dream about the time when the prince went away to go to church. Losing no time, she took and killed her child and collected the blood and put the body in the oven. Now the oven had been well fired the evening before when people were making their butter cakes and their egg rolls for Easter, so the child was quickly reduced to ashes. She took the blood and anointed the marble figure all over from the head right down to the feet; then she sprinkled it with the ashes. Then what a sight to see the pieces of stone fall off it to the ground! But it was not yet alive. She said to herself: 'But what is the matter? This was what the All-holy Virgin told me to do.' But she had forgotten to anoint the soles of the feet below. Well, of this she became aware and she still had a little blood left. So she anointed the soles of the feet as well as the rest of the body. Then the slave came alive again, and was even more handsome than he had been before. He said to her: 'Now dress in your fine clothes and we will go together to the church.' So they went, and the prince saw his wife coming in with a handsome fellow: they were standing in the church close to one another, side by side. How was he to imagine that this was his brother? At once he thought that something was wrong and said to himself: 'Oh, this daughter of the devil! She has a lover and is not ashamed to bring him with her to the church.' He was bitterly enraged, but they were in the church. He waited angrily for the service to end, and then he would go off to the house and catch her.

Well, the service came to an end. The prince did not wait, not even to take the Blessed Bread; he went off home full of rage: indeed the house was too small to hold him. Following him came his wife and the slave, both full of happiness. At once he rushed to seize her: 'Woman, are you not ashamed? Who is this man whom you are bringing along with you?' She said: 'Who is he? Why, he is your brother.' The prince turned expecting to see the marble figure. It was not there. Then he recognized the slave and fell upon him and embraced and kissed him. He asked him how he had come to life again. His wife told him how it had all happened. She took him to show him the cradle and that the baby was not in it. But what was before their eyes? They saw the baby lying in the cradle alive and asleep. Then there were indeed rejoicings.

All the same I was not there and you are not to believe the story.

38

The younger Brother rescues the elder

THIS is a rare story and the only well-told versions are three from Pontos: from Kerasund, from Ordoú, and from Kromni. It has the opening of *The Child given and claimed*, for which see No. 7. A childless father was given by a mysterious visitor—at Kromni and Ordoú by a dervish; at Kerasund by a devil—an Apple of Fertility. He and his wife ate it and twin sons were born to them. From the peelings the mare produced twin foals. The mysterious visitor reappeared and in accordance with his bargain claimed one of the boys. One son—if they are not twins, the elder—went off; if he were in trouble his brother would know it from a sympathetic token: at Kromni an olive-tree would wither; at Kerasund a club, and at Ordoú a sword, would drip blood. The boy who went off with the visitor escaped all the attempts to kill him; at Ordoú warned by an old woman, presumably his Fate. He found a beautiful girl and married her. Then he strove with some strange opponent; either at card-playing or at wrestling or in a test which of them should eat a plate of pilaf. The opponent is at Kromni a fairy, and at Kerasund and Ordoú a blackamoor. In this contest he was defeated and his brother, knowing from the sympathetic token that some ill-fortune had happened, went out to the rescue. He came to his brother's house where from their resemblance he was taken for his brother; in bed he set a sword between himself and his sister-in-law. Then he went forward and vanquished the opponent, the fairy or the blackamoor. If it was a fairy, he married her; if it was a blackamoor, he still had a bride, for the blackamoor changed into a beautiful girl. All four returned to their father's palace.

The hero, in killing his opponent, must strike one blow only; a second would undo the effect of the first. For this there is a note in *M.G. in A.M.*, p. 226. See also No. 35*b* above.

Of this story there are also two not very good versions from Thrace, in which a third brother rescues the two elder, though both miss many of the points of the Pontic versions. From Euboia Hahn has a rather similar story. A childless couple were on their way to the Holy Sepulchre when a devil appeared and promised them a son, who must, however, in due time be handed over to him. The boy met an old man who was Christ and by His help he made his escape. The story goes on that he met some fairy sisters who were daughters of the devil who had claimed him. He married the youngest and she helped him to perform the tasks set him by her father. Finally he paid a visit to his home, his fairy wife having bidden him never to kiss his mother: if he did he would forget her. But his mother kissed him in his sleep and he forgot his fairy wife. He was just marrying a mortal woman as arranged by his mother when the fairy wife appeared and claimed him. All this latter part rather belongs to the Fiorendino story, No. 49, in which the kiss of forgetfulness plays a part; for which kiss see also No. 25, *The Girl in the Bay-tree.*

This story belongs to a series of the widest range examined by BP. in their notes, i. 528–56, to Grimm, No. 60, *The two Brothers.*[1] To their numerous references may now be added a not very close Albanian parallel from Prizren,[2] and a variant with a tragic ending recorded from the Serbo-Croatian gipsies.[3] Also the 'Arabian Nights' *Story of the Prince Sayf-al-Muluk and the Princess Badi'a al-Jamal* has a very similar beginning with the birth of two sons, one to the king and the other to the vizier, although their subsequent adventures are not like those in the Pontic stories.[4] Yet there is a general resemblance, and it is to be noted that like many of the stories of this wide group the *Arabian Nights* tale contains the episode of the sword set in the bed between the man and the woman who was not his but his brother's wife. This Sword of Chastity may even be said to be an integral part of the Two Brothers story.[5]

Belonging to the same cycle of the two brothers, the younger helping the elder, are two simpler stories from the Greek mainland, much like the Thracian versions.[6] It is, however, these versions from Pontos that present a special form of *The two Brothers*, which may be regarded as the Greek, or rather the Pontic oikotype of the story.

The references are:

1, 2, 3. PONTOS: district of Kerasund, here translated; from Kromni, an unpublished version; from Ordoú in *Arkheíon Pontou*, xi. 83.

4, 5. THRACE: *Thrakiká*, xvi. 130 and 154.

6. EUBOIA: Hahn, i. 295, No. 54.

[1] Something further may be found in the references to the Aarne–Thompson Type 303.

[2] *Folklore*, liv. 34.

[3] Yates, *Gypsy Folk-Tales*, p. 86.

[4] Burton's Library edition, vi. 100.

[5] Funk and Wagnall's *Dictionary of Folklore*, *s.v.* Separating Sword. We meet it again in No. 46.

[6] From Epeiros in Pio, p. 60, which is Hahn, i. 166, No. 22, and translated in Geldart, p. 74. The other is Legrand, p. 161, which is taken from Buchon's *La Morée et la Grèce continentale*, p. 263.

NO. 38. THE YOUNGER BROTHER RESCUES THE ELDER[1]

There was a king and he had no son; he grew angry with God and went off to complain to Him. As he was on his way a devil came up to him and said: 'Where are you going?' The king said: 'I cannot beget a son and for this I am on my way to complain to God. Neither I nor my mare have any offspring.' The devil said to him: 'I will make you have two sons and your mare shall have two foals, if you will give over to me one of the sons and one of the colts.' 'Very well,' said the king. 'One of each is enough for me.' The devil gave him an apple saying: 'This apple you must peel, and one half of it you must eat yourself and the other half you must give your wife to eat, and the peel you must give the mare.' The king went and did as the devil had told him, and after nine months the queen gave birth to two beautiful boys, the two of them just alike; the mare too dropped two fine black foals; they too just alike. In one day the boys and the colts too made a year's growth; the boys used to mount the colts and go for rides.

Then the devil came and said to the king: 'Give me that to which I have a right.' The king said: 'And what is your right?' The devil said: 'Did I not give you the two boys and the two colts and you were to let me have one of the boys and one of the colts? Hand them over to me and let me go my way.' The king said: 'Say not a word to me of a son or of a horse; whatever else you may want let me know, be it money or anything else.' The devil grew angry and said: 'Did you not give me them? You shall lose everything.' So he cursed the king and went off. Then the boys and the horses fell sick and were like to die. The king sent for the devil, not knowing that he was a devil, and said: 'Take one boy and one foal; one of each is enough for me.' Then the devil roused the boys and the horses, and one boy he took away and one horse. Before the boy went off he said to his brother: 'You must hang my club up inside the hall and when you see blood dripping from it, then come to me; I shall have fallen into some trouble. 'Then he mounted his horse and followed as the devil led him.

The horse had the gift of a man's voice, and he said to the lad:

[1] Translation of a story from the neighbourhood of Kerasund recorded by I. Valavánis.

'This fellow will lead you by very ugly paths to try to make you dismount; if you do, he will devour you. But you must not dismount; I, your horse, wherever he may take you will carry you and make my way. And if he says to you, "Get down, my lad, not to be hard upon the horse," then you must say to him, "Be easy, master; never mind if the horse does break down. If he breaks down, then we must get another." ' The devil brought him along very ugly roads to try to make him dismount; then he could devour him. The boy did not dismount. The devil said: 'My boy, you must dismount here; the road is very bad and I fear the horse may break down.' The boy said: 'This horse of ours is strong and brave and it will come to no harm. And even if he does break down, be at ease, master; we will get another one.' So they went on and on; at last as they were on their way the devil pointed out to him his sister's house, and said: 'Over there is your poor old auntie's house.' Then the horse again spoke to the boy and said: 'If it is, she will do you much mischief.' 'I must go and meet my aunt.' Saying this he turned the horse towards the house. Then the devil went into the house without the boy seeing him. As soon as the boy had come into the house, he looked, and what did he see? A very beautiful girl. The girl said: 'Is it you, my cousin? And why have you come here? The snake will devour you.' Now the snake was in fact that very same devil. The boy came out of the house and the horse said: 'The devil has turned into a snake down there by the sheepfold, and he will say to you: "Come; go in by way of the door and then come out again." and if you go in and come out again three times, then he will devour you. But when he says to you "Go in and come out again," you must say to him: "I have been wont to go in and come out by doors so great and wide that by this narrow gate I cannot go in and come out again. You lead, and come out and go in for me to learn how." When the third time the snake comes out and goes back in again, you must smite him on his neck with your sword one single stroke. If you give him a second stroke he will recover his life.' The devil shouted to the boy: 'Why do you not come in and go out again by the door here?' The boy said: 'I have been wont to go in and come out by such big doors that by this narrow gate I cannot pass in and out. You must lead and come out and go in for me to learn how.' So the devil came out and went in again, and the third time the boy struck that snake a blow with his sword. The snake cried out: 'May your hand be broken! Smite me yet another blow.' Then said the boy: 'Once was I born of my mother and once do I strike.' The snake died and the boy went in and said to the girl: 'Come here and see; I have cut the snake all into pieces.' The girl was full of joy, for it was the snake who had carried her off and brought her to that place.

When it was evening the girl made ready a bed for the two of them. When it was fully night as his hand strayed it came upon her head; there were two keys tied up in the girl's hair. Very gently the boy untied the keys and took them away. He went and opened one of the rooms and inside it were two dogs, the pair of them exactly alike. There was also a small fountain running with a silver stream. Then he opened the next room and inside it there was a fountain running with gold. He took one of the dogs and brought it under the flow of silver and so made it all of silver. Then he brought a dog [this should be 'the other dog'?] and set it under the flow of gold and made it gold all over. In the morning he rose up, mounted his horse, and took also one of the dogs. While he was riding back again to the house he saw in the forest a wild goat. He chased after it and with him the dog, but he could not come up with it. The wild goat was really a black woman. She went off into a cave and presently a blackamoor came out and said to the boy: 'Come; let us play cards and see who wins. If you win, I will give you as against yourself a man, as against your horse a horse, and for your dog another dog. If I win, then I will take all the three of you, you and your horse and your dog.' So they played their game and the blackamoor won, and so for all the three wagers. The blackamoor took all the three of them down into the cave.

Then the club hanging up in the house began to drip blood, and when the boy's brother saw it he said: 'My brother has fallen into some ill plight.' He went and brought his horse out of the stable and mounted to go and find his brother. He gave his horse his head and the horse by the scent followed after the other horse. He rode along the ugly paths and thinking of his brother he said: 'Alas, for my brother, what trouble he had!' As the horse went on and on over these ugly roads, he came to the place where his brother's house was. He went in and as soon as the girl saw him, he was so like his brother that she thought it was he and was full of joy. When it became evening she prepared a bed for the two of them and the man set his sword between them and lay down. Then he took the dog and mounted his horse and went off to find his brother.

He too came upon the wild goat and chased after it, he and the dog. The wild goat went and entered the cave and presently the blackamoor came out and said to him: 'Come, let us play cards and see who wins. If I win I will take down with me into the cave all three of you, and if you win, I will give you as against yourself a man, as against your horse a horse, and for your dog another dog like your own dog. Then the boy understood that his brother was down there in the cave. He played cards with the blackamoor and all three times he won. Then the blackamoor went down into the cave and brought out his brother and his horse and his dog. When the two brothers saw one another they embraced and fell down in a swoon. The blackamoor poured water upon them and brought them to life again. Then the blackamoor turned into a girl and the second brother took her for his own, and the first brother went and took the first girl, and took his dog and they all went to their home.

NOTE. The text says that the first brother lays a sword between himself and the girl whom he wins and that the second brother does the same. The sword is, of course, only in place when the second brother comes out to the rescue and, being taken for his brother-in-law, sleeps with the girl who is his brother's wife. In the translation I have made the necessary slight alteration.

39

The Prince in Disguise

THIS is another story of the child given to a couple, a type of story discussed in the notes to No. 7, *The Child from the Sea*. In *The Prince in Disguise* the young man to be handed over to the dervish or to the ogre escapes and comes to great fortune. First in a castle he wins treasures or talismans by gaining the favour of the guardian animals. This he does by the common device of redistributing their food in a way that suits their capacity: in the Thracian example, translated, by giving the grass to the lamb and the flesh to the lion; in the example from Sozópolis by giving the soft meat to the eagle and the bones again to the lion, this being the commoner case: with the food the other way the animals had been starving. Next he found himself in a town and the princess fell in love with him. Disguised as a man with a scabby head, he did various services to the king and so won the hand of the princess. In the version translated, he fetched the Water of Immortality to cure the king's blindness, but the commonest turn to this part of the story is that he serves in the palace as a gardener, secretly destroying and then restoring the garden; then, still disguised as a buffoon, he goes to the war on a sorry nag and performs prodigies of valour, being ultimately recognized by the kerchief with which the king has bound up his wounded hand.

This story seems to me rather Turkish in style. Lorimer in his *Persian Tales*, p. 33, has a version, *The Colt Qéytās*, and in the Chian version the hero is given the Turkish name *O Bilimes*, the *Know Nothing*, from the Turkish *bilmem, I do not know*. The general tone of buffoonery points the same way. Also the Turkish love of gardens and of all that pertains to war may be noted.

The version translated is a little incoherent. If the hero's disguise was assumed at will, what need had he of the kindly animals to make him appear as a handsome youth?

The episode of the hero going to war in a buffoonish disguise and being at last recognized by having his wounded hand tied up with the king's kerchief is found in other stories: for example in a long, wandering tale from Samos; also in Astypálaia it is worked in at the end of a version of No. 53, the story of the boy who dreams that his father will one day serve him with water to wash his hands.[1]

[1] Stamatiádis, *Samiaká*, v. 523; for Astypálaia, Pio, p. 179.

The versions of *The Prince in Disguise* are seven:

1. CYPRUS: I have read an unpublished version.
2. KÁRPATHOS: in Kretschmer, *Neugr. Märchen*, p. 157.
3, 4. CHIOS: Argenti and Rose, *Folklore of Chios*, p. 500; and an unpublished version collected by Kanellakis.
5, 6, 7. THRACE: *Thrakiká*, xvi. 150, translated; and xvii. 164; also from Sozópolis, in *Laographía*, v. 452.

NO. 39. THE PRINCE IN DISGUISE[1]

Once upon a time there was a king, who lived happily with his queen and his people. He had no heir to leave behind him and this was a great sorrow to him. One day coming back from hunting he met a gipsy woman: she was his Fate. The gipsy told him that the queen would have a son, but hardly would he be ten years old than the ogre would carry him off. The king laughed at the gipsy's words. Time passed and the queen gave birth to a fair prince: the king could not believe his eyes. He ordered money to be distributed to the poor in all his kingdom, and that all men should hold festival. In the palace were very great rejoicings. The king remembered what the gipsy had said, that the ogre would carry off the boy as soon as he was ten years old. So from that time he heightened the walls all round the palace and fenced it all round with iron; night and day soldiers guarded the door of the palace.

The prince grew big and on the day when he was ten years old, as he was playing with the other boys, he disappeared. People ran everywhere to find him but he was nowhere to be found. The king died of grief: the queen too died.

All this time the prince was growing up in the ogre's tower. When he was eighteen he wanted to leave the tower, but how could he, when the door was locked and the ogre always had the key on him? It came to the prince's mind that there was a certain herb that if you put it into water and drank of it, you would go to sleep for weeks: this herb he put into the water which the ogre drank and so he fell into this deep sleep. The prince took the key and opened the door. He locked it again and went off. As he was on the way he came to a bridge: at one end

[1] Text from Thrace in *Thrakiká*, xvi. 150, with the title *The Prince and the Water of Life*.

of it there was a lamb and at the other a lion: in front of the lion there was a heap of grass and in front of the lamb there was flesh. The prince took the flesh and set it before the lion and took the grass and set it before the lamb. The animals thanked him for the kindness he had done them and each gave him one of their hairs and said: 'If ever you have need of anything, singe one of these two hairs and you shall have it.' 'I thank you,' said the prince and hid the hairs away in his pocket and went off.

He found himself outside a great city. There he met a poor man. To him he gave his royal dress and put on the poor man's clothes, and to hide his golden hair he bought an animal's paunch and covered it up. Boys who saw him shouted out: 'Come and look at scabby head.' In the palace some one was wanted to help in the garden and he was hired for this work.

Every year there was a great festival to which all the royal household went; only the young princess remained in the palace; from her window she used to look out to see the people. That year as she was gazing here and there she saw in the garden a handsome prince with golden hair: he was riding on a white horse and with his sword he was cutting at the flowers. From this time a year passed, and the princess could not find out anything about the prince. The day came when the festival would be held again, and the princess pretended that she was ill. As she was sitting at her window gazing out upon the people, she again saw the prince with the golden hair riding on a white horse, and with his sword cutting at the flowers. The princess asked him who he was and where he came from, and he told her all his story. When he chose he used to singe the hairs given him by the lion and the lamb, and then appear not as a scabby head but as a fine prince.

The king wanted to get his daughters married and he sent for all the princes in the world and told the princesses that they should throw the golden apple at whichever one of them they pleased. The two elder princesses threw the apple at princes, but the youngest princess at the scabby head. At this the king was angry and ordered her once more to throw the golden apple. Again she threw it at the boy with a scabby head. So she had him as her husband and they lived together in his cottage.

Years passed and the king lost his sight. The doctors said that only by the Water of Life could he be cured, and his sons-in-law said that they would go off to find it. To mock the scabby head they gave him a wretched feeble horse, one which could hardly lifts its feet. The scabby head singed a hair: a horse came for him, a horse for a prince, and he went and fetched the Water of Life. On the way he met the two princes and they said that they had gone to fetch the Water for the king and had not found it. The prince told them that he had it and in a little bottle he gave them some water. By way of thanks they gave him a ring they had.

The prince turned back and presently disguised as a scabby head sat on his miserable nag. The two princes passed by and spat at him for still staying there while they had brought the Water of Life. They went to the palace and gave the king the Water to bathe his eyes, but his sight did not come back; it had just been plain water. Then the scabby head turned back to go to the king and he gave him the Water of Life; as soon as he had bathed his eyes, he regained his sight. The king was delighted. The scabby head singed a hair and turned into a fine prince and told the whole story to the king, and the princess jumped for joy. The king brought them to the palace to live and he gave them all the kingdom and so they lived well and may we live yet better.

40

The Girl whose Father wanted to marry her

AARNE–THOMPSON TYPE 706

THE story begins with a widower who wanted to marry again, but it must be a woman who is fitted by his dead wife's slipper: the only woman it fits is his own daughter. In the version from Thrace translated this opening incident is omitted and we are told only that her parents wanted to marry her against her will to an old man. In the Chian version the sin which the girl will go to all ends to avoid is not incest but apostasy: the girl had been brought up by her mother as a Christian and the father who was a Turk wished her to go over to Islam. This would go down very well in Chios where there was a large Christian Greek population and a minority of Turks, often wealthy but naturally unpopular.

In the standard beginning the father, like many people who have resolved to go their own way but are of uneasy conscience about it, tries to get some sort of moral support by asking, but in a hidden form, the advice of some higher authority, a priest or a bishop. In the version from Epeiros a bishop is consulted. A man has brought up a lamb: is it better that he eat it himself or let some one else have it? The bishop gives the desired answer: It is better that the man himself eat it. The episode is not in the Chian version of the story, but it does occur in a Chian poem, a *Eulogy of Saint Markella*, in which the wicked father of the saint asked the confessor whether he might not eat of the fruit of a tree which he had himself planted.[1] In a variant of the allied story, *The Girl who had her Hands cut off*,[2] from Roccaforte in Calabria, the father asks a priest: 'I have a little pig; may I eat it myself?' And the priest answers that it is better to eat the pig than to sell it.[3] Sometimes the question is asked about an apple-tree which a man has planted in his own garden: who deserves the fruit more than he does? This weakness of human nature, to desire to cast a plausible veil over what is known to be wrong, must have been recognized everywhere, and we are safe in seeing an independent invention when we read that in Cambodia a king asked his mandarins: a man who had planted a garden, should he eat from it

[1] Argenti and Rose, *Folklore of Chios*, p. 820.

[2] *Forty-five Stories*, No. 9, and p. 131.

[3] *Rivista d. tradizioni popolari italiane*, i. (1893), p. 51.

himself or give the fruit to another? The mandarins of course returned the desired obsequious answer.[1]

The girl resolved to escape from her father's wicked intentions and persuaded him to give her two gifts. One must be three splendid dresses, the dresses so familiar in Greek stories: one embroidered with the sky and its stars; the next with the sea and the fish in it; the third with the earth and all the flowers. The other gift is some sort of disguise in which she can move about freely and not be recognized. In the versions from Chios and Mitylene she asks for a dog's skin in which she can disguise herself. More often she asks for a box or the wooden figure of a human being. Thus in the Smyrna version she demands a kind of portable chest; in Mýkonos the wooden figure of a girl; in Thrace of a man; in the version from Thrace here translated it is a wooden chest with wings so that she can fly about.[2] At Phárasa she asks for a large portable lampstand in which she can conceal herself. The golden deer-skin in the version from Kos is midway between the dog's skin and the idea of a box. These two forms of disguise may be taken as symbols of the means by which a woman in trouble and danger can protect herself: the dresses stand for her beauty and the wooden box for her powers of withdrawal and concealment.

Then a prince saw her, on each of three occasions wearing one of her dresses; this comes very close to the way in which the prince saw Cinderella in her beauty, either in a church or at a dance. At last by taking a token off her as she was making her escape the prince pierced her disguise and married her.

The story is very close to *Forty-five Stories*, No. 9, *The Girl with her Hands cut off*, where the points of contact have been discussed. The variant from Vourla has the persecution of the heroine and her babies which belongs properly to the *Girl with her Hands cut off*. In this variant the wicked father is a priest, and it is he who, disguised as a woman, murders the babies, who at the end are brought to life again by the Water of Life.

Of this story there are many European variants with very good parallels in Turkey, Sicily, and Naples, but the eleven Greek versions are enough to establish a Greek type of the story spread all the way from Phárasa to Epeiros.[3]

[1] Cosquin, *Études folkloriques*, p. 9, quoting from Aymonier, *Textes Khmers*, p. 11. I find the episode also in Leclère, *Contes laotiens*, p. 225.

[2] The Greek calls her the 'Wooden Angel', *Ξυλάγγελος*: I translate 'the box with wings'.

[3] Halliday in *M.G. in A.M.*, p. 260, gives references, and there are many more in BP.'s notes to Grimm, No. 21, i. 165, and to the allied No. 65, ii. 45. See also Politis' notes to an Attic–Albanian version in *Laographía*, i. 119. The Turkish ver-

The references for this story are:

1. PHÁRASA IN THE TAURUS: *M.G. in A.M.*, p. 511.
2. SMYRNA: Legrand, *Recueil de contes pop. grecs*, p. 217.
3. VOURLA, near Smyrna: *Mikrasiatiká Khroniká*, iv. 257.
4. MITYLENE: *Z.A.* ii. 24.
5. CHIOS: Argenti and Rose, *Folklore of Chios*, p. 508.
6. KOS: *Forty-five Stories*, No. 14, p. 181.

7, 8. MÝKONOS: Roussel, *Contes de Mycono*, pp. 107, 109.

9, 10. THRACE: *Thrakiká*, xvi. 92, translated, and *Arkheíon Thrakikoú Laogr.* vi. 263.

11. EPEIROS: Hahn, i. 191, No. 27.

NO. 40. THE GIRL WHOSE FATHER WANTED TO MARRY HER[1]

Once upon a time there were a king and a queen and they had a daughter, twenty years old. They wanted to marry her to an old man, a king. The princess was not willing. One day she said to the king: 'Father, I want you to make me a wooden chest; it must be fitted with wings, and in it there must be three compartments; it must shut from the inside and from the inside it must open, and at the top there must be a hole. Make me also three dresses: one worked with the sky and the stars, the second with the earth and its flowers, and the third with the sea and the fish.' In three days' time they brought her the chest and the dresses. The princess opened the chest and into each compartment she put a dress. She went inside the chest and shut herself in; only her head remained outside. Then she called upon God: 'O God, give me wings that I may fly.' The sky was clear and she flew off.

So she flew and flew and flew, until she came down in another kingdom, resting high up on a mountain. Three days later the king's son went out hunting with his servants; they saw in front of them a strange object. The prince said to them: 'Do not shoot at it; we must take it alive and see if it is a wild beast or some apparition.' The prince went up close and asked the girl: 'Are you an apparition? What are you?'—'I am a human being, as you are.' 'Won't you come and let me bring you to my mother?'

sion is in *Istanbul Masallari*, p. 78; the Neapolitan in Basile, *Pentamerone*, ii. 6; and the Sicilian in Gonzenbach's *Sizilianische Märchen*, i. 261, No. 38.

[1] Text from Thrace in *Thrakiká*, xvi. 92, with the title *The flying Princess.*

'I will come.' The prince took her and brought her to his mother. 'Mother,' said he, 'I have brought you a servant.' 'But could not they get me servants with women's bodies and not women like this one, made of wood? Well; let her stay since you have brought her.' And she was known as the Box with Wings.

Easter came and the king and the queen and the prince went to the church; they told the Box with Wings to come and hear the happy message of Easter. When they had gone out, the Box with Wings opened her chest; she soaped herself and combed herself and put on the dress worked with the sky and the stars, and so went to the church: there she stood by the side of the queen. Scarcely had the Good Message been announced, than she went back to the palace, took off the dress worked with the sky and the stars and went again into the box. The king and the queen and the prince came back from church, and the queen said: 'Today a princess came to church and stood by me; she was wearing a dress worked with the sky and the stars. So fair a girl I never saw and I wish I knew where she lives that I could make haste to find her and have her for my son's wife.' The king said: 'She will come again to the church tomorrow. We must set soldiers on guard at the door to see where she goes.'

The Box with Wings heard this. In the morning the king and the queen and the prince again went to the church. The Box with Wings soaped herself and combed herself and put on the dress worked with the sea and the fish: also she took in her pocket a handful of gold coins. Then she went to the church and stood near the queen. Before the service was over, she went out. The soldiers started to follow her to see where she went. The Box with Wings threw the coins in their faces; when they were picking them up, they lost track of her. The prince asked the soldiers what way the princess went. 'What excuse can we make to you, Sir Prince? She threw coins in our faces and while we were picking them up we lost track of her.' The prince said: 'Tomorrow I will keep guard myself.'

Next morning again the king and the queen and the prince all together went to the church. The Box with Wings soaped herself and combed herself and put on the dress worked with the earth and the flowers; also she took a handful of sand in her pocket and so she went to the church. The moment came when the Box with Wings went out of the church. The prince was on guard at the door and began to follow her. The princess turned round and flung the sand in his face. Then she plucked the ring off his finger and ran off to the palace.

The prince was brought to the palace and doctors sent for to heal his eyes. When he was well, he said to his mother the queen: 'I, my mother, will go to find the princess.' The queen brought together all the girls between eighteen and twenty-one and set them to make ring biscuits for the prince to take with him. The girls joined together: one of them crushed the sugar, another the cinnamon, another was working the butter, another did the kneading: they began to shape the biscuits. The prince was out taking a walk. The Box with Wings said: 'Give me a morsel of dough that I too may shape a little cake for the prince.' The girls refused and the Box with Wings complained to the prince. He said to the girls: 'There are so many of you. Each of you give her a morsel that she may shape her little cake.' Then they gave her some dough and she kneaded it and put into it the prince's ring. She mixed it all well, baked the cake and hid it away. They filled the bags with the biscuits and loaded them all on the ship. The Box with Wings went and said to the prince: 'Take my little cake as well and lay it in a corner; it may be of use to you.' They laid it in a corner in the prow of the ship.

The anchor was raised and they went off, voyaging to cities and harbours. The prince was always full of thought. One day he said: 'Boys, look there in the prow. There was a little cake put there made by the Box with Wings. If you can find it bring it to me.' He cut the cake to eat it, and in it he found his ring. Scarcely had he seen it than he said to the sailors: 'Start off and back home again.' The ship came into the harbour. Cannons began firing off and the Box with Wings was aware that the prince had come back. There were great rejoicings in all the kingdom that the prince had returned; all the people great and small went to bid him welcome. The king and the queen full of joy embraced the prince; he showed them the ring and told them that he had found it in the cake made by the Box with Wings. 'We must send for her,' said the queen. The girl went to them, just as she always was, inside her wooden chest, only she had not wrapped up her head as she had done the other times. She combed her hair as she had done the three times she had gone to the church, and she was so fair that her face shone brightly. The people saw her and were amazed. The prince took his sword and with great care cut off one wing; then he cut off the other. Then he slit the front plank of the box, and there was the princess fully to be seen wearing the dress worked with the sky and the stars.

The queen embraced and kissed her. 'You are the princess who has been teasing us for so long, are you?' The king kissed her and announced that the wedding should now begin. A joyous wedding was held with great festivities; the feast lasted for forty days and forty nights and the two of them lived happily and we here yet better.

41

The Underworld Marriage

THIS is the story of a girl who found her way into the World Below; there she witnessed the wickedness of a woman who deceived her husband with a negro paramour. At this she was so much scandalized that she threw something at the woman and put out her eye. The husband, to find out who had done this, came up into the Upper World; he found the girl and married her and brought her back with him into the World Below. The version from Zákynthos here translated begins with the marriages of two elder sisters, and this shape of the story, beginning with the two elder sisters and their marriages, and going on to the marriage of the youngest sister to a mysterious man from underground, reminds us a good deal of the Lord of the World Below in the version from Melos of No. 17, the story called *Human Flesh to eat*.

The passage of the girl into the World Below is managed in several ways; in the Leros story by the girl wandering away by herself when her companions were gathering herbs, and coming by accident to the head of the stairs which led down to an underworld garden. Of this story I find five Greek variants; one from Zákynthos, and the rest from the Aegean islands. The Turks have a similar story and from its general tone the tale may well be of oriental origin.[1] Richard Burton has remarked that in oriental fiction the negro lover appears almost symbolically to express the extreme depravity of the woman.[2]

This underworld, the World Below, has no connexion with the world of the dead; it is represented as a sort of separate and parallel country lying below the ordinary world of men. It is the world which the hero of No. 26, *The Underworld Adventure*, finds when he is carried down under the earth by the black sheep. It is hardly perhaps the World Below of No. 17, *Human Flesh to eat*, for this has a certain charnel-house flavour, and the Lord of the World Below and his human wife are so very much like Pluto and Persephone. In the Athens version of No. 32, *The Prince in a Swoon*, we are told that the way into the palace where the prince is lying in his swoon is down through a cistern, and the heroine has the slave girl she buys let down to her 'by way of the cistern'. Here again we have a suggestion of the World Below.

[1] The Turkish story is in *Istanbul Masallari*, p. 4, and in Mrs. Kent's *Fairy Tales from Turkey*, p. 159.

[2] *Arabian Nights*, Library edition, i. 5.

We read very clearly of this World Below in a story from Astypálaia called *The Magic of Solomon*, which is a longer variant of No. 8 above, *The Boy and the Box.*[1] Loaded with treasure from some mysterious palace the hero returned to his wife. She said: 'And where have you come from?' 'I am coming', said he, 'from the World Below.' 'What! From Hades?' 'No, not from there; that is where the dead are.' 'Then from where?' The husband said: 'From the other place; the men there are alive." 'And where is this place?' 'Down below, but I don't know how to get there.' Then he went on to tell his wife that, by the aid of the forty girls who come at his command from out of the talismanic box, he can go there and take her with him.

The references for this story are:

1. LEROS: *Forty-five Stories*, p. 200.
2. KÁLYMNOS: *Folklore*, xi. 454.
3, 4. MÝKONOS: Roussel, *Contes de Mycono*, pp. 125, 126.
5. ZÁKYNTHOS: *Laographía*, x. 386, translated.

NO. 41. THE UNDERWORLD MARRIAGE[2]

Win your father's blessing you may climb a mountain.

Once there was a family living in the country: father, mother, and three girls. The father had been dead for some time and the girls were left with their mother. Two years later the mother also fell sick and by the weakening of her senses she knew that she was going to die. She called her three daughters to her and besought them by all her blessings to be good girls; that they should in quietness await their marriage, for if they were patient and peaceful all three of them would be married. Then she died and the girls were left alone. They lived very modestly and made their living by their handiwork. The eldest [here the text by an error reads *the youngest*] used to walk out on the road. That country was a kingdom and the king had a son; also a negro servant. Every day the negro used to conduct the prince to school, while the eldest of the three girls used to walk about as she pleased. The negro gave the prince a buffet, and he fell down as if dead. He was taken up and brought home. The girl out walking had seen all that had happened to the boy.

They brought the prince to the palace and at once made every effort to bring him round, but no remedy could be discovered. The king made an order that whoever knew what had been done

[1] Dieterich, p. 504. [2] Text from Zákynthos in *Laographía*, x. 386.

to the boy, whoever he was, should be given money; if it were a girl, then he would give her the boy to be her husband. The girl and her sisters heard this, and she said to them: 'I saw what was done to the boy.' The sisters took her to the palace, and she said to the king: 'I saw it all. The negro gave the boy a buffet and felled him to the ground senseless like a dead man.' The negro was a magician. Then the king sent for the negro and said: 'You must give him another buffet on the other side.' When the negro gave him the buffet, the boy at once came to his senses. The king punished the negro and kept the girl in the palace. As soon as she came of age, according to his promise he made a marriage between her and the prince, and so she became a queen.

Now we must leave the queen and tell of the other two girls. The place where they lived was near the sea, and one day as they were doing their washing a ship with her captain sailed by: a storm was blowing. The girl was pounding her washing on the stone. The captain thought she was making a sign to him to change his course, so he sailed forward and came to shore at the place where the girls were washing. He looked at the girl and she seemed to him the most beautiful in all the world: at once he asked who she was and if she were unmarried. He was told much good of her and that she had a sister who was a queen. The whole place was set in a stir and the marriage was celebrated. The festival lasted for ten days, and with joy and honour he took her off, and they went to his own country.

Thus there was only the youngest sister left, and she stayed there working all by herself, poor girl. Not knowing what to do left alone like this, she went one day to her mother's room, which she had never opened since her mother died. She opened it and began to bring out the furniture. Then as she was cleaning the room she found a big paving slab with an iron ring set in it. This frightened her, but she was also very curious to raise the slab and see what it was. She lifted it, and underneath she saw steps: that was the way to the World Below. In that world there lived only a king and a queen; they had a servant, a negro. Scarcely had the girl seen all this, than she came up again. After some time she thought one day of going down there again: she saw the king at table and with him the queen and the negro. She perceived that this was the whole family; then she went away. Yet another day she went down. Then she saw the queen in the king's arms, and understood that he was her husband and the negro was the servant. Then one day she went down again; the king was away and the negro had the queen in his arms. The girl was much troubled, and said: 'Look at that! To think that she has the negro as a lover!' So she took an apple and threw it at the woman's face and put out her eye. The girl was frightened; she picked some flowers, sorts that were not in the World Above, and went up the steps and shut the place carefully. Some of these flowers she took to her sister the queen.

Now we must leave the girl and tell of the queen with her eye put out. Her husband came and saw that she had lost her eye. 'Who knocked your eye out?' he said. 'I don't know,' she said: 'I suddenly found it like that.' The king said: 'Here in this World Below there is no one at all, so who can have struck you?' Then he said: 'I shall go as a priest and confessor up into the World Above to hear men's confessions, and in this way I shall find out who struck you.' So he turned himself into a priest and went up into the World Above. It became known that a new confessor had come and he was brought to the king, for men to make their confessions. There he saw the flowers, and he said to the queen: 'From where are these flowers?' She said: 'A sister of mine brought them to me.' Then said the priest: 'Would she be willing for me to hear her confession?' The queen sent the priest to her sister; there he saw the rest of the flowers that she had. At once he heard the girl's confession, and she told him the whole story, how she had seen the queen with the negro. Then the priest said: 'Can you show me the steps by which you went down?' The girl said 'No,' because she was afraid, not knowing that the priest was the husband of the woman whose eye she had knocked out. 'Come,' said he, 'show me; you need not be afraid; I am a priest.' Then she lifted up the slab and the priest went down. He saw the queen his wife in the embraces of the negro. At once he seized his sword and hewed at the two of them. Then he came up quickly and went to the palace and made everything known: he said to them: 'I want to take this sister of yours to be my wife.' This was told to the girl. The wedding was held in the palace and he took her down with him to the World Below. So she too became a queen and by the blessing of their mother they lived, all the three daughters, in great good fortune.

42

The Son of the Hunter

THE essence of this story is that according to her husband's dying wish a widow refused to tell her son what his trade had been: at last she admitted that he had been a hunter, and in this occupation the boy became so skilled that he incurred the jealousy of the vizier who persuaded the king to get rid of him by sending him out on impossible and perilous tasks. The last quest was to fetch a closely-guarded fair maiden.

Under the heading *Le métier du pére* Cosquin has studied this story especially in connexion with variants in India,[1] but whether he is right in seeing its origin in India or not, *The Son of the Hunter* is in the Greek area a well-defined story, and I find variants in Pontos, Cyprus, Chios, Astypálaia, Syra, Tenos, Mýkonos, Mitylene, and the Peloponnese. Behind all these variants we find the essential elements of the story: the father's mysterious trade, the jealous vizier, the tyrannous king, the hero's helpers, the last mission which is to fetch the girl for the king, and at the end the hero's marriage to her. The final quest is worked out in several ways: the hero is helped by an elder, or by a Lamia, or by grateful animals, or as in the variants from Syra and Kerasund, by the Gifted Champions; details are given in the Astypálaia version in *Forty-five Stories*.[2] Here it need only be said that versions in the neighbouring countries are not common. In the notes in *Forty-five Stories* Albanian, Russian, Turkish, and Armenian versions are quoted, and a friend tells me he has found a very similar story among the Arabs at Acre, but they are not numerous and never very close or very complete. The story as it stands seems to me to be specifically Greek. By far the best version is the one from Syra, but as this has been translated by Geldart I have preferred an unpublished version from Kerasund. But as the beginning of the Kerasund version is extremely inadequate, I have begun with the opening of the Syra version and then gone on to the Kerasund version complete. This Syra version is the only one which explains why the mother wanted to conceal her husband's business; it was because it had brought him into the vizier's bad books.

In the two passages about the man who made leaps by the aid of stones held in his hands, the language I find very obscure, and I can

[1] Cosquin, *Contes indiens*, p. 395. [2] p. 72.

only give an approximate translation. It seems to me plain that in making his leaps the champion was helped by stones which he held in his hands and flung back at the moment of taking off: in fact he made use of the jumping weights which the ancients used and called *haltēres*. Whether these are used in modern times I do not know.

The versions are:

1. From Kerasund in Pontos: recorded by Valavánis. This is translated below.
2. Cyprus: an unpublished version.
3. Chios: unpublished version collected by Kanellakis.
4. Astypálaia: *Forty-five Stories*, No. 3, p. 56.
5. Syra: Pio, p. 212, translated by Geldart, p. 144.
6. Tenos: Hahn, ii. 3, No. 63. This is in German in Kretschmer's *Neugr. Märchen*, p. 246.
7, 8. Mýkonos: Roussell, *Contes de Mycono*, pp. 33, 35. Also in a periodical *Mykoniatiká Khroniká*, for 6 Nov. 1934.
9. Mitylene: Georgeakis et Pineau, *Folklore de Lesbos*, p. 20.
10. Peloponnese: *N.A.* i. 46.

A story from Mitylene, *The Waterseller's Son*, translated by W. R. Paton in *Folklore*, xi. 452, begins like this but works round to a rather poor version of *The Underworld Adventure*.

NO. 42*a*. THE SON OF THE HUNTER[1]

The beginning of the tale and a good evening to your lordships.

Once there was a king and he had in his pay a hunter; he gave him his rations, his butter and his oil, but all the birds he shot he had to bring to the king. One day when he was on his way to the king with birds, he had to pass by where the vizier was. The vizier asked him for the birds; the hunter being a faithful servant refused him. The vizier came to hate him very much and in every way he could tried to ruin him. However the hunter was a clever man and the vizier could never find an occasion against him. The time came when the hunter grew old and near to death. He sent for his wife and said: 'Wife, I am about to die. Only this: let my son be to you as your eyes. Go on keeping him at school, and if ever he asks you what was his father's business, you must not let him know, for it may be that the vizier because of his spite against me will find some occasion

[1] Text from Syra printed in Pio, p. 212, with the title *Johnnie, the Son of the Widow*.

against him and bring him to ruin.' When he had said this, he died.

Now the boy as long as his father was alive, used to go to school nicely dressed. When he was dead the pay from the king ceased, and so the boy went barefoot and in rags. In his hearing the neighbours would say: 'If his father were alive, would this boy be in such rags?' Next day he asked his mother, what had been his father's business. She remembered her husband's orders, and to put him off, said that his father had been a tailor. As the boy was again on his way to school, he heard the same thing said. Then again he asked his mother what had been his father's business. She made a thousand excuses to keep him quiet, but when she could not, she took and said: 'Your father's business was hunting, and the king gave us rations and pay and we lived very well.' All the week the boy went to school, and on Sunday he told his mother to give him his father's arrows, because he would go for a walk. So in the morning he went off hunting and had the luck to shoot a great many birds: he took them at once to the king. He continued every day to bring him birds. He enjoyed hunting and shot many birds which he used to take at once to the king. When the king asked who the man was who brought the birds, he was told that it was the widow's boy Johnnie, the son of the hunter whom he had had formerly. Then he sent for him: 'Are you the son of the man I had before as a hunter?' He answered 'Yes.' The king said: 'I will take you to succeed to your father.' He had given the father a ration of five pounds; of everything he gave to Johnnie the double. So the boy began to bring in game every day

One day as he was on the way to the king's palace, the vizier saw him passing by his house: he took a fancy to the birds he had and asked for them. The boy, even more faithful than his father had been, would not let him have them, but brought them to the king. So the vizier had a great quarrel with him and tried in many ways to find an occasion to bring him to ruin.

NOTE. The story goes on with the shooting of the wonderful animal, the fetching of the ivory, and the search for the beautiful girl, the hero being helped by the Gifted Champions: it is all translated in Geldart, so I give no more here, but go on to the version from Kerasund.

NO. 42*b*. THE SON OF THE HUNTER[1]

There was a hunter who had a son. When the hunter was about to die he said to his wife: 'Wife, my son is not to learn my business.' When the boy grew big he said: 'Mother, where is my father's gun?' The woman was unwilling to let him have it, but he was a bold lad and took it. He went out into the wood, and wandering about until the morning he shot a deer. Then when he was walking up and down in the bazaar, the king's vizier met him and said: 'How many piastres must I give you for the deer?' The Son of the Hunter said: 'And you: how many will you offer me?' The vizier said: 'Ten piastres.' When the Son of the Hunter would not accept this price, the vizier grew angry and did what he could to ruin him, and in his anger he went to the king and said: 'My king, there is a man here selling a deer: you buy it, but do not go beyond a piastre and a half.' The king sent for the Son of the Hunter and he came with the deer. The king said: 'How much am I to give you for the deer here?' The boy said: 'You know the price.' The king said to his vizier: 'What is the deer worth?' The vizier said: 'A top price would be a piastre and a half.' The boy took his piastre and a half and went off.

Early in the morning the king's servant came to the door and carried the Son of the Hunter off to the palace. The king said to him: 'You, since you have brought me this deer, you are the man to bring me ivory as well and to build me a palace of ivory.' The boy began thinking about this a little, and the king said: 'What are you thinking about? If you can do it, then say you can. And if you can't; then the headsman!' What was the boy to do? He said to the king: 'I can do it.' He went to his house weeping and said to his mother: 'Mother,' said he, and so he told her all the story. And when he had told his mother, he said: 'Now I must go right away. Give me my knapsack with a little bread in it.' 'And where are you going?' said his mother. 'Come now; your father used to say to me, "Ah, if only the king had given me a party of men! Up there on the mountain every Friday the elephants come and I would have gone and done the deed." Then I would say to him: "And how would you have caught them?" Then my husband used to say to me: "I would

[1] Text from Kerasund.

drain off the lake and fill it up with wine, and when the elephants came to drink, they would get drunk and tumble into the lake." '

When he had heard this the boy in the morning went off and said to the king: 'Grant me a company of men and forty barrels of wine and I will go and bring you the ivory and build you the palace.' So he took the company of men and the wine and went up on the mountain. He drained the lake and poured in the wine and waited for Friday when the elephants would come and drink and get drunk. In this way he got the ivory and went back and built the palace.

When the vizier saw that the boy had not been killed, he said to the king: 'O king, send off this Son of the Hunter to go to such and such a mountain: seven brothers live there and they have a sister. You ought to have her here in the palace which the boy has built for you.' When the king had given him this command, the Son of the Hunter took his knapsack and went right off in despair. As he was on his way, he came upon a man who was sitting on the brink of the river drinking and going on drinking, saying all the time: 'Thirsty, I am thirsty.' The Son of the Hunter said to him: 'You there; and what kind of fine fellow are you?' The man said: 'I am no fine fellow. There is a man, the Son of the Hunter, he who has built the king his palace of ivory, it is he who is the fine fellow. You should have seen his doings: him I would have taken for a brother.' 'I am he,' said the boy, and did become the man's brother. And so they went on together.

On their way they came across another man and he was in a bath-house and saying: 'Cold, I am very cold.' The boy took him also for a brother.

As they were on their way he came upon yet another man and he was devouring food by the plateful, saying all the time: 'Hungry, I am very hungry.' Him too they took as a brother.

As they were on their way they met a man who was holding his ear to the ground listening to all that was happening in the world. Him too they took as a brother and went forward on their way.

They came upon yet another man, and he was one who by gripping big stones by the side of his legs and throwing them behind him could leap from here even to the city of Constantine. Him too they made a brother and so went on.

They met another man who could make the earth to shake: with this man they made up six brothers, and counting the Son of the Hunter seven.

When they came to the frontier and the seven brothers of the sister saw them, they ran right up to devour them. But seeing that they were fine strong fellows they were in some fear and said: 'What is it you seek?' The men said: 'We seek your sister.' Then the seven brothers went to their house and agreed that if the men could eat seven cauldronsful of food, then they might have their sister. Then the Son of the Hunter said to the man who could put his ear to the ground and hear everything: 'What are they saying?' The man said: 'They are saying: "Let us say to them that if they can eat the seven cauldronsful of food, then we will let them have our sister; if they can't we will not let them have her."' When this was heard by the man who used to eat and eat and yet never be full, he said: 'Oh, Oh, I am here and what are you talking about? Has it ever happened that I could not eat all the lot? At one gulp I will swallow it all.' The others all ate their fill, but the man who was always hungry could not get enough just with his spoon; he began with the platters heaped with food and ate his own share and the shares of all the rest of them.

In the morning seven jars of water were brought. The man who was always thirsty said: 'Oh, Oh, and has it ever happened that I could not drink the lot?' The others could not drink it all, and the man set to work drinking from the jar and drank his own share and the water of all the rest of them.

Again the brothers spoke: 'One of you we must put into the fiery heat of the bath, and if he can endure it, then we will let you have our sister; if he cannot we will not let her go.' The man who was always cold went into the bath-house saying: 'I am cold, I am cold.' The brothers brought him out of the bath, saying: 'O you men, whatever we have told you you must do, that you have done. Yet one more thing we will bid you do, and if you can do it we will let you have our sister. One of you must go for the Water of Immortality, and we for our part will send our sister to fetch it, to see which of the two will fetch it the more quickly. If you can fetch it first, then we will give you our sister, but if our sister is the quicker then we will not give her to you.'

Then the man who could hold stones by his legs, fling them

back and leap forward, made a leap right all the way to the Water of Immortality. On his way back he met the girl who was still on her way to it. He cried out to her and said: 'And now we have won you: come, let us sit and talk together a little.' They sat down, and as they were talking the man who flung the stones fell asleep and was left behind by her. The girl emptied the Water of Immortality into her own flask and went back with it. The Son of the Hunter said to the man who had the ear to listen: 'You listen and find out what our brother is doing.' The man listened and heard that the brother was asleep. 'It is all up with us,' he said. 'What is the matter with him?' 'The lad went off to sleep and then the girl took the water and is coming back here with it.' As soon as the Son of the Hunter heard this he said to his brother: 'Come, you must shake the earth and make the lad wake up.' Then the man made the earth shake, and when the boy woke up he looked round, and what did he see? The girl had taken the Water and gone off. With one leap he reached her and took the Water from her and got back before she could come. As everything had been done which they had been bidden to do, the Son of the Hunter and his men took the girl and brought her to the king.

The girl asked the king: 'Who built this palace?' 'The Son of the Hunter.' 'And this deer, who brought it?' 'The Son of the Hunter.' 'And who has brought me here?' 'The Son of the Hunter.' Then when the girl had learned what the vizier had done against the Son of the Hunter she flew out against him and said: 'May this vizier be changed to a mouse and the king to a cat and chase the mouse.' Her curse came to pass. And the Son of the Hunter took the girl and lived there as king and all his brothers were great lords.

43

The young Man and his three Friends

THE very long and artfully constructed story from Skyros to which I have given this name seems to have no full parallels, though several elements which go to its construction can be recognized. It begins with a boy going out with his mother to the mountain where she was cutting wood for her oven. He found himself in a perilous castle. He overcame the ogre of the castle, who fitted him out with magical equipment: shoes of silence, cap of darkness, an invincible sword, and a horse with the gift of speech. Up to now he is presented as a child, later as a young man; and the rest of the story is concerned with how he went out to seek his lady and on the way met with three friends for each of whom he won a wife. He attained his own love and then was killed by a king who had seen her picture and fallen in love with her. The three friends then came to his aid. He was brought to life again, rescued his wife from the king, and the story ends happily.

The story is worth examining in more detail. The ogre in the castle gave him the keys of forty rooms; the fortieth he must not open. He did so and in it he saw a fair girl; she was that Fair One of the World whose love is the central thread of the story. She said he must prove himself worthy of her by seeking her in the Wood of the Golden Trees. She turned into a spirit of the air and disappeared. On the way to find the mysterious wood he met three men: the first was the Son of the Sun, riding on his white horse; the second the Son of the Moon on his silver horse; the third rider was the Son of the Sea. The four of them on their horses pursued the quest, and the hero found wives for all his three friends. First for the Son of the Sun by succeeding in leaping over a very wide ditch; he left his friend with his wife and the others went on. Then he found a princess held under the enchantment of a blackamoor lover; the hero broke the charm and married her to the Son of the Moon. Then with only the Son of the Sea he went forward, and they came to a land where the princess, of age to be married, would do nothing but preserve an obstinate silence; the king her father would give her in marriage to whatever suitor could make her speak. Here we recognize No. 48, the common story of *The silent Princess*, provoked to break her silence by stories told her by her clever suitor. Here the successful story is not one usually found in the framework of *The silent Princess*: it is roughly the story of *The*

Master and Pupil, our No. 24. In this way the hero won a bride for his third friend, the Son of the Sea. These subsidiary stories make up together rather more than a quarter of the whole.

The hero after thus finding wives for his three friends came at last to the Wood of the Golden Boughs and the castle of the Fair One, these at the very edge of the world. She accepted him as her lover, but she had by now, I think by virtue of her love for a mortal, ceased to be a spirit of the air and had become a woman, and as such had the sense to know that they must go back into the world of men. The sentimental idea of a permanent life in the Venusberg has very little attraction for the Greek intelligence; the Greeks know what men and women really are, and the Fair One transported her castle and the Golden Wood and the garden, all of them, into the world where men live. To keep in good health the hero, like other young men living pleasantly, every day rode out hunting. But to have his wife always in his mind he carried with him a picture of her.

One day the picture fell from his pocket and in a strange manner came into the hands of a king who fell in love with so fair a woman. By the aid of a cunning old crone the king carried off the Fair One, and with his own sword the old woman killed the hero. This episode of the picture and the amorous king carrying off the lady occurs also in a story from Kos, No. 10 in *Forty-five Stories*, *The darling Son*, but I do not find it elsewhere in Greece, and the parallels to the Kos story are both of them from Armenia.

At this point of the tale the three friends learned from the sympathetic tokens which the hero had left with them that he was in some ill plight. Their fathers, the Sun and the Moon and the Sea, showed them how to find the body of the hero, and how to get the Water of Life to restore him again, and the Son of the Sea recovered the sword. Then the hero said farewell to his three friends and went off to rescue his wife and with the sword to kill the king and the wicked old woman. By this time we may suppose that the life of the happy pair in the world was over, for the Fair One carried the tower and the Wood of the Golden Trees back again into fairyland, and there at the edge of the world they lived and 'may still be living' in joy and love.

Although this story so far as I know stands by itself, it has for all that in its structure a close resemblance to the second version of No. 23, *The magic Brothers-in-law*. The hero of the brothers-in-law story finds wives, his own sisters, for the three suitors, just as the Skyros hero does for his three friends. In both stories when the hero has brought off the three marriages he himself has his own wife carried away: in the brothers-in-law story by the strange monster; in the

Skyros story by the king who desires her beauty. Then the hero wins her back by the aid of the three grateful brothers-in-law, or in the Skyros story by the aid of his three friends, the Sons of the Sun, of the Moon, and of the Sea. The Skyros story is in fact *The magic Brothers-in-law* with the three friends acting the part of the brothers-in-law; both have a hero who first finds wives for his friends, and then when he loses his own is helped to regain her by the men who owe their wives to his good services. This, kindness rewarded, is the theme common to the two stories.

It seems to me likely that some gifted story-teller in Skyros, perhaps the very man, Manoli Stamelos, who gave Madame Pérdika the story, perceived the true theme of *The magic Brothers-in-law*, and on its lines constructed a new story, not yet spread abroad. It is of interest to contrast its plausible neatness of construction, as if it were brand new from the mint, with the roughnesses of some of the old-established and widely-spread fairy romances of the same sort: they have had time to get untidy. The story-teller must have been well acquainted with the general *corpus* of Greek folktales, and so been able to insert the subsidiary stories; neatly enough, but not very accurately, because as we have seen he sets *The Master and Pupil* in the framework of *The silent Princess*, where it has no such nice suitability as the normal three sub-stories have.

NO. 43. THE YOUNG MAN AND HIS THREE FRIENDS[1]

Once upon a time there was a woman who was a baker; she had one son. Left a widow and a poor woman, she had her oven, and she used to go to the mountain to cut wood and bring it to the village and heat the oven: thus for one woman she would bake her bread and for another her meat. They paid her and so she and her son made their living.

One day she rose up to go to the mountain. The boy began to cry: 'I want to go too; I want to go too.' His mother did not want to take him and said: 'I won't take you; you can't come because there is no water there. You will get thirsty and there will be nothing for you to drink.' 'No, no,' said the boy, 'I shan't get thirsty, and if I am, I won't ask you for water. You shall do your work and I'll do without drinking until we come back to the village. Let me come and you shall see.'

Finally she took the boy and they went off. When they came

[1] Text from Skyros, Pérdika, ii, Nos. 25 and 26; printed with the titles: *The golden Boughs* and *Woe is Me*.

to the mountain the boy ran about and played till he was tired. He sat down to eat a couple of olives and a little piece of bread his mother gave him. When he had eaten he was thirsty. He said nothing to his mother but rose up and began to look to see if he could find water anywhere. Then a little lower down on the other side of the mountain he saw a tower. The door was open and there was a fine garden, and among the trees and flowers there was a stream flowing. Full of delight he went to his mother and said: 'Look, mother, I have found water inside the castle; I am going there to drink.' His mother began to cry and told him not to go: the tower was haunted. If anyone went there to drink, the door shut and the man was lost: no one ever came back again. She went on entreating the boy and told him that they would go off back again to the village. 'Just let me tie up the wood and make it into faggots,' said she. 'Then we can make up our loads and go off at once. Don't go into the tower, my boy, for I shall lose you.' The boy made as if he would not go, and his mother set to tying up the faggots, but he tricked her and went to the castle and drank of the water. As he was going out after quenching his thirst, the door shut. He wept and called out for his mother. She ran up and banged at the door but there was no reply to her entreaties.

The mother went all round and round the castle crying out to her son. When the boy saw that the door would not open, he said that he must go farther and perhaps he might find some other door to go out by. Straying a long way from his mother he lost her. The mother stayed there until late in the evening, and when she saw that the boy was lost she went back to the village with a sore heart.

Now we must leave the mother lamenting her fate—she had lost her son and was left desolate like a reed in the field—and we must see what happened to the boy. He turned and walked about to find a way out. Night fell and he was tired; what with walking and weeping he had no more strength. He lay down under a tree, stretched himself out and went to sleep. At dawn there came up to him a monster, a haunting spirit from the castle. He saw the boy and went up close and looked at him. He laid hold of his arms and his body, and said: 'A little feeble; I must feed him up and then I can eat him.' He pushed the boy and said: 'Get up and come inside with me.' Johnnie was angry and said: 'Why are you pushing me? Why must I get up? I am sleepy. Leave me to sleep.' 'Get up quickly, you who think so much of yourself,' said the ogre. The boy without losing his wits at all sat down under the tree and said: 'I won't go. I am very well here. And if you dare, you may come and fetch me away.'

The ogre rushed at him and they began their struggle. The ogre seized the boy and drove him down into the earth to his ankles. Johnnie seized the ogre and dealt him a stroke and pushed him down into the earth as far as his knees. The ogre said: 'Enough! You have conquered me. Now I must go hence; everything here will be left as yours. Take these keys: there are forty of them and you are to open the thirty-nine cupboards you will find in the castle. All that you find shall be yours. Only, the last cupboard you must not open: if you do it will be your death. All those who have opened it have gone on the road by which there is no returning. They have never been seen again. In the first little cupboard you will find the shoes: if you put them on no one will hear your steps. Also the cap: if you wear it no one can see you. Also the sword unconquerable: when you draw it you will victoriously slay every one. Put on all these and go to the stable and there you will find the horse with the gift of speech. When he sees you with the sword, he will know you for his master and carry you wherever you please.' As soon as he had said all this, the ogre disappeared from sight.

Johnnie was left all dazed. He could not well understand what all this was that the ogre had said to him. He took the keys and thought a little; perhaps it was a dream. Then he said: 'Come, I must open these cupboards and see what I shall find.' He opened the first and the second; he found the sword and the cap and the shoes. Also he found sweets and fruit and food; he found golden clothes, gold coins and diamonds: every kind of fine thing. He found also four golden apples, of which the ogre had said that they were enchanted and were the apples of his fate. As long as he was well, the apples would remain rosy red, and their leaves green and fresh. But if he were sick or in danger the apples would wither and the leaves fall. He took the apples as well as the other things.

Thus he opened all the thirty-nine cupboards. Then he came to the last one; he still had the key in his hand and was thinking:

'Shall I open it? Shall I not open it?' He was of two minds. Then said he: 'And why should I not open it? Think of all the things I found in the thirty-nine other cupboards! I must try to see what treasures the ogre had stored up in it. Also the ogre told me that I might have everything; why should I sparc only what is here? Come, I will open it and see what is inside?'

He put in the key and opened the cupboard. As soon as he opened it, the place was flooded with brightness. It was a girl, the Fair One of the World; she was shut in there and looking at him. He thrust forward to take her. She with her hands pushed him away, saying: 'Do not lay hands on me. You have not yet proved yourself worthy to be mine. I must go off to where the Golden Boughs are. If you prove worthy and can find out where that is, then I will be yours.' She turned into a spirit of the air, a puff of smoke, and vanished from his sight.

Losing her, Johnnie came near to losing his senses: such beauty as never was! He said: 'I must go and find the Golden Boughs even if I have to search over all the world. I will never give her up.' He girt on the sword, put on the shoes, and took the cap. Then he went down to the stable and found the horse and greeted him and to please him gave him some of the sugar buns he had found in the cupboards. He said: 'My good horse, I want you to carry me to find the Golden Boughs; I know you know all about it.' 'I will carry you where you please,' said the horse. 'All the world I know well, but of the Golden Boughs I know nothing. Give up this intent; it will not be for your good. We shall never be able to find this place.' But Johnnie was firm in his intent and kept saying: 'I want to go there, my good horse, I do indeed; we must go and find the Golden Boughs. I do beg of you, carry me there.' Then the horse said: 'Since you wish it, let us go, and may God help us.'

They went on and on and on. The horse loved Johnnie and was highly pleased to have a man as his master and not the ogre. He used to talk to him and tell him what was the right thing, what he ought to do. One day at dawn they came to a place, and as the sun rose they saw a man riding on a white horse and coming towards them. The horse said: 'Do you see that rider? He is the Son of the Sun. When he comes near us you must hit him in the eye and then say good day.' This seemed strange to Johnnie, but he said nothing because he knew that the horse was always right. When the rider came near Johnnie gave him a blow, and then said: 'Good day to you, brother.' 'Good day, brother; where are you going?' said the Son of the Sun. 'I am on my way to find the Golden Boughs and I don't know where they are,' said Johnnie. 'I will come with you, brother,' said the Son of the Sun: 'The sad thing is that neither do I know where they are.'

So they became brothers. The Son of the Sun followed Johnnie and accepted him as his leader; by the lightning blow he had given him he had recognized him as his master. They went on all day together, and on and on and on. Then in the evening when the sun was setting, they saw a rider on a silver horse coming in their direction. Again the horse spoke to Johnnie: 'Do you know this rider? This one is the Son of the Moon. Give him too a blow, for if you do not he will not recognize you as his leader, and will try to fight with you to see which will overcome the other.' Again Johnnie gave the rider a blow saying: 'Good evening, brother.' This man too joined him and that made them three.

When they reached the sea-shore they met another rider: he was the Son of the Sea. Again the horse spoke to Johnnie, and he gave this man too a buffet and made him his brother. He too went with them, so they were now four and Johnnie was their leader. Then they fared from place to place to find out where the Golden Boughs were. But wherever they went and wherever they asked no one could tell them. Time passed and Johnnie was much vexed to think of these three fellows of his; he was giving them all the toil of going round with him on the quest.

One day they came to a town and they heard a crier making a proclamation: 'Whoever can on his horse cross over this ditch, leap over it and turn and come back again, that man shall have the princess as his wife.' When Johnnie heard this he said: 'It would be fine if I could set up one of my brothers here; he would marry the princess and stay here to become king. Think of all these years he has been toiling with me!'

Johnnie went to the horse and caressed him lovingly and asked: 'What do you say to this, my good horse? Could you leap over the ditch and then we could get the princess to be a wife for my brother?' The horse said: 'It is no easy matter but yet I can leap over the ditch.' Then Johnnie said to the king:

'I will leap the ditch, and if I succeed my brother, the Son of the Sun, shall have the princess.' The king consented.

Johnnie on his horse went and leaped right across the ditch; then he leaped back again. What rejoicings, cries of hurray, clappings of hands! Everyone was there and the wedding took place among the greatest rejoicings. About a month passed and Johnnie said: 'Brother, I must go forward. I leave with you this apple. As long as you see it whole and fresh that will mean that I am well. When you see it withered and the leafage yellow, that will mean that some ill fortune has befallen me. If you love me, take the eastwards road, the road facing the sun, and search until you find me, alive or dead.' The three of them started off, and went on and on and on, seeking for the Golden Boughs, but in vain. Some time passed and again they came to a city. They met a crier proclaiming: 'Whoever can watch by the princess all night without sleeping and see where she goes and what she does every evening when she lies down to sleep, that man shall have her as his wife.' This princess was under an enchantment; she was not willing to be married. It was a blackamoor who had enchanted her and she had no eyes for any other man in the world. Every evening he came and carried her away and no one knew where they went and what they did all night. The father tried to find her a husband but she would not listen to him. She and the king had made an agreement that she would marry whoever could succeed in following her and seeing where she went every night. But whoever was overcome by sleep, he should have his head cut off.

Up to the day when Johnnie came thirty-nine princes had come forward, and with their heads the princess had built a fine big tower. When she could cut off one more head and make up the forty then the tower would be finished, and the king had promised that he would leave her at peace, and talk to her no more of marriage. When Johnnie heard the crier he said: 'A fine thing it would be to marry my brother the Son of the Moon to this princess.' Johnnie went to the king and said that he himself wanted to stay there and keep watch to see if he could find out where the princess went, and his brother the Son of the Moon could marry her. The king was grieved about Johnnie and told him not to go; it would be a sin that so fine and handsome a youth should lose his life. Johnnie would not listen to him. Then they agreed that he should go there in the evening and if he succeeded his brother should marry the princess.

Johnnie went off to his horse and asked him what he was to do to manage to stay awake. The horse told him to take good care not to drink the coffee they would serve him; only to pretend to drink it and to pour it away. Then he must pretend to have gone to sleep, and when the princess rose up to go away then he too must follow behind her and be careful to take some token from the place where she went, and in this way be able to get the better of the princess. For she might say that he was telling lies and he not be able to prove what he had said. 'In order that she may not hear you when you are going after her you must wear the shoes which make no sound when you walk, and the cap so that you cannot be seen.' These were the horse's last orders. 'I thank you, my good horse,' said Johnnie and caressed him and gave him sweets and kissed him and then went off. In the evening Johnnie came to the princess's room, and she gave him some coffee to drink. Johnnie poured it inside the neck of his shirt where he had put a sponge. A little time passed and he pretended to yawn as if he could not stay awake. He lay down and began seemingly to snore. 'Ah, he's off like the rest!' said the princess.

At midnight Johnnie heard thunder; the fire-place split open in two parts and into the room there came a blackamoor, a terror to behold. He said: 'Good evening, my little dove; Good evening my golden dear.' 'Good evening, my love,' said the princess. 'Well, what about it? It is time now,' and they embraced and kissed one another and out they went through the split in the fire-place. Johnnie rose up and put on his cap and went with them. They entered a carriage, Johnnie following them.

They came to a beautiful garden. They got down and went to a table set ready for them. They sat down to eat, Johnnie at the side of the princess. The blackamoor set food before her; he set it down and Johnnie ate it from off her plate. Before you could turn round and look, lo, the plate was empty. The blackamoor said: 'What an appetite you have tonight, my love! I can't bring the food quickly enough for you.' 'It is because of my joy,' said the princess. 'Tonight is the end of the term granted by my father. Counting the fool who is now asleep in my room, the heads are forty. So I can finish building the tower and my father has given me his word he will speak to me no more of marriage. Now you will be able to come every night and sleep with me in the palace. There will be no one to stand in our way.' The blackamoor said: 'We shall be all the night together. I shall have you as my wife. In case you ever want me to come to you by day as well, I will give you this egg. When you want me, break it and at once I will be with you.' The princess took the egg and put it in her pocket and went on caressing the blackamoor, saying: 'Whatever you want for your pleasure that I will do. I will throw myself into the fire if you tell me.' As she was caressing him like this, Johnnie stooped down and took the egg from her pocket and hid it in his bosom: they did not notice him.

When dawn was near they rose up and went away again in the carriage to go to the palace. They went into her room by the way of the fire-place. Johnnie passed in in front of them and went and lay down; he took off his cap and pretended to be asleep The princess lay down and went to sleep and so did Johnnie until the dawn. In the morning the king came; he unlocked the door and found his daughter already awake. She said: 'Come, father; take this fellow too; get him up and go and cut off his head and so I can finish my tower. I have won the wager.'

The king was much distressed but he pushed Johnnie to wake him up. Johnnie opened his eyes and he saw the king and his soldiers all round him. He rose up and said: 'Pardon me, my king. All night long I was following round after your daughter; this tired me and sleep came upon me.' 'What are you saying?' said the king. 'You went sound asleep and all night long never woke up. You must have seen all this in your sleep.' Johnnie began to tell the king how the fire-place had split and about the blackamoor and everything else. The princess denied it. Johnnie told about the garden and about the dinner. The princess was trembling with dismay. How had Johnnie seen all this when she had never seen him there? She went on with her denials. 'And to show you that all this is true,' said Johnnie, 'take this egg, O king, and break it and you will see that the blackamoor will come here: you shall see him for yourself and then you will believe my story.' When the princess heard about the egg, she felt in her pocket but she could not find it. She fell fainting. The king took the egg and broke it: a blackamoor presented himself: a real monster. When they saw him everyone's blood froze. When he saw the princess in a faint in his eager desire the blackamoor ran to embrace her; Johnnie was before him and drew his sword and with one stroke hewed off his head. When the princess came to, she opened her eyes and fell into the arms of her father, delivered from her enchantment. All rejoiced and with pleasure fell to laughing; in a few days the princess was married to the Son of the Moon with songs, dances, music and all manner of rejoicings.

About a month passed and with the Son of the Sea Johnnie rose up and took with him his sword and his horse and all his gear. He said farewell to the king and also to his brother and his wife the princess. With him he left an enchanted apple, saying that if it withered he must wait for his other brother the Son of the Sun and the two must go off together to find him. He kissed him good-bye and was off.

They went on and on, the two of them by themselves, and going this way and that they came to a kingdom where the princess was refusing to speak and the king had sent out a crier to proclaim: 'Whoever can succeed in making the princess speak may have her as his wife. If he fails he must be slain.' Again Johnnie asked his horse: 'What am I to do, my good horse, to get the princess to speak so that I may marry her to my brother here, and he too find rest and be no more at the pains of travelling about with us?' 'This is the most difficult task of all,' said the horse. 'In one way only can you succeed. You must tell the king to make you a double-faced mirror and inside it you must conceal the Son of the Sea, and when you see that you can't get the princess to speak, then at dawn you must speak to the mirror and say: 'Mirror, my little mirror, since the princess will not talk to me, will *you* not talk to me and console me, for this is my very last night. Tell me some story that I may forget my grief.' Then the Son of the Sea will begin to talk to you from inside the mirror and perhaps the princess will become curious and speak herself to question you and find out how it is that the mirror talks. Johnnie did as the horse told him. The king made him the mirror. His companion was shut up inside it, and when in the evening the mirror was carried into the princess's room Johnnie went in with it. Then Johnnie began to talk to her; he besought her and also told her amusing stories. But from the princess, not a word! You would have said she wasn't there.

When it was near dawn and he saw that all his talking was to no purpose, Johnnie turned and said to the mirror: 'My good mirror, since the people here are so hard of heart that they have no pity for me, I who am so young and must die, and yet they won't speak a word to me, speak to me yourself, I pray you, you who have no life in you, you give me your company.' The Son of the Sea started and spoke from inside the mirror: 'And what do you want me to say to you?' 'Tell me a story to pass the time a little until the day comes and they put me to death,' said Johnnie. The mirror said: 'With pleasure I will tell you a story: Once upon a time there was a poor man and he had only one son, and him he loved dearly. But how poor he was and no work to do! He was in despair and said to his wife: "I will take our son off to the town that he may learn some craft so as not to starve when he is grown up." He took the boy; they had no money and so they started off on foot. On the way when they came to Alortho Pouri they were tired and sat down to eat a little and refresh themselves. The father, feeling very sad that he would be leaving his son in the hands of strangers, said with a sigh: "Woe is me! Woe is me!" As he said this he saw the sea swelling up and a wave coming down over him, a wave as high as a mountain. He was afraid and wanted to run away. As this was in his mind, the wave opened and from the midst of it there came an angry spirit which said to him: "Why did you call for me? What do you want?" The poor father was frightened and said: "I said nothing to you, master. I only sighed and said: Oh alas and thrice alas for my cruel fortune and for my poverty which deprives me of my son, for I must leave him all alone in the hands of strangers, all for him to learn a craft." The spirit said: "As you have called for me, be patient and I will help you; I will take your son with me and teach him a craft. After two years come here to this same place, call for me, and take your son back again." The spirit took the boy with him, and one two, he drew him down under the sea to his palace. There he had with him other children as well, whom he had carried off long before: from the waist downwards they had been turned to stone. He put the boy there to wait upon the others and told him what he had to do. He told him he must be careful not to open a cupboard which stood there in the corner; above all he must not touch the books there; if he did, he would suffer grievous trouble.

'The boy was lively and clever and he said: "Why should I not try to read the books and see what is written in them? Then I too might learn and have my eyes opened." So he began to read. The books were of magic and Woe-is-me had told him not to read them to prevent him learning this art. But the boy was clever and read the books and learned magic arts, and not only what Woe-is-me knew but yet one thing more. He learned to know another man's thoughts.

'The two years passed. The father came to Alortho Pouri and cried aloud. Woe-is-me came out from the sea and caught hold of him saying: "Come, and you shall see your son." They went down into the palace. Woe-is-me called for the boy: Oh what delight; kisses and caresses! But the boy who had learned to know what another man was thinking understood what Woe-is-me had in his mind to do. So he said to his father: "Father, that one there is not willing to let you have me. He will turn me into a horse with all the other boys whom he has brought together and locked up here. He will say to you that you may have me if you can recognize me. Now you must know that I will be right in the front and be the first horse to arrive. When he asks you which of them is your son, then you will be able to point to me."

'Presently Woe-is-me came and said to the father: "Eh? Isn't it time for you to go away?" The father said: "I will go, but I must have my son to take him with me." "If you know which is your son and can pick him out from the rest when I show them to you all together, then I will let you have him.' So said Woe-is-me.

'Then he took the father and brought him into a big field. Presently there came into the field some hundred young horses. Woe-is-me then said: "All these horses are boys; I enchanted them and turned them into horses. Which of them is your son?" The old man went round and looked at all the horses; he pretended to be searching, and presently he pointed at the horse who was in front of the others and said: "This one is my son," and so in truth he was. Since the father had recognized him Woe-is-me could do nothing. He brought them up out of the sea and let them go, and off they went.

'As they were on the road to the village they saw a shepherd going in front of them. The boy said to his father: "Father, I have learned the magic art and I will now turn into a horse for you to sell me to the shepherd and we will have ten pounds from him. Then I will leave him and turn back into a man again and so we shall have the money." On this they agreed, and the boy turned into a horse. The old man led him by the halter. The shepherd said: "I say, friend, will you sell me your horse?" "Yes, gladly I will sell him: if you give me ten pounds, he is yours." The shepherd paid the ten pounds and went off with the horse. The father followed them secretly to see what would happen. The boy, tied and led by the shepherd, began to rub himself against his hands and to lick them. The shepherd said: "Now he knows me, and I will let him loose a little." Scarcely had he loosed him when the horse dropped behind and turned into a boy again and went to his father, saying: "Forward; time to be off." And thus they went on. The shepherd ran back to look; he searched but to no purpose.

'Then Woe-is-me came intending to find the boy and take him back again; he had changed his mind and was sorry he had let him go. As soon as the shepherd asked him if he had seen a horse, Woe-is-me understood that this horse was the boy and that he had learnt the art of magic.

'At once Woe-is-me turned into a hawk and flew off to find the boy. When the boy saw him coming he turned into an eagle and swooped down on Woe-is-me. Woe-is-me turned into some bigger bird and tried to devour the eagle. The boy turned into two grains of corn: one fell into the lap of the princess as she sat there in the garden; the other fell to the ground. Woe-is me at once turned into a dove and perched on the princess's lap and swallowed the grain that was there. As the dove was hopping down to eat the other grain, the one that had the boy in it, the boy turned into a hawk, caught the dove in his talons, and tore it all to pieces. This was the death of Woe-is-me. The boy was delivered; so too were all of them set free from his enchantments and lived happily.'

'Well, do you like my story?' said the mirror. 'Thank you,

my dear little mirror,' said Johnnie, 'it was a fine story.' When the mirror began to talk, the princess left her place and came near and looked: once at the mirror and once at Johnnie. How this marvel had happened she could not understand. As she looked at Johnnie and saw how handsome he was she began to like him and to find it a pity that he should be put to death. Yet she did not want it to appear that he pleased her so well. She acted as though she could not restrain her curiosity about the mirror, and looking in the mirror she could keep watch on Johnnie. When the story came to an end she said: 'But how is it that the mirror talks?' Johnnie rose and went up to her and said: 'I have conquered you, my princess.' She was loath to admit this, and he had scarcely spoken when she changed her mind and again shut her mouth and sat down where she was with not a word said. Johnnie said: 'I have conquered you for you have spoken a word and I have a witness too.' He went and opened the mirror and brought out the Son of the Sea, saying: 'This is he who has conquered you for it was he inside the mirror speaking. He shall be your husband.' And now what could the princess do? She was forced to accept. Together they went out of her room and went off to the king. Johnnie made the marriage of this couple also and with the man he left an apple. Then he went off, he and the horse. His only companion now was the horse, and with him he talked and the horse told him what he must do.

They went on and on, and one morning they stood at the very edge of the world. Away beyond the boundary of the world the horse saw something shining in the sunshine. He said to Johnnie: 'Here I think, are the Golden Boughs; what do you say? Shall we go there?' 'Let us go,' said Johnnie.

They passed right beyond the world and as they went forward they saw they were approaching a whole forest of Golden Boughs. In the midst was a tower with a garden, and all round it were trees, all with Golden Boughs: it was a real paradise. Outside the door of the tower an old woman was sitting. When she saw Johnnie she was astonished and said: 'How have you come here?' Johnnie said: 'I have come to find the Golden Boughs, that I may win the Fair One of the World. Do you know where she is?' 'She is here,' said the old woman. 'Wait for me to tell her that you have come.' She went and told the Fair

One and then brought Johnnie into the tower. Johnnie could never have his fill of gazing at her. Then said the Fair One of the World: 'Now that you have shown yourself worthy to come here and have succeeded in finding me, you shall be my husband.'

Then they lived there together, and she fell in love with him and to give him pleasure became his wife even as women do: she ceased to be a spirit of the air. She transported the garden and the Golden Boughs and the tower all of them near to where men dwell in this world. Johnnie was mad with love of her; he could not stay a moment away from her. She used to tell him to go out of the tower and go hunting, lest his health should fail, always shut up in the tower. He must go and mix with other men now that they were back again in the world. His answer was that he could not endure a moment without seeing her. 'Is that all?' said the girl. 'Stay a moment and I will give you my picture and that you can have with you wherever you go.' She gave him her picture and he put it into his bosom and went off hunting. He went hunting all over the mountain going up and coming down. Then he became tired and thirsty. He came to a spring and stooped down to drink; then he sat down to rest. When he was stooping to drink the picture fell out without his noticing it. He rose up and went back to the palace and to his wife.

In the evening the king's servants went to water the horses at the spring. The horses would not drink; they took fright and were off. The servants went back to the palace and the king asked them if they had watered the horses. They told him what had happened. The king took the horses and himself led them to the spring. He stooped down to see what was in the water to prevent them from drinking. So he found the picture. He had hardly seen it when he fell madly in love. Then the king sent out a crier: 'Whoever could be found to tell him who the girl was and where he could find her, to that man he would give a half of his kingdom. An old woman sent out by the Fair One of the World went down to the grocer's to do her shopping. She heard the crier and went to the king and said: 'Be at rest; I will bring her to you. Only your servants must come with me to carry her off because she will be unwilling and they must help me and be at my orders.' The servants went with the old woman and she hid them in the tower.

Next day Johnnie went off hunting. When he came back tired he had a meal and lay down to sleep. His wife was sitting by him at her embroidery and the old woman said to her: 'Come and do your embroidery downstairs, my lady; you may wake him up.' She went down and the old woman went off and called the king's servants. They killed the horse to prevent him from telling Johnnie; then they took and bound the Fair One. The old woman went upstairs and took Johnnie's sword; she went to him as he slept and with a single stroke she killed him. The old woman called for the king's servants and they cut the boy into three pieces and the horse too into three pieces. They dug a deep hole and threw the pieces into it, and with them the shoes and the cap: they buried them all together. The sword they threw into the sea. They carried off the Fair One and locked up the tower; with the old woman they went off to the king's palace. The king was full of joy. To the old woman he gave a half of his kingdom. The Fair One he placed in a chamber all of gold with servants and handmaids to attend upon her. Every morning he went and looked at her. She would neither look at him nor listen to him; all the time she sat crying.

Now we must leave the princess and tell of Johnnie's three brothers. They were living in their kingdoms with their wives all in great good fortune. One morning the Son of the Sun woke up and went to look at the apple which Johnnie had left with him in order to see how his brother was. He saw the apple all withered and its leafage yellow and dry. He went to his wife and said: 'My brother Johnnie is in some evil plight; I must go and find him.' He mounted his horse and went off and joined the two other brothers. They went on and on asking if anyone could tell them where Johnnie was. The Son of the Sun said: 'Stay; we must ask my father.' So they asked the Sun and he said: 'You must go to such and such a place and you will find the tower. Then dig and you will find him.' They dug and found Johnnie and the horse. They brought the pieces of the bodies together, but they had none of the Water of Life.

Again they questioned the Sun and he said: 'All day I make my circle, yet that Water have I seen nowhere. Go and ask the Moon; it may be that he has seen it at night.' The Son of the Moon went and asked the Moon. The Moon said: 'I know where it is. It is behind yonder mountain, in the place where it opens and closes again. Tie a little vessel to a dove's tail and let it loose. The dove will pass through and dip the bottle into the Water and be in time to come out before the mountain shuts again.' With the vessel tied to its tail the dove passed through the mountain and brought them the Water of Life. They took it and sprinkled it over Johnnie and over the horse, and they came to life again. What joy! What embracings and kissings! Then said Johnnie: 'I thank you, my brothers, for delivering me. Now I want to find my sword to slay all these people who have carried away my wife and brought me to death.'

Then the three went off and the Son of the Sun asked his father. The Sun said: 'I can't see it; I don't know where it is.' The Son of the Moon asked his father and the Moon replied: 'I have not seen it.' The Son of the Sea asked and the Sea answered her son: 'I have the sword.' The Son of the Sea dived down into the embraces of his mother; he searched and found the sword and gave it to Johnnie. Then Johnnie thanked his brothers and again they kissed one another. The brothers went off to their kingdoms and their wives.

Johnnie mounted his horse and leaning forward to caress him he said: 'Well, my good horse, now we must go and set free our lady.' So he said, and the horse darted forward and in two moments was standing outside the king's palace. Scarcely had the soldiers seen Johnnie than they trembled: how could he be alive again? They had buried him; they had seen him dead. They went to bar the door against his entry, but Johnnie drew his sword, hewing this way and that, and he killed them all. He went into the palace and killed the king; he found the old woman and cut her all into little pieces. He went to the room where his wife was and took her. They mounted the horse and went to their tower. The Fair One of the World by her magic arts removed the tower and the Golden Boughs and carried it far away from the world back to the place where it had been before. The two of them, Johnnie and his wife, lived in joy and love and it may be they are still alive to this day.

44

The destined Girl wins her Place as the Prince's Bride

AARNE–THOMPSON TYPE 870A

THERE was a girl of whom it was foretold that she should marry a prince.[1] In the Chian version translated below the girl quotes the prophecy: 'Thus said the witch, thus said the bird; if it be God's will, so shall it be.' The king, however, arranged a marriage between his son and a lady of high position: but the lady was no longer a maid. To get out of her difficulty the bride persuaded the destined girl to take her place on the wedding night. The prince gave her gifts and tokens, and she had a child by him; by the tokens the prince recognized the child and the justice of the mother's claims. Faced by the problem which of the two girls he would take as his wife, the prince at his wedding banquet produced two cups: one was of gold but the bottom was broken out; the other of lesser value, of clay or of silver, but whole. The company agreed that the unbroken cup was the better; so the prince dismissed the high lady and married the girl of the prophecy. Considering the princess's earlier lapse the episode of the two cups is clearly a true part of the story, yet it appears only in the versions from Chios and Kos. No. 55, *The fated Bridegroom*, is a kind of opposite number to this story, but the situation is handled quite differently.

The tale enforces the moral that if only it be the will of God, anything, however unlikely, may come to pass: nothing could stand in the way of the girl's destiny. The tale has been studied in *Forty-five Stories*, No. 29. The tone is perhaps rather Islamic, but besides these seven Greek versions it is found also in Sicily in Pitrè's collection, though with some differences in detail.[2]

We can see how it was that the prince fell in love with Marouditsa as she sat weaving, if we remember that in island cottages the loom stands close to a window for a good light, and a young man standing outside sees the girl inside at her work. This is the subject of a widely spread popular couplet, a *matináda*; I have heard it in Crete.

[1] The same prophecy is at the beginning of No. 32, *The Prince in a Swoon.*

[2] Pitrè, *Fiabe . . . siciliani*, i. 32.

Alas, alas, I have gone mad
for the love of a Roman maid;
And I saw her but for a moment
by the window as I strayed.

Also a well-known ballad begins:

The comb was white as ivory,
the loom with gold was red;
A girl shaped like an angel
sat there and plied the thread.

Of this story we have eight versions:

1, 2. PONTOS: from Ordoú in Akoglou, *Laographiká Kotyóron*, p. 406; and from Oinoi in *Pontiakí Estía*, ii, part 16, p. 905.
3. KOS: *Forty-five Stories*, p. 299.
4. RHODES IN MIKH.-NOUÁROS: *Πῶς νὰ γνωρίζουμε τὴ Δωδεκάνησο*, p. 156.
5. CHIOS: Pernot, *Études de linguistique*, iii. 196, translated.
6. NAXOS: *N.A.* ii. 25.
7. THRACE: *Thrakiká*, xvii. 142.
8. ZÁKYNTHOS: *Laographía*, x. 444.

NO. 44. THE DESTINED GIRL WINS HER PLACE AS THE PRINCE'S BRIDE[1]

There was once a king with a son; also he had a serving girl called Marouditsa. The prince fell in love with Marouditsa. As she sat at the loom she would deck her head with flowers, and the prince would greet her:

'Good evening, Marouditsa, with leaves all garlanded;
It makes me love you madly, the parsley on your head.'

Then Marouditsa would answer: 'Good evening, my royal lord prince. Thus said the witch; thus said the bird; if it be God's will, so shall it be.' And thus it befell every morning and every evening.

'Good evening, Marouditsa, with leaves all garlanded;
It makes me love you madly, the parsley on your head.'

'Good evening, my royal lord. Thus said the witch; thus said the bird; if it be God's will, so shall it be.' Well: need I tell

[1] From Pernot, *Études de linguistique*, iii. 196.

you? In one word, thus they fared with one another; they were in love.

After a time the king understood that his son had fallen in love with the servant, and so he went off and brought a girl to marry him to: yes, he brought a girl to be his son's wife. 'I have brought a girl for you to marry, my son.' Then the youth—what else could he do?—said: 'Whatever you say, father; I am in your hands.' Then came the servants, a whole army of them, to bring everything for the wedding: to sweep and all. Marouditsa started ironing and sweeping and doing all the rest of the work like a servant: but ah! how she suffered! For the two were in love with one another. So the gifts of betrothal were brought and everything else for the wedding. The poor serving girl went on sweeping and ironing and doing all as she was bidden.

Then came the time for setting on the crowns of marriage. The bride was in a difficulty and she went to Marouditsa and said: 'Marouditsa, Marouditsa,' said she, 'I have something to say to you. I want you to do me a favour. On the evening of my wedding day I will take all the royal gifts which the king has given me, and I will give them all to you, and when I am to sleep with the prince, then you shall come instead and the gifts shall be yours to have what you will of them.' The poor servant girl was delighted and said: 'Well, give me the presents he has given you and then I will come.' So the bride gave the presents to Marouditsa. Now you know that Turkish women wear veils, so the prince did not know clearly what woman it was. It was Marouditsa who came to him. Now what do you think happened? I don't have to explain it all to you clearly. Marouditsa then rose up and went away and the bride came and lay down by the bridegroom.

It was a devilish business, our enemy at work, but Marouditsa became with child by the prince and everyone heard of it: everyone heard that Marouditsa was with child. 'But how has it come about that such a thing should befall a girl who never comes outside the palace?' The king too heard of it, and the prince went to visit Marouditsa to see if it were really true.

> *'Good evening, Marouditsa, with leaves all garlanded,*
> *It makes me love you madly, the parsley on your head.'*

'Good evening, my royal lord. Thus said the witch; thus said the bird; if it be God's will, so shall it be.' And so the matter went on and on and Marouditsa had a child, a son. As soon as he was born Marouditsa took the gifts she had had from the prince and decked the child with them.

The prince said: 'I must go and find Marouditsa.' When he came and saw the child, he saw that he had on him the royal gifts which he had given to his wife. So he went home and said to his wife: 'This child now born is wearing the presents I gave you; how has this come about?' Also to Marouditsa he said: 'Will you not tell me? What about these gifts? Where did you get them to adorn your child with them?' Marouditsa said: 'The child is yours and the presents are those very ones you gave me. Thus said the witch; thus said the bird; it was God's will and it has so come to pass.' So said Marouditsa to the prince.

The prince then had to deal with his royal wife, the princess whom he had married. He arranged a banquet and had two drinking-vessels set out: one was of gold, but—pardon my plain speaking—it had no bottom; the other was of silver and all complete and whole. He set the banquet and invited the royal personages, his father-in-law and all of them. The drinking-vessels he set on the table. When all had eaten and the feast was at its end, he said to the king; to his father-in-law: 'Here you have this golden cup, but why should you pay so high a price for it? It has no bottom to it. Choose which of the two cups you will have.' And the king said: 'I will have the silver cup complete with all its parts, and in it pour wine for my drinking. The gold cup for all its high price I do not want; it is no good to me.' 'And that is what the girl is like, the one you gave me for my wife. She was just like this cup, and so you can have your daughter and the cup with her and be off: good-bye.' So the king took the royal bride and went off and the prince took Marouditsa and they lived as man and wife.

And now I have no more to say than that may we meet again and may the good God grant you to lie down happily for the night, and meet us again here, and we have joy and jollity and much happy entertainment.

45

The three Measures of Salt

THIS story is a novel on a small scale. The full beginning is of two kings who had one of them three or nine sons and the other three or nine daughters. The two kings gibed at one another about the slowness of their children to marry.[1] Then one daughter—in the Naxian version translated she is not the youngest but the eldest—says she will show herself a match for the eldest son of the rival king, and not only that but she will rub on his head three measures of salt and he know nothing about it. From this point the versions from Naxos and Skyros follow the same lines. The son and the daughter married, and when the bride would not tell her husband what she meant by the three measures of salt, he was so angry that he left her, undertaking three journeys in succession: in the Naxian version to Salonika, to Aigina, and to Venice. At each of these places his wife contrived to arrive before him and presented herself to him in disguise; thus she had by him without his knowing it three children. Still she refused to tell him the meaning of the salt, and in his annoyance he thought of taking another wife. Then she brought her three children before him and with them the tokens which showed that he was their father, and told him that these three tricks she had played upon him so successfully were the three measures of salt.

The versions from Smyrna and from Mitylene are very like these, except that the Smyrna version begins with a poor girl destined to marry a prince and a prophetic beggar-man foretells not only her wedding but the three measures of salt.

For the woman's remark in the version translated that 'likenesses there are everywhere', see the note to No. 60 on the divine unity and the multiplicity of created things.

The other two versions, from Crete and Thrace, begin not with a general prophecy, but with a meeting with the Three Fates at the time when the girl is born. In the Cretan version the father and mother find themselves benighted and spend the night in the house of the Fates, where, as in a Thracian version of No. 79, *The Search for Luck*, they find Luck distributing to the newly born whatever she happens to have at the moment.[2] A poor woman has a child: to her she gives from her hands a skein of gold thread; a princess is born,

[1] The same bickering of the fathers is in No. 47*b*. [2] *Thrakiká*, xvii. 150.

but the Fate had then in her hands nothing but ashes. The child of the wanderers is to be born at the monastery as the parents have vowed; but she will wear out three shifts in harlotry. Knowing this doom the father had her locked up in a tower like the jealously loved daughter in No. 30. Of course she escaped and fell in love with the prince by whom she had three children. These the prince in due time recognized by the tokens he had given to their mother whom he then married. The mother was recognized by the lullabies she was singing to her baby; the same incident occurs in a different story from Kos, No. 36, in *Forty-five Stories*. Of the three measures of salt this version makes no express mention.

Of this story we have six versions:

1. SMYRNA: Legrand, *Recueil de contes pop. grecs*, p. 263.
2. MITYLENE: *Folklore*, xi. 336.
3. NAXOS: *N.A.* ii. 40, translated.
4. SKYROS: Pérdika, *Skyros*, ii. 212.
5. CRETE: *Myson*, vii. 151.
6. THRACE: *Arkheíon Thrakikoú Laogr.* viii. 191.

NO. 45. THE THREE MEASURES OF SALT[1]

There was once a king with nine sons; he was faced by another king with nine daughters: in those days everyone was a king. Every morning each king used to go out to his frontier to greet the other. Once as they met at the frontier and greeted one another the king with the nine daughters said to the other: 'Good day, my lord king, you with your nine boys, and may you never get a wife for any of them!' When the other heard this he was smitten to the heart, and sat in a corner of his palace deep in thought. One of his sons came up: 'What is the matter, father, that you are so sorrowful?' 'Nothing, my son.' The next brother asked him: 'Nothing, my son; I have a headache.' The third one came: 'But why won't you tell us what is the matter?' The king said not a word. Not to make too long a story, they all asked him and to none of them would he say what was the matter. The boys left him. Midday came and the king had no appetite to eat. God brought the day to its evening; then the dawn; but the king was still wrapt in thought. The eldest son came to him again: 'But, father, this cannot be endured; a day and a night you are here fasting and sorrowful,

[1] Text from Naxos, printed in *N.A.* ii. 40.

and yet you won't tell us what is the matter.' He said: 'But what can I say, my son?' He told him what had happened between him and the other king: 'When he saw me yesterday morning he said to me: "Good day, king, with your nine sons and may you never get a wife for any of them!" ' 'And is it this that has filled you with such great bitterness, father? Tomorrow when you meet, you must say to him: "Good morning, my lord king, with your nine daughters, and may you never get a husband for any of them." ' Next day very early the king went out to his frontier and when he saw the other king he said: 'Good day, my lord king, with your nine daughters, and may you never get a husband for any of them.' When the other king heard this, how vexed he was! He too went and sat in a corner of his palace all full of trouble.

One of his daughters came and said: 'What is the matter, father?' 'Nothing, my daughter.' Then the next daughter asked him: 'Nothing at all but a headache.' Then came the third. The king said: 'I told you there is nothing the matter.' Thus not to make a long story, all the nine came and asked him and he would tell none of them. Then his daughters left him. Midday came, but he would not eat. God brought the day to its evening; then the dawn; still he was wrapt in care. Then at last his daughters said: 'But this cannot be endured: for him to sit all by himself a day and a night; to put not even a crumb of church bread in his mouth, and to refuse to breathe a word of what is the matter, but just to put us off with stories!' The eldest went again to her father: 'Dear father, why please won't you tell us what is the matter?' 'If you want to know, my daughter, the king over the way said to me: "Good day, my lord king, with your nine daughters and a husband for none of them may you never have!" ' She was a clever girl and said: 'Are you grieved for that, father? Tomorrow you must answer him and say: "Since I have no husband for my girls, why, give me one of your sons: my eldest daughter can very easily rub three measures of salt on his face and he be none the wiser." ' As the girl had told him, so he did.

Next day when they greeted one another very early, he said to the other king: 'Since I have no husband for any of my girls, give me one of your sons; my eldest daughter is a match for him; very easily can she rub three measures of salt on his face and he be none the wiser.' So they made the match and married the eldest son with the eldest daughter. When they lay down in bed the first evening the prince said to his newly wed princess: 'You have managed it very well, you clever girl, and now we are married; but tell me what are these three measures of salt which you would rub on my head and I be none the wiser?' She said: 'I won't tell you.' 'Tell me or I will go away and leave you.' 'Go then; only let me know where you are going so that I can send you a letter sometimes.' 'I am going to Salonika.' So the youth made all ready. She too went off in a ship and reached that same place before him.

By the shore she met an old woman who said to her: 'You must be newly come here. If you like, I have a house I can let you have near the sea, a house for a king's daughter.' The girl went up into the house and then she said to the old woman: 'A prince will be coming here in a day or two and you must bring him here.' 'At your orders, my lady,' said the old woman. Next day the prince arrived. The old woman went down to the shore and said to him: 'I can bring you to a house fit for a prince; you will also have there a girl to kiss.' He went up into the house and saw the princess. 'Good day, and you are very much like my wife: what am I to think of it?' 'Well, well, my good Christian': says she: 'Man to man and thing to thing, likenesses there are everywhere.' But of course the woman was the wife herself. All day they talked and in the evening they lay down together. She became with child and had a boy baby: when he was born the room was full of light, for on his brow was the star of morning. Within the year the prince wanted to go away, and she said: 'And won't you leave some present for your child?' Then he took out his gold watch and hung it on the baby, and to the old woman he gave a present of a thousand gold pieces. When he had gone, his wife embarked in a ship and came to her country before him. The boy she handed over to a nurse and he was brought up in a golden room below the earth which she had constructed in her father's palace. She warned all the maidservants that they must say nothing to the prince when he came back about her being away; only that she had had a cold and been ill all the year. Next day the prince arrived; he asked how his wife was. They said: 'As I could wish your ill-wishers were, and this all because of your absence.'

Then he came to find her and they kissed one another, and he said: 'I am told that you have been ill because of our separation, but it was all your fault because you would not tell me about those three measures of salt which you said you would rub on me and I be none the wiser. Now tell me,' said he. 'No, I won't tell you.' 'Obstinate are you? Well, so am I. Either you will tell me or I shall go away and leave you.' 'Go then; only tell me where you will be that I may be able some time to send you a letter.' 'In Aigina,' said he.

When he went off, she too went by another way and took ship and came to Aigina before him. There on the shore she found the same old woman—it was really her Fate—and again she went with her to a house on the shore. Next day the prince also arrived and the old woman took him to the same house and left him there and then went off. As soon as the prince saw the woman in the house he ran and kissed her. She said: 'And what makes you so passionate just from seeing me?' 'I have a wife just like you and she came to my mind.' 'Man to man and thing to thing, likenesses there are everywhere.' All day they were there talking and in the evening they lay down together and so every evening, until she was with child and had a boy baby; when he was born the room was full of light for on his brow was the shining moon. Before a year was over he gave the boy his gold walking-stick for a remembrance: he kissed him; gave the old woman another thousand gold pieces as a present and went away. Thus he went off and his wife after him. She came first to her house and handed over this second child to the same nurse and gave the servants a present not to tell that she had been away; in the palace she again played the part of the sorrowful woman. When her husband came next day, he questioned the servants about his wife, and they told him that all the year she had shut herself up in sorrow. The servants went back again and the prince came to his wife and said: 'Whatever you may have suffered, it is all the fault of your ladyship. But now do tell me what are those three measures of salt you would rub on my face and I be none the wiser: if you won't, I shall be off again.' 'And a good journey to you; only tell me where you are going and I shall know if at any time I want to send you any news.' 'I'm going to Venice.'

Again he took ship and she followed, arriving before him.

The same old woman appeared and took her to a great big palace on the shore. In two or three days the prince arrived. The old woman said to him: 'You are welcome, prince. Pray be so good as to come to my house and stay there as long as you please, because I have a girl there for you.' 'Wonderful,' said he. Then he went and again he saw the woman: he said: 'Oh, how like you are to my wife!' 'Man to man and thing to thing, likenesses there are everywhere.' Not to make a long story, she became with child and bore a daughter; the room was full of light for on her forehead was the shining of the sun. They christened the child and called her Alexandra. Before the year was out the prince wanted to go away and the princess said to him: 'Won't you at least make the baby some present for her to remember you?' Says he: 'Of course. Even without you telling me I had been thinking of it.' He went to the shops and bought a string of precious stones of all sorts, a thing beyond price—when you say from Venice, you can imagine what it was—and he hung it on the baby's neck; also he bought a dress all of gold, and he took off his ring and gave it to her. Then he kissed the baby and gave the old woman a thousand gold pieces as a present and went off. The princess starting after him arrived at her house before him; she handed the child over to the nurse with money for her trouble and made a present to the women servants not to tell of her. Again she shut herself up in the palace pretending to be full of grief. In two or three days her husband came and asked the servants: 'How is my wife?' said he. 'As I would wish your ill-wishers were, and all for your absence.' He went and found her in a sad state. He said: 'And whom can you blame? You have asked for what has happened to you. Why wouldn't you tell me what are those three measures of salt which you would smear over my face and I be none the wiser? But tell me now.' 'I won't tell you.' 'This cannot be endured. Tell me or I will leave you and take another wife.' 'Well, go and marry again and I will come and give you my blessing.' Then he made up a match with another princess near-by and fixed say next Sunday for the wedding.

All the world went to give them their blessing and the instruments of music were playing. Then his first wife dressed herself in her best and fitted out her three children finely; to the eldest she gave the watch, to the second the walking-stick, and the youngest she adorned with the string of jewels and the ring. The nurse brought them and they all went to join in the blessings at the marriage service. All the women danced in the hall and their eyes were upon the children and the mother because all the room was bright as lightning from the morning star and the sun and the moon, all on the children's foreheads. All said: 'Joy and delight to the mother who bore them!' The prince too left the girl whom he was going to marry and stared at the children; the young bride was full of jealousy. Then the two boys were heard talking to their sister, who was not yet I suppose a year old and was being carried by the nurse, the boys being in front of her: 'Little lady, little lady,' said the boys, 'little Alexandra, listen to the watch, tick tick tick: mother in the room all decked with gold.' When the prince heard this he could endure no longer and right in the middle of the marriage service he left his new bride and ran up to the children. He looked at them and saw the string of jewels and the watch and the ring, and so he recognized them.

His former wife was standing by and he asked whose children these were. 'Yours and mine; one of them we had at Salonika, the second at Aigina, and the youngest at Venice. The woman whom you met in all those three places, each of them was I, and when I left the place I always got ahead of you. And to think that you should not know your own children! These were the three measures of salt which I was to smear on your face and you be none the wiser.' He lifted up the children and in his delight kissed them all. He took them to his former house and their mother too with them. And so the new bride was left there with the bath grown cold and she half-married.

46

The Girl who went to War

AARNE–THOMPSON TYPE 514

Of this story there are two variants from Pontos; one from Ordoú, and the other, not so well told, from Argyrópolis.[1] In general outline the story is that there was a father with three daughters; the king summoned him to join the army and each of the three daughters volunteered to go in his place. The eldest and the second daughter failed in the tests for bravery imposed on them by their father, but the youngest showed herself capable of playing the warrior and dressed as a youth she went off to the war, helped always by her faithful horse who possessed, as in so many stories, the gift of speech. In the war the girl acquitted herself so manfully that the king and queen chose her as the husband for their daughter. The marriage was naturally a failure and when the supposed bridegroom set a sword between himself and his bride as they lay together, the king and still more the queen decided to get rid of him. This they tried to do in the usual way, by sending her off on quests supposed to be impossible and fatal. In the version from Ordoú here translated the girl is sent first to fetch an Apple of Paradise; then to collect taxes from a recalcitrant village, and thirdly to destroy a savage mare. Then in a last attempt to get rid of her she is sent to fetch fire from the one-eyed giants. She fought the giants, and when they were defeated they cursed her: 'If you are a boy you shall be turned into a girl; if you are a girl you shall be turned into a boy.' The curse worked; the heroine became a boy and her marriage was happily concluded.

For what may lie behind the fire to be fetched from the one-eyed giants I have a pointer in a version of *The Son of the Hunter*, No. 42 above, recently recorded by my friend Major G. C. Campbell from the Arabs in Acre. The hero is sent to fetch the Water of Life and a Brand of the Flame which can never be quenched. As the Water of Life or of Immortality is a universal panacea, so it may be that the Fire of Hell is the most deadly of all possible weapons of offence. This can be no more than a suggestion.

Of this story I find only one variant in Greece and even this has

[1] From Ordoú in *Khroniká tou Pontou*, i. (1943), pp. 13, 44, here translated. From Argyrópolis in *Arkheíon Pontou*, vii. 93. See also Aarne–Thompson's Type 514.

some important differences. It is from Euboia.[1] There was a man skilled in playing the zither, but unfortunately he offended first one fairy, Neraïda, and then another by not playing to their dancing, and we may infer still worse by not responding to their embraces. The second fairy said she would either kill him or curse him. He chose the curse, and it was: *If you are a man you shall become a woman and if you are a woman you shall become a man.* The man broke his zither, and though now a woman went off as a warrior to a foreign land. He rescued first one princess and then another, but neither of them could he marry because he was now, not a man, but a woman. The king, the father of the second princess, determined to get rid of him and so, like the brave heroine in the Pontic stories, he was sent off to meet his death on various quests, one after the other: first to fetch a golden treasure; then to kill a monster. In both of these he was successful. The third quest was to get a magic apple from a gigantic negro. As he was conquered the negro cursed the hero: *If you are a man be a woman; if a woman, then become a man.* Which of course brings about the happy ending.

The story from Euboia, though with a fresh opening and the use of the curse to fit a hero who begins as a man, is clearly the same as the Pontic stories, and it is the only variant I can find in Greek lands. But outside Greece there are variants at each end of the Hellenic area: in Albania and in the Caucasus, and having the same opening they are really closer to the Pontic stories. The Albanian story runs:[2] A man asked his two elder daughters to take his place in the army. They could not for they were both married. The third daughter went off as a soldier and such were her acts of prowess that she was compelled to marry the king's daughter; with the usual results. She was sent out on quests. First she overcame and brought back a man-devouring Lamia; next as in the Pontic stories she brought a savage mare, and lastly she collected tribute, not from reluctant villagers but from a company of serpents. The serpents cursed her: *If you are a boy become a girl; if a girl become a boy.* So the marriage was turned into a success.

The very close parallel from the Caucasus is recorded by Dirr as a Kabardian story.[3] A man had three daughters and wanted to test their courage. The two elder sisters broke down under his test, but the youngest approved herself as a warrior. She rode off and came

[1] In Hahn, i. 307, No. 58. The same story is in Kretschmer, *Neugr. Märchen*, p. 240, but there said to be from the Cyclades. See also BP., ii. 58.

[2] Dozon, *Contes albanais*, No. 4. The girl who lives like a man is a well known and curious feature of Albanian life.

[3] From A. Dirr, *Kaukasische Märchen*, p. 110, No. 25: *Die tapfere Tochter*. The same story is in Lucy Menzies, *Caucasian Folktales*, p. 117, No. 23.

to a land where there was a girl to be saved from a snake that she might be made the bride of a son of the Khan. The heroine is sent on the usual quests to get rid of her, the last being that she must fetch the milk of a buffalo which lived in the sea. This she did, but incurred the curse of the buffalo: *He who drives me from the sea, if he be a man shall become a woman, and if he be a woman shall become a man.* And this of course the heroine does. In the somewhat obscure and, to me, chaotic ending the son of the Khan is in some way drowned in the milk, but the girl saved from the snake swims through it, of course to be the bride of the heroine, now by the buffalo's curse become a man.

A story from Epeiros can hardly be said to be a variant, as it contains no more than the opening incident of the third daughter volunteering for the war.[1] In a story, from Thrace, otherwise quite different, we have the incident of a girl disguised as a boy getting out of the difficulty of a marriage by a curse which brings about her change from a girl to a boy, and there is a very similar story in Turkish.[2] An Italian story has hardly more than the third daughter going to the war and the prince being sure that she is a girl and not a boy; in the end he marries her.[3]

An Albanian story twice recorded by Mrs. Hasluck has the sex-changing curse. There was a king who much wanted a son and a daughter was born to him. To save the girl's life the angry and disappointed king was induced to believe that she was really a boy. The girl helped by her horse of the Jinn breed contrived to get cursed by the Jinn: '*If you are a boy become a girl, and if you are a girl become a boy*'. So she did become a boy and so saved her life.

NO. 46. THE GIRL WHO WENT TO WAR[1]

In the early ages and in the years of silver there was an old man with three daughters. The daughters grew up, with no prospects before them.

At that time a war broke out with the neighbouring kingdom and the king mustered his army and went off to fight. The girls said to their father: 'It was not our fortune that we should marry. We will go to the war to fight for our country.' Their

[1] *Z.A.* i. 195, No. 3.

[2] *Arkheion Thrakikoú Laogr.* ix. 201; the Turkish story in Kent, p. 136.

[3] *Ueber italienische Märchen*, in *Festgabe für Hermann Suchier*, p. 336.

[4] Pontic text from Ordoú, printed with the title *The youngest Child* in *Khroniká tou Pontou*, i. 13.

father was not willing to let them go.' 'Shall you girls go to the war?' said he; 'This is no work for you.'

The eldest daughter insisted: indeed she wanted very much to go to the war. Her father then bade her farewell, and when she had changed her dress, she took a sword and went off to a cross-road. There was there a spring with beautiful cold water. Whoever went away out of the village would pass by this cross-road. The old man went and waited by the spring. Presently his eldest daughter passed by. She was wearing boys' clothes and carried weapons. The father called upon her to stop. He changed his voice so as not to be recognized and questioned her. 'Where are you going, my lad?' 'I am going to the war,' said she, changing her voice and making it like a boy's. 'You, my girl, have no business there. Come, turn back quickly and go to your nice little house. Do you think I did not know you were a girl?' said the father to her. He threatened her once and again with his sword, and the girl rose up and turned to go home. Presently the father himself came home and questioned her. 'Why have you come back?' She told him her story. 'Yes, my girl,' said her father. 'Is this the way you wanted to go and fight for your country? You would have been knocked to pieces. Sit quietly at home. You have no business there.'

Next day his second daughter rose up and went off. Her father did the same thing to her and she too turned back home.

Finally his youngest daughter rose up and went off. This girl when she was thirteen years old had found down by the sea a young colt and had taken him and brought him home. There all by herself she had groomed him and all by herself had given him fodder and water. The colt had grown big, but the sun had never been allowed to shine on him; she used to bring him his fodder and his water all inside the stable. He had become a fine big horse; from his nostrils he breathed fire. The young horse said to the girl: 'He who frightened your sisters and made them turn back home was your father. You be careful; he will do the same to you. But you mustn't be frightened. Draw my saddle girths tightly, and whatever he says to you and however much he threatens you, you must not give way. Also he will have a sword and draw it to hew at us. We will flee away. If we cannot avoid it, we too will hit out at him and be off.'

Then the girl put on boys' clothes and armed herself fully and mounted on the horse: 'In the name of the Lord,' said she, and rode off on him. This girl, the youngest of his daughters, the father loved far more than the others: all the world could be set on one side and on the other this youngest and most beloved daughter. He said good-bye to her and at once arrayed himself like a fine young warrior; he armed himself from head to foot and waited for her at the cross-road close to the spring of water. When his daughter came he said: 'Good day, my good girl; whence and whither?' he asked her. 'And how do you know that I am a girl?' said she. 'Your clothes,' said he, 'are a boy's and you are riding your horse very sturdily, but from your face I can see that you are a girl. Come, tell me, where have you come from?' 'I am going to the war. I am going off to fight for my country,' said she. Then her father said to her: 'You turn and go home quickly. What can you do there at the war, you who are a girl? How can you live night and day with young men? This is not work for girls. Come; go back home at once,' said he, and he drew his sword to frighten her. Then the girl said: 'All this is no good with me. Come if you will and let us fight and see which of the two of us is the finer warrior.' Then at once she drew her sword and made to attack him. The horse pushed him and threw him to the ground, but without trampling on him. Then the man let her know that he was her father. At his entreaty she dismounted and he said: 'Your good health, my dear daughter! Now I give you my leave to go. I can see that you will be able to fight for the country and will not bring disgrace upon us. Go and farewell as God bids you.' He embraced her and kissed her once and once again and gave her his blessing. Then she kissed his hand and again mounted the horse and was off like the wind.

When she came up to the armies the war had hardly begun. At once she drew her sword and attacked the enemy. Her sword was a blade with two edges; her horse was swimming up to his knees in blood. The enemy were in flight and she all by herself was pursuing them on her horse. The king and his army and his followers were left behind. They could not keep up with her. When the enemy had retreated and come near the place where their king had his royal seat they asked for peace: they were beaten.

Later the king asked who was the man who had pursued

after the enemy. 'Whoever he is, let him come before me,' he said, 'and whatever he asks I will give him.' They looked here and they looked there; they could not find the girl anywhere. Then the king gave a command that whoever could find this man, he should be given a fine present. It so happened that someone saw the bloody marks of the horse's hooves and he went and told the king. At once the king sent his men and they went and brought the girl before him. The girl was wearing boys' clothes and was fully armed. She had her hair covered and there was no sign that she was a girl. The king said: 'I am very well pleased with you for the bravery which you showed in the battle. Now, whatever your heart desires and whatever you may ask, that I will give you. Ask what you like.' 'My king and many be your years! My wish is for the prosperity of your kingdom,' she answered. 'I have done my duty to you and to the country. I want nothing. As I came, so will I go away again. Come, pray let me go away to my poor home.' The queen looked at her and saw that she was a young and handsome lad; she felt moved towards him and told the king to take the lad as a husband for their daughter. 'That is well said,' said the king, and at once they began to prepare for the wedding. After a month the wedding was celebrated and the feast lasted forty days and forty nights.

Two weeks went by after the wedding, and the queen one day asked her daughter if she were pleased with her husband. The girl answered: 'He is a very fine, handsome, pleasant young man. He looks after me very well. All the thousand dainties he brings me to eat and to drink! He has bought for me the most beautiful clothes and bracelets and rings and ear-rings. But, oh, how can I tell you, mother?' 'What is it, my darling?' said the queen. 'You mustn't keep anything hidden from your mother. You must tell me everything. Should a married girl be too shy with her mother to speak of such matters?' The girl sighed and said: 'Oh, mother, but how can I say it? He is a very fine lad, but when we lie down. . . .' 'Come,' said the queen, 'tell me what you have to say. Tell me, my dear. You must hide nothing from me; you must not be shy of me.' Then the girl began to cry with all her heart and she hugged her mother and went on crying dolefully. 'Don't cry, my dear, don't cry,' said her mother. 'Tell me freely what you have in your heart.' When she had cried for a while her heart was relieved and she said: 'How can I say it, mother? Endearments and kisses and embracings; all these he gives me; for this I have nothing to complain of. But when the time comes for bed, he lays his sword between me and himself saying: "To this side of the sword you must not come!" '

The queen at once understood her daughter's trouble and she went and told it all to the king. He said: 'With the youth I find no fault. He wanted to go away off to his own home, and we pressed him—tell me if we didn't—to marry our daughter. It is we who are to blame. Now let us see what we must do.' They thought again and again how they could no longer have to worry their heads about him, and at last they said they would send him to go and fetch them an apple from Paradise. 'Thus,' they said, 'he will go and lose his life and never come back again.' They told her this, and the girl fell to thinking how she could go and get the apple from Paradise and bring it to them.

Every day she used to go all by herself and water the horse and by herself bring him fodder; all by herself too she used to groom him. When she went that day with his fodder the horse saw that she was full of care and he questioned her. The girl told him the reason. 'Don't be afraid,' said the horse. 'We will go and fetch the apple. You must take and nail my shoes on backwards that they may not know where we are going. Also take provisions for forty days and let us be off.' The girl did as the horse told her and they started off. They travelled night and day; they went on and on and on, and came out near a great lake. To that lake every day the girls from Paradise used to come down and bathe. Each one brought an apple and a slice of bread and these they ate after their bathe. The horse told the girl that while all the girls were bathing together she must seize the clothes of one of them and hide them. She did as the horse told her. When the girls from Paradise saw her and the horse, at once they came up out of the lake and took their clothes and ran off. One of them remained behind because the girl had hidden her clothes. She besought the girl and said to her: 'Give me my clothes and whatever you want I will give you.' She then asked for an apple. At once the girl gave her her apple and her slice of bread as well. The girl then gave her back her clothes and took the apple and at once mounted the horse and went off like the wind. The slice of bread she did not take with her. She went straight to the palace and gave the apple to the king. When the king saw it he was astonished. The apple had on it the mark of a cross and it was plain that it came from Paradise.

So the girl came back and the queen and her daughter were still vexed for the same thing began all over again: in the bed was the sword. To tell the truth the king was sorry for his son-in-law because he was a fine and worthy fellow, but the queen and her daughter were resolute: in some way they must destroy him and be at peace again. The king thought and thought again and a week later he said to his son-in-law: 'In such and such a village for now seven years they have not paid me their taxes. See; you must go there and collect them for me.' Everyone knew that if he went there the people would kill him. The girl went at once and told the horse; he said: 'This is a very difficult piece of work but again we can manage it. See; you must take two hundred okes of wine and some three hundred okes of big iron bullets and provisions for forty days and let us start on the road.' The girl asked the king for these things; he made them all ready and they started off.

When they came to the boundary of the village, she saw an armed man on guard and he asked her if she had leave to pass: if not he would not allow them to go on. 'We know nothing of such things as leaves and permits,' said the girl. She smote at him and killed him and presently she came to the centre of the village. When the villagers saw her they were astonished and all collected together and asked her where she came from and what business she had in their village. She told them her business: 'I am come to collect the taxes you owe to the king.' Then the men grew angry and began to threaten her and made ready to kill her. She drew her sword and attacked them savagely. Some of them she killed, and the others brought out their swords from their houses and came at her to kill her. Then the horse told her to open the wine and to sprinkle it over them and to throw the iron bullets at them. The girl did as the horse told her, and at once the villagers began to entreat her saying: 'Stay, we will pay you whatever you ask.' They saw the red wine, and as the weather was cloudy they thought there had been a rain of blood. Also they heard the bullets falling on the ground and they took the sound for an earthquake. They said too: 'This man for sure has been sent here from God.' Then they all became quiet and rose up and paid him the taxes which they had been owing for seven years. They put the money in a golden carriage and escorted her out to the boundary of their village. When the carriage was near the palace the people gathered together wondering at the success of the king's son-in-law. 'Such a fine fellow,' said they, 'is not to be found in all the world; may God give him many years! If it had not been for him,' said they, 'who knows how many of us would have gone and been killed; also we should never have been able to get the taxes.' The king and the queen were amazed when they saw the girl and began to fear that if they got her killed the people would do them some mischief.

But again the queen and her daughter could never be at rest; somehow or other they must get rid of her; then only would they be at rest. The king, poor man, loved his son-in-law well: 'Where shall I find such a lad?' he used to say. But the queen and her daughter had made up their minds, and one day the queen rose and said to her son-in-law: 'In our kingdom there is a piece of land of some ten thousand acres: some fields there, they yield a crop twice a year. The land is very fertile. But a savage mare keeps guard over those fields; on her neck she has a band plaited all of diamonds and brilliants, and they shine so brightly that no one can go close to them.' The girl went and told this to the horse. Then the horse said: 'Now we have something to weep for; we are doomed. This mare is of far greater power than I am.' Then the girl threw her arms round the horse's neck and began to weep. The horse too was moved with grief and turned and said to her; 'Hush, do not cry. We can manage something about this too. Ask the king to give you bread for forty days, and fifty okes of old wine and a hundred ells of woollen cloth. The cloth you must take and sew me a sevenfold covering of it. When the mare bites me she will tear the cloth, and when I bite her I shall tear off her flesh. In this way it may be that we shall have the better of her. This mare once a week, every Saturday, goes to a spring to drink water. You must pour the wine into the water, and then I will tell you what we must do.' The girl did as the horse told her, and then they started on their way to go to find the mare. On Saturday at very early dawn they approached the spring, and the horse said to the girl: 'Now you must pour the wine into the spring and go and hide yourself; I will stay here and wait the coming of the mare.'

At full day the sun shone and the heat began; it was scorching hot. Presently the mare came and she was so thirsty that as soon as she came she dipped into the water without looking to see what it was; she drank to her fill. When she had thus drunk the wine she was dizzy and began to stumble. Then the horse came out into the open and began to strike at her. The mare bit him, tearing off the cloth coverings: the horse bit her and tore off flesh. The blood came flowing like a river from the mare's wounds, and she was in a sad stress; she was dizzy too with the wine and fell down flat. 'There is a scent here of a son of man,' said she. 'Set me free, and whatever you wish I will give you.' Then the girl too came out into the open and she seized the neck-band, and mounted the horse and was off like the wind. When they at last arrived at the royal capital it was night, and from the bright shining of the neck-band even from a long way off the whole city and the palaces were lit up. All the people rose up full of amazement. The king came and utterly lost his head. On the one hand he was delighted, and on the other he was wondering what he was now to do. The queen and her daughter were delighted when they saw the neck-band; they had never seen such a thing in their lives. Again in the evening when the bridegroom went to lie down, he set his sword between himself and the princess.

Next day his mother-in-law asked him: 'My son, why do you do this? Are you never going to take away the sword from between the two of you?' He said to her: 'I do not wish to lose my strength. Then too there is no need for us to act in haste. Let me perform one or two more brave deeds and then we will see.' 'Now what is this talk of his?' said the queen to herself, and she went and told the king. Then the king called for his son-in-law and said to him: 'My son, I am very much pleased with you. You have done everything I told you. One more thing I will tell you to do, and if you do this, then you will be sent nowhere else. We shall stay and live here all at rest. Now you must go and fetch me fire from the one-eyed giants.' The girl went and told this to the horse. When she told him this the horse wept. 'This is a very hard task,' he said. 'From the one-eyed giants no one at all can escape. Nor do I know where they are. But my mother knows this. Now we must go to the sea, down to the beach, to the place where you found me, and you must take my bridle and throw it into the sea. Then at once my mother will come out from the sea and we will tell her of this and she will tell us what we must do.'

They rose up and went down to the beach and the girl did as the horse had told her. As soon as she had thrown the bridle into the sea, there came out of the sea a very old mare who went to them and would have all but devoured the girl, but the horse would not let her. Then the horse told his dam about it all and asked her to go with the girl and so they could fetch the fire from the one-eyed giants. The mare said to the girl: 'I am by now old and I cannot help you in this business. The one-eyed giants are many and they can run swiftly; no one can overtake them. Also they are so savage that whoever goes into their country can never escape from their hands: out of their own country they never go at all. Nor do they ever give anyone of the fire they have. But you do as I tell you, and we will go and see what we can do. Now go and ask the king for two hundred okes of wine and a hundred okes of soap, and combs to the weight of a hundred okes, and provisions for a hundred days, and then let us start off.' The girl went and got all these things from the king; she came down to the sea and mounted on the old mare and started on the way. The horse stayed there waiting for their return.

In forty days and forty nights they reached the frontier of the one-eyed giants. They saw that there was no one on guard. The giants were holding a festival and they were all away at it. The girl and the mare came to where the giants lived and saw all the houses standing open. Then the mare pointed out a house to the girl and said: 'Go into that house and put some fire into your kerchief and hide it in your bosom. Come out at once and mount and we will be off. Do not be afraid; the fire of the one-eyed giants does not burn.' The girl at once dismounted and went into the house. She put some fire into her kerchief and hid it deep in her bosom; then she ran off and again mounted the mare. At that moment an old giant had come out of a house; he had a vessel of water in his hand to go to the jakes. When he saw them he knew that they had stolen the fire and he stopped and set up a loud shout. At once all the one-eyed giants ran up and the place was full of them and they began to chase after the girl.

The mare ran fast and the giants ran fast. All of them running, the giants came up near her. The mare said to the girl: 'Tell me; are they very near us?' 'In about two strides they have us,' said the girl. 'I am now old and I can't go fast. Quick; pour the wine out behind us,' said the mare. The girl poured out the wine and the giants very fond of wine stopped a little to drink and then again in a crowd pursued them. Before the mare had gone far, again she asked the girl: 'See if they are very close to us.' 'In about two strides they have us,' said the girl. 'Throw down the soap and quickly too,' said the mare. At once the girl threw down the soap. The giants began slipping about; close behind at first; then they dropped farther back. A little time passed and again the mare asked the girl? 'What has happened? Look well; now they are very near us; I can hear their steps.' 'Yes,' said the girl. 'If they stretch out their hands they can catch us.' 'Throw down the combs at once,' said the mare. Then the girl threw down the combs; the giants were tangled in them and the combs ran into their feet and so they dropped behind. The girl and the mare had not gone far when they crossed the frontier of the one-eyed giants. The giants made a stop at the frontier, for beyond their frontier they never went, and they cursed the girl saying: 'For stealing our fire: if you are a boy you shall turn into a girl, and if you are a girl you shall turn into a boy.' Then the mare said to the girl: 'The curse of the one-eyed giants is never in vain. Now tell me: are you a girl or are you a boy?' 'I am a girl,' said she. 'If that is so you have now turned into a boy,' said the mare. 'Look well at yourself and you will see that you are now a boy.' The girl found that she had in fact become a boy. Then said the mare: 'Never have I had on my back a boy, and now that this has befallen, I have to die at once. Let us go quickly down to the sea.' They went there and found the horse and presently the mare died. Then the boy mounted the horse and returned to the city.

When his son-in-law was a long time in coming back the king thought that the giants had killed him. But when he saw him in the palace and with the fire of the giants he was struck with amazement: what to do he knew not.

Then the girl—but now she was a boy—went to the house and told them to get water ready for a bath. She went into the bath-house and had a good bath and then went to her wife. She let down her hair and said to her wife: 'A long time since I had my hair combed; come and comb it.' When the wife saw the hair she thought it must be a girl. But when they went to lie down the sword at once disappeared from between them. Next day she went full of joy and told her mother. The queen went and told the king and they were so delighted they did not know what to do. Then the king gave orders for another forty days and forty nights of wedding celebrations.

So we are here and they are there and we are better off than they are.

47

Is it a Girl? Is it a Boy?

THIS title I have chosen as fitting a story the centre of which is the question whether the heroine, who is dressed as a man, is really a man or a girl. This theme, a girl playing the part of a youth, naturally forms a contact between this story and No. 46, *The Girl who went to War*, and in fact two of our four versions, those from Epeiros and Thrace, have the beginning of the girl volunteering to take her father's place in the army, but the centre of the two groups of tales is different: here we have the debate as to the heroine's sex, and in *The Girl who went to War* we have a tangle which is solved by her being changed from a girl to a boy. For translation I have chosen a short version from Thrace and a longer one from Thera, printed with the title of *Sir Northwind*, the outline of which is as follows:

There were two men, kings; one had nine sons and the other, the senior king, nine daughters. The fathers bickered, and so far we are on the lines of No. 45, *The three Measures of Salt*. The two fathers then proposed a test for the quality of their children: they would see which could bring the Water of Life; one of the boys or one of the girls. To the delight of her father the youngest girl was successful. Her quest led her to the castle of Sir Northwind and his mother. He fell in love with her, being quite sure that in spite of her dress she was really a girl. The mother set various tests for her sex, but the girl always, in this version by invoking the blessing of her parents, evaded being proved to be a girl. When in the end she and Sir Northwind are married, the story has a suggestion of *Beauty and the Beast*, for Sir Northwind tells his wife that he was a king's son, but under a compelling doom to live as a wild monster unless some girl were found to love him.

The closest parallel to this story which I can find is in Sicily.[1] Two fathers disputed about their families, and a test of worth is proposed: which of the two, a son of the one or a daughter of the other, can steal the prince's crown. The boy, as in the Sir Northwind story, is left behind by the girl as he is foolishly trying to cross a stream by bailing out the water in a nutshell. The girl then met the prince who fell in love, being sure that she was really a girl, though she evaded all tests that might reveal her sex: in the garden she picked a rose, as

[1] Gonzenbach, *Sizilianische Märchen*, i. 114, No. 17.

we are told a boy would do, and not a pink, as a girl would. She stole the crown and the prince then came to her father's house and married her.

Another close parallel comes from Turkey;[1] it has been printed by Kunos, but not yet translated. It begins with the two bickering fathers, one with three sons and the other with three daughters. The test of worth is to see who can steal the ring of the bey of Kirez. The girl went out on the quest and came to the bey and his mother. The bey suspected her sex and his mother applied several tests. She put roses under her bed; if they withered, then she would be a girl. Then she tried if the girl would be interested in boys' or in girls' clothes. A third test was whether she was fond of jewels. At last the mother told the bey that he must take her to the bath: in the bath-house the girl fulfilled the quest by stealing his ring, and made her escape. In the end she and the bey were married.

Parallels to a Greek story found in Sicily and in Turkey can really tell us nothing as to its place of origin, though the Sicilian story is in some details so remarkably close to the Greek that the Turkish story is not likely to be the prototype.

The tests for sex which are in all the versions except the one from Zákynthos have some interest.[2] We may ask why the grass and flowers upon which a girl has slept would be found in the morning withered, while if the sleeper be a boy, they would be found still fresh. Here I am inclined to see the old idea that the temperature of a woman's body is higher than that of a man, and this again is connected with the idea that her passions are more violent. If we ask why a girl would choose to gather a pink and a boy a rose, we may observe that the same idea is in the Sicilian story quoted above from Gonzenbach, where in a note we read that a boy would pick a rose because boys are more attracted by beauty, whereas girls like a sweet scent. We get a less fanciful and a more concrete explanation if we turn to a book called *The Turkish Secretary*, in which the art of corresponding by tokens is expounded.[3] Here we are told that to send a pink means: 'You are a beauty beyond compare; a long, long time have I loved you without daring to let you know it;' and to send a rose means: 'I weep continually, but you make a mock of my tears.' It is plain that the pink suits the modest reticence of an enamoured girl, while the rose expresses the feelings of an ardent youth pressing his suit with tears.

[1] Kunos, *Oszmán-török Népköltési Gyüjtemény*, i. 275, No. 64.

[2] The reference to Gonzenbach is in Stith Thompson's *Motif-Index*, but all the other tests of sex he gives under H 1578 are not relevant here. See also BP. ii. 57.

[3] The book is *The Turkish Secretary*, London, 1688; p. 35, for which see note on No. 65.

'Brides are not supposed to speak.' Notably among the Greeks of Cappadocia this silence of brides was carried, I was told, to unbelievable extents. The strongest prohibition was against the young married woman speaking to her father- or her mother-in-law; if she had anything to say, it must be conveyed by one of her sisters-in-law. Nor might she eat in their presence; even when this was conceded, she must keep her hand before her mouth. After the birth of her first child these rules were relaxed. At the wedding festivities modesty demanded that the bridegroom as well as the bride should keep silence; at least when the groom was very young.[1]

The references for this story are:

1. THERA: *Parnassós*, vii (1885), p. 555, translated.
2. THRACE: *Thrakiká*, xvii. 170, translated.
3. EPEIROS: Pio, p. 57, which is Hahn, i. 114, No. 10, translated by Geldart, p. 70.
4. ZÁKYNTHOS: *Laographía*, xi. 3. 459.

NO. 47*a*. IS IT A GIRL? IS IT A BOY?[2]

Once upon a time there was a father who had three daughters, and an order came to him that he should go to join the army; at this he was much disquieted. His eldest daughter questioned him: 'What is the matter, father, that you are so much troubled?' 'How could I not be? News has come that I must go to the army.' 'And I thought that it was that you were anxious about arranging for my marriage!' The second daughter saw him full of trouble and she too questioned him: 'Father, why are you so much troubled?' 'Don't ask me, my dear daughter. I have told your elder sister.' 'Tell me too; it may be that I can do something to relieve you.' 'News has come that I must go to the army.' 'And I thought you were anxious about having me married.' The youngest daughter saw him and questioned him: 'Father, why are you so much troubled?' 'Don't ask me, my daughter; I have told your sisters.' 'Tell me too; it may be I can do something to lighten your trouble.' 'News has come that I must join the army.' 'Is that what is troubling you? Give me your clothes and your gun and your horse and I will go in your place.'

Her father would not consent. The girl insisted; she cut off

[1] See Halliday in *Folklore*, xxiii. 81.

[2] Thracian text from *Thrakiká*, xvii. 170, under the title *Theodora in the Army*.

her hair; put on men's clothes; took the gun, mounted the horse and went off to the army; she said her name was Theodore. Theodore found a companion and they became friends, and this friend was quite sure that Theodore was not a man. When he went to his village he said to his mother:

'Theodora it is, not Theodore,
And for her my heart is sore.'

'Since you think it is a girl, take your friend one day to the place where they sell bracelets and pins.' So they went there, but Theodore wanted to look at pistols and said to the other: 'What do you want with bracelets? Are you a girl?' Yet he thought still that Theodore was not a man, and he said:

'Theodora it is, not Theodore,
And for her my heart is sore.'

Three years they passed in the army, and when the men were to go back home to the village her companion, very well aware that Theodore was in fact Theodora, ran to overtake her. In the night he went into her house, and as they were all asleep, he put a charm upon her and carried her off to his house. When Theodora opened her eyes and instead of her father and her sisters saw her companion in the army, and herself in a strange place, she blushed all red. The man made her a thousand speeches; that he loved her, that he wanted to make her his wife. Theodora said not a word. Everyone thought she was dumb; she never opened her mouth to say a word.

Her companion from the army betrothed himself to another girl, and his marriage was to take place. As they were on their way to church to be crowned in marriage, they had with them Theodora, the dumb girl never saying a word. Then this dumb girl lit a taper and set fire to her sleeve. The bride saw this and cried out—although brides are not supposed to speak: 'The dumb girl will be burned; put out the flame.' 'Well' said Theodora, 'I was three years and never spoke and you are beginning to talk very quickly.' Then the bridegroom said: 'Bring forward Theodora for the crown of marriage; so modest was she that for three years she said not a word.' So they lived happily and may we live yet better.

NO. 47*b*. IS IT A GIRL? IS IT A BOY?[1]

There were two kings, two brothers, both married. The palace had many rooms, and one king occupied one half of it and the other the other half: the roof-terraces of both halves were in one. The first king was as it were the greater of the two; his kingdom was bigger. On his terrace he had two thrones; one of silver and one of gold, and when this greater king was in good mood he used to sit on the golden throne, and when he was ill-disposed on the silver one. Now the first king had nine daughters and the second nine sons. Every morning the kings used to walk out on the terrace; the second king was jealous of the first. Every morning then they used to go out on the terrace and take, let us say, their coffee, and the lesser king would tease the other one.

The king with the nine daughters used to keep each of them shut up in her room. The youngest of them all he loved very much; she was the beauty, and when the king chose to go out for a walk he used to come back with some gift for his little daughter. Well, one morning he came out on the terrace and sat down on the golden throne. His brother also came out on the terrace, and when he saw the other king he was jealous and thought what he could do to cool him down; he too was in high spirits. So he said: 'Good day, my brother, to you and your nine sows.' So his morning greeting was to call the nine daughters sows; then he sat himself down on the silver throne. The other king just sat there. Next day he came out in a very bad humour and his brother again said the same thing. The daughter got no more presents and she begged her father to tell her what was the matter. He would not tell her. Three mornings the other king rose up and said the same thing to him. Then said the daughter: 'Father, tell me,' and she pressed him and caressed him until he told her. 'How can I tell you, my daughter?' said he. 'Now three times your uncle has said to me: "Good day, brother, you and your nine sows."'

She said: 'But, my dear father, do you not see that you should say to him: "Good day, my brother, you and your nine boars?"' 'Well said, my daughter,' said he. Then he came out

[1] Text from Thera printed in *Parnassós*, vii (1885), p. 555, with the title *Sir Northwind*.

on the terrace and they talked both of them together; the king was in very ill humour but nothing happened. The next day the lesser king came out and said: 'Even if mine are boars, they are men enough to bring me the Water of Life, and I have sent the finest of my lads to go to fetch it for me. And you can send your sows.' The greater king was sitting on the golden throne; at this he rose and sat on the silver one. Then he went down into the house and his daughter came to him and said: 'Tell me what is the matter, father, that you are again vexed.' She pressed him and he told her. 'Do not be vexed, my father.' She bade her father have two or three suits of men's clothes made for her, and then she said: 'Now we shall see, father, who will bring the Water, that fellow or I.' Her father was afraid and not willing to let her go.

The girl rose up and took a good horse and her sword and with the blessing of her parents started off. She went on and on towards the place where the Water of Life was. Half-way there was a river. When the girl came to the river, she saw a youth bailing out the water with a nutshell to bring the water low enough for him to cross over. She greeted him and said: 'What are you doing there?' He told her and she said, 'Good.' She pulled out an arrow and shot it into the river; it dried up and she crossed over. Then said he: 'And won't you take me too with you?' She said: 'As I passed over, so can you pass over yourself.' So she went off and left him there.

She went on and on, and came to a land where Sir Northwind lived, and it was he who had the Water of Life. In that land there was but one palace and to it she went. She found a lady in the palace: 'Good day, my lady.' 'Good day, my daughter, and what do you want?' She said: 'The king, my father, is at his last breath and I am come to ask you to give me the Water of Life.' 'My daughter, I cannot let you have it, for I have a son; his name is Sir Northwind. He is out hunting and you must wait for him to come and let you have the Water.' She gave the girl a slap and this turned her into a cup and the cup she set on a table. Sir Northwind came; she had set the table for him with abundance of food and he sat down and ate. Then his mother came and caressed him: 'O my son, suppose you saw some prince here, would you do anything to him?' 'By the strength of my arm, O my mother, I will do him no harm.' Then she let him see the girl. Said he: 'And what are you doing here, boy?' 'I am a prince'—she gave the name—'and I am come here for you to give me the Water of Life.' 'Oh, a prince: then I must give it to you. But you have come a long way and you must stay here a while and rest.' So the girl remained there.

Next day Sir Northwind said to his mother: 'Do you know, mother, but this young man is a girl?' 'My dear good son, he is as you are.' He said: 'Never, never, mother; it is a girl.' 'Take him, my son, into the garden; then if he picks a flower, it is a girl; but if not, he is as you are.' He took the girl and they went into the garden. When she came down into the garden, she said to herself: 'Be with me, blessing of my father and of my mother, and do not let me be made known.' They went into the garden and she picked nothing at all. He said: 'Won't you pick a flower?' She said: 'Flowers! flowers are for girls, not for such as us.' He went up to the house again: 'My son, how did you fare?' He said: 'Nothing happened at all.' 'He is as you are, my good lad.' 'Never,' said he. Then his mother said: 'To-morrow go and take her to the shop; on one side there are women's clothes and on the other men's; if he looks first at the women's things, then it is a girl; otherwise he is such as you are.' In the morning he said: 'Come, my friend, and let us go to my shop and you shall see what it is like.' On the way there the girl said three times: 'Be with me, blessing of my father and my mother, and do not let me be made known.' Now how did she know to say this? When they came to the shop all her eyes were on the men's clothes. He was vexed to see that she did not look at the women's clothes at all, and said: 'My friend, don't you see how pretty these things are?' 'These things are all for young women; they are not for such as us.' Much vexed he took her back. His mother questioned him: 'Nothing at all, mother,' said he. Next day and the same thing again. 'But mother, never is she a boy. She is a girl whatever you can say.' Said his mother: 'Nothing more can I do, my boy.'

The two of them used to sleep in one bed, this youth and Sir Northwind, and on Sir Northwind's side his mother laid down flowers. 'Well, my boy, I shall set flowers below this youth also: I shall strew the whole bed with flowers, and if the flowers beneath him wither, then he is indeed a girl.' On Sir Northwind's side of the bed the flowers stayed always as fresh as when his mother set them there. When the girl came to lie down she saw the flowers; then said she: 'Be with me, blessing of my father and of my mother, and do not let me be made known.' Then she lay down and went to sleep and in the morning when they rose up, what was to be seen? The flowers on her side were even fresher than those on his. Then his mother said: 'My boy, the lad is even as you are.' He said: 'No, mother.' Then the girl pressed to be given the Water of Life and suffered to depart.

Then said his mother: 'My son, nothing is left but this to try the matter. You must go together up on the terrace,'—now the terrace was very lofty and from it the whole land was to be seen below you. 'Then, my son, if she is a girl it will be plain because half-way up the stairs blood will come from her.' He took her and said: 'Come, my friend, and look at the country, and this will be some pleasure to you now that you must be in such haste to go away from us.' The girl went and when she saw all the height of the stairs, she said three times: 'Be with me, blessing of my father and of my mother, and do not let me be made known.' Then she went up the stairs even better than he did; half-way up blood came; then the blessing of her parents in the form of a little dog licked up the blood and Sir Northwind saw nothing of it. His mother came with chocolate for them to drink. She said: 'And how did you fare, my son?' Said he: 'Nothing happened at all.' The girl gazed at the palaces and at the country and she was well pleased. Then they came down the stairs and the same thing happened; he saw nothing. When they were down, his mother said: 'Well, my son, now your mind can be made up about this.' Then said Sir Northwind: 'Mother, I am going hunting, and if this boy presses you, give him the Water of Life to take away and I never see him again.' Northwind went off hunting, and the girl said: 'Let me have the Water of Life.' The mother went off to get it, and while she was away fetching the Water, the girl took pen and paper and wrote this: 'With my honour saved I came; with my honour saved I go; my defiance to Sir Northwind. We lay down together and he never knew me what I was.' She stuck the paper on the pillows of the bed in which they had slept and set it opposite to the door of the room. Then they brought her the Water of Life; she said good-bye and went off.

She went on and on and half-way she found the son of her uncle still there by the river. She shot an arrow and the river became dry ground; she passed over it. 'Oh, my friend,' said he, 'don't you see my plight? Help me to cross over.' She said: 'As I crossed over, so must you.' Enough said of him.

The girl came home and gave her father the Water of Life, saying: 'My father, as I went so have I come back, and here is for you the Water of Life. Tell my uncle to send to fetch his son, and unless he makes haste it will be all over with the boy.' So the king was told; he sent companies of men and the youth was picked up and carried home. Then the king cherished his daughter; no rain should fall upon her and wet her; such was his care for her. He kept her shut up in her room. But because it was summer the windows were left open. However, let us leave her and speak of Sir Northwind.

Soon he came back from hunting, and his mother said: 'My son, he has gone away; he was very pressing with me.' Said he: 'He did well.' He was quite calm and said: 'He did well to go off without my seeing him.' In the evening when he went to lie down on his bed, he set the table and his book and the lamp all by his side to read: then by the wall he saw the paper. When he saw it he dropped everything and took the paper and read it. Then he shouted to his mother: 'Mother, come and look.' He fell down groaning and moaning, a very sick man. But there in his room where he lay sick was the dove-cot with two pairs of doves. One pair his mother was feeding up; the other she was leaving without food, for they were to stay where they were. Sir Northwind was at his last gasp. Then one day he heard the doves talking. One pair said: 'Our mistress is feeding us up, but not you.' The other pair said: 'But you have a journey to make.' Sir Northwind heard this and took comfort, but when the days passed and nothing happened his sickness increased. Then his mother took the doves and said to them: 'You I shall feed with stones of price and you who are fasting I shall feed with pearls, and you must go and bring here to me the daughter of a king,' and she told them the name. Then she again gave them food and water and sprinkled them—it seemed she was a witch—and sent them forth, a fine pair of doves and gave them their orders. When the doves went off Sir Northwind was at his last breath.

It was summer and the royal girl had her windows open and was sitting on her throne all by herself. Then the doves came and perched on the window. She saw the doves and sent away her chambermaid and sat there in her room by herself with the beautiful golden doves. She said: 'They are quite tame and gentle and I will let them come inside.' The doves came and perched on her and at last they lulled her to sleep. When she was asleep they lifted her up on their wings and out of the window. Then, one, two, off they went on their way to the house of Sir Northwind. They laid her down in the room, all asleep as she was. The mother of Sir Northwind came and sprinkled her and gave her to drink and woke her up and then called for him; he came and saw the girl. When he saw her in his delight he plumped himself up like a great cat; then he fell writhing on the ground. Like a flash he split open and out from him came a prince; one to amaze the very sun himself. He threw his arms round the royal lady and said: 'I was a king's son and this was my compelling doom: to live a savage monster if no girl were found to love me.' The wedding was made ready and they were married and passed their lives in all good fortune.

48

The silent Princess

THIS is the story of a princess who was so reluctant to marry that she was dumb to all proposals; but if a man could make her break silence, then she would regard all as lost and take him. The successful suitor told her, or in some way let her hear from the mouth of a magic talisman, three successive stories, in each version the same stories, each of them ending in a problem: which of three suitors deserved to be married to a girl. At the end of each story the suitor, and in the full form of the story the teller as well, gives his answer, an answer framed in such a way as to appear to the princess so absurd that she cannot but break out with her own solution. Thus she has to yield to the suitor who has so successfully played on the desire natural to most people, and perhaps to all Greeks, to set someone else right. It is the same method by which in so many stories an old woman makes a girl come down from her perch on a tree by sieving corn or kneading dough in a way so ridiculous that the girl cannot but come down to show her how it ought to be done.[1]

If we ask why the suitor needs a talisman; why cannot he achieve his ends by his own native capacity? the answer may be that in moments of stress a man is apt to go beyond his usual capacity, to, as we say, excel himself, and this excess power is symbolized by the assistance of the talisman, which in fact does most of the work of making the lady speak.

As the whole story can very well stand with less than the full set of sub-stories, and as each of the three can well be told quite independently of the silent princess framework, it is not surprising that we often, and indeed most usually, find incomplete versions, and in fact I find the story complete only twice: one version from the Smyrna district here translated, and the other, an immensely padded version, from Astypálaia, and as in these the order of the sub-stories is not the same, it must be admitted that of any primitive sequence nothing can be said. The second version from Thrace has two sub-stories; the other versions one each, *The Louse Skin* being the commonest.

The Smyrna version is both complete and neatly told with no gaps and no digressions. The stories are told to the princess in the presence of her suitor by a magic bird which the hero conceals, first in a cup-

[1] For which see No. 2 above, *The little Boy and his elder Sister*.

board, then under a stool, and the third time under a sofa. For witnesses the first two nights he has some old women hidden, but they went to sleep and could give no evidence; the third night he set some young girls to listen and their curiosity kept them awake. By this device it is arranged that there shall be the threefold action demanded by the conventions of the Greek folktale.

The first story in this Smyrna version may be called *The Makers of the Image*. There were three men; one shaped a log into the figure of a girl; one made clothes for it; the third, a priest, gave the figure the breath of life. In the second Thracian version the figure is made of snow; Thrace has a hard Balkan winter. Then came the question: which of the three was entitled to her; the suitor said she should belong to the carpenter; the magic bird said to the tailor; the indignant princess burst out that it belonged to the monk by whose prayers a soul had been given to the senseless log.

The next story is conveniently called *The Louse Skin*. A king preserved the skin of a louse which had been kept and fed until it reached a prodigious size: he would give his daughter in marriage to the man who could say what skin it was. A demon knew the answer and was given the girl. He carried her off and kept her in a cave and sucked her blood.[1] She let her friends know her plight by releasing a pigeon with a letter, and she was rescued by a band of gifted brothers. The problem again is which of the three brothers should have her.[2] The suitor said it should be the brother who had bottled the devil up in a wine skin; the magic bird said she should go to the swift runner. Whereupon the princess could not refrain from saying that she was the due of the man who had caught her as she was dropped from the clouds by the devil when he was carrying her away.

The third story may be called *The Cure of the sick Girl*. Three men desired a girl, but she either fell sick or died. One of the men knew by a magic mirror, that she was ill; the second had the means of reaching her rapidly on a magic carpet, and the third a medicine by which to cure her. Which should have her? The suitor said the man who saw her; the bird said the man who brought them to her on his carpet; but the princess would have it that he deserved her who had cured her.

This third story branches off into a story which might be called *The most valuable Object*. In a version of this from Samos a father would

[1] Just as Death does to the dead girl in the song in Passow, No. 411. She says of Death: 'On my knees I hold him clasped and on my breast he leans; and when he is hungry my body is his meat, and when he is athirst he drinks from my two eyes.'

[2] For this part of the story see Aarne–Thompson's Types 621 and 653.

give his daughter to the youth who can bring him the greatest treasure. Her suitors brought him, one a mirror in which everything could be seen, the second a healing apple, and the third a flying carpet. The girl fell sick; she was seen by the mirror; reached by the carpet; and cured by the apple, which was then adjudged to be the most valuable object, and to the youth who brought it she was given as his bride.

BP.'s notes to Grimm, No. 129, *Die vier kunstreichen Brüder*, and No. 212, *Die Laus*, contain abundant references by which it appears that the whole complex of *The silent Princess*, and above all the sub-stories I and II, is of Indian origin.[1] Yet the extremely neat dovetailing of the three stories into the frame of *The silent Princess* seems to me rather specially Greek. In a Turkish story from Constantinople —but here Greek influence may well be suspected—we have the frame and the three sub-stories. They are, however, not quite the same sub-stories as the Greek, and not so ingeniously planned.[2]

In these references for *The silent Princess* the numbers in brackets indicate which of the three sub-stories it contains: I, *The Makers of the Image*; II, *The Louse Skin*; III, *The Cure of the sick Girl.*

1, 2. TAURUS MOUNTAINS: at Phárasa, *M.G. in A.M.*, p. 465 (I); at Afshár-köi, ibid., p. 575 (II).

3, 4. SMYRNA DISTRICT: *Mikrasiatiká Khroniká*, iv. 225 (I, II, III), translated. Also ibid. iv. 283, there is a story very close to *The Louse Skin.*

5. BUDRUM: *Folklore*, xii. 317 (I).

6. NISYROS: *Z.A.* i. 427 (II).

7. ASTYPÁLAIA: Pio, p. 93 (III, I, II) = Geldart, p. 106.

8. NAXOS: *N.A.* ii. 118 (II).

9. MÝKONOS: Roussel, *Contes de Mycono*, p. 143 (II).

10. SYRA: Pio, p. 230 (I) = Garnett, p. 138.

11, 12. THRACE: *Thrakiká*, xvi. 148 (II); and *Arkheíon Thrakikoú Laogr.* v. 176 (III, I).

13. ZÁKYNTHOS: *Laographía*, xi. 520 (II).

Of *The most valuable Object*, the development of the third sub-story, we have three versions:

1. PONTOS: *Pontiakí Estía*, i, Part I, p. 21.

2. SAMOS: Stamatiádis, *Samiaká*, v. 590.

3. EPEIROS: Hahn, i. 263, No. 47.

This is also found in Turkish in *Istanbul Masallari*, p. 8; not translated by Kent and too recent for BP.

[1] BP., *Anmerkungen*, iii. 45 and 483. For Indian variants see also Penzer-Tawney, *Ocean of Story*, vi. 261, 273. See also *M.G. in A.M.*, p. 277.

[2] Kunos, *Stambul*, p. 45.

NO. 48. THE SILENT PRINCESS[1]

There was once a prince and he and a dervish were very great friends; every day they ate and drank together. One day while they were eating and drinking, the dervish brought something out of his wallet, kissing it and weeping. The prince said to him: 'What is this which you are looking at and weeping; I want to see it myself.' 'O my prince, you cannot; it is not right that you should see it.' But the prince was so pressing in his entreaty that the dervish made up his mind to let him see it. Well, what he showed him was a girl; beautiful, O so beautiful that scarcely had the prince seen her than he fell sick of love for her; off his head. He went to his father and said: 'Father, what you have that it is right you should give me, let me have it, because I am going away.' The king was unwilling to let him go, yet since he was his only son he did him this kindness. So the prince rose up and went away to the city of Constantine.

As he was on his way he saw a great crowd gathered together. He went to ask what it was, and they told him that there was a bird which was for sale. So the prince came up and bid fifty gold pieces; others however bid fifty-five; others sixty. Well, the prince at once bid two hundred gold pieces and took the bird and the cage in which it was. But when he came to the inn he changed his mind and was sorry he had bought the bird, saying to himself; 'What have I done? I was a fool to give all that money for this little sparrow.' The bird had the voice of a man; also it could read men's hearts, and he said to the prince: 'You have changed your mind, have you, my master, and are sorry you bought me? But don't think you have been swindled. You were in luck, and you will be a winner in what you came here for.' 'O no, my bird,' said the prince, 'I have not changed my mind.'

The bird knew why the prince had come there, and he also knew that this girl whom he was seeking refused to speak. The king her father had therefore made an order that whoever could make her speak should have her for his wife; but if he failed his head should be taken off. So the bird who knew all this said to the prince: 'Now when you go to her whom you seek, you must put me in a little cupboard which there is there. So you will

[1] Text from near Smyrna, in *Mikrasiatiká Khroniká*, v. 225.

speak to her and she will say nothing to you. When you see that she won't speak, then you must say "good evening" to the cupboard. Then I will answer you and tell you a little story to pass away the time.'

So the prince went off and he and the king agreed that he should go there in the evening to make the princess speak. In the evening they took two or three old women to stay outside and bear witness next day if she had said anything. So when the prince came there he said: 'A good evening to you.' She said not a word. Again he said: 'A good evening to you.' Again she said not a word. Then the prince said: 'Let me talk to the cupboard there and see if it will talk to me and so I shall pass the time.' 'Oh yes,' said she to herself. 'You stay here; but it shall be the cupboard that talks to you.' Then the prince turned and said to the cupboard: 'A good evening to you, my cupboard.' Not a word from the cupboard. So he said once more: 'A good evening to you, my cupboard.' And again the cupboard said nothing. But when he had said the third time: 'A good evening to you, my cupboard,' then the cupboard spoke and said: 'Welcome, and welcome here like a good new year. All this time, my master, and to me you said nothing but stayed talking to this bad girl?' 'And won't you tell me some little story to pass the time together, you and me?' 'With pleasure I will tell you a story,' said the little cupboard.

'Once upon a time there were three brothers and they went into a far distant land to find work. When these three had come a great distance, right out in the country, they said: "Here at this place we will meet one another again," and each one went his way. Three years later they came back to this same place and turned to go to their own country. On the way night came upon them, and they found a cave and went into it to rest. When it was time for them to go to sleep, they said that every two hours one of them should keep watch. They drew lots and the lot fell upon the carpenter: for one of them was a carpenter. At the mouth of the cave there was a great log of wood. To pass the time he started on it with his axe and shaped it into the body of a woman. The time passed and it was the turn of the next brother to rise and keep watch. He was a tailor. When he was up he saw the log and understood what had happened; so he said: "My brother set his axe to the log and made it into a woman. Now it is for me to make it clothes to wear." So he started and made a dress for it. Then after two hours came the turn of the other brother: this other brother was a monk. So the monk saw the log of wood dressed in its clothes, and he said: "Now it is my turn; let me make a prayer to God and perhaps He will give it a soul." So he fell to praying to God. And God heard him and brought the log to life; it became a woman all complete.' 'Now,' said the cupboard, 'to which of them should the woman belong?'

'To the one who shaped the wood with his axe,' said the prince. 'No, no,' said the bird. 'She ought to be for the man who made her clothes.' 'Oh, this is too much; it will kill me,' broke out the girl who never spoke. 'She belongs to the man by whose prayers a living soul came to her.' The old women outside had gone to sleep, so they did not hear that the girl had spoken. In the morning when the king came he asked the prince if his daughter had spoken. 'She did speak,' said the prince. Then he said to his daughter: 'Did you speak?' She said: 'I did not speak.' They asked the women and they said: 'We did not hear her.'

What could the prince do then? He was compelled to go again the next evening to make the princess speak. But before they went the bird said to him: 'This time when we go there you will find the little cupboard all broken in pieces. Look for some other place where you can put me.'

The prince started off; he put the bird in his bosom and went to where the princess was. When he went in her eyes were downcast. He took the bird carefully and set it underneath a stool. The prince spoke to her but she did not say a word. So when he saw and saw clearly that the princess would give him no answer he said: 'I shall talk to this stool here; you need say nothing and so the time will pass.' 'Oh yes,' said she to herself, 'you stay here and let the stool talk to you.' Then the prince turned and said to the stool: 'A good evening to you, my little stool.' Not a word from the stool. Once again he said: 'A good evening to you, my little stool.' Again the stool said not a word. But when he had said the third time: 'A good evening to you, my little stool,' then the stool spoke and said: 'Welcome, and welcome here, like a good new year. All this time, my master, and to me you said nothing, but stayed talking to this bad girl?' 'And won't you tell me some little story, to pass the time together, you and me?' 'With pleasure I will tell you a story,' said the little stool.

'Once there was a king and he had a louse and he put this louse into a jar and there he gave it blood to drink. With all this blood the louse grew very fat, and the jar was not big enough to hold it, and it died. The king took its skin and had it dried and hung it up in front of the door of the palace, and he said that if anyone could tell him of what animal this was the skin, he should have his daughter as his wife: if not he would be put to death. Many men came but none of them could find out; one said it was the skin of a cat, another of a dog, but no one could find out. So the king cut off their heads. After a long time the devil came there, changed into the shape of a handsome young man. But even he did not know. So he thought out a device. He took a golden apple and went below the windows of the palace and played with the apple. The king's daughter was there at the window. When she saw the golden apple she longed to have it. So she said to the devil: "Won't you let me have this golden apple?" "With pleasure I will let you have it," said he, "if you also will tell me of what animal this is the skin." It seemed to the girl that the young man pleased her and so she said to him: "It is the skin of a louse." He went to the king and said to him: "What you have here is the skin of a louse." The king said: "My daughter is yours; take her."

'When it was the time for his daughter to leave him he gave her three pigeons, so if any time she needed she could send him her news. So the devil took the beautiful girl and went to the side of a mountain where there was a cave. It was difficult for a man to get up there for the path was very steep. In that cave he kept her and brought her whatever came to hand. When she saw that her husband was no man, she took and wrote a letter to her father: "Father, save me, for he whom you gave me is not a man." She tied the letter to the foot of one of the pigeons and let it fly off. When the devil saw this he turned into a cloud and seized the pigeon and devoured it. The girl wrote another letter and sent it by the next pigeon. The devil turned into a cloud and devoured this pigeon also. Then the girl wrote a third letter and tied it to the foot of the third pigeon. "Up, my pigeon," said she: "You are my last hope. See to it that you escape from my husband and reach my father's palace." The third pigeon succeeded in escaping and reached her father's palace.

'When her father read the letter, he sat down and thought: how could he save her from the hands of the devil? He took and sent out an order that whoever could help him should come and present himself. After some days an old woman appeared before him. "I, my king," said she, "will help you. I have a son and you could load him like a camel and he would run like a hare. And I have another son: he puts his ear to the ground and knows what is happening in all the world. I have yet another son and he can clap the devil into a wineskin and he not know what has happened. I have another son; he with his arrow can pierce a flea's eye. Also I have yet another who if a cup of oil should fall from the sky, he can catch it and the oil be not spilled." "It is you," said he, "who can save my daughter."

'So they all mounted on the back of the man who could run like a hare, and when they had gone a very long way they said: "Come here, you who know what is happening in all the world, and use your ear that we may know where we are." The man put his ear to the ground and said: "We are not there yet." Again they mounted on the man who ran like a hare. Again when they had gone some way they said to the second brother: "Dismount and see where we are." The man dismounted and said: "See, the place is up there." "Come here, you who can clap the devil into a wineskin." So the man went and put the devil into the wineskin the very moment when he was asleep; then he took the girl and came down to them. A long while passed and then the devil understood what had happened; at one stroke he broke the wineskin, and as they were on their way he turned into a black cloud and carried the girl away. "Now," they cried, "You with the arrow, look out." The man with the arrow took his stand and killed the devil. The other brother, the one who could catch the oil without its being spilled, caught the girl so that she did not fall down and be killed.'

'Well,' said the little stool: 'to which of them should the girl belong?' 'To the man who put the devil into the wineskin,' said the prince. 'No, no,' said the bird. 'She ought to be for the man who could run like a hare.' 'Oh, this is too much; it will kill me,' broke out the girl who never spoke. 'She belongs to the man who caught her as she was falling and so she was not killed.' But again the old women outside had gone to sleep, so they did not hear that the girl had spoken. In the morning when the king came he asked the prince if his daughter had spoken. 'She did speak,' said the prince. Then he asked his daughter: 'Did you speak?' She said: 'I did not speak.' They asked the women, and they said: 'We did not hear her.'

So it was agreed that the prince should go there yet one more evening, but outside the door there should be girls and not old women, because the old women just slept and snored. But before they went the bird said to the prince: 'This time when we go there you will find the little stool all broken to pieces. Look for some other place where you can put me.'

The prince started off; he put the bird in his bosom, and went to where the princess was. When he went in her eyes were downcast. He took the bird carefully and set it underneath a little sofa. The prince spoke to her, but to him she did not say a word. When he saw and saw clearly that the princess would give him no answer, he said: 'I shall talk to this little sofa; perhaps it will talk to me and so I shall pass the time.' 'Oh yes,' said she to herself, 'You stay here and let the sofa talk to you.' So the prince turned and said to the sofa: 'A good evening to you, my little sofa.' Not a word from the sofa. Once again he said: 'A good evening to you, my little sofa.' And again the sofa said not a word. But when he had said the third time: 'A good evening to you, my little sofa,' then the sofa spoke and said to him: 'Welcome, and welcome here, like a good new year. All this time, my master, and to me you said nothing but stayed talking to this bad girl?' 'And won't you tell me some little story to pass the time together, you and me.' 'With pleasure I will tell you a story,' said the little sofa.

'Once there were three brothers, three princes. The three brothers were in love with their cousin. To make them forget her their father sent them on a far journey. When they had gone a long way they wished to separate. So they heaved up a flat slab and put their rings underneath it and agreed that whoever was the first to come back should wait for his brothers and they would return home together. When the time came for returning the three met and they began to ask one another what they had bought on their journey. One of them said: "I found and bought a little looking-glass." "And I", said the next one, "found and bought a little carpet." "And I", said the third brother, "found and bought an apple, and a dead man when he smells this apple will rise up again." "And my little carpet," said the other, "if we mount on it will carry us in two minutes to the very end of the world." "And in my little mirror," said the man who had the glass, "we may see what is happening at the other end of the world, whatever we may think of." "Let us look at our cousin," at once said the two others. They bent over it and what did they see? They saw their cousin dead. Then they mounted on the little carpet. "My little carpet, carry us to our father's palace." When they came there the brother with the apple ran and held it to the nose of the dead girl. And so the girl rose up alive again.'

'Well, now,' said the little sofa, 'to which of them should the woman belong?' 'To the man who had the little mirror.' 'No, no,' said the bird; 'she ought to be for the man who had the little carpet.' 'Oh, this is too much; this will kill me,' broke out the girl who never spoke, 'Why do you not say the man who brought her to life?'

At that moment the king came in, for the girls who were watching outside the door had told him the news. 'Ah ha,' he said: 'So you have spoken have you? Well, you shall marry this young man.' So the youth took the princess and went back to his own place and celebrated a joyous wedding.

49

The Story of Fiorendino

AARNE–THOMPSON TYPE 313

THIS story has been studied at some length in *Forty-five Stories*, where it is No. 44, and the version from Kos there translated is so much better than any of the other eleven that it is hardly necessary to do more here than give an outline of the story.

The only remedy for a sick king was that he should eat the heart of a prince; specially dieted for forty days. His daughter, very often called Dolcetta, ensnared a prince, the hero Fiorendino, and caused herself to be shut up with him for the forty days of preparation. This was too much for them; womanly pity and the fire of love played their inevitable part, and Fiorendino and Dolcetta fell in love with one another. They ran away together baffling pursuit by the well-known device of the magical escape.[1] When they were happy together, Fiorendino went to visit his mother, the princess warning him that he must on no account allow her to kiss him: if she did he would forget all about his love for her. And his mother did kiss him, though only when he was asleep and off his guard; he thereupon forgot his bride. To win her husband back Dolcetta disguised herself as a nun and went to the town where Fiorendino was living. Underneath her black robe she wore the richest dresses, and the young men of the place all fell in love with her, and for them she kept a seemingly open house. She was visited by the son of the general, by the son of the vizier, and finally by her forgetful husband. All the young men were thrown out of the house by her servants with every circumstance of humiliation. The youths then very unsportingly denounced the supposed nun for her loose life. The girl with great spirit defended herself in the court; then she showed herself in her royal robes and was recognized by Fiorendino.

It is curious that in all the versions the latter part of the story is for the most part told in verse. The lines differ in every version nor can I find any poem of Fiorendino. This simple versification comes very easily in Greek, and a good many other stories are apt at moments of special tension to break out into verse. For some reason it would seem that the final dramatic scene of the Fiorendino story was specially suitable for this treatment.

[1] For which see *Forty-five Stories*, p. 484.

The story is well established in Italy. The names, Fiorendino and Dolcetta, are plainly Italian. The story is not found at all east of the Aegean; that is to say it is confined to those parts of Greece which have been under Italian influence. Wherever else it may now be found it can hardly be doubted that it came to Greece from Italy.

The notion that a mother's kiss will bring about the forgetfulness of love is very common; we have it in Nos. 25 and 38, and many references will be found for this in *Forty-five Stories*, p. 484.[1] The mother's kiss is a symbol for a man's early feeling for his home and his parents which must now give way to a fresh set of relations with his wife; the kiss blocks his passage from the earlier to the later phase of his life. In another story, No. 36 in *Forty-five Stories*, we see that the man enchanted by the fairies is forbidden even to approach his mother: the fairies know too well how easily their power over him may be broken by this earlier association.

The references to the Greek versions of Fiorendino are:

1. LEROS: *Forty-five Stories*, No. 44, p. 478.
2. RHODES: P. Gneftos, *Τραγούδια δημοτικὰ τῆς Ρόδου*, p. 137.
3. SAMOS: Stamatiádis, *Samiaká*, v. 525.
4. MITYLENE: Kretschmer, *Heut. lesbische Dialekt*, p. 485.
5. IOS: Thumb, *Handbuch d. neugr. Volkssprache*, 2nd ed., p. 280.
6. NAXOS: M. K. Krispis, *Khorta diáphora*, ii. 211.

7, 8. CRETE: *Kritikós Laós*, pp. 78, 104, and 135, 167.

9. ATHENS: Kamboúroglou in *Deltíon*, i. 138 = Garnett, p. 53.
10. SPARTA: *Σπαρτιατικὸν Ἡμερολόγιον*, 1910, and in outline in *Laographía*, ii. 146.

11, 12. ZÁKYNTHOS: *Laographía*, xi. 415, 418.

[1] See also BP.'s index, *s.v. küss.*

50

The Man born to be King

AARNE—THOMPSON TYPE 930

THIS is one of the numerous stories on the impossibility of escaping from the inexplicable decrees of destiny. A rich man is by some accident lodging in a poor cottage when a son is born to the people in the house. From the Fates or from the aspect of the stars the rich man learns that the newly-born boy is to marry his daughter and so become his heir. He tries to kill the child but his effort is always in vain. First he exposes him as a baby; later he sends the lad off with a 'kill bearer' letter; the letter is changed for an injunction to his wife to marry the bearer to their daughter, and too late the father comes and finds that the marriage has already taken place. In the finest form of the story the change in the letter is worked by a mysterious old man to be taken as the hero's personal Fate. In the version here translated the mother's injunction to her son to rest awhile and not drink while he is sweating is a natural incident used to make sure that the meeting with the fateful old man will not fail to take place. But the agent is not always Fate: in the version from Mýkonos it is the boy who reads and changes the letter; in the first Thracian version it is the girl herself. This has a certain piquancy and we find it again in the Old French version mentioned below. In three of our versions, the first one from Thrace, the Macedonian one here translated, and in Abbott's version, the father after the marriage makes a further attempt to get rid of the hero by another 'kill bearer' letter, but this is worse than frustrated because it is his own son who in the end delivers the letter and is killed. In the second version from Thrace the rich man, after the attempt to get rid of the boy by the letter, plots to have him shot and is shot himself. In the version from Epeiros the boy's life is saved because he delays delivering the letter, like the page of St. Elizabeth of Portugal: for whom I refer to No. 71 in this book, *The fortunate Delay*.

This story is spread over the whole European field and Cosquin has called attention to its appearance in the Middle Ages:[1] in Godfrey of Viterbo of the late twelfth century; in the *Gesta Romanorum*; and in the thirteenth-century French romance, *Le dit de l'empereur Constant*, which last may be read in William Morris's translation.

[1] Cosquin, *Études folkloriques*, p. 142.

From this I have borrowed my title, although in Greece the story is told of a rich man.

BP.'s notes to Grimm, No. 29, *The Devil with the three golden Hairs*, i. 276, show that *The Man born to be King* has been made a part of this story. The father of the girl refuses to grant his daughter to the destined hero until he has brought as a test of his worth either three hairs from the devil or three feathers from the phoenix. In none of the Greek versions is there any trace of this: the father after his attempts to get rid of his unwelcome son-in-law acquiesces in his fate.[1]

As to the following translation, no doubt the hearers knew about the miser Gavrilasko, and that the Kalamaria Gate is the eastern gate of Salonika.

The references are:

1. PHÁRASA IN THE TAURUS: *M.G. in A.M.*, p. 492.
2. SMYRNA: *Laographía*, i. 115.
3. MÝKONOS: ibid. i. 117.
4. ATTICA: Albanian text, ibid. i. 92.
5, 6. THRACE: *Arkheíon Thrakikoú Laogr.* v. 190; ibid. xiii. 183.
7, 8, 9. MACEDONIA: *Laographía*, Slav text, ii. 576; *ibid.* ii. 584, translated; Abbott, *Macedonian Folklore*, p. 347.
10. EPEIROS: Hahn, i. 161, No. 20.
11. PHOKIS: B. Schmidt, *Griechische Märchen*, p. 67.

NO. 50. THE MAN BORN TO BE KING[2]

There was a boy and there was another boy as well, and they had hold of a little pair of breeks: one pulled and the other pulled, and Johnnie tore the breeks.

Once upon a time there was a very rich man; his house was full of gear; household stuff and every treasure you could mention; good stock of all the fine things in the world; the very milk of the birds. How can I tell you of it all? For all his wealth he was very fond of money: well, like Gavrilasko; for when he had friends at his table he gave them first of all water to drink so that they could fill up on that and then eat the less.

This man had need to go to some big town, to Salonika let us say, and not to spend any money, he did not go to an inn or to any rich man's house, where he might have had to pay out

[1] Here see Aarne–Thompson Type 461.

[2] Macedonian text from *Loagraphía*, ii. 584.

money: he went to the cottage of a poor man of his acquaintance. The poor man's house had only one room and so they put him to sleep in one corner, and in another the man of the house and his wife slept. His horse and his servant passed the night in the court outside. I forgot to tell you that the poor man's wife was for the third day in bed, because she had had a baby. In the evening when they lay down, the poor man and his wife at once fell asleep, because they had no trouble to vex them. But the rich man thinking about his money and his wealth could not sleep: all night he never closed an eye.

About midnight the door opened and three women came in, dressed in white. They were the three Fates, coming to fix the luck of the little one, the good and the evil he would pass through in the course of his whole life. When the Fates came in they began to consider what good and what evil they should allot to him. Then the eldest turned to the others and said that they should grant him this boon: it should be his destiny to be the heir of the man asleep in the corner. They all agreed; they assigned this lot to him and went away. The rich man, who was not asleep but just crouching in the corner, was trembling with fear when he heard them, and all through the night was thinking what he could do to kill the baby, not to have him as his heir.

In the morning the poor man rose up, and the rich man said: 'Today I must go to the village. God has given me no children. If you are willing, give me this little one to bring up and I shall hold him as my own son. You are still young and God will give you other children.' When the poor man heard this he jumped for joy and went to tell his wife what the rich man had said. But she, being a mother, was at first unwilling. At last however, not to stand in the way of the child's fortune, she consented. She took the baby and dressed him in new clothes and gave him suck abundantly; she went with him right out of the village. When they were outside, as one might say at the Kalamaria gate, she kissed him and handed him over to the rich man, who took him and went off.

They came to a wood and the rich man said to his servant: 'Take this little one and carry him right up there in the wood and kill him.' The servant was a man who feared God; he trembled at this and did not want to go. But he could do no otherwise, for this was an order from his master. He took the baby and carried him up and away to a place where his master could not see him. There he took a stone and banged it against another stone, but the baby he left there on the ground. Then off he ran as though someone were pursuing him. When the master had witnessed all this, he whipped up his horse and went off.

The wood where the baby was lying belonged to an honest householder, to whom God had given no children. Day and night he and his wife used to pray God to give them a child to be the delight of their married state. Meanwhile on that evening God showed them His marvellous doings. As the man late in the evening was walking round his fields, he heard nearby in the wood the voice of a young child. At first he was frightened; then he went quietly to see what it was. When he came to the place where the servant had left the baby, he saw a tiny child left there deserted in the grass. When he saw how beautiful and neat he was, he could not for pity leave him there, and so he took him and brought him to his wife. 'See, my wife,' said he, 'we have begged for a child from heaven, and now in our own field God has given us one. Look at the baby, and this is how I found him in the field. From now onwards he shall be our child.' His wife like a woman was at first a little suspicious, thinking that her husband had had the child by another woman, and was not willing to accept it as her own. But when he had besought her much, she accepted the child and sent for a nurse to bring him up.

Many years passed and the boy, as of a poor but good family, grew big and became the finest boy in the village: all loved him like a brother. One day it chanced by luck that the above-mentioned rich man came to the village and would lodge in the father's house. When he saw that they had a boy, he was astonished; he knew that they had no children, and asked them how they came to have a boy. 'It is now eighteen years,' said the boy's mother, 'since my husband found this boy of ours in the grass near the wood, and now here he is. As we had no children, we took him and brought him up and we hold him as our own son.' When the rich man heard this, he was full of bitterness, for he saw clearly that this boy was the one whom he had taken from the poor man to kill, and that the servant had not killed him but told him a lie. He thought what he could still do to kill him. At last an idea came into his head. He turned and said that he wanted to send a most important letter to his village and wanted a very trusty man to carry it. 'If that is it, our own son shall take it,' said the boy's father, and so the matter was settled.

Then the rich man sat down and wrote a letter to his wife, enjoining her that when the boy reached the village, she should send him up to the mountain for the shepherds to kill him and throw him into the cistern. As soon as the letter was written, the boy made ready and took it and mounted his horse. His mother then kissed him and told him not to drink water when he was tired.

When he came to a spring which was on the road, he dismounted and sat down a little; first to dry off his sweat and then to drink some water, exactly as his mother had told him. And lo, an old man passed by. 'Good day, my lad, and where are you going?' 'I am taking this letter to the village, father. It was that rich man who gave it to me.' 'Give it to me, my lad, to look at, because I think I know the man.' The boy gave him the letter. The old man took it and turned it about a little in his hand and then gave it back to the boy and went about his business. He went on by one road and the boy by another.

In the evening the boy came to the rich man's house. When the mistress saw a stranger, she ran to give him a welcome. As the boy dismounted he looked up and saw at the window a very beautiful girl. Straightway his heart was cloven, just as though it had been written for him by fate that he should fall in love with her. The girl was a child of the rich man. When the boy had gone into the house and up to the main room, he gave the letter to the lady. But the letter was not then as the rich man had written it, because the old man who had met him on the way had been his Fate, and by his magic art had altered the letter; instead of saying that he should be sent to the shepherds for them to kill him, it said that as soon as the boy arrived they should marry him to his daughter, and after a week he himself would come back home. In the morning the wife made everything ready for the wedding and sent for the priest, and he put on their heads the crowns of marriage.

When the rich man came back to his house a week later he

saw up at the window the boy sitting by the side of his daughter. He fell to the ground all dizzy. When after many remedies he came to himself, his wife asked him what had been the matter. 'Nothing, my dear; I was tired by the journey and the sun went to my head. But do tell me why you did not do what I told you in the letter I wrote.' 'But, husband, I did do as you wrote to me. There! Look at your letter.' And she gave him the letter to read.

When he had read the letter, he was amazed and could not understand who had altered the letter. He rubbed his eyes hard and read the letter again and again; he saw it was his own writing and did not know what to say. 'Anyhow,' he said to his wife, 'what has happened, has happened. I will now go and lie down for I am tired, and you, very early in the morning before dawn must send your son-in-law up to the shepherds to take the letter which I shall now write.' He sat down and wrote a letter to the shepherds like the first letter, and then he lay down and went to sleep.

In the morning his wife went to wake up her son-in-law, but when she saw him asleep in her daughter's arms, she for pity would not wake him up and sent the letter off by her own son. When her husband got up, he asked her if her son-in-law had gone up to the sheep-fold with the letter. She said: 'Husband, I thought it was a pity to wake him up so early in the morning. But do not be vexed about the letter: I sent it off by our son.' 'Oh, and what have you done, my wife?' he cried out, and, one, two, he ran off like a madman to catch up the boy, so that the shepherds should not kill him as he had written in his letter. His wife thought he had lost his senses and she too ran off after him.

When they came to the mountain it was too late: the shepherds had killed the boy and thrown him into the well. Then in his grief the rich man threw himself into the well with him and was drowned. His wife, seeing what trouble had come to her house, went mad and she too fell into the well and was drowned, and so the son-in-law was left as their sole heir and inherited the wealth of the man who had loved his money so well, even as the Fates had written his destiny.

This story is to show that no one can escape his destiny.

51

The Ordering of the Fates

THIS story may be taken as an appendage to *The Man born to be King*; it is the same story with the sex changed. A man is present when the Fates give their gifts to a newly-born girl and hears that he is to be her husband. Not desiring to submit, he does what he can to destroy the girl; but of course in vain. In a version from Kérkyra the man first threw the baby girl into a bramble bush, for which reason the story is called *The Girl thrown into the Bramble Bush*. Later he found her still alive and threw her into the sea in a box. Finally he found that he could not avoid marrying her, and after this submission he lived happily with her. This variant of *The Man born to be King* is not confined to Greece: Halliday finds it in Bohemian and even in English folktales.[1]

In the Thracian text translated we read that when the queen saw the chest floating in the sea, she told her servants that if there was money in it, it should be theirs; if there was a child in it, she would keep it for herself. This idea is common; we find it for example in No. 62, *The Curse laid on Rosa*. When a town is taken by siege, I have read somewhere of the conqueror granting the buildings and the loot to his soldiers but reserving the people in the town for himself. The idea seems the same: that human life is on a higher level than material wealth.

The Greek versions are:

1. MÝKONOS: Roussel, *Contes de Mycono*, p. 99.
2, 3. THRACE: *Thrakiká*, xvii. 157 and 158; the latter translated.
4. MACEDONIA: from Velvendós, in *Laographía*, ii. 589.
5. KÉRKYRA: Bernhard Schmidt, *Griech. Märchen*, No. 2.

NO. 51. THE ORDERING OF THE FATES[2]

Once upon a time there was a king and one day his young son the prince took his gun and went off to shoot birds. The young hunter went beyond the palace garden and when he was on the mountain night came upon him. The weather broke and he

[1] *M.G. in A.M.*, p. 256.

[2] Text from Thrace, *Thrakiká*, xvii. 158, with the title *Soused in the Cistern*.

lost the way. In the distance he saw a light in a cottage. He went and knocked at the door: a shepherd lived there with his wife. They were good people and took him in and made him warm in a corner of the house. They gave him a meal and laid a mattress on the floor for him to sleep on. The prince was well content and stayed on with them. At that time the shepherd's wife had a baby, and on the third day at midnight the door opened of itself and three women came in, the three Fates; they went straight to the baby's cradle to set down her destiny. One of them said: 'Your beauty shall have no match.' The next: 'Your husband shall be the prince who is sleeping there on the mattress.' The third said: 'You are to be a queen and you shall sit on a royal throne.' The prince, a man of keen sense and lively spirit,[1] heard what the Fates said: he said to himself that he would see about her marrying him.

When he rose in the morning, he said to the mother of the baby, that he would go back to his house, and he asked them to give him the baby for him to take her to his father and mother; they would rear the child and teach her letters; and 'from time to time you may come to see her'. The parents thought this over and were uncertain as to what they should do. The shepherd said to his wife: 'Let us give him the baby; the young man for sure is of a good family and of a wealthy house; in the town our daughter will be well educated; here in the desert with us poor folk, what will be made of her? Signing her with the cross, let us give him the baby; once a month we can go and look at her.' At last the mother was persuaded; she wrapped her up carefully in clean clothes and swaddled her tight in woollen stuff and, weeping all the time, kissed her baby; so did the father; then they handed her over to the prince. He was very well pleased and went away with her. When he had gone some way he saw a ditch and was minded to throw her into it. 'Shall I throw her in? Yes or No? Shall I? And suppose I don't? To do this would be a sin.' He took her along with him. Next he came to a garden and there he saw a great cistern. 'I will leave the baby here on the edge; the birds will come to drink and they will push her in and so she will be drowned.' He left her there and went hastily off as though he were being chased. In the morning the

[1] The Greek word here is *elaphroïskiotos*, 'of light spirit', for which see note on No. 16 above.

gardener went to fill the cistern; he heard a baby crying; full of joy he took it off to his wife and they made it their own child. When six years had passed, the prince said: 'I must go and see if the baby is still alive,' and he started to go to the garden. Scarcely had he arrived than he saw a pretty little girl about six years old, and she took him in to her father. When he had sat down, the mother said: 'Come, little girl from the cistern, come here and pour out for us.' The prince saw that this was the baby whom he had left by the cistern. Then he asked her parents: 'Will you not let me have your daughter, and I can take her to the town to my mother who will send her to school? Here she cannot learn letters. I could bring her here to see you, and for you to see her.'

For a long time they thought over this. The gardener said to his wife: 'The youth says well; let us hand her over to him, and then she will be educated.' As soon as the prince had left the garden, he put her into a little chest and threw it into the sea, saying to himself: 'This time you won't escape me.' The chest floated and floated and so came to Constantinople. There his aunt was queen, and when she saw the chest floating on the sea, she said to her servants: 'Go and get it: if there is money in it, that shall be yours; if there is a child, it shall be mine.' The serving women ran and took the chest; they opened it and saw inside a beautiful little girl. They took her to the queen, and the queen having no children was much delighted and accepted her as a daughter. Years passed and the girl grew big; she was like a real princess; her beauty had no equal and she was adorned with every grace. The queen loved her much, and said: 'Why should I not send for my young nephew, not to make a stranger my son-in-law, and then I can leave them my kingdom?' She wrote him a letter and he came. The queen saw him with great delight; she embraced him and kissed him and said: 'I shall show you my daughter and you will see how beautiful she is.' The prince was puzzled, for he knew that his aunt had no children. Then the queen told him the whole story; how many years before she had seen one day a chest floating on the sea in front of the palace; she had sent her servants to pick it up, and told them that if it had money in it, that should be for them, and if it were a child, she would take it herself. The chest had in it a beautiful girl; she had loved her so much that she had made her her daughter. Now that the girl was grown up, she wanted to marry her and that was why she had sent for him, to take the girl as his wife. Then as years passed by she would give them the kingdom. The prince gave his promise and they were betrothed, but to himself he said: 'No success for you this time!' He ordered two rings just alike, and he gave her one for her betrothal, saying: 'I am going away and in a year I shall return; if you lose your ring, I shall not take you as my wife.'

The last day before he was to go, he went by night secretly and stole the ring from her; then as he was going off in the ship, he threw the ring into the sea. The princess woke up in the morning and saw that her ring was missing. She searched everywhere but it was nowhere to be found, and she made a great wail. The time for the wedding was coming near and the princess was very sad: she could not find her ring, and the prince had said: 'In a year I shall come; if you have lost your ring, I shall not make you my wife.'

For some days food was being got ready in the kitchen for a banquet to be given to the whole town. A servant was cutting open a big fish, and in it the princess saw her ring: in her delight she ran off to tell the queen. Now all the time that the prince had been away, he had been thinking of the princess and he could not forget her charm and her beauty: he was in love with her, but he did not want to marry her and let things turn out as the Fates had decreed. The girl thrown into the cistern had not her ring and the marriage was not to take place even though everything had been made ready for it. Then when the prince came the princess full of joy ran up and showed him the ring.

At this the prince saw clearly that what has been written by fate can never be unwritten. They were married and the festivities lasted for forty days and forty nights, and they reigned for many years and lived happily and we here still better.

52

The forty Thieves

THIS story is very popular in Greece and most of the cheap books of popular tales contain a version of it. The exhaustive references given by BP., iii. 137, to the Grimm version, make it unnecessary to say much more of a story so well known from the *Arabian Nights*, '*Ali Baba and the forty Thieves*'. In Greece it runs all the way from Zákynthos to Pontos, where in the summer of 1914 I recorded a version from the Christian village of Giga in the Of valley, the eastern limit of Pontic Hellenism.

Of a story so well known it is hardly necessary to print a text. The outline of the story is that there were two men, one rich and one poor. The poor man found his way into the treasure house of the Forty Thieves and came back rich. His companion went for his share, and at this point the story takes two lines. Either he calls upon the door to open by a magic word, which he afterwards forgets and so cannot get out and is killed by the thieves; or he watches the thieves coming out and counts them: he makes a mistake, and going into the treasure house finds that one thief is still there and so he is killed. The story winds up by the thieves discovering who it is that has robbed them and they introduce themselves into the house hidden in chests or jars. But the householder discovers them and kills them. In the *Arabian Nights* version the discovery is made by the clever slave girl Margiana,[1] Coral, and she kills them by pouring boiling oil into the jars. These two types of the story were first pointed out by Halliday who suggested that the form with the magic words is the older.[2] In Greece both forms are widely spread. In our list the magic words are in Nos. 2, 5, 8, 10, 11, 12?, 14?, 15, 16, and the error in counting in Nos. 1, 3, 4, 7, 9, 13. No. 6 from Mitylene combines the two types.

Accustomed to the *Arabian Nights* version of the story with its magic words 'Open Sesame', a version which BP. point out had by the end of the eighteenth century spread in chap-books all over Europe, English readers may expect to find them in the Greek versions. But although often the words of command look very magical, 'Open Sesame' is never found at all and seems in fact to belong exclusively

[1] Slaves are often named after precious stones.

[2] *Folklore*, xxxi. 321.

to the Arabian recension of the story. In detail: at Sinasós in Cappadocia, in Skyros, and in Thrace, the summons is simply, 'Open, my door'. The Phárasa version is a little nearer the Arab idea with 'Open, hyacinth'. Kanellakis's version from Chios has 'Open, spice tree'. In the Mitylene version in *Folklore* the words are Turkish, 'Ach, karakiz,' and 'Kapla, karakiz' which is 'Open, Black eye', and 'Shut, Black eye'.[1] In Samos the word is 'Open, tree', and in Nísyros 'Lift up, stone', as if the treasure house were entered by a way down through the earth. In the Mýkonos version we read: 'The man went up on the mountain and cried *Isknize*, and the mountain opened for him.' In *Isknize* I would see σχίζε, 'Split open'. The Zákynthos form is of some interest for us in this country, for the words in Greek are *bents*, μπέντς, and *set*, σέτ, and I think it not fanciful to recognize in them the English *open* and *shut*, as if the story had been told in the Ionian islands during the nineteenth-century British occupation by some English narrator familiar with the *Arabian Nights*.

A digression may be permitted on 'Open Sesame'; why sesame? F. W. Hasluck suggested that sesame is an ordinary oil-producing plant, the oil being used *inter alia* for oiling locks, and so the name is supposed to act magically on enchanted doors. Hasluck arrived at this idea by finding *madjun*, the name in Turkish of a very sticky sweet, used as a magic word to immobilize people. He is probably right.[2]

The references for the story are:

1. PONTOS: *Arkheíon Pontou*, iii. 113.
2. PHÁRASA IN THE TAURUS; *M.G. in A.M.*, p. 515.
3, 4, 5. CAPPADOCIA: from Ulaghátsh, ibid., p. 363; from Sílata, ibid., p. 447; from Sinasós, in Arkhélaos's *Sinasós*, p. 211.
6, 7. MITYLENE: *Folklore*, vii. 155; and Kretschmer, *Heut. lesbische Dialekt*, p. 514, and translated in his *Neugr. Märchen*, No. 7, p. 28.
8. SAMOS: Stamatiádis, *Samiaká*, v. 598.
9, 10. CHIOS: Pernot, *Études de linguistique*, iii. 294, and an unpublished version recorded by Kanellakis.
11. NÍSYROS: *Z.A.* i. 418.
12. MÝKONOS: Roussel, *Contes de Mycono*, p. 82.
13. SYRA: *Parnassós*, iv. 228, which is in Geldart, p. 9.
14. SKYROS: Pérdika, ii. 178.
15. THRACE: *Thrakiká*, xvii. 135.
16. ZÁKYNTHOS: *Laographía*, x. 416.

[1] *Karakiz* may be either *Kara kiz*, Black girl, or *Kara göz*, Black eye. For several reasons I prefer the latter.

[2] Here I quote from F. W. Hasluck, *Letters on Religion and Folklore*, p. 116.

53

The Boy's Dream

AARNE–THOMPSON TYPE 725

FOR this story of the son's dream and its triumphant fulfilment BP. give abundant references, mostly from the Slav world. Halliday quotes Armenian and Hungarian versions and refers to the story as occurring in Wallachia and among Turkish tribes in Siberia.[1] In the Greek area it clearly belongs to the eastern half, the farthest west example as yet recorded being from Astypálaia. A story from Epeiros in Hahn, i. 258, No. 45, is scarcely to the point; it contains hardly more than a dream that the boy will one day take his father's throne.

In Greece the story falls into two types.[2] In the first, Nos. 1, 2, and 3 of our list, respectively from Pontos, Cappadocia, and Astypálaia, the boy dreams that some day, when he washes his hands, his father will serve him with water and his mother hold the towel. He is driven out by his father, either because he refuses to tell his dream or because his father is angry at its presumption. After various adventures he returns in the guise of a man so rich and important that his parents, not knowing who he is, zealously offer this humble service.

Of this first type the good version from Astypálaia has been translated by Geldart and it need hardly be repeated here.

The second type, that of Nos. 4, 5, and 6, with its very Islamic touch of the two wives, is also from Asia Minor; Nos. 4 and 5 from Phárasa in the Taurus and No. 6 from Indje-Sou. The boy's dream concerns his marriage with two brides, and it is only at the end of the story, when after many troubles he is happily united with both of them, one with a child and the other an expectant mother, that he relates his dream as he sits in the pleasant company of his two wives and the baby: he had been driven away by his father for refusing to reveal what he had seen.

Of this second type the version translated was recorded by Anastasios Levidis, a schoolmaster at the Greek school of the Prodromos at Zindji Dere near Talass. I saw him in 1909; he was then a very old man, blind, and partly paralysed. He had collected and partly

[1] BP. i. 324; *M.G. in A.M.*, p. 256.

[2] It would be of interest to trace these two types in the regions outside Greece. For this it would be necessary to use the Slav versions, and this I cannot do. An Armenian version in *Folklore*, xxii. 476, is of the second type.

published a great deal of material about the Greeks of Cappadocia and the Taurus, and after his death I bought from his son a manuscript book of what he had brought together. From this I have published proverbs and songs,[1] but this is the first appearance of *The Boy's Dream.* In the rather incoherent innocence of the narrative and the amount of children's chatter this story has a close kinship to most of the Phárasa stories in *M.G. in A.M.*

In No. 4, also from Phárasa, the dream is not of three roses but of the sun, the moon, and a star. It has this form: 'In my dream the sun struck me on one side and on the other the moon; from my head there hung a star.' To which the second bride answers: 'I am the moon; the sun is the first bride; that which hung from your head is the baby boy.'

The Indje-Sou version is not good. The hero has only one bride and the story is much padded-out by the insertion of the theme of the Six Gifted Companions.

A few points in the Levidis version deserve notes. The final paragraph about the three apples gives us in the form of an image the whole idea of what oral tradition is. The story is put before us as told by a man who has heard it from the man who made the story, and now passes it on to a third person: upon all three of them the blessing of heaven. This has also a further interest. In an eighteenth-century manuscript book of hymns and prayers in the monastery of Vatopédi on Mount Athos there is a colophon which runs: *The man who wrote this book with toil; the man who reads it with a pious heart; the man who has it in his possession: may the Holy Trinity guard all three of them.*[2] The connexion is obvious between the formula closing the folktale and the colophon written by the scribe at the end of his labours. We are in that border country where literary writing and oral tradition touch one another.

The ending with the three apples seems to be Armenian: at least I find it in some Armenian stories published in *Folklore*, xxii. This same story, on p. 481, ends: *Three apples came down from God; one for the man who told the story; one for the man who asked for it to be told; and one for the man who gave ear to it.*[3] Another example is ibid., p. 484. Cosquin finding the formula in Armenian and also in Turkish stories thinks it is of Turkish origin;[4] to me the Christian colophon on Athos

[1] In *Laographía*, xi. 131; *Annuaire de l'Institut* (*Mélanges Bidez*), ii. 185; *American Journal of Archaeology*, xxxviii. 112.

[2] The colophon is in MS. No. 1015 on p. 182 of Eustratiadis and Arcadios's *Catalogue of the Greek MSS. of Vatopédi*, Harvard Theological Studies, xi. 1924.

[3] I have very slightly altered the wording, though not the sense.

[4] Cosquin, *Études folkloriques*, p. 535, referring to Kunos, *Stambul*, pp. 86, 180, and to Kunos, *Volksmärchen aus Adakale*, i. 184.

and the occurrence of it at Phárasa, where there was a good deal of Armenian influence, rather points the other way and I would take it as Armenian.

It is noticeable that the reason why the boy would not tell his dream was that his father did not offer to bless the dream if it were told to him. But this his wife, the daughter of Kirali, expressly does: 'May this be for good; tell us your dream.'

Who is Kirali? I suggest that it is Köroglou, the Turkish Anatolian hero, who appears also in No. 14, a story from Skyros, where there is a note on him with references.

Lastly, on the incident in which the hero sets the blind men on to kill the dogs in the village. These dogs in the village were not to blame for the damage done by the wolves to the sheep on the hills: it was no business of theirs; they were dogs of the village, not sheep dogs. In the same way it was no business of the daughter of Kirali that the hero was in love also with the daughter of the king. When this was pointed out to her, she had nothing more to say, and consented to share him as a husband with the king's daughter.

The references for versions are these:

1. PONTOS, from Amisós-Samsoún: *Arkheíon Pontou*, i. 185.
2. CAPPADOCIA, from Ulaghátsh: *M.G. in A.M.*, p. 359.
3. ASTYPÁLAIA: Pio, p. 159 = Geldart, p. 154.
4. PHÁRASA IN THE TAURUS: *M.G. in A.M.*, p. 537.
5. PHÁRASA: recorded by Levidis, translated below.
6. INDJE-SOU, in Asia Minor: Carnoy-Nicolaïdes, p. 43, No. 2.

As an appendage to this story a tale from Nísyros (*Z.A.* i. 421) may be mentioned, in which the dreamer is a girl. She had a dream of the moon washing a star and as she would not reveal it her father drove her out. After many adventures she became rich and prosperous and her dream was fulfilled by her father pouring water for her to wash her hands, he the moon and she the star.

NO. 53. THE BOY'S DREAM[1]

The story goes on and goes on, and in the beginning of time there were a man and his wife; they had a little boy. The man was a ploughman; he used to go out with his yoke of oxen. One day came and then another, and on one day he went at dawn to his ploughing. The little boy saw a dream. As he was putting on his clothes he rose and said to his mother: 'Mother, I have

[1] Translated from an unpublished text recorded at Phárasa by Anastasios Levidis with the title *The young Son of the Ploughman.*

had a dream.' His mother said: 'Tell it to me that I may see what your dream was.' But the boy would not tell her. Said his mother: 'May your dream be for good.' He would not tell her. Then said his mother: 'Come, tell me.' 'I won't tell you.' So they quarrelled, and his mother rose and beat him. With his waist-belt in his hand the boy went off crying to find his father in the field to tell him about it. 'I have had a dream; I wouldn't tell it to my mother and she rose and beat me.' Until that day the boy had never gone from home and he did not know where the field was. He went out of the village and walked some way along the path; he saw that the path divided. Here the boy stayed, for he thought: 'If I go one way perhaps my father will come by the other; I will wait here until the evening because my father will come by one path or the other.' The field his father tilled was small and so he finished his work early and came back, driving his oxen before him. He saw his son sitting at the fork of the road and in his haste he pressed on his oxen: 'I must see why he is sitting there, the place where the path divides.' When he was near he said: 'Why have you come here, my son?' The boy had not yet girt himself when his father came. Fastening his belt he rose to his feet saying: 'Father, I got up this morning and as I was girding myself I said to my mother: "I have had a dream!" Then she said: "Tell me your dream." But I would not tell her and she rose up and beat me. Then I said: "I will go to the field and tell my father and he will come and beat you." I walked off and here I am. I saw that the path forked and I did not know where our field was, so not to go astray I sat down here, saying that for sure my father will come. So now here you are, and I have told you about it.' His father said: 'Tell me your dream, my son, and then I can see what it is.' His son said: 'I won't tell you either.' His father said: 'My son, you wouldn't tell your mother your dream and now won't you tell me either?' In his heart the boy felt that his father might have said about his dream: 'May God write it all down for good, and so tell me your dream that I may see what manner of dream it is.' But as his father did not say anything of this sort, the boy refused to tell him what it was. Then said his father: 'My son, why will you not tell me your dream?' The boy said: 'I won't tell you anything at all.' The father gave the boy two slaps and pushed his oxen forward and went off saying to his son: 'Don't dare to come home; since you won't tell me your dream you are no longer my son.' So he went off to their house.

Then his wife rose up and drove the oxen into the stable, fed them, and came and set out the table. She said to her husband: 'Your boy went off to find you: have you seen him?' Her husband said: 'He came to the fork in the path and waited there. I came back from the field and said: "Why are you waiting here, my son?" He said: "I got up in the morning and when I was dressing I said to my mother that I had had a dream. She said: "Tell me your dream." But I would not tell her. Then my mother got up and beat me. I did not know where our field was and so I came here and saw that the path forked and I said: Surely by one or the other of these paths my father will come." I quickly finished ploughing and came and found him sitting at the fork of the path. I said: "Why are you waiting here, my son?" Then he said: "I have had a dream." I said: "Tell me your dream." But he would not tell me. Then I gave him a couple of slaps and left him there and drove on with the oxen. As I was going I said: "Don't dare to come home: I won't have you." ' Then said his wife: 'How could it be well for our son to have a dream and to make it known neither to his mother nor to his father? But we will let time pass and see what God will grant us to see.'

Now let us come to the boy. He followed the path and, walking a lot and walking a little, he saw before him a village. He entered the village and as he was walking in the market-place, so too were the king and his vizier with him. The king saw a fine boy there and with the vizier he went up to him. Said the king to the vizier: 'This boy is from some other place; let us ask him where he is going.' So when they came to the palace, the king sent off a policeman: 'Go to the market-place; there by the fountain a boy is sitting. Tell him that the king wants him. Take him and bring him here.' The man went off and found the boy by the fountain, and said: 'Come you with me: the king wants you.' The boy said: 'I am but a young boy and what can the king want of me?' The man who had come for him said: 'I do not know what the king wants of you, only I am to bring you to him.' The boy rose up and they went off. The man who was leading him said to the king: 'I have brought the boy for whom you sent me.' The king saw that it was the same boy and said to him: 'You do not belong to this place? Tell me from where you are.' Then the boy said: 'I *am* from here.' The king said: 'You are *not* from here. Tell me, or I will cut off your head.' The boy thought to himself: not to tell him is impossible. So he said: 'How can I hide it? I am from another place.' 'And why have you come here?' said the king. The boy said, 'I had a dream, and I would not tell my dream to my mother or to my father and they beat me. Then I walked off and happened upon this village here.' The king said: 'You did well. Tell me the dream you had, and we shall see what it means.' Then the boy said: 'Nor will I tell you my dream.' The king said: 'Two headsmen to come here!' He spoke to the man on guard and the headsmen came. 'Take this boy; lead him outside the village and cut off his head.' As they were taking him away they passed by in front of the door of the king's youngest daughter. The girl saw that he was a handsome boy and said to those who were leading him: 'Where are you taking this boy?' The men said: 'This boy had a dream; this dream he would not tell to your father, and your father has ordered us to cut off his head.' The girl told them to come into her house. They went in, and the girl said: 'See, here are a hundred piastres for each of you; let the boy stay here and tell no one anything about it. Now take his shirt and this puppy; spread out the shirt and cut off the puppy's head and let the blood run down over the shirt; then take the shirt to my father and he too will pay you something.' They took the money and went and did as she had told them. They spread out the shirt and cut off the puppy's head and the blood ran down, and they took the shirt off to the king. The king saw it and gave them their pay. Then they went off.

The girl sent the little boy to go to learn reading. The girl saw to their food for when the boy should come back from his lesson; when he came home from his lesson they ate their meal together and he went off again.

One day passed; two days, and the king and Kirali had a quarrel; they would have nothing to do one with the other. On a day Kirali rose up and groomed two mares and sent them to the king saying: he must distinguish which of these two is the dam and which is the foal and send them back to him. The king rose up and brought together his men, great and small, and said: 'Kirali must let me have a term of three days in which to find the answer to this question.' The man who had brought the mares went off. Then the king brought together the people great and small; every one of them. No one could tell which was which. At midday the boy came back from his lesson for them to eat together; he saw that the girl was full of thought. He sat down and said: 'Bring the bread and we will eat.' The girl said: 'There is the food; fetch it, eat it, and go off to your lessons.' The boy said: 'Why are you acting in such a way? Before, I used to fetch the food and eat it; now must I go off and before I have eaten?' The girl said: 'Fetch your food and eat it and then go to your work. Today there is something here for us to think about.' The boy said: Tell me; I want to see what it is you are thinking about.' The girl said: 'Kirali has sent two mares to my father to say which of them is the dam and which is the foal. We cannot distinguish them and that is what fills us with trouble.' The boy said: 'Bring us the food for our meal and I will go off for my reading lesson. When I come back you must have the mares here.' They ate and the boy went off for his lesson. The girl rose up and went to her father and said: 'My father, send the mares to our house and we will see if I can find the answer.' Then she went home. Her father sent the mares after her to her house. When it was towards evening the boy said to his teacher: 'Give me leave to go off home; we have a little piece of work there.' The master said: 'Since you have work there, go.' When the boy reached home he said: 'Have you brought the mares?' And the man said: 'I have brought them.' 'Go and give the boys five farthings apiece and bid them collect half a bushel of pebbles. When the lads brought the pebbles he mixed them up with the barley and put them into the nose-bags hung on the necks of the mares. The dam picked out the barley grain by grain and ate it but the colt ate all and everything. Then the boy said to the girl: 'The bay there is the dam and the grey is the colt.' The king sent the mares back to Kirali. Kirali said: 'Now that he has distinguished them he must come in the morning to Pavletsi and we can drink a coffee together.'

The man who had brought the mares came and told the king that that Kirali greeted him and would he come in the morning to Pavletsi to drink a coffee, bringing his daughter with him. Then the king said to his daughter: 'Make all ready for us to go to Pavletsi in the morning.' His daughter said: 'I will not go, and give me leave to tell you how it was I distinguished the two mares. You sent off a boy and with him two men with orders to cut off his head; I kept him in my house and it was he who distinguished the two mares.'

Her father said to her: 'Go and bring me the boy.' They brought the boy and the king set apart two horses; the king mounted on one of them and the boy on the other and they rode off. On the way the boy found a flint stone; he dismounted and picked it up and they went on. They went straight on and dismounted at Kirali's palace. There they drank their coffee. Kirali had a daughter: she was a powerful witch, and by casting lots she knew everything that would happen. One day she cast the lots and found that the boy was in love with the daughter of the king. The boy had much wisdom granted him by God. The girl by agreement with her father proposed that the boy should come with him and if he came she should have him as her husband: 'I want him,' said she. So when she saw the boy coming with the king she was much pleased. Then they drank their coffee.

When the girl—the daughter of Kirali—came she brought three stones and said to the boy: 'Look at these stones and tell me which of them is a stone of value.' The boy took the stones and looked at them and when he had tested them with the flint which he had in his pocket he threw the stones aside saying: 'These are not worth anything at all.' At this the girl was angry and she told her father, and her father and the king resolved on a fight. At these words the king rose up and the boy with him and the king went to his palace. And as they were making ready for the battle the boy said to the king: 'You stand aside and give me leave and let me have the boldness to go myself to contend with Kirali.' At this the king was pleased and gave him leave and encouraged him. Then one day the boy brought together as many as fifty Kurds, men who did not know their language. To each one of them he gave a club as a weapon; they went to Kirali's village. The boy said to the Kurds: 'Now wherever you come upon a dog, big or small, you must hit him hard and kill him.' The Kurds did as he told them. All this while Kirali's daughter was sitting at her window and when she saw what the Kurds were doing she sent an army of men to seize them and throw them into prison. But the boy said: 'I will not go into the prison; I will go to see Kirali.' They seized him and brought him to Kirali, but before Kirali could say anything the girl said to the boy: 'What have the dogs done amiss that you command the Kurds to kill them?' The boy said: 'How have they done nothing amiss? Why did they not guard my sheep which graze on our mountains and the wolves devour them?' The girl said: 'The dogs here, how can they act as guards for the sheep up on the hills?' The boy said: 'It is the same with you; you are here and are making trouble because I love the king's daughter who is in the village, and are trying what you can to bring about a quarrel.' And when he had said this the girl had nothing more to say, but she said: 'If you will marry me as well then I will tell my father and he and the king will no longer be enemies.' The boy was well pleased and he took as his wife the daughter of Kirali and brought her to the king's palace, and there for forty days the wedding was celebrated. So he married both the daughter of Kirali and the daughter of the king.

Nine months later the daughter of Kirali gave birth to a little girl. One day the boy had taken his little girl in his arms and as they were thus sitting his dream came into his mind and he said: 'One time I had a dream.' When he said this the daughter of Kirali said to him: 'May this be for good; tell us your dream that we may see what it was.' The boy began and said: 'In my dream I saw three roses; one rose was open; the second was about to open and the third seemed like a bud. This was my dream and now tell me what it signified.' The girl said: 'These three roses signify the three of us. The open rose is for me for I have had a child. The rose to open is the king's daughter for she has not yet had her child. The rose in bud is the baby girl whom you have in your arms.'

From heaven there fell three apples: one apple was for the man who made the story; the next apple was for him who told the story; the third was for him who has heard and understood it. Now it is at an end.

54

The rejected Bride, or *He who will not when he may*

THIS is the story of two men who agreed that their children should marry one another. But when the time came, the father of the boy was rich and the girl was poor, so the rich people cried off the bargain; even if the boy was willing, his friends dissuaded him and he jilted the girl. Her father then married her to the first suitor who turned up. Then the rich youth changed his mind, but 'he who will not when he may, and so on,' and the girl refused to desert her rather unpromising husband. Her rich suitor brought the case into court, and it was revealed that the seemingly poor husband was in fact the king, who was at the moment sitting in judgement on the case. The girl did not know him until he reappeared in the court in his rags; then she recognized him, and he reassumed his royal robes and brought her to the palace.

The story has two very close Turkish parallels: one is in Kent's *Fairy Tales from Turkey*, p. 110, and the other is from Ada-Kale, printed in Kunos' *Adakale*, No. 22, i. 97, and ii. 136. Whether the story is of Greek or of Turkish origin or neither is no clearer to me now than when I discussed the Astypálaia variant in *Forty-five Stories*.

The references are:

1. ASTYPÁLAIA: *Forty-five Stories*, p. 288: *What Luck may send.*
2. SMYRNA: Legrand, *Recueil de contes pop. grecs*, p. 233.
3. MÝKONOS: Roussel, *Contes de Mycono*, p. 94, translated below.
4. MACEDONIA: *Laographía*, vi. 510. Also translated.

NO. 54*a*. THE REJECTED BRIDE[1]

Once upon a time there were two neighbours, one rich and one poor. The rich man had a son and the poor man had a daughter. One day the rich man's son said to his mother: 'Mother, I want to have our neighbour's daughter as my wife.' 'What are you talking about?' said his mother. 'Have you thought what you

[1] Text from Macedonia in *Laographía*, vi. 510, with the title, *The poor Girl's Luck.*

are saying? Why, tomorrow the daughters of rich men will be coming to ask for you; girls with dowries.' 'No,' said he, 'It is she I want to have.' On the next day his mother started and went off to her neighbour and knocked at the door. 'Bah, what is the matter with her?' said the poor man's wife; 'our neighbour coming and knocking at our door?' Well, she went and opened the door. 'Good day to you, neighbour.' 'Good day to you.' 'Do you know why I have come here, neighbour?' 'And how should I know?' 'Well, listen. My son wants your daughter as his wife.' 'Very well said, neighbour,' said the poor man's wife, 'I thank you for your good intentions, but do you know that we are poor people and I have nothing to give her more than the smock she stands up in.' 'Bah,' said the other, 'that is not worth talking about. My son wants her just as she is.' 'Very well; when my husband comes in the evening I will tell him.' In the evening her husband came and she told him all about it. 'Well, since he wants her, let him have her.' Next day the two wives met and made the exchange of rings. So the betrothal was heard of all over the town.

When the young man's friends heard of it, they went and talked to him and made him change his mind. So the youth went home and said to his mother: 'I have changed my mind. I will not marry our neighbour's daughter.' 'What is this you are saying, my son? I told you from the very beginning that the girl is not suitable for you; but now as things are how can I go and tell this to my neighbour, now that everybody knows about it? What? Do you want the poor girl put to shame?' 'You go and say plainly and clearly that I don't want her daughter.' So his mother went off to her neighbour. 'Good day.' 'And good day to you.' 'Well, neighbour, and how am I to put it? My son has changed his mind and does not want your daughter. See; here is your ring; take it back again and give me mine.' In the evening her husband came and she said: 'Our young neighbour doesn't want to marry our daughter.' 'Bah, and is it for that that you are so much vexed? For our daughter it will be all right. You just give her a bath and comb her hair that she look smart on Saturday evening, and I will take her by the hand and we will go to the cross-roads; then whatever man I meet there, him I will accept as her husband.' So on Saturday evening he took the girl to the cross-roads. It happened that just then the king was passing by. The man stopped him and without recognizing him, for it was dark, said to him: 'I will take you as my daughter's husband because I have said that whomsoever I meet here I will take as my son-in-law.' 'Very well,' answered the king, 'Let us go to your house and fetch the priest; but the wedding must be performed with no lights lit.' So they were crowned in marriage and went to bed. In the morning the bridegroom before dawn got up and gave the girl some money, saying: 'Your father must go and have three sets of clothes cut out for you, and then he must go to the bazaar and buy you jewellery of the finest; also he must find the master builder and go with him to the king's palace and measure the plan of it to build another palace like it.'

When the son of the rich man heard of all this he wanted to have the poor man's daughter back again, but she refused because she was married to another man. So they went to the king to have their case judged. The rich man's son began the pleading saying: 'At the beginning I had this girl betrothed to me; we broke it off and now I want her again, to marry her.' 'And how can he have me?' said the girl, 'seeing that I am married to another man?' And this she said not knowing that the king was her husband. 'Do you know who your husband is?' said the king. 'No, I do not know, but taking his hand in mine then I shall know if it is he.'

Next day there was a royal command that all the men of the town should assemble; they were to pass by a place where the girl was, she putting out only her hand and not seeing them. So all the people began to pass by and to take her hand; but she recognized no one. At last the king said: 'I too must pass by.' So he passed by; she took his hand and said: 'This is he.' Then said the king to the rich man's son: 'Behold; this girl was destined for me and not for you.' So the king took her to his palace, and they lived well and may we live yet better.

NO. 54*b*. THE REJECTED BRIDE[1]

There were two girls, orphans, and they went to fetch water. Two merchants chanced to be there and one of them said: 'I wish I had her as my wife, the fair one: I should like her well.'

[1] Text from Mýkonos, in Roussel's *Contes de Mycono*, p. 94.

The other said: 'And I should like to have the dark one; her I would choose.' The girls drew the water and went home, and the merchants followed them. They questioned an old woman: 'Are those girls married?' 'They are not.' 'Will you not go and ask if they are willing to be married?' 'I will go.'

The old woman went and said to the girls: 'My dears, these merchants are asking for you.' One said: 'We have no means of marriage for we are poor.' The merchants said: 'We want you.' One married the fair girl and the other the dark girl. 'Well, friend, here we are, married. When our wives have children, let us make a marriage alliance together.' The fair bride had a baby, a girl, and the dark one a boy.

Time passed, and the girl was now twenty years old, but the dark woman was not willing for her to be married to her son. The girl's mother went to her and said: 'Friend, we arranged to have an alliance of marriage.' 'I do not want your daughter; in truth my son is to marry a princess.' The woman at this rose up and went back home.

In the evening her husband went down to shut up the ground floor, and at the door he found a young man dressed in rags. He said: 'What do you want here?' Then he said to his wife: 'Here is a man come to marry our daughter.' Said his wife: 'Up then, my husband; go off and get the licence and we can make the marriage, and this will teach our friend a lesson.' The father went off and took out the licence.

Thus they made the young man her husband. In the night he rose up and said to his wife: 'I must be off. Underneath your pillow you will find something.' In the morning the girl rose up and she found three hundred gold coins wrapped in a silk kerchief. Then her mother said: 'Where is your husband?' She said: 'He went away in the night and left me this money.' 'Oh, my daughter; the man must be a robber.' The girl said: 'Is it I who made the marriage? It was you; you gave him to me.'

Then the son of the dark woman changed his mind and sought the girl in marriage, but she said to him: 'I am now married. Let your mother go find you a queen.' He said: 'I will bring you before the law court.' In the evening when her husband came to her, she said: 'Don't you see what a trouble I am in now with the son of the dark lady? He says he will bring me before the law court to make me marry him.' The man said: 'Well, wife, why not marry him?' 'And how can I marry him now that I am already married and am your wife? Yours and not his.' 'Well, then he will take it to the law court.' 'Do please come to the court with me.' 'I can't come; anyhow you can go by yourself.'

In the morning the husband rose up and went off. About ten o'clock the wife heard music. There came a carriage all decked with gold and in it twelve girls; it came up to the house. One of the girls said: 'Come, my lady; we want to dress you and we can go to the law court.' The girls dressed her and they went into the carriage and so to the law court. The son of the dark woman was there.

The president of the court said to her: 'How is it, my lady, that you have got married and will not accept this young man here?' 'Because, your worship, his mother wanted to give him a queen for a wife; not me, but a queen.' 'Now you ought to leave your husband and marry this youth.' 'This is not well said, your worship. I am married; he too must go and find a wife and marry her.' 'This is not well said, my lady; you are bound to marry him, even against your will.' She said: 'No, your worship.' She turned to the young man: 'Indeed I cannot bear the sight of you. I shall retire.'

Then said the president: 'Stay, my lady.' Then he said to the youth: 'See, she will not have you, and that because she is married.' Then the president rose up and went into the palace and put on his ragged clothes. Then he came out again and took the girl's arm and led her into the royal palace and set her on the throne. Then he went and took off the ragged clothes and put on his royal robes, and so they are living in the palace and ruling their kingdom even to the present day.

55

The fated Bridegroom

THIS is a story of destiny; it is fated that the daughter of a rich man shall marry a servant in her father's house, a blackamoor. Yet in the Greek view it seems that to those who in the words of the Cretan version here translated 'leave all to the power of God', things may turn out better than might seem possible: in this case the young blackamoor is turned into a white man. That in the hero's search for Christ he should be asked questions in the hope that on his return he may bring helpful answers is a conspicuous part of No. 79, *The Search for Luck*, and can in fact be fitted into any story of a man going to consult a higher power. The present story is a variant of No. 27 in *Forty-five Stories*, *What is written is not to be unwritten*—what has once been written stands good for ever—and beyond the notes there nothing more need be said of it.

One of Hahn's stories from Epeiros, ii. 159, No. 113, is on the same theme: a rich father refused to allow his daughter to marry her betrothed because he was poor. But the story is worked out quite differently, and the boy wins the girl by a mixture of bribery and persistence. There is also a story from Silli near Konia, in *M.G. in A.M.*, p. 240, of a girl who in accordance with the prophecy of a wise man married much below her, a man who sold ashes. Her father, learning that two children whom he saw were called, one of them 'In Predestination that which is written', and the other 'In Mutability is hardly found', recognized his daughter's children and submitted to the decree of fate.

The references for this story are:

1. ASIA MINOR, FROM MOUDANIÁ: *Mikrasiatiká Khroniká*, iv. 284.
2. KOS: *Forty-five Stories*, p. 281.
3, 4. CRETE: *Myson*, vii. 152, here translated, and from Rétimo in Kretschmer's *Neugr. Märchen*, p. 84.
5. THRACE: *Arkheíon Thrakikoú Laogr.* v. 188.

NO. 55. THE FATED BRIDEGROOM[1]

Once upon a time there was a rich man and he had no children. Every day he used to beseech God to send them children, and

[1] Text from Zyros in East Crete, printed *Myson*, vii. 152, with the title *What is written cannot be unwritten.*

He sent them a girl. One day there came a woman who told fortunes, and she told the little girl's fortune: she would be married to the young blackamoor who served in the house.

The parents suggested to her everyone possible. 'Indeed, indeed,' said the girl, 'The man for me is the blackamoor and no one else at all.' At once the parents took steps either to banish him or to kill him; yet they were sorry for him. So they gave him some money and said: 'Go, my lad, and try to find Christ and ask Him whether what has been written is ever unwritten.' 'And where am I to find Him?' 'Go off; when you search you will find Him.'

The young blackamoor started off; he went to towns and villages and wild woods, but never did he find Christ. He went all the way to Hell and to all the boiling pitch in it. There he saw a man half plunged in the cauldron, seething in torment. The man said to him: 'Where are you going, my lad?' 'I am on my way to find Christ.' 'Speak to Him, my boy: Oh, curse and blast Him; how long will He keep me burning here?'

As the boy went on and on he met a blind man. 'Where are you going, my boy?' 'I am on my way to find Christ.' 'Ask Him how long He will keep me here in the misery of blindness; He must deliver me; I can endure no longer.' The boy went on farther and saw a rich woman, 'You are welcome; come and have a meal and a lodging.' She too questioned him and he answered in the same way. 'Tell Him, my boy, to send His good gifts to someone else than me for I have all I can desire.' At last he met with a little old man, and this was Christ. 'My master has sent me for you to tell me whether what is written can be unwritten.' He said: 'Come and let me wash you with this medicine I have, and I will leave nothing but a black cross on your belly, and this shall be a sign. Here too is a lot of money and this little bottle.' 'But I have been meeting people, and they said to me. . . .' And so he told Christ the whole story. 'You can go tell the woman that as long as she remembers me, I shall send her what will be for her good. Tell the blind man to anoint himself with this medicine and he will have his sight. Tell the other man that I shall keep him there as long as he blasphemes. Tell your master that what is written is not unwritten.' The blackamoor went back again, now young and handsome and rich; he kept a shop.

The boy's master with his wife and his daughter went to this shop, and the girl fell in love with the boy: she could neither eat nor drink nor in peace give glory to God. 'What is the matter with you, my daughter?' said her mother. 'Mother, I love that young man and I want you to give him to me; if not, I shall die.' 'My girl, this is a great thing you ask; he will not accept you.' At last when his daughter insisted the father made up his mind to invite the young man to a meal, and when they met he would tell him and leave all the matter to the power of God. So the man went and invited the youth, and he accepted and went to the meal. Passing from one subject to another, the father made up his mind and told the youth: 'We wanted to talk to you like this to see if you would accept the proposal.' 'What is all this talk? Why are you saying this? How am I better than her?' So first they made the betrothal and when all was ready they held the marriage.

On the morning after the wedding people spoke of the telling of fortunes, and the bride's father said: 'See, my children, what they say about fortune-telling. I myself among many things, I once had with me a young blackamoor. . . .' So he told all the story. The bridegroom burst out and said: 'And I am that young blackamoor. Am I lying?' He opened his shirt and showed the mark of the cross and told them all the story. Then to his father-in-law he said: 'What is written cannot be unwritten.' Then they lived in good hap and we still more happily.

56

The Thief in the King's Treasury

AARNE–THOMPSON TYPE 950

THIS is the well-known story in Herodotus of the thief in the treasury of the Pharaoh Rhampsinitus, and in these five variants we can see the Greek oikotype of this very widely-distributed story, for which full references are given by BP. iii. 395, in their notes to the allied story in Grimm, No. 192, *The Master Thief*. For translation there is not much difference: I choose the version from Zákynthos, although it is very untidily told.

The third boy makes the ring-rolls of bread fall down by softening them, in the same way as the princess in No. 6 rots the chain and so brings down the shoes by throwing on it as acid 'stinking water and rotten lemons'.

The Greek versions I find are:

1. CYPRUS: Sakellarios, ii. 320, which has been borrowed by Legrand, *Recueil de contes pop. grecs*, p. 205.
2. DEMIRDESH IN BITHYNIA: Danguitsis, *Étude descriptive du dialecte de Démirdési*, p. 206.
3. MITYLENE: Kretschmer, *Heut. lesbische Dialekt.*, p. 481, and also in his *Neugr. Märchen*, p. 54, No. 16.
4. KÁLYMNOS: Dieterich, p. 470.
5. ZÁKYNTHOS: *Laographía*, x. 410, translated.

NO. 56. THE THIEF IN THE KING'S TREASURY[1]

Once there was a robber with three nephews; he wanted to pick out among them one who as a robber would be his equal. So he called for one of the three and shut him up in a room, where hanging from a rafter there was a forked stick with rings of bread on it. 'There is the bread,' said he, 'and now you may eat of it.' In the morning he came back; said he: 'Have you eaten?' 'No,' said the boy; 'how could I? I could not reach up to the bread.' Next day he shut the second boy in the room and he too was found to have eaten nothing. Next day he called for the

[1] Text from Zákynthos, printed in *Laographía*, x. 410.

third. This boy steeped a sponge in water, and by throwing it up against the ring rolls, soaked them and softened them so that they fell down. At dawn his uncle came: 'Have you eaten?' said he. 'I have; there was bread up there and of course I ate it.' 'Ah,' said he, 'you're the boy for me.'

They started and went off on the road. In the distance they saw a priest with a lamb. The nephew said: 'I will contrive to get the lamb from him.' 'But how can that be done?' 'Leave it to me and you shall see.' He took off one of his shoes and set it on the road. The priest passed by. 'Oh,' said he, 'if only there were the other shoe as well, then I would pick it up.' The robber nimbly took off his other shoe and put it down a little farther on. The priest left the lamb in order to go back and take the first shoe. Right off the robber seized the lamb. 'Now,' said he, 'we can go and make a meal of it.'

While the robbers were in the wood cooking the lamb, they were saying that they would go and steal the king's gold. And in fact the young robber did go and steal some gold; he put it in his pocket. Next evening he did the same. The third evening he said to his uncle: 'You too must go.' Now the king was anxious by any means possible to discover the thief. So he ordered his men to smear pitch on the floor. The elder robber came and fell into the pitch. His nephew waited for him and waited, but in vain. At the end of his patience he went into the treasury. He drew his sword and cut off the robber's head that the king might not know who it was. The king was at a loss: 'I must see,' said he, 'who it is.' Then he had a proclamation made; anyone weeping and lamenting must be a kinsman of the robber. The man's unfortunate wife began her lamentations. 'Hush, hush,' said the nephew. 'Go to the spring with a pitcher to fetch water, and when you are holding it up to fill it, just manage to let it fall. Then your lamentations will seem to be for your pitcher.' So next morning the king's officers went out and all round the city, and they could find no one making lamentation, no one at all but the old woman crying for her pitcher. How could it ever enter their minds that she was the wife of the robber? They turned back to the palace and told the king. 'Oh,' said he, 'and didn't you seize her? She must be the one.'

By the king's orders the square of the city was spread with gold; whoever gazed at the gold with savage rapacity, he would be the robber. But what did the robber do? He took his shoes and covered them with fish glue; then he walked over the gold and by means of the glue he collected all the gold. The soldiers came back having achieved nothing. 'Everybody,' they said, 'walked by, O king, with their eyes cast down.'

Yet the king did not give up; he was set upon discovering the thief. He set in the city square a number of camels loaded with gold, and whoever should buy them he could be taken as the robber. But the robber had a little knife, and as he passed by he cut the tie-ropes and drew the camels after him. The king almost died of vexation. 'Oh,' said he, 'this is indeed a strange happening.'

Then he ordered an old woman to go round all the houses in the town asking for a little piece of camel meat for her sick child. So she went to one house and then to another, and then to the house of the robber. She said: 'A piece of camel's meat, pray; my child is sick and weak.' The robber's aunt took and gave her a piece. The old woman marked a big cross on the door and went away. But as she was going out the robber was approaching. 'Oh,' said he, 'stop a moment and I will give you a lot, for we have any amount,' The old woman was deceived by this and went into the house; the robber gave her one blow and cut off her head. But before he could cut it off, she just had time to set a mark on his nose. 'And now,' said the robber, 'what can I do, for she has marked the house with a cross?' He set fire to it. Everyone ran up to put out the fire. He stood by the door and with a seal marked each one of them on the nose. As they went in, they said: 'You are the robber surely? Are you not?' He said: 'Look at your own mug.' The king did not know what he could then do.

Now all this time the king of Turkey was laughing at our king, the king of Greece, because he could not catch the robber. The robber presented himself to the king of Greece: 'Your Majesty,' said he, 'I will bring you the man, this king of Turkey. I ask you to commission a big ship and give me a dress all hung with bells, and announce to the king of Turkey the coming of the crown prince of Greece.' This was done as he directed. The Turk received him with bands of music and with festivities. In the evening when they were all asleep, the robber put on the dress with the bells and went to the king's room. Ting a ling, ting a ling ling! The king woke up. The robber said: 'I am the Lord's angel. I am to take you to Paradise; shall it be quick or dead?' The king was quite dazed; he said: 'Quick, alive! But please wait for tomorrow for me to say goodbye to my family.' Then in just the same way the robber came the next night and put the king into a chest and nailed it up and took it straight to his steamer. But the robber had before this sent a telegram to the king of Greece that he must sit on a golden throne to receive them, just as though he were God. They arrived, and the king of Turkey fell at the feet of our king, thinking him to be God. Then he said: 'I am the king of Greece and I can show you that I can hold in captivity if not the robber yet certainly you.' The robber acknowledged his fault and the king gave him his hand. The robber took the princess as his wife and they lived well and may we live yet better.

57

The Girl who was left at home

AARNE–THOMPSON TYPE 883A

UNDER the title of *The beautiful Girl Sweetmeatmaker* this story has been studied by Halliday, who regards it as of Balkan origin.[1] This cumbrous title proves to be of little value, and the one I have devised at least gives some idea of the story, which is of a girl left at home by her father in charge of a villain who presently assaults her. The girl escaped and was married; later on she was attacked again by the same villain. She then dressed as a boy and gathering an audience together narrated to them the history of her sufferings and denounced her persecutor.

The management of the end of the story is interesting.[2] In order to proclaim her sufferings and her innocence and the wickedness of her enemy in as dramatic a manner as possible, the heroine calls together behind closed doors all the people concerned, including above all the villain: before beginning her story she demands that no one shall on any pretext leave the room, so that the villain cannot sneak away and escape. This manner of the final vindication of the heroine is found in other stories—e.g. Nos. 1 and 11, above—but it is here that it seems most properly to belong. It is all the more effective as it seems to have been the regular almost formal way in which story-tellers did begin their stories, using precisely this form of preface. Thus in describing how stories were told at Ordoú on the Black Sea Akoglou writes: 'When everything was ready in the room, the story-teller assumed his professional style and introduced the matter by this declaration: *He who is in the room, let him stay in the room; he who is outside let him stay outside; who wants to go out for any purpose, let him go now and come back again.* Then came the fixed formula for the beginning of a story: *In those first ages and in those years of silver, there was*, and so on.'[3]

It is just in this way that the heroine of the present story prefaced her account of herself: shutting the door and putting the key in her pocket, and then starting her story.

[1] *M.G. in A.M.*, p. 267.

[2] A Turkish example in Kunos, *Stambul*, p. 383. The text is in *Oszmán-török népköltési gyüjtemény*, i. p. 294, No. 68.

[3] See Xenophon Akoglou, *Laographiká Kotyóron*, p. 386. See also BP. ii. 255, 505.

As this story has already been printed three times in English—the versions from Cappadocia, from Chios, and from Athens—it seems unnecessary to do more here than give this outline of it.

The references are:

1, 2. PONTOS: *Arkheíon Pontou,* iii. 80 and ix. 179.

3. CAPPADOCIA: from Ulaghátsh, *M.G. in A.M.*, p. 360.

4. CHIOS: Argenti and Rose, *Folklore of Chios,* p. 429; *Hadji Nicholas's Daughter.*

5. ASTYPÁLAIA: Pio, p. 143.

6. SKYROS: Pérdika, ii. 173.

7. ATHENS: Kamboúroglou, p. 106 = Garnett, p. 368.

8, 9. THRACE: *Thrakiká,* xvi. 160, and *Arkheíon Thrakikoú Laogr.*, v. 174.

58

The virtuous Wife

AARNE–THOMPSON TYPE 712

IN *Forty-five Stories* No. 45, *The Story of Jack*, from Kos, is a version of the old Greek novel of Apollonios of Tyre; it has returned to Greece by way of a rhymed version in popular Greek, first printed at Venice in 1534. But the last scenes of the story as presented in this version differ a good deal from the denouement of the Apollonios story and have been remodelled on a folktale of which the present story from Thrace, to which I have given the title *The virtuous Wife*, is the better of the Greek versions yet brought to light: the other one is from Epeiros.[1] Outside Greece this tale of *The virtuous Wife* is found in the *Gesta Romanorum*,[2] and from this source it may be supposed that it was carried into Greece, where it now survives in these two versions and in the fresh ending which the Koan narrator gave to the Apollonios story.

We have to go to the Epeiros version to learn that why the blackamoor needed crutches, when he went to the supposed monk to confess his sins and be cured, was that he had become a leper. Nor does our version say anything definite of the cure of the husband's blindness.

NO. 58. THE VIRTUOUS WIFE[3]

Once upon a time there was a great merchant who had a wife, very beautiful and also good; her name was Myrtle. The merchant went off to a distant country trading, entrusting his wife to a friend of his. The friend wanted to take her as his mistress; Myrtle was a woman of honour and refused and drove him out of her house. The man at once took and wrote a letter to his friend: 'When you had gone away your wife went right out of

[1] Pio is p. 66, Hahn, i. 140, No. 16. The wanderings in Greece of the Apollonios story I have discussed in a paper in *The Modern Language Review*, xxxvii, 1942, p. 169.

[2] *Gesta Romanorum*, Oesterley's edition, Chap. 249, app. 53, p. 648.

[3] Text from Phanari in Thrace, printed in *Thrakiká*, xvii. 180, with the title *Mersina, Myrtle.*

her mind, mad, first for one man and then for another, and of you she never thinks at all.' Her husband without looking any further wrote to his friend that he must bury her alive.

To wreak his vengeance, as soon as ever he received the letter the man made a chest; he took it out to the mountain, and in spite of all her weeping put Myrtle into the chest and buried her. Shepherds passing that way saw that the earth had been dug up and they also heard her cries. They dug her up and took her out of the chest and took her off with them. On the way they saw a great crowd of people running. Myrtle asked what it was. They told her that it was a certain man who owed five hundred piastres, and because he had not the money to pay his debt he was being taken to be hanged. Myrtle was grieved that he should be hanged and she brought out the five hundred piastres and paid the debt and delivered the man.

She thanked the shepherds who had dug her up and took up her package of clothes to embark in a ship. The man, whose debt she had paid and had delivered him, asked her for her package to carry it himself on board the ship: when he had seen what a beautiful woman she was, he had sold her to the captain of the ship, and he himself went away. When the ship had the sails set and was on her course, the captain was always by her saying: 'So now you are mine.' Myrtle did not know what she could do to escape and she besought God with all her heart for a storm to blow up. God heard her, and at midnight there came a great storm and the ship was all in pieces. Myrtle did not lose heart; she mounted on a plank and was cast up on an island. On the shore of the island there were people; among them was a blackamoor who was a servant in the house of a rich man where they wanted a nurse for the child, and he brought her to the house. The blackamoor saw how beautiful she was and he desired her and wanted her for his wife. She would not have him, and to revenge himself on her he one night strangled the child to make the master think that it was the nurse who had strangled him. The next day she was driven out, the blackamoor saying that she should be killed. This her master would not do, and they agreed to let what was due to her come to her from God. Sorrowfully the girl went her way. She met a nun and revealed to her all her sufferings. The nun said: 'Fast and pray, my daughter; so shall all men be at your feet.'

Myrtle put on monastic dress and went to another village; there she heard people's confessions, saving them from their sins. Her husband, who had lost his sight, heard that there was a monk confessing people and curing the sick. He determined to go to the monk himself: he went and told him of his sin. The monk said: 'Your sin is a great one.' She recognized that the man was her husband, but did not make herself known; rather, in order that she might hear what they all had to say she did as the nun had told her: she put him in a room alongside of her cell and told him that he must fast and pray and so his sin be forgiven. In a few days time his friend arrived with his hands paralysed. He confessed that he had buried his friend's wife alive.

'To bury a human being alive! Your sin is a great one. You must fall to crying peccavi; you must have faith in God; you must make prostrations; your cure rests in the hands of God. I can do nothing for you. You must hope in God and it may be He will pardon you.' Under all the cloaks he had on him she could see who it was, and she was pleased to see him in such a plight. Her husband she could hear inside saying with tears: 'O, my Myrtle, what she suffered! And where can she be? Is she alive or dead?' Some days passed. Then the man who had sold her to the captain arrived; he was in a sad state. He made his confession; namely that he had sold to a sea captain a woman who had saved him from the gallows.

'Your sin is a great one; you must fall to making prostrations, and perchance God may pardon you.' Her husband heard all this and with tears said: 'O my God, pardon me for what I did to Myrtle; if she is alive may I be counted worthy to see her.' Some days passed: then came the blackamoor with his crutches. He told how he had strangled his master's child because the nurse had refused him, and he had put the blame on the innocent woman. 'You have committed a great sin. You must entreat God to pardon you.'

Her husband could eat nothing; day and night he wept saying: 'I did this unrighteous deed to my wife, ignorantly and rashly. Would I could see her but once and then die.' This went on for days. Then Myrtle had pity on him and opened the door and went in to comfort him. She said: 'God has sent you your Myrtle.' Then she took off her monk's robes. When he saw her before him he thought it an illusion; he could not believe that the light had come again to his eyes.

'Have you heard what befell me? I am your Myrtle,' and she stooped down and kissed him. All the time he was weeping and begging her forgiveness for having been the cause of all her so great sufferings.

So they lived well and may we live yet better.

59

The Clerk Theophilos

It is at once plain that this story from Crete is the legend of the clerk Theophilos widely spread all over Europe in the Middle Ages, the clerk who in return for worldly position and wealth handed over his soul to the devil, giving him a bond signed with his blood. As years went on Theophilos repented and in answer to his prayers the Virgin recovered the bond and the man's soul was saved. This story of the bond given to Satan and recovered is Greek in origin, and Strohmayer has shown that it appears for the first time in the eighth- or ninth-century life of St. Basil of Caesarea, erroneously attributed to the saint's contemporary Amphilochius, Bishop of Iconium.[1] Here it is St. Basil who recovers the bond.

Theophilos is mentioned by many medieval writers, the story usually being that he was vidame of the church of Adana in Cilicia. He refused the honour of being made bishop, but was so badly treated by the new bishop that he had recourse to a sorcerer called Salatins and struck his terrible bargain with the devil. Jubinal has discussed at length the Theophilos legend as it appears in medieval French literature.[2] It is mentioned in the *Golden Legend*, on the authority, which I cannot check, of Fulcher of Chartres, as having happened in Sicily with the very precise date, A.D. 537.[3] We may suppose here a confusion between the names Cilicia and Sicilia.

This Theophilos legend I find nowhere else in Greek folktale and it may very well have reached Crete by way of the Venetian settlers. It has, however, been given a very odd twist. In the European form of the story the devil keeps his bargain and gives Theophilos all the pleasures he has promised him; the clerk's repentance is to save his soul from hell. But in the Cretan version the devil simply swindles the man who has been so foolish as to trust him, and the man invokes the help of the Virgin, not to save his soul but to give him relief from the devil, who not only refuses to keep his promise but makes himself

[1] Strohmayer in *Romania*, xxiii (1894), p. 601. In *Amphilochii Opera*, Paris, 1644, p. 88 is a chapter: 'De iuvene qui Christum negaverat.'

[2] For the legend see *Le miracle de Théophile par Rutebeuf trouvère du treizième siècle*, published by Achille Jubinal, Paris, 1838, p. 40, and Jubinal's *Œuvres complètes de Rutebeuf*, ii. p. 79. Also *Theophilus in Icelandic, Low German, and other Tongues*, by G. W. Dasent, 1845.

[3] *Aurea Legenda*, ed. Graesse, chap. cxxxi, p. 593.

a great nuisance as well. It is the same story as the European but with the other world element entirely omitted and the story brought down from the theological and religious plane to the level of such bargains as are commonly made in the world of men. The Cretan peasant is not repenting of a deadly sin but going to a good friend to help him to slip out of an ill-considered bargain. A similar translation from the theological to the earthly may be seen in the second version of No. 75, *The three Words of Advice*, the Greek version of the *Gesta Romanorum* story *Of a young Knight who had three Friends.*

The notion of the bond is familiar in Greece, and such a general bond is held to have been cancelled at the Crucifixion. In the Easter Vespers we have the verse: *Christ our Saviour nailing it to His Cross cancelled the bond written against us and brought to nought the power of Death.* *Χριστὸς ὁ Σωτὴρ ἡμῶν τὸ καθ' ἡμῶν χειρόγραφον προσηλώσας τῷ Σταυρῷ ἐξήλειψε καὶ τοῦ θανάτου τὸ κράτος κατήργησε.*

NO. 59. THE CLERK THEOPHILOS[1]

Once upon a time there was a poor man who constantly besought God to make him rich. When he saw and saw very clearly that God would never make him rich, he thought to turn his supplications to the Devil. So one morning he rose up and went off to find the Devil. On the way he saw a man riding on a grey horse. When they met, the rider said: 'Where are you going?' 'How does that concern you?' answered the poor man. The rider said: 'I am he whom you seek.' 'And can you, you being the Devil, make me rich?' 'Well, of course I can,' answered the Devil. 'All that is needed is that you sign an agreement with me that with God you will have no dealings.' The poor man consented and drew up the agreement; then he pricked his little finger and brought three drops of blood: thus he sealed the paper.

From that hour the Devil was never away from the poor man's side; yet he did not make him rich.

The poor man began to repent of his bargain, for he had much to endure, hungry and tired. But the Devil had no intention of allowing him any rest. The poor fellow wept but the Devil, far from having mercy on him, clouted him on the head into the bargain.

His life was a martyrdom. His tongue was all roughened with

[1] From Siteia in Crete, with title *The Poor Man who wanted to become rich*; in *Myson*, vii. 157.

hunger and thirst. It seems that the Holy Virgin had pity on him and one day when the pair of them were passing a second time by her church, the door was open and the poor man went in. The Devil leaped into the church and the Holy Virgin tried to push him out. The poor man fell to prayer and penitential prostrations. For three days and three nights he continued praying until he was so much tired that he fell asleep. In his sleep he had a dream that the Holy Virgin came and said to him: 'What can *I* do for you, seeing that you have delivered yourself over to him with a sealed bond?' The man woke up and began again to pray and so for yet three days and three nights. He was so much tired that again he fell asleep. This time in his dream he saw the Holy Virgin bringing him the bond. He woke up and saw that it was in his hand. At once he set it on fire and burned it. He went back to his house and told his wife and his children all that he had seen and suffered.

60

The Goldsmith's Wife

WHAT may be regarded as the full form of this story begins with two friends, one of whom contrived to procure for the other the wife of a very jealous man, generally a goldsmith. The husband kept his wife always locked up in her house, and the friends began their siege by digging a tunnel so that the wife could dodge in and out of the house without her husband knowing of it. The young men took from the house some jewel or a golden slipper and then showed it to the goldsmith, ordering a duplicate to be made. The goldsmith recognized the object which had, of course, been abstracted from his house by means of the secret tunnel; he was much surprised, as he had supposed that it had never left his own house. This device was to accustom the husband to the idea that all things, women included, are made by God in pairs. When therefore he saw a woman who seemed to be his wife in company with one of the young men, and even being married to him, he was ready to believe that it was not really her but her double. His wife he had left at home and could not know that she had come out to join the youth by way of the secret tunnel.

That all things are made in pairs is probably a common enough notion in eastern folktales and in theological thought, pointing the contrast between the Divine Unity and the confused multiplicity of created things. To begin with folktales: I find in a novel from Pontos, the theme of which is a confusion between two men who resembled one another very closely, that the man to be deceived says to himself: 'It is well said that every man in the world has another one just like him.'[1] Also in the Naxos version of *The three Measures of Salt*, No. 45, we have the same idea. The story in the *Arabian Nights*, '*Kamar al-Zaman and the Jeweller's Wife*' is an immensely drawn-out version of the present tale, and the unfortunate jeweller says of his wife:[2] 'If she be at home, this slave-girl must be her counterpart, and glory be to Him who alone hath no counterpart.' In the *Mirror of Princes*, a Persian book dated to A.D. 1082, we have a philosophic discussion of the 'Oneness' of God: all created things partake in some way of

[1] *Arkheíon Pontou*, xii. 177.

[2] Burton's *Arabian Nights*, library edition, vii. 342.

the nature of 'Twoness', of duality. 'The One, in verity, is God Almighty; all else is dual.'[1]

Halliday has given references for this story of the goldsmith's wife and concludes that it is one of 'those oriental tales of intrigue which passed into European literature with the Sindibad cycle of stories'.[2]

The variants differ in details and the subtleties of the story are not always very clear. In the second version from Zákynthos the husband is a tailor and the place of the pimping friend is taken by an old woman. In the Pontic version the husband is a priest and he is beguiled into reading the wedding service for his wife and her lover. In the Mýkonos version he is forced to be the best man at her wedding. The version from Athens takes the form of a long story of intrigue in which a tunnel from a bath to the lady's house plays a part. In the first of the two versions from Zákynthos, the one I have chosen for translation the story begins and ends like the *Faithful John* story, No. 37 above, beginning with the fertility charm and ending with the turning of the friend to stone.

The references to this story are:

1. PONTOS: *Pontiaká Phylla*, iii, Part 25, p. 26, No. 2.
2. ASIA MINOR: Silli near Konia; *M.G. in A.M.*, p. 296.
3. MÝKONOS: Roussel, *Contes de Mycono*, p. 136.
4. ATHENS: Kamboúroglou, p. 98.
5. EPEIROS: Hahn, i. 201, No. 29 and this is the same as Kretschmer, *Neugr. Märchen*, No. 63, p. 305.

6, 7. ZÁKYNTHOS: *Laographía*, xi. 444, translated, and 450.

NO. 60. THE GOLDSMITH'S WIFE[3]

Once upon a time there were a king and queen; they had a maidservant. Now the queen had no children. Then she made a marriage for her servant, and she too had no children. The queen was full of bitter sorrow. One day a beggar came that way and asked her why she was so sorrowful; she said it was because she had no children. The beggar said: 'I will give you a pear; just eat it and you will have children.' This beggar was Christ. So the queen ate the pear and became with child. She called for the servant to wash the plates, and on the plates the girl found the

[1] *A Mirror of Princes*, translated from the Persian by Reuben Levy, London, 1951, p. 8.

[2] *M.G. in A.M.*, p. 236.

[3] Text from Zákynthos, printed in *Laographía*, xi. 444, with the title *The two loving Friends.*

peelings. 'My mistress had a pear and she never gave me any,' she said to herself: 'Well, I will eat the peelings.' So she did, and thus the servant too became with child. The queen had a baby; it was a boy and she called him George. The servant also had a boy and he was called Paul. They were brought up together in the same way; like two brothers, loving one another from their hearts.

When the boys grew big, the queen said to the king: 'It is wrong not to make a distinction between George and Paul. George should be as a prince and Paul as a servant. Buy them clothes and for George a fine suit.' The king got the boys' clothes and for George a fine outfit. As soon as the prince saw the clothes, he said to his father: 'Why have you bought these ugly clothes for Paul? Either you will get him fine ones, or I shall take these ugly ones myself.' 'Very well, my son,' said the king, 'I will get some fine clothes for Paul as well.'

When the boys were grown up, George said to his father: 'I want to make a marriage for Paul.' So he called for Paul and told him they must start off. 'We must go,' said he, 'to find a fair woman to be your wife, because I want to have you married.' Then what they did was this: they took a ship and started off. They went round from place to place to find some fair woman. At last they came to a certain place and landed. They questioned an old woman: 'Can you tell us? Is there any fair woman here where you live?' The old woman said: 'There is; the beautiful wife of a goldsmith, but he keeps her shut up and no eye ever sees her.' They said: 'If you can manage for us to carry her off, we will pay you well.' The old woman said: 'Don't you worry. She wants to get away, because she can't endure any longer being kept shut up. I can see her, because my house has a window opposite the tower where she lives, and we chat together, and she has told me about it.' 'Very well,' said the two boys: 'we will go off together, and you must manage it all.' 'Don't you worry, my lads; your job is done already.'

So the old woman went home and the first thing she did was to chat with the goldsmith's wife. Scarcely had the wife seen the old woman, than she greeted her and asked what was the ship in the harbour and why she had come. The old woman said it was two princes who had come to the country to find a wife for one of them. 'They are looking out for a beautiful woman and they have been told of your ladyship. They were told that you are married, but they don't mind about that. Only: is your ladyship willing to go off with them?' 'Oh, my dear dame, if you can do me this good turn and I get away from here, I will be indebted to you for a great kindness.' Next day the old woman met the princes and said: 'The fair woman consents to go away any time you wish. But she doesn't know how she can get out.' The princes said that she need have no care about that, for they would make an underground passage from the sea to her tower so that not an eye should see her when she went off.

Next day they began to dig the underground passage; by the time they had finished it a year had passed. As soon as they had finished it all the way to the tower, George told the woman to let him have her slippers, which were made of gold, and he would make her another pair just the same. She gave them to him. Then George went to the husband and said: 'Make me a pair of golden slippers like these. Look at them; look at them carefully. I want them exactly like these.' 'Let me have them here in my hands: I want to have them before me when I make your pair. But I can't make them like these.' 'Not like these! Please make them just like, or I shall have to go elsewhere for them.' 'Very well, my boy; I will make them for you.'

Then the prince took the slippers back to the house by way of the underground passage. As soon as the prince had left him the goldsmith shut up his shop and went to the tower. By the time he had opened the forty rooms there, the slippers were back in their place. 'Wife,' said he, 'bring me here the keys.' 'But, my dear husband, why do you want them?' 'Bring them here; what business is it of yours?' She brought him the keys and he opened the chest of drawers and as soon as he saw the slippers, he said: 'Oh wife, if only you knew! A man came and told me to make him a pair of slippers like these of yours, absolutely the same.' 'O my husband, human beings have each their fellow; each thing is a pair with some other.'

Next day George told her to give him her ear-ring that he may make her one like it. He took the ear-ring to the goldsmith and said: 'I want you to make me an ear-ring like this one.' 'Well, let me have it here to look at.' 'No, no; if you will make it for me, good; if you can't, I must go somewhere else.' 'Very well; I will make it for you, and if you are pleased with my work, I will set the crown on your head when you are married.' 'Thank you very much,' said the prince. The prince then brought back the ear-ring by way of the underground passage. As soon as the prince had left, the goldsmith shut up his shop and went home to his tower. As soon as he had opened the door he took his keys and opened the chest of drawers. He saw the ear-ring and at once said to his wife: 'The same young man came again to me and brought me an ear-ring for me to make one for him, but it was exactly like yours.' 'But didn't I tell you, husband, that human beings have each their fellow; each thing is a pair with another.' 'My interest in it all was so great, wife, that I told him I would set the crown of marriage on his head.' 'You did well, my husband, and will you not take me with you?' 'Oh no, that is impossible; I can't take you.'

The prince went to the goldsmith and said: 'Next Sunday, my gossip, my brother is to be married, and as you invited me I am come to call upon you to set the crown upon his head.' 'Good; I will come.' On Sunday the goldsmith dressed himself and went down to the ship, and George went up by the underground passage and brought away his wife. As soon as the goldsmith saw her at the wedding he said to the best man: 'I have forgotten something, and I must go home.' 'All right, gossip; go your way.' As soon as the goldsmith had started, his wife went off by the underground passage. The goldsmith went into his tower and found his wife sitting and looking out of the window at the ship. 'What have you forgotten, husband?' He said:

> 'Thy whiteness and beauty, O wife most fair,
> Are those of the bride: yet thou art here.'

'But, my poor man, did I not tell you that all are in pairs, thing and thing and man and man, just alike? What do you mean talking like this? Here am I in the tower and there is she in the ship, and yet you say that I am she.' 'Very well, my wife; then I am off.' Before he could get out by way of the tower, she had gone through the underground passage and arrived before him. As soon as the goldsmith saw her, he said to the best man that he had forgotten his wedding gift and must go to fetch it. 'Well, go this time, but you shan't go another time; be careful to see that you don't forget anything else.' Before he could get to his house, his wife had come by way of the passage. 'Have you forgotten something again?' said she. 'I had in mind your fair eyes and your bright beauty and the manner of your dress, my fairest lady.' 'My husband, are you in your senses? How should I get away from here? Take me with you; there are plenty of women there.' 'Oh, impossible.' 'Take me, husband.' 'I won't.' 'Well then, to make you quite sure that I am really here, I shall let you see my hand out of the window.' 'Very well, wife. So I am going off.' Then she took a reed which she had hidden away, and put a sleeve on it and set it at the window: then she went off to the ship again by the underground passage. As soon as the goldsmith went and saw her there at the window, he could not sit down in quiet but kept looking at the window to see her hand.

So the young man put the marriage crown upon her and the people left the ship and she sailed off. As soon as the goldsmith landed, he went straight to the tower. When he opened the door, at once he saw the sleeve set on the reed. He took a glass of wine and said: 'Your health and again your health and a fair voyage; these are my deserts. Oh, unhappy me!'

While the princes were travelling round from place to place three years passed. The king died and the queen too, and their servant, the serving woman (Paul's mother), was left alone by herself awaiting the return of the princes. As they were on their voyage, a bird came at night and perched on the mast; it said: 'If a man whoever he be can make fair the path for the bride and the bridegroom to pass over, then they and all their kinsmen will live long. Whoever hears this and tells, that man shall be turned to stone even to the knees.' George was there and he heard this. Next night George went there again to see if he might hear the bird. The bird came and said: 'If a man, whoever he may be, can take away the food that is in the hand of the (bride's) mother-in-law and himself give food to the bride, then the bride and the bridegroom and all their kinsmen will live long. Whoever hears this and tells, that man shall be turned to stone even to the middle.' The bird came again the third evening and said: 'If a man, whoever he may be, can stay that evening in their room when a monster will come to devour the bride and the bridegroom, and can kill the monster, then the bride and the bridegroom and all their kinsmen will live long. Whoever hears this and tells, that man shall be turned to stone.'

The ship arrived at their country, and George told the bridegroom not to land with the bride until he had laid down velvet along their path. So George laid down the velvet, and they landed and went to their house. Then the mother-in-law came forward to give them refreshments, and George went and took away the food that was in her hand and gave food to them himself. So too in the evening the bride and the bridegroom lay down to sleep, and George came into their room and killed the monster.

The mother-in-law began her gnawing curiosity: Why had George taken and given them the refreshments himself, and why had he stayed in their room? Since she was so very curious, George made up his mind to tell her the whole story. So he said: 'If I tell you why I gave the refreshments to the bride myself and why I stayed in their room, I shall be turned to stone.' 'Tell me, even if you do turn to stone.' 'Oh, don't speak,' said the bride. Yet because of the gnawing curiosity of the mother-in-law he ordered that in the middle of the city there should be set up a column and when this was done, he mounted on it and said: 'To the ship as we were on our way here, there came a bird; it perched on the mast and said: "If a man whoever he be, can make fair the path for the bride and bridegroom to pass over, then the bride and the bridegroom and all their kinsmen will live long. Whoever hears this and tells that man shall be turned to marble even to the knees."' So George turned to stone even to the knees. The bride said to him: 'Do not tell any more.' But the mother-in-law grumbled out: 'Tell, tell, even if you do turn to stone.' 'Next evening the bird said: 'If a man, whoever he may be, can take the food that is in the hand of the mother-in-law and himself give food to the bride, then the bride and the bridegroom and all their kinsmen will live long. And whoever hears this and tells, that man shall be turned to stone even to the middle."' So George turned to stone even to the middle. 'Oh, tell no more,' said the bride: 'not why you came to our room.' But would George listen to her? 'On the third night the bird came again and said: "If a man, whoever he be, can go to their room when a monster rushes upon them to devour the bride and the bridegroom and can kill the monster, then the bride and the bridegroom and all their kinsmen will live long. Whoever hears this and tells, that man shall be turned to stone."'

Then George was turned to stone, his whole body. The bride said: 'Oh, if it were possible for George to be restored to life, whatever she were ordered she would do; she would give even her own life.

One day Christ was passing by, dressed as a beggar. He said to her: 'If I could tell you how George might come to life, what would you do for this end?' 'Three sons I have: I would slay them all.' 'Now slay the three of them, and George will come back again.' Then she went into the room and killed them. As she came out, she saw George coming towards her. She embraced him and said: 'Come; let us go into the room and you shall see how for the love of you I have killed my three sons.' They went into the room and there they found the three boys sitting reading out of golden books. So they all lived well and may we here live yet better.

61

St. Alexios the Man of God

THIS 'Story of Johnnie' recorded either at Kerasund or at one of the Greek villages in the district may at once be recognized as the legend of St. Alexios, known as the Man of God, whose fame is spread all over Europe. It is also under the date, March the 17, in the Greek collection of lives of the saints, the *Synaxarion*. The legend is ultimately of Syrian origin.[1]

The *Synaxarion* says that the saint was a native of 'Old Rome' in the days of Theodosios the Great. On the very day of his wedding he left home to live the ascetic life; first at Edessa, then at Tarsus, and finally at Rome. The account goes on to say that on his death-bed the saint wrote a letter to be given to his parents only after his death telling them that he was their lost son. This is different from the current legend and from the Kerasund version which agrees in saying that the recognition was brought about because on his body was found a book of prayers or some such object given him by his parents.

It would seem therefore that the Kerasund version comes not as might be expected from the Greek *Synaxarion*, but from some current oral form of the legend more in agreement with the legend as found in Europe. I know no other version of the St. Alexios legend in Greek folktales.

The Holy Mountain is of course Athos.

In the notes on Nos. 59 and 75 I have spoken of the tendency of the Greeks to transfer theological stories to the everyday world of human relations. In this story of the boy-monk Johnnie and his homesickness there is a human touch not to be found at all in the theological pages of the *Synaxarion*.

NO. 61. ST. ALEXIOS, THE MAN OF GOD[2]

There was a very rich man and he had a son. This son used to go to the school. The other boys of his company had each of them a Gospel book, and he had not. One day he said to his

[1] For the story of St. Alexios see *Folklore*, lix. 1940.
[2] Text from Kerasund under the title of *Yannétsis, Johnnie*.

mother: 'Mother, all the boys with me have Gospel books, and I have not. Won't you tell my father to get me too a Book of the Gospels?' His mother told her husband and he bought a book and sent it to be bound. And when it was bound he brought it to a jeweller who from five hundred gold pieces made a cover for the book: then he gave it to his son, for him to take to school with him.

One day a monk came to the house of the rich man, and the man asked him: 'Whence do you come and whither are you going?' The monk said: 'I am coming from the Holy Mountain and am on my way to the Holy Sepulchre.' In the morning Johnnie—this was the rich man's son—said to him: 'Father, when you are on your way back from the Holy Sepulchre, come this way again, and then I can go with you to the Holy Mountain.' 'Good,' said the monk, 'so I will.' Johnnie made him take an oath that he would come and take him away to the Holy Mountain. The monk went to the Holy Sepulchre and came again. He said to Johnnie: 'In the morning we can go off.' At that time a ship came to take in cargo, and Johnnie said to the monk: 'Why do we not sail in her? For what are we waiting?' Then the monk said: 'Let the ship take in her cargo, and after that.' Johnnie then said: 'Why don't you go and talk to the captain? Won't he sail just with us? We can give him as much passage money as he wants.' Then the monk went off and said to the captain: 'There is a boy here who says: "We will give the captain as much passage money as he likes and will he not carry us to the Holy Mountain?"' 'Very well,' said the captain. The monk made the bargain for a hundred gold pieces and came and told the boy.

At this time Johnnie had no money and he went and said to his mother: 'Mother, all the boys are friendly to me and they all take me to their houses; why may not I too invite them here?' And his mother said: 'Why, surely invite them.' He spoke to his mother and she asked his father for a hundred gold pieces to go to the shops and buy one thing and another. His mother gave him the money saying: 'My son, take the servant with you, and don't load yourself with the things.' She sent the servant with him and they went off marketing. Johnnie did what he could to escape from the company of the servant, and said to him: 'Up; go and see if the boys have yet gone to the school.' The servant went after the boys and Johnnie jumped into the boat and went off. The servant came but could not find Johnnie: he was not there. He went to the house and said: 'I can't find Johnnie. Has he been here?' Then his mother said: 'Run off and look for him: someone is maltreating him somewhere.' The servant came back and said: 'I have been over all the market and I could not find him.' Then his mother went to the school; again he was not to be found. Also she called for her husband and they searched up and down: again Johnnie was not to be found. This went on for two months and more, and then they gave it up.

The monk took Johnnie and brought him to the Holy Mountain. When the abbot saw that the boy was young, he said to the monk: 'What did you think we could do with him here? Is the boy fit to stop here with us?' Then said the monk: 'He wanted to come and he said he could stay here.' Johnnie was sent for and questioned; he said: 'I am fit for the life here.' So they made him a monk and there he stayed.

But when a year had passed he began to think of his father and of his mother and he became very unhappy. They asked him: 'What is the matter that you have become so miserable?' He said: 'There is nothing the matter; I am quite well.' When he had been there three years, he became yet more miserable and was quite undone. Again they questioned him, and he said: 'There is nothing the matter with me. The devil is tempting me sorely and he says to me: "Why do you not go to your mother and your father?" ' The abbot understood that the boy was melancholy from thinking of his parents and he summoned all the monks and asked them that permission should be given for Johnnie to go to his own people. The abbot obtained the authorization and sent Johnnie off to his own country.

As Johnnie was on his way he met an old man who was wearing a mantle patched all over. Said Johnnie: 'Uncle, you are an old man and your mantle is heavy and weighs on you. Let me give you my good clothes and let me have the mantle to wear.' So he put on the old man's mantle; the old man disappeared. Johnnie went on to his home, and came to the door of the house and said to the servant: 'In the name of God, give me something to help me.' His father was a good man and used to give help to the poor. The servant was bringing him something to eat, but Johnnie said: 'I have no need of cooked food; just give me a little bread.' The servant gave him some bread, but Johnnie did not go away: he stayed there at the door. The servant went and told the master of the house: 'There is a beggar down below and I gave him some bread and he does not go away: he stays by the gate.' Johnnie's father came down and questioned him: 'Why do you stay down there? Come up into the house.' Johnnie said: 'I don't want to come inside. Tell the servant to build me a little hut to live in.' The servant built a little hut and Johnnie lived in it: the people there put food into his mouth.

One day the sun shone, and Johnnie went out and sat behind his hut and sunned himself. His mother came out of the house on her way somewhere. When she saw Johnnie her bowels were so much stirred with emotion that she went into the house again and said to the servant: 'Go and tell that man to go into his hut. I have to go on my affairs and he moves me to yearning.' The servant went and told Johnnie of this. When Johnnie had gone into his hut and his mother had gone her way, he said: 'I thank Thee, my God; my mother saw me; the sight of me her son made her sick with yearning.'

At this time a voice from heaven came to Johnnie and said to him: 'John, you are to live three days more. I am about to take your soul.' When that day came Johnnie said to the servant: 'Go and tell your mistress to come here.' The servant went and told his mistress. She said: 'That man stirs my bowels even to sickness; how can I go to see him?' The servant came and told Johnnie: 'She does not want to come.' Again Johnnie said: 'Go and tell her to come; if she does not her head will ache for it.' The servant went and told his mistress: ' "She must come", said the beggar man; "otherwise your head will ache for it." ' 'But, fellow, how can I go?' said she. 'He makes me feel sick. But go, wrap him up in a cloth and cover his face, and then I will go.' The servant went and wrapped Johnnie up and his mother came. She said to him: 'What have you to say to me?' He said: 'I have nothing to say to you. When I am dead, I beg you to bury me here inside the hut. And do not change my clothes; in these very clothes you shall bury me. If you do not do what I tell you, your head will ache for it.' Then he took the Gospel book out of his bosom and gave it to her. As soon as the mother saw the book, she said: 'Go tell the master to come quickly.' The servant went and told him. When he came his wife said to him: 'Is not this our Johnnie's Gospel book?' 'It is,' said her husband, 'and who had it?' She said: 'It was this beggar man.' Her husband said: 'Stay; the jeweller too will recognize it.' The servant went and fetched the jeweller. And when he saw the Gospel book the man said: 'It is your book.' Then the master asked Johnnie: 'This Gospel book, where did you get it?' He said: 'It is mine.' 'How is it yours?' said they; 'Whence did you get it?' 'My father gave it to me,' said he, 'when I was a little boy.' Then his father said to him: 'And your father is . . .?' 'You are my father and she is my mother,' said he, and his soul passed away. Then his mother, she whose bowels had been moved at the sight of him, fell and embraced him, weeping bitterly. They dressed him all in gold. But when they had set the golden dress upon him, lo, his mother's tongue was held; no longer could she lament. She cast a glance at her husband and he changed Johnnie's clothes and put on him again the old mantle: then was her tongue loosed. They buried Johnnie inside his hut.

62

The Curse laid on Rosa

To judge from Dunlop's *History of prose Fiction*—I quote from vol. i, p. 463—there are in European literature quite a number of stories of these incestuous complications. Dunlop quotes from Bandello, ii, No. 35, a title: *Un gentiluomo navarrese sposa una che era sua sorella e figliuola non lo sapendo.* Further he gives an epitaph, apparently in the Bourbonnais, on the grave of a man and a woman: *Cy gist la fille—Cy gist le pere—Cy gist la sœur—Cy gist le frere—Cy gist la femme—Et le mary—Si n'y a que—Deux corps icy.* The man had married first his mother and secondly the woman with whom he was buried, she being his daughter by his own mother, and therefore his sister.

The present story from Cyprus[1] is a sort of exercise on this theme, but rather expressed in the language of Fairyland, by the conventions of which the marriage with the father is presented as the eating of an apple from a tree springing from his grave. In this apple-tree which is really a man, and in the three sisters, the Cyprus story shows a general adaptation to the traditions of Greek and other story-telling. The woman's identification of her husband by the scars which she has herself inflicted is rather like the identification of Oidipous by the cuts on his feet, although I see no specific descent of one story from the other. Further, the identification by scars is rather a commonplace in story-telling: it occurs for example in the Macedonian version of No. 51, *The Ordering of the Fates.*

An Albanian Oidipous story has been published by Mrs. Hasluck in *Folklore*, lx. 340. A man heard a fairy pronouncing the doom of his new-born son: the boy is to kill his father and marry his mother. The tragic ending is that the doomed man killed first the woman who was his mother and wife; then his son by her; and lastly himself. On the basis of this horrible story a riddle of relationships has been constructed, and, very extraordinarily, a lullaby for babies.

It is worth while to compare a Maratha story published in *Man*, l, p. 71, by Dr. Karye. The Goddess of Fate, Satwai, had a daughter; the goddess told her that her fate was to marry her own son. The girl of set intention remained unmarried, but one day she drank from a lake into which a king had gargled, and from this she became with child. She exposed her baby, a boy, but he was saved and brought

[1] Translated also in Garnett, p. 194.

up by a gardener, and in due time married his mother. She found out what had happened by observing that he had on him a piece of the very cloth in which she had wrapped her baby. Then, very unexpectedly, we are told that he and she disregarded the discovery and continued to live together happily.

If we take it that the king who gargled into the lake was the father of the heroine, we have here an exact parallel with the story of Rosa from Cyprus, always with the very remarkable difference springing from social ideas. In the story from Cyprus the affair is taken tragically and Rosa kills herself; the Maratha story ends, as Dr. Karye puts it, 'in a good-humoured acceptance of a queer fate'. He tells us that in Hindu, in Buddhist, and especially in Jain literature, these incest stories are found in two connexions: 'to show the sinfulness of all worldly relationships and as conundrums to set an intellectual exercise about kinships arising from such a union.' The French epitaph shows the conundrum side of the matter; the tragic ending is everywhere; the Maratha acquiescence I have not met with elsewhere. It would be hazardous to suggest any historical connexion between all these stories. It may be rather that such unnatural situations have always had a certain tragic attraction of terror and horror.

For the distinction between objects found in the chest, objects of value or a living soul, see note on No. 51 above.

NO. 62. THE CURSE LAID ON ROSA[1]

Once upon a time there was a rich man who had three daughters. They grew up; he could not get them married and he did not know what he was to do. So, my lady, he had a plan: he would have portraits made of his daughters and display them at the door of his house, so that whoever passed by might see them, and thus perhaps he could get the girls married. The place where the rich man lived was by the sea, and many ships from other lands used to come and anchor there. At last, my lady, a captain one day saw these pictures, and he fancied the youngest of the three; he went and asked her father for her. But the father would not let him have her, because he wanted to marry off the elder girls first, and after them the youngest, and it was the youngest whom this son-in-law wanted. However the father was advised by his friends to let the young man have

[1] A story from Cyprus, printed by Sakellarios, *Kypriaká*, ii. 311, under the title *The Story of the Rich Man and his three Daughters.*

the youngest, and so he would make a good start in marrying them all off. So finally, my lady, he did make up his mind to let him have the youngest, and after a few days the wedding took place.

When they had been crowned in marriage, all their kinsmen and friends went away and left the bridegroom and the bride by themselves. The bride lay down for the night on her bedstead; then when the bridegroom was coming to her, the wall opened and a shape came out of it and said to him: 'Keep far from Rosa,'—Rosa was the bride's name—'for Rosa is to marry her father, and of him she will have a son, and later on she will take this son as her husband.' Without telling anyone anything of this, the bridegroom, as soon as he heard these words, went to his father-in-law and said that he had made a mistake and that he wanted the eldest daughter and not the youngest to be his wife. The father-in-law was well pleased because he wanted to get his eldest daughter married first. So he set the crowns of marriage on them, and the bridegroom took his wife and went off to his own country.

A little while afterwards another son-in-law appeared, and he too favoured the youngest daughter. Not to make a long story of it, the same thing happened to him as had happened to the first bridegroom, and poor Rosa who had been married to two men, was left without a husband. When some time had passed, Rosa fell to thinking over it and she could not understand why it was that both of the two men who had crowned her in marriage had left her. She thought of a plan: she would ask her father's leave to go to visit her sisters; she could say she was longing to see them; in this way she might learn why her husbands had left her. Her father gave her leave and she went. When she came to the place where her eldest sister lived, she saw her servant at the well, where she had gone to fill her jar. She recognized her and said: 'Take this ring and give it to your mistress, and I will wait outside for you to bring me an answer.' After a little while the servant returned and asked her to be so good as to come in, because her mistress wanted her. She found her sister sitting by herself. 'My sister,' she said, 'I felt a desire for you, and now I have come to see you: will you do me a favour? At night when you go to sleep with your husband, put out the light; then leave your bed and let me come to it.' Her sister said: 'With pleasure; why not? Whatever you like I am ready to do.'

When it was night her sister did as she had been asked and left her husband; Rosa then went and lay down by her brother-in-law. Presently, just as if she were his wife, she said: 'All the time you have been my husband I have forgotten to ask you why you married my youngest sister and then left her.' Then he told her all that had happened. As soon as she had heard this, Rosa left the bed and her sister returned to it. Next day she went away to find her second sister, and after hearing the same story from her other brother-in-law, she went back home, saying to herself: 'No, I will not take my father for my husband as the apparition said I should. No, I will hire men to kill him.'

Well, my lady, after a few days she hired the men, and they killed her father and took him away and buried him in a field outside the town. Then out of the tomb where her father was buried there grew an apple-tree and on it were fine apples. One day, my lady, Rosa saw a man selling apples. She called for him and bought some apples and ate them: she conceived a child. After a little while she began to grow heavy and did not know why, but later she was aware that on her father's tomb an apple-tree had grown up, and it came to her mind that she had eaten some of the apples. Then she said to herself: 'And once more I will not let it be that the apparition spoke truth; when the baby is born, I will manage to kill it.' Then as soon as it was born she took the baby and slashed it on the breast several times with a knife. She put it into a chest; this she nailed up well and threw into the sea. The wind blowing off the mainland carried the chest right out into the open sea. It chanced that a merchant ship well out at sea was passing that way, and the captain saw the chest. He said to his crew: 'Launch the boat and pick up that chest. If there are any objects of value in it, you may have them for yourselves; but if there be in it any living soul, that shall be mine.'[1] They lowered the boat and picked up the chest; inside it they found a baby soaked in its own blood. The captain took the baby for himself and reared it as his own son. Many years later the captain died, and his adopted son was the heir to all his goods. When the boy had grown up he followed his father's business, voyaging from place to place.

[1] For which see note on No. 51.

It happened that on one of his many voyages he went to his mother's country, and there he saw the door of his mother's house: he asked what were those pictures at the door. He was told the story of the three sisters; also that the youngest of them was not married. Then said he: 'I will take her as my wife.' Then he married her. When many years had passed and they had had children, one day as he was changing his linen and she was handing him a shirt, on his breast she saw the marks of the knife, the cuts which she had given him when she put him into the chest. Then she had a suspicion and questioned him: 'Will you not tell me what are the scars you have on your breast?' He told her that he had known neither father nor mother, but a ship's captain had found him in a chest in the open sea and had taken him and reared him as his son. 'Then when my father died I inherited from him and followed his business. So I came to this place and took you as my wife. I know no more.' She said to him: 'Behold how my unhappy fate has run me down. You are my son, and now that everything the apparition told me has come true, I leave you to your sorrow and my children as orphans. I go to my death; all that has happened was in my destiny.' She went and threw herself down from the roof of a house and was killed.

63

The Man who found the Pea

THE hero of this story, of which a general outline will give a better idea than any one of the seven available versions, chanced to pick up a pea, and from this pea he calculated that he would become immensely rich: so hopeful was he that he asked for the king's daughter in marriage. To test whether he was really a man of delicate breeding the king put him to sleep in a not very comfortable bed. The man remained all the night sleepless; not because of the bed but from anxiety about the pea. The king, however, supposed that it was because he had been brought up to every comfort and luxury, and so thought him fit to be married to the princess. That his wealth was entirely non-existent put the hero into a difficulty, and from this he was rescued by the devil or by an ogre, who promised him great wealth if only he could answer a riddle: if he should fail, then the usual forfeit was to be paid. The hero, by the special help of God, answered the riddle and the story ends happily.

The riddle generally takes the form of the first few items of 'The Riddle of the Hundred Words', of which the questions are: One, what is One? Two, what is Two? and so on. For instance, in the Naxos version it begins: *One of a sort; what is it? The answer is God.*[1] *Two of a sort? The devil, for he has a pair of horns. Three of a sort? A table with its three legs;* and so on. These riddles based on a series of numbers are called *Songs of the Hundred Words*, *'Εκατάλογα*, and Hesseling and Pernot have devoted a book to them, in which these folktales of the man who found the pea are specially mentioned.[2] The Pontic version has a different riddle which I find nowhere else. The last paragraph runs:

> The youth stayed in the palace for a year, always wondering what would happen if the devil should come. One day before the year was up, the youth again took his gun, intending to run away. As he was on his way he met an old man: this was Jesus Christ, and He said to him: 'Come, do not be afraid; to what the devil will ask you I know the answer. Come therefore, let us go to your house.' So they went, and Christ lay down to sleep near the door.

[1] For the unity of God see the notes on No. 60.

[2] Rather oddly called *'Ερωτοπαίγνια*, *Chansons d'amour*. The riddle is on p. xii.

The boy was afraid and set a rope hanging down from a window so that he might make his escape in case the Elder could not solve the riddle. When day dawned the devil came and thundered at the door and asked his riddle: 'What can this be: It is above and then it will be below, and then it will be above again?' Then Christ said: 'The answer is Man: he is in the world above; he will die and go down into the tomb; and again he will rise at the Second Coming.' Then the devil in his bitter wrath dashed his head against the wall and so died. The bridegroom in his delight gave fifty gold pieces to the noble old man and said farewell to him. The Elder gave the money to three poor men and so went out of sight.

The man who counts his chickens before they are hatched and the test for delicate breeding are both well known. The central idea of the present story is that a simple and foolishly self-confident young man allows himself to fall into the power of the devil, but God is merciful and the young man is helped to give the devil his answer.

The references for this story are:

1. PONTOS: *Arkheíon Pontou*, i. 193.
2. DEMIRDESH, NEAR BRUSA: Danguitsis, *Étude descriptive du dialecte de Démirtési*, p. 180.
3. KÁRPATHOS: Mikh.-Nouáros, *L. S. Karpáthou*, i. 285.
4. TENOS: Pio, p. 193, which is Hahn, ii. 210, No. 17.
5. THERA: Kretschmer, *Neugr. Märchen*, p. 190.
6. NAXOS: *N.A.* ii. 26 = Garnett, p. 94.
7. EPEIROS: Hahn, i. 148, No. 17.

64

The simpleton Brother, or *The Incense and the magic Pipe*

STORIES of a pair of brothers or of a family of brothers of which the youngest is a sort of clever buffoon are common enough everywhere, and there is no lack of them in Greece. Most of what is needed has been said by Halliday in his notes on *The mad Brother*.[1] Yet it is worth while to give an example of a rather special type of this story, of which I find four full examples: from Chios, Thrace, Epeiros, and Zákynthos; I have translated the version from Thrace. The special feature of this form of the story is that the fool brother, after being the death of his mother and doing a good deal more mischief, finds a great quantity of incense. This he takes, generally up a mountain, apparently to be nearer to God, and there offers it. He is rewarded by the gift of a magic pipe to the sound of which everyone must dance, and by this he makes his living. There is a version from Kárpathos, which has all the other episodes but not that of the incense, and a Cappadocian story from Malakopí has most of the story. Two other versions from Cappadocia, from Araván and Delmesó, are rather different; they begin with the two brothers dividing their animals according to whether they go into the old or the new stable: the clever brother knew that they would go into the stable to which they are accustomed. On the pipe to which everyone must dance a note is hardly needed; the references in Stith Thompson's *Motif-Index*, D 1415, may be consulted. In conclusion, all these stories are often dished up with a certain amount of the scatological buffoonery fortunately rare in Greek stories.

The references are:

1, 2, 3. CAPPADOCIA: *M.G. in A.M.*: Malakopí, p. 405; Araván, p. 331; Delmesó, p. 327.
4. CHIOS: Argenti and Rose, *Folklore of Chios*, p. 532.
5. KÁRPATHOS: Mikh.-Nouáros, *L. S. Karpáthou*, i. 271.
6. THRACE: *Thrakiká*, xvii. 132, translated.
7. EPEIROS: Hahn, i. 219, No. 34.
8. ZÁKYNTHOS: *Laographía*, xi. 490.

[1] *M.G. in A.M.*, p. 231. To his references add *Pontiakí Estía*. ii. 517.

NO. 64. THE SIMPLETON BROTHER, *or* THE INCENSE AND THE MAGIC PIPE[1]

Once upon a time there were three brothers and they had an old mother; also hens and an ox. The elder brothers worked hard and looked after their mother. One day they left their youngest brother, who was a simpleton, to look after their mother and to feed the fowls; to feed the ox too.

The youngest brother fetched water for the fowls; as they drank they threw up their heads. Then said he: 'Don't be mocking God, you fowls.' The fowls went on drinking with their heads held high: 'Don't be mocking God, you fowls,' and he took up a stick and killed them. The ox was chewing, and the simpleton asked it for some mastich gum for himself to chew. Once he said it and twice he said it: 'Give me some mastich gum; mastich, mastich.' The third time he killed the ox and put its head on the pitchfork and set it up in the sheep-fold. Then he put water in the kettle and boiled it and gave his mother a wash, scalding her with the boiling water; so she died. Then he changed her clothes and combed her hair and set her up in the corner. He boiled an egg and peeled it and set it in her mouth; in front of her he put her distaff and her spindle, for her to spin wool.

In the evening his brothers came and asked him where the fowls were. 'There they are: they mocked at God and I killed them.' 'Where is the ox?' 'He was chewing mastich; I asked him for some. "Give me some mastich." He wouldn't, and I killed him.' Then he showed them the ox's head, stuck on the pitchfork. 'Where is our mother?' 'She is sitting in the house. I gave her a wash and combed her hair and put her to sit in the corner; I gave her her distaff and spindle to spin; then I boiled an egg and set it in her mouth.' The brothers went to find their mother and saw her there dead. They began to lament and left the house crying. The simpleton shouted out: 'Where are you going?' 'You shut the door and come with us.'

The simpleton tore up the door and set it on his back. They went on and on and came to a high tree; they climbed up it to pass the night there. The simpleton too climbed up, carrying the door. In the morning the elder brothers went away; the

[1] Text from Thrace in *Thrakiká*, xvii. 132.

simpleton stayed there up in the tree. In the evening the king came there with all his men; they sat there to rest and eat some bread. The simpleton up in the tree was hungry and from the bottle he had he rained a little water down on them to make the king go away. When he saw that the king did not move, he began to drum on the door with his feet as if it were thundering. The king was alarmed and with all his people went off, leaving behind them the food and the cauldrons. The simpleton climbed down and ate and ate. Then he found a sack of incense and this he burned to the honour of God. The angel of God descended and asked him: 'What reward would you choose to have for the good deed you have done me?' Then the simpleton asked for a pipe for him to play on, and all trees and all beasts and all men should dance to its music: with that pipe he made his living. God gave it to him because he had a simple soul.

65

The clever Peasant Girl

THIS group of stories has been discussed by BP. ii. 349, with wide parallels in their notes to Grimm, No. 94, *The Peasant's wise Daughter*, and in the notes to Nos. 20 and 21 of *Forty-five Stories*. I translate a version from Cyprus, and in the wide range of Greek variants, for which it is not necessary to repeat the references,[1] the same riddling turns of language occur again and again, the commonest perhaps being the enigmatic presents, where the cheese stands for the moon and the twelve loaves for the twelve months, and it is to be guessed that what has been flayed from the goat is the wine-skin, which ought to be, and is not, full and tight when it is brought to the girl by the servant.

This riddling way of talking appeals to the Greeks, who call it *korakistiká, the language of crows*: it is assumed that the chattering of birds *has* some meaning, but to understand it a man must be very quick-witted. The matter has been discussed by Kyriakidis.[2]

The enigmatic presents are akin to the system of carrying on a correspondence not by letters but by the exchange of conventional tokens. This did away with the inconvenience of not being able to read and write; also the tokens were not compromising, and not even known to everybody. This I gather from a little book printed in London in 1688 with the title: *The Turkish Secretary, containing the Art of expressing one's Thoughts without seeing, speaking, or writing to one another*. It contains a long list of tokens and their meaning: for example, a cat's whisker means 'come secretly like a cat in the night'. How far such an elaboration of the 'Rosemary, that's for remembrance' idea could have been very serious it is hard to say.

NO. 65. THE CLEVER PEASANT GIRL[3]

There was once a king with a son. This prince did not wish to marry unless he could find a girl whose ways of speech were a

[1] *The clever Peasant Girl* references given in *Forty-five Stories* are from Pontos, Cyprus, Constantinople (this translated by Garnett, p. 301), Mitylene, Chios, Kos, Melos, Crete; nothing from the mainland or the west.

[2] *Laographía*, i. 683 and ii. 172.

[3] Text from Cyprus, in Sakellarios' *Kypriaká*, ii. 314.

match for his own. Now one day a herb seller came to deliver herbs at the palace and he heard the king's son talking in this way; he could see that what the king's son was saying was very like what his daughter would say, and this he told to the king's servants. That the king himself should hear the old man who had been saying this, the prince sent for him and said: 'What were you saying, old man?' The old man answered: 'If what I said, O king, is not the truth, then you may cut off my head.' 'Well, old man, I will go with you and you can take me to your house.' 'I will take you with pleasure, my lord.' So they started off. When they had gone some way, they came to a hill. The prince said: 'You help me, old man, and I'll help you, and so we will climb the hill.' The old man said: 'My son, you are young and I am old, and how can I help you in climbing the hill?' 'Well, push on, old man; you didn't understand what I meant.' They went some way farther and came to a field of corn ready for reaping. The prince said: 'Now for this corn, old man; has the owner eaten it or is he going to eat it some time?' 'Of course he hasn't eaten it, my son; the corn is not yet harvested, so how can a man have eaten it?' 'Push on, old man, you don't understand what I meant.'

Well, they went on and on and came to the old man's house. When they came there, the old man invited the prince to go in first. The prince said: 'You go in, old man, and I will come in after you.' At once the old man pulled the door to and the prince was shut out. The girl said to him: 'We had a dog but he is dead now. Good evening, my lord; open the door and come in.' The prince at once opened the door and went in.

When the prince came in he asked to have 'sweet fruits laid in a privy place'. The old man's daughter said in answer: 'They came and barked and ate the cock-a-doodle-doos, and the nests are scattered abroad.' At once the prince saw that she understood the way he talked. Then as they were having a meal the prince said: 'What you have at the top is good but it is a little weak.' The girl answered: 'Weak it is, but full of good grain.' They ate and rose up from the table and went to lie down. The old man said to her: 'If you will have my blessing on you, my daughter; what was it you and the prince were saying?' She said: 'You have only to ask me, my father, and I will tell you.' 'When I and the prince were on the road, we came to a hill, and he said to me: "You help me and I will help you, and so we shall climb the hill." Then I said: "You are young and I am an old man, and how can I be a help to you?" ' Then the girl said to him: 'My father, this meant that you should support yourselves on staffs: I carry you, my staff, and you carry me; thus you would both climb the hill.' 'Very well, my daughter. Then presently as we were going farther on our way, we came to a field of corn ready for the harvest, and the prince said: "Now this corn: Has the owner eaten it, or is he in some time to come going to eat it?" Then I said: "The corn is not yet harvested, and how could a man have eaten it?" The prince said to me: "You don't understand what I meant."' Then the girl said: 'The meaning was: does the man owe it as a debt and will he have to hand it over in payment, or will he be able to consume it himself?' 'Very well, my daughter. Then when we came home and he was shut out, you said: "We had a dog but he is dead now: good evening, my lord, come in."' 'This meant,' said the girl, 'we had a dog and he is now dead, and I said this meaning that he should open the door and come in, and have no fear.' 'Very well, my daughter. But what about when he said to you: "Sweet fruits and laid in a privy place, a place apart," and you answered: "They came and barked and ate the cock-a-doodle-doos and the nests are scattered abroad." ' 'This meant,' she said, 'he asked for eggs and I told him that the foxes had come and the nests were scattered abroad.' 'Very well, my daughter. And now this also: When he said to you: "What you have at the top is good, but it is a little weak." ' She answered: 'I said to him: "Weak it is but it is full of good grain." And to this the prince said to me: "Is this what you mean: that you are a good girl but your eye is weak?" Then said I to the prince: "My eye may in truth be weak, but I myself have much good wit."' 'Oh, my daughter,' said the old man, 'I understand none of these things.'

They went to sleep and rose up in the morning and at once an engagement was made that the prince should have the girl as his wife. So the prince said farewell and went off to his royal dwelling to make all ready for the wedding. When the prince arrived he called for his black servant and gave him twelve loaves; he gave him also cheeses and two skins of wine and told him to give this message to his betrothed: 'Twelve months are in the year; round is the moon; what is flayed from the goat is full as full, and so are the wine-skins from one end to the other.' Also she must tell him what her mother is doing and her father and her sister. The negro came to the girl betrothed to the prince and told her all that he had said. The girl told him for his message back to the prince: 'Greet your master from me and say to him: "The year has eleven months, and the moon is at the half; what is flayed from the goat is as empty as a drum. My mother has been to fetch a soul to earth from the heights of heaven, and my father has gone to pick roses in May, and my sister is at her embroidery frame, and I myself am making old things new again." When you tell him all this, if he rushes at you to beat you, you must say to him that if he is to have pleasure with the partridge he must not beat the crow.'

When her father heard her saying this he asked her to explain it to him. She said: 'Sir, the prince sent me twelve loaves; the cheeses were not cut and the skins, the wine-skins flayed from goats, were full of wine from ear to ear. Then the negro, I suppose with some friends, sat down to eat and to drink the wine, and my message to the prince was to let him know in what state his present reached me. Then I was sorry for the negro and sent word that if he wished to have pleasure in me he must not beat the negro. As for my mother, what I told him was that she had gone to deliver a woman with child, and you yourself had gone to fetch fire, a thing as common as roses in May. As for my sister I said—and this was plain—that she was working patterns on her embroidery frame; I myself was patching old clothes.' Then her father said: 'My daughter, take my blessing; of all this talk I understood nothing at all.'

Finally the negro came to his master and told him what his betrothed had said. At once the prince rushed at him to beat him. 'Alas, my master, if you are to enjoy the partridge, you must not beat the poor crow.' At last, my lady, all the king's preparations were finished, and the horses were yoked to the carriages to go to fetch the bride. Then with fiddling and with dancing the marriage was celebrated and we too came home again.

66

The foolish Women

THIS story Ralston has called 'one of the most popular simpleton-tales in the world,' and this absolves from the necessity of doing more than pointing to the references in BP., and mentioning Clouston's *Book of Noodles*.[1] An example from Kos is printed in *Forty-five Stories*, No. 13, where I have also given references to versions from Crete. Astypálaia, Mitylene, Skyros, and to two versions from Pontos.

The essence of the story is that a woman, generally going to fetch water, sees a handsome young man and wishes she was married to him: but then she thinks that if she were, either he or their son might have an accident and die. This imaginary trouble causes her to weep so much that she cannot do her work; the other women sympathize and even have a funeral feast for the supposed death of the non-existent son. Here sometimes the story ends, but in the fuller version the man of the house is so angry at their folly that he leaves the house and vows that he will return only if he finds women in other places equally silly. In a Pontic version he then finds a woman parting with money to a man who says he will use it for journey money to bring back from death her first husband and his dead son. This seems so silly that the man goes home again: his womenkind are no sillier than women elsewhere.[2]

In this Pontic version the foolish women to make the funeral feast for the supposed death of the non-existent boy kill an ox. Some light is cast on this in the book by Loukópoulos and Petrópoulos, on the popular religion of Phárasa, *Ἡ λαϊκὴ θρησκεία τῶν Φαράσων*, p. 45. Here we are told that at Phárasa sacrifices, by which is meant animals killed for ritual purposes in a ritual way, were common, but that the people took an ox for the victim only when making a memorial for the dead. Our story is from Pontos and it is with the Greeks of Pontos that the people of Phárasa seem to have had their closest contact with the outside world.

[1] Ralston, *Russian Folk-Tales*, p. 53. BP., i. 335, on Grimm, No. 34, *Die kluge Elsa*.

[2] The text is in *Pontiaká Phylla*, i (1936), Part III, p. 20, under the title *The old Woman, her Son, and his Wife*.

67

The Riddle

THE Greeks love riddles of all sorts. Politis and Kyriakídis have both written of them at length and they are also discussed in *Forty-five Stories*, No. 22, where the symbolic carving of the fowl is also found.[1] This actual riddle of the eyes, teeth, and skull is found again in Kos, Symi, Mitylene, and Crete, and is probably very widely spread, perhaps from Italy to Russia.

The Greek references for this riddle story are:

1. KOS: *Forty-five Stories*, No. 22.
2. NÍSYROS: *Z.A.* i. 424, here translated.
3. SYMI: *Z.A.* i. 238.
4. MELOS: *N.A.* i. 29.
5. CRETE: *Myson*, vii. 149.

This version from Nísyros contains the enigmatic presents of 'The clever Peasant Girl' stories (No. 65) and also the symbolic carving of the fowl. There are in fact several contacts between this story and the Clever Girl series.

NO. 67. THE RIDDLE[2]

In those days there was a king. This king had a negro servant; with him his wife had been for seven years in love. After these seven years the negro died, and on the fortieth day after his death the queen went and dug him up and carried away his teeth and his eyes and his skull: the eyes and skull she took to the goldsmith, who set the eyes in rings as precious stones; of his skull a cup was made for drinking water. His teeth she took to the shoemaker, and he made her a pair of shoes with the teeth set in them as nails. Then after a year she thought of letting her husband know of this. So one day as they were at table she said to the king: 'I should like to ask you a riddle.' He said: 'Ask me.'

[1] Politis in *Sýllogos*, viii. 513, and in *Laographía*, ii. 371; Kyriakídis, *Ἑλληνικὴ Λαογραφία*, p. 341. For the symbolic carving of the fowl see Clouston, *Popular Tales*, ii, 329 and 493. He finds it in the Talmud. See also BP. ii. 360.

[2] Text from Nísyros, in *Z.A.* i. 424.

Then she said: '*What I see with, I wear; what I chew with, I tread upon; and from my brain I drink water.*' The king fell into deep thought and pondered night and day, but he could not make plain the riddle. Then he summoned his Council of Twelve and told them to think of the answer to the riddle, but they could no more solve it than he could.

The king thought to go to some other land to find the answer to the riddle and be free from this puzzle. So he took with him his Council of Twelve and went his way. On the way they saw a field sown with corn, corn of Roumelia. Then the king said: 'Look now at this field: the man who has sown it; is it his own or not?' His people said: 'If it is not his own field, would he sow it?' Then said the king: 'You did not take my meaning: I asked whether he owes it as a debt or not.' So they went on and on and came to a village; as they went into the village they came to a house. The king knocked at the door and an old man opened it. The king said: 'Good evening, old man.' 'You are welcome, O king.' The king said to the old man: 'Will you not be kind and take us into your house this evening, for it is late?' The old man said: 'O my king, how can we take you in? We are poor folk here and have no bedclothes for you.' 'That doesn't matter; make up a bed on the ground for me to sleep.' This old man had a daughter, a very sharp girl, and she was sitting in the recess weaving. The king went in and saw her weaving. He said: 'A happy day at the harvest!' And the girl said: 'A happy day at the harvest and at binding the sheaves also!' The king said to himself: 'This girl will surely be able to answer the riddle for me.' So the king went up to the house. The old woman there had a hen; she killed it and cooked it for their supper. The old woman set the table for the meal. The king took and divided the fowl; before the father he set the head, before the mother the keel bone, that is the bone of the breast, and before the girl he set all the meat, and he himself took the feet. They ate and then lay down to sleep.

In the night the old woman woke up and said to the old man: 'My dear old gaffer, I don't see what the king meant when he gave you the head and me the breast bone, we who are the seniors, and to the girl all the meat. Why did he do this? He ought to have given the meat to us and the bones to the girl.' Now the girl was awake and heard them, and she said to her mother: 'Don't you know that my father is the head of the house and that is why the king gave him the head; and to you he gave the keel bone because you are the keel of our ship; and he gave me the tender meat because I am a young girl; and he took the legs for himself because he is a stranger and will walk away.' Now the king was awake listening to all that the girl said, and he said to himself that she was a girl capable of solving his riddle.

Next day dawned and the girl went to her recess and sat weaving. The king too rose up and he found her in the recess and said: 'Let me ask you a riddle to see if you can answer it.' The girl said: 'Ask me and I will see.' Then the king told her the riddle: '*What I see with, I wear; what I chew with, I tread upon; and from my brain I drink water.*' Then the girl laughed and said: 'Good; I can explain it to you, but I don't know whether it was a man or a woman. The person, either a man or a woman, had a lover and when this lover died, the person went and dug up the body and took out the teeth, the skull and the eyes. Then shoes were made and the teeth set in them as nails; of the skull a vessel was made from which to drink water, and for the eyes rings were made and the eyes set in them as stones.'

Then the king went off to his palace. On the queen's hands he saw the rings and in them as precious stones the eyes of the negro: he saw the shoes and that the negro's teeth were set in them as nails. Then he went and took the drinking bowl and scraped it with his knife and saw that it was the skull. Then he believed the girl, and he took his wife and cut her into little pieces; for all in the court to see her.

Then he called for his servant and gave him thirty gold pieces and a loaf and a skin of wine, and said: 'You must take these to the house where we were and give them to the girl and say: "The moon is full; the month is at its thirtieth day and the wine-skin is full up."' The servant took the king's gifts. On his way he was hungry and cut half the loaf and ate it. Then he said: 'I must also have a gold piece, just for pocket money.' Then he said: 'I must drink a little wine, and how will this be found out?' Then he went to the village and knocked at the door and gave the presents to the girl saying: 'The moon is full, the month is at its thirtieth day and the wine-skin is full up.' First the girl laughed and then she said: 'Go to the king and say: "The moon is at the half, the month at twenty-nine days, and the wine-skin is slack and shaking." ' He said: 'Very well,' and so he went off. She called out to him and said: 'You must tell the king that if he loves the partridge he must not beat the crow.' So he went off to the king and said: 'The moon is at the half; the month is at the twenty-ninth day and the wine-skin is slack and shaking.' When the king saw what had happened he started to beat him. Then the servant remembered the other thing which the girl had told him, and he said to the king: 'If you love the partridge you must not beat the crow.' Then the king said: 'Why did you not say this to me but kept it to yourself and waited for me to beat you before you would tell me?' Then the king sent him off again and he went and brought the girl and they were married and so the poor girl was made a queen.

68

The rival Liars

AARNE–THOMPSON TYPE 920

THE competition between two men as to which of them can tell the most extravagant lie is so widely spread—BP.'s references are innumerable[1]—that it is strange not to find it commoner in Greece. The six examples I have found show that the specifically Greek form of the story is that the youngest son of three is sent to a mill to have the corn ground. The miller is a *spanós*, that is a man without a beard, the rascally hero of the stories collected under No. 69, and the two enter into rivalry, the prize being a cake, which of them can tell the biggest lie. The youngest son defeats the beardless man. I note that beans, uncooked, notoriously produce not quench thirst.

The opportunities of millers for stealing part of the corn sent to them to grind are so great that everywhere they have a bad name. We have the rhyme:

> Take a webster that is leal,
> Take a miller that will not steal;
> Take a lawyer that will not lie,
> And lay the three a dead corpse by;
> Then by the virtue of those three
> The said dead corpse shall quick'ned be.

The examples of this story are:

1. TAURUS MOUNTAINS, FROM PHÁRASA: *M.G. in A.M.*, p. 535.
2. PONTOS: *Arkheíon Pontou*, vi. 228.
3. MITYLENE: Georgeakis et Pineau, *Folklore de Lesbos*, p. 140.
4. SKYROS: Pérdika, ii. 163, translated.
5. EUBOIA: Hahn, i. 313, No. 59.
6. EPEIROS: *Laographía*, ii. 475.

NO. 68. THE RIVAL LIARS[2]

Once upon a time there were an old man and an old woman and they had an adopted son. The time came for them to send the barley to the mill. They got all ready for the milling and gave

[1] BP. ii. 506 to Grimm, No. 112.

[2] Text from Skyros in Pérdika, ii. 163, with the title, *The Beardless Man and the Cake*.

the boy the barley and told him to go and grind it. They told him not to go to the nearest mill, the one at Kaliméri, nor to Mármara, but he must go to the beardless man Constandí the son of Pandelí, for he was a man of honour and would not steal the flour. Also he must not leave the barley there, but wait for it to be ground and then load it up and come back home.

The boy went off and found the miller and gave him the barley to be ground. The miller poured the barley into the great hopper and said to the boy: 'Sit here until the grinding is finished and my wife will make us a cake, and whichever of us can tell the biggest lie, he shall have the cake to eat.' When they had sat down, the miller began and said: 'My honoured father had a Turkey oak and it was so big that in its shade five hundred sheep could lie down. This is what I have to say; now it is your turn.'

Then the boy began; and he said: 'When my mother gave birth to my father, they sent me off to go and call the priest to come and read the wedding service over them. I went to the priest, Father George, and he sent me to Father Francis and he sent me to Father Alexander. Father Alexander said: "I can't go unless you bring me a licence written out by Uncle God." Off I went to find Uncle God, and so, on and on and on. On the way I grew thirsty; I had a few beans in my pocket and I began to eat them. One bean fell on the ground and a bean plant grew up. I hooked myself up from leaf to leaf and scrambled up and came to Uncle God. I said to him: "Uncle God, Father Alexander has sent me for you to grant me a licence for him to read the wedding service over my mother, who has just given birth to my father and is even now in her bed." Uncle God gave me the licence; I did him reverence for his grace and went off. And there by the road I came to a well. I stooped down to drink a little water and my head fell off and dropped into the water. I went down to get hold of my head and I let the licence drop. Then out came a fox. The fox snatched the licence. I ran this way and that to catch the fox and get back the licence from her. This made me tired and out of breath: but no licence. I could do nothing at all and how was I to get it again?' The miller said: 'But what writing had the licence on it?' The boy said: 'O my uncle, it wrote that the boy should eat the cake and the beardless man eat dung and then go and wipe his mouth.'

69

The Man with no Beard

IT is a part of the Greek admiration for physical perfection and distaste for anything which mars it that they strongly dislike all such personal blemishes as birth-marks and so on. On the days, the first to the third of February, *Ta Symóyiorta*, dedicated to St. Symeón, women with child and their husbands abstain from work lest the child to be born have a mark, a *simeíon*, on his body. This is of course a pun on the name of the saint, who is naturally connected with children as it was he who took the infant Christ in his arms and sang the *Nunc dimittis*; hence his name the *Theodókhos*, he who received Christ. In the same way a mule or horse with a cut ear loses much in value. The same feeling is to the fore in the way a man is regarded who by physical defect can grow no beard, who is what is called a *spanós*. These people are not uncommon in many parts of Greece and from their defect are generally an object of contempt and dislike; often too of fear, for they are supposed to have the evil eye. In our story, as in No. 34, the hero, after meeting the beardless man and refusing his greeting, 'turned back', to make a fresh start after this inauspicious meeting. I remember a workman at an excavation in Crete who was a jovial, buffoonish character, drank too much, and was a general favourite; yet he had the evil eye. Two brothers I knew, men of some education, if they met this man on the road as they were going out, say, shooting, would go back home, like the boy in our story, and make a fresh start to avoid the ill luck his evil eye would bring upon whatever they were starting to do.

In stories the beardless man is one very much to be avoided, being, as Halliday has put it, a despicable and merciless villain. The boy out on his adventures is often warned to have nothing to do with a beardless man. In Greek stories he appears in several connexions. First; in the story of *The rival Liars*, No. 68, a *spanós* is often one of the liars, in the end defeated by generally the youngest of three brothers. In a second set of stories the stupidity of ogres is emphasized by introducing a *spanós* to outwit the blundering monster: here comes No. 5, the story I have called *The Ogre outwitted.* In yet a third set of stories, one of which from Pontos is here translated, the beardless man is swindled in a variety of ways, being induced to buy a mule supposed to drop gold, a hare or a dog which he is made to believe is able to run messages, and so on.

Examples of this third kind are:

1. PONTOS: *Arkheíon Pontou*, iii. 108. My own record translated below.
2, 3. MITYLENE: Anagnóstis, *Lesbiaká*, p. 194; *Folklore*, xi. 117.
4. NAXOS: *N.A.* ii. 93.
5. ASTYPÁLAIA: Pio, p. 112 = Geldart, p. 126.
6. EPEIROS: Hahn, i. 249, No. 42.

In a fourth set of stories the hero makes an agreement with the beardless man that whichever of the two first loses his temper shall pay a forfeit: his head or a piece of flesh cut from his body. This story has been studied by Halliday in *Journal Gypsy Lore Society*, N.S. ii. 151.[1]

The following Greek instances are found:

1. TAURUS MOUNTAINS, at Afshár-Köi, *M.G. in A.M.*, p. 575.
2. CAPPADOCIA: from Ulaghátsh, ibid., p. 371.
3. MÝKONOS: Roussel, *Contes de Mycono*, p. 47.
4. THRACE: *Arkheíon Thrakikoú Laogr.* ix. 204.
5. EPEIROS: Pio, p. 48, which is Hahn, i. 118, No. 11.

There are in addition a few stories in which a boy, as a rule the youngest of three brothers, outwits a beardless man by some means or another. Here I would reckon two stories from Pontos in *Arkheíon Pontou*, iii. 96, and vi. 228, and a story from Naxos in *N.A.* ii. 108.

NO. 69. THE MAN WITH NO BEARD[2]

There was a man who had a son. He called for the boy: 'My son, I shall give you a piece of advice and do you pay heed to it. When you are going anywhere, and meet on the road a man without a beard, you must not accept his greeting; turn back again.' The father died.

The boy used to go on the roads with his horse laden with charcoal. He met a man with no beard. The man said: 'Good day.' The boy said: 'Your Good Day and you too may go and be buried together.' The boy turned back. Next day again he passed along the road with a load of charcoal; again he fell in with the beardless man. 'Good day,' said the man. 'Good day,' said the boy. 'This charcoal, is it not for sale?' The boy said: 'It is for sale, but I don't trade with a beardless man. This my

[1] Halliday gives references to *M.G. in A.M.*, p. 234; Cosquin, *Contes de Lorraine*, ii. 47; BP. ii. 293; Jacobs, *Celtic Fairy Tales*, i. 181.

[2] Text from the Of valley in Pontos, printed in *Arkheíon Pontou*, iii. 108.

father told me.' The man said: 'This is a place all full of beardless men; no others are to be found. Now will you not let me have it?' So they made a bargain, and the boy sold him the charcoal for eighty piastres. They went to the house of the beardless man, and the boy unloaded and then took his horse to go his way. The beardless man said: 'I bought the charcoal, and for my eighty piastres I bought the horse as well.' The boy could make no way against the beardless man; he took his money and went off.

The boy went home. He took a mule and again made up a load of charcoal. He took in his hand some three pounds, some five medjids, and went along the road. From a distance he saw the beardless man coming. He pushed the gold coins and the medjids into the mule's hind parts. The beardless man had a fancy to buy the mule, and said: 'Will you not sell me this load?' The boy said: 'Are you aware what a treasure this beast is? This one is not like the former animal.' As they were talking, in the mule's droppings the gold coins were to be seen and the medjids too. The beardless man said: 'What is the price of this mule?' The boy said: 'His droppings are gold; he costs a lot.' 'Well, what do you want for him?' 'For three hundred pounds I will let you have him,' said the boy. They struck the bargain for three hundred pounds. The beardless man took the mule and paid over the money. The boy said: 'He will drop gold all the time, but you must put him into the cellar and for forty days not open the door; nail it up.' Inside the house you must dig a hole and down this hole pour the water for the mule to drink and put the fodder for him to eat; afterwards go and open the cellar and you will find it full of gold coins and crown pieces.' The beardless man was too impatient to wait. After ten days he went and peeped in through the crack of the door and looked: the mule was lying on its back dead; in the darkness there was a bright shining; it was the mule's shoes. The man went and said to his wife: 'The cellar is all bright with crown pieces.' After forty days he went joyfully to open the cellar and he found the mule dead: no money or anything else.

Then the boy heard that the beardless man was coming back to ask: 'What trick is this you have played me?' So the boy said to his wife: 'If he asks you, "Where is your husband?" you must say: "He has gone out to the field." If he says: "I wanted him," then you must say: "Let me send this dog to go to him, and then he will come." ' The beardless man said: 'Can a dog go and tell him to come?' The wife said: 'This dog is our serving boy; we give him food and he takes it off to the harvest field.' The boy was standing a little way from the house. The wife hit at the dog and he ran out of the courtyard. 'Go and tell my husband to come; this man here wants him.' When the dog ran down to the cellar; the boy saw him and called to him to come where he was. The dog came and the boy stayed there for a while and then came to the house and the dog with him. He said: 'Good day, you with no beard.' He said: 'A fine trick you have played me!' 'And what have I done to you?' 'What have you done to me?' said the beardless man. 'The mule is dead and there are no gold coins or crowns either.' The boy said: 'How did you manage that?' He said: 'I put the mule in the cellar and poured down the water and gave him the fodder.' He said: 'You ought not to have done it that way. Have you ever heard of people pouring out water like that? That is why the mule died.'

'Well, we can leave all that,' said the beardless man. 'Sell me this dog.' The boy said: 'I can't sell him; he is my servant, and besides that he is the dog I keep here.' However for fifty pounds he did sell the dog. The beardless man went home. When his wife saw the dog, she said: 'He has swindled you again.' He said: 'What are you talking about, wife? As for this dog, when I go to the field, you must make my food ready and hang it on his neck and send him off to me in the field. We have no serving boy at hand; the dog shall be our boy.' So one day the beardless man went to the field. His wife made his food ready and put it in the bag and hung it on the dog's neck; she gave him a blow to drive him from the courtyard and said: 'Take this food and carry it to the field for the beardless man.' The dog took the bag and went down to the cellar; there he stayed and ate all the food. The beardless man was in the field and there he waited hungry; neither food nor anything else. In the evening the beardless man came home and said: 'Wife, why did you not send me any food?' She said: 'I gave the food to the dog and he stayed down by the cellar and ate it all. That boy swindles you every day and gets your money for nothing. You must go at once to the boy and get your money back.'

The boy was aware that the beardless man was coming. He said to his wife: 'We must play him a master trick. Take a bladder and fill it with blood and hang it round your neck. When the beardless man comes, you must say to me: "Why do you swindle people and take their money for nothing?" I shall say to you: "Get out of my sight." Then I shall take my knife and cut your throat'. The woman said to him: 'Cut my throat, if you can: you *do* swindle men and take their money for nothing.' In his fury the youth plunged his knife into the bladder and the blood ran out. The beardless man said: 'The woman is dead.' She lay there stretched out. The beardless man said: 'We need have no more talk about the money; you have killed your wife and for nothing.' The boy said: 'I will restore her life.' 'How can you restore her life?' said the beardless man. The boy went into the house and brought out a pipe and began to play, *toot toot toot*. The woman began to stir her feet. The beardless man said: 'He is bringing her back to life.' The wife rose up. At this the beardless man said: 'What has passed between us has passed. You swindled me, but let it all be pardoned. Come, sell me this pipe.' He said: 'I can't let it go.' The man said: 'I will give you as much as you like, but let me have it.' He said: 'Give me two hundred pounds and I will let you have it.' The boy accepted the two hundred pounds and gave the man the pipe.

The beardless man went home. His wife said: 'What have you done?' He said: 'I have bought this pipe for two hundred pounds.' His wife said: 'Oh! Alas for the money! He has swindled you again.' He said: 'Don't worry me; get away from here.' Certain other people were there. He said to his wife: 'I will hit you and kill you; get away.' The woman said: 'Alas for the money! We shall perish from hunger.' He pulled out his knife and plunged it into her throat. His wife was killed. The people there said: 'What have you done?' He said: 'It is quite simple; I can raise her up and restore her to life again.' He took out the pipe and began, *toot toot toot*. But the woman did not get up. The men said: 'What have you done?' He said: 'I will raise her up.' Again he began, *toot toot toot*. To no purpose. The policemen were summoned and the beardless man was put in prison. The boy escaped from the hands of the beardless man and spent the money. The boy's horse had cost the beardless man five hundred and fifty pounds.

After that I came here.

70

Only one Brother was grateful

IN a recent paper Dr. Winstedt has called attention to the story to which I have given this name.[1] It has also been studied by Halliday and they have found parallels in Armenia and in Slav countries; Halliday adds one from the Berbers.[2] An Albanian version from Prizrend is in *Folklore*, liv. 37. I can find only three Greek versions; two from Asia Minor and one from Samos, which I have translated.

The machinery of the three brothers of whom the youngest alone acts well or is successful is of course familiar, and about the sacrifice of a child for the sake of a friend much has been written: some of it will be found in the note on No. 37 in this book, *Faithful John*.

The references are:

1. THE TAURUS: from Phárasa; *M.G. in A.M.*, p. 523.
2. CAPPADOCIA, from Ulaghátsh; a poor version in Kesisoglou, *Glossikòn idíoma t. Oulagats*, p. 154.
3. SAMOS: Stamatiádis, *Samiaká*, v. 535.

NO. 70. ONLY ONE BROTHER WAS GRATEFUL[3]

Once upon a time there was a man and he was poor; he used to work at a daily wage and so he kept his family, his wife and his three children. As long as he was in health we need say nothing; he would bring home a piece of bread for his family to eat. But no long time passed before he fell sick; from day to day his sickness grew worse. Not to make a long story of it, soon from being rich and well-to-do all their living was scattered. Now when the man was still alive his children saw food no more often than at no moon and at full moon, so you may imagine what happened to them when their father was gone; they sat as empty as so many sieves. They looked at the matter and looked again, and they made up their minds to go away from home to

[1] *Folklore*, lvii. 143. [2] *M.G. in A.M.*, p. 253.
[3] Text from Samos, *Samiaká*, v. 535.

make a living. This they told their mother: what could the poor old woman do? She gave them her blessing and put a piece of bread and a couple of shirts into a package and sent them off to find their luck.

The boys started off, but where were they to go? They did not know; they had no one to help them; in front of them was an open well, behind them the deep sea. They followed a path blindly and went off. Then on their way they met an old man and he asked them where they were going. 'Where are we going?' said the boys. 'We are going, my uncle, to find some rich house where we may win a living; we are orphans and we have even left our mother at home with no bread in the house.' Then the old man told the boys to follow him and he would find them a rich house. As they were on the way, a number of crows flew out. When the eldest boy saw them flying out, he said to the old man: 'Tell me, uncle, what is the good of those crows? Wouldn't it be better for them to be sheep for me to have them for my livelihood as a shepherd and the others could live with me?' The old man said: 'Then, my boy, would you like the crows to be turned into sheep?' 'Wouldn't I, uncle?' said the boy. 'What a pity they can't be.' 'Don't trouble about that,' said the old man: 'I will turn them into sheep. But whoever passes by your dairy you must give him something to eat; milk or cheese or whatever you have.' 'And may this turn to your pleasure,' said the boy. Then the old man pronounced certain words and at once the crows turned into sheep. So the eldest son took them off to graze, and the old man went on his way and the other two boys with him.

On the way they came to a spring and they sat there a while to drink and refresh themselves. One of the boys said to the old man: 'Uncle, wouldn't it be still better if the spring were an oilpress and all the trees round about olive-trees?' The old man said: 'Would you like the spring to turn into an oilpress, my boy, and the trees be olive-trees? This I would do, but whoever passes by the oilpress to him you must give some oil as a free gift.' 'As you wish, my uncle,' said the boy. 'You make it into an oilpress and turn all the trees into olive-trees, and whoever passes by, to him I will give oil to last him a whole year.' Again the old man pronounced some secret words, and the spring became an oilpress and all the trees turned into olive-trees. So the second boy stayed there by the oilpress and the old man went off with the third boy.

As they were on the way the old man said to the boy: 'You saw your two brothers, how to one of them I gave sheep for him to be a shepherd, and the other I put in charge of an oilpress. And now you: what would you like me to do for you?' The boy said: 'I don't want anything. I want to go on with you, wherever you go.' 'Very well,' said the old man; 'let us be off then.' On their way they came into a city, and there they saw a great house with many servants; music too and lights: it was a marriage being held there. The old man went in. 'Good day.' 'You are welcome, old man.' 'What are you doing here?' 'We are making a marriage. Sit down with us, my poor old man, and take your pleasure.' 'I won't stay,' said the old man, 'but please me, I beg you, by not making the marriage today; you will be sorry for it.' 'Why should we not have the marriage today?' 'Because I tell you so,' said the elder. 'See; now I am going away, and for whatever may come upon you any blame is on your own heads.' So he made ready to depart.

When the company at the wedding heard this, they were afraid and said to one another: 'This man must surely be some sort of wizard. Let us call for him to tell us what we ought to do.' So they ran and came up with him and said: 'Old man, old man, even as you said to us, we are not holding the wedding today; but do give us some counsel about what we ought to do.' Then the elder said to them: 'Let the bridegroom take a burning brand and this boy I have here with me shall take another; the two must plant the brands in the courtyard and to the one whose brand shall be found tomorrow with leaves on it, to him shall the bride be given.' So they did as the elder told them, and the burning brands were planted by the bridegroom and by the boy, and they waited for the next day to see whose brand would have put out leaves. God brought the day, and what did they see? The bridegroom's brand was still as when it had been planted and the boy's brand had grown into a very fine tree with branches and with fruit such as a man would delight to behold. Then the boy took the bride for himself and the unlucky bridegroom was left like the poor mouse drenched in the oil.

After the wedding and the feasting and drinking, the elder gave the boy his counsel: he must be kindly, and feel for the sufferings of the poor. After this he thought to go and find the other two boys, the shepherd and the one with the oilpress, and see what they were doing. When he was close to the dairy he began to cry out: 'Help an old man, a poor leper with nothing to eat, and so may all your dead find pardon for their sins.' Then the shepherd ran out from the dairy and gave him his answer: 'Get away from here; we don't want to catch your leprosy.' So he drove the old man away roughly: tears came into his eyes. Then as he was starting to go off the old man said to the shepherd: 'Crows they were and crows they shall again be.' And immediately the sheep turned into crows and the shepherd was left with his crook in his hand and nothing else.

From there the elder went and visited the man with the oilpress and again began his requests, asking him for a driblet of oil. But this man too fell to insulting him and drove him away even more roughly than the other one. Then the old man said: 'A spring of water it was and a spring again it shall be for men to come and drink water.' Immediately the oilpress turned into a spring of water and the olive-trees became wild olives; wild trees of all sorts. The elder went away and came to the third youth, the one for whom he had found a wife. He knocked at the door and a serving woman looked out of the window and asked him what he wanted. 'I want a little bread to eat and a lodging here for the night: I am a poor leper and very tired.' 'Stay,' said she, 'and I will go and tell my mistress, because the master is not here.' So the servant went and told her mistress that there was a leper knocking at the door and asking for bread and a lodging for the night, because he had nowhere to sleep. 'Stay,' said her mistress, 'I will go down myself and invite him in,' and she went herself to the old man and told him to come in and eat and to take a rest after his toils. 'Oh no, my daughter,' said the elder. 'Give me a little bread to eat and I can sleep here outside because I am a leper and it may be your husband would drive me away.' 'Come in, come inside,' said the woman. 'My husband is a man of merciful heart and would scold me if he heard that I had left you outside. Come in; we have room for you to sleep wherever you like.' When the old man saw the lady's kindly disposition he went into the house and lay down in a basement room. The woman sent him a mattress there and a coverlet and whatever cooked food she had, and when her husband came in the evening she told him that an old leper had come and she had asked him to lodge in their house, but he was unwilling and had gone into the basement and there lain down. When her husband heard this he went down into the basement and took the leper, willing or unwilling, and brought him up into the house and set a table for him; dishes to make a man's mouth water. When they had eaten well he said to the elder: 'Tell me, old man, why have you not looked out for a cure for your leprosy? Perhaps you have no money? I can give you as much as is needed.' 'Ah, my lad,' said the elder, 'and how can I be cured? The remedy I need is a very hard matter and no one will grant me to have it.' 'But what is this remedy that no one will give you?' 'A very great doctor told me,' said the old man, 'that I could be cured at once by killing a boy three years old and anointing myself with his blood; further I should burn his body and make powder of it and with that dust sprinkle myself. Now who will give me one of his sons and let me have his life?' 'You are right, my poor friend,' said the man, 'Yet God is great and governs all things. I shall give you my child; he was yours from the moment you came and told me your trouble.' The elder took the child and killed him and anointed himself with the blood; then he put the body into the oven to be charred to powder for him to sprinkle himself with. After the day God brought the night; the child's parents rose up but they could not find the old man. Then the woman said to her husband: 'It seems as if the old man was afraid that we might change our minds about letting him have our child: he kill him and then we make trouble; so he must have risen in the night and gone off. But let us go to the oven and see if he took the dust and sprinkled himself with it.' So they went in and opened the oven and what did they see? There was the boy all alive and in one hand he held a basket all full of diamonds and brilliants, of gold and of silver, and in the other little hand was a golden book lying open and the boy writing in it in fine big letters: *He who receives in his house and serves the stranger and the poor man, he receives and serves God Himself.* For it seems that the old man was an angel and did all these things to show us that the worst of all actions is ingratitude and hardness of heart, and also that whoever does good, to him in recompense God grants the same and even more.

Is this a good story?

71

The fortunate Delay

THIS story belongs to a group which has been studied by Cosquin under the title of *The Legend of the Page of St. Elizabeth of Portugal.*[1] In Greece I find only this one version from Thrace, which is translated here, and a story in the Cretan writer Agapios Landos, though there are two good parallels in the Nearer East.

Of these the better is perhaps a Georgian story.[2] A father let his son go out into the world on his adventures, bidding him never to commit or connive at an adultery dishonouring the house of his host or of his master, and never to fail to go into a church when he hears the bell ring and remain there until the end of the service. The wife of his master, the Duke of Bechi, tempted him, but he refused her advances. The lady had another lover and the hero caught the guilty pair. In order to get rid of a man now so dangerous, the lady told the duke that the young man had insulted her. The duke sent the youth, unconscious of his danger, off to the executioner, ordering the man to behead his first visitor and to give the head to the second man who came to his house. On the way our hero heard a church bell and went in to the service. In the meanwhile the king's messenger, who chanced to be the lady's lover, came on his errand to the executioner to find out if the king's orders had been fulfilled. He was in this way the first man to arrive, and the executioner duly cut off his head, and when the hero left the church and came to the house of the executioner he was given the unfortunate messenger's head to carry it to the duke. Then the hero told the duke the whole story.

The second Near East variant is from Bulgaria; in it St. John the Baptist plays the leading part.[3] He was at the king's court, and the queen wanted to get rid of him because he had discovered that she had a lover. She had a daughter by a previous marriage, and this girl was a dancer; her mother persuaded her to claim as her reward the head of St. John; and so far the story is just that of Herod

[1] Cosquin, *Études folkloriques*, pp. 73 ff.

[2] In *Contes et légendes du Caucase*, by J. Mourier, No. vii, p. 19. It is a Georgian story, and Mourier points out that it comes from the *Book of Wisdom and Lies*; in Wardrop's translation it is on p. 26.

[3] Lydia Schischmanoff, *Légendes religieuses bulgares*, No. 46, p. 97: St. Jean le Décapité.

and Herodias and the Baptist. The king yielded to the girl's request and ordered his executioner to cut off the head of the first man who came to his house: he sent the saint. But on the way St. John turned aside into a church to hear Mass. To find out if his order had been obeyed the king sent his wife's lover, and the man, coming first, was at once beheaded. After his death St. John arrived and was given the head to carry to the king. This is not the end of the story. The stepdaughter, Salome, said that she had wanted St. John's head, and the king then had the saint beheaded. A miracle was worked: a fresh head grew on the saint's body, and given his choice of the two he said he preferred the new head, as the old one had been the head of a sinner. All this seems to me likely to be an explanation offered of some icon of the saint on which he was painted with his head on his shoulders, but also carrying it on a charger.

The Cretan parallel is in the seventeenth-century book by the Cretan monk Agapios Landos, called *The Salvation of Sinners*.[1] In the days of Theodosios the Great there was a man who became very poor: he asked two things of his son; to allow himself for his father's benefit to be sold as a slave, and never to miss hearing Mass. Like Joseph by Potiphar's wife the young man was tempted by a lady. She denounced him to her husband and as in the other versions the lady's lover was beheaded in place of the virtuous hero who came late to the house of the executioner, having delayed to attend church. Here the story, entirely turned to a moral use, ends with an exhortation not to talk in church, but still more not to go out before the end of the service. A man who does this is acting like Judas who rose up from the supper table to go out to betray Christ: Oh, the graceless wretch!

The resemblance of these three stories to the Thracian tale of adventures of Handsome Johnnie with his master's wife and his escape by going to church and hearing the singing of the Six Psalms is very clear. The main difference is that in the Thracian story it is not a lover who is beheaded but the temptress who loses her life by being made into soap, and so quickly that when the master who had hoped to destroy Johnnie came to the factory the foreman could proudly show him the bags already filled with the soap made from the fat of his wicked wife's body.

The earlier part of our story, the adventures of Handsome Johnnie, when the princess falls in love with him hardly belongs at all to the story of the 'Fortunate Delay', and the rather incoherent episode when he goes down the well to set free the flow of water and his companions draw up two beautiful girls is a clumsy borrowing from our

[1] In the 1681 Venice edition, p. 435.

No. 26, *The Underworld Adventure.* It is only after the account of Johnnie's prosperity that the 'Fortunate Delay' theme really begins with the tempting of the hero by the wife of the man who owned the soap factory.

The gist of Cosquin's paper is the essential identity of these Near East stories with the legend of the page in the service of St. Elizabeth of Portugal, a thirteenth-century queen of that country. She had a virtuous page, and another page who was jealous of him spread the scandal that he and the queen were lovers. The king sent the virtuous page to the executioner who had orders to behead the first man who presented himself. But the virtuous page had gone into the church by the road to hear Mass and the first to arrive was the wicked page who had slandered him who at once lost his head.

This story, says Cosquin, appeared first in 1562 in a Franciscan chronicle by Brother Mark of Lisbon and spread all over western Europe in numerous books of Exempla. It differs very notably from the Nearer East stories in this, that the lady is innocent. The one constant factor is that the hero escapes death by coming late owing to his attention to his religious duties. This too is the link of the St. Elizabeth legend and the Near East stories with a group of Indian tales adduced by Cosquin, of which the essential point is that the hero escapes the death which threatens him by coming late for the same reason. How far this episode can be held to make a genetic link between stories in other respects so different is a very difficult question. I am inclined to think that the episode might have been invented separately. In countries where life is regulated by nature and the sun rather than by the clock and the time-table such an idea might have occurred in different places quite spontaneously.

NO. 71. THE FORTUNATE DELAY[1]

Red thread spun so well;
  Wind it tightly on the reel.
Kick the reel to make it spin;
  Then the tale may well begin.

Once upon a time there was a man of learning, and he was with the king to write his letters; his wife too was a well-lettered woman. They had a son, and the very evening the son was born the father died. After the father's death the king employed his wife to do the washing: he did not know that she had a son, and she brought him up secretly; until he was eighteen years old she

[1] Printed under the title of Handsome Johnnie in *Arkheíon Thrakikoú Laogr.*, v. 180.

never let him out of the house. Whatever of letters she knew she taught the boy. He was so handsome and so clever that there was no one to match him. He was called Handsome Johnnie.

When this boy was eighteen he begged his mother to let him too go freely about the town. His mother made him some fine clothes and filled his pocket with money and said: 'Go as you will, but be careful. Let no one do you a mischief, and don't you do a mischief to anyone else.' When the boy had gone off, it happened that he passed outside the king's palace. When the princess saw him she went mad with love, and called out to her mother, the queen: 'Quick, mother, come and look.' The mother who would not thwart her, for she loved her daughter fondly, ran quickly to the window and asked: 'What do you want, my daughter?' 'That is what I want, mother,' and she pointed with her finger at Handsome Johnnie. 'I want you to tell my father and we can take the boy and put him to school.' 'And then what will happen, my daughter?' 'But, mother, don't you see what will happen?' 'Very well, my dear, but your father will not consent.' 'But I want him, I want him; I do, I do. You can persuade him, mother, that the boy be taken into our house.'

The poor mother went and told the father, and not to cross his daughter the father sent and called the boy. No one knew that he was the son of the washerwoman. When the man sent to summon him saw his house, he saw that it was the washerwoman's house and he would not go in; he hesitated. He went back and told the king it was the washerwoman's house: 'I didn't like to go in.' The king said: 'In such a house what can the boy be doing?' He sent a policeman with the man and ordered them to force the boy to come. So they went and knocked at the door and the washerwoman came out and asked: 'What do you want?' 'We want a boy you have in the house here.' 'And what do you want the boy for?' 'The king wants him.' 'I will bring him myself; you can go away now.' They went away, and the washerwoman took the boy to the king. 'Good day, my king, and many be your years: what do you want of my son?' The king stroked his beard with surprise; 'Where did you get this boy?' 'He is my own boy, O king of many years.' 'If he is yours, what is his name?' 'Handsome Johnnie.'

'Come here, my girl,' said the king to his daughter. 'Is this the boy you spoke of?' 'Yes, father, it is he.' 'Won't you leave this boy with me?' said the king to the washerwoman, 'and I will send him to school.' 'If you wish, take him; I can say nothing against the king's will.'

The king had him taught letters well. When he had done learning, the boy went back to his mother, and then he and his mother together went to the king for him to kiss the king's hand in thanks. The king gave him a very fine dinner, and then the princess said to her mother: 'I want to have this man as my husband.' 'This cannot be, my child; he has no royal blood; your father will not consent.' The girl fell down fainting. The queen went and said to the king: 'Come and see what has happened.' When the king saw that things were thus, he called for all the doctors to look at the girl. The doctors found she had had a shock. The king asked the queen: 'Do you know what shock this is that our daughter has had? Ask her quietly to tell you.' 'Very well,' said the queen and went off. In the evening she questioned her daughter, and told the king that she was in love with Handsome Johnnie: 'Impossible to part them; the girl has set her heart on him.' Then the king said: 'I will accept him, but she must keep house with the washerwoman; ask her how she likes that.' 'I asked her,' said the queen; 'and she told me she wants him and is quite content even if they must keep house with the washerwoman.' Then the king sent for the washerwoman and said: 'I will make this marriage for my daughter and give her to your son, but you must have them living in your house.' The marriage was made, and Handsome Johnnie took his wife home.

All the money his mother had they spent very quickly, for the princess must have food fit for her rank. So Handsome Johnnie began to go out to work for daily wages, and the poor fellow did whatever work he could find.

Between the city of Constantine and Adrianople there was a factory where soap was made and sent into all parts of the realm. By the road there was a well with water; to set the water flowing for people to drink a man had to be let down into the well, and in this way on every journey a man lost his life.

One day a man was being sought to work at a daily wage: Handsome Johnnie made up his mind to go. He went and asked his mother about it: 'Mother, I have found work by the day, and I must go away from home.' 'If you like, go,' said his mother; 'only this: don't dishonour the bread of your own house; tell the truth; and never neglect church-going. Now make your cross and go your way.'

So all the men went off and they came to the mill. The old workmen knew well that whoever went down for water would be lost, so they wanted to cast lots. Johnnie would not wait for this and said: 'I will go down; keep a look out; tie me with the cord and let me down.' They tied him with the cord and let him down. The well was very dark, and he could not see where he was. When he reached the slabs at the bottom there was a double door standing open. There he saw a stout lad with a black face holding two girls, one on each side of him: one was black and one was white. The fellow asked Handsome Johnnie: 'Which of these ought I to have?' Handsome Johnnie said: 'You should take whichever pleases you.' 'Good,' said the fellow and took out of his pocket three apples and gave them to Handsome Johnnie. 'Put them in your pocket and they will be for your good,' said he and disappeared. The girls were left there and Handsome Johnnie tied them to the rope and pulled at it for his companions to draw them up out of the well.

When the men saw the girl coming up from the well, her beauty drove them mad. The girl said: 'Untie the rope and draw up the other girl.' Then they drew up the other girl. 'Untie the rope,' said she, 'and draw up the man left in the well.' As the rope went down, so the water began to rise, and Handsome Johnnie cried out: 'Be quick, or the water will drown me.' They brought him up from the well and out flowed the water and with it came Handsome Johnnie. After that there was abundance of water.

They took the girls and with their mules they went to the factory, all full of delight. When the owner saw them, forty men and with them two girls, the most graceful in the world, he jumped for joy. 'What has happened, foreman?' he asked. 'Never mind, master; all is well with us. This man has set the water flowing.' When the master saw how handsome the youth was and that he had done them all this benefit, he gave him a present and told him to send it off to his children. In with the present Handsome Johnnie put one of the apples which the ogre down the well had given him, and sent it off to his wife. Now his wife knew that these apples were of great value and she sold the apple for many millions. Then she built a palace bigger than her father's and in each and every village all the way from the city of Constantine to Adrianople she built an inn and a bakehouse, all marked 'Handsome Johnnie'. Also in every village she made a place outside for the cows and sheep.

One day the owner's wife went to the factory. When she saw Handsome Johnnie with his good looks and his fine singing voice, she began to desire him, and she said to her husband, the master: 'Send me this gay fellow to our house tomorrow; I want him for chopping wood to heat the cauldron.' The master said: 'Johnnie, tomorrow you must go and chop up wood for heating the cauldron.' So Handsome Johnnie started off to go to the house. He said to the mistress: 'Where is the axe for me to chop up the wood?' She said: 'Come upstairs first and you can chop the wood later on.' So he went up, and she had ready for him roasted pigeons[1] and good wine, and told him to eat and he could do his work afterwards. The poor lad was hungry and he sat down and ate. When he had done eating the mistress said: 'Come this way; I have something to say to you.' Then she went into the next room and made ready. 'Come, Johnnie, and you can go and chop wood later on.' Johnnie said: 'My mother told me not to do dishonour to the bread I am eating.' 'I will tell the master and it will be the worse for you.' 'Whatever ill may befall me, I will heed my mother's saying.' So there the poor woman was left and the bath had all gone cold.

The woman was all full of spite and determined to ruin Johnnie. Johnnie took the axe and went off to chop the wood. The master came home and his wife was waiting for him and told him that Johnnie had insulted her. 'Never mind, wife; tomorrow we will boil him up for soap.' So said the master, and he went to the factory and said to the foreman: 'Tomorrow morning the first man you open the door to—cut him down with an axe and then into the soap boiler with him.' 'Very good, master.' The master went back again to his house. Johnnie knew nothing at all of this; he was singing and chopping the wood. The master called for him and said: 'Tomorrow morning at three o'clock you must rise and go to the factory to wake up the

[1] From the amorous character of the turtledove its flesh has aphrodisiac virtue.

foreman.' Johnnie rose up at three o'clock; by the time he had washed and put on his clothes it was four o'clock, and then he left the house to go to the factory. But listen; the church bell was going ding-dong. Then Johnnie thought of his mother's word that he must not neglect church-going. 'It is still early,' said he, 'I will go to the church and light a candle.' He went and lit a candle as the Six Psalms were being chanted. 'When the Six Psalms are over then I will go,' said he. Meanwhile the mistress repented of what she had said to her husband; she was sorry for Handsome Johnnie. So she rose up to go to the factory to tell them not to kill the man. The master was asleep and did not notice when she went away. She went flying off to the factory and knocked at the door. The foreman heard the noise; the men got ready the axes and opened the door and hewed at her and threw her into the soapworks without seeing at all who it was. But see, after her came Handsome Johnnie singing on the way. He started his tasks and worked away cheerfully. When the master woke up and found that his wife was not by his side he shouted out: 'Where are you?' But the mistress was neither here nor there; neither in the jakes nor in any nearby house; she was nowhere. The hour came for him to go to the factory. There he saw Handsome Johnnie working away, and saw that there had been a mistake. He called for the foreman: 'Where is the man I told you about? Have you done it?' 'There are the bags of soap, master, all finished; I did what you told me to do.' Then the master went home and looked again for his wife; she was not there, and he saw what had happened. He went to the factory and called for Handsome Johnnie and questioned him. 'You must tell me the truth,' he said. 'Certainly, master, that is what my mother also said to me, that I must tell the truth.' 'Yesterday when you went to the house what did the mistress say to you, and what did you do?' Johnnie told him briefly what had taken place.

The master was highly pleased with Johnnie's honesty and paid him what was owing to him; also he gave him a present of still greater value than his due, saying: 'Come, my lad, now go home to your wife.' With no feelings but joy Johnnie took up his things and started off. 'May many years yet be yours, my master; now I am off.' As he was on the way he saw an inn, marked *Handsome Johnnie*; a bakehouse, *Handsome Johnnie.*

'Whose sheep are those?' he asked. 'They belong to Handsome Johnnie.' 'Whose are those cows?' 'They belong to Handsome Johnnie.' He went mad with vexation, thinking there must be someone else called Handsome Johnnie.

He came to the city of Constantine and went to the place of their house, and there he saw a palace; written on it was *Handsome Johnnie.* He could not recognize his house and went farther on; then he turned back: it was the right place but it wasn't the house. His wife was looking at him from the window; she could not refrain herself and came down and said: 'Come here, come here.' When he knew it was she, they embraced and kissed one another. 'What is this, my wife? Did your father repent and build you a house like this?' 'Oh no, Johnnie; to think of my father repenting! This is the doing of Handsome Johnnie.' 'What Handsome Johnnie? Is there some other Handsome Johnnie?' 'You are the one and only Handsome Johnnie. All this is your doing. It was the apple you sent me: I sold it for ten millions.' 'What are you telling me, my dear wife? And I have two more apples.' 'See, now even my father will be friends with us; have no fear, Johnnie.'

The princess went to her mother and told her everything. She also showed her the two apples and they told the king. He saw the apples, and took the pair to his palace, and set Handsome Johnnie on the throne and made him king. I was there and in the king's service.

72

The three Brothers and the Umpire

THIS story, of which a version from Symi is here translated, has been studied in *Forty-five Stories*, No. 31.[1] The central theme is how of three brothers the one guilty of a theft was discovered by the wisdom of the umpire, being forced to condemn himself out of his own mouth by an ignoble and ungenerous comment on a story told them as a test of their characters. In this version from Symi the youngest brother said that he for his part would never have repelled from his room a girl in the story, and she the wife of the master of the house. This was a very base comment; in acting in this way he would in fact be disobeying the command given by his mother to the youth in *The fortunate Delay*, No. 71 above, never to commit an adultery dishonouring the house of his host: that he was capable of such a wickedness was enough to show the umpire that he only could have been guilty of stealing his brothers inheritance.

In Greece the story is rare. I find only this version from Symi and the version from Kos in *Forty-five Stories*. It is found among the Ossetes of the Caucasus, and there is a Hebrew version which is very likely to be the origin of them all. There is a close parallel in the Novels of Sercambi, where the story is located in the Moslem world. The umpire, 'the wisest of all men in the law of Mahomet', is called the Cali, that is the Caliph, of Mangi, which is taken to be China. All this suggests that it is an eastern story, which has found its way into Greece with a further extension into the Italian of Sercambi.

There is besides these a set of versions which contain the deductions about the lost camel, about the food offered to the brothers by the umpire, and how they are convinced that he is a bastard, but the testing story told them by the umpire is not given; the guilty brother is detected in some other way. This version is found in Greece in Zákynthos; among the Turks of Constantinople and the Turks of South Siberia; in Georgian; in Armenian, and even in Tamil. Also my friend Major C. G. Campbell tells me that he has heard it in Irak, and that it is in a book printed in Cairo for the use of children. I have never found a version containing the umpire's testing story

[1] All the references will be found in *Forty-five Stories*, p. 324, from which it is hardly necessary to reprint them. For the Hebrew version see BP. iv. 328; it is of the eleventh century.

and not the detective deductions, though the latter occur so often without the former, and it would seem that there has been some amalgamation of two originally distinct stories: the story of the ingenious deductions and the story of how the thief is compelled to give himself away by his comments on a story told by the umpire to test the three brothers. They go well together, but neither is necessary to the other.

NO. 72. THE THREE BROTHERS AND THE UMPIRE[1]

In those days things were and things were not, yet there was a king, an old man, with three sons. Two of them were a good deal older; the youngest was still a boy going to school. The king was not very rich: he had nothing but a chest full of gold coins. He called his three sons to him and said: 'My sons, all my substance is what I have in this chest: in a little while I am likely to die. I shall seal up the chest, and you are to keep it safely, and when the youngest of you leaves school and is of age, then you can open it and divide the gold fairly among the three of you, like the good brothers you are.' The sons said: 'May this be to your happiness, Sir.'

Well; the king was an old man and in a little while he died. The elder brothers waited for their youngest brother to come of age like them, and then they would open the chest to divide the treasure in it according to their father's last directions. But the youngest one, a lively lad, even before he had left school started and made an opening in the bottom of the chest and took out all the money and hid it. Then he filled the chest with stones, made it look all right and put it back again in its place. It seemed still sealed up and precisely as it had been before.

What shall I say next? The youngest brother himself too came of age and left school. One day the eldest one said: 'Well, brothers, it is now time for us to open the chest to make the division, much or little, of what our father has left us.' They unsealed the chest and opened it; and what did they see? The chest was full of stones: of gold not a single piece. The youngest brother was cunning and began accusing his elder brothers: 'You have stolen the money. You saw that I was a little boy and have dealt with me as you pleased.' So he cried and bewailed

[1] Text from Symi, in *Z.A.* i. 252.

himself and filled the whole world with his complaints. The elder brothers amazed at this did not know what to say. One said: 'You have taken it yourself, boy.' The other said: 'No; it is you who have stolen it.' So they disputed and to tell the story shortly they resolved to go to the judge to get his decision.

The judge lived out in a village and they went off to find him. On their way first of all the eldest brother met a man who seemed to have lost something. 'Have you lost a camel, my friend?' he asked. The man said: 'Yes; have you seen it? Tell me where it is and then I can go and get it again.' The eldest brother said: 'I have not seen your camel; it is for you to think how to find it again.' After this came the second brother: 'My man, was the camel laden with vinegar?' 'Yes, it was. Now tell me where it is and I will go and get it again.' Then he said: 'I don't know; I have never seen it. It is for you to look about and find it.' The youngest brother came up; he too met the man and said: 'My man; this camel you have lost: was it blind in one eye?' He answered: 'Yes. But tell me and don't torment me; tell me where it is and I can go and get it back again.' Then the youngest brother said: 'I don't know; it is for you to think how to get it back again.' Then the man who had lost the camel said to them: 'It is plain you know where my camel is; or maybe it is you who have stolen it? There is nothing for it but for me to take you before the judge and bring an accusation against you.'

It was about evening when they reached the village and came before the judge. He received them as befitted princes and sent a servant to go and fetch a kid and another to bring grapes. He questioned them and they told him their story. The judge heard them and perceived that it was a difficult matter; he could not make such a decision at once. So he said: 'Tomorrow at dawn I will give a verdict.' Then he questioned them about the owner of the camel: 'But what does the man want?' They said: 'You question him, my lord judge, and let him tell you.' The judge questioned the man and he said: 'I, my lord judge, had a train of camels tied one to another loaded with vinegar. As they were going on the road one of the ropes parted; the camel strayed off and I lost it. The eldest of these men met me and asked: "Have you lost a camel?" I said: "Yes." How did he know that I had lost a camel? I asked him: "Where is my camel?" He said: "I have not seen it." The second brother met me and asked me: "Was the camel loaded with vinegar?" I said: "Yes." Then I told him to tell me where it was. He said: "It is for you to think how to find it; I have not seen it." After them the youngest brother came; he asked me: "Was the camel blind in one eye?" I said: "Yes." I begged him not to tease me but to tell me where my camel was. He said: "I don't know." But, my lord judge, how did they know that I had lost a camel? Also that it was laden with vinegar and that it was blind in one eye? They must surely know where my camel is, and you must order them to give it back to me.' The judge questioned the brothers. The eldest said: 'I, my lord, knew it was a camel from its footprints.' The second brother said: 'The skin bottles must have had holes in them and the vinegar dripped down so that the ground was wet with it, and that is how I know.' The judge asked the youngest: 'But how did you know the camel was blind in one eye?' He said: 'On one side of the path the grass was all eaten and on the other it was not touched; therefore I could see that it was blind in one eye; with the good eye it saw the one side of the path and ate the grass there. The other eye, the blind one, saw nothing, and so on the other side the grass was not eaten.' The judge heard them with amazement and said to the man: 'You go now and think how to get your camel back again; these young men have not got it.' What could the man do? He went off.

Dinner was made ready. A table was set in the room and the princes sat down to eat. The judge sat below listening, hoping to catch some word that would enable him to give his verdict. As he listened the eldest brother said: 'I say, brothers, my idea is we ought not to eat of this kid; it has sucked a bitch and stinks of dog.' The second brother said: 'And I too must tell you, brothers; we must not eat of these grapes because as I think the vine grows from out of the tombs, and they have a nasty taste.' The youngest brother said: 'And I too must tell you, brothers: this judge I think is a bastard.' The judge heard this and said to himself: 'Ha ha!' Then at once he ran off to go and find the man whom he had sent to bring the kid; he questioned him: 'Come, fellow, tell me the truth; where did you get that kid you brought me?' The man said: 'What am I to say, my lord judge? You sent me off and it was already evening; I had no time to go to the sheepfold and back. However we had a kid whose mother had died and the bitch was giving it suck, and this was the kid I brought you.' Off went the judge and ran to find the other man, the one whom he had sent to bring grapes. He questioned him: 'Tell me the truth; where did you get the grapes?' The man said: 'What am I to say, my lord judge? When you sent me it was already night and I had no time to go to the garden and back again. What was I to do? I cut some grapes from the graveyard.' Then the judge was ready to burst from vexation, saying to himself: 'Now I have to look and see how it is that I can be shown a bastard as the youngest of these three said I was.' In a tearing hurry he ran to his mother and pressed her hard saying: 'My poor mother, you are now an old woman and ready for the grave, and I want you to tell me all the truth. Who was my father? Your husband or some stranger?' What was she to do? She said: 'What answer can I make, my son? From your father no children came to me; another man was your father.' The judge heard all this and was amazed. 'Well, here I am, a bastard indeed! The devil is in these fellows.'

All the night he was thinking in what way he could determine on his verdict. At dawn the brothers came again into his presence. As soon as they had drunk their coffee and smoked their pipe, the judge said to them: 'Now I shall tell you a story.'

'In those days there was a daughter of a rich man; then a man of no worth, a common fellow, fell in love with her. She too loved him and vowed to him that she would accept no other man as her husband. To this her father would not consent; he wanted to give her in marriage to some great lord, a man who would be her equal. So he constrained her and married her to a rich man. The wedding was held with dances and music and all the world was there, and among the rest her sweetheart. He came up to the bride and made his complaint to her: "But you promised to accept no one else and to marry me?" Then she said to him: "But what could I do? I did not want to do this; it is my father who is to blame." And what then? She promised that in the night she would go to him: first she would sleep with her lover and then with her husband. He said not a word. Well, the wedding came to an end. In the night when there was no one on foot, the lover heard a knocking at the door. He rose from the place where he was lying and opened the door: he saw the bride. She said: "Did not I tell you? Here I have come to you." He said to her: "I did indeed desire to marry you, but now you belong to another man: go your way." And he shut the door upon her.'

The youngest prince at once said: 'Ah, my lord judge, let me speak. If it had been me, never would I have let her go.' Then said the judge: 'So you must be the man who stole the money. You must bring out the money and then the three of you divide it like good brothers even as your father left you his commands.'

73

Truth or Lies? Which pays best?

AARNE-THOMPSON TYPE 613

THIS moral tale, spread widely over the world and probably of Indian origin, has been discussed by Stith Thompson; abundant references to variants are given by BP.[1] The story is found all over the Greek world from Pontos to Epeiros: the version translated here I recorded in 1914 in the Christian village of Giga in the Of valley east of Trebizond. The lazy liar with a strong sense of his own merits and deserts is well touched off.

On the basis of this tale an ingenious story-teller constructed a novel of contemporary life, of which a version was collected in Kos by Jacob Zarraftis somewhere about 1905. With the title of *The Boatman* it has been printed in *Forty-five Stories* with notes on the process of remodelling the folktale.[2]

The Greek variants seem to be eight:

1, 2. PONTOS, *Arkheíon Pontou*, iii. 105 translated; and from Kromni, in Parkharídis' *Ἱστορία τῆς Κρώμνης*, p. 101.

3. SILLI, near Konia: *Journal of Hellenic Studies*, xxx. 128.

4. KÁRPATHOS: Kretschmer, *Neugr. Märchen*, p. 187, No. 3.

5. SYRA: Pio, p. 227 = Garnett, p. 283.

6. MÝKONOS: Roussel, *Contes de Mycono*, p. 7.

7. CRETE: in the periodical *Myson*, vii. 155.

8. EPEIROS; Hahn, i. 209, No. 30, which is Kretschmer's *Neugr. Märchen*, No. 64 on p. 313.

NO. 73. TRUTH OR LIES? WHICH PAYS BEST?[3]

There were once two widows, each with a son. They sent the boys away to work. One said to her son: 'Never sit doing nothing. Even for a wage of a farthing, set to work.' The other said to her son: 'For less than twenty farthings, don't you work.' Both boys sought for work. The one who was willing to work for a

[1] Stith Thompson, *The Folktale*, p. 30; BP. ii. 473, on Grimm, No. 107. Guterman, p. 202, has a Russian variant.

[2] *Forty-five Stories*, No. 32, p. 327; also *Folklore*, lix. 62.

[3] Text from *Arkheíon Pontou*, iii. 105.

wage of a farthing made no loss. The other found no work to do and be paid his twenty farthings. After a year they turned back home again. On the way they said: 'Let us count our money.' They counted it: one had but little; the other had much. The man who had the little said to the other: 'In this world which has the mastery, lying or telling the truth?' His fellow said, 'Truth.' The other said: 'Lying.' They made an agreement; one said: 'If lying be master, then I will give you the money.' The other one said: 'If truth be the master, then I will yield you the money.' They said: 'Whomever we meet on the way we will ask which has the mastery.'

They went on and met a young priest. He said: 'Lies have the mastery.' The man said: 'Let us ask two people more.' They questioned a priest in middle life: he too said 'Lying'. Last they questioned an old priest; he too said, 'Lying has the mastery.' Then the lad gave his money to the other one, to the idle man, and himself turned back for he had no money to take home. The idle one took the money and brought it to his mother. The other one was overtaken by evening on the way. He came upon a rotten boat and went under it to sleep. That night the devils came there and questioned one another. One said: 'Tomorrow is Sunday. There are two brothers. I will set them to quarrel about their boundaries and so they will miss going to church.' The next one said: 'I have set an enchantment on the king's daughter, and now she is seven years in her bed and cannot move. In the chest there is a stick; if they would take it and give her a dose of it, then she would be cured. But no one knows this.' The man there under the boat heard them. In the morning he went to the two brothers and reconciled them and sent them off to church. He went himself to the town, crying out: 'I am a doctor.' The king heard him and sent his servant to fetch him. He asked: 'Can you cure my daughter?' Said he: 'I can.' He went into the room and opened the chest and brought out the stick and gave the girl a dose; at once she was cured. Then the king loaded two horses with money and gave them to him and sent him home. When his mother saw him she jumped with joy. He took the money to count it. Then said he to his mother: 'Bring me the measure for me to count the money.' His mother had no measure. She said to her daughter-in-law: 'Go to our neighbour and fetch me their measure. When they ask you what you want it for, say that we need it.' The son cried out: 'Don't be telling lies: in this world truth has the mastery. When they ask you, you must say: "The master wants the measure to count his money." ' The house she went to was his companion's and when the man heard all this he went right off his head. He went with the girl to see if she were telling him the truth. He questioned his companion who told him what had befallen him. Then he asked: 'If I should go there and get in underneath the boat, might not I too gain something?' 'God knows', said the other. Then the man went and crept in under the boat. Again the devils came and questioned one another: 'What have you done today?' One said: 'I today set two brothers quarrelling about their boundaries, and they would never have gone to church unless someone had come and talked to them about it so that their quarrel was made up.' The next one said: 'For seven years I have set an enchantment on the king's daughter and today someone has cured her: one of us must have gone and told her.' The next devil said: 'It may be that there is someone here underneath the boat listening and going and telling? Let us look.' They lifted up the boat and saw a man underneath it. 'So it is you who goes and tells?' said they. They threw him into the sea and drowned him.

74

The Woman granted to see the Angel of Death

Of this story, which I do not know of elsewhere, I find in Greece only two versions: one is from Euboia[1] and the other, here translated, was recorded by Madame Pérdika in the adjacent island of Skyros. In it we have a picture of the Greek woman at her best: charitable to the poor, in her house industrious and patient, and with these virtues a firm and resolute spirit and the very Greek quality of inquiry. So charitable was she that her gifts to the poor were accepted by God and by a symbol changed to incense to be offered to Him in a fresh act of worship. Being asked by the angel what reward she would have, she chose an increase of knowledge, an insight into the mystery of death; to know the fate of each soul. With this knowledge we see her at the death-bed, first of the good and then of the wicked man, one of which fills her with joy and the other with horror. Her laughter when the good man died was not, as her neighbours illnaturedly supposed, any laughter of derision, but that laughter which can in innocent souls well up from the depths of sheer happiness; although after the age of childhood not often. Her noble searching into the mystery is well brought out by the contrast with the stupid inquisitiveness of her husband.

NO. 74. THE WOMAN GRANTED TO SEE THE ANGEL OF DEATH[2]

Once there was a girl of noble nature; constant in works of charity. She was married and had a mother-in-law always vexing her and complaining of her to her husband, saying that she was a bad housewife and one who was wasteful with the flour. But the bride did not trouble herself, whatever they might say about her; when she did her cooking, she first set a portion aside to give to the poor and the rest she would serve for her family to eat.

The mother-in-law went on complaining to her son that his wife would bring the house to ruin; that she was wasteful. This

[1] Hahn, i. 314, No. 60. [2] Text from Skyros in Pérdika, ii. 223.

she kept on saying; also she kept a watch over the young wife to prevent her taking anything out of the house. The wife was annoyed, but she did what she could and would take a little food and put it aside in the outhouse where her mother-in-law never went in order presently to give it to the poor.

Some days had passed, and she said: 'I must go and see that the food I have put there is not stale.' She went, and what did she see? The food had all of it been changed into a great quantity of fragrant incense. This incense she put into a bag, laid it on her shoulder, and went far away to a cleft between two mountains. She lit a fire of twigs and threw the incense on it, to burn it without anyone seeing her. As soon as the incense was alight the whole place was fragrant, and the smoke and the sweet reek went up to heaven.

Then she saw the heavens opening; three angels came down and stood before her and said: 'God told us to say: "What would you have us do in return for your good deed?" Whatever you wish we are to give you. Do you want long life? Do you want riches?' 'No,' said she, but trembling with fear so that the very dust fell from her feet. 'What do you want?' the angels again said. 'Tell us, and do not be afraid.' Then she said: 'When a man is to die, I should like to see in what manner the angel carries away his soul.' The angels said: 'Do not ask for this; it will not be for your good. Also, if you let anyone else know, you will die.' The woman would not listen, but said: 'This is what I want, even if I am to die for it.' Then the angel said: 'Since this is what you want, so let it be.'

A little while afterwards to a man in the neighbourhood—a good man but very poor—there came the hour when he should die. All went to visit him and to weep, for they were sorry at his death. The woman too went there, and as soon as she came into the house she looked and saw the angel: he was standing by the sick man's head, caressing him and smiling, and all round him were young angels with pipes and viols, singing to lull him to sleep and to soothe his pain. When the woman saw all the people weeping, while she could see with what bliss he was giving over his soul into the hands of the angel, she began to laugh happily, and in this mood she went to her house, all the way laughing for joy. Her mother-in-law saw her laughing, and when the husband came she began complaining and telling him what a wicked woman his wife was: when all the others were full of sorrow for the poor man she was crazy with laughter to see him dying.

Again, after a few days an old man took to his bed to die; a rich man; and he had tormented many with his wickedness. All who heard that he was breathing his last, hugged themselves, mocking and cursing his dirty soul, wishing him pain until his soul left him, so cruel had he been to the poor. The woman went into the house. All round the bed where the rich man was lying she saw demons big and little with daggers and knives tearing at his soul to carry it away, and the man himself holding on to it with his teeth, trying not to let it depart from his body, because he saw what was awaiting him; he lay there in agony, with his eyes starting from his head. Her soul was filled with compassion, and she went off home crying all along the way.

When her mother-in-law saw her, she asked why she was crying, and when her son came, she began to abuse her daughter-in-law roundly: a hellish creature; one to point at in scorn; a monster; she used to sleep with the man and now there she was weeping and crying for him. Her son could stand this no longer, and he went and asked his wife why she laughed when the poor man died and now at the rich man's death she was weeping. 'I want you to tell me this; why do you do thus?' So said he again and again. His wife wept and said: 'Do not torment me; if I tell you the secret you will lose me.' He persisted: 'I want you to tell me, even if I do lose you.' Then the woman said: 'First you must order a bier to be made and brought here for me.' Her measure was taken and the bier was made; when the men had brought it and set it down before the door, the woman went and lay down on it. Then she called for her husband and told him of the gift which God had given her. That same hour she saw the angel descending with singing and the music of viols to take her soul. Her eyes closed and with a smile she committed her soul to the angel, as he stood before her ready to receive it.

75

The three Words of Advice

AARNE–THOMPSON TYPES 910–14

THIS story of the 'Three Words of Advice', either so dearly bought and so well worth the money, or as a legacy from a dying father to his son, has been studied by Halliday and again in *Forty-five Stories.*[1] Halliday thinks it of eastern origin and diffused all over Europe by the influence of the *Gesta Romanorum*. How early and how wide was this diffusion is witnessed by its appearance in the Irish *Wandering of Ulysses* as written down in the year A.D. 1300.[2] Seeking advice on his wanderings Ulysses came to the 'Judge of Right', who for three payments sold him the Three Words: the first was not to slay a man rashly; the second to avoid bypaths; and the third—this I do not find elsewhere—was not to start earlier than when the sun was in the position in which it was at that moment. As the third word of advice is typically *Don't act in a hurry; restrain your anger*, this third counsel seems likely to mean *Don't be too quick to get into action.*

The first word of advice in the Pontic version here translated: *Never mix yourself up in other people's affairs; you have seen nothing, you know nothing*, brings to my mind a story I have heard in Crete told of the Sultan Abdul Hamid. He was seeking for a man to be a confidential servant. The candidates were ranged before him on the deck of a ship. The Sultan ordered a sailor to be thrown overboard and drowned. He then said to the first candidate: 'What did you see?' 'Your Majesty drowned a man.' And so too for the second candidate. When the third candidate saw a third sailor drowned and was asked what he had seen, he answered: 'Your Majesty, I saw nothing.' The third man was chosen for the imperial service.

The story has also been dealt with by Cosquin in his essay on the legend of the page of St. Elizabeth of Portugal: he speaks very definitely of 'ce thème très indien des Bons Conseils'.[3] This view I accept, though I do not see that Cosquin has shown any real connexion between the words of advice which are the core of the present story and the quite differently given other pieces of advice in the quite

[1] *M.G. in A.M.*, p. 238; in *Forty-five Stories*, No. 19. To the references there add Wardrop's *Georgian Folk Tales*, p. 109, a Mingrelian story, and BP. iv. 149.

[2] *Merugud Uilix Maicc Leirtis*, translated by Kuno Meyer, p. 22.

[3] Cosquin, *Études folkloriques*, p. 121.

separate story of the page of St. Elizabeth: this latter is studied in this book under No. 71, *The fortunate Delay*. In the widest sense too the story of the Three Words is treated by Stith Thompson in his *Motif-Index* under the heading *Wisdom, Knowledge, acquired by Experience*. Wesselski remarks that even a superficial account of these stories, all based on the Three, or Two, Words of Advice, would fill a big volume.[1] In these circumstances I need do no more than point out that in Greece the story appears in two quite distinct forms.

Of these two by far the commoner is that a servant at the close of his period of service accepted in lieu of wages three words of advice from his master. These are as a rule: *Keep to the main road, the straight path; Mind your own business; Think before you act in anger*. In the *Gesta Romanorum* we find a similar story told of the emperor Domitian; he bought from a merchant three words of advice: *In all your actions be prudent, having regard to the end; Never leave the highway to walk on a side path; Never lodge in the house where the master is an old man and the wife a young woman*.[2] By observing these three precepts the emperor saved his life three times from the attacks of his enemies.

The Greek variants of this form of the story are as follows:

1, 2. PONTIC: *Pontiaká Phylla*, ii, No. 23, p. 460; here translated; also from the Of valley in *Arkheíon Pontou*, iii. 111.

3. SILLI, near KONIA: *M.G. in A.M.*, p. 293.

4. DEMIRDESH, near BRUSA: Danguitsis, *Étude descriptive du dialect de Démirdési*, p. 202.

5, 6. CHIOS: Argenti and Rose, *Folklore of Chios*, p. 574, and an unpublished version by Kanellakis.

7. KOS: *Forty-five Stories*, p. 237.

8. SYRA: Pio, p. 222 = Garnett, p. 374.

9. CRETE: *Epetirís et. kritikón spoudón*, iv. 202.

10. ZÁKYNTHOS: *Laographía*, x. 431.

11. TERRA D'OTRANTO: Vito Palumbo in 1884 number of *Le Muséon*, Louvain.

The other form of the story is in Greece found only in three versions:

1. SAMOS: *Samiaká*, v. 570, translated below.

2. NÍSYROS: *Z.A.* i. 419.

3. VELVENDÓS in MACEDONIA: in Boudonas, *Μελέτη*, p. 118.

[1] Wesselski, *Märchen des Mittelalters*, p. 219.

[2] Oesterley's edition, p. 431, chap. 103 (95). The third piece of advice, not to lodge where the husband is old and the wife is young, recalls the mother's advice to the hero in No. 71, *The fortunate Delay*, above: 'Don't dishonour the bread of your house'. The same piece of advice is in the eleventh-century Latin narrative poem *Ruodlieb*, as analysed by F. J. E. Raby, *Secular Latin Poetry*, i. 395. The counsels here are: *Don't trust a man with red hair; Don't avoid a muddy village street by riding*

Apart from the fact that there are three words of advice the story here and the actual words are quite different. A father on his death-bed gives his son three words of advice. The Nísyros version runs: *Never make a Turk your friend; Never tell your wife a secret; Do not rear up a bastard, or a child cast out by his parents.* The Samos version here translated is much the same; we may remember that a soldier of the Sultan would naturally be a Turk. The Velvendós variant is: *Don't sow beans with a man bigger than yourself; Don't tell a secret to your wife; Don't take an adopted son.* The 'man bigger than yourself' is like the Turk or in the Samos version the colonel, and the meaning is: *Don't be too fond of and rely upon people in high places.* The man then tests these three pieces of advice by pretending to have committed a murder, the corpse being really that of an animal. His wife reveals the supposed murder; the Turkish officer refuses to protect him from the rigour of the law; the only person who will volunteer to act as executioner is the boy whom he has befriended.

Whatever may be the general distribution of this type of the story, it is interesting to find it also in the *Gesta Romanorum*; at its best in the English translation edited by Herrtage.[1] It is called *Of the young Knight who had three Friends.* Domitian a wise emperor ruled in the city of Rome. His son went out on his travels and came and told his father that he had made three friends: one he loved more than himself; the second as himself; the third but little in comparison with the others. His father told him to test these three friends. 'Kill a pig and put it into a sack; go to your friends and say that you have killed a man and see what they will say, when you ask them to hide the body for you.' The first friend refused his help but said he would give the man two ells of cloth for his shroud when he was hanged. The second also refused but said that for his love to him he would bear him company to the gibbet; then go and find himself another friend. The third also refused to hide the body but would take his place on the gallows. The *moralitas* is that the emperor is the Father of Heaven; the son is every Christian man; the first friend is the world and its goods; the second is his wife and children; the third friend is Christ.

In a less effective form this same story appears in the Latin *Gesta*.[2] A man had three friends: a rich friend he served always; a second friend he served sometimes; a third friend he served seldom or never. To test them he did actually commit a murder. The first friend told him he deserved to be hanged, and on being pressed said he would give him a kerchief to bind his eyes. The second friend said he would

across the cornfields; Don't lodge with an old man with a young wife. In BP. iv. 353, the *Ruodlieb* Three Words are given differently.

[1] Early English Text Society's *Early English Versions of the Gesta Romanorum*, 1879, p. 127.

[2] Oesterley's edition, p. 637, chap. 238, app. 42.

accompany him to the gallows; the third, who was a poor man, saved him from death: we are not told that he died for him. The rich friend is the world; the second figures his kinsfolk; the third is God who redeemed us.

In considering the stories in the *Gesta* we may, I think, confine ourselves to the chapter in the English version, *Of the young Knight who had three Friends*, so obviously superior to the shorter chapter in the Latin. The kinship to the story of the 'Three Words' as it appears in Samos and Nísyros and at Velvendós is at once plain: we find the same sham murder and the same three friends. The Turkish colonel, all powerful in this world, corresponds to the first friend of the *Gesta*, explained as the world and its goods: in the Velvendós version it is simply 'a man bigger than yourself'; the second is, as in the Greek stories, the man's wife; the third is, however, in these rationalized versions no longer the Son of Man but the youth who as an adopted son had a special duty of love and respect. The three allegorical figures of the *Gesta* are thus rearranged to fit the three human relations of a man: with the world; with his wife; and with his son: so far are we carried by the Greek feeling for human rather than for theological interest. Then comes the influence of the usual type of the story of the *Three Words of Advice*, and three fresh words are invented to fit this new story: as far as the world is concerned don't take a Turk for a friend; as far as your house is concerned don't tell your wife too much; as far as your family is concerned avoid adopted sons, whose ingratitude is proverbial; for example, in No. 26 of *Forty-five Stories*, 'The High King', we meet with the boy brought up out of charity, who alone was ready to act as the executioner of his father. Even adopting a cast-out baby is dangerous, as we see from a story from Vourla near Smyrna with a variant in Legrand:[1] with the title *Neither Good nor Ill*: to be too righteous and too kindly may be dangerous. In this story the adopted baby is a girl who, married to her benefactor, sets the whole family at odds.

The version of the story of the Clerk Theophilos, No. 59 in this book, is another example of the Greek capacity for transferring a theological story into this world of men and human doings.

NO. 75*a*. THE THREE WORDS OF ADVICE[2]

There was a tinsmith who was out of work. He saw that his family would go hungry, and so one day he said to his wife: 'Wife, I can find no work here and we shall die of hunger. I

[1] Legrand, p. 227; *Mikrasiatiká Khroniká*, iv. 270. See also *Folklore*, lix. 53.
[2] Text from Pontos, in *Pontiaká Phylla*, ii. No. 23, p. 460.

must go abroad; it may be that there my luck will clear and we too shall behold turned towards us the face of God. As I wish to see you again, look well after our child. Now knead up a little maize flour and make me a few biscuits and let me go off with God's blessing.' This his wife did and let her husband depart.

The man went off on his way and after ten days he came upon a great city. He looked here and he looked there; anyhow he found work on a farm. After fifteen years he said to his master: 'I want to go back home again.' His master took out two hundred gold pieces and gave them to him and sent him off on his way. The man was on the road when his master once more called after him: 'Come,' said he, 'I want to say something to you. Give me ten pieces and I will give you a word of advice.' The man took the ten pieces out of his pocket and handed them over: 'Now tell me your word of advice.' His master said: 'Never mix yourself up in other people's affairs: you have seen nothing; you know nothing.' 'All good be with you, master,' said the man and set out on the road.

'Hi, where are you? Stop, I want to tell you something else,' his master shouted after him. 'Give me ten more gold pieces and I will give you another word of advice.' Again the man gave him the ten pieces and waited for the advice. 'Never leave the king's highway.' 'All good be with you, master,' said he and set out on the road.

'Hi, where are you? Stop, I want to tell you something else,' his master shouted after him. 'Give me another ten gold pieces and I will give you the last word of advice.' The man grumbled: 'This man with his words of advice will be taking back all the money he gave me. For all that I must hear the last advice.' Saying this he gave his master the ten pieces. 'First think and afterwards act.' 'All good be with you, master,' said he and very quickly indeed was off on the road.

As he was on the road he met a young man and they went on together. They spent the evening at an inn. The innkeeper had no place to lodge them and he put them into the stable. To a manger there were tied three Persian horses munching their barley. The men lay down on the straw and went to sleep. At midnight they heard a little noise: both of them woke up and listened. They saw three men coming to make the horses ready; they were going to mount and ride away. With ten ears apiece the two companions listened to their talk. 'There are three hours left before dawn,' said one of them. 'Let us get on the road quickly to be in time to cut in in front of them. At the big turn in the road we shall be in time to catch the guards with their load of treasure.' The men at once mounted and set out on the road.

The young man rose and said to the tinsmith: 'Let us go and tell the innkeeper.' 'Go to sleep,' said the tinsmith: 'Don't mix yourself up in other people's business. You have neither seen nor heard; this is no affair of ours.' The youth would not listen to him and went and told the innkeeper. The innkeeper was a man in with the gang, and he was afraid that the youth might go and tell someone else. At once he seized the youth and hanged him on a poplar-tree. In the morning the tinsmith woke up and saw his companion hanged; he pretended to have seen nothing and went off. On the road he bethought him: 'A piece of good luck those ten gold pieces I paid my master.'

He went on and on, and on the road he met two camel-drivers with ten camels loaded with Persian shawls and silk cloth. He joined company with them and they went on together. When they had gone some way they were hungry. What were they to do? The camel-drivers said to him: 'Here we must leave the king's highway; here behind the hill there is a big inn; there we shall find something and have a meal and come back again.' 'For my part,' said the tinsmith, 'I will never leave the king's highway. If you like you may go and I will wait for you.' The camel-drivers left their camels and went to the inn behind the hill. Before long the tinsmith heard a noise as of thunder; the ground shook. What had happened? The people of the inn had a store of powder and cartridges. A fire had been lit, and somehow it happened that sparks flew out and the place caught fire and everything there was burned up with the inn. So the camels were left with the tinsmith. Was there anything he could do? It was the will of God. So he took the camels and went off.

Ten days later he came to his house; the night was dark as pitch. He came close to the door and peering through a crack he saw: Oh, what did he see? His wife and a fine young man were sitting there by the side of the fire. He suspected something. In a rage he took up his gun to shoot and kill the youth. At that moment he remembered the third word of advice; he lowered his gun and bethought him who the lad might be. As he was thinking, he heard the youth saying: 'Mother, in the morning I shall go to the field: you set the food by the fireside and go and fetch a load of wood.' 'Very well,' said she, 'I will go to fetch wood, my dear, but as for food, what am I to do? we have nothing here to cook. Your father, my darling, went off abroad; he is lost and has forgotten all about us.' 'What shall we do, Mother, do you ask? God is good and He will not forget us.' At that moment his father opened the door and with tears rushed into the house and embraced them and kissed them, and from that time they lived happily.

NO. 75*b*. THE THREE WORDS OF ADVICE[1]

There was once an old man, and when he was about to die he called for his son, the only son he had, and said to him: 'My son, I am dying and you will live yet many years. But if you wish for a happy life, keep yourself from three things. Tell no secret to your wife; Do not make a friend of a soldier of the Sultan; Never rear up a castaway bastard.'

When the old man was dead his son felt inquisitive and wanted to test these three words of advice. He made a Turkish colonel his bosom friend; he married a girl who had loved him for many years, and he found a bastard child who had been cast out and took him to his house. Two or three years passed; his wife loved him as at first; he continued his friendship with the colonel; the bastard was as loving as possible. Very often the colonel would say to him: 'If ever you get into any trouble, even if you are in danger of death, I will get you off.' Our fine fellow thought that his father's injunctions had no reason to them. However, he determined to put them to the test.

Fifteen years after his father's death he met a shepherd and asked him to let him have a fat lamb. 'Very well', said the shepherd, 'But you must pay me fifty piastres.' 'Fifty, brother, fifty?' He bought the lamb agreeing that the shepherd should keep the head and the hide and that he should pay fifty piastres. And what do you think he did then? He took the flayed carcase and put it into a bag and went home all pale and in a tremble. 'How comes it that you look so changed?' his wife asked. 'Oh, my poor

[1] Text from Samos in Stamatiadis, *Samiaká*, v. 570.

wife, haven't you heard? Just now as I was coming home I met a drunken man and he came and attacked me. I caught him one on the head with a stick and felled him to the ground. When I saw that he had had it, I got a bag from the cellar and put him into it and left him down there. Come; let us go and bury him.' 'Very well,' said his wife, and they went down to the cellar. The poor woman saw the bag all covered with blood, but there was nothing she could say. They dug a hole with the pick and put the bag into it just as it was and covered it up. 'I say, my poor wife, don't you say anything about it; if you do I too shall lose my life and you be left a widow.' 'Well, husband,' said the wife, 'and do you think me so silly as to go and betray you? If they cut me all to little pieces, even then never would I do such a thing.' 'To our happy meeting!' said the man. 'Now I am off to the café and shall be drunk there until the morning so that no suspicion may rest upon me. You stop here alone in the house, and if anyone comes thundering to be let in, don't you open the door.' 'A pleasant time and don't worry.' In the morning an hour or two after dawn our good friend came home. 'Good day, wife.' 'Good day to you,' she answered. 'What news?' 'All well.' 'Did anyone come last night?' 'No, I saw no one.' 'Have you cooked a meal?' 'And how should I have cooked anything? It is not time yet.' 'Not time? I am hungry. Last evening I ate nothing. Do you remember or don't you? There, that's to teach you another time to do your cooking early.' And he caught her two or three smacks on the face. 'Come, neighbours, quick, quick,' cried the woman. 'This murderer! Last night he killed a man and now he wants to kill me as well.' The neighbours ran up and asked what was the matter. Our good woman stood there and told them her story from the beginning: How her husband the evening before had killed a man and they had buried him down in the cellar; how he had come home early in the morning and because she had no food cooked he was trying to kill her. When the man's enemies heard all this they went straight off to the Cadi and told him that So and so the evening before had killed a man and had buried him down in his cellar. 'Quick,' said the Cadi to the colonel, the man who was the friend of the murderer: 'Go and fetch him here for us to hang the rascal.' The colonel ran at once to the man's house—he knew it because every day they used to eat and drink together—and he found him there. 'Come with me, and quickly, the Cadi wants you.' The man said to his friend: 'Gently, gently, brother; I must eat a little bread and I am with you.' 'The Cadi has given me orders to bring you now at once,' said the colonel, 'and we must go now.' The other man, poor fellow, thought that the colonel was joking with him. 'My dear friend,' he said, 'wasn't it you who told me that even if I were condemned to death you would get me off? Have you forgotten all that you promised me, and only yesterday? Where is the friendship we had together?' 'I know nothing of that. The Cadi told me you have committed a great crime and I am bound to take you off to him; if not I shall be in trouble myself.' 'Well, brother, since you have forgotten how one day we ate bread and salt together; come then, let us be off.' So they went to the Cadi, and the Cadi ordered him at once to be taken off to the deepest dungeon. Then he set a court and they examined the murderer's wife and she bore witness that down under the cellar the two of them together had buried the dead man in a sack. Finally without going to the house to dig up the dead man to see who it was, they gave sentence to hang the murderer. At that time the executioner who used to hang condemned men was dead, and the Cadi looked for someone else, but he could find no one. He offered as much as five hundred piastres as a present to the man who would haul the rope to hang the murderer. At last the bastard whom the man had brought up went to the Cadi and said: 'My lord the Cadi, I will haul the rope to hang my father. Why should anyone else have the five hundred piastres? Why should I let them slip by me and lose the profit?'

Then the poor man who was condemned remembered his father's words and his commands. This made him burst out laughing loudly so that everyone said he had gone mad. 'I say, they are taking him off to be hanged and he is laughing. What sort of man can he be? For sure he is mad.' So said all those who were standing by looking on. 'I am not mad,' said the condemned man, 'and now I will show you. Fetch the Cadi here.' They ran off and told the Cadi that the condemned man wanted him. The Cadi came and the man said to him: 'My lord Cadi, why are you going to hang me?' 'Because you are a murderer,' said the Cadi. 'Whom have I murdered?' Then the Cadi saw that he had acted rashly and that before giving his verdict he ought to have gone and seen who the dead man was. 'Come,' said the man to the Cadi, and to the rest of them; 'let us go to my cellar and I will show you who the dead man is.' Then they took the noose off his neck and brought him to his house. They opened the cellar and found the sack. They untied it and saw inside it a very fine fat lamb, flayed. 'What is this?' said the Cadi. 'This lamb, my lord? This is the man whom I killed.'

Then he sat down and told them the story: the commands which his father had given him when he was dying, and how in order to put them to the test he had bought the lamb from such and such a shepherd and in this way had tested the three commands his father had given him, and all three of them were sound. Then the Cadi released the man and he went to his house and drove out his wife and the bastard. He took another wife and never told her any secrets, and when he met on the road either a bastard or soldiers of the Sultan he fled from them as if they had been the plague.

76

The two Women and the twelve Months

THIS story Halliday has very fitly called *Virtue rewarded*, because the essence of it is that two women, one good and one bad, go out from home successively and meet a company of twelve men: the first woman treats them with respect and kindliness and is rewarded; the second with rudeness and ingratitude, and is correspondingly punished.[1] The typical form of this story in Greece is that the women meet the Twelve Months, the good woman being always contented with what each month brings her. The best version I find is the one from Imera in Pontos, and I have chosen it for translation. It was dictated to me in the summer of 1914 by a young man in the Monastery of the Forerunner outside the village, and for my benefit the teller was very precise and full on the names of the months and the seasons. The Months occur also in the versions from Melos, Thrace, and Zákynthos; at Stavrín in Pontos they appear as twelve young men sitting warming themselves by a fire in a cave: the 'interlunar cave' of Milton and Shelley. In the version from Athens the women meet a company of cats; at Soúrmena in Pontos a band of angels; in the Ulaghátsh version they meet the Archangel Gabriel; at Axó in Cappadocia the Twelve Apostles. In the Cretan version the women cleanse the head of Christ; the first one graciously, the second one grudgingly. The Araván version has this same incident.

In the *Pentamerone*, v, No. 2, we hear of two brothers going out and finding the Twelve Months sitting round a fire, but most of the references in BP. are from the Slav world; here the place of the months is often taken by elves, fairies, water sprites, the four winds or the four seasons; sometimes by saints of the Christian calendar.

The Greek versions are:

1, 2, 3. PONTOS: from Soúrmena, *Arkheíon Pontou*, iii. 97; from Imera, *Laographía*, vii. 285 with the translation reprinted below; from Stavrín, *Arkheíon Pontou*, xii. 171.

4, 5, 6. CAPPADOCIA: from Ulaghátsh in *M.G. in A.M.*, p. 347; from Axó, ibid., p. 399; from Araván, ibid., p. 335.

7. THRACE: *Thrakiká*, xvii. 168.

8. MELOS: *N.A.* i. 12, which is Garnett, p. 348.

[1] *M.G. in A.M.*, p. 254; BP. i. 102 ff.

9. ATHENS: Kamboúroglou, p. 82; also in Garnett, p. 351.
10. CRETE: *Z.A.* ii, 1896, p. 58.
11. ZÁKYNTHOS: *Laographía*, xi. 477.

NO. 76. THE TWO WOMEN AND THE TWELVE MONTHS[1]

There were two sisters-in-law; one was rich but wicked, and the other was poor but good. The poor woman in the evening used to go to the rich woman's house and spin her wool. After one or two days the rich woman drove her away, and the wretched poor woman, because she had no oil, used to go and sit outside the rich woman's house, and opposite the light of the window used to spin her wool. The rich woman found this out, and to drive her away she put curtains in the windows. The next day the poor woman, because she could do nothing else, sat pondering upon her threshold. All at once she saw on the mountain opposite a light. 'Let me go,' she said, 'and sit with them and spin my wool.' She went there, and when she looked, she saw twelve men sitting round the fire. 'Come, mother,' they said to her, 'sit down with us.' And she too sat there and was spinning. And then one of them asked her, 'Aunt, what do you think of the months?' And she said, 'March, April and the Fair Month of May bring the spring, the flowers bloom, and I think them very beautiful. The Month of Cherries, the Month of Hay Harvest and August bring the harvest, and we reap it, and these also I think very beautiful. The Month of the Cross, the Month of Vintage and the Month of St. George bring the apples and pears, and these too I love well. The Month of the Birth of Christ, the Month of the New Year and the Clipped Month of February bring stoves and we warm ourselves; for this I love them also very much.' The twelve men were pleased, and finally, when the woman would go away, said to her, 'Aunt, spread out your apron, and let us fill it with coals.' 'But I shall be burned,' said the old woman. 'Do not be afraid,' the twelve men said to her. They filled her apron with coals and sent her away. She, when she came to her house, opened it and looked to see what had become of the coals. And when she looked, she saw her apron full of gold pieces. She brought them in, and next day she bought all manner of fine things.

[1] Translation reprinted from *Laographía*, vii. 285.

Her sister-in-law found this out, and asked her, how she got so many gold pieces. And she said to her that thus and thus it happened. The next evening the rich woman also went, and did as her sister-in-law. When he asked her what she thought of the months, she said, 'The Season of Opening, the spring, comes with much evil, because there are its gloomy days. The Season of Harvest, the summer, comes with evil, because it brings the heat, and I cannot walk a step. The Season of Fruit, the autumn, brings the apples, but, because I have no orchard, sad and short be his years! The Season of Storms, the winter, brings the cold and the snow, and a curse upon him when he comes out of his door!' When she also would go away, they filled her apron also with coals. She looked for them to become gold pieces, but when she came to her house and poured them out on the ground, there came out from the midst scorpions and snakes and twined round her neck and strangled her.

This is the fate of the wicked, who do not desire the good of others.

77

The Princess who loved her Father like Salt

AARNE–THOMPSON TYPE 923

IT is curious that of a story which sounds so familiar and obvious as this one I can find only this one Greek version. Stith Thompson, *Motif-Index*, H 592, and BP. ii. 47 and iii. 303 give references, and the theme has been discussed by Cosquin, *Contes indiens*, p. 103. The Thracian story is simple enough; the only point calling for remark is that the episode of the man coming near to killing his wife when he finds her kissing their son whom he now sees for the first time, has been borrowed from No. 75, *The three Words of Advice*, where the last word is often, *First think and afterwards act*; that a man should restrain his hasty anger.

NO. 77. THE PRINCESS WHO LOVED HER FATHER LIKE SALT[1]

Red thread twisted on the wheel,
Neatly wind it on the reel;
Kick the reel to make it spin,
Then the tale can well begin.

At the beginning of the story: a good evening to you. Once upon a time there was a king with three daughters; he sent for them all and asked them how much they loved him. The eldest said that she loved him like honey; the second like sugar; and the third like salt. The king was angry with the youngest princess, she who had told him that she loved him like salt. Then still angry he went and stood at the gate of the palace: he saw an old man passing by and declared that he would make him his son-in-law. 'My king and many be your years! shall I who am a poor man, marry the princess?' 'That is my wish,' and the king gave him his youngest daughter to be his wife.

The poor man accepted the princess; he took her to his mother and they lived all of them good friends but in great poverty;

[1] Thracian text from *Thrakiká*, xvi. 189.

scarcely could the man earn their daily needs. Some rich merchants were about to go on a distant journey and they wanted to take him with them. So he said Good-bye to his wife and his mother and went off. As they were on the way they came to a well; the poor man was sent to fetch water. Scarcely had he begun drawing the water when the spirit of the well showed himself. The poor man said: 'Good day, friend.' 'Because of the kind word you have spoken I shall not devour you as it has been my wont to devour all those who came to draw water. I shall give you three pomegranates; do not cut them when you are with your companions.' The poor man thanked him; he hid the pomegranates in his bosom and went off. One pomegranate he sent home to his house. His mother said: 'My daughter, why not cut the pomegranate and freshen our lips with it?' They cut the pomegranate, and what did they see? From it fell nothing but diamonds. The poor women were amazed. A little while after her husband had gone away the princess bore a son; he grew big and in him they took very great delight. They sold the diamonds and built a house like a palace. Also they made a fountain at which passers by could quench their thirst.

Many years passed and the poor man came back to his village; where his hut had stood he saw a house like a palace: this puzzled him. Also he saw his wife sitting at the window with a handsome youth. This filled him with anger and his intent was to kill both his wife and the youth. His wife full of joy came out and greeted him: 'A long time you have been away from us.' Then to the youth she said: 'Come and kiss your father's hand.' Then the man understood; he kissed his wife; he also kissed his son. Then he asked how she had come to build such a house. She thought it strange that he should ask her this, but she said: 'It was from your own diamonds, those you sent us in the pomegranate.' In his bosom the man had the next pomegranate; he brought it out and opened it and from it there poured out diamonds to dazzle the eyes of anyone who saw them. They built another still finer palace with large gardens. Also they did much charity to the poor and set up a sweetshop where everyone who liked could come and eat sweets and not pay a halfpenny. Their acts of charity and the sweetshop came to the ears of the king and he said to his vizier: 'Who is this man who is doing so much kindness to the poor and whoever likes can go and eat sweets and nothing to pay? Let us go and see.'

The princess recognized her father the king, and to her husband she said: 'This evening we shall make friends with these people.' She ordered the cook to prepare dishes, half of them to be without salt and half of them to be salted. First the dishes without salt were served at the table: neither the king could eat them nor yet the vizier. Then they were removed and the other dishes with salt were served; these they then ate with a good appetite. The king was asked how he liked the food; he said: 'The first had no salt and was uneatable; food without salt is no good.' 'Oh,' said his daughter, 'and when I told you, father, that I loved you like salt, you drove me away. Yet now God has given me what my heart desired.' The king admitted that his daughter was in the right; he kissed her and said: 'You were in the right; salt is better than honey and better than sugar.' And so they lived with good hap and we yet more happily.

78

The Man who went to find Fear

AARNE–THOMPSON TYPE 326

ONE of the best known of the Grimm stories is No. 4, *The Man who went out to find what Fear was.*[1] Spread over the whole of the Old World this story is rare in Greece, and I find it only at Samsoún in Pontos, in Chios and in Samos. In a very Italianate form it has been recorded from the Saracatsans, nomad Greek shepherds who range over the mountains of Epeiros. Of the story as it occurs in Greece I have made a study in a volume printed at Athens as an offering to M. Merlier.

The story as found in Europe is of a young man so fearless that he must go out into the world to find out what everybody but himself knows: what fear is. After a series of macabre tricks played on him which quite fail to terrify him, he is at last by some rather grotesque device made to understand at least the physical aspect of fear: water is poured over him as he is sleeping, or a fish or a hedgehog is put in his bed. In Greece, however, the story takes a much more subtle turn. It is combined in various proportions with a story which we find at its best in Georgia of a hero who victoriously survived his struggles with three successive mysterious women.[2] The combination of these two stories, this and the European fear story, gives a tale in which we have a hero who does not know fear. First he shows that he has no fear of men; then by the three contests with women, one of them being a Gorgon of the sea, that the feminine has no terrors for him. Then at the end he does show fear, but it is at nothing human: he feels fear at seeing the unexplained passage of a shadow over the sea; the shadow of a flight of birds.

The best of the Greek versions is the one printed by Argenti and Rose; the Samos version and that from Pontos are so far inferior that it seems useless to do more than give this outline of the story and refer to *The Folklore of Chios.*

The references are:

1. PONTOS: *Arkheíon Pontou*, vii. 113.
2. CHIOS: Argenti and Rose, *Folklore of Chios*, p. 548.
3. SAMOS: Stamatiádis, *Samiaká*, v. 561.
4. SARACATSANS: Höeg, *Les Saracatsans*, ii. 41, No. viii.

[1] BP. i. 22; Grimm No. 4.

[2] Wardrop, *Georgian Folk Tales*, p. 52.

79

The Search for Luck

AARNE–THOMPSON TYPE 460B

THE translations here given of stories from Mitylene, and Pontos, are chosen from ten Greek stories about the man who goes out to find his Luck or his Fate: in his troubles he wants to see face to face this mysterious power. In these stories we see the various, often incompatible, ideas by which men try to explain why it is that one man is happy and successful, another poor and miserable. We are shown Destiny; we see in her house the personification of Luck, the luck of men, who distributes good or ill at random; we see the Will of God; and lastly we see in the answers to the traveller's questions, how each man can do much to improve his fortune. Logically these ideas exclude one another; practically they are all present to some degree in the puzzled mind of man contemplating the mysteries of human life.

One such story, from Kos, has appeared in *Forty-five Stories*, No. 35, with references and comparisons with similar tales covering the wide area from Italy to Russia and in the east to Persia and Armenia. Cosquin shows that the earliest forms of the story are to be found in India.[1] The two examples given here, although neither of them comes up to the story as recorded in Kos, contain most of the points in the Greek tradition and the ideas the Greeks have of luck.

In many stories luck is a sort of goddess of Fortune in general; she who distributes to all men good or ill fortune. In the first of the three versions from Thrace a young man chose as his wife the youngest of three sisters, for all that she was extremely idle, doing nothing all day but fiddle with matches. But her personal Luck used to come to her house and do everything for her, and when she and her husband found their way to Luck's house, she let them know that she gave to everyone according as she herself was rich or poor, industrious or, like the man's wife, just sitting idle, and so each child's good or ill fortune was fixed.

A Bulgarian legend combines this idea of the dependence of Luck herself on her own state of wealth or poverty with the notion that favours are dispensed in accordance with the omnipotent will of God.[2] There was, we are told, a young man working for God on the

[1] *Contes indiens*, p. 126.
[2] Lydia Schischmanoff, *Légendes religieuses bulgares*, p. 232, No. lxxxviii.

task of making a ladder from earth to heaven. On three successive nights God gave a feast to all his workmen: on the first night the dinner was good and opulent; on the second it was a good but plain meal; on the third night the food was very scanty. All this it would seem by the will of God, and we are told that on each of these three nights the souls of the newly born had similar proportional allotments of worldly goods. In the story here translated from Imera in Pontos Luck is presented as a sort of arbiter of man's fortune in the semblance of the sun, the Undying Sun, for so I would render the confessedly difficult Pontic Greek phrase, *ὁ Ἥλεν μάραντον*.

In another set of stories we have the idea of each man's individual fortune; to every man belongs a separate luck. This appears sometimes as almost a man's personal guardian, and a man's luck may be heard of as lying asleep under a tree; a man out to seek for him must wake him up before he can hope to repair his fortunes. Sometimes again a man's luck is presented by a sort of figurative image. Thus in the story from Mitylene here translated each man's individual fortune is presented as the spout of a fountain; for the lucky man the water flows freely; for the man of ill fortune the flow is no more than a scanty dropping of water. From this same Mitylene story we learn that some men are so extremely unlucky that nothing can be done to help them: the unfortunate hero sells or even gives away the goose or the part of the cake stuffed with gold coins that the kindly king has given him. There is a similar idea that some men are always lucky, so lucky as to feel uneasy about it. In a story from Thrace we hear of a man whose luck never failed him:[1] it was based on his parents' blessing, who had said to him: 'Take earth in your hands and it will turn to gold.' Like Polycrates of Samos the man felt that so much good fortune was dangerous and might bring some form of retribution. He did not, like the tyrant of Samos, throw a valuable ring into the sea, but he determined on a trading venture which would surely result in a loss. Carrying, as it were, coals to Newcastle, he loaded up a cargo of dates, buying them where they were dear and bringing them to Egypt where they are naturally very cheap. Questioned by the King of Egypt, he told him of his parents' blessing, and to illustrate it he took up a little sand in his hand: in the sand there was the ring which the king had lately lost. Neither then or ever could anything interfere with the good fortune brought him by his parents' blessing.

Among the unpublished stories collected by Kanellakis in Chios there is one called *The Blessing of my Father and my Mother*. With his parents' blessing a youth went off to sea and while he was away the

[1] In *Arkheíon Thrakikoú Laogr.* ii. 173.

city was destroyed by an earthquake. When he came back to the ruins of his house, he managed to dig out a gold horse, which in the voice of a man told him to mount, for he was 'the blessing of his father and of his mother'. The horse, this incarnate blessing, acted as his protector all through the story, which has in general lines a certain likeness to *The Son of the Hunter*.

In most of these stories the searcher for luck, like the old woman in our story from Pontos, 79 *b*, meets people on the way who ask questions about their difficulties and beg him to bring back answers from the power he is on the way to find. This has been discussed in the notes to No. 35 in *Forty-five Stories*, and here 79 *b* will serve as a sample. Also a legend from Bulgaria may be added. A man with a large family went out to find God to be his helper. On his way various questions were put to him that he might bring back whatever answers God would give him. To remedy his own troubles with his family he was given good advice about the training of his children.[1]

In the Pontic story translated we hear of the rock and the river which could never be at rest till they had been the death of a passer-by. On this curious idea that nothing can be at ease unless it achieves that for which it came into being, however mischievous that end may be, there are some remarks in *Forty-five Stories*, p. 366.

The Greek references are:

1. PONTOS: from Imera in *Arkheíon Pontou*, viii. 181, translated.
2. CYPRUS: *Kypriaká Khroniká*, ix. 285.
3. KOS: *Forty-five Stories*, No. 35.
4. MITYLENE: Kretschmer, *Heut. lesbische Dialekt*, p. 536, translated.
5, 6. CRETE: Kretschmer, *Neugr. Märchen*, p. 84. Also *Myson*, vii. 151, for which see No. 45, *The three Measures of Salt*. These two stories I have reckoned also as variants of No. 55, *The fated Bridegroom*.
7. THESSALY: epitomized in *Laographía*, i. 668.
8, 9, 10. THRACE: *Thrakiká*, xvii. 150, 152, and 174, which last contains only the traveller's questions of Christ, whom he is out to seek.

NO. 79*a*. THE SEARCH FOR LUCK[2]

Once there was a poor man who lived by making cloth for sacks, and he came to such a pitch of poverty that he had not even bread to eat. One day as he was twisting the thread for his work, he said: 'At the very least I must go off and find my Luck.' He went off along whatever path he saw in front of him. On the

[1] Lydia Schischmanoff, *Légendes religieuses bulgares*, p. 249, No. xc.

[2] Text from Mitylene in P. Kretschmer's *Heut. lesbische Dialekt*, p. 536; with the title *Blocked up*.

way he came to an inn and there he found little fountains of water: one just dripping and the next one running with a full stream. There was an old man sitting there and he said: 'These fountains are the lucks of men.' The poor man said: 'Come then and tell me which of them is mine.' The old man said: 'That little fountain there, just dripping: that one is your luck.' The man said: 'But this one here flowing with a full stream, whose luck is it?' 'This fountain,' said the old man, 'is the luck of the king.'

The man then went to his luck—to the fountain I mean—waiting for the water to flow; but it did no more than drip. An hour passed by: one little drop! Another hour passed: drip! just one more drop! The man said: 'I must take a stick and clear the passage.' So he took a stick and pushed it into the spout to clear it. The stick broke off inside, so instead of the one drop there had been before there was then no water at all. The man sat weeping: 'It must be blocked up, blocked up; yes, blocked up!'

Then one day the king and the vizier passed in disguise outside the man's shop. They heard him saying: 'It must be blocked up, blocked up!' When they were back in the palace the king sent for the man. When he came the king asked him: 'Why every day do you cry out, "It must be blocked, blocked up?"' Then the man told him all the truth. Then said the king: 'What of my luck? Did you get any sight of it?' 'Your luck,' said the man. 'It is a flowing river.' 'Be not vexed,' said the king. 'Your luck too shall flow with a full stream.' In the morning the king prepared a stuffed goose and baked it well in the oven. Then he put inside it a handful of gold coins and sewed it up so that nothing was to be seen. Then he sent it to the man as a present.

Precisely at the moment when the goose was brought, two strangers happened to be in the man's shop. 'What does your honour want with the goose?' said one of them. 'Let us have it to eat, for we are strangers here with no houses and we will pay you a crown for it.' When the man heard them say a crown, thinking of his poverty, he let them have the goose and took the money. The strangers took the goose and left the shop.

In the morning the king again sent for the man and asked him about the goose. The man said he had not eaten it but had sold it for a crown. The king marvelled at the trick Luck had played on the man, but he said nothing. Again in the morning the king sent him a cake, and half of it was stuffed with gold coins. At the very moment when the cake from the king was brought to him it happened by chance that an old woman passed by begging. The man cut off the half of the cake that had the coins in it and gave it to the old woman. In the morning again the king called for him: 'What have you done with the cake?' 'Half of it,' said the man, 'I gave to an old woman, and the other half I ate myself.' 'But anyhow did you not find something inside the cake?' 'What do you mean?' said he. 'What do you think I would find inside the cake? All my luck is blocked up and cut off.' Then the king was sorry for him and said: 'Well, you have been unlucky with the goose and with the cake. Now take this golden apple here and throw it with all your strength, and all the houses which the apple passes over shall be yours.' The man prepared to throw the apple; he threw it so that it struck a wall and bounced back and hit him on the forehead. They left him as he was, lying there. Never again did the poor fellow say: 'My luck is blocked up.'

NO. 79*b*. THE SEARCH FOR LUCK[1]

To go on and on with the story: there was an old woman and she had a hen. Like her the hen was well on in years and a good worker: every day she laid an egg. The old woman had a neighbour, an old man, a plague-stricken old fellow, and whenever the old woman went off anywhere he used to steal the egg. The poor old woman kept a lookout to catch the thief, but she could never succeed, nor did she want to make accusations against anyone, so she had the idea of going to ask the Undying Sun.

As she was on the way she met three sisters: all three of them were old maids. When they saw her they ran after her to find out where she was going. She told them what her trouble had been. 'And now,' said she, 'I am on my way to ask the Undying Sun and find out what son of a bitch this can be who steals my eggs and does such cruelty to a poor tired old woman.' When the girls heard this they threw themselves upon her shoulders:

[1] Text from Imera in Pontos; printed in *Arkheíon Pontou*, viii. 181, under the title *The Undying Sun.*

'O auntie, I beg you, ask him about us; what is the matter with us that we can't get married.' 'Very well,' said the old woman. 'I will ask him, and perhaps he may attend to what I say.'

So she went on and on and she met an old woman shivering with cold. When the old woman saw her and heard where she was going, she began to entreat her: 'I beg you, old woman, to question him about me too; what is the matter with me that I can never be warm although I wear three fur coats, all one on top of the other.' 'Very well,' said the old woman, 'I will ask him, but how can I help you?'

So she went on and on and she came to a river; it ran turbid and dark as blood. From a long way off she heard its rushing sound and her knees shook with fear. When the river saw her he too asked her in a savage and angry voice where she was going. She said to him what she had to say. The river said to her: 'If this is so, ask him about me too: what plague is this upon me that I can never flow at ease.' 'Very well, my dear river; very well,' said the old woman in such terror that she hardly knew how to go on.

So she went on and on, and came to a monstrous great rock; it had for very many years been hanging suspended and could neither fall nor not fall. The rock begged the old woman to ask what was oppressing it so that it could not fall and be at rest and passers-by be free from fear. 'Very well,' said the old woman, 'I will ask him; it is not much to ask and I will take it upon me.'

Talking in this way the old woman found it was very late and so she lifted up her feet and how she did run! When she came up to the crest of the mountain, there she saw the Undying Sun combing his beard with his golden comb. As soon as he saw her he bade her welcome and gave her a stool and then asked her why she had come. The old woman told him what she had suffered about the eggs laid by her hen: 'And I throw myself at your feet,' said she: 'tell me who the thief is. I wish I knew for then I should not be cursing him so madly and laying a burden on my soul. Also, please see here: I have brought you a kerchief full of pears from my garden and a basket full of baked rolls.' Then the Undying Sun said to her: 'The man who steals your eggs is that neighbour of yours. Yet see that you say nothing to him; leave him to God and the man will come by his deserts.'

'As I was on my way,' said the old woman to the Undying

Sun, 'I came upon three girls, unmarried, and how they did entreat me! "Ask about us; what is the matter with us that we get no husbands."' 'I know who you mean. They are not girls anyone will marry. They are like to be idle; they have no mother to guide them nor father either, and so it happens that every day they start and sweep the house out without sprinkling water and then use the broom and fill my eyes with dust and how sick I am of them! I can't bear them. Tell them that from henceforth they must rise before dawn and sprinkle the house and then sweep, and very soon they will get husbands. You need have no more thought about them as you go your way.'

'Then an old woman made a request of me: "Ask him on my behalf what is the matter with me that I cannot keep warm although I wear three fur coats one on top of the other." ' 'You must tell her to give away two in charity for the sake of her soul and then she will keep warm.'

'Also I saw a river turbid and dark as blood; its flow entangled with eddies. The river requested me: "Ask him about me; what can I do to flow at ease?" ' 'The river must drown a man and so it will be at ease. When you get there, first cross over the stream and then say what I have said to you; otherwise the river will take you as its prey.'

'Also I saw a rock: years and years have passed and all the time it has hung like this suspended and cannot fall.' 'This rock too must bring a man to death and thus it will be at ease. When you go there pass by the rock, and not till then, say what I have said to you.'

The old woman arose and kissed his hand and said Farewell and went down from the mountain. On her way she came to the rock, and the rock was waiting for her coming as it were with five eyes. She made haste and passed beyond and then she said what she had been told to say to the rock. When the rock heard how he must fall and that to the death of a man, he grew angry; what to do he knew not. 'Ah,' said he to the old woman: 'If you had told me that before, then I would have made you my prey.' 'May all my troubles be yours,' said the old woman and she—pray excuse me—slapped her behind.

On her way she came close to the river and from the roar it was making she saw how troubled it was and that it was just waiting for her to hear what the Undying Sun had said to her.

She made haste and crossed over the stream, and then she said what he had told her. When the river heard this, it was enraged, and such was its evil mood that the water was more turbid than ever. 'Ah,' said the river, 'Why did I not know this? Then I would have had your life, you who are an old woman whom nobody wants.' The old woman was so much frightened that she never turned round to look at the river.

Before she had gone much farther she could see the reek coming up from the roofs of the village and the savour of cooking came across to her. She made no delay but went to the old woman, she who could never keep warm and said to her what she had been told to say. The table was set all fresh and she sat down and ate with them: they had fine lenten fare and you would have eaten and licked your fingers, so good it was.

Then she went to find the old maids. From the time the old woman had left them their minds had been on her; they were neither lighting the fire in their house nor putting it out: all the time they had their eyes on the road to see the old woman when she came by. As soon as the old woman saw them, she went and sat down and explained to them that they must do what the Undying Sun had told her to tell them. After this they rose up always when it was still night and sprinkled the floor and swept it, and then suitors began to come again, some from one place and some from another; all to ask them in marriage. So they got husbands and lived and were happy.

As for the old woman who could never keep warm, she gave away two of her fur coats for the good of her soul and at once found herself warm. The river and the rock each took a man's life and so they were at rest.

When the old woman came back home she found the old man at the very gate of death. When she had gone off to find the Undying Sun he was so much frightened that a terrible thing happened to him: the hen's feathers grew out of his face. No long time passed before he went off to that big village whence no man ever returns. After that the eggs were never missing and the old woman ate them until she died and when she died the hen died too.

80

A just Man for a Godfather

THIS story is a version of Grimm, No. 4, *Der Gevatter Tod*, *Death the Godfather*, for which BP. i. 377, give references. In Greece I find Mr. Akoglou's version from Ordoú (Kotýora) here translated, and a good version from Mitylene.[1] The story is of a peasant who seeks a godfather for his son; he must be a man of perfect justice and impartiality. No one could be found but Death; in this Ordoú version presented as the Archangel Michael, who in common Greek belief comes to carry away the soul of a dying man. As a return Michael gave the father the power to know if a sick man would recover or must die; in the first case he would be seen sitting by the man's feet, in the second case by his head. So the man set up as a doctor and became rich. At last the time came for his own soul to be carried away and from this there was no escape; the godfather showed himself indeed impartial.

In a version of this story from Majorca the sign is given by the buzzing of a fly; at the sick man's head or by his feet.[2]

The hero is made a peasant, because it is the peasant who is the typical plain man, a little like our Piers the Ploughman; simple, and in his simplicity seeing deeply into man's nature. There is a version of the *Truth or Lies?* story in a fifteenth-century Franciscan writer, where the humble peasant knows that Truth is better than lies though all the great ones of the earth, a merchant, a judge, a bishop, and a king, have all asserted the opposite.[3]

In Greece the father of a child and the sponsor at the font, the godfather, call each other gossip, *koumbáros*, *compère*; or else *synteknoi*, the men who share in the paternity of the child; one the physical the other the spiritual father. In the same way a bridegroom and his best man call one another *koumbaros*, gossip, and these relations are taken more seriously than they generally are with us, carrying with them the spiritual affinities that are a bar to marriage.

[1] Translated in Carnoy-Nicolaïdes, p. 144. See also Politis, *Melétai*, i. 293, and Bernhard Schmidt's *Griech. Märchen*, p. 117.

[2] David Huelin, *Folktales of Mallorca*, Buenos Aires, 1945, p. 26.

[3] *Sermones Pomerii Fratris Pelbarti de Themesvar, De tempore*; Pars paschalis, Sermo viii; quoted in *Forty-five Stories*, p. 332.

NO. 80. A JUST MAN FOR A GODFATHER[1]

In the very early years there were a man and his wife; they had a baby boy. One man and then another asked to be the godfather. The man said to his wife: 'Not one of them will I allow to take the child to the font. Whoever is a man of just dealings, him', said he, 'I will accept as his godfather.'

One day as they were sitting at home a man came and knocked at the door. They opened to him. 'Who are you and what do you want?' they said. 'I have come,' said the man, 'to be godfather to your baby. I am God.' 'I won't let you have the baby,' said the man. 'You are a doer of unjust dealings. Some you make rich and others you make poor; some you make handsome and others you make ugly: that is, there is no justice in your doings. I will not let my baby be baptized by a doer of unjust dealings.' So he drove God away.

Some days later another man came and knocked at his door and asked to be godfather to the child. 'And who are you?' said the father. 'I,' said the man, 'I am the Devil.' 'Go away from here,' said the man: 'you deal unjustly and are wicked too. You act wickedly and do wicked deeds; you speak evil of men and set them one against the other. I will not have you as his godfather.' This one too he drove away.

Some days later yet another man came to the door. They opened to him. 'You are welcome.' 'I am glad to have met you. I have come', said the man, 'to ask you to let me take your baby to the font.' At once the father said to him: 'Tell me who you are. Then I will let you have my baby to baptize him.' 'I am the Archangel Michael,' said the man, 'and it is I who carry away the souls of men.' 'Ha!' said he, 'You are one who deals justly. You have regard neither to rich nor yet to poor. Of all men alike you carry away the souls. To you I will give my child for you to take him to the font.' So said he. So the angel took the child to baptism and the two men were united in this bond.

'Well now,' said the Archangel, 'O father of my godson, take a bag in your hands and go to work as a doctor. When they send for you to visit a sick man and you go into his room and see me sitting at the sick man's head, then,' said the Archangel, 'you

[1] Text from Kotýora in Pontos, printed in *Laographiká Kotyóron* by Xenophón K. Akoglou, p. 410.

must say to them there: "I will do what I can, but whatever you do, I do not think that this sick man of yours will get well." But when you see me sitting at his feet, then,' said he, 'just mix up water and a little sugar and say to the man that he will be well quite soon.' Well then, the father became a great person, and earned a great deal of money. He was a doctor and a very good doctor; they used to send from the villages for him to come. The man grew very rich; all goods and all good things were in his house.

Years went by, many of them, and one day the godfather of his son made himself visible. He had come to carry away his soul. The man besought him: 'At once, gossip; you understand these things, yet grant me a respite of fifteen days to go to my house and then come and carry away my soul.' He rose up and went to his house and said to his wife: 'My wife; this is what has happened; the godfather has come to carry away my soul. Now I must go away from here and from the people here, and go where I am not known and so my gossip will not find me and carry off my soul.' What he said that he did; exactly. He put on old clothes and went off to another place. When the fifteen days were over, Michael the Archangel came and found him and clapped him on the shoulders and said: 'My gossip, here I am; the time granted you is over.' 'What do you mean, calling me your gossip?' said the man. 'Tell me who you are and how you know me?' 'Come, my gossip, you know that I am one who deals justly. What you wanted I have given you. The fifteen days I granted you are now at an end. Did you think to hide yourself? These doings do not pass with me.' 'Oh, woe is me, gossip,' said the man. 'Now you have recognized me it brings me no profit to hide. Let me go to my house and in the morning come and take my soul.' So he went to his house and the next day the godfather, his gossip, came and carried away his soul.

81

God will provide

THIS simple but ingenious story is not common. Halliday under the title *I ask Boons of God* has discussed a version from Phárasa, then the only Greek version published, and by way of variants could point only to a Persian story:[1] on the general relations of the story I can go no farther, though we have now five more Greek versions: from Pontos, Mitylene, Chios, Kos, and Thrace.

One point arises. The version from Pontos translated here has as a heading and as a summary of the whole: 'When God gives it is in this manner He gives.' What lies behind this we may see from a story in the Georgian *Book of Wisdom and Lies*,[2] the fifth story entitled *The Man who puts Water into a Sieve.* It begins: *A man sat on the river-bank and held in his hands a sieve. He dipped the sieve in the water, and when it filled with water, he said: 'When God giveth to a man, thus doth He give.' Then he lifted up the sieve, and when all the water had run out he said: 'When He taketh away, thus doth He take away.'* Behind the sentence in our story 'When God gives it is in this manner He gives', we may therefore see the idea that the gifts of God come to a man as freely and as abundantly as water flows into a sieve, but with the warning that as freely as they have come so may they at any moment go.

The rest of the Georgian story is to show that a man should for all that make some effort to help himself: 'Did food ever fall into anyone's mouth without the help of hands?'

The references are:

1. PONTOS: *Pontiaká Phylla*, iii, No. 25, p. 25, here translated.
2. PHÁRASA in the Taurus: *M.G. in A.M.*, p. 529.
3. MITYLENE: Kretschmer, *Heut. lesbische Dialekt*, p. 519.
4. CHIOS: an unpublished version collected by Kanellakis.
5. KOS: *Forty-five Stories*, p. 270, *The High King.*
6. THRACE: *Arkheíon Thrakikoú Laogr.* xiii. 179.

[1] *M.G. in A.M.*, p. 240, quoting Clouston, *A Group of Eastern Romances.*
[2] Translated by Oliver Wardrop, p. 14.

NO. 81. GOD WILL PROVIDE[1]

When God gives it is in this manner He gives.

In the early ages three companions once went off to a foreign land; there they worked and gained a few piastres, and then turned back to go to their own village. When they came to the city where the king had his throne, it was evening; where they could lodge they did not know. They saw the king's palace and by it the garden; they went and settled in a corner of the garden, saying: 'Here we can sleep.' But the weather was cold and they began to be chilly. They gathered a few sticks and lit a fire and warmed themselves.

On that evening the king had given an order: 'In no place may men kindle fire or light.' When he saw that below the palace men were making a fire, he went to see who it was: he saw those three men sitting round the fire warming themselves. He stayed and waited to see what they would be talking of. One of them said: 'Were the king to give me a nice sum of money in my pocket, then I would go home as a man should.' The next one said: 'As for me, if he would give me his daughter, then I could live always as I would wish. If he gave me money, that would all be spent again.' The third one said: 'I don't want the king's money: who is the king? What is given to me, I would have from God.'

The king listened to all this, and in the morning early he sent and brought the men before him. He said: 'Where you were last night and all that you said, I know well: if you tell me lies, I will cut off your heads.' The men were afraid and told him all the truth. About the one who had asked for money the king said: 'Load him with as much money as he needs.' To the one who had asked for the girl he gave his daughter, and to the third one he said: 'Go away, let it be for God to care for you.' The king gave him nothing. Thus he sent them off to their village.

As they were on the way, the one with the load of money grew tired and said to his fellow: 'You carry the money and I will pay you.' So he gave him the load, and they went on. The king, left standing there, regretted not having killed the man who had given him that rough and reproachful answer, and so

[1] Text from Pontos in *Pontiaká Phylla*, iii, No. 25, p. 25.

he sent his men after them with the order: 'Go now and kill the man who has no burden.' So they went and did so. But the man they killed was the one to whom the king had given the money, because at that moment it was the other who was carrying it, and thus the money remained in his possession.

For awhile the men went on. Then some other accident befell the man who had married the king's daughter, and he too lost his life.[1] So the bride and the money too both remained with the man who had made his entreaty to God.

The pair went to a certain place and spent the evening below the village in a cottage by the road. In it there was a poor man who made his living by selling what he could. When they had eaten and rested themselves, it became dark, and the man said to them: 'Come; let us go and lodge in the village; you may come here again very early in the morning.' The two were not willing. The man said: 'He who lodges in this house dies.' As they were still unwilling, the man left them and went off to the village.

Down below the cottage there was a big cave with a flat slab covering the entrance. When night came, the man was tired out by carrying the load of money and went to sleep. The woman was watching, and in her hand she had an enchanted knife; she kept it with her and it had been given her by her father. She saw the slab lifted and out came a black man. Before he was well out, the woman smote him and his head was one half cut off. The black man then besought her: 'Of this stroke I can never be healed. Down here I have a great treasure. Finish the job and carry me outside and throw me out into the well, and all the treasure will be yours.' Then the woman cut his head right off, and dragged him away and threw him into the well. She took the light and went down and saw that in the cave there were forty chambers full of all sorts of fine things and golden treasures, such as were not to be found even in the king's palace.

Then she came up and set the slab on the hole and woke up her husband; she took him down and showed him everything. In the morning the keeper of the tavern came: he thought they would be dead and it would be for him to bury them. When he came and saw them sitting there, he was amazed and asked them if nothing had happened. 'We have not seen anything,'

[1] In other versions he was drowned crossing a river.

they said: 'What could we have seen?' Then the keeper of the tavern told them that the cottage was unlucky: 'No one can live in it; they all die. I would like to find someone to sell it to, and be free of the place.' They said: 'Sell it to us.' He accepted the offer and demanded ten gold pieces. They gave him twenty and bought the place, and from that time whoever came used to eat and drink and lodge there, and then when he went away they would give him a gold piece as a present and send him off.

This came to the king's ears, and he said to the queen: 'Let us go and see what place this is and the people who own it.' They went, and the man who had asked a gift from God—the king did not recognize him—came and showed them round the rooms. The king saw all the fine things and was amazed, for he who was a king had not such treasures. One room only the man did not show him. 'Why will you not show me that one?' said the king. 'That room may not be opened,' said the man. They finished their round, and the king said to the queen: 'Do whatever you can to get that room opened and see what there is in it.' The queen went round all the rooms and told the man to open that room as well. He said: 'In there is my wife.' 'Very well; let me see her.' Then he opened the room and the queen to her great amazement saw her daughter. They embraced the one the other, and the girl said: 'All these things belong to us, and this man is the one of the three strangers who desired to have his gift from God.' The king rejoiced much, and took them into his palace, and when the king died the man was made king.

In that land there were of old royal palaces: in later years other kings captured and destroyed them all, and it is in this way that chambers have been preserved underneath the earth all filled with golden treasures, and of these God gave to the man, who rested his hope in Him, and whatever was given to him would have it from God.

82

The greater Sinner

AARNE–THOMPSON TYPE 756C

THIS story has been discussed exhaustively by N. P. Andrejev and these notes are drawn largely from his paper.[1]

The essence of the story is always that a penitent sinner, as a rule a robber or a murderer, sometimes a parricide or a man guilty of incest, is given what seems an impossible penance: generally to make a dead branch put out leaves and blossoms; less often to graze black sheep till they turn white. While he is watering the log or grazing the sheep, some greater sinner comes by and in some way insults him; the penitent turns and kills him. Then to his astonishment he finds his apparently impossible task fulfilled and he has won his pardon. The priest explains to him that the man he has just killed has been so great a sinner that to rid the earth of him has been taken as an atonement for all his own crimes: this one additional murder has wiped out the guilt of all the ninety and nine he had committed.

The story is in origin Slav and Andrejev has collected more than forty examples, all from Slav lands, except a very few strays to Armenia and Palestine. Distinguishing four main recensions of the story, he thinks it arose in some southern Slav region, probably in Bulgaria.

The greater sin, greater than all the crimes of the penitent, varies a good deal. In most of the Russian versions the sin is social: the man has been a tyrannical overseer, a hard landlord, a money grabber of some sort; in one story simply a lawyer. There is an odd frequency of tobacco smuggling and a good many instances of necrophily, probably connected with the Slav interest in vampires. In the Ukraine the sinner is often a man who insults the dead and tries to use them for some impious purpose, or he is a devil who mocks at the thunder. In Greece the sin is very different: it is either keeping back the supply of water from those who need it, or hindering a happy marriage, breaking up a betrothal in some way. That these should be very specially heinous sins seems to me very much a Greek idea. The Greek does not ask, as the Slav does, to be protected from swindling lawyers and oppressors; he can look after himself. What seems to

[1] *Die Legende von den zwei Erzsündern*, by N. F. Andrejev, in *FF Communications*, No. 54, 1924, in vol. xvi of *FF C*. See also Stith Thompson's *The Folktale*, p. 132.

him dreadful is that anyone should by his wickedness interfere with the goodness of God to mankind by hindering the natural blessings of abundant water and of happy marriage.

In Roumanian, Bulgarian, and Servian versions we are brought close to the Greek; for example in one Roumanian version the sin is that of keeping back water. There is also a Bulgarian legend in which breaking off a marriage appears as the greatest of all sins.[1] A story, no doubt as Andrejev holds, by origin Slav seems in Greece and in the neighbourhood of Greece to have taken on this peculiarly Greek dress.

Equally from Thrace is another mention of the sin of cutting off a marriage. In a short account of a visit by the Virgin on Holy Saturday to look at the souls of the wicked, we are told that she came upon a soul so deeply sunk in hell as hardly to be seen. He was a man who had stood in the way of another man on his way to being betrothed: for this sin the earth had opened and swallowed him up.[2]

Beyond these two stories from Thrace here translated I find no other Greek versions of this story, nor have any Turkish stories of this type come my way.

NO. 82*a*. THE GREATER SINNER[3]

A wicked man had killed thirty-nine men. After all this he repented and went to the priest to confess and to ask for pardon. The priest told him to see to it that he sinned no more: morning and evening he must pray to God for pardon. Also he must plant a twig, scorched and dry; then he must water it; when the twig puts forth leaves, then will his sins be pardoned. The man rented a field close to a spring of water; he tilled it and dug it three spades deep and sowed it as a garden. In it he planted the dried up twig as the confessor had told him, praying the while for the pardon of God. The garden flourished: the melons and the pumpkins were many and sweet, and to everyone who came to the spring to drink and take rest he would give each of them a pumpkin or a melon. When they offered to pay him, he would say that he was doing it for the good of his soul, that his sins might be pardoned. The twig he watered regularly, but how was it possible that it should bear leaves?

One day he saw a man passing by in a hurry and called out to him: 'Come here; come and rest yourself and eat some melon.'

[1] Schischmanoff, *Légendes réligieuses des Bulgares*, p. 227.
[2] Madame Elpiniki Sarandí in *Thrakiká*, ii. 146.
[3] Thracian text from *Thrakiká*, xvii. 173, No. 84.

The man neither turned to look at him nor gave him any answer. This made him so angry that he ran after him and killed him. Then he was sorry and began to weep and beat his breast, saying: 'Oh, what a wicked thing I have done! A thing for which I can never find consolation.' Then he went to water the twig which he had planted, and what did he see? The twig had put out leaves. He told this to the priest. The priest found the matter difficult and told him to look and find out what man this was whom he had killed. He asked and found that he was a man who cut off supplies of water. At that very time he had been going in haste to break up a water conduit that the people in the village and their beasts might have no water; in their trouble they would send for him and pay him money: then he would let the water flow. This they told the man, and he went and told the priest. The priest said: 'In killing this man who cut off the supply of water, not only did you commit no sin, but all your sins have been pardoned because you delivered the men of the village from his wickedness.'

NO. 82*b*. THE GREATER SINNER[1]

Whoever dissuades a man who wants to get married by making unjust accusations against the bride, that man in the next world must abide burning in the pitch for ever. There was a man who killed nine and ninety men, and then he repented and went and confessed to the priest and begged for forgiveness. The confessor said: 'If you have truly repented of what you have done, your sins shall be pardoned, but your pardon shall be even when this dry stick which you are to plant on the hill shall bring forth leaves.'

The man went and planted the dry stick: every day he brought water to pour upon it; it produced no leaves. One day when he was in the field he saw a man passing by in a hurry: he asked him: 'Where are you going that way?' The man made no answer. Again he asked him: 'Where are you going that way?' Again he did not answer, and the man said to himself: 'I shall kill that man; I speak to him and he will not speak to me.' Then he killed him. Next day he went to water the stick, and what did he see? It had produced leaves. He went off and told the priest:

[1] Thracian text from *Thrakiká*, xvii. 173, No. 83.

'For all these many days I have been watering the dry twig and never did it produce leaves. Yesterday I killed yet another man: I had spoken to him and he would not speak to me. Then I went to water the twig and saw it all green leafage.' 'Ah,' said the priest: 'the man whom you killed was on his way to break up a betrothal and stop it, and therefore it has come about that your sins have been forgiven you.'

83

The Mercy of God

SEVERAL other stories in this book, Nos. 7, 38, 39, begin with the grant of a child to childless persons by some mysterious person, often a dervish, who gives them an Apple of Fertility; then at a later period the child is to be given up. This theme, we have seen, is developed in several ways. In the two stories from Thrace here translated it is given a religious turn. The childless mother eats no apple but prays to God and her prayer is granted, always, however, with the usual condition that when she is twelve years old her little girl will be taken from her. At the appointed time the claim was made, but both the child and the mother accepted the condition with so much piety and resignation that God relented.

The second story has the complaints against man of the wheat and the barley and the flax; these are companion pieces to our complaint of John Barleycorn. It also contains 'just so' explanations of why the rye has no blessing on it; why there is a patch of white on a deer's hoof; and why the deer is the most innocent of creatures. Of these fancies about plants we have a good number. Several occur in a charm against the Yiloú, the ancient Gelló, the demon who devours babies. The charm takes the form of a narrative. The demon Yiloú was being pursued by the brothers of the injured mother; these are St. Sisýnios and St. Synódoros. The saints asked the willow to guide them. The willow would tell them nothing and was therefore cursed: 'Never shall she bear fruit for man to eat.' And the same thing with the bramble: 'Thy root shall spring up into thy topmost spray and thy topmost spray take root; thy fruit shall be useless and from it no man shall live.' The Greeks avoid blackberries, and the branches do fall over to the ground and strike fresh roots. Then the olive helped the saints in their pursuit and received their blessing: 'Thy fruit shall abound and from it shall the saints enjoy light.'[1]

For 'roses and pearls' see No. 11.

NO. 83*a*. THE MERCY OF GOD[2]

Once upon a time there were a king and a queen. They had no children and besought God to give them a child. God had pity

[1] The charm, of which I have an eighteenth century copy, was printed by Leo Allatius in his *De quorundam Graecorum opinionibus*, 1645, chap. viii, p. 126.

[2] Thracian text from *Thrakiká*, xvii. 160.

on them and gave them a little girl, saying: 'When she is twelve years old, you must give her to Me.' 'Very well,' said the king and the queen.

The little princess grew big and went to school. When she was twelve years old, one day as she was coming back from school, three angels met her and said: 'You must tell your mother to send us the gift which she promised us.' The princess went to the queen and said: 'Mother, three angels have come to me and said that you must give them the gift you promised them.' When the queen heard this, she wept. She bathed her daughter and changed her clothes and sent her off to school saying: 'When the angels come to you, you must say: "My mother has said you must take the gift." ' As the princess was on her way, the angels met her; she said: 'My mother said you must take the gift which she promised you.' 'Tell your mother that we will not take this gift from her, because she has sent it to us with a pure heart.' Then each of the angels gave her a blessing. One said: 'As you talk golden roses shall fall from you.' The next said: 'Your tears shall turn to pearls.' The third gave her a golden cross.

When the princess came home, she found her mother weeping. She said: 'The three angels told me to tell you that they will not claim the gift because you sent it to them with a pure heart, and each one of them gave me a blessing: one said that when I talk golden roses shall fall from me; the next one said that my tears shall turn to pearls; and the third one gave me a golden cross.

The king and the queen wept for joy and gave glory to God who had granted them their daughter. They did many deeds of kindness to the poor, and in the palace they held feasts and many rejoicings. When the princess grew up they married her to a prince and they all lived well and may we live yet better.

NO. 83*b*. THE MERCY OF GOD[1]

'Grant me, O God, a child; let me have him for twelve years and then take him from me.' God listened to the mother as she prayed with all her heart, and He gave her a little girl: she called her Maroulitsa. Maroulitsa grew big and was her mother's joy; she sent her to school. When she was twelve years old, as

[1] Thracian text from *Thrakiká*, xvii. 161.

she was on her way back from school, an old man often used to look at her; he said: 'You must tell your mother not to forget the vow she made to me.' Maroulitsa played with her toys and forgot to tell her mother. Again the old man looked at her and questioned her: 'Have you told your mother?' 'I forgot, granddad.' 'Tell her not to forget the vow she made to me.' Maroulitsa always forgot to tell her mother, and one day the old man said: 'I will tie a thread on your finger, so that you won't forget to tell her this evening.' Her mother saw the thread tied to Maroulitsa's finger and asked her why she had put it there. 'Now for some time when I am coming back from school, an old man has been telling me to bid you not forget the vow you made to him. I used to forget, and now he has tied the little thread on me for me to remember to tell you.'

Then the unhappy mother remembered the vow which she had made to God at the time when she used to pray to Him and say: 'Give me, O God, a child; let me have him for twelve years and then You may take him from me.' She wept and with tears and prayers beat her breast, holding Maroulitsa tightly in her arms so that she might not lose her. 'O God, I did not know that the years would go so quickly. Grant me this grace and do not take my child.' God was in the right to ask her to fulfil her vow, because He had given her the child for Him to take it away in twelve years, and if she had refused to give her up, the Almighty might well have afflicted the child to punish the sinful woman. The mother made her cross and her prayer before the icons in the house; she kissed Maroulitsa, saying with a sad heart: 'Tell the old man that what he has found he may take.'

As Maroulitsa was on her way to school, the old man—and this was God—carried her away to gardens of verdure: in them were beautiful flowers and trees. Maroulitsa took no delight in them; she remembered her mother and wept all the time. God gave her crisp herbs to cook and gave her too a ration of salt; yet it was with her tears that the food was salted, for they fell into the food as she wept, saying: 'Cut like these herbs is the tender heart of my mother, as she weeps for me, for Maroulitsa.' Next day too the food was salt, and every day the herbs were salty with Maroulitsa's tears, as she wept continually saying: 'Cut like these herbs is the tender heart of my mother, as she weeps for me, for Maroulitsa.'

Nor did the mother forget Maroulitsa; always was she weeping and crying: 'O God, Thou hast taken my daughter, yet it was even so that I prayed to have her. My God, I thank Thee; yet can I never forget her. O grant me this grace.' And so she shed bitter tears.

God had pity on her and said: 'I must send the girl back to her mother.' So He questioned the wolf: 'O wolf, what do you eat?' 'I eat flesh and I drink water.' 'It is not for you to carry a child to her mother.' Then God questioned the fox: 'O fox, what do you eat?' 'I eat flesh and drink water.' 'Nor are you one to carry a child back to her mother.' Then He questioned the deer: 'O deer, what do you eat?' 'I eat grass and I drink water.' 'It is for you to carry the child back to her mother.' So God set Maroulitsa on the deer's back for her to be carried to her mother.

The deer went on, but behind him ran the wolf, hoping to devour the little girl. On the way the wolf questioned the wheat: 'Have you seen a deer passing by this way?' 'Stop, O wolf; I want to tell you of my own troubles. Men sow me and reap me and winnow me and sift me and grind me and knead me; they make me into bread and eat me, and use my stubble to burn as brushwood, and all this is very bitter to me.' The wolf went farther and questioned the barley. 'O barley, have you seen a deer passing this way?' 'Stop, O wolf; I want to tell you of my troubles. Men sow me, they reap me and winnow me and carry me to the barn, and grind me and knead me; they make me into bread and then men eat me; so do animals too.' The wolf went farther and questioned the flax. 'O flax, have you seen a deer pass by this way?' 'Stop, O wolf; I want to tell you my troubles. Men sow me and when I am grown up tall, they tear me up from the earth, and pound me with the head of the mallet to separate out the seed; then they steep me in water for days, and wash me and dry me and pound me with the mallet to make ready my fibres; then they make thread of me and weave me and then they bleach me in the stream.' The wolf went farther and met the rye. 'O rye, have you seen a deer pass this way?' 'Run quickly; that is the way he went; you are hardly in time.' As soon as ever the deer had reached the mother's house and gone in and set Maroulitsa down, the wolf came and just bit his hind hoof. The mother tied some cotton-wool on the hoof and to this very day every deer has a little white patch there.

The mother gave thanks to God who had given her back her daughter. They kept the deer there and he stayed always with them and was the companion of Maroulitsa: nothing parted them. The rye which had shown the wolf the way has no blessing on it, nor is it allowed to pass the door of the church. From its flour the bread for Mass may not be made, and when anyone asks why it cannot enter the church, the rye gives as its answer: 'I grow tall; so very tall that I can see the church from where I am.'

84

Shall not the Judge of all the Earth do right?

THE story from Cyprus here presented under this title was told near Famagusta by a man who could neither read nor write. It very clearly falls into three distinct and as stories separable parts or themes: the first may be called *The Traveller and his mysterious Guide*; the second, *The Ascetic by the Fountain*; and the third, *The Difference between the Best and the Worst of Men.* Of the three themes the first is by far the commonest and occurs by itself in the versions from Ordoú, Kos, Naxos, and Mýkonos. The Mýkonos version is remarkable in that the traveller has seemingly no companion, but at the end goes to a monastery where Christ gives him the needed explanations. All the three themes have also been given me by a young man at Imera in Pontos, who recounted the first theme and then after a pause the second and third. He was a man of some education but knew the stories as current in the village from which he used to come to tell me stories in the Monastery of the Forerunner where I was spending a few days in 1914. The version from Kos with a study of all the three themes is printed in *Forty-five Stories*: it is No. 24, 'The Schoolmaster and the Holy Elder'.[1]

Of the three, the first theme seems certainly to be of Jewish origin. BP. iv. 325 say that its oldest version is that of Rabbi Nissim in the first half of the eleventh century. Hasluck regarded the story as a Jewish apophthegm on the verse in Genesis xviii. 25, which I have ventured to take as a general title.[2]

As it is the commonest in Greece, so the first theme is much the most widely spread. We have seen its appearance in Jewish writing. In the west it appears in the *Gesta Romanorum* and in the *Exempla* of Jacques de Vitry. Crane in his edition of the *Exempla* has collected numerous references to it as occurring in Europe. From Jacques de Vitry it has passed into Pauli's *Schimpf und Ernst.* It is hardly necessary to do more than allude to the later European versions of this theme. Its presence in Voltaire's *Zadig* and in Parnell's *Hermit* mark the popularity of oriental stories at that period.

The second theme, *The Ascetic by the Fountain*, appears at least among the neighbours of Greece. It is one of the tales in the Slav

[1] With all the references.

[2] Hasluck, *Christianity and Islam*, p. 700. It is the Aarne–Thompson Type 759.

dialect of Macedonia printed by Mazòn,[1] who has pointed out its kinship with *The Traveller and his mysterious Guide.* Indeed one of Mazon's Slav versions combines the two themes, the first and the second. Told of God and St. Peter, the second theme, the doings at the fountain, has been recorded from the Turkish-speaking Gagaüzy of Bessarabia.[2] It appears to be of Talmudic origin.[3]

The third theme I do not know elsewhere.

That it was a special mark of sanctity to be able to carry about water in a kerchief as if in a normal vessel we can see from a Pontic story.[4] An ascetic went to visit his brother who was in the world, working as a shoemaker. He could find no other gift to bring but some water from his own spring; by his sanctity he was able to tie up the water in a cloth and bring it to his brother. But to the brother's shop there came a woman to buy shoes, and she was so beautiful that he was tempted. At this loss of his sanctity all the water ran out, and the ascetic learned the lesson that in spite of all appearances his brother in the world was a better man than he was.

The Greek versions, of which Nos. 2, 4, 5, and 7 have the first theme only, are:

1. IMERA IN PONTOS: a translation of the first theme is in *Medium Ævum*, vi. 181, and of the second and third in *Forty-five Stories*, p. 262.
2. ORDOÚ IN PONTOS: Xenophon Akoglou, *Laographiká Kotyóron*, p. 412.
3. CYPRUS: *Kypriaká Khroniká*, ix. 280. Translated below.
4. KOS: *Forty-five Stories*, p. 257.
5. NAXOS: *N.A.* ii. 1. Translated by Garnett, p. 290.
6. NAXOS: *N.A.* ii. 5. Translated by Garnett, p. 288. This has the theme of *The Ascetic by the Fountain.*
7. MÝKONOS: Roussel, *Contes de Mycono*, p. 6.

NO. 84. SHALL NOT THE JUDGE OF ALL THE EARTH DO RIGHT?[5]

There was once an ascetic; three days and three nights he fasted, praying God to reveal to him His hidden secrets. At the end of the three days there came to him an angel, sent by God to ask for what reason he was so importunate. The ascetic said to the angel: 'I want to know the hidden secrets of God.' 'But,' said the angel, 'do you not know that the hidden secrets of God are

[1] Mazon, *Contes slaves*, pp. 82, 172.

[2] C. F. Coxwell, *Siberian and other Folktales*, p. 417. The story is from one of Radloff's volumes written in Russian.

[3] Clouston, *Popular Tales*, i. 25.

[4] *Khroniká tou Pontou*, i. 265.

[5] Text from Cyprus in *Kypriaká Khroniká*, ix. 280.

very many?' Said the ascetic: 'I want to see with my eyes the judgements of God.' 'Very well,' said the angel; 'then come with me.' The angel carried him off to the house of a rich man: the angel had changed himself into a man. They went to the rich man's house. 'Good day to you.' 'You are welcome.' 'Have you not some little corner where we who are strangers can find a lodging?' 'No, my son,' said the rich man. 'Go from here in peace; I have nothing for you, and it may be you will find a lodging somewhere else.' 'And where are we to go?' said the angel. 'We have come here; find us a lodging and so you will do a good deed for the sake of your soul.' 'Well,' said the rich man, 'over there is a place where I keep straw; if it suits you, you may stay there.' 'Very well, my son,' said the angel. So there they lodged. When night came, the rich man gave them no water; neither bread nor anything to eat, nor rugs, nor anything. There was a wall there ready to fall down, and in the night the angel rose and built it up strongly and carefully to prevent it from falling. 'Hold in awe what I do,' said the angel. 'Whatever you see me do, you must say nothing.' When the day dawned they rose up and went away.

Then they came to another village. 'Now,' said the angel, 'we are going to the house of a very rich man, a man very well disposed.' They went to the rich man's house and as soon as he saw them he and his wife, they cried out: 'You are very welcome, and we have here a house for you to lodge in. There you may eat and refresh yourselves.' Well, to make a long story short, he gave them abundant attention and care. For the night beds were laid down for them to sleep. As soon as men were asleep, the angel rose up: the baby of the people of the house was in his cradle; the angel took him by the throat and strangled him. All the time the ascetic was looking on. In the morning they rose up and went their way.

Then they came to another village. Again they lodged in the house of a rich man: Oh, what richness in Thy mercies, O God! Again they were given food and whatever else they needed. As the people were asleep in the night, the ascetic saw the angel rise and take up a gold cup which they had been given to drink from. The angel threw it away. Then they left this house also.

They came to a very big olive-tree; its trunk was all hollow. The angel said to the ascetic: 'Come; let me hide you inside the tree and you shall see strange doings.' The angel hid the man and then went away. Presently there came up a very wealthy man riding on his horse; he tied the horse to the tree and dismounted. He drank of the spring in the place and began to count out the gold pieces he had in his wallet to see how much money he had with him for going to the festival. He had picked up the money in his house at random and wanted to see what sum he had taken. As he was counting it, his horse shied and broke into a gallop and was off. As soon as the rich man saw his horse galloping off he left the money there on the ground and ran off himself to catch the horse. Presently another man came up, and he took the wallet and the money and went off to the hills to hide himself from pursuit. Some time passed by and a poor unhappy man, a beggar, came up; as soon as he saw the spring of water and the shade of the tree, he sat down to rest himself and drink a little water. The rich man had caught his horse and came galloping back to the olive-tree to take up his money. He looked for it; he could not see it anywhere. 'You wicked old man,' he said to the beggar, 'what have you done with my money that was on the ground here?' 'With your money? I have seen nothing here, my son, nothing at all.' 'You've seen nothing, you rascal?' said the man. 'No one has been this way and who else can have taken it?' Again the old man said that he had taken nothing. The rich man brought out his gun and shot him dead and then went off. 'Oh!' said the ascetic, 'and is this the righteous judgement of God which he told me he would show me?' As soon as the ascetic had uttered these words which came from his heart; behold and see! all the water which he had tied up in his kerchief had dripped right away. I forgot to tell you that the ascetic was a righteous man and had the power to tie up water in his kerchief without a drop being lost. So when he saw that the water had run out he knew well that he had sinned.

Then the angel came again and said to him: 'Now I shall take you and show you the man who is the greatest sinner and the man who is the most righteous. You must stay here by that door through which people will be coming out. The man who comes out first is the greatest sinner, and he who shall go in last of all in the evening, that man is the most righteous.'

At dawn the man went and sat down by the door and the

first man who came out he saw was a fisherman and with him a little boy, his son, and the man was on his way to his fishing. So the fisherman went and cast his line to catch fish. 'Oh, daddy,' cried his little son, 'are the waves of the sea the most in number, or is it the sand, or is it the stars in the sky?' 'No, my son,' said the fisherman, 'neither the waves of the sea are most in number nor yet the sand nor yet the stars in the sky. The loving mercy of God is more than them all.' When night came the ascetic was waiting; waiting for the most righteous man to pass through the door. The fisherman came. 'Oh,' cried the ascetic, 'so the greatest sinner and the most righteous man are one and the same man?' Then the angel came. 'Ah,' said he, 'so you have seen both the sinner and also the most righteous man?' The man said: 'But I do not understand. How can it have been that the same man should come out in the morning a sinner and by night-time become righteous? Within one day did he save his soul?' 'He did,' said the angel to the ascetic, 'and this because he told his son that the most in number are neither the waves of the sea nor the sand nor yet the stars, but the loving mercies of God, and it was this one word that saved his soul.'[1]

'Well,' said the ascetic, 'and about that rich man who gave us neither food nor drink: why did you save his wall from falling down?' 'Ah,' said the angel, 'hidden in it there was a jar full of gold coins and if the wall had fallen the rich man would have found them and done much harm in the world. I stayed up the wall that some good man of his family may find the treasure and do good with it.' Then said the ascetic: 'And what of the man who treated us with such hospitality and you strangled his baby?' 'That man and his wife are good people, but that child of theirs would have grown into a bad man, and his parents would have lost all the rewards of their good deeds, and so I killed their child that their good deeds might still avail them.' 'And what of the other man whose golden cup you threw away?' 'This I did,' said the angel, 'because those two, the man and his wife, are good folk, but the cup was someone else's and had been stolen; I threw it away to save them from the guilt of owning it.' 'Well,' said the ascetic, 'and what of the rich man

[1] The Imera version—*Forty-five Stories*, p. 263—ends: The ascetic went to his house, thinking within himself: 'For us men, one single word is enough to win us paradise; one word is enough to lose it.'

who killed the old man, who was innocent, for it was not he who had taken the money?' 'As for the man whom you saw carrying off the money; some people belonging to the rich man had stolen it from his people, and that is why he stole it from the rich man that the debt should be settled. Also the relations of the man who was killed; they had killed relations of the man who then killed him, and this is why this slaughter was done that this debt too might be paid.'

Index